# Jules Verne
## Four Novels

*FIVE WEEKS IN A BALLOON*

*A JOURNEY TO THE CENTER OF THE EARTH*

*TWENTY THOUSAND LEAGUES UNDER THE SEA*

*AROUND THE WORLD IN EIGHTY DAYS*

*Introduction by Ernest Hilbert*

**Canterbury Classics**

San Diego

Canterbury Classics
An imprint of Printers Row Publishing Group
10350 Barnes Canyon Road, Suite 100, San Diego, CA 92121
www.canterburyclassicsbooks.com

Printers Row Publishing Group is a division of Readerlink Distribution Services, LLC.
Canterbury Classics is a registered trademark of Readerlink Distribution Services, LLC.

All correspondence concerning the content of this book should be addressed to
Canterbury Classics, Editorial Department, at the above address.

Publisher: Peter Norton
Associate Publisher: Ana Parker
Publishing/Editorial Team: April Farr, Kelly Larsen, Kathryn C. Dalby
Editorial Team: JoAnn Padgett, Melinda Allman, Dan Mansfield, Traci Douglas
Production Team: Jonathan Lopes, Rusty von Dyl

Library of Congress Cataloging-in-Publication Data

Verne, Jules, 1828-1905.
  [Novels. English. Selections]
  Jules Verne / introduction by Ernest Hilbert.
    p. cm.
  ISBN 978-1-60710-317-2 -- ISBN 1-60710-317-6
1.  Verne, Jules, 1828-1905--Translations into English. 2.  Science fiction,
French--Translations into English.  I. Hilbert, Ernest, 1970- II. Title.
PQ2469.A2 2012
843'.8--dc23

2012004785

Printed in China
22 21 20 19 18  8 9 10 11 12

# CONTENTS

# Introduction

## *LIFE*

Jules Verne is one of the most famous authors of all time. He has been a best-seller for nearly a century and a half, in both his native French and many other languages, particularly English. According to UNESCO's Index Translationum, only Agatha Christie is more frequently translated than Verne. Two of his most famous characters, the enigmatic Captain Nemo of *Twenty Thousand Leagues Under the Sea* and the resolute Englishman Phileas Fogg of *Around the World in Eighty Days*, are commonly known to both children and adults the world over. Verne is celebrated as a pioneer of the science-fiction genre, a spinner of timeless adventure stories, and an endlessly readable chronicler of the last age of European exploration. He expressed the powerful and sometimes destructive Victorian faith in science as a means of surmounting obstacles and transforming the natural world. His stories endure today in movies, television, comics, cartoons, video games, and even amusement park rides.

Verne was born in 1828 in Nantes, France, a bustling harbor city on the Loire River near the Atlantic Ocean. Ships from around the world made fast at the wharves, and the air bristled with masts. As boys, Jules and his brother Paul explored the docks and riverbanks. From his earliest years, Jules watched vessels raise anchors for distant ports, and these departures sparked his imagination. At a young age, he developed an appetite for books about travel and exploration, and began writing for enjoyment. Poetry was "a family pastime" according to biographer Herbert R. Lottman, and Verne was attracted to literature from the start. His father was a successful attorney and hoped his son would follow him into the profession. When Verne moved to Paris to study law in 1848—a turbulent year of revolutions that began in Paris and spread across Europe—he quickly befriended other aspiring writers. With his friend Michel Carré he wrote opera libretti. He also composed poetry and plays and soon abandoned his law studies. His father was incensed and severed family support, but Verne continued to write while earning a living as a stockbroker, a profession he would practice until 1862. In 1857 he married Honorine de Viane Morel, a widow and mother of two. Unlike Verne's father, she supported his writing and urged him to find a publisher. In time he met Pierre-Jules Hetzel, one of the most distinguished publishers of the age—and also one of the most demanding.

At age thirty-four, Verne sent the manuscript of his first novel, *Five Weeks in a Balloon*, to Hetzel. As critic Roger Cardinal explains, "Hetzel was delighted with Verne's approach and at once offered him a long-term contract: the arrangement, involving a commitment to produce two books a year, was to last for the rest of the author's life and established his financial security." Thus began the Voyages

Extraordinaires, or Extraordinary Voyages, the works for which Verne is best known. He would go on to write dozens of these novels and works of nonfiction, with more appearing after his death. The novelist Jane Smiley writes that Hetzel was "strong, almost dictatorial" as an editor, and he resisted any attempt on "Verne's part to depict France, to have a less than happy ending," or to "include any sort of sex or complex male-female relations." Hetzel knew his audience, and he understood the bottom line. Lottman writes that "Hetzel would nurture Verne, making sure that his writing contained just the right mix of erudition and discovery."

Hetzel's domineering influence on Verne's work may have inhibited the author in some regards, but as with any constraint placed on a great artist, it also enhanced his work in surprising ways. For instance, Verne originally conceived Captain Nemo as a Polish exile seeking revenge for the loss of his family in the Polish January Uprising against imperial Russia in 1863 (some of this hidden story remains, as when we see "the portrait of a woman, still young, and two little children . . . Nemo looked at them for some moments, stretched his arms toward them, and, kneeling down, burst into deep sobs"). Ever the businessman, Hetzel wanted to avoid ruffling political feathers and forced Verne to scour Nemo of nationality and motivation, which had the beneficial effect of transforming Nemo into an alluring enigma while adding a much-needed aura of inscrutability to the novel in which he appears. Although Hetzel "had a reputation as the publisher of serious writers like Balzac, Hugo, and Proudhon," Cardinal insists that "it has to be acknowledged that Verne's books were largely conceived as money-spinners targeting a wide popular audience." Yet it is hardly to Verne's detriment that he made money from his books, many of which have endured in a manner that few of the self-consciously literary novels of his time have not.

Verne's life nicely matches that of the Victorian era of the late nineteenth century. The British established an empire that spanned North America, Australia, India, and Africa. The French colonial empire of the time—diminished from its height—included swathes of western Africa, Madagascar, and Southeast Asia. The industrial revolution spurred expansion of cities, brought about new technologies, and drove a golden age of invention. Verne lived to see the fantastic tales he pioneered taken up by others. H. Rider Haggard's outlandish African epic *King Solomon's Mines* appeared in 1885. The English author H. G. Wells (another contender to the title "father of science fiction") arrived in 1895 with *The Time Machine*, followed by *The Island of Dr. Moreau* (1896), *The Invisible Man* (1897), *The War of the Worlds* (1898), and *The First Men in the Moon* (1901), though Verne felt Wells failed to ground his stories in established scientific fact. In 1912 Sir Arthur Conan Doyle published *The Lost World*, about a South American plateau where dinosaurs still reigned. H. P. Lovecraft mimicked Verne's journeys to the poles in his terrifying scientific novella *At the Mountains of Madness* in 1931, long after the regions themselves had been explored.

Verne created a new type of character to populate his new type of novel. Cardinal labels his heroes "cerebral" adventurers. They are scholars, scientists, and cultured gentlemen, not soldiers, pirates, or knights. Still, they are heroic after the fashion of the time. Men like Verne and his characters—who deem conquest of the unknown to be among the highest virtues—belong to what the historian Oswald Spengler called "Faustian civilization," endlessly and tragically striving for new frontiers. While these frontiers lasted, they piqued Verne's curiosity. He was perfectly at home in the industrial age. He delightedly announced that the Victorian era was "witness to the most astonishing discoveries" and once declared, "I get as much pleasure out of watching a steam engine or a beautiful locomotive in motion as I do contemplating a painting by Raphael or Correggio."

Jules Verne's characters span the globe in search of knowledge, revenge, or merely to win a bet, but Verne himself never strayed far from France. He saw Italy and Scandinavia, Scotland, and other countries in Europe. He visited the north coast of Africa and made a brief trip to America on the SS *Great Eastern*, the largest ship ever built at the time; the ship inspired his 1871 novel *A Floating City*, and was used to lay the first lasting transatlantic telegraph cable. He toured New York City and made a short jaunt by rail to Niagara Falls. The globe-spanning journeys of the novels occurred only in his mind. It is a testament to his abilities, and to his everlasting credit, that they appear so credible to us even today.

## *SCIENCE FICTION OR FACT?*

Translator and biographer William Butcher insists that "Verne is *not* a science-fiction writer: most of his books contain *no* innovative science. He did not write for children." Smiley agrees, noting that "because his plots were exciting and exotic, he was pegged as a boy's novelist," though Verne "did not see his work as 'science-fiction.'" This is true, to a point. Verne's most famous "invention," the submarine *Nautilus*, was inspired by early prototype submarines such as Robert Fulton's 1800 *Nautilus* and the experimental *Plongeur*, exhibited at the 1867 Exposition Universelle. However, primitive submarines of one sort or another had been around for some time when Verne dreamed up the *Nautilus*. Nevertheless, it is hard to argue that Verne was not a science-fiction writer, even if the term itself usually refers to a later genre. It is true that much of the science Verne deployed was already commonly known, but it is rarely the main point, even if science—whether geography, oceanography, astronomy, or new applications in engineering, ballistics, and transportation—is essential to his method of storytelling. Smiley adds that "what Verne was always interested in was not exactly the goal (the center of the earth, for example) but the journey. He is writing in the tradition of *Candide* and even *Don Quixote*." He wrote episodic adventures, a style as old as literature. His great innovation was the use of science and technology to move his stories forward and make them believable.

Verne was also at times a futurist. In 1863 he wrote *Paris in the Twentieth Century*, which Hetzel suppressed on the grounds that it was preposterous and not commercially viable. The novel was not published until 1994, 131 years after it was written. Verne envisioned Paris in 1960 packed with skyscrapers (perhaps not Paris, but many cities would spawn such prodigious skylines), where society is dominated by the demands of business and technology. In his 1865 novel *From the Earth to the Moon* and its 1870 sequel *Around the Moon*, Verne launches his heroes in a capsule from Florida. They visit the moon and eventually splash down in the ocean to be picked up by a U.S. Navy vessel. This prefigures NASA's Mercury, Gemini, and Apollo missions in the

1960s with one significant difference: Verne's characters are shot out of a giant gun. Novelists are not prophets; they are storytellers. Verne used science to excite readers. His love of technical detail, awareness of contemporary scientific theories, and trust in scientific advancement saturate his books, as one finds when the imperturbable Professor Liedenbrock of *A Journey to the Center of the Earth* proclaims: "When science has uttered her voice, let babblers hold their peace." It is worth noting, however, that later in life Verne took a grimmer view of scientific progress in novels like *Robur the Conqueror* (1886) and its sequel *Master of the World* (1904).

Verne's fame and wealth grew throughout his life. He earned considerable income from stage adaptations of his novels. He purchased a yacht, the *Saint-Michel*, which he would upgrade with the larger *Saint-Michel II* and even larger *Saint-Michel III*. He enjoyed leisurely cruises, during which he would take copious notes for his works. Most of his life is believed to have been spent in productive domestic tranquility. Sadly, in 1886 events turned against Verne. His deranged twenty-five-year-old nephew Gaston shot him in the leg; Gaston was dispatched to an asylum for the remainder of his life while the family tried to keep the affair quiet. The following year, both his mother Sophie and publisher Hetzel died. Verne turned to local politics in Amiens, where he lived the remainder of his life, and served admirably as town councilor for fifteen years, even as he continued to write and publish. He died at home in 1905.

## FIVE WEEKS IN A BALLOON

Jules Verne's first novel, *Five Weeks in a Balloon*, was published in 1863 as *Cinq semaines en ballon* and translated into English for the first time six years later. Edgar Allan Poe's stories "The Balloon Hoax" and "The Unparalleled Adventures of One Hans Pfaal," translated in 1856 by the poet Charles Baudelaire, may have served as inspiration for *Five Weeks in a Balloon*, but nothing prepared readers for Verne's maiden Extraordinary Voyage. It is the first novel of its kind, joining exhilarating adventure with persuasive (though speculative) scientific theory. Lottman believes Verne wrote "the 'new kind of novel,' a book so different from anything he or anyone else had done or tried to do until then, it seems an amazing achievement." It was an overnight success and was adapted into a long-running play in Paris, celebrated for its extravagant sets and the use of a live elephant. Of his many novels, only *Around the World in Eighty Days* would sell more copies.

As with many of Verne's works, the heroes of *Five Weeks in a Balloon* start out in rather tame surroundings—the Royal Geographical Society of London—only to journey into what were then considered wild, uncivilized regions. Dr. Ferguson, a scientific genius and intrepid explorer, recruits his "easy, logical, [and] natural" manservant Joe and the "open, resolute, and headstrong" (but reluctant) Scottish sportsman Kennedy for a bold attempt to traverse Africa—then only partly explored and barely understood by Europeans—by balloon from the island of Zanzibar on the east coast to the French territories on the Atlantic Ocean in the west. For this purpose, Ferguson invents a device that allows his balloon—the *Victoria*, named after Britain's queen—to easily change altitude without relieving the craft of ballast or increasing the amount of gas. Like Verne, Ferguson sees progress as inevitable, or, as he puts it, "because, what cannot be done in one way, should be tried in another."

Ferguson is a man of fate. "He claimed that he was impelled, rather than drawn by his own volition, to journey as he did," like a "locomotive, which does not direct itself, but is guided and directed by the track it runs on." His motto "Excelsior!" (meaning "ever higher") captures the sense of unbridled progress that marked the thinking of the age. The principal goal of his expedition is to link the voyages of Sir Richard Burton and John Hanning Speke in East Africa with those of the German explorer Heinrich Barth in the Sahara in order to locate the fabled and long-sought source of the Nile River, which had thus far eluded explorers, many of whom died trying to find it. Readers would have known that a trip across Africa in a balloon could hardly be accomplished without some danger. In fact, Verne provides an African martyrology, a gruesome catalog of explorers who died of thirst, disease, or at the hands of native African populations, who were understandably less than pleased with European incursions.

> The tribes inhabiting the region seemed excited and hostile; they
> manifested more anger than adoration, and evidently saw in the aeronauts
> only obtrusive strangers, and not condescending deities. It appeared as
> though, in approaching the sources of the Nile, these men came to rob
> them of something.

During their journey Ferguson and crew cross over the great lakes of Africa (including Lake Victoria), treacherous mountain peaks, and the legendary ancient city of Timbuktu. Because so much of the journey takes place over then-unmapped territory, Verne was obliged to invent landscapes. He incorrectly compares the lush grassland of the savanna to the surface of the moon. Verne may be forgiven this, as the book is, after all, a work of imaginative literature, speculating about worlds unknown.

Along the way, the trio finds itself ensnared in a variety of perilous situations, as when their anchor inadvertently hooks a bull elephant in high grass, or when they descend to liberate a missionary about to be ritually sacrificed by a cannibal tribe. They are harassed by squadrons of giant condors and find themselves drifting listlessly, like the Ancient Mariner, without wind or water over an endless wasteland. *Five Weeks in a Balloon* contains action scenes worthy of a blockbuster Hollywood film, as when Joe, pursued on horseback by a regiment of enraged and heavily armed Arab horsemen, leaps in the nick of time from his exhausted horse directly onto a rope ladder dangling from the balloon.

> Joe clung with all his strength to the ladder during the wide oscillations that
> it had to describe, and then making an indescribable gesture to the Arabs,
> and climbing with the agility of a monkey, he sprang up to his companions,
> who received him with open arms.

Amusingly, the novel anticipates news of the actual discovery of the source of the Nile. In fact, Speke's book *Journal of the Discovery of the Source of the Nile* appeared only a few months after the fictional Ferguson is credited with the feat.

*Five Weeks in a Balloon* is an astounding first novel, but it is not without defects. Verne's labored descriptions of the balloon sometimes slows the novel's pace, and his depictions of native African cultures—of which he would have known little or nothing—may seem coarse and even, at times, repugnant to modern sensibilities. Nonetheless, Verne forged a lasting story of perseverance that changed expectations of what a novel could achieve. After several false starts, he had also begun on one of the most spectacular and successful literary careers of all time.

# A JOURNEY TO THE CENTER
# OF THE EARTH

A*Journey to the Center of the Earth*, the third Extraordinary Voyage, was published by Hetzel in 1864 as *Voyage au centre de la Terre*, appearing in English translation in 1871. Brian Taves and Jean-Michel Margot describe it as "one of Verne's most enduring and mythically powerful works." Indeed, the novel displays affinities with ancient stories about travel to the underworld, such as Homer's *Odyssey*, Virgil's *Aeneid*, the myths of Persephone and Orpheus, and, later, Dante's *Inferno*, though in Verne's vision the underworld has been scrubbed, for the most part, of any specific mythical and religious significance. Rather, it is perceived geologically by Professor Liedenbrock, a German who hopes to be the first to publish a book on the subject. Hollow-earth theories are as old as human civilization and persist to this day. Verne would have known of prominent advocates such as the Scottish physicist Sir John Leslie, who suggested that two suns resided at the earth's core. Another, the American John Cleves Symmes Jr., believed the earth consisted of several concentric shells with openings at each pole. Although modern science has completely disproven such notions, it hardly detracts from the wonderful tension Verne crafts as Liedenbrock and his skeptical nephew Axel (who tells the story) penetrate ever deeper into the earth's core and discover all manner of peculiar and seemingly impossible phenomena.

The story begins when Professor Liedenbrock happens upon a runic cryptogram concealed in an antiquarian volume of the poet of Snorre Turlleson's Icelandic saga *Heims Kringla*. After translating the runes into Latin letters, he is driven nearly mad in his efforts to decode the apparently meaningless words. Axel begins to worry for his uncle's health.

> When I awoke next morning that indefatigable worker was still at his post.
> His red eyes, his pale complexion, his hair tangled between his feverish
> fingers, the red spots on his cheeks, revealed his desperate struggle with
> impossibilities, and the weariness of spirit, the mental wrestlings he must
> have undergone all through that unhappy night.

Out of desperation Liedenbrock locks the house, with Axel and their maid Martha inside, until he can crack the code, but he meets with no success. In the first of several comic flourishes, young Axel discovers, while casually fanning himself with the parchment before a bright fire, that the bizarre characters reveal themselves as rough Latin sentences when viewed from the back. Read in reverse, they tell of a passage into the earth's center.

> Descend, bold traveler, into the crater of the jokul of Sneffels, which the shadow of Scartaris touches before the kalends of July, and you will attain the center of the earth; which I have done, Arne Saknussemm.

Liedenbrock is determined to retrace Saknussemm's steps, against all known scientific learning and common sense. Axel fears the message is a hoax, but he is enlisted by his unshakably confident uncle. As the ominous journey looms, Verne keeps his sense of humor, as when Martha inquires in a concerned way about the trip:

> "Is master mad?" she asked.
> I nodded my head.
> "And is he going to take you with him?"
> I nodded again.
> "Where to?"
> I pointed with my finger downward.
> "Down into the cellar?" cried the old servant.
> "No," I said. "Lower down than that."

Liedenbrock and Axel set out for Iceland, where they acquire a guide, Hans Bjelke, a "grave, phlegmatic, and silent individual" who leads them to the extinct volcano Sneffels. At the end of June, the shadow of the neighboring peak Scartaris points to the cave entrance. As they descend ever further they nearly expire of thirst before Hans locates a subterranean river and breaks through to it (it is boiling hot). At last, they emerge into an impossibly vast cavern that cradles an underground sea, with a ceiling so high that it contains clouds, all bathed in an eerie light supplied by electrically charged gas.

Liedenbrock indulges the European explorer's penchant for baptizing new discoveries (the boiling river is named the "Hansbach" in honor of Hans; he claims the sea as "Liedenbrock Sea" and later a small geyser island for Axel). They stroll beneath tree-sized mushrooms as Hans fashions a raft from petrified trees, then set sail on the Liedenbrock Sea, which they suspect may be "as wide as the Mediterranean." They witness a terrifying battle between an ichthyosaurus and a plesiosaurus, two colossal marine reptiles believed long extinct:

> Those huge creatures attacked each other with the greatest animosity. They heaved around them liquid mountains, which rolled even to our raft and rocked it perilously. Twenty times we were near capsizing.

Later, they drift helplessly into a titanic and terrifying storm:

> The most vivid flashes of lightning are mingled with the violent crash
> of continuous thunder. Ceaseless fiery arrows dart in and out among the
> flying thunderclouds; the vaporous mass soon glows with incandescent
> heat; hailstones rattle fiercely down, and as they dash upon our iron
> tools they too emit gleams and flashes of lurid light. The heaving waves
> resemble fiery volcanic hills, each belching forth its own interior flames,
> and every crest is plumed with dancing fire.

Verne is never more prone to fabulous contrivances than in *A Journey to the Center of the Earth*. In one chapter, Axel glimpses a colossal primitive man who shepherds woolly mammoths, a figure reminiscent of the Cyclops from the *Odyssey*. This is a rare example of Verne describing something that is simply not scientifically possible even by the standards of his own age. However, as Lottman points out, Verne includes an escape clause: "When Axel later recalls the discovery—for it is he who writes the log of their odyssey—he wonders whether they really saw this twelve-foot-tall superhuman specimen."

Like Odysseus and his crew, the three finally arrive back at the earth's surface, near Sicily, a great distance from the frozen volcano they entered.

> There were those who envied [Liedenbrock] his fame; and as his theories,
> resting upon known facts, were in opposition to the systems of science
> upon the question of the central fire, he sustained with his pen and by his
> voice remarkable discussions with the learned of every country.

Having trekked through the very bowels of the earth, meeting terrible monsters and suffering unthinkable deprivations, the professor is met with his just reward of scholarly recognition—a truly Vernian ending.

# TWENTY THOUSAND LEAGUES UNDER THE SEA

*Twenty Thousand Leagues Under the Sea* was first published in 1870 as *Vingt mille lieues sous les mers*, the sixth of Verne's Extraordinary Voyages. William Butcher recognizes it as "Verne's most ambitious novel in terms of the breadth and diversity of its themes and psychology." Indeed, it deserves to be considered his masterpiece, the novel with which he is most closely associated and which continues to exert the strongest pull on the popular imagination. It is more sweeping, lyrical, and elegiac than his other novels. It is where his imagination grows truly oceanic. Verne himself admitted, "I've never held a better thing in my hands." Part of his chronicle may have been shaped by Victor Hugo's 1866 novel *Toilers of the Sea*, which contains a battle with a massive octopus. It also exhibits certain kinships with Herman Melville's *Moby-Dick* (1851), a maritime epic whose principal character, Ahab, is, like Nemo, driven by madness toward his doom (both *Moby-Dick* and *Twenty Thousand Leagues Under the Sea* end with enormous whirlpools).

The novel begins with worldwide hysteria triggered by an "extraordinary creature" that defies all scientific explanation. "For some time past vessels had been met by 'an enormous thing,' a long object, spindle-shaped, occasionally phosphorescent, and infinitely larger and more rapid in its movements than a whale." The mythical depths of Verne's darkest novel are present from the start.

> In every place of great resort the monster was the fashion. They sang of it
> in the cafés, ridiculed it in the papers, and represented it on the stage. All
> kinds of stories were circulated regarding it. There appeared in the papers
> caricatures of every gigantic and imaginary creature, from the white whale,
> the terrible "Moby Dick" of sub-arctic regions, to the immense kraken,
> whose tentacles could entangle a ship of five hundred tons and hurry it into
> the abyss of the ocean. The legends of ancient times were even revived.

Dr. Arronax, a French marine scientist and author of *Mysteries of the Great Submarine Grounds*, is invited to join the crew of the American steam frigate *Abraham Lincoln*, a warship "of great speed" commissioned by the U.S. government to hunt down and destroy the monster. Unable to resist an opportunity to add to his store of aquatic knowledge, Arronax accepts the offer and brings his servant Conseil, who possesses a Linnaean ability to place animals according to zoological classification. Onboard, they meet Ned Land, a robust, broad-shouldered Canadian, "prince of harpooners," who is determined to add to his impressive tally of kills.

When the *Abraham Lincoln* finally confronts the monster, Ned Land hurls a harpoon that bounces from its side. Arronax recounts "a fearful shock followed, and, thrown over the rail without having time to stop myself, I fell into the sea." Land is also knocked overboard, while Conseil, ever loyal, dives after his master. As the stricken frigate drifts away, the three find themselves clinging for life to the metal shell of a submarine. They are soon taken captive by its crew (which speaks an unknown language) and meet the mysterious Captain Nemo, who agrees to allow them aboard his submarine, the *Nautilus*, as captive guests.

They proceed to travel around the globe—the 20,000 leagues of the title, which equals about 50,000 miles—astounded both by real and mythical wonders (it is actually helpful to have an atlas or globe handy while reading the book, in order to trace the progress of the *Nautilus*). Nemo's submarine is more of a gentleman's ancestral manor than a machine-age vessel, distinguished by what the *Encyclopedia of Science Fiction* describes as "Second Empire plushness . . . ornate luxury enabled by advanced technology." Unlike real submarines, the *Nautilus* is quite roomy, appointed with a library, parlors, and Nemo's pipe organ. Arronax describes Nemo's private museum:

> A luminous ceiling, decorated with light arabesques, shed a soft clear
> light over all the marvels accumulated in this museum. For it was in fact
> a museum, in which an intelligent and prodigal hand had gathered all the

treasures of nature and art, with the artistic confusion which distinguishes a painter's studio.

Arronax is drawn to the research possibilities of the *Nautilus* and begins to feel comfortable in its shell, like a snail, even as Ned Land doggedly pursues any possible avenue of escape. Together with Conseil, they attend undersea hunting excursions, reconnoiter sunken wrecks, cower as the *Nautilus* is boarded by curious cannibals, observe a solemn undersea burial in a coral grove, harvest coconut-sized pearls from giant clams, clash with sharks, visit the lost city of Atlantis (perched on the edge of an active underwater volcano that lights it in the darkness), attain the South Pole (Nemo plants a black flag emblazoned with an "N" more than forty years before the Norwegian Roald Amundsen actually set foot there), find themselves trapped inside a capsized iceberg (one of the novel's most powerful scenes), and battle gigantic squids.

Nemo, whose name means "no man" in Latin, is moody, prone to disappear for days at a time, his motives never properly understood by his guests.

> "Professor," replied the commander, quickly, "I am not what you call a civilized man! I have done with society entirely, for reasons which I alone have the right of appreciating. I do not, therefore, obey its laws, and I desire you never to allude to them before me again!"

When Arronax, Conseil, and Land are forced into their cabin and drugged, they realize that the *Nautilus* is being used not only for scientific good but also for violence: "Captain Nemo was not satisfied with shunning man. His formidable apparatus not only suited his instinct of freedom, but perhaps also the design of some terrible retaliation." Nemo's hatred of the surface world is matched by a devotion to the sea, as he expounds in one of the novel's finest passages.

> "Yes; I love it! The sea is everything. It covers seven tenths of the terrestrial globe. Its breath is pure and healthy . . . The sea is only the embodiment of a supernatural and wonderful existence. It is nothing but love and emotion; it is the 'Living Infinite,' as one of your poets has said . . . In it is supreme tranquility. The sea does not belong to despots. Upon its surface men can still exercise unjust laws, fight, tear one another to pieces, and be carried away with terrestrial horrors. But at thirty feet below its level, their reign ceases, their influence is quenched, and their power disappears."

We see the story through Aronnax's eyes, but it is quite possible that Verne saw something of himself in Nemo. Lottman suggests that "amateur psychologists would have a field day comparing the curiously withdrawn Jules Verne, who would become increasingly solitary, with this submarine captain, whose eccentricity the author had yet to explain." Verne's grandson Jean Jules-Verne once remarked that the author's three loves were "freedom, music, and the sea." Indeed, Nemo dedicates himself to the sea, cherishes his independence (his motto is "Mobilis in mobili," which can be translated from the Latin as "mobile in the mobile element"), and enjoys thundering away on his private pipe organ (he plays only the black keys, which gives his music a dark resonance).

The ocean world is at times placid, as when Conseil itemizes schools of flamboyantly colored fish through the observation window, and at other times downright terrifying. One of the book's most famous scenes is the attack of the giant squids, referred to as "poulps" in the present translation (*poulp* means "octopus" in French, but what Verne describes are squid). They are terrifyingly large and manage to carry off a crewmember; Verne may have been inspired by naturalist Pierre Denys de Montfort, who was fascinated by the idea of giant octopuses and claimed that some had pulled down whole ships.

> Before my eyes was a horrible monster worthy to figure in the legends
> of the marvelous. It was an immense cuttlefish, being eight yards long. It
> swam crossways in the direction of the *Nautilus* with great speed, watching
> us with its enormous staring green eyes. Its eight arms, or rather feet, fixed
> to its head, that have given the name of cephalopod to these animals, were
> twice as long as its body, and were twisted like the furies' hair.

At the novel's climax, the *Nautilus* is attacked by a warship that flies no national flag. When urged by Arronax not to sink it, Nemo's lashes out.

> "I am the law, and I am the judge! I am the oppressed, and there is the
> oppressor! Through him I have lost all that I loved, cherished, and
> venerated—country, wife, children, father, and mother. I saw all perish!
> All that I hate is there! Say no more!"

Nemo identifies with the downtrodden and seeks to help them. In the course of the novel he gives a bag of pearls to an exploited Ceylonese diver and later delivers a cache of gold, recovered from sunken ships, to Greeks, presumably to fund their uprising against Ottoman rule in the 1866–69 Cretan Revolt. As the emotional depth of Nemo's character is revealed, Arronax begins to see him in heroic and even mythical terms.

> Then Captain Nemo seemed to grow enormously, his features to assume
> superhuman proportions. He was no longer my equal, but a man of the
> waters, the genie of the sea.

At the novel's end, the *Nautilus* is dragged into a huge whirlpool off the coast of Norway, just after Arronax, Conseil, and Land finally manage to escape. The mysteries of Nemo's past, his motives, and the bizarre language used by his crew remain unexplained. Arronax muses on Nemo and wonders, almost hopefully, if he survived.

> But what has become of the *Nautilus*? Did it resist the pressure of the
> maelstrom? Does Captain Nemo still live? And does he still follow under
> the ocean those frightful retaliations? . . . Will the waves one day carry to
> him this manuscript containing the history of his life?

Nemo lives on as one of the most famous—and infamous—characters of the nineteenth century (he also appears in Verne's 1874 sequel, *The Mysterious Island*). He still intrigues us. We are disgusted by his violence yet charmed by his intelligence and moved by his sympathy for the oppressed. Like Arronax, we find ourselves forever lured back onto the *Nautilus*.

## AROUND THE WORLD IN EIGHTY DAYS

Verne's eleventh Extraordinary Voyage is *Around the World in Eighty Days*, published in 1873 as *Le tour dumonde en quatre-vingts jour*. *Twenty Thousand Leagues Under the Sea* may be Verne's masterpiece, but *Around the World in Eighty Days* remains his most popular. A comic novel inhabited by memorable characters, it speeds along at breakneck pace. It is the novel that sold best during Verne's lifetime. In fact, it was a sensation. Many readers believed that the journey was actually taking place as they read newspaper excerpts that preceded book publication. The final excerpt was cunningly scheduled to appear on December 22, 1872, the day the story ends. By the 1870s, Verne's heroes had journeyed to the moon and the seafloor, the icy poles and across Africa. There seemed to be no place left to map. The age of exploration had given way to the age of tourism. Instead of legendary discoveries, Verne is forced to convey the frantic and lonely pace of the modern world. As Butcher points out, "under its gay abandon . . . *Around the World in Eighty Days* is streaked with the melancholy of transitoriness."

The novel's hero, Phileas Fogg, is as inflexible and secretive as Nemo in his own way. He is a proper English gentleman who never deviates from his precise daily routine, which takes him from his home in Saville Row to the Reform Club, where he spends the day reading newspapers and playing whist, and then back home again. Nothing is known about him or how he acquired his fortune. "Phileas Fogg was a member of the Reform, and that was all."

> Was Phileas Fogg rich? Undoubtedly. But those who knew him best could not imagine how he had made his fortune, and Mr. Fogg was the last person to whom to apply for the information. He was not lavish, nor, on the contrary, avaricious . . . He was, in short, the least communicative of men.

His life is so exacting that he dismisses his servant "because that luckless youth had brought him shaving-water at eighty-four degrees Fahrenheit instead of eighty-six." The hapless valet is replaced by Passepartout, a Frenchman of many trades, including gymnastics instructor. He is "well-built, his body muscular, and his physical powers fully developed by the exercises of his younger days." He hopes to settle down to a quiet life as a gentleman's gentleman in London.

While playing whist, his only known pastime, Fogg finds himself embroiled in a debate about a recent bank robbery. A "gentleman of polished manners, and with a well-to-do air" has made off with a great deal of money from the Bank of England.

While a banker insists that the robber will be easily apprehended, others are less certain. They suggest that the world has "grown smaller" and that, consequently, a robber could avoid capture by moving to the far side of the globe very quickly. Fogg agrees and wagers that he can travel around the world in exactly eighty days. To the astonishment of his fellow clubmen, who accept his challenge, he dashes off straightaway. Passepartout, who "mechanically set about making the preparations for departure," wonders if his master is a fool, or if it is all an elaborate joke.

The wager may seem a frivolous reason to travel around the world, but it is more than a gimmick. It is important for two reasons. First, Fogg is an emblem of humdrum English life, a middle-aged bachelor without purpose. He seeks any justification to break out of his routine before it is too late to do so. Second, the world was, in a sense, shrinking in the Victorian era due to several developments: telegraph cables (news of Fogg's progress excites gamblers across England), canals (the Suez Canal opened in 1869), steamships, and railways such as the Great Indian Peninsula Railway and the American transcontinental railroad. Fogg, "calm and phlegmatic, with a clear eye" and "English composure" seems utterly isolated from his surroundings as he travels. Foreign cultures may not serve as impediments to his progress, but they do not have an appreciable effect on him either. In other words, he remains unmoved as he moves, a living symbol of British fortitude.

By the time Fogg reaches Suez, he is shadowed by a bumbling and persistently frustrated detective named Fix, who is convinced that Fogg is the gentlemanly bank robber. Unfortunately for Fix, he must adhere to the British rule of law in the empire's dominions, and the arrest warrants he requests from London invariably appear too late in each stage of the journey to be of any use. Delays and cancelations threaten Fogg's timetable, but at each setback he calmly proceeds by another method. The first major setback occurs when he learns that the train from Bombay (Mumbai) to Calcutta has not actually been completed as reported in the newspapers. Passengers are invited to disembark and walk fifty miles to the nearest railhead. Faced with a looming deadline, Fogg acquires an elephant and starts off again through the jungle. With the help of a British officer, Sir Francis Cromarty, who is on his way to rejoin a garrison at Benares, they rescue a young Indian woman, Aouda, about to be burned on the funeral pyre of her husband. Following a daring escape from the infuriated congregation, Fogg, Passepartout, and Aouda continue to make their way across Asia and America, moving steadily from one mishap to another, with the ever-determined Fix in tow.

*Around the World in Eighty Days* is defined by tensions between the ideal and the real. It shows how best-laid plans go astray. It is quite an achievement to conjure so much animated adventure from steamship timetables and railway delays, but it works splendidly. It is a sketch of the British Empire at its peak, envisioned by a Frenchman who never saw the regions himself. (Gonzague Saint Bris declares, "Jules Verne is the great bard of Victorian England.") Additionally, *Around the World in Eighty Days* allows Verne to venture one last great prediction. He saw an age in which tourists would dash from place to place, hardly absorbing their surroundings, before returning home again.

## *LEGACY*

Jules Verne is one of those rare authors whose creations have long outlived their creator. His stories have entered our minds from many directions. Even those who have never read his books will recognize the name Nemo. Verne foresaw a world obsessed with technology, where even those who choose to avoid it cannot escape its influence. John Derbyshire comments that "perhaps a better title for Verne is 'Father of Tech-Fi,' of stories that revolve around the fanciful possibilities of technology to harness nature's powers, to aid human adventure, and to rescue men from terrible perils." Some suggest that Verne profoundly changed the very ways in which we think. In a 1975 address to the U.S. Congress, the famed science-fiction writer Arthur C. Clarke observed that "we would not have had men on the moon if it had not been for Wells and Verne and the people who write about this and made people think about it."

On the occasion of a 2006 Smithsonian Institution Libraries exhibit dedicated to Verne, Norman Wolcott wrote that Verne was the first "to recognize that the new world of nineteenth-century scientific discovery offered a framework for adventure novels where the science of the day played an important role."

> Indeed the science was accurate, but it required a hundred years or more for technology to advance to the point where his inventions and adventures became reality. The traversal of the Arctic Ocean under the ice in 1959 by the USS *Nautilus* made a reality of the undersea adventures of Captain Nemo and his *Nautilus*. The Apollo project made *From the Earth to the Moon* . . . a preliminary exercise. Even the fanciful balloon voyage across Africa in *Five Weeks in a Balloon* pales in comparison with current around-the-world balloon exploits.

Verne's first novel imagined men floating almost helplessly across a largely unmapped Africa in search of the still-undiscovered sources of the Nile. By the time *Around the World in Eighty Days* was published, the planet had been crossed, demarcated, conquered, and exploited. The wonders Verne captured in *Five Weeks in a Balloon* were essentially gone by the end of his life. To this day, however, Verne challenges readers to explore new worlds while also mourning the passing of older, quieter ones, those immersed in mystery and ennobled by myth, which, like ours, are made up of stories. His novels may chart the disappearance of a world, but they also bring us the beginnings of a new one, the one we inherited from him.

Ernest Hilbert, PhD
Philadelphia, Pennsylvania
April 9, 2012

# Five Weeks in a Balloon

## CHAPTER I

There was a large audience assembled on the 14th of January, 1862, at the session of the Royal Geographical Society, No. 3 Waterloo Place, London. The president, Sir Francis M———, made an important communication to his colleagues, in an address that was frequently interrupted by applause.

This rare specimen of eloquence terminated with the following sonorous phrases bubbling over with patriotism:

"England has always marched at the head of nations" (for, the reader will observe, the nations always march at the head of each other), "by the intrepidity of her explorers in the line of geographical discovery." (General assent.) "Dr. Samuel Ferguson, one of her most glorious sons, will not reflect discredit on his origin." ("No, indeed!" from all parts of the hall.)

"This attempt, should it succeed" ("It will succeed!"), "will complete and link together the notions, as yet disjointed, which the world entertains of African cartology" (vehement applause); "and, should it fail, it will, at least, remain on record as one of the most daring conceptions of human genius!" (Tremendous cheering.)

"Huzza! Huzza!" shouted the immense audience, completely electrified by these inspiring words.

"Huzza for the intrepid Ferguson!" cried one of the most excitable of the enthusiastic crowd.

The wildest cheering resounded on all sides; the name of Ferguson was in every mouth, and we may safely believe that it lost nothing in passing through English throats. Indeed, the hall fairly shook with it.

And there were present, also, those fearless travelers and explorers whose energetic temperaments had borne them through every quarter of the globe, many of them grown old and worn out in the service of science. All had, in some degree, physically or morally, undergone the sorest trials. They had escaped shipwreck; conflagration; Indian tomahawks and war clubs; the fagot and the stake; nay, even the cannibal maws of the South Sea islanders. But still their hearts beat high during Sir Francis M———'s address, which certainly was the finest oratorical success that the Royal Geographical Society of London had yet achieved.

But, in England, enthusiasm does not stop short with mere words. It strikes off money faster than the dies of the Royal Mint itself. So a subscription to encourage Dr. Ferguson was voted there and then, and it at once attained the handsome amount of two thousand five hundred pounds. The sum was made commensurate with the importance of the enterprise.

A member of the Society then inquired of the president whether Dr. Ferguson was not to be officially introduced.

"The doctor is at the disposition of the meeting," replied Sir Francis.

"Let him come in, then! Bring him in!" shouted the audience. "We'd like to see a man of such extraordinary daring, face to face!"

"Perhaps this incredible proposition of his is only intended to mystify us," growled an apoplectic old admiral.

"Suppose that there should turn out to be no such person as Dr. Ferguson?" exclaimed another voice, with a malicious twang.

"Why, then, we'd have to invent one!" replied a facetious member of this grave Society.

"Ask Dr. Ferguson to come in," was the quiet remark of Sir Francis M——.

And come in the doctor did, and stood there, quite unmoved by the thunders of applause that greeted his appearance.

He was a man of about forty years of age, of medium height and physique. His sanguine temperament was disclosed in the deep color of his cheeks. His countenance was coldly expressive, with regular features, and a large nose—one of those noses that resemble the prow of a ship, and stamp the faces of men predestined to accomplish great discoveries. His eyes, which were gentle and intelligent, rather than bold, lent a peculiar charm to his physiognomy. His arms were long, and his feet were planted with that solidity which indicates a great pedestrian.

A calm gravity seemed to surround the doctor's entire person, and no one would dream that he could become the agent of any mystification, however harmless.

Hence, the applause that greeted him at the outset continued until he, with a friendly gesture, claimed silence on his own behalf. He stepped toward the seat that had been prepared for him on his presentation, and then, standing erect and motionless, he, with a determined glance, pointed his right forefinger upward, and pronounced aloud the single word—

"Excelsior!"

Never had one of Bright's or Cobden's sudden onslaughts, never had one of Palmerston's abrupt demands for funds to plate the rocks of the English coast with iron, made such a sensation. Sir Francis M——'s address was completely overshadowed. The doctor had shown himself moderate, sublime, and self-contained, in one; he had uttered the word of the situation—

"Excelsior!"

The gouty old admiral who had been finding fault was completely won over by the singular man before him, and immediately moved the insertion of Dr. Ferguson's speech in "The Proceedings of the Royal Geographical Society of London."

Who, then, was this person, and what was the enterprise that he proposed?

Ferguson's father, a brave and worthy captain in the English Navy, had associated his son with him, from the young man's earliest years, in the perils and adventures of his profession. The fine little fellow, who seemed to have never known the meaning of fear, early revealed a keen and active mind, an investigating intelligence, and a remarkable turn for scientific study; moreover, he disclosed uncommon address in extricating himself from difficulty; he was never perplexed, not even in handling his fork for the first time—an exercise in which children generally have so little success.

His fancy kindled early at the recitals he read of daring enterprise and maritime adventure, and he followed with enthusiasm the discoveries that signalized the first part of the nineteenth century. He mused over the glory of the Mungo Parks, the Bruces, the Caillies, the Levaillants, and to some extent, I verily believe, of Selkirk (Robinson Crusoe), whom he considered in no wise inferior to the rest. How many a well-employed hour he passed with that hero on his isle of Juan Fernandez! Often he criticized the ideas of the shipwrecked sailor, and sometimes discussed his plans and projects. He would have done differently, in such and such a case, or quite as well at least—of that he felt assured. But of one thing he was satisfied, that he never should have left that pleasant island, where he was as happy as a king without subjects—no, not if the inducement held out had been promotion to the first lordship in the admiralty!

It may readily be conjectured whether these tendencies were developed during a youth of adventure, spent in every nook and corner of the globe. Moreover, his father, who was a man of thorough instruction, omitted no opportunity to consolidate this keen intelligence by serious studies in hydrography, physics, and mechanics, along with a slight tincture of botany, medicine, and astronomy.

Upon the death of the estimable captain, Samuel Ferguson, then twenty-two years of age, had already made his voyage around the world. He had enlisted in the Bengalese Corps of Engineers, and distinguished himself in several affairs; but this soldier's life had not exactly suited him; caring but little for command, he had not been fond of obeying. He therefore sent in his resignation, and half botanizing, half playing the hunter, he made his way toward the north of the Indian Peninsula, and crossed it from Calcutta to Surat—a mere amateur trip for him.

From Surat we see him going over to Australia, and in 1845 participating in Captain Sturt's expedition, which had been sent out to explore the new Caspian Sea, supposed to exist in the center of New Holland.

Samuel Ferguson returned to England about 1850, and, more than ever possessed by the demon of discovery, he spent the intervening time, until 1853, in accompanying Captain McClure on the expedition that went around the American continent from Behring's Straits to Cape Farewell.

Notwithstanding fatigues of every description, and in all climates, Ferguson's constitution continued marvelously sound. He felt at ease in the midst of the most complete privations; in fine, he was the very type of the thoroughly accomplished explorer whose stomach expands or contracts at will; whose limbs grow longer or shorter according to the resting place that each stage of a journey may bring; who can fall asleep at any hour of the day or awake at any hour of the night.

Nothing, then, was less surprising, after that, than to find our traveler, in the period from 1855 to 1857, visiting the whole region west of the Thibet, in company with the brothers Schlagintweit, and bringing back some curious ethnographic observations from that expedition.

During these different journeys, Ferguson had been the most active and interesting correspondent of the *Daily Telegraph*, the penny newspaper whose circulation amounts to 140,000 copies, and yet scarcely suffices for its many legions of readers. Thus, the doctor had become well known to the public, although he could not claim membership in either of the Royal Geographical Societies of London, Paris, Berlin, Vienna, or St. Petersburg, or yet with the Travelers' Club, or even the Royal Polytechnic Institute, where his friend the statistician Cockburn ruled in state.

The latter savant had, one day, gone so far as to propose to him the following problem: Given the number of miles traveled by the doctor in making the circuit of the globe, how many more had his head described than his feet, by reason of the different lengths of the radii? Or, the number of miles traversed by the doctor's head and feet respectively being given, required the exact height of that gentleman?

This was done with the idea of complimenting him, but the doctor had held himself aloof from all the learned bodies—belonging, as he did, to the church militant and not to the church polemical. He found his time better employed in seeking than in discussing, in discovering rather than discoursing.

There is a story told of an Englishman who came one day to Geneva, intending to visit the lake. He was placed in one of those odd vehicles in which the passengers sit side by side, as they do in an omnibus. Well, it so happened that the Englishman got a seat that left him with his back turned toward the lake. The vehicle completed its circular trip without his thinking to turn around once, and he went back to London delighted with the Lake of Geneva.

Doctor Ferguson, however, had turned around to look about him on his journeyings, and turned to such good purpose that he had seen a great deal. In doing so, he had simply obeyed the laws of his nature, and we have good reason to believe that he was, to some extent, a fatalist, but of an orthodox school of fatalism withal, that led him to rely upon himself and even upon Providence. He claimed that he was impelled, rather than drawn by his own volition, to journey as he did, and that he traversed the world like the locomotive, which does not direct itself, but is guided and directed by the track it runs on.

"I do not follow my route;" he often said, "it is my route that follows me."

The reader will not be surprised, then, at the calmness with which the doctor received the applause that welcomed him in the Royal Society. He was above all such trifles, having no pride, and less vanity. He looked upon the proposition addressed to him by Sir Francis M—— as the simplest thing in the world, and scarcely noticed the immense effect that it produced.

When the session closed, the doctor was escorted to the rooms of the Travelers' Club, in Pall Mall. A superb entertainment had been prepared there in his honor. The dimensions of the dishes served were made to correspond with the importance of the personage entertained, and the boiled sturgeon that figured at this magnificent repast was not an inch shorter than Dr. Ferguson himself.

Numerous toasts were offered and quaffed, in the wines of France, to the celebrated travelers who had made their names illustrious by their explorations of

African territory. The guests drank to their health or to their memory, in alphabetical order, a good old English way of doing the thing. Among those remembered thus, were: Abbadie, Adams, Adamson, Anderson, Arnaud, Baikie, Baldwin, Barth, Batouda, Beke, Beltram, Du Berba, Bimbachi, Bolognesi, Bolwik, Belzoni, Bonnemain, Brisson, Browne, Bruce, Brun-Rollet, Burchell, Burckhardt, Burton, Cailland, Caillie, Campbell, Chapman, Clapperton, Clot-Bey, Colomieu, Courval, Cumming, Cuny, Debono, Decken, Denham, Desavanchers, Dicksen, Dickson, Dochard, Du Chaillu, Duncan, Durand, Duroule, Duveyrier, D'Escayrac, De Lauture, Erhardt, Ferret, Fresnel, Galinier, Galton, Geoffroy, Golberry, Hahn, Halm, Harnier, Hecquart, Heuglin, Hornemann, Houghton, Imbert, Kauffmann, Knoblecher, Krapf, Kummer, Lafargue, Laing, Lafaille, Lambert, Lamiral, Lampriere, John Lander, Richard Lander, Lefebvre, Lejean, Levaillant, Livingstone, MacCarthy, Maggiar, Maizan, Malzac, Moffat, Mollien, Monteiro, Morrison, Mungo Park, Neimans, Overweg, Panet, Partarrieau, Pascal, Pearse, Peddie, Penney, Petherick, Poncet, Prax, Raffenel, Rabh, Rebmann, Richardson, Riley, Ritchey, Rochet d'Hericourt, Rongawi, Roscher, Ruppel, Saugnier, Speke, Steidner, Thibaud, Thompson, Thornton, Toole, Tousny, Trotter, Tuckey, Tyrwhitt, Vaudey, Veyssiere, Vincent, Vinco, Vogel, Wahlberg, Warrington, Washington, Werne, Wild, and last, but not least, Dr. Ferguson, who, by his incredible attempt, was to link together the achievements of all these explorers, and complete the series of African discovery.

# CHAPTER II

The Article in the *Daily Telegraph*—War Between the Scientific Journals—Mr. Petermann Backs His Friend Dr. Ferguson—Reply of the Savant Koner—Bets Made—Sundry Propositions Offered to the Doctor

On the next day, in its number of January 15th, the *Daily Telegraph* published an article couched in the following terms:

"Africa is, at length, about to surrender the secret of her vast solitudes; a modern Oedipus is to give us the key to that enigma which the learned men of sixty centuries have not been able to decipher. In other days, to seek the sources of the Nile—*fontes Nili quoerere*—was regarded as a mad endeavor, a chimera that could not be realized.

"Dr. Barth, in following out to Sudan the track traced by Denham and Clapperton; Dr. Livingstone, in multiplying his fearless explorations from the Cape of Good Hope to the basin of the Zambesi; Captains Burton and Speke, in the discovery of the great interior lakes, have opened three highways to modern civilization. *Their point of intersection*, which no traveler has yet been able to reach, is the very heart of Africa, and it is thither that all efforts should now be directed.

"The labors of these hardy pioneers of science are now about to be knit together by the daring project of Dr. Samuel Ferguson, whose fine explorations our readers have frequently had the opportunity of appreciating.

"This intrepid discoverer proposes to traverse all Africa from east to west *in a balloon*. If we are well informed, the point of departure for this surprising journey is to be the island of Zanzibar, upon the eastern coast. As for the point of arrival, it is reserved for Providence alone to designate.

"The proposal for this scientific undertaking was officially made, yesterday, at the rooms of the Royal Geographical Society, and the sum of twenty-five hundred pounds was voted to defray the expenses of the enterprise.

"We shall keep our readers informed as to the progress of this enterprise, which has no precedent in the annals of exploration."

As may be supposed, the foregoing article had an enormous echo among scientific people. At first, it stirred up a storm of incredulity; Dr. Ferguson passed for a purely chimerical personage of the Barnum stamp, who, after having gone through the United States, proposed to "do" the British Isles.

A humorous reply appeared in the February number of the *Bulletins de la Société Geographique* of Geneva, which very wittily showed up the Royal Society of London and their phenomenal sturgeon.

But Herr Petermann, in his *Mittheilungen*, published at Gotha, reduced the Geneva journal to the most absolute silence. Herr Petermann knew Dr. Ferguson personally, and guaranteed the intrepidity of his dauntless friend.

Besides, all manner of doubt was quickly put out of the question: preparations for the trip were set on foot at London; the factories of Lyons received a heavy order for the silk required for the body of the balloon; and, finally, the British government placed the transport ship *Resolute*, Captain Bennett, at the disposal of the expedition.

At once, upon word of all this, a thousand encouragements were offered, and felicitations came pouring in from all quarters. The details of the undertaking were published in full in the bulletins of the Geographical Society of Paris; a remarkable article appeared in the *Nouvelles Annales des Voyages, de la Géographie, de l'Histoire, et de l'Archaeologie de M. V. A. Malte-Brun* ("New Annals of Travels, Geography, History, and Archaeology, by M. V. A. Malte-Brun"); and a searching essay in the *Zeitschrift für Allgemeine Erdkunde*, by Dr. W. Koner, triumphantly demonstrated the feasibility of the journey, its chances of success, the nature of the obstacles existing, the immense advantages of the aerial mode of locomotion, and found fault with nothing but the selected point of departure, which it contended should be Massowah, a small port in Abyssinia, whence James Bruce, in 1768, started upon his explorations in search of the sources of the Nile. Apart from that, it mentioned, in terms of unreserved admiration, the energetic character of Dr. Ferguson, and the heart, thrice panoplied in bronze, that could conceive and undertake such an enterprise.

The North American Review could not, without some displeasure, contemplate so much glory monopolized by England. It therefore rather ridiculed the doctor's scheme, and urged him, by all means, to push his explorations as far as America, while he was about it.

In a word, without going over all the journals in the world, there was not a scientific publication, from the *Journal of Evangelical Missions* to the *Revue Algérienne et Coloniale*, from the *Annales de la Propagation de la Foi* to the *Church Missionary Intelligencer*, that had not something to say about the affair in all its phases.

Many large bets were made at London and throughout England generally, first, as to the real or supposititious existence of Dr. Ferguson; secondly, as to the trip itself, which, some contended, would not be undertaken at all, and which was really contemplated, according to others; thirdly, upon the success or failure of the enterprise; and fourthly, upon the probabilities of Dr. Ferguson's return. The betting books were covered with entries of immense sums, as though the Epsom races were at stake.

Thus, believers and unbelievers, the learned and the ignorant, alike had their eyes fixed on the doctor, and he became the lion of the day, without knowing that he carried such a mane. On his part, he willingly gave the most accurate information touching his project. He was very easily approached, being naturally the most affable man in the world. More than one bold adventurer presented himself, offering to share the dangers as well as the glory of the undertaking; but he refused them all, without giving his reasons for rejecting them.

Numerous inventors of mechanism applicable to the guidance of balloons came to propose their systems, but he would accept none; and, when he was asked whether he had discovered something of his own for that purpose, he constantly refused to give any explanation, and merely busied himself more actively than ever with the preparations for his journey.

## CHAPTER III

Dr. Ferguson had a friend—not another self, indeed, an alter ego, for friendship could not exist between two beings exactly alike.

But, if they possessed different qualities, aptitudes, and temperaments, Dick Kennedy and Samuel Ferguson lived with one and the same heart, and that gave them no great trouble. In fact, quite the reverse.

Dick Kennedy was a Scotchman, in the full acceptation of the word—open, resolute, and headstrong. He lived in the town of Leith, which is near Edinburgh, and, in truth, is a mere suburb of *Auld Reekie*. Sometimes he was a fisherman, but he was always and everywhere a determined hunter, and that was nothing remarkable for a son of Caledonia, who had known some little climbing among the Highland mountains. He was cited as a wonderful shot with the rifle, since not only could he split a bullet on a knife blade, but he could divide it into two such equal parts that, upon weighing them, scarcely any difference would be perceptible.

Kennedy's countenance strikingly recalled that of Herbert Glendinning, as Sir Walter Scott has depicted it in "The Monastery"; his stature was above six feet; full of grace and easy movement, he yet seemed gifted with herculean strength; a face embrowned by the sun; eyes keen and black; a natural air of daring courage; in fine, something sound, solid, and reliable in his entire person, spoke, at first glance, in favor of the bonny Scot.

The acquaintanceship of these two friends had been formed in India, when they belonged to the same regiment. While Dick would be out in pursuit of the tiger and the elephant, Samuel would be in search of plants and insects. Each could call himself expert in his own province, and more than one rare botanical specimen, that to science was as great a victory won as the conquest of a pair of ivory tusks, became the doctor's booty.

These two young men, moreover, never had occasion to save each other's lives, or to render any reciprocal service. Hence, an unalterable friendship. Destiny sometimes bore them apart, but sympathy always united them again.

Since their return to England they had been frequently separated by the doctor's distant expeditions; but, on his return, the latter never failed to go, not to *ask* for hospitality, but to bestow some weeks of his presence at the home of his crony Dick.

The Scot talked of the past; the doctor busily prepared for the future. The one looked back, the other forward. Hence, a restless spirit personified in Ferguson; perfect calmness typified in Kennedy—such was the contrast.

After his journey to the Thibet, the doctor had remained nearly two years without hinting at new explorations; and Dick, supposing that his friend's instinct for travel and thirst for adventure had at length died out, was perfectly enchanted. They would have ended badly, some day or other, he thought to himself; no matter what experience one has with men, one does not travel always with impunity among cannibals and wild beasts. So, Kennedy besought the doctor to tie up his bark for life, having done enough for science, and too much for the gratitude of men.

The doctor contented himself with making no reply to this. He remained absorbed in his own reflections, giving himself up to secret calculations, passing his nights among heaps of figures, and making experiments with the strangest-looking machinery, inexplicable to everybody but himself. It could readily be guessed, though, that some great thought was fermenting in his brain.

"What can he have been planning?" wondered Kennedy, when, in the month of January, his friend quitted him to return to London.

He found out one morning when he looked into the *Daily Telegraph*.

"Merciful Heaven!" he exclaimed. "The lunatic! The madman! Cross Africa in a balloon! Nothing but that was wanted to cap the climax! That's what he's been bothering his wits about these two years past!"

Now, reader, substitute for all these exclamation points, as many ringing thumps with a brawny fist upon the table, and you have some idea of the manual exercise that Dick went through while he thus spoke.

When his confidential maid-of-all-work, the aged Elspeth, tried to insinuate that the whole thing might be a hoax—

"Not a bit of it!" said he. "Don't I know my man? Isn't it just like him? Travel through the air! There, now, he's jealous of the eagles, next! No! I warrant you, he'll not do it! I'll find a way to stop him! He! Why if they'd let him alone, he'd start someday for the moon!"

On that very evening Kennedy, half alarmed, and half exasperated, took the train for London, where he arrived next morning.

Three-quarters of an hour later a cab deposited him at the door of the doctor's modest dwelling, in Soho Square, Greek Street. Forthwith he bounded up the steps and announced his arrival with five good, hearty, sounding raps at the door.

Ferguson opened, in person.

"Dick! You here?" he exclaimed, but with no great expression of surprise, after all.

"Dick himself!" was the response.

"What, my dear boy, you at London, and this the midseason of the winter shooting?"

"Yes! Here I am, at London!"

"And what have you come to town for?"

"To prevent the greatest piece of folly that ever was conceived."

"Folly!" said the doctor.

"Is what this paper says, the truth?" rejoined Kennedy, holding out the copy of the *Daily Telegraph*, mentioned above.

"Ah! That's what you mean, is it? These newspapers are great tattlers! But, sit down, my dear Dick."

"No, I won't sit down! Then, you really intend to attempt this journey?"

"Most certainly! All my preparations are getting along finely, and I—"

"Where are your traps? Let me have a chance at them! I'll make them fly! I'll put your preparations in fine order." And so saying, the gallant Scot gave way to a genuine explosion of wrath.

"Come, be calm, my dear Dick!" resumed the doctor. "You're angry at me because I did not acquaint you with my new project."

"He calls this his new project!"

"I have been very busy," the doctor went on, without heeding the interruption; "I have had so much to look after! But rest assured that I should not have started without writing to you."

"Oh, indeed! I'm highly honored."

"Because it is my intention to take you with me."

Upon this, the Scotchman gave a leap that a wild goat would not have been ashamed of among his native crags.

"Ah! Really, then, you want them to send us both to Bedlam!"

"I have counted positively upon you, my dear Dick, and I have picked you out from all the rest."

Kennedy stood speechless with amazement.

"After listening to me for ten minutes," said the doctor, "you will thank me!"

"Are you speaking seriously?"

"Very seriously."

"And suppose that I refuse to go with you?"

"But you won't refuse."

"But, suppose that I were to refuse?"

"Well, I'd go alone."

"Let us sit down," said Kennedy, "and talk without excitement. The moment you give up jesting about it, we can discuss the thing."

"Let us discuss it, then, at breakfast, if you have no objections, my dear Dick."

The two friends took their seats opposite to each other, at a little table with a plate of toast and a huge tea urn before them.

"My dear Samuel," said the sportsman, "your project is insane! It is impossible! It has no resemblance to anything reasonable or practicable!"

"That's for us to find out when we shall have tried it!"

"But trying it is exactly what you ought not to attempt."

"Why so, if you please?"

"Well, the risks, the difficulty of the thing."

"As for difficulties," replied Ferguson, in a serious tone, "they were made to be overcome; as for risks and dangers, who can flatter himself that he is to escape them? Everything in life involves danger; it may even be dangerous to sit down at one's own table, or to put one's hat on one's own head. Moreover, we must look upon what is to occur as having already occurred, and see nothing but the present in the future, for the future is but the present a little farther on."

"There it is!" exclaimed Kennedy, with a shrug. "As great a fatalist as ever!"

"Yes! But in the good sense of the word. Let us not trouble ourselves, then, about what fate has in store for us, and let us not forget our good old English proverb: 'The man who was born to be hung will never be drowned!'"

There was no reply to make, but that did not prevent Kennedy from resuming a series of arguments which may be readily conjectured, but which were too long for us to repeat.

"Well, then," he said, after an hour's discussion, "if you are absolutely determined to make this trip across the African continent—if it is necessary for your happiness, why not pursue the ordinary routes?"

"Why?" ejaculated the doctor, growing animated. "Because, all attempts to do so, up to this time, have utterly failed. Because, from Mungo Park, assassinated on the Niger, to Vogel, who disappeared in the Wadai country; from Oudney, who died at Murmur, and Clapperton, lost at Sackatou, to the Frenchman Maizan, who was cut to pieces; from Major Laing, killed by the Touaregs, to Roscher, from Hamburg, massacred in the beginning of 1860, the names of victim after victim have been inscribed on the lists of African martyrdom! Because, to contend successfully against the elements; against hunger, and thirst, and fever; against savage beasts, and still more savage men, is impossible! Because, what cannot be done in one way, should be tried in another. In fine, because what one cannot pass through directly in the middle, must be passed by going to one side or overhead!"

"If passing over it were the only question!" interposed Kennedy. "But passing high up in the air, doctor, there's the rub!"

"Come, then," said the doctor, "what have I to fear? You will admit that I have taken my precautions in such manner as to be certain that my balloon will not fall; but, should it disappoint me, I should find myself on the ground in the normal conditions imposed upon other explorers. But, my balloon will not deceive me, and we need make no such calculations."

"Yes, but you must take them into view."

"No, Dick. I intend not to be separated from the balloon until I reach the western coast of Africa. With it, everything is possible; without it, I fall back into the dangers and difficulties as well as the natural obstacles that ordinarily attend such an expedition: with it, neither heat, nor torrents, nor tempests, nor the simoom, nor unhealthy climates, nor wild animals, nor savage men, are to be feared! If I feel too hot, I can ascend; if too cold, I can come down. Should there be a mountain, I can pass over it; a precipice, I can sweep across it; a river, I can sail beyond it; a storm, I can rise away above it; a torrent, I can skim it like a bird! I can advance without fatigue, I can halt without need of repose! I can soar above the nascent cities! I can speed onward with the rapidity of a tornado, sometimes at the loftiest heights, sometimes only a hundred feet above the soil, while the map of Africa unrolls itself beneath my gaze in the great atlas of the world."

Even the stubborn Kennedy began to feel moved, and yet the spectacle thus conjured up before him gave him the vertigo. He riveted his eyes upon the doctor with wonder and admiration, and yet with fear, for he already felt himself swinging aloft in space.

"Come, come," said he, at last. "Let us see, Samuel. Then you have discovered the means of guiding a balloon?"

"Not by any means. That is a Utopian idea."

"Then, you will go—"

"Whithersoever Providence wills; but, at all events, from east to west."

"Why so?"

"Because I expect to avail myself of the trade winds, the direction of which is always the same."

"Ah! Yes, indeed!" said Kennedy, reflecting. "The trade winds—yes—truly—one might—there's something in that!"

"Something in it—yes, my excellent friend—there's *everything* in it. The English government has placed a transport at my disposal, and three or four vessels are to cruise off the western coast of Africa, about the presumed period of my arrival. In three months, at most, I shall be at Zanzibar, where I will inflate my balloon, and from that point we shall launch ourselves."

"We!" said Dick.

"Have you still a shadow of an objection to offer? Speak, friend Kennedy."

"An objection! I have a thousand; but among other things, tell me, if you expect to see the country. If you expect to mount and descend at pleasure, you cannot do so, without losing your gas. Up to this time no other means have been devised, and it is this that has always prevented long journeys in the air."

"My dear Dick, I have only one word to answer—I shall not lose one particle of gas."

"And yet you can descend when you please?"

"I shall descend when I please."

"And how will you do that?"

"Ah, ha! Therein lies my secret, friend Dick. Have faith, and let my device be yours—'Excelsior!'"

"'Excelsior' be it then," said the sportsman, who did not understand a word of Latin.

But he made up his mind to oppose his friend's departure by all means in his power, and so pretended to give in, at the same time keeping on the watch. As for the doctor, he went on diligently with his preparations.

## CHAPTER IV

The aerial line which Dr. Ferguson counted upon following had not been chosen at random; his point of departure had been carefully studied, and it was not without good cause that he had resolved to ascend at the island of Zanzibar. This island, lying near to the eastern coast of Africa, is in the sixth degree of south latitude, that is to say, four hundred and thirty geographical miles below the equator.

From this island the latest expedition, sent by way of the great lakes to explore the sources of the Nile, had just set out.

But it would be well to indicate what explorations Dr. Ferguson hoped to link together. The two principal ones were those of Dr. Barth in 1849, and of Lieutenants Burton and Speke in 1858.

Dr. Barth is a Hamburger, who obtained permission for himself and for his countryman Overweg to join the expedition of the Englishman Richardson. The latter was charged with a mission in the Soudan.

This vast region is situated between the fifteenth and tenth degrees of north latitude; that is to say, that, in order to approach it, the explorer must penetrate fifteen hundred miles into the interior of Africa.

Until then, the country in question had been known only through the journeys of Denham, of Clapperton, and of Oudney, made from 1822 to 1824. Richardson, Barth, and Overweg, jealously anxious to push their investigations farther, arrived at Tunis and Tripoli, like their predecessors, and got as far as Mourzouk, the capital of Fezzan.

They then abandoned the perpendicular line, and made a sharp turn westward toward Ghât, guided, with difficulty, by the Touaregs. After a thousand scenes of pillage, of vexation, and attacks by armed forces, their caravan arrived, in October, at the vast oasis of Asben. Dr. Barth separated from his companions, made an excursion to the town of Aghades, and rejoined the expedition, which resumed its march on the 12th of December. At length it reached the province of Damerghou; there the three travelers parted, and Barth took the road to Kano, where he arrived by dint of perseverance, and after paying considerable tribute.

In spite of an intense fever, he quitted that place on the 7th of March, accompanied by a single servant. The principal aim of his journey was to reconnoiter Lake Tchad, from which he was still three hundred and fifty miles distant. He therefore advanced toward the east, and reached the town of Zouricolo, in the Bornou country, which is the core of the great central empire of Africa. There he heard of the death of Richardson, who had succumbed to fatigue and privation. He next arrived at Kouka, the capital of Bornou, on the borders of the lake. Finally, at the end of three weeks, on the 14th of April, twelve months after having quitted Tripoli, he reached the town of Ngornou.

We find him again setting forth on the 29th of March, 1851, with Overweg, to visit the kingdom of Adamaoua, to the south of the lake, and from there he pushed on as far as the town of Yola, a little below nine degrees north latitude. This was the extreme southern limit reached by that daring traveler.

He returned in the month of August to Kouka; from there he successively traversed the Mandara, Barghimi, and Klanem countries, and reached his extreme limit in the east, the town of Masena, situated at seventeen degrees twenty minutes west longitude.

On the 25th of November, 1852, after the death of Overweg, his last companion, he plunged into the west, visited Sockoto, crossed the Niger, and finally reached Timbuctoo, where he had to languish, during eight long months, under vexations inflicted upon him by the sheik, and all kinds of ill treatment and wretchedness. But the presence of a Christian in the city could not long be tolerated, and the Foullans threatened to besiege it. The doctor, therefore, left it on the 17th of March, 1854, and fled to the frontier, where he remained for thirty-three days in the most abject destitution. He then managed to get back to Kano in November, thence to Kouka, where he resumed Denham's route after four months' delay. He regained Tripoli toward the close of August, 1855, and arrived in London on the 6th of September, the only survivor of his party.

Such was the venturesome journey of Dr. Barth.

Dr. Ferguson carefully noted the fact, that he had stopped at four degrees north latitude and seventeen degrees west longitude.

Now let us see what Lieutenants Burton and Speke accomplished in eastern Africa.

The various expeditions that had ascended the Nile could never manage to reach the mysterious source of that river. According to the narrative of the German doctor, Ferdinand Werne, the expedition attempted in 1840, under the auspices of Mehemet Ali, stopped at Gondokoro, between the fourth and fifth parallels of north latitude.

In 1855, Brun-Rollet, a native of Savoy, appointed consul for Sardinia in eastern Soudan, to take the place of Vaudey, who had just died, set out from Karthoum, and, under the name of Yacoub the merchant, trading in gums and ivory, got as far as Belenia, beyond the fourth degree, but had to return in ill health to Karthoum, where he died in 1857.

Neither Dr. Penney—the head of the Egyptian medical service, who, in a small steamer, penetrated one degree beyond Gondokoro, and then came back to die of exhaustion at Karthoum—nor Miani, the Venetian, who, turning the cataracts below Gondokoro, reached the second parallel—nor the Maltese trader, Andrea Debono, who pushed his journey up the Nile still farther—could work their way beyond the apparently impassable limit.

In 1859, M. Guillaume Lejean, intrusted with a mission by the French government, reached Karthoum by way of the Red Sea, and embarked upon the Nile with a retinue of twenty-one hired men and twenty soldiers, but he could not get past Gondokoro, and ran extreme risk of his life among the negro tribes, who were in full revolt. The expedition directed by M. d'Escayrac de Lauture made an equally unsuccessful attempt to reach the famous sources of the Nile.

This fatal limit invariably brought every traveler to a halt. In ancient times, the ambassadors of Nero reached the ninth degree of latitude, but in eighteen centuries only from five to six degrees, or from three hundred to three hundred and sixty geographical miles, were gained.

Many travelers endeavored to reach the sources of the Nile by taking their point of departure on the eastern coast of Africa.

Between 1768 and 1772 the Scotch traveler, Bruce, set out from Massowah, a port of Abyssinia, traversed the Tigre, visited the ruins of Axum, saw the sources of the Nile where they did not exist, and obtained no serious result.

In 1844, Dr. Krapf, an Anglican missionary, founded an establishment at Monbaz, on the coast of Zanguebar, and, in company with the Rev. Dr. Rebmann, discovered two mountain ranges three hundred miles from the coast. These were the mountains of Kilimandjaro and Kenia, which Messrs. de Heuglin and Thornton have partly scaled so recently.

In 1845, Maizan, the French explorer, disembarked, alone, at Bagamayo, directly opposite to Zanzibar, and got as far as Deje-la-Mhora, where the chief caused him to be put to death in the most cruel torment.

In 1859, in the month of August, the young traveler, Roscher, from Hamburg, set out with a caravan of Arab merchants, reached Lake Nyassa, and was there assassinated while he slept.

Finally, in 1857, Lieutenants Burton and Speke, both officers in the Bengal army, were sent by the London Geographical Society to explore the great African lakes, and on the 17th of June they quitted Zanzibar, and plunged directly into the west.

After four months of incredible suffering, their baggage having been pillaged, and their attendants beaten and slain, they arrived at Kazeh, a sort of central rendezvous for traders and caravans. They were in the midst of the country of the Moon, and there they collected some precious documents concerning the manners, government, religion, fauna, and flora of the region. They next made for the first of the great lakes, the one named Tanganayika, situated between the third and eighth degrees of south latitude. They reached it on the 14th of February, 1858, and visited the various tribes residing on its banks, the most of whom are cannibals.

They departed again on the 26th of May, and reentered Kazeh on the 20th of June. There Burton, who was completely worn out, lay ill for several months, during which time Speke made a push to the northward of more than three hundred miles, going as far as Lake Ukéréoué, which he came in sight of on the 3rd of August; but he could descry only the opening of it at latitude two degrees thirty minutes.

He reached Kazeh, on his return, on the 25th of August, and, in company with Burton, again took up the route to Zanzibar, where they arrived in the month of March in the following year. These two daring explorers then reembarked for England; and the Geographical Society of Paris decreed them its annual prize medal.

Dr. Ferguson carefully remarked that they had not gone beyond the second degree of south latitude, nor the twenty-ninth of east longitude.

The problem, therefore, was how to link the explorations of Burton and Speke with those of Dr. Barth, since to do so was to undertake to traverse an extent of more than twelve degrees of territory.

# CHAPTER V

KENNEDY'S DREAMS—ARTICLES AND PRONOUNS IN THE PLURAL—DICK'S
INSINUATIONS—A PROMENADE OVER THE MAP OF AFRICA—WHAT IS
CONTAINED BETWEEN TWO POINTS OF THE COMPASS—EXPEDITIONS NOW
ON FOOT—SPEKE AND GRANT—KRAPF, DE DECKEN, AND DE HEUGLIN

Dr. Ferguson energetically pushed the preparations for his departure, and in person superintended the construction of his balloon, with certain modifications; in regard to which he observed the most absolute silence. For a long time past he had been applying himself to the study of the Arab language and the various Mandingoe idioms, and, thanks to his talents as a polyglot, he had made rapid progress.

In the meanwhile his friend, the sportsman, never let him out of his sight—afraid, no doubt, that the doctor might take his departure, without saying a word to anybody. On this subject, he regaled him with the most persuasive arguments, which, however, did *not* persuade Samuel Ferguson, and wasted his breath in pathetic entreaties, by which the latter seemed to be but slightly moved. In fine, Dick felt that the doctor was slipping through his fingers.

The poor Scot was really to be pitied. He could not look upon the azure vault without a somber terror: when asleep, he felt oscillations that made his head reel; and every night he had visions of being swung aloft at immeasurable heights.

We must add that, during these fearful nightmares, he once or twice fell out of bed. His first care then was to show Ferguson a severe contusion that he had received on the cranium. "And yet," he would add, with warmth, "that was at the height of only three feet—not an inch more—and such a bump as this! Only think, then!"

This insinuation, full of sad meaning as it was, did not seem to touch the doctor's heart.

"We'll not fall," was his invariable reply.

"But, still, suppose that we *were* to fall!"

"We will *not* fall!"

This was decisive, and Kennedy had nothing more to say.

What particularly exasperated Dick was, that the doctor seemed completely to lose sight of his personality—of his—Kennedy's—and to look upon him as irrevocably destined to become his aerial companion. Not even the shadow of a doubt was ever suggested; and Samuel made an intolerable misuse of the first person plural:

"'We' are getting along; 'we' shall be ready on the ——; 'we' shall start on the ——," etc., etc.

And then there was the singular possessive adjective:

"'Our' balloon; 'our' car; 'our' expedition."

And the same in the plural, too:

"'Our' preparations; 'our' discoveries; 'our' ascensions."

Dick shuddered at them, although he was determined not to go; but he did not want to annoy his friend. Let us also disclose the fact that, without knowing exactly why himself, he had sent to Edinburgh for a certain selection of heavy clothing, and his best hunting gear and firearms.

One day, after having admitted that, with an overwhelming run of good luck, there *might* be one chance of success in a thousand, he pretended to yield entirely to the doctor's wishes; but, in order to still put off the journey, he opened the most varied series of subterfuges. He threw himself back upon questioning the utility of the expedition—its opportuneness, etc. This discovery of the sources of the Nile, was it likely to be of any use? Would one have really labored for the welfare of humanity? When, after all, the African tribes should have been civilized, would they be any happier? Were folks certain that civilization had not its chosen abode there rather than in Europe? Perhaps! And then, couldn't one wait a little longer? The trip across Africa would certainly be accomplished someday, and in a less hazardous manner—in another month, or in six months before the year was over, some explorer would undoubtedly come in—etc., etc.

These hints produced an effect exactly opposite to what was desired or intended, and the doctor trembled with impatience.

"Are you willing, then, wretched Dick—are you willing, false friend—that this glory should belong to another? Must I then be untrue to my past history; recoil before obstacles that are not serious; requite with cowardly hesitation what both the English government and the Royal Society of London have done for me?"

"But," resumed Kennedy, who made great use of that conjunction.

"But," said the doctor, "are you not aware that my journey is to compete with the success of the expeditions now on foot? Don't you know that fresh explorers are advancing toward the center of Africa?"

"Still—"

"Listen to me, Dick, and cast your eyes over that map."

Dick glanced over it, with resignation.

"Now, ascend the course of the Nile."

"I have ascended it," replied the Scotchman, with docility.

"Stop at Gondokoro."

"I am there."

And Kennedy thought to himself how easy such a trip was—on the map!

"Now, take one of the points of these dividers and let it rest upon that place beyond which the most daring explorers have scarcely gone."

"I have done so."

"And now look along the coast for the island of Zanzibar, in latitude six degrees south."

"I have it."

"Now, follow the same parallel and arrive at Kazeh."

"I have done so."

"Run up again along the thirty-third degree of longitude to the opening of Lake Ukéréoué, at the point where Lieutenant Speke had to halt."

"I am there; a little more, and I should have tumbled into the lake."

"Very good! Now, do you know what we have the right to suppose, according to the information given by the tribes that live along its shores?"

"I haven't the least idea."

"Why, that this lake, the lower extremity of which is in two degrees and thirty minutes, must extend also two degrees and a half above the equator."

"Really!"

"Well from this northern extremity there flows a stream which must necessarily join the Nile, if it be not the Nile itself."

"That is, indeed, curious."

"Then, let the other point of your dividers rest upon that extremity of Lake Ukéréoué."

"It is done, friend Ferguson."

"Now, how many degrees can you count between the two points?"

"Scarcely two."

"And do you know what that means, Dick?"

"Not the least in the world."

"Why, that makes scarcely one hundred and twenty miles—in other words, a nothing."

"Almost nothing, Samuel."

"Well, do you know what is taking place at this moment?"

"No, upon my honor, I do not."

"Very well, then, I'll tell you. The Geographical Society regards as very important the exploration of this lake of which Speke caught a glimpse. Under their auspices, Lieutenant (now Captain) Speke has associated with him Captain Grant, of the army in India; they have put themselves at the head of a numerous and well-equipped expedition; their mission is to ascend the lake and return to Gondokoro; they have received a subsidy of more than five thousand pounds, and the governor of the Cape of Good Hope has placed Hottentot soldiers at their disposal; they set out from Zanzibar at the close of October, 1860. In the meanwhile John Petherick, the English consul at the city of Karthoum, has received about seven hundred pounds from the foreign office; he is to equip a steamer at Karthoum, stock it with sufficient provisions, and make his way to Gondokoro; there, he will await Captain Speke's caravan, and be able to replenish its supplies to some extent."

"Well planned," said Kennedy.

"You can easily see, then, that time presses if we are to take part in these exploring labors. And that is not all, since, while some are thus advancing with sure steps to the discovery of the sources of the Nile, others are penetrating to the very heart of Africa."

"On foot?" said Kennedy.

"Yes, on foot," rejoined the doctor, without noticing the insinuation. "Doctor Krapf proposes to push forward, in the west, by way of the Djob, a river lying under the equator. Baron de Decken has already set out from Monbaz, has reconnoitered the mountains of Kenaia and Kilimandjaro, and is now plunging in toward the center."

"But all this time on foot?"

"On foot or on mules."

"Exactly the same, so far as I am concerned," ejaculated Kennedy.

"Lastly," resumed the doctor, "M. de Heuglin, the Austrian vice-consul at Karthoum, has just organized a very important expedition, the first aim of which is to search for the traveler Vogel, who, in 1853, was sent into the Soudan to associate himself with the labors of Dr. Barth. In 1856, he quitted Bornou, and determined to explore the unknown country that lies between Lake Tchad and Darfur. Nothing has been seen of him since that time. Letters that were received in Alexandria, in 1860, said that he was killed at the order of the king of Wadai; but other letters, addressed by Dr. Hartmann to the traveler's father, relate that, according to the recital of a felatah of Bornou, Vogel was merely held as a prisoner at Wara. All hope is not then lost. Hence, a committee has been organized under the presidency of the regent of Saxe-Cogurg-Gotha; my friend Petermann is its secretary; a national subscription has provided for the expense of the expedition, whose strength has been increased by the voluntary accession of several learned men, and M. de Heuglin set out from Massowah, in the month of June. While engaged in looking for Vogel, he is also to explore all the country between the Nile and Lake Tchad, that is to say, to knit together the operations of Captain Speke and those of Dr. Barth, and then Africa will have been traversed from east to west."*

"Well," said the canny Scot, "since everything is getting on so well, what's the use of our going down there?"

Dr. Ferguson made no reply, but contented himself with a significant shrug of the shoulders.

---

* After the departure of Dr. Ferguson, it was ascertained that M. de Heuglin, owing to some disagreement, took a route different from the one assigned to his expedition, the command of the latter having been transferred to Mr. Muntzinger.

## CHAPTER VI

A Servant—Match Him!—He Can See the Satellites of Jupiter—
Dick and Joe Hard at It—Doubt and Faith—The Weighing
Ceremony—Joe and Wellington—He Gets a Half-crown.

Dr. Ferguson had a servant who answered with alacrity to the name of Joe. He was an excellent fellow, who testified the most absolute confidence in his master, and the most unlimited devotion to his interests, even anticipating his wishes and orders, which were always intelligently executed. In fine, he was a Caleb without the growling, and a perfect pattern of constant good humor. Had he been made on purpose for the place, it could not have been better done. Ferguson put himself entirely in his hands, so far as the ordinary details of existence were concerned, and he did well. Incomparable, whole-souled Joe! A servant who orders your dinner; who likes what you like; who packs your trunk, without forgetting your socks or your linen; who has charge of your keys and your secrets, and takes no advantage of all this!

But then, what a man the doctor was in the eyes of this worthy Joe! With what respect and what confidence the latter received all his decisions! When Ferguson had spoken, he would be a fool who should attempt to question the matter. Everything he thought was exactly right; everything he said, the perfection of wisdom; everything he ordered to be done, quite feasible; all that he undertook, practicable; all that he accomplished, admirable. You might have cut Joe to pieces—not an agreeable operation, to be sure—and yet he would not have altered his opinion of his master.

So, when the doctor conceived the project of crossing Africa through the air, for Joe the thing was already done; obstacles no longer existed; from the moment when the doctor had made up his mind to start, he had arrived—along with his faithful attendant, too, for the noble fellow knew, without a word uttered about it, that he would be one of the party.

Moreover, he was just the man to render the greatest service by his intelligence and his wonderful agility. Had the occasion arisen to name a professor of gymnastics for the monkeys in the Zoological Garden (who are smart enough, by the way!), Joe would certainly have received the appointment. Leaping, climbing, almost flying— these were all sport to him.

If Ferguson was the head and Kennedy the arm, Joe was to be the right hand of the expedition. He had, already, accompanied his master on several journeys, and had a smattering of science appropriate to his condition and style of mind, but he was especially remarkable for a sort of mild philosophy, a charming turn of optimism. In his sight everything was easy, logical, natural, and, consequently, he could see no use in complaining or grumbling.

Among other gifts, he possessed a strength and range of vision that were perfectly surprising. He enjoyed, in common with Moestlin, Kepler's professor, the rare faculty of distinguishing the satellites of Jupiter with the naked eye, and of counting fourteen of the stars in the group of Pleiades, the remotest of them being only of the ninth magnitude. He presumed none the more for that; on the contrary, he made his bow to you, at a distance, and when occasion arose he bravely knew how to use his eyes.

With such profound faith as Joe felt in the doctor, it is not to be wondered at that incessant discussions sprang up between him and Kennedy, without any lack of respect to the latter, however.

One doubted, the other believed; one had a prudent foresight, the other blind confidence. The doctor, however, vibrated between doubt and confidence; that is to say, he troubled his head with neither one nor the other.

"Well, Mr. Kennedy," Joe would say.

"Well, my boy?"

"The moment's at hand. It seems that we are to sail for the moon."

"You mean the Mountains of the Moon, which are not quite so far off. But, never mind, one trip is just as dangerous as the other!"

"Dangerous! What! With a man like Dr. Ferguson?"

"I don't want to spoil your illusions, my good Joe; but this undertaking of his is nothing more nor less than the act of a madman. He won't go, though!"

"He won't go, eh? Then you haven't seen his balloon at Mitchell's factory in the Borough?"

"I'll take precious good care to keep away from it!"

"Well, you'll lose a fine sight, sir. What a splendid thing it is! What a pretty shape! What a nice car! How snug we'll feel in it!"

"Then you really think of going with your master?"

"I?" answered Joe, with an accent of profound conviction. "Why, I'd go with him wherever he pleases! Who ever heard of such a thing? Leave him to go off alone, after we've been all over the world together! Who would help him, when he was tired? Who would give him a hand in climbing over the rocks? Who would attend him when he was sick? No, Mr. Kennedy, Joe will always stick to the doctor!"

"You're a fine fellow, Joe!"

"But, then, you're coming with us!"

"Oh! Certainly," said Kennedy; "that is to say, I will go with you up to the last moment, to prevent Samuel even then from being guilty of such an act of folly! I will follow him as far as Zanzibar, so as to stop him there, if possible."

"You'll stop nothing at all, Mr. Kennedy, with all respect to you, sir. My master is no harebrained person; he takes a long time to think over what he means to do, and then, when he once gets started, the Evil One himself couldn't make him give it up."

"Well, we'll see about that."

"Don't flatter yourself, sir—but then, the main thing is, to have you with us. For a hunter like you, sir, Africa's a great country. So, either way, you won't be sorry for the trip."

"No, that's a fact, I shan't be sorry for it, if I can get this crazy man to give up his scheme."

"By the way," said Joe, "you know that the weighing comes off today."

"The weighing—what weighing?"

"Why, my master, and you, and I, are all to be weighed today!"

"What! Like horse jockeys?"

"Yes, like jockeys. Only, never fear, you won't be expected to make yourself lean, if you're found to be heavy. You'll go as you are."

"Well, I can tell you, I am not going to let myself be weighed," said Kennedy, firmly.

"But, sir, it seems that the doctor's machine requires it."

"Well, his machine will have to do without it."

"Humph! And suppose that it couldn't go up, then?"

"Egad! That's all I want!"

"Come! Come, Mr. Kennedy! My master will be sending for us directly."

"I shan't go."

"Oh! Now, you won't vex the doctor in that way!"

"Aye! That I will."

"Well!" said Joe with a laugh. "You say that because he's not here; but when he says to your face, 'Dick!' (with all respect to you, sir) 'Dick, I want to know exactly how much you weigh,' you'll go, I warrant it."

"No, I will *not* go!"

At this moment the doctor entered his study, where this discussion had been taking place; and, as he came in, cast a glance at Kennedy, who did not feel altogether at his ease.

"Dick," said the doctor, "come with Joe; I want to know how much you both weigh."

"But—"

"You may keep your hat on. Come!" And Kennedy went.

They repaired in company to the workshop of the Messrs. Mitchell, where one of those so-called Roman scales was in readiness. It was necessary, by the way, for the doctor to know the weight of his companions, so as to fix the equilibrium of his balloon; so he made Dick get up on the platform of the scales. The latter, without making any resistance, said, in an undertone:

"Oh! Well, that doesn't bind me to anything."

"One hundred and fifty-three pounds," said the doctor, noting it down on his tablets.

"Am I too heavy?"

"Why, no, Mr. Kennedy!" said Joe. "And then, you know, I am light to make up for it."

So saying, Joe, with enthusiasm, took his place on the scales, and very nearly upset them in his ready haste. He struck the attitude of Wellington where he is made to ape Achilles, at Hyde Park entrance, and was superb in it, without the shield.

"One hundred and twenty pounds," wrote the doctor.

"Ah! Ha!" said Joe, with a smile of satisfaction And why did he smile? He never could tell himself.

"It's my turn now," said Ferguson—and he put down one hundred and thirty-five pounds to his own account.

"All three of us," said he, "do not weigh much more than four hundred pounds."

"But, sir," said Joe, "if it was necessary for your expedition, I could make myself thinner by twenty pounds, by not eating so much."

"Useless, my boy!" replied the doctor. "You may eat as much as you like, and here's half a crown to buy you the ballast."

## CHAPTER VII

GEOMETRICAL DETAILS—CALCULATION OF THE CAPACITY OF THE BALLOON—
THE DOUBLE RECEPTACLE—THE COVERING—THE CAR—THE MYSTERIOUS
APPARATUS—THE PROVISIONS AND STORES—THE FINAL SUMMING UP

Dr. Ferguson had long been engaged upon the details of his expedition. It is easy to comprehend that the balloon—that marvelous vehicle which was to convey him through the air—was the constant object of his solicitude.

At the outset, in order not to give the balloon too ponderous dimensions, he had decided to fill it with hydrogen gas, which is fourteen and a half times lighter than common air. The production of this gas is easy, and it has given the greatest satisfaction hitherto in aerostatic experiments.

The doctor, according to very accurate calculations, found that, including the articles indispensable to his journey and his apparatus, he should have to carry a weight of 4,000 pounds; therefore he had to find out what would be the ascensional force of a balloon capable of raising such a weight, and, consequently, what would be its capacity.

A weight of four thousand pounds is represented by a displacement of the air amounting to forty-four thousand eight hundred and forty-seven cubic feet; or, in other words, forty-four thousand eight hundred and forty-seven cubic feet of air weigh about four thousand pounds.

By giving the balloon these cubic dimensions, and filling it with hydrogen gas, instead of common air—the former being fourteen and a half times lighter and weighing therefore only two hundred and seventy-six pounds—a difference of three thousand seven hundred and twenty-four pounds in equilibrium is produced; and it is this difference between the weight of the gas contained in the balloon and the weight of the surrounding atmosphere that constitutes the ascensional force of the former.

However, were the forty-four thousand eight hundred and forty-seven cubic feet of gas of which we speak, all introduced into the balloon, it would be entirely filled; but that would not do, because, as the balloon continued to mount into the more rarefied layers of the atmosphere, the gas within would dilate, and soon burst the cover containing it. Balloons, then, are usually only two-thirds filled.

But the doctor, in carrying out a project known only to himself, resolved to fill his balloon only one-half; and, since he had to carry forty-four thousand eight hundred and forty-seven cubic feet of gas, to give his balloon nearly double capacity he arranged it in that elongated, oval shape which has come to be preferred. The horizontal diameter was fifty feet, and the vertical diameter seventy-five feet. He thus obtained a spheroid, the capacity of which amounted, in round numbers, to ninety thousand cubic feet.

Could Dr. Ferguson have used two balloons, his chances of success would have been increased; for, should one burst in the air, he could, by throwing out ballast, keep himself up with the other. But the management of two balloons would, necessarily, be very difficult, in view of the problem how to keep them both at an equal ascensional force.

After having pondered the matter carefully, Dr. Ferguson, by an ingenious arrangement, combined the advantages of two balloons, without incurring their inconveniences. He constructed two of different sizes, and enclosed the smaller in the larger one. His external balloon, which had the dimensions given above, contained a less one of the same shape, which was only forty-five feet in horizontal, and sixty-eight feet in vertical diameter. The capacity of this interior balloon was only sixty-seven thousand cubic feet: it was to float in the fluid surrounding it. A valve opened from one balloon into the other, and thus enabled the aeronaut to communicate with both.

This arrangement offered the advantage, that if gas had to be let off, so as to descend, that which was in the outer balloon would go first; and, were it completely emptied, the smaller one would still remain intact. The outer envelope might then be cast off as a useless encumbrance; and the second balloon, left free to itself, would not offer the same hold to the currents of air as a half-inflated one must needs present.

Moreover, in case of an accident happening to the outside balloon, such as getting torn, for instance, the other would remain intact.

The balloons were made of a strong but light Lyons silk, coated with gutta-percha. This gummy, resinous substance is absolutely waterproof, and also resists acids and gas perfectly. The silk was doubled, at the upper extremity of the oval, where most of the strain would come.

Such an envelope as this could retain the inflating fluid for any length of time. It weighed half a pound per nine square feet. Hence the surface of the outside balloon being about eleven thousand six hundred square feet, its envelope weighed six hundred and fifty pounds. The envelope of the second, or inner, balloon, having nine thousand two hundred square feet of surface, weighed only about five hundred and ten pounds, or say eleven hundred and sixty pounds for both.

The network that supported the car was made of very strong hempen cord, and the two valves were the object of the most minute and careful attention, as the rudder of a ship would be.

The car, which was of a circular form and fifteen feet in diameter, was made of wickerwork, strengthened with a slight covering of iron, and protected below by a system of elastic springs, to deaden the shock of collision. Its weight, along with that of the network, did not exceed two hundred and fifty pounds.

In addition to the above, the doctor caused to be constructed two sheet-iron chests two lines in thickness. These were connected by means of pipes furnished with stopcocks. He joined to these a spiral, two inches in diameter, which terminated in two branch pieces of unequal length, the longer of which, however, was twenty-five feet in height and the shorter only fifteen feet.

These sheet-iron chests were embedded in the car in such a way as to take up the least possible amount of space. The spiral, which was not to be adjusted until some future moment, was packed up, separately, along with a very strong Buntzen electric battery. This apparatus had been so ingeniously combined that it did not weigh more than seven hundred pounds, even including twenty-five gallons of water in another receptacle.

The instruments provided for the journey consisted of two barometers, two thermometers, two compasses, a sextant, two chronometers, an artificial horizon, and an altazimuth, to throw out the height of distant and inaccessible objects.

The Greenwich Observatory had placed itself at the doctor's disposal. The latter, however, did not intend to make experiments in physics; he merely wanted to be able to know in what direction he was passing, and to determine the position of the principal rivers, mountains, and towns.

He also provided himself with three thoroughly tested iron anchors, and a light but strong silk ladder fifty feet in length.

He at the same time carefully weighed his stores of provision, which consisted of tea, coffee, biscuit, salted meat, and *pemmican*, a preparation which comprises many nutritive elements in a small space. Besides a sufficient stock of pure brandy, he arranged two water tanks, each of which contained twenty-two gallons.

The consumption of these articles would necessarily, little by little, diminish the weight to be sustained, for it must be remembered that the equilibrium of a balloon floating in the atmosphere is extremely sensitive. The loss of an almost insignificant weight suffices to produce a very noticeable displacement.

Nor did the doctor forget an awning to shelter the car, nor the coverings and blankets that were to be the bedding of the journey, nor some fowling pieces and rifles, with their requisite supply of powder and ball.

Here is the summing up of his various items, and their weight, as he computed it:

| | |
|---|---:|
| Ferguson | 135 pounds |
| Kennedy | 153 " |
| Joe | 120 " |
| Weight of the outside balloon | 650 " |
| Weight of the second balloon | 510 " |
| Car and network | 280 " |
| Anchors, instruments, awnings, and sundry utensils, guns, coverings, etc. | 190 " |
| Meat, *pemmican*, biscuits, tea, coffee, brandy | 386 " |
| Water | 400 " |
| Apparatus | 700 " |
| Weight of the hydrogen | 276 " |
| Ballast | 200 " |

4,000 pounds

Such were the items of the four thousand pounds that Dr. Ferguson proposed to carry up with him. He took only two hundred pounds of ballast for "unforeseen emergencies," as he remarked, since otherwise he did not expect to use any, thanks to the peculiarity of his apparatus.

## CHAPTER VIII

About the 10th of February, the preparations were pretty well completed; and the balloons, firmly secured, one within the other, were altogether finished. They had been subjected to a powerful pneumatic pressure in all parts, and the test gave excellent evidence of their solidity and of the care applied in their construction.

Joe hardly knew what he was about, with delight. He trotted incessantly to and fro between his home in Greek Street, and the Mitchell establishment, always full of business, but always in the highest spirits, giving details of the affair to people who did not even ask him, so proud was he, above all things, of being permitted to accompany his master. I have even a shrewd suspicion that what with showing the balloon, explaining the plans and views of the doctor, giving folks a glimpse of the latter, through a half-opened window, or pointing him out as he passed along the streets, the clever scamp earned a few half-crowns, but we must not find fault with him for that. He had as much right as anybody else to speculate upon the admiration and curiosity of his contemporaries.

On the 16th of February, the *Resolute* cast anchor near Greenwich. She was a screw propeller of eight hundred tons, a fast sailer, and the very vessel that had been sent out to the polar regions, to revictual the last expedition of Sir James Ross. Her commander, Captain Bennet, had the name of being a very amiable person, and he took a particular interest in the doctor's expedition, having been one of that gentleman's admirers for a long time. Bennet was rather a man of science than a man of war, which did not, however, prevent his vessel from carrying four carronades, that had never hurt anybody, to be sure, but had performed the most pacific duty in the world.

The hold of the *Resolute* was so arranged as to find a stowing place for the balloon. The latter was shipped with the greatest precaution on the 18th of February, and was then carefully deposited at the bottom of the vessel in such a way as to prevent accident. The car and its accessories, the anchors, the cords, the supplies, the water tanks, which were to be filled on arriving, all were embarked and put away under Ferguson's own eyes.

Ten tons of sulfuric acid and ten tons of iron filings were put on board for the future production of the hydrogen gas. The quantity was more than enough, but it was well to be provided against accident. The apparatus to be employed in manufacturing the gas, including some thirty empty casks, was also stowed away in the hold.

These various preparations were terminated on the 18th of February, in the evening. Two staterooms, comfortably fitted up, were ready for the reception of Dr.

Ferguson and his friend Kennedy. The latter, all the while swearing that he would not go, went on board with a regular arsenal of hunting weapons, among which were two double-barreled breech-loading fowling-pieces, and a rifle that had withstood every test, of the make of Purdey, Moore & Dickson, at Edinburgh. With such a weapon a marksman would find no difficulty in lodging a bullet in the eye of a chamois at the distance of two thousand paces. Along with these implements, he had two of Colt's six-shooters, for unforeseen emergencies. His powder case, his cartridge pouch, his lead, and his bullets did not exceed a certain weight prescribed by the doctor.

The three travelers got themselves to rights on board during the working hours of February 19th. They were received with much distinction by the captain and his officers, the doctor continuing as reserved as ever, and thinking of nothing but his expedition. Dick seemed a good deal moved, but was unwilling to betray it; while Joe was fairly dancing and breaking out in laughable remarks. The worthy fellow soon became the jester and merry-andrew of the boatswain's mess, where a berth had been kept for him.

On the 20th, a grand farewell dinner was given to Dr. Ferguson and Kennedy by the Royal Geographical Society. Commander Bennet and his officers were present at the entertainment, which was signalized by copious libations and numerous toasts. Healths were drunk, in sufficient abundance to guarantee all the guests a lifetime of centuries. Sir Francis M—— presided, with restrained but dignified feeling.

To his own supreme confusion, Dick Kennedy came in for a large share in the jovial felicitations of the night. After having drunk to the "intrepid Ferguson, the glory of England," they had to drink to "the no less courageous Kennedy, his daring companion."

Dick blushed a good deal, and that passed for modesty; whereupon the applause redoubled, and Dick blushed again.

A message from the queen arrived while they were at dessert. Her Majesty offered her compliments to the two travelers, and expressed her wishes for their safe and successful journey. This, of course, rendered imperative fresh toasts to "Her most gracious Majesty."

At midnight, after touching farewells and warm shaking of hands, the guests separated.

The boats of the *Resolute* were in waiting at the stairs of Westminster Bridge. The captain leaped in, accompanied by his officers and passengers, and the rapid current of the Thames, aiding the strong arms of the rowers, bore them swiftly to Greenwich. In an hour's time all were asleep on board.

The next morning, February 21st, at three o'clock, the furnaces began to roar; at five, the anchors were weighed, and the *Resolute*, powerfully driven by her screw, began to plow the water toward the mouth of the Thames.

It is needless to say that the topic of conversation with everyone on board was Dr. Ferguson's enterprise. Seeing and hearing the doctor soon inspired everybody with such confidence that, in a very short time, there was no one, excepting the incredulous Scotchman, on the steamer who had the least doubt of the perfect feasibility and success of the expedition.

During the long, unoccupied hours of the voyage, the doctor held regular sittings, with lectures on geographical science, in the officers' mess room. These young men felt an intense interest in the discoveries made during the last forty years in Africa; and the doctor related to them the explorations of Barth, Burton, Speke, and Grant, and depicted the wonders of this vast, mysterious country, now thrown open on all sides to the investigations of science. On the north, the young Duveyrier was exploring Sahara, and bringing the chiefs of the Touaregs to Paris. Under the inspiration of the French government, two expeditions were preparing, which, descending from the north, and coming from the west, would cross each other at Timbuctoo. In the south, the indefatigable Livingstone was still advancing toward the equator; and, since March, 1862, he had, in company with Mackenzie, ascended the river Rovoonia. The nineteenth century would, assuredly, not pass, contended the doctor, without Africa having been compelled to surrender the secrets she has kept locked up in her bosom for six thousand years.

But the interest of Dr. Ferguson's hearers was excited to the highest pitch when he made known to them, in detail, the preparations for his own journey. They took pleasure in verifying his calculations; they discussed them; and the doctor frankly took part in the discussion.

As a general thing, they were surprised at the limited quantity of provision that he took with him; and one day one of the officers questioned him on that subject.

"That peculiar point astonishes you, does it?" said Ferguson.

"It does, indeed."

"But how long do you think my trip is going to last? Whole months? If so, you are greatly mistaken. Were it to be a long one, we should be lost; we should never get back. But you must know that the distance from Zanzibar to the coast of Senegal is only thirty-five hundred—say four thousand miles. Well, at the rate of two hundred and forty miles every twelve hours, which does not come near the rapidity of our railroad trains, by traveling day and night, it would take only seven days to cross Africa!"

"But then you could see nothing, make no geographical observations, or reconnoiter the face of the country."

"Ah!" replied the doctor. "If I am master of my balloon—if I can ascend and descend at will, I shall stop when I please, especially when too violent currents of air threaten to carry me out of my way with them."

"And you will encounter such," said Captain Bennet. "There are tornadoes that sweep at the rate of more than two hundred and forty miles per hour."

"You see, then, that with such speed as that, we could cross Africa in twelve hours. One would rise at Zanzibar, and go to bed at St. Louis!"

"But," rejoined the officer, "could any balloon withstand the wear and tear of such velocity?"

"It has happened before," replied Ferguson.

"And the balloon withstood it?"

"Perfectly well. It was at the time of the coronation of Napoleon, in 1804. The aeronaut, Gernerin, sent up a balloon at Paris, about eleven o'clock in the evening. It bore the following inscription, in letters of gold: 'Paris, 25 Frimaire; year XIII; Coronation of the Emperor Napoleon by His Holiness, Pius VII.' On the next morning, the inhabitants of Rome saw the same balloon soaring above the Vatican, whence it crossed the Campagna, and finally fluttered down into the lake of Bracciano. So you see, gentlemen, that a balloon can resist such velocities."

"A balloon—that might be; but a man?" insinuated Kennedy.

"Yes, a man, too! For the balloon is always motionless with reference to the air that surrounds it. What moves is the mass of the atmosphere itself: for instance, one may light a taper in the car, and the flame will not even waver. An aeronaut in Garnerin's balloon would not have suffered in the least from the speed. But then I have no occasion to attempt such velocity; and if I can anchor to some tree, or some favorable inequality of the ground, at night, I shall not fail to do so. Besides, we take provision for two months with us, after all; and there is nothing to prevent our skillful huntsman here from furnishing game in abundance when we come to alight."

"Ah! Mr. Kennedy," said a young midshipman, with envious eyes, "what splendid shots you'll have!"

"Without counting," said another, "that you'll have the glory as well as the sport!"

"Gentlemen," replied the hunter, stammering with confusion, "I greatly—appreciate—your compliments—but they—don't—belong to me."

"You!" exclaimed everybody. "Don't you intend to go?"

"I am not going!"

"You won't accompany Dr. Ferguson?"

"Not only shall I not accompany him, but I am here so as to be present at the last moment to prevent his going."

Every eye was now turned to the doctor.

"Never mind him!" said the latter, calmly. "This is a matter that we can't argue with him. At heart he knows perfectly well that he is going."

"By Saint Andrew!" said Kennedy. "I swear—"

"Swear to nothing, friend Dick; you have been ganged and weighed—you and your powder, your guns, and your bullets; so don't let us say anything more about it."

And, in fact, from that day until the arrival at Zanzibar, Dick never opened his mouth. He talked neither about that nor about anything else. He kept absolutely silent.

## CHAPTER IX

THEY DOUBLE THE CAPE—THE FORECASTLE—A COURSE OF COSMOGRAPHY
BY PROFESSOR JOE—CONCERNING THE METHOD OF GUIDING BALLOONS—
HOW TO SEEK OUT ATMOSPHERIC CURRENTS—EUREKA

The *Resolute* plunged along rapidly toward the Cape of Good Hope, the weather continuing fine, although the sea ran heavier.

On the 30th of March, twenty-seven days after the departure from London, the Table Mountain loomed up on the horizon. Cape City, lying at the foot of an amphitheater of hills, could be distinguished through the ship's glasses, and soon the *Resolute* cast anchor in the port. But the captain touched there only to replenish his coal bunkers, and that was but a day's job. On the morrow, he steered away to the south'ard, so as to double the southernmost point of Africa, and enter the Mozambique Channel.

This was not Joe's first sea voyage, and so, for his part, he soon found himself at home on board; everybody liked him for his frankness and good humor. A considerable share of his master's renown was reflected upon him. He was listened to as an oracle, and he made no more mistakes than the next one.

So, while the doctor was pursuing his descriptive course of lecturing in the officers' mess, Joe reigned supreme on the forecastle, holding forth in his own peculiar manner, and making history to suit himself—a style of procedure pursued, by the way, by the greatest historians of all ages and nations.

The topic of discourse was, naturally, the aerial voyage. Joe had experienced some trouble in getting the rebellious spirits to believe in it; but, once accepted by them, nothing connected with it was any longer an impossibility to the imaginations of the seamen stimulated by Joe's harangues.

Our dazzling narrator persuaded his hearers that, after this trip, many others still more wonderful would be undertaken. In fact, it was to be but the first of a long series of superhuman expeditions.

"You see, my friends, when a man has had a taste of that kind of traveling, he can't get along afterward with any other; so, on our next expedition, instead of going off to one side, we'll go right ahead, going up, too, all the time."

"Humph! Then you'll go to the moon!" said one of the crowd, with a stare of amazement.

"To the moon!" exclaimed Joe. "To the moon! Pooh! That's too common. Everybody might go to the moon, that way. Besides, there's no water there, and you have to carry such a lot of it along with you. Then you have to take air along in bottles, so as to breathe."

"Ay! Ay! That's all right! But can a man get a drop of the real stuff there?" said a sailor who liked his toddy.

"Not a drop!" was Joe's answer. "No! Old fellow, not in the moon. But we're going to skip round among those little twinklers up there—the stars—and the splendid planets that my old man so often talks about. For instance, we'll commence with Saturn—"

"That one with the ring?" asked the boatswain.

"Yes! The wedding ring—only no one knows what's become of his wife!"

"What? Will you go so high up as that?" said one of the ship boys, gaping with wonder. "Why, your master must be Old Nick himself."

"Oh! No, he's too good for that."

"But, after Saturn—what then?" was the next inquiry of his impatient audience.

"After Saturn? Well, we'll visit Jupiter. A funny place that is, too, where the days are only nine hours and a half long—a good thing for the lazy fellows—and the years, would you believe it—last twelve of ours, which is fine for folks who have only six months to live. They get off a little longer by that."

"Twelve years!" ejaculated the boy.

"Yes, my youngster; so that in that country you'd be toddling after your mammy yet, and that old chap yonder, who looks about fifty, would only be a little shaver of four and a half."

"Blazes! That's a good 'un!" shouted the whole forecastle together.

"Solemn truth!" said Joe, stoutly.

"But what can you expect? When people will stay in this world, they learn nothing and keep as ignorant as bears. But just come along to Jupiter and you'll see. But they have to look out up there, for he's got satellites that are not just the easiest things to pass."

All the men laughed, but they more than half believed him. Then he went on to talk about Neptune, where seafaring men get a jovial reception, and Mars, where the military get the best of the sidewalk to such an extent that folks can hardly stand it. Finally, he drew them a heavenly picture of the delights of Venus.

"And when we get back from that expedition," said the indefatigable narrator, "they'll decorate us with the Southern Cross that shines up there in the Creator's button-hole."

"Ay, and you'd have well earned it!" said the sailors.

Thus passed the long evenings on the forecastle in merry chat, and during the same time the doctor went on with his instructive discourses.

One day the conversation turned upon the means of directing balloons, and the doctor was asked his opinion about it.

"I don't think," said he, "that we shall succeed in finding out a system of directing them. I am familiar with all the plans attempted and proposed, and not one has succeeded, not one is practicable. You may readily understand that I have occupied my mind with this subject, which was, necessarily, so interesting to me, but I have not been able to solve the problem with the appliances now known to mechanical science. We would have to discover a motive power of extraordinary force, and almost impossible lightness of machinery. And, even then, we could not resist atmospheric currents of any considerable strength. Until now, the effort has been rather to direct the car than the balloon, and that has been one great error."

"Still there are many points of resemblance between a balloon and a ship which is directed at will."

"Not at all," retorted the doctor, "there is little or no similarity between the two cases. Air is infinitely less dense than water, in which the ship is only half submerged, while the whole bulk of a balloon is plunged in the atmosphere, and remains motionless with reference to the element that surrounds it."

"You think, then, that aerostatic science has said its last word?"

"Not at all! Not at all! But we must look for another point in the case, and if we cannot manage to guide our balloon, we must, at least, try to keep it in favorable aerial currents. In proportion as we ascend, the latter become much more uniform and flow more constantly in one direction. They are no longer disturbed by the mountains and valleys that traverse the surface of the globe, and these, you know, are the chief cause of the variations of the wind and the inequality of their force. Therefore, these zones having been once determined, the balloon will merely have to be placed in the currents best adapted to its destination."

"But then," continued Captain Bennet, "in order to reach them, you must keep constantly ascending or descending. That is the real difficulty, doctor."

"And why, my dear captain?"

"Let us understand one another. It would be a difficulty and an obstacle only for long journeys, and not for short aerial excursions."

"And why so, if you please?"

"Because you can ascend only by throwing out ballast; you can descend only after letting off gas, and by these processes your ballast and your gas are soon exhausted."

"My dear sir, that's the whole question. There is the only difficulty that science need now seek to overcome. The problem is not how to guide the balloon, but how to take it up and down without expending the gas which is its strength, its lifeblood, its soul, if I may use the expression."

"You are right, my dear doctor; but this problem is not yet solved; this means has not yet been discovered."

"I beg your pardon, it *has* been discovered."

"By whom?"

"By me!"

"By you?"

"You may readily believe that otherwise I should not have risked this expedition across Africa in a balloon. In twenty-four hours I should have been without gas!"

"But you said nothing about that in England?"

"No! I did not want to have myself overhauled in public. I saw no use in that. I made my preparatory experiments in secret and was satisfied. I have no occasion, then, to learn anything more from them."

"Well! Doctor, would it be proper to ask what is your secret?"

"Here it is, gentlemen—the simplest thing in the world!"

The attention of his auditory was now directed to the doctor in the utmost degree as he quietly proceeded with his explanation.

# CHAPTER X

### FORMER EXPERIMENTS—THE DOCTOR'S FIVE RECEPTACLES— THE GAS CYLINDER—THE CALORIFERE—THE SYSTEM OF MANEUVERING—SUCCESS CERTAIN

"The attempt has often been made, gentlemen," said the doctor, "to rise and descend at will, without losing ballast or gas from the balloon. A French aeronaut, M. Meunier, tried to accomplish this by compressing air in an inner receptacle. A Belgian, Dr. Van Hecke, by means of wings and paddles, obtained a vertical power that would have sufficed in most cases, but the practical results secured from these experiments have been insignificant.

"I therefore resolved to go about the thing more directly; so, at the start, I dispensed with ballast altogether, excepting as a provision for cases of special emergency, such as the breakage of my apparatus, or the necessity of ascending very suddenly, so as to avoid unforeseen obstacles.

"My means of ascent and descent consist simply in dilating or contracting the gas that is in the balloon by the application of different temperatures, and here is the method of obtaining that result.

"You saw me bring on board with the car several cases or receptacles, the use of which you may not have understood. They are five in number.

"The first contains about twenty-five gallons of water, to which I add a few drops of sulfuric acid, so as to augment its capacity as a conductor of electricity, and then I decompose it by means of a powerful Buntzen battery. Water, as you know, consists of two parts of hydrogen to one of oxygen gas.

"The latter, through the action of the battery, passes at its positive pole into the second receptacle. A third receptacle, placed above the second one, and of double its capacity, receives the hydrogen passing into it by the negative pole.

"Stopcocks, of which one has an orifice twice the size of the other, communicate between these receptacles and a fourth one, which is called the *mixture reservoir*, since in it the two gases obtained by the decomposition of the water do really commingle. The capacity of this fourth tank is about forty-one cubic feet.

"On the upper part of this tank is a platinum tube provided with a stopcock.

"You will now readily understand, gentlemen, the apparatus that I have described to you is really a gas cylinder and blowpipe for oxygen and hydrogen, the heat of which exceeds that of a forge fire.

"This much established, I proceed to the second part of my apparatus. From the lowest part of my balloon, which is hermetically closed, issue two tubes a little distance apart. The one starts among the upper layers of the hydrogen gas, the other amid the lower layers.

"These two pipes are provided at intervals with strong jointings of india rubber, which enable them to move in harmony with the oscillations of the balloon.

"Both of them run down as far as the car, and lose themselves in an iron receptacle of cylindrical form, which is called the heat tank. The latter is closed at its two ends by two strong plates of the same metal.

"The pipe running from the lower part of the balloon runs into this cylindrical receptacle through the lower plate; it penetrates the latter and then takes the form of a helicoidal, or screw-shaped, spiral, the rings of which, rising one over the other, occupy nearly the whole of the height of the tank. Before again issuing from it, this spiral runs into a small cone with a concave base that is turned downward in the shape of a spherical cap.

"It is from the top of this cone that the second pipe issues, and it runs, as I have said, into the upper beds of the balloon.

"The spherical cap of the small cone is of platinum, so as not to melt by the action of the cylinder and blowpipe, for the latter are placed upon the bottom of the iron tank in the midst of the helicoidal spiral, and the extremity of their flame will slightly touch the cap in question.

"You all know, gentlemen, what a calorifere, to heat apartments, is. You know how it acts. The air of the apartments is forced to pass through its pipes, and is then released with a heightened temperature. Well, what I have just described to you is nothing more nor less than a calorifere.

"In fact, what is it that takes place? The cylinder once lighted, the hydrogen in the spiral and in the concave cone becomes heated, and rapidly ascends through the pipe that leads to the upper part of the balloon. A vacuum is created below, and it attracts the gas in the lower parts; this becomes heated in its turn, and is continually replaced; thus, an extremely rapid current of gas is established in the pipes and in the spiral, which issues from the balloon and then returns to it, and is heated over again, incessantly.

"Now, the cases increase 1/480 of their volume for each degree of heat applied. If, then, I force the temperature 18 degrees, the hydrogen of the balloon will dilate 18/480 or 1,614 cubic feet, and will, therefore, displace 1,614 more cubic feet of air, which will increase its ascensional power by 160 pounds. This is equivalent to throwing out that weight of ballast. If I augment the temperature by 180 degrees, the gas will dilate 180/480 and will displace 16,740 cubic feet more, and its ascensional force will be augmented by 1,600 pounds.

"Thus, you see, gentlemen, that I can easily effect very considerable changes of equilibrium. The volume of the balloon has been calculated in such manner that, when half inflated, it displaces a weight of air exactly equal to that of the envelope containing the hydrogen gas, and of the car occupied by the passengers, and all its apparatus and accessories. At this point of inflation, it is in exact equilibrium with the air, and neither mounts nor descends.

"In order, then, to effect an ascent, I give the gas a temperature superior to the temperature of the surrounding air by means of my cylinder. By this excess of heat it obtains a larger distention, and inflates the balloon more. The latter, then, ascends in proportion as I heat the hydrogen.

"The descent, of course, is effected by lowering the heat of the cylinder, and letting the temperature abate. The ascent would be, usually, more rapid than the descent; but that is a fortunate circumstance, since it is of no importance to me to descend rapidly, while, on the other hand, it is by a very rapid ascent that I avoid obstacles. The real danger lurks below, and not above.

"Besides, as I have said, I have a certain quantity of ballast, which will enable me to ascend more rapidly still, when necessary. My valve, at the top of the balloon, is nothing more nor less than a safety valve. The balloon always retains the same quantity of hydrogen, and the variations of temperature that I produce in the midst of this shut-up gas are, of themselves, sufficient to provide for all these ascending and descending movements.

"Now, gentlemen, as a practical detail, let me add this:

"The combustion of the hydrogen and of the oxygen at the point of the cylinder produces solely the vapor or steam of water. I have, therefore, provided the lower part of the cylindrical iron box with a scape-pipe, with a valve operating by means of a pressure of two atmospheres; consequently, so soon as this amount of pressure is attained, the steam escapes of itself.

"Here are the exact figures: 25 gallons of water, separated into its constituent elements, yield 200 pounds of oxygen and 25 pounds of hydrogen. This represents, at atmospheric tension, 1,800 cubic feet of the former and 3,780 cubic feet of the latter, or 5,670 cubic feet, in all, of the mixture. Hence, the stopcock of my cylinder, when fully open, expends 27 cubic feet per hour, with a flame at least six times as strong as that of the large lamps used for lighting streets. On an average, then, and in order to keep myself at a very moderate elevation, I should not burn more than nine cubic feet per hour, so that my twenty-five gallons of water represent six hundred and thirty-six hours of aerial navigation, or a little more than twenty-six days.

"Well, as I can descend when I please, to replenish my stock of water on the way, my trip might be indefinitely prolonged.

"Such, gentlemen, is my secret. It is simple, and, like most simple things, it cannot fail to succeed. The dilation and contraction of the gas in the balloon is my means of locomotion, which calls for neither cumbersome wings, nor any other mechanical motor. A calorifere to produce the changes of temperature, and a cylinder to generate the heat, are neither inconvenient nor heavy. I think, therefore, that I have combined all the elements of success."

Dr. Ferguson here terminated his discourse, and was most heartily applauded. There was not an objection to make to it; all had been foreseen and decided.

"However," said the captain, "the thing may prove dangerous."

"What matters that," replied the doctor, "provided that it be practicable?"

# CHAPTER XI

An invariably favorable wind had accelerated the progress of the *Resolute* toward the place of her destination. The navigation of the Mozambique Channel was especially calm and pleasant. The agreeable character of the trip by sea was regarded as a good omen of the probable issue of the trip through the air. Everyone looked forward to the hour of arrival, and sought to give the last touch to the doctor's preparations.

At length the vessel hove in sight of the town of Zanzibar, upon the island of the same name, and, on the 15th of April, at 11 o'clock in the morning, she anchored in the port.

The island of Zanzibar belongs to the imam of Muscat, an ally of France and England, and is, undoubtedly, his finest settlement. The port is frequented by a great many vessels from the neighboring countries.

The island is separated from the African coast only by a channel, the greatest width of which is but thirty miles.

It has a large trade in gums, ivory, and, above all, in "ebony," for Zanzibar is the great slave market. Thither converges all the booty captured in the battles which the chiefs of the interior are continually fighting. This traffic extends along the whole eastern coast, and as far as the Nile latitudes. Mr. G. Lejean even reports that he has seen it carried on, openly, under the French flag.

Upon the arrival of the *Resolute*, the English consul at Zanzibar came on board to offer his services to the doctor, of whose projects the European newspapers had made him aware for a month past. But, up to that moment, he had remained with the numerous phalanx of the incredulous.

"I doubted," said he, holding out his hand to Dr. Ferguson, "but now I doubt no longer."

He invited the doctor, Kennedy, and the faithful Joe, of course, to his own dwelling. Through his courtesy, the doctor was enabled to have knowledge of the various letters that he had received from Captain Speke. The captain and his companions had suffered dreadfully from hunger and bad weather before reaching the Ugogo country. They could advance only with extreme difficulty, and did not expect to be able to communicate again for a long time.

"Those are perils and privations which we shall manage to avoid," said the doctor.

The baggage of the three travelers was conveyed to the consul's residence. Arrangements were made for disembarking the balloon upon the beach at Zanzibar. There was a convenient spot, near the signal mast, close by an immense building, that would serve to shelter it from the east winds. This huge tower, resembling a tun standing on one end, beside which the famous Heidelberg tun would have seemed but a very ordinary barrel, served as a fortification, and on its platform were stationed Belootchees, armed with lances. These Belootchees are a kind of brawling, good-for-nothing Janizaries.

But, when about to land the balloon, the consul was informed that the population of the island would oppose their doing so by force. Nothing is so blind as fanatical passion. The news of the arrival of a Christian, who was to ascend into the air, was received with rage. The negroes, more exasperated than the Arabs, saw in this project an attack upon their religion. They took it into their heads that some mischief was meant to the sun and the moon. Now, these two luminaries are objects of veneration to the African tribes, and they determined to oppose so sacrilegious an enterprise.

The consul, informed of their intentions, conferred with Dr. Ferguson and Captain Bennet on the subject. The latter was unwilling to yield to threats, but his friend dissuaded him from any idea of violent retaliation.

"We shall certainly come out winners," he said. "Even the imam's soldiers will lend us a hand, if we need it. But, my dear captain, an accident may happen in a moment, and it would require but one unlucky blow to do the balloon an irreparable injury, so that the trip would be totally defeated; therefore we must act with the greatest caution."

"But what are we to do? If we land on the coast of Africa, we shall encounter the same difficulties. What are we to do?"

"Nothing is more simple," replied the consul. "You observe those small islands outside of the port; land your balloon on one of them; surround it with a guard of sailors, and you will have no risk to run."

"Just the thing!" said the doctor. "And we shall be entirely at our ease in completing our preparations."

The captain yielded to these suggestions, and the *Resolute* was headed for the island of Koumbeni. During the morning of the 16th April, the balloon was placed in safety in the middle of a clearing in the great woods, with which the soil is studded.

Two masts, eighty feet in height, were raised at the same distance from each other. Blocks and tackle, placed at their extremities, afforded the means of elevating the balloon, by the aid of a transverse rope. It was then entirely uninflated. The interior balloon was fastened to the exterior one, in such manner as to be lifted up in the same way. To the lower end of each balloon were fixed the pipes that served to introduce the hydrogen gas.

The whole day, on the 17th, was spent in arranging the apparatus destined to produce the gas; it consisted of some thirty casks, in which the decomposition of water was effected by means of iron filings and sulfuric acid placed together in a large quantity of the first-named fluid. The hydrogen passed into a huge central cask, after having been washed on the way, and thence into each balloon by the conduit pipes. In this manner each of them received a certain accurately ascertained quantity of gas. For this purpose, there had to be employed eighteen hundred and sixty-six pounds of sulfuric acid, sixteen thousand and fifty pounds of iron, and nine thousand one hundred and sixty-six gallons of water. This operation commenced on the following night, about three A.M., and lasted nearly eight hours. The next day, the balloon, covered with its network, undulated gracefully above its car, which was held to the ground by numerous sacks of earth. The inflating apparatus was put together with extreme care, and the pipes issuing from the balloon were securely fitted to the cylindrical case.

The anchors, the cordage, the instruments, the traveling wraps, the awning, the provisions, and the arms were put in the place assigned to them in the car. The supply of water was procured at Zanzibar. The two hundred pounds of ballast were distributed in fifty bags placed at the bottom of the car, but within arm's reach.

These preparations were concluded about five o'clock in the evening, while sentinels kept close watch around the island, and the boats of the *Resolute* patrolled the channel.

The blacks continued to show their displeasure by grimaces and contortions. Their *obi-men*, or wizards, went up and down among the angry throngs, pouring fuel on the flame of their fanaticism; and some of the excited wretches, more furious and daring than the rest, attempted to get to the island by swimming, but they were easily driven off.

Thereupon the sorceries and incantations commenced; the "rainmakers," who pretend to have control over the clouds, invoked the storms and the "stone showers," as the blacks call hail, to their aid. To compel them to do so, they plucked leaves of all the different trees that grow in that country, and boiled them over a slow fire, while, at the same time, a sheep was killed by thrusting a long needle into its heart. But, in spite of all their ceremonies, the sky remained clear and beautiful, and they profited nothing by their slaughtered sheep and their ugly grimaces.

The blacks then abandoned themselves to the most furious orgies, and got fearfully drunk on "tembo," a kind of ardent spirits drawn from the cocoa-nut tree, and an extremely heady sort of beer called "togwa." Their chants, which were destitute of all melody, but were sung in excellent time, continued until far into the night.

About six o'clock in the evening, the captain assembled the travelers and the officers of the ship at a farewell repast in his cabin. Kennedy, whom nobody ventured to question now, sat with his eyes riveted on Dr. Ferguson, murmuring indistinguishable words. In other respects, the dinner was a gloomy one. The approach of the final moment filled everybody with the most serious reflections. What had fate in store for these daring adventurers? Should they ever again find themselves in the midst of their friends, or seated at the domestic hearth? Were their traveling apparatus to fail, what would become of them, among those ferocious savage tribes, in regions that had never been explored, and in the midst of boundless deserts?

Such thoughts as these, which had been dim and vague until then, or but slightly regarded when they came up, returned upon their excited fancies with intense force at this parting moment. Dr. Ferguson, still cold and impassible, talked of this, that, and the other; but he strove in vain to overcome this infectious gloominess. He utterly failed.

As some demonstration against the personal safety of the doctor and his companions was feared, all three slept that night on board the *Resolute*. At six o'clock in the morning they left their cabin, and landed on the island of Koumbeni.

The balloon was swaying gently to and fro in the morning breeze; the sandbags that had held it down were now replaced by some twenty strong-armed sailors, and Captain Bennet and his officers were present to witness the solemn departure of their friends.

At this moment Kennedy went right up to the doctor, grasped his hand, and said:

"Samuel, have you absolutely determined to go?"

"Solemnly determined, my dear Dick."

"I have done everything that I could to prevent this expedition, have I not?"

"Everything!"

"Well, then, my conscience is clear on that score, and I will go with you."

"I was sure you would!" said the doctor, betraying in his features swift traces of emotion.

At last the moment of final leave-taking arrived. The captain and his officers embraced their dauntless friends with great feeling, not excepting even Joe, who, worthy fellow, was as proud and happy as a prince. Everyone in the party insisted upon having a final shake of the doctor's hand.

At nine o'clock the three travelers got into their car. The doctor lit the combustible in his cylinder and turned the flame so as to produce a rapid heat, and the balloon, which had rested on the ground in perfect equipoise, began to rise in a few minutes, so that the seamen had to slacken the ropes they held it by. The car then rose about twenty feet above their heads.

"My friends!" exclaimed the doctor, standing up between his two companions, and taking off his hat. "Let us give our aerial ship a name that will bring her good luck! Let us christen her *Victoria*!"

This speech was answered with stentorian cheers of "Huzza for the queen! Huzza for old England!"

At this moment the ascensional force of the balloon increased prodigiously, and Ferguson, Kennedy, and Joe waved a last good-bye to their friends.

"Let go all!" shouted the doctor, and at the word the *Victoria* shot rapidly up into the sky, while the four carronades on board the *Resolute* thundered forth a parting salute in her honor.

# CHAPTER XII

CROSSING THE STRAIT—THE MRIMA—DICK'S REMARK AND
JOE'S PROPOSITION—A RECIPE FOR COFFEEMAKING—THE UZARAMO—
THE UNFORTUNATE MAIZAN—MOUNT DATHUMI—THE DOCTOR'S
CARDS—NIGHT UNDER A NOPAL

The air was pure, the wind moderate, and the balloon ascended almost perpendicularly to a height of fifteen hundred feet, as indicated by a depression of two inches in the barometric column.

At this height a more decided current carried the balloon toward the southwest. What a magnificent spectacle was then outspread beneath the gaze of the travelers! The island of Zanzibar could be seen in its entire extent, marked out by its deeper color upon a vast planisphere; the fields had the appearance of patterns of different colors, and thick clumps of green indicated the groves and thickets.

The inhabitants of the island looked no larger than insects. The huzzaing and shouting were little by little lost in the distance, and only the discharge of the ship's guns could be heard in the concavity beneath the balloon, as the latter sped on its flight.

"How fine that is!" said Joe, breaking silence for the first time.

He got no reply. The doctor was busy observing the variations of the barometer and noting down the details of his ascent.

Kennedy looked on, and had not eyes enough to take in all that he saw.

The rays of the sun coming to the aid of the heating cylinder, the tension of the gas increased, and the *Victoria* attained the height of twenty-five hundred feet.

The *Resolute* looked like a mere cockleshell, and the African coast could be distinctly seen in the west marked out by a fringe of foam.

"You don't talk?" said Joe, again.

"We are looking!" said the doctor, directing his spyglass toward the mainland.

"For my part, I must talk!"

"As much as you please, Joe; talk as much as you like!"

And Joe went on alone with a tremendous volley of exclamations. The "ohs!" and the "ahs!" exploded one after the other, incessantly, from his lips.

During his passage over the sea the doctor deemed it best to keep at his present elevation. He could thus reconnoiter a greater stretch of the coast. The thermometer and the barometer, hanging up inside of the half-opened awning, were always within sight, and a second barometer suspended outside was to serve during the night watches.

At the end of about two hours the *Victoria*, driven along at a speed of a little more than eight miles, very visibly neared the coast of the mainland. The doctor, thereupon, determined to descend a little nearer to the ground. So he moderated the flame of his cylinder, and the balloon, in a few moments, had descended to an altitude only three hundred feet above the soil.

It was then found to be passing just over the Mrima country, the name of this part of the eastern coast of Africa. Dense borders of mango trees protected its margin, and the ebb tide disclosed to view their thick roots, chafed and gnawed by the teeth of the Indian Ocean. The sands which, at an earlier period, formed the coastline, rounded away along the distant horizon, and Mount Nguru reared aloft its sharp summit in the northwest.

The *Victoria* passed near to a village which the doctor found marked upon his chart as Kaole. Its entire population had assembled in crowds, and were yelling with anger and fear, at the same time vainly directing their arrows against this monster of the air that swept along so majestically away above all their powerless fury.

The wind was setting to the southward, but the doctor felt no concern on that score, since it enabled him the better to follow the route traced by Captains Burton and Speke.

Kennedy had, at length, become as talkative as Joe, and the two kept up a continual interchange of admiring interjections and exclamations.

"Out upon stagecoaches!" said one.

"Steamers indeed!" said the other.

"Railroads! Eh? Rubbish!" put in Kennedy. "That you travel on, without seeing the country!"

"Balloons! They're the sort for me!" Joe would add. "Why, you don't feel yourself going, and Nature takes the trouble to spread herself out before one's eyes!"

"What a splendid sight! What a spectacle! What a delight! A dream in a hammock!"

"Suppose we take our breakfast?" was Joe's unpoetical change of tune, at last, for the keen, open air had mightily sharpened his appetite.

"Good idea, my boy!"

"Oh! It won't take us long to do the cooking—biscuit and potted meat?"

"And as much coffee as you like," said the doctor. "I give you leave to borrow a little heat from my cylinder. There's enough and to spare, for that matter, and so we shall avoid the risk of a conflagration."

"That would be a dreadful misfortune!" ejaculated Kennedy. "It's the same as a powder magazine suspended over our heads."

"Not precisely," said Ferguson, "but still if the gas were to take fire it would burn up gradually, and we should settle down on the ground, which would be disagreeable; but never fear—our balloon is hermetically sealed."

"Let us eat a bite, then," replied Kennedy.

"Now, gentlemen," put in Joe, "while doing the same as you, I'm going to get you up a cup of coffee that I think you'll have something to say about."

"The fact is," added the doctor, "that Joe, along with a thousand other virtues, has a remarkable talent for the preparation of that delicious beverage: he compounds it of a mixture of various origin, but he never would reveal to me the ingredients."

"Well, master, since we are so far aboveground, I can tell you the secret. It is just to mix equal quantities of Mocha, of Bourbon coffee, and of Rio Nunez."

A few moments later, three steaming cups of coffee were served, and topped off a substantial breakfast, which was additionally seasoned by the jokes and repartees of the guests. Each one then resumed his post of observation.

The country over which they were passing was remarkable for its fertility. Narrow, winding paths plunged in beneath the overarching verdure. They swept along above cultivated fields of tobacco, maize, and barley, at full maturity, and here and there immense rice fields, full of straight stalks and purple blossoms. They could distinguish sheep and goats too, confined in large cages, set up on piles to keep them out of reach of the leopards' fangs. Luxuriant vegetation spread in wild profuseness over this prodigal soil.

Village after village rang with yells of terror and astonishment at the sight of the *Victoria*, and Dr. Ferguson prudently kept her above the reach of the barbarian arrows. The savages below, thus baffled, ran together from their huddle of huts and followed the travelers with their vain imprecations while they remained in sight.

At noon, the doctor, upon consulting his map, calculated that they were passing over the Uzaramo* country. The soil was thickly studded with coconut, pawpaw, and cottonwood trees, above which the balloon seemed to disport itself like a bird. Joe found this splendid vegetation a matter of course, seeing that they were in Africa. Kennedy descried some hares and quails that asked nothing better than to get a good shot from his fowling-piece, but it would have been powder wasted, since there was no time to pick up the game.

The aeronauts swept on with the speed of twelve miles per hour, and soon were passing in thirty-eight degrees twenty minutes east longitude, over the village of Tounda.

"It was there," said the doctor, "that Burton and Speke were seized with violent fevers, and for a moment thought their expedition ruined. And yet they were only a short distance from the coast, but fatigue and privation were beginning to tell upon them severely."

In fact, there is a perpetual malaria reigning throughout the country in question. Even the doctor could hope to escape its effects only by rising above the range of the miasma that exhales from this damp region whence the blazing rays of the sun pump up its poisonous vapors. Once in a while they could descry a caravan resting in a "kraal," awaiting the freshness and cool of the evening to resume its route. These kraals are wide patches of cleared land, surrounded by hedges and jungles, where traders take shelter against not only the wild beasts, but also the robber tribes of the country. They could see the natives running and scattering in all directions at the sight of the *Victoria*. Kennedy was keen to get a closer look at them, but the doctor invariably held out against the idea.

"The chiefs are armed with muskets," he said, "and our balloon would be too conspicuous a mark for their bullets."

"Would a bullet hole bring us down?" asked Joe.

"Not immediately; but such a hole would soon become a large torn orifice through which our gas would escape."

"Then, let us keep at a respectful distance from yon miscreants. What must they think as they see us sailing in the air? I'm sure they must feel like worshipping us!"

"Let them worship away, then," replied the doctor, "but at a distance. There is no harm done in getting as far away from them as possible. See! The country is already

---

* *U* and *Ou* signify country in the language of that region.

changing its aspect: the villages are fewer and farther between; the mango trees have disappeared, for their growth ceases at this latitude. The soil is becoming hilly and portends mountains not far off."

"Yes," said Kennedy, "it seems to me that I can see some high land on this side."

"In the west—those are the nearest ranges of the Ourizara—Mount Duthumi, no doubt, behind which I hope to find shelter for the night. I'll stir up the heat in the cylinder a little, for we must keep at an elevation of five or six hundred feet."

"That was a grant idea of yours, sir," said Joe. "It's mighty easy to manage it; you turn a cock, and the thing's done."

"Ah! Here we are more at our ease," said the sportsman, as the balloon ascended; "the reflection of the sun on those red sands was getting to be insupportable."

"What splendid trees!" cried Joe. "They're quite natural, but they are very fine! Why, a dozen of them would make a forest!"

"Those are baobabs," replied Dr. Ferguson. "See, there's one with a trunk fully one hundred feet in circumference. It was, perhaps, at the foot of that very tree that Maizan, the French traveler, expired in 1845, for we are over the village of Deje-la-Mhora, to which he pushed on alone. He was seized by the chief of this region, fastened to the foot of a baobab, and the ferocious black then severed all his joints while the war song of his tribe was chanted; he then made a gash in the prisoner's neck, stopped to sharpen his knife, and fairly tore away the poor wretch's head before it had been cut from the body. The unfortunate Frenchman was but twenty-six years of age."

"And France has never avenged so hideous a crime?" said Kennedy.

"France did demand satisfaction, and the Said of Zanzibar did all in his power to capture the murderer, but in vain."

"I move that we don't stop here!" urged Joe. "Let us go up, master, let us go up higher by all means."

"All the more willingly, Joe, that there is Mount Duthumi right ahead of us. If my calculations be right, we shall have passed it before seven o'clock in the evening."

"Shall we not travel at night?" asked the Scotchman.

"No, as little as possible. With care and vigilance we might do so safely, but it is not enough to sweep across Africa. We want to see it."

"Up to this time we have nothing to complain of, master. The best cultivated and most fertile country in the world instead of a desert! Believe the geographers after that!"

Let us wait, Joe! We shall see by and by."

About half-past six in the evening the *Victoria* was directly opposite Mount Duthumi; in order to pass, it had to ascend to a height of more than three thousand feet, and to accomplish that the doctor had only to raise the temperature of his gas eighteen degrees. It might have been correctly said that he held his balloon in his hand. Kennedy had only to indicate to him the obstacles to be surmounted, and the *Victoria* sped through the air, skimming the summits of the range.

At eight o'clock it descended the farther slope, the acclivity of which was much less abrupt. The anchors were thrown out from the car and one of them, coming in contact with the branches of an enormous nopal, caught on it firmly. Joe at once let himself slide down the rope and secured it. The silk ladder was then lowered to him and he remounted to the car with agility. The balloon now remained perfectly at rest sheltered from the eastern winds.

The evening meal was got ready, and the aeronauts, excited by their day's journey, made a heavy onslaught upon the provisions.

"What distance have we traversed today?" asked Kennedy, disposing of some alarming mouthfuls.

The doctor took his bearings, by means of lunar observations, and consulted the excellent map that he had with him for his guidance. It belonged to the atlas of *Der Neuester Endeckungen in Afrika* (*The Latest Discoveries in Africa*), published at Gotha by his learned friend Dr. Petermann, and by that savant sent to him. This atlas was to serve the doctor on his whole journey; for it contained the itinerary of Burton and Speke to the great lakes; the Soudan, according to Dr. Barth; the Lower Senegal, according to Guillaume Lejean; and the Delta of the Niger, by Dr. Blaikie.

Ferguson had also provided himself with a work which combined in one compilation all the notions already acquired concerning the Nile. It was entitled *The Sources of the Nile; Being a General Survey of the Basin of That River and of Its Head-Stream, with the History of the Nilotic Discovery*, by Charles Beke, D.D.

He also had the excellent charts published in the *Bulletins of the Geographical Society of London*; and not a single point of the countries already discovered could, therefore, escape his notice.

Upon tracing on his maps, he found that his latitudinal route had been two degrees, or one hundred and twenty miles, to the westward.

Kennedy remarked that the route tended toward the south; but this direction was satisfactory to the doctor, who desired to reconnoiter the tracks of his predecessors as much as possible. It was agreed that the night should be divided into three watches, so that each of the party should take his turn in watching over the safety of the rest. The doctor took the watch commencing at nine o'clock; Kennedy, the one commencing at midnight; and Joe, the three o'clock morning watch.

So Kennedy and Joe, well wrapped in their blankets, stretched themselves at full length under the awning, and slept quietly; while Dr. Ferguson kept on the lookout.

## CHAPTER XIII

CHANGE OF WEATHER—KENNEDY HAS THE FEVER—THE DOCTOR'S
MEDICINE—TRAVELS ON LAND—THE BASIN OF IMENGÉ—MOUNT RUBEHO—
SIX THOUSAND FEET ELEVATION—A HALT IN THE DAYTIME

The night was calm. However, on Saturday morning, Kennedy, as he awoke, complained of lassitude and feverish chills. The weather was changing. The sky, covered with clouds, seemed to be laying in supplies for a fresh deluge. A gloomy region is that Zungomoro country, where it rains continually, excepting, perhaps, for a couple of weeks in the month of January.

A violent shower was not long in drenching our travelers. Below them, the roads, intersected by "nullahs," a sort of instantaneous torrent, were soon rendered impracticable, entangled as they were, besides, with thorny thickets and gigantic lianas, or creeping vines. The sulfuretted hydrogen emanations, which Captain Burton mentions, could be distinctly smelled.

"According to his statement, and I think he's right," said the doctor, "one could readily believe that there is a corpse hidden behind every thicket."

"An ugly country this!" sighed Joe. "And it seems to me that Mr. Kennedy is none the better for having passed the night in it."

"To tell the truth, I have quite a high fever," said the sportsman.

"There's nothing remarkable about that, my dear Dick, for we are in one of the most unhealthy regions in Africa; but we shall not remain here long; so let's be off."

Thanks to a skillful maneuver achieved by Joe, the anchor was disengaged, and Joe reascended to the car by means of the ladder. The doctor vigorously dilated the gas, and the *Victoria* resumed her flight, driven along by a spanking breeze.

Only a few scattered huts could be seen through the pestilential mists; but the appearance of the country soon changed, for it often happens in Africa that some of the unhealthiest districts lie close beside others that are perfectly salubrious.

Kennedy was visibly suffering, and the fever was mastering his vigorous constitution.

"It won't do to fall ill, though," he grumbled; and so saying, he wrapped himself in a blanket, and lay down under the awning.

"A little patience, Dick, and you'll soon get over this," said the doctor.

"Get over it! Egad, Samuel, if you've any drug in your traveling chest that will set me on my feet again, bring it without delay. I'll swallow it with my eyes shut!"

"Oh, I can do better than that, friend Dick; for I can give you a febrifuge that won't cost anything."

"And how will you do that?"

"Very easily. I am simply going to take you up above these clouds that are now deluging us, and remove you from this pestilential atmosphere. I ask for only ten minutes, in order to dilate the hydrogen."

The ten minutes had scarcely elapsed ere the travelers were beyond the rainy belt of country.

"Wait a little, now, Dick, and you'll begin to feel the effect of pure air and sunshine."

"There's a cure for you!" said Joe. "Why, it's wonderful!"

"No, it's merely natural."

"Oh! Natural; yes, no doubt of that!"

"I bring Dick into good air, as the doctors do, every day, in Europe, or, as I would send a patient at Martinique to the Pitons, a lofty mountain on that island, to get clear of the yellow fever."

"Ah! By Jove, this balloon is a paradise!" exclaimed Kennedy, feeling much better already.

"It leads to it, anyhow!" replied Joe, quite gravely.

It was a curious spectacle—that mass of clouds piled up, at the moment, away below them! The vapors rolled over each other, and mingled together in confused masses of superb brilliance, as they reflected the rays of the sun. The *Victoria* had attained an altitude of four thousand feet, and the thermometer indicated a certain diminution of temperature. The land below could no longer be seen. Fifty miles away to the westward, Mount Rubeho raised its sparkling crest, marking the limit of the Ugogo country in east longitude thirty-six degrees twenty minutes. The wind was blowing at the rate of twenty miles an hour, but the aeronauts felt nothing of this increased speed. They observed no jar, and had scarcely any sense of motion at all.

Three hours later, the doctor's prediction was fully verified. Kennedy no longer felt a single shiver of the fever, but partook of some breakfast with an excellent appetite.

"That beats sulfate of quinine!" said the energetic Scot, with hearty emphasis and much satisfaction.

"Positively," said Joe, "this is where I'll have to retire to when I get old!"

About ten o'clock in the morning the atmosphere cleared up, the clouds parted, and the country beneath could again be seen, the *Victoria* meanwhile rapidly descending. Dr. Ferguson was in search of a current that would carry him more to the northeast, and he found it about six hundred feet from the ground. The country was becoming more broken, and even mountainous. The Zungomoro district was fading out of sight in the east with the last coconut trees of that latitude.

Ere long, the crests of a mountain range assumed a more decided prominence. A few peaks rose here and there, and it became necessary to keep a sharp lookout for the pointed cones that seemed to spring up every moment.

"We're right among the breakers!" said Kennedy.

"Keep cool, Dick. We shan't touch them," was the doctor's quiet answer.

"It's a jolly way to travel, anyhow!" said Joe, with his usual flow of spirits.

In fact, the doctor managed his balloon with wondrous dexterity.

"Now, if we had been compelled to go afoot over that drenched soil," said he, "we should still be dragging along in a pestilential mire. Since our departure from Zanzibar, half our beasts of burden would have died with fatigue. We should be looking like ghosts ourselves, and despair would be seizing on our hearts. We should be in continual squabbles with our guides and porters, and completely exposed to their unbridled brutality. During the daytime, a damp, penetrating, unendurable humidity! At night, a cold frequently intolerable, and the stings of a kind of fly whose bite pierces the thickest cloth, and drives the victim crazy! All this, too, without saying anything about wild beasts and ferocious native tribes!"

"I move that we don't try it!" said Joe, in his droll way.

"I exaggerate nothing," continued Ferguson, "for, upon reading the narratives of such travelers as have had the hardihood to venture into these regions, your eyes would fill with tears."

About eleven o'clock they were passing over the basin of Imengé, and the tribes scattered over the adjacent hills were impotently menacing the *Victoria* with their weapons. Finally, she sped along as far as the last undulations of the country which precede Rubeho. These form the last and loftiest chain of the mountains of Usagara.

The aeronauts took careful and complete note of the orographic conformation of the country. The three ramifications mentioned, of which the Duthumi forms the first link, are separated by immense longitudinal plains. These elevated summits consist of rounded cones, between which the soil is bestrewn with erratic blocks of stone and gravelly boulders. The most abrupt declivity of these mountains confronts the Zanzibar coast, but the western slopes are merely inclined planes. The depressions in the soil are covered with a black, rich loam, on which there is a vigorous vegetation. Various watercourses filter through, toward the east, and work their way onward to flow into the Kingani, in the midst of gigantic clumps of sycamore, tamarind, calabash, and palmyra trees.

"Attention!" said Dr. Ferguson. "We are approaching Rubeho, the name of which signifies, in the language of the country, the 'Passage of the Winds,' and we would do well to double its jagged pinnacles at a certain height. If my chart be exact, we are going to ascend to an elevation of five thousand feet."

"Shall we often have occasion to reach those far upper belts of the atmosphere?"

"Very seldom: the height of the African mountains appears to be quite moderate compared with that of the European and Asiatic ranges; but, in any case, our good *Victoria* will find no difficulty in passing over them."

In a very little while, the gas expanded under the action of the heat, and the balloon took a very decided ascensional movement. Besides, the dilation of the hydrogen involved no danger, and only three-fourths of the vast capacity of the balloon was filled when the barometer, by a depression of eight inches, announced an elevation of six thousand feet.

"Shall we go this high very long?" asked Joe.

"The atmosphere of the earth has a height of six thousand fathoms," said the doctor; "and, with a very large balloon, one might go far. That is what Messrs. Brioschi and Gay-Lussac did; but then the blood burst from their mouths and ears. Respirable air was wanting. Some years ago, two fearless Frenchmen, Messrs. Barral and Bixio, also ventured into the very lofty regions; but their balloon burst—"

"And they fell?" asked Kennedy, abruptly.

"Certainly they did; but as learned men should always fall—namely, without hurting themselves."

"Well, gentlemen," said Joe, "you may try their fall over again, if you like; but, as for me, who am but a dolt, I prefer keeping at the medium height—neither too far up, nor too low down. It won't do to be too ambitious."

At the height of six thousand feet, the density of the atmosphere has already greatly diminished; sound is conveyed with difficulty, and the voice is not so easily heard. The view of objects becomes confused; the gaze no longer takes in any but large, quite ill-distinguishable masses; men and animals on the surface become absolutely invisible; the roads and rivers get to look like threads, and the lakes dwindle to ponds.

The doctor and his friends felt themselves in a very anomalous condition; an atmospheric current of extreme velocity was bearing them away beyond arid mountains, upon whose summits vast fields of snow surprised the gaze; while their convulsed appearance told of titanic travail in the earliest epoch of the world's existence.

The sun shone at the zenith, and his rays fell perpendicularly upon those lonely summits. The doctor took an accurate design of these mountains, which form four distinct ridges almost in a straight line, the northernmost being the longest.

The *Victoria* soon descended the slope opposite to the Rubeho, skirting an acclivity covered with woods, and dotted with trees of very deep-green foliage. Then came crests and ravines, in a sort of desert which preceded the Ugogo country; and lower down were yellow plains, parched and fissured by the intense heat, and, here and there, bestrewn with saline plants and brambly thickets.

Some underbrush, which, farther on, became forests, embellished the horizon. The doctor went nearer to the ground; the anchors were thrown out, and one of them soon caught in the boughs of a huge sycamore.

Joe, slipping nimbly down the tree, carefully attached the anchor, and the doctor left his cylinder at work to a certain degree in order to retain sufficient ascensional force in the balloon to keep it in the air. Meanwhile the wind had suddenly died away.

"Now," said Ferguson, "take two guns, friend Dick—one for yourself and one for Joe—and both of you try to bring back some nice cuts of antelope meat; they will make us a good dinner."

"Off to the hunt!" exclaimed Kennedy, joyously.

He climbed briskly out of the car and descended. Joe had swung himself down from branch to branch, and was waiting for him below, stretching his limbs in the meantime.

"Don't fly away without us, doctor!" shouted Joe.

"Never fear, my boy! I am securely lashed. I'll spend the time getting my notes into shape. A good hunt to you! But be careful. Besides, from my post here, I can observe the face of the country, and, at the least suspicious thing I notice, I'll fire a signal shot, and with that you must rally home."

"Agreed!" said Kennedy; and off they went.

## CHAPTER XIV

The Forest of Gum Trees—The Blue Antelope—The Rallying Signal—
An Unexpected Attack—The Kanyemé—A Night in the Open Air—
The Mabunguru—Jihoue-la-Mkoa—A Supply of Water—Arrival at Kazeh

The country, dry and parched as it was, consisting of a clayey soil that cracked open with the heat, seemed, indeed, a desert: here and there were a few traces of caravans; the bones of men and animals, that had been half-gnawed away, moldering together in the same dust.

After half an hour's walking, Dick and Joe plunged into a forest of gum trees, their eyes alert on all sides, and their fingers on the trigger. There was no foreseeing what they might encounter. Without being a rifleman, Joe could handle firearms with no trifling dexterity.

"A walk does one good, Mr. Kennedy, but this isn't the easiest ground in the world," he said, kicking aside some fragments of quartz with which the soil was bestrewn.

Kennedy motioned to his companion to be silent and to halt. The present case compelled them to dispense with hunting dogs, and, no matter what Joe's agility might be, he could not be expected to have the scent of a setter or a greyhound.

A herd of a dozen antelopes were quenching their thirst in the bed of a torrent where some pools of water had lodged. The graceful creatures, snuffing danger in the breeze, seemed to be disturbed and uneasy. Their beautiful heads could be seen between every draft, raised in the air with quick and sudden motion as they sniffed the wind in the direction of our two hunters, with their flexible nostrils.

Kennedy stole around behind some clumps of shrubbery, while Joe remained motionless where he was. The former, at length, got within gunshot and fired.

The herd disappeared in the twinkling of an eye; one male antelope only, that was hit just behind the shoulder joint, fell headlong to the ground, and Kennedy leaped toward his booty.

It was a *blauwbok*, a superb animal of a pale bluish color shading upon the gray, but with the belly and the inside of the legs as white as the driven snow.

"A splendid shot!" exclaimed the hunter. "It's a very rare species of the antelope, and I hope to be able to prepare his skin in such a way as to keep it."

"Indeed!" said Joe. "Do you think of doing that, Mr. Kennedy?"

"Why, certainly I do! Just see what a fine hide it is!"

"But Dr. Ferguson will never allow us to take such an extra weight!"

"You're right, Joe. Still, it is a pity to have to leave such a noble animal."

"The whole of it? Oh, we won't do that, sir; we'll take all the good eatable parts of it, and, if you'll let me, I'll cut him up just as well as the chairman of the honorable corporation of butchers of the city of London could do."

"As you please, my boy! But you know that in my hunter's way I can just as easily skin and cut up a piece of game as kill it."

"I'm sure of that, Mr. Kennedy. Well, then, you can build a fireplace with a few stones; there's plenty of dry deadwood, and I can make the hot coals tell in a few minutes."

"Oh! That won't take long," said Kennedy, going to work on the fireplace, where he had a brisk flame crackling and sparkling in a minute or two.

Joe had cut some of the nicest steaks and the best parts of the tenderloin from the carcass of the antelope, and these were quickly transformed to the most savory of broils.

"There, those will tickle the doctor!" said Kennedy.

"Do you know what I was thinking about?" said Joe.

"Why, about the steaks you're broiling, to be sure!" replied Dick.

"Not the least in the world. I was thinking what a figure we'd cut if we couldn't find the balloon again."

"By George, what an idea! Why, do you think the doctor would desert us?"

"No; but suppose his anchor were to slip!"

"Impossible! And, besides, the doctor would find no difficulty in coming down again with his balloon; he handles it at his ease."

"But suppose the wind were to sweep it off, so that he couldn't come back toward us?"

"Come, come, Joe! A truce to your suppositions; they're anything but pleasant."

"Ah! Sir, everything that happens in this world is natural, of course; but, then, anything may happen, and we ought to look out beforehand."

At this moment the report of a gun rang out upon the air.

"What's that?" exclaimed Joe.

"It's my rifle, I know the ring of her!" said Kennedy.

"A signal!"

"Yes; danger for us!"

"For him, too, perhaps."

"Let's be off!"

And the hunters, having gathered up the product of their expedition, rapidly made their way back along the path that they had marked by breaking boughs and bushes when they came. The density of the underbrush prevented their seeing the balloon, although they could not be far from it.

A second shot was heard.

"We must hurry!" said Joe.

"There! A third report!"

"Why, it sounds to me as if he was defending himself against something."

"Let us make haste!"

They now began to run at the top of their speed. When they reached the outskirts of the forest, they, at first glance, saw the balloon in its place and the doctor in the car.

"What's the matter?" shouted Kennedy.

"Good God!" suddenly exclaimed Joe.

"What do you see?"

"Down there! Look! A crowd of blacks surrounding the balloon!"

And, in fact, there, two miles from where they were, they saw some thirty wild natives close together, yelling, gesticulating, and cutting all kinds of antics at the foot of the sycamore. Some, climbing into the tree itself, were making their way to the topmost branches. The danger seemed pressing.

"My master is lost!" cried Joe.

"Come! A little more coolness, Joe, and let us see how we stand. We hold the lives of four of those villains in our hands. Forward, then!"

They had made a mile with headlong speed, when another report was heard from the car. The shot had, evidently, told upon a huge black demon, who had been hoisting himself up by the anchor rope. A lifeless body fell from bough to bough, and hung about twenty feet from the ground, its arms and legs swaying to and fro in the air.

"Ha!" said Joe, halting. "What does that fellow hold by?"

"No matter what!" said Kennedy. "Let us run! Let us run!"

"Ah! Mr. Kennedy," said Joe, again, in a roar of laughter, "by his tail! By his tail! It's an ape! They're all apes!"

"Well, they're worse than men!" said Kennedy, as he dashed into the midst of the howling crowd.

It was, indeed, a troop of very formidable baboons of the dog-faced species. These creatures are brutal, ferocious, and horrible to look upon, with their doglike muzzles and savage expression. However, a few shots scattered them, and the chattering horde scampered off, leaving several of their number on the ground.

In a moment Kennedy was on the ladder, and Joe, clambering up the branches, detached the anchor; the car then dipped to where he was, and he got into it without difficulty. A few minutes later, the *Victoria* slowly ascended and soared away to the eastward, wafted by a moderate wind.

"That was an attack for you!" said Joe.

"We thought you were surrounded by natives."

"Well, fortunately, they were only apes," said the doctor.

"At a distance there's no great difference," remarked Kennedy.

"Nor close at hand, either," added Joe.

"Well, however that may be," resumed Ferguson, "this attack of apes might have had the most serious consequences. Had the anchor yielded to their repeated efforts, who knows whither the wind would have carried me?"

"What did I tell you, Mr. Kennedy?"

"You were right, Joe; but, even right as you may have been, you were, at that moment, preparing some antelope steaks, the very sight of which gave me a monstrous appetite."

"I believe you!" said the doctor. "The flesh of the antelope is exquisite."

"You may judge of that yourself, now, sir, for supper's ready."

"Upon my word as a sportsman, those venison steaks have a gamy flavor that's not to be sneezed at, I tell you."

"Good!" said Joe, with his mouth full. "I could live on antelope all the days of my life; and all the better with a glass of grog to wash it down."

So saying, the good fellow went to work to prepare a jorum of that fragrant beverage, and all hands tasted it with satisfaction.

"Everything has gone well thus far," said he.

"Very well indeed!" assented Kennedy.

"Come, now, Mr. Kennedy, are you sorry that you came with us?"

"I'd like to see anybody prevent my coming!"

It was now four o'clock in the afternoon. The *Victoria* had struck a more rapid current. The face of the country was gradually rising, and, ere long, the barometer indicated a height of fifteen hundred feet above the level of the sea. The doctor was, therefore, obliged to keep his balloon up by a quite considerable dilation of gas, and the cylinder was hard at work all the time.

Toward seven o'clock, the balloon was sailing over the basin of Kanyemé. The doctor immediately recognized that immense clearing, ten miles in extent, with its villages buried in the midst of baobab and calabash trees. It is the residence of one of the sultans of the Ugogo country, where civilization is, perhaps, the least backward. The natives there are less addicted to selling members of their own families, but still, men and animals all live together in round huts, without frames, that look like haystacks.

Beyond Kanyemé the soil becomes arid and stony, but in an hour's journey, in a fertile dip of the soil, vegetation had resumed all its vigor at some distance from Mdaburu. The wind fell with the close of the day, and the atmosphere seemed to sleep. The doctor vainly sought for a current of air at different heights, and, at last, seeing this calm of all nature, he resolved to pass the night afloat, and, for greater safety, rose to the height of one thousand feet, where the balloon remained motionless. The night was magnificent, the heavens glittering with stars, and profoundly silent in the upper air.

Dick and Joe stretched themselves on their peaceful couch, and were soon sound asleep, the doctor keeping the first watch. At twelve o'clock the latter was relieved by Kennedy.

"Should the slightest accident happen, waken me," said Ferguson, "and, above all things, don't lose sight of the barometer. To us it is the compass!"

The night was cold. There were twenty-seven degrees of difference between its temperature and that of the daytime. With nightfall had begun the nocturnal concert of animals driven from their hiding places by hunger and thirst. The frogs struck in their guttural soprano, redoubled by the yelping of the jackals, while the imposing bass of the African lion sustained the accords of this living orchestra.

Upon resuming his post, in the morning, the doctor consulted his compass, and found that the wind had changed during the night. The balloon had been bearing about thirty miles to the northwest during the last two hours. It was then passing over Mabunguru, a stony country, strewn with blocks of syenite of a fine polish, and knobbed with huge boulders and angular ridges of rock; conic masses, like the rocks of Karnak, studded the soil like so many Druidic dolmens; the bones of buffaloes and elephants whitened it here and there; but few trees could be seen, excepting in the east, where there were dense woods, among which a few villages lay half concealed.

Toward seven o'clock they saw a huge round rock nearly two miles in extent, like an immense tortoise.

"We are on the right track," said Dr. Ferguson. "There's Jihoue-la-Mkoa, where we must halt for a few minutes. I am going to renew the supply of water necessary for my cylinder, and so let us try to anchor somewhere."

"There are very few trees," replied the hunger.

"Never mind, let us try. Joe, throw out the anchors!"

The balloon, gradually losing its ascensional force, approached the ground; the anchors ran along until, at last, one of them caught in the fissure of a rock, and the balloon remained motionless.

It must not be supposed that the doctor could entirely extinguish his cylinder, during these halts. The equilibrium of the balloon had been calculated at the level of the sea; and, as the country was continually ascending, and had reached an elevation of from six to seven hundred feet, the balloon would have had a tendency to go lower than the surface of the soil itself. It was, therefore, necessary to sustain it by a certain dilation of the gas. But, in case the doctor, in the absence of all wind, had let the car rest upon the ground, the balloon, thus relieved of a considerable weight, would have kept up of itself, without the aid of the cylinder.

The maps indicated extensive ponds on the western slope of the Jihoue-la-Mkoa. Joe went thither alone with a cask that would hold about ten gallons. He found the place pointed out to him, without difficulty, near to a deserted village; got his stock of water, and returned in less than three-quarters of an hour. He had seen nothing particular excepting some immense elephant pits. In fact, he came very near falling into one of them, at the bottom of which lay a half-eaten carcass.

He brought back with him a sort of clover which the apes eat with avidity. The doctor recognized the fruit of the "mbenbu" tree which grows in profusion, on the western part of Jihoue-la-Mkoa. Ferguson waited for Joe with a certain feeling of impatience, for even a short halt in this inhospitable region always inspires a degree of fear.

The water was got aboard without trouble, as the car was nearly resting on the ground. Joe then found it easy to loosen the anchor and leaped lightly to his place beside the doctor. The latter then replenished the flame in the cylinder, and the balloon majestically soared into the air.

It was then about one hundred miles from Kazeh, an important establishment in the interior of Africa, where, thanks to a south-southeasterly current, the travelers might hope to arrive on that same day. They were moving at the rate of fourteen miles per hour, and the guidance of the balloon was becoming difficult, as they dared not rise very high without extreme dilation of the gas, the country itself being at an average height of three thousand feet. Hence, the doctor preferred not to force the dilation, and so adroitly followed the sinuosities of a pretty sharply inclined plane, and swept very close to the villages of Thembo and Tura-Wels. The latter forms part of the Unyamwezy, a magnificent country, where the trees attain enormous dimensions; among them the cactus, which grows to gigantic size.

About two o'clock, in magnificent weather, but under a fiery sun that devoured the least breath of air, the balloon was floating over the town of Kazeh, situated about three hundred and fifty miles from the coast.

"We left Zanzibar at nine o'clock in the morning," said the doctor, consulting his notes, "and, after two days' passage, we have, including our deviations, traveled nearly five hundred geographical miles. Captains Burton and Speke took four months and a half to make the same distance!"

## CHAPTER XV

KAZEH—The Noisy Marketplace—The Appearance of the Balloon—
The Wangaga—The Sons of the Moon—The Doctor's Walk—The
Population of the Place—The Royal Tembé—The Sultan's Wives—
A Royal Drunken Bout—Joe an Object of Worship—How They
Dance in the Moon—A Reaction—Two Moons in One Sky—
The Instability of Divine Honors

Kazeh, an important point in Central Africa, is not a city; in truth, there are no cities in the interior. Kazeh is but a collection of six extensive excavations. There are enclosed a few houses and slave huts, with little courtyards and small gardens, carefully cultivated with onions, potatoes, cucumbers, pumpkins, and mushrooms, of perfect flavor, growing most luxuriantly.

The Unyamwezy is the country of the Moon—above all the rest, the fertile and magnificent garden spot of Africa. In its center is the district of Unyanembé—a delicious region, where some families of Omani, who are of very pure Arabic origin, live in luxurious idleness.

They have, for a long period, held the commerce between the interior of Africa and Arabia: they trade in gums, ivory, fine muslin, and slaves. Their caravans traverse these equatorial regions on all sides; and they even make their way to the coast in search of those articles of luxury and enjoyment which the wealthy merchants covet; while the latter, surrounded by their wives and their attendants, lead in this charming country the least disturbed and most horizontal of lives—always stretched at full length, laughing, smoking, or sleeping.

Around these excavations are numerous native dwellings; wide, open spaces for the markets; fields of *cannabis* and *datura*; superb trees and depths of freshest shade—such is Kazeh!

There, too, is held the general rendezvous of the caravans—those of the south, with their slaves and their freightage of ivory; and those of the west, which export cotton, glassware, and trinkets to the tribes of the great lakes.

So in the marketplace there reigns perpetual excitement, a nameless hubbub, made up of the cries of mixed-breed porters and carriers, the beating of drums, and the twanging of horns, the neighing of mules, the braying of donkeys, the singing of women, the squalling of children, and the banging of the huge rattan, wielded by the jemadar, or leader of the caravans, who beats time to this pastoral symphony.

There, spread forth, without regard to order—indeed, we may say, in charming disorder—are the showy stuffs, the glass beads, the ivory tusks, the rhinoceros' teeth, the shark's teeth, the honey, the tobacco, and the cotton of these regions, to be purchased at the strangest of bargains by customers in whose eyes each article has a price only in proportion to the desire it excites to possess it.

All at once this agitation, movement, and noise stopped as though by magic. The balloon had just come in sight, far aloft in the sky, where it hovered majestically for a few moments, and then descended slowly, without deviating from its perpendicular. Men, women, children, merchants and slaves, Arabs and negroes, as suddenly disappeared within the "tembes" and the huts.

"My dear doctor," said Kennedy, "if we continue to produce such a sensation as this, we shall find some difficulty in establishing commercial relations with the people hereabouts."

"There's one kind of trade that we might carry on, though, easily enough," said Joe; "and that would be to go down there quietly, and walk off with the best of the goods, without troubling our heads about the merchants; we'd get rich that way!"

"Ah!" said the doctor. "These natives are a little scared at first; but they won't be long in coming back, either through suspicion or through curiosity."

"Do you really think so, doctor?"

"Well, we'll see pretty soon. But it wouldn't be prudent to go too near to them, for the balloon is not iron-clad, and is, therefore, not proof against either an arrow or a bullet."

"Then you expect to hold a parley with these blacks?"

"If we can do so safely, why should we not? There must be some Arab merchants here at Kazeh, who are better informed than the rest, and not so barbarous. I remember that Burton and Speke had nothing but praises to utter concerning the hospitality of these people; so we might, at least, make the venture."

The balloon having, meanwhile, gradually approached the ground, one of the anchors lodged in the top of a tree near the marketplace.

By this time the whole population had emerged from their hiding places stealthily, thrusting their heads out first. Several "waganga," recognizable by their badges of conical shellwork, came boldly forward. They were the sorcerers of the place. They bore in their girdles small gourds, coated with tallow, and several other articles of witchcraft, all of them, by the way, most professionally filthy.

Little by little the crowd gathered beside them, the women and children grouped around them, the drums renewed their deafening uproar, hands were violently clapped together, and then raised toward the sky.

"That's their style of praying," said the doctor; "and, if I'm not mistaken, we're going to be called upon to play a great part."

"Well, sir, play it!"

"You, too, my good Joe—perhaps you're to be a god!"

"Well, master, that won't trouble me much. I like a little flattery!"

At this moment, one of the sorcerers, a "myanga," made a sign, and all the clamor died away into the profoundest silence. He then addressed a few words to the strangers, but in an unknown tongue.

Dr. Ferguson, not having understood them, shouted some sentences in Arabic, at a venture, and was immediately answered in that language.

The speaker below then delivered himself of a very copious harangue, which was also very flowery and very gravely listened to by his audience. From it the doctor was not slow in learning that the balloon was mistaken for nothing less than the moon in person, and that the amiable goddess in question had condescended to approach the town with her three sons—an honor that would never be forgotten in this land so greatly loved by the god of day.

The doctor responded, with much dignity, that the moon made her provincial tour every thousand years, feeling the necessity of showing herself nearer at hand to her worshippers. He, therefore, begged them not to be disturbed by her presence, but to take advantage of it to make known all their wants and longings.

The sorcerer, in his turn, replied that the sultan, the "mwani," who had been sick for many years, implored the aid of heaven, and he invited the son of the moon to visit him.

The doctor acquainted his companions with the invitation.

"And you are going to call upon this negro king?" asked Kennedy.

"Undoubtedly so; these people appear well disposed; the air is calm; there is not a breath of wind, and we have nothing to fear for the balloon?"

"But, what will you do?"

"Be quiet on that score, my dear Dick. With a little medicine, I shall work my way through the affair!"

Then, addressing the crowd, he said:

"The moon, taking compassion on the sovereign who is so dear to the children of Unyamwezy, has charged us to restore him to health. Let him prepare to receive us!"

The clamor, the songs and demonstrations of all kinds increased twofold, and the whole immense ants' nest of black heads was again in motion.

"Now, my friends," said Dr. Ferguson, "we must look out for everything beforehand; we may be forced to leave this at any moment, unexpectedly, and be off with extra speed. Dick had better remain, therefore, in the car, and keep the cylinder warm so as to secure a sufficient ascensional force for the balloon. The anchor is solidly fastened, and there is nothing to fear in that respect. I shall descend, and Joe will go with me, only that he must remain at the foot of the ladder."

"What! Are you going alone into that blackamoor's den?"

"How! Doctor, am I not to go with you?"

"No! I shall go alone; these good folks imagine that the goddess of the moon has come to see them, and their superstition protects me; so have no fear, and each one remain at the post that I have assigned to him."

"Well, since you wish it," sighed Kennedy.

"Look closely to the dilation of the gas."

"Agreed!"

By this time the shouts of the natives had swelled to double volume as they vehemently implored the aid of the heavenly powers.

"There, there," said Joe, "they're rather rough in their orders to their good moon and her divine sons."

The doctor, equipped with his traveling medicine chest, descended to the ground, preceded by Joe, who kept a straight countenance and looked as grave and knowing as the circumstances of the case required. He then seated himself at the foot of the ladder in the Arab fashion, with his legs crossed under him, and a portion of the crowd collected around him in a circle, at respectful distances.

In the meanwhile the doctor, escorted to the sound of savage instruments, and with wild religious dances, slowly proceeded toward the royal "tembé," situated a considerable distance outside of the town. It was about three o'clock, and the sun was shining brilliantly. In fact, what less could it do upon so grand an occasion!

The doctor stepped along with great dignity, the waganga surrounding him and keeping off the crowd. He was soon joined by the natural son of the sultan, a handsomely built young fellow, who, according to the custom of the country, was the sole heir of the paternal goods, to the exclusion of the old man's legitimate children. He prostrated himself before the son of the moon, but the latter graciously raised him to his feet.

Three-quarters of an hour later, through shady paths, surrounded by all the luxuriance of tropical vegetation, this enthusiastic procession arrived at the sultan's palace, a sort of square edifice called *ititénya*, and situated on the slope of a hill.

A kind of veranda, formed by the thatched roof, adorned the outside, supported upon wooden pillars, which had some pretensions to being carved. Long lines of dark red clay decorated the walls in characters that strove to reproduce the forms of men and serpents, the latter better imitated, of course, than the former. The roofing of this abode did not rest directly upon the walls, and the air could, therefore, circulate freely, but windows there were none, and the door hardly deserved the name.

Dr. Ferguson was received with all the honors by the guards and favorites of the sultan; these were men of a fine race, the Wanyamwezi so-called, a pure type of the central African populations, strong, robust, well-made, and in splendid condition. Their hair, divided into a great number of small tresses, fell over their shoulders, and by means of black-and-blue incisions they had tattooed their cheeks from the temples to the mouth. Their ears, frightfully distended, held dangling to them disks of wood and plates of gum copal. They were clad in brilliantly painted cloths, and the soldiers were armed with the sawtoothed war club, the bow and arrows barbed and poisoned with the juice of the euphorbium, the cutlass, the "sima," a long saber (also with sawlike teeth), and some small battle-axes.

The doctor advanced into the palace, and there, notwithstanding the sultan's illness, the din, which was terrific before, redoubled the instant that he arrived. He noticed, at the lintels of the door, some rabbits' tails and zebras' manes, suspended as talismans. He was received by the whole troop of his majesty's wives, to the harmonious accords of the "upatu," a sort of cymbal made of the bottom of a copper kettle, and to the uproar of the "kilindo," a drum five feet high, hollowed out from the trunk of a tree, and hammered by the ponderous, horny fists of two jet-black *virtuosi*.

Most of the women were rather good looking, and they laughed and chattered merrily as they smoked their tobacco and "thang" in huge black pipes. They seemed to be well made, too, under the long robes that they wore gracefully flung about their persons, and carried a sort of "kilt" woven from the fibers of calabash fastened around their girdles.

Six of them were not the least merry of the party, although put aside from the rest, and reserved for a cruel fate. On the death of the sultan, they were to be buried alive with him, so as to occupy and divert his mind during the period of eternal solitude.

Dr. Ferguson, taking in the whole scene at a rapid glance, approached the wooden couch on which the sultan lay reclining. There he saw a man of about forty, completely brutalized by orgies of every description, and in a condition that left little or nothing to be done. The sickness that had afflicted him for so many years was simply perpetual drunkenness. The royal sot had nearly lost all consciousness, and all the ammonia in the world would not have set him on his feet again.

His favorites and the women kept on bended knees during this solemn visit. By means of a few drops of powerful cordial, the doctor for a moment reanimated the imbruted carcass that lay before him. The sultan stirred, and, for a dead body that had given no sign whatever of life for several hours previously, this symptom was received with a tremendous repetition of shouts and cries in the doctor's honor.

The latter, who had seen enough of it by this time, by a rapid motion put aside his too-demonstrative admirers and went out of the palace, directing his steps immediately toward the balloon, for it was now six o'clock in the evening.

Joe, during his absence, had been quietly waiting at the foot of the ladder, where the crowd paid him their most humble respects. Like a genuine son of the moon, he let them keep on. For a divinity, he had the air of a very clever sort of fellow, by no means proud, nay, even pleasingly familiar with the young negresses, who seemed never to tire of looking at him. Besides, he went so far as to chat agreeably with them.

"Worship me, ladies! Worship me!" he said to them. "I'm a clever sort of devil, if I am the son of a goddess."

They brought him propitiatory gifts, such as are usually deposited in the *fetich* huts or *mᶎimu*. These gifts consisted of stalks of barley and of "pombé." Joe considered himself in duty bound to taste the latter species of strong beer, but his palate, although accustomed to gin and whiskey, could not withstand the strength of the new beverage, and he had to make a horrible grimace, which his dusky friends took to be a benevolent smile.

Thereupon, the young damsels, conjoining their voices in a drawling chant, began to dance around him with the utmost gravity.

"Ah! You're dancing, are you?" said he. "Well, I won't be behind you in politeness, and so I'll give you one of my country reels."

So at it he went, in one of the wildest jigs that ever was seen, twisting, turning, and jerking himself in all directions; dancing with his hands, dancing with his body, dancing with his knees, dancing with his feet; describing the most fearful contortions and extravagant evolutions; throwing himself into incredible attitudes; grimacing beyond all belief, and, in fine giving his savage admirers a strange idea of the style of ballet adopted by the deities in the moon.

Then, the whole collection of blacks, naturally as imitative as monkeys, at once reproduced all his airs and graces, his leaps and shakes and contortions; they did not lose a single gesticulation; they did not forget an attitude; and the result was, such a pandemonium of movement, noise, and excitement, as it would be out of the question even feebly to describe. But, in the very midst of the fun, Joe saw the doctor approaching.

The latter was coming at full speed, surrounded by a yelling and disorderly throng. The chiefs and sorcerers seemed to be highly excited. They were close upon the doctor's heels, crowding and threatening him.

Singular reaction! What had happened? Had the sultan unluckily perished in the hands of his celestial physician?

Kennedy, from his post of observation, saw the danger without knowing what had caused it, and the balloon, powerfully urged by the dilation of the gas, strained and tugged at the ropes that held it as though impatient to soar away.

The doctor had got as far as the foot of the ladder. A superstitious fear still held the crowd aloof and hindered them from committing any violence on his person. He rapidly scaled the ladder, and Joe followed him with his usual agility.

"Not a moment to lose!" said the doctor. "Don't attempt to let go the anchor! We'll cut the cord! Follow me!"

"But what's the matter?" asked Joe, clambering into the car.

"What's happened?" questioned Kennedy, rifle in hand.

"Look!" replied the doctor, pointing to the horizon.

"Well?" ejaculated the Scot.

"Well! The moon!"

And, in fact, there was the moon rising red and magnificent, a globe of fire in a field of blue! It was she, indeed—she and the balloon!—both in one sky!

Either there were two moons, then, or these strangers were impostors, designing scamps, false deities!

Such were the very natural reflections of the crowd, and hence the reaction in their feelings.

Joe could not, for the life of him, keep in a roar of laughter; and the population of Kazeh, comprehending that their prey was slipping through their clutches, set up prolonged howlings, aiming, the while, their bows and muskets at the balloon.

But one of the sorcerers made a sign, and all the weapons were lowered. He then began to climb into the tree, intending to seize the rope and bring the machine to the ground.

Joe leaned out with a hatchet ready. "Shall I cut away?" said he.

"No; wait a moment," replied the doctor.

"But this black?"

"We may, perhaps, save our anchor—and I hold a great deal by that. There'll always be time enough to cut loose."

The sorcerer, having climbed to the right place, worked so vigorously that he succeeded in detaching the anchor, and the latter, violently jerked, at that moment, by the start of the balloon, caught the rascal between the limbs, and carried him off astride of it through the air.

The stupefaction of the crowd was indescribable as they saw one of their waganga thus whirled away into space.

"Huzza!" roared Joe, as the balloon—thanks to its ascensional force—shot up higher into the sky, with increased rapidity.

"He holds on well," said Kennedy; "a little trip will do him good."

"Shall we let this darky drop all at once?" inquired Joe.

"Oh no," replied the doctor, "we'll let him down easily; and I warrant me that, after such an adventure, the power of the wizard will be enormously enhanced in the sight of his comrades."

"Why, I wouldn't put it past them to make a god of him!" said Joe, with a laugh.

The *Victoria*, by this time, had risen to the height of one thousand feet, and the black hung to the rope with desperate energy. He had become completely silent, and his eyes were fixed, for his terror was blended with amazement. A light west wind was sweeping the balloon right over the town, and far beyond it.

Half an hour later, the doctor, seeing the country deserted, moderated the flame of his cylinder, and descended toward the ground. At twenty feet above the turf, the affrighted sorcerer made up his mind in a twinkling: he let himself drop, fell on his feet, and scampered off at a furious pace toward Kazeh; while the balloon, suddenly relieved of his weight, again shot up on her course.

# CHAPTER XVI

SYMPTOMS OF A STORM—THE COUNTRY OF THE MOON—THE FUTURE OF
THE AFRICAN CONTINENT—THE LAST MACHINE OF ALL—A VIEW OF THE
COUNTRY AT SUNSET—FLORA AND FAUNA—THE TEMPEST—THE ZONE
OF FIRE—THE STARRY HEAVENS

"See," said Joe, "what comes of playing the sons of the moon without her leave! She came near serving us an ugly trick. But say, master, did you damage your credit as a physician?"

"Yes, indeed," chimed in the sportsman. "What kind of a dignitary was this Sultan of Kazeh?"

"An old half-dead sot," replied the doctor, "whose loss will not be very severely felt. But the moral of all this is that honors are fleeting, and we must not take too great a fancy to them."

"So much the worse!" rejoined Joe. "I liked the thing—to be worshipped! Play the god as you like! Why, what would anyone ask more than that? By the way, the moon did come up, too, and all red, as if she was in a rage."

While the three friends went on chatting of this and other things, and Joe examined the luminary of night from an entirely novel point of view, the heavens became covered with heavy clouds to the northward, and the lowering masses assumed a most sinister and threatening look. Quite a smart breeze, found about three hundred feet from the earth, drove the balloon toward the north-northeast; and above it the blue vault was clear; but the atmosphere felt close and dull.

The aeronauts found themselves, at about eight in the evening, in thirty-two degrees forty minutes east longitude, and four degrees seventeen minutes latitude. The atmospheric currents, under the influence of a tempest not far off, were driving them at the rate of from thirty to thirty-five miles an hour; the undulating and fertile plains of Mfuto were passing swiftly beneath them. The spectacle was one worthy of admiration—and admire it they did.

"We are now right in the country of the Moon," said Dr. Ferguson; "for it has retained the name that antiquity gave it, undoubtedly, because the moon has been worshipped there in all ages. It is, really, a superb country."

"It would be hard to find more splendid vegetation."

"If we found the like of it around London it would not be natural, but it would be very pleasant," put in Joe. "Why is it that such savage countries get all these fine things?"

"And who knows," said the doctor, "that this country may not, one day, become the center of civilization? The races of the future may repair hither, when Europe shall have become exhausted in the effort to feed her inhabitants."

"Do you think so, really?" asked Kennedy.

"Undoubtedly, my dear Dick. Just note the progress of events: consider the migrations of races, and you will arrive at the same conclusion assuredly. Asia was the first nurse of the world, was she not? For about four thousand years she travailed, she grew pregnant, she produced, and then, when stones began to cover the soil where the golden harvests sung by Homer had flourished, her children abandoned her exhausted and barren bosom. You next see them precipitating themselves upon young and vigorous Europe, which has nourished them for the last two thousand years. But already her fertility is beginning to die out; her productive powers are diminishing every day. Those new diseases that annually attack the products of the soil, those defective crops, those insufficient resources, are all signs of a vitality that is rapidly wearing out and of an approaching exhaustion. Thus, we already see the millions rushing to the luxuriant bosom of America, as a source of help, not inexhaustible indeed, but not yet exhausted. In its turn, that new continent will grow old; its virgin forests will fall before the axe of industry, and its soil will become weak through having too fully produced what had been demanded of it. Where two harvests bloomed every year, hardly one will be gathered from a soil completely drained of its strength. Then, Africa will be there to offer to new races the treasures that for centuries have been accumulating in her breast. Those climates now so fatal to strangers will be purified by cultivation and by drainage of the soil, and those scattered water supplies will be gathered into one common bed to form an artery of navigation. Then this country over which we are now passing, more fertile, richer, and fuller of vitality than the rest, will become some grand realm where more astonishing discoveries than steam and electricity will be brought to light."

"Ah! Sir," said Joe, "I'd like to see all that."

"You got up too early in the morning, my boy!"

"Besides," said Kennedy, "that may prove to be a very dull period when industry will swallow up everything for its own profit. By dint of inventing machinery, men will end in being eaten up by it! I have always fancied that the end of the earth will be when some enormous boiler, heated to three thousand millions of atmospheric pressure, shall explode and blow up our globe!"

"And I add that the Americans," said Joe, "will not have been the last to work at the machine!"

"In fact," assented the doctor, "they are great boilermakers! But, without allowing ourselves to be carried away by such speculations, let us rest content with enjoying the beauties of this country of the Moon, since we have been permitted to see it."

The sun, darting his last rays beneath the masses of heaped-up cloud, adorned with a crest of gold the slightest inequalities of the ground below; gigantic trees, arborescent bushes, mosses on the even surface—all had their share of this luminous effulgence. The soil, slightly undulating, here and there rose into little conical hills; there were no mountains visible on the horizon; immense brambly palisades, impenetrable hedges of thorny jungle, separated the clearings dotted with numerous villages, and immense euphorbiae surrounded them with natural fortifications, interlacing their trunks with the coral-shaped branches of the shrubbery and undergrowth.

Ere long, the Malagazeri, the chief tributary of Lake Tanganayika, was seen winding between heavy thickets of verdure, offering an asylum to many watercourses that spring from the torrents formed in the season of freshets, or from ponds hollowed in the clayey soil. To observers looking from a height, it was a chain of waterfalls thrown across the whole western face of the country.

Animals with huge humps were feeding in the luxuriant prairies, and were half hidden, sometimes, in the tall grass; spreading forests in bloom redolent of spicy perfumes presented themselves to the gaze like immense bouquets; but, in these bouquets, lions, leopards, hyenas, and tigers were then crouching for shelter from the last hot rays of the setting sun. From time to time, an elephant made the tall tops of the undergrowth sway to and fro, and you could hear the crackling of huge branches as his ponderous ivory tusks broke them in his way.

"What a sporting country!" exclaimed Dick, unable longer to restrain his enthusiasm. "Why, a single ball fired at random into those forests would bring down game worthy of it. Suppose we try it once!"

"No, my dear Dick; the night is close at hand—a threatening night with a tempest in the background—and the storms are awful in this country, where the heated soil is like one vast electric battery."

"You are right, sir," said Joe, "the heat has got to be enough to choke one, and the breeze has died away. One can feel that something's coming."

"The atmosphere is saturated with electricity," replied the doctor; "every living creature is sensible that this state of the air portends a struggle of the elements, and I confess that I never before was so full of the fluid myself."

"Well, then," suggested Dick, "would it not be advisable to alight?"

"On the contrary, Dick, I'd rather go up, only that I am afraid of being carried out of my course by these countercurrents contending in the atmosphere."

"Have you any idea, then, of abandoning the route that we have followed since we left the coast?"

"If I can manage to do so," replied the doctor, "I will turn more directly northward, by from seven to eight degrees; I shall then endeavor to ascend toward the presumed latitudes of the sources of the Nile; perhaps we may discover some traces of Captain Speke's expedition or of M. de Heuglin's caravan. Unless I am mistaken, we are at thirty-two degrees forty minutes east longitude, and I should like to ascend directly north of the equator."

"Look there!" exclaimed Kennedy, suddenly. "See those hippopotami sliding out of the pools—those masses of blood-colored flesh—and those crocodiles snuffing the air aloud!"

"They're choking!" ejaculated Joe. "Ah! What a fine way to travel this is; and how one can snap his fingers at all that vermin! Doctor! Mr. Kennedy! See those packs of wild animals hurrying along close together. There are fully two hundred. Those are wolves."

"No! Joe, not wolves, but wild dogs; a famous breed that does not hesitate to attack the lion himself. They are the worst customers a traveler could meet, for they would instantly tear him to pieces."

"Well, it isn't Joe that'll undertake to muzzle them!" responded that amiable youth. "After all, though, if that's the nature of the beast, we mustn't be too hard on them for it!"

Silence gradually settled down under the influence of the impending storm: the thickened air actually seemed no longer adapted to the transmission of sound; the atmosphere appeared muffled, and, like a room hung with tapestry, lost all its sonorous reverberation. The "rover bird" so-called, the coroneted crane, the red and blue jays, the mockingbird, the flycatcher, disappeared among the foliage of the immense trees, and all nature revealed symptoms of some approaching catastrophe.

At nine o'clock the *Victoria* hung motionless over Msene, an extensive group of villages scarcely distinguishable in the gloom. Once in a while, the reflection of a wandering ray of light in the dull water disclosed a succession of ditches regularly arranged, and, by one last gleam, the eye could make out the calm and somber forms of palm trees, sycamores, and gigantic euphorbiae.

"I am stifling!" said the Scot, inhaling, with all the power of his lungs, as much as possible of the rarefied air. "We are not moving an inch! Let us descend!"

"But the tempest!" said the doctor, with much uneasiness.

"If you are afraid of being carried away by the wind, it seems to me that there is no other course to pursue."

"Perhaps the storm won't burst tonight," said Joe; "the clouds are very high."

"That is just the thing that makes me hesitate about going beyond them; we should have to rise still higher, lose sight of the earth, and not know all night whether we were moving forward or not, or in what direction we were going."

"Make up your mind, dear doctor, for time presses!"

"It's a pity that the wind has fallen," said Joe, again; "it would have carried us clear of the storm."

"It is, indeed, a pity, my friends," rejoined the doctor. "The clouds are dangerous for us; they contain opposing currents which might catch us in their eddies, and lightnings that might set on fire. Again, those perils avoided, the force of the tempest might hurl us to the ground, were we to cast our anchor in the treetops."

"Then what shall we do?"

"Well, we must try to get the balloon into a medium zone of the atmosphere, and there keep her suspended between the perils of the heavens and those of the earth. We have enough water for the cylinder, and our two hundred pounds of ballast are untouched. In case of emergency I can use them."

"We will keep watch with you," said the hunter.

"No, my friends, put the provisions under shelter, and lie down; I will rouse you, if it becomes necessary."

"But, master, wouldn't you do well to take some rest yourself, as there's no danger close on us just now?" insisted poor Joe.

"No, thank you, my good fellow, I prefer to keep awake. We are not moving, and should circumstances not change, we'll find ourselves tomorrow in exactly the same place."

"Good night, then, sir!"

"Good night, if you can only find it so!"

Kennedy and Joe stretched themselves out under their blankets, and the doctor remained alone in the immensity of space.

However, the huge dome of clouds visibly descended, and the darkness became profound. The black vault closed in upon the earth as if to crush it in its embrace.

All at once a violent, rapid, incisive flash of lightning pierced the gloom, and the rent it made had not closed ere a frightful clap of thunder shook the celestial depths.

"Up! Up! Turn out!" shouted Ferguson.

The two sleepers, aroused by the terrible concussion, were at the doctor's orders in a moment.

"Shall we descend?" said Kennedy.

"No! The balloon could not stand it. Let us go up before those clouds dissolve in water, and the wind is let loose!" And, so saying, the doctor actively stirred up the flame of the cylinder, and turned it on the spirals of the serpentine siphon.

The tempests of the tropics develop with a rapidity equaled only by their violence. A second flash of lightning rent the darkness, and was followed by a score of others in quick succession. The sky was crossed and dotted, like the zebra's hide, with electric sparks, which danced and flickered beneath the great drops of rain.

"We have delayed too long," exclaimed the doctor; "we must now pass through a zone of fire, with our balloon filled as it is with inflammable gas!"

"But let us descend, then! Let us descend!" urged Kennedy.

"The risk of being struck would be just about even, and we should soon be torn to pieces by the branches of the trees!"

"We are going up, doctor!"

"Quicker, quicker still!"

In this part of Africa, during the equatorial storms, it is not rare to count from thirty to thirty-five flashes of lightning per minute. The sky is literally on fire, and the crashes of thunder are continuous.

The wind burst forth with frightful violence in this burning atmosphere; it twisted the blazing clouds; one might have compared it to the breath of some gigantic bellows, fanning all this conflagration.

Dr. Ferguson kept his cylinder at full heat, and the balloon dilated and went up, while Kennedy, on his knees, held together the curtains of the awning. The balloon whirled round wildly enough to make their heads turn, and the aeronauts got some very alarming jolts, indeed, as their machine swung and swayed in all directions. Huge cavities would form in the silk of the balloon as the wind fiercely bent it in, and the stuff fairly cracked like a pistol as it flew back from the pressure. A sort of hail, preceded by a rumbling noise, hissed through the air and rattled on the covering of the *Victoria*. The latter, however, continued to ascend, while the lightning described tangents to the convexity of her circumference; but she bore on, right through the midst of the fire.

"God protect us!" said Dr. Ferguson, solemnly. "We are in His hands; He alone can save us—but let us be ready for every event, even for fire—our fall could not be very rapid."

The doctor's voice could scarcely be heard by his companions; but they could see his countenance calm as ever even amid the flashing of the lightnings; he was watching the phenomena of phosphorescence produced by the fires of St. Elmo that were now skipping to and fro along the network of the balloon.

The latter whirled and swung, but steadily ascended, and, ere the hour was over, it had passed the stormy belt. The electric display was going on below it like a vast crown of artificial fireworks suspended from the car.

Then they enjoyed one of the grandest spectacles that Nature can offer to the gaze of man. Below them, the tempest; above them, the starry firmament, tranquil, mute, impassible, with the moon projecting her peaceful rays over these angry clouds.

Dr. Ferguson consulted the barometer; it announced twelve thousand feet of elevation. It was then eleven o'clock at night.

"Thank Heaven, all danger is past; all we have to do now, is, to keep ourselves at this height," said the doctor.

"It was frightful!" remarked Kennedy.

"Oh!" said Joe. "It gives a little variety to the trip, and I'm not sorry to have seen a storm from a trifling distance up in the air. It's a fine sight!"

## CHAPTER XVII

THE MOUNTAINS OF THE MOON—AN OCEAN OF VERDURE—THEY
CAST ANCHOR—THE TOWING ELEPHANT—A RUNNING FIRE—DEATH
OF THE MONSTER—THE FIELD OVEN—A MEAL ON THE GRASS—
A NIGHT ON THE GROUND

About four in the morning, Monday, the sun reappeared in the horizon; the clouds had dispersed, and a cheery breeze refreshed the morning dawn.

The earth, all redolent with fragrant exhalations, reappeared to the gaze of our travelers. The balloon, whirled about by opposing currents, had hardly budged from its place, and the doctor, letting the gas contract, descended so as to get a more northerly direction. For a long while his quest was fruitless; the wind carried him toward the west until he came in sight of the famous Mountains of the Moon, which grouped themselves in a semicircle around the extremity of Lake Tanganayika; their ridges, but slightly indented, stood out against the bluish horizon, so that they might have been mistaken for a natural fortification, not to be passed by the explorers of the center of Africa. Among them were a few isolated cones, revealing the mark of the eternal snows.

"Here we are at last," said the doctor, "in an unexplored country! Captain Burton pushed very far to the westward, but he could not reach those celebrated mountains; he even denied their existence, strongly as it was affirmed by Speke, his companion. He pretended that they were born in the latter's fancy; but for us, my friends, there is no further doubt possible."

"Shall we cross them?" asked Kennedy.

"Not, if it please God. I am looking for a wind that will take me back toward the equator. I will even wait for one, if necessary, and will make the balloon like a ship that casts anchor, until favorable breezes come up."

But the foresight of the doctor was not long in bringing its reward; for, after having tried different heights, the *Victoria* at length began to sail off to the northeastward with medium speed.

"We are in the right track," said the doctor, consulting his compass, "and scarcely two hundred feet from the surface; lucky circumstances for us, enabling us, as they do, to reconnoiter these new regions. When Captain Speke set out to discover Lake Ukéréoué, he ascended more to the eastward in a straight line above Kazeh."

"Shall we keep on long in this way?" inquired the Scot.

"Perhaps. Our object is to push a point in the direction of the sources of the Nile; and we have more than six hundred miles to make before we get to the extreme limit reached by the explorers who came from the north."

"And we shan't set foot on the solid ground?" murmured Joe. "It's enough to cramp a fellow's legs!"

"Oh, yes, indeed, my good Joe," said the doctor, reassuring him; "we have to economize our provisions, you know; and on the way, Dick, you must get us some fresh meat."

"Whenever you like, doctor."

"We shall also have to replenish our stock of water. Who knows but we may be carried to some of the dried-up regions? So we cannot take too many precautions."

At noon the *Victoria* was at twenty-nine degrees fifteen minutes east longitude, and three degrees fifteen minutes south latitude. She passed the village of Uyofu, the last northern limit of the Unyamwezi, opposite to the Lake Ukéréoué, which could still be seen.

The tribes living near to the equator seem to be a little more civilized, and are governed by absolute monarchs, whose control is an unlimited despotism. Their most compact union of power constitutes the province of Karagwah.

It was decided by the aeronauts that they would alight at the first favorable place. They found that they should have to make a prolonged halt, and take a careful inspection of the balloon: so the flame of the cylinder was moderated, and the anchors, flung out from the car, ere long began to sweep the grass of an immense prairie, that, from a certain height, looked like a shaven lawn, but the growth of which, in reality, was from seven to eight feet in height.

The balloon skimmed this tall grass without bending it, like a gigantic butterfly: not an obstacle was in sight; it was an ocean of verdure without a single breaker.

"We might proceed a long time in this style," remarked Kennedy. "I don't see one tree that we could approach, and I'm afraid that our hunt's over."

"Wait, Dick; you could not hunt anyhow in this grass, that grows higher than your head. We'll find a favorable place presently."

In truth, it was a charming excursion that they were making now—a veritable navigation on this green, almost transparent sea, gently undulating in the breath of the wind. The little car seemed to cleave the waves of verdure, and, from time to time, coveys of birds of magnificent plumage would rise fluttering from the tall herbage, and speed away with joyous cries. The anchors plunged into this lake of flowers, and traced a furrow that closed behind them, like the wake of a ship.

All at once a sharp shock was felt—the anchor had caught in the fissure of some rock hidden in the high grass.

"We are fast!" exclaimed Joe.

These words had scarcely been uttered when a shrill cry rang through the air, and the following phrases, mingled with exclamations, escaped from the lips of our travelers:

"What's that?"

"A strange cry!"

"Look! Why, we're moving!"

"The anchor has slipped!"

"No; it holds, and holds fast too!" said Joe, who was tugging at the rope.

"It's the rock, then, that's moving!"

An immense rustling was noticed in the grass, and soon an elongated, winding shape was seen rising above it.

"A serpent!" shouted Joe.

"A serpent!" repeated Kennedy, handling his rifle.

"No," said the doctor, "it's an elephant's trunk!"

"An elephant, Samuel?"

And, as Kennedy said this, he drew his rifle to his shoulder.

"Wait, Dick; wait!"

"That's a fact! The animal's towing us!"

"And in the right direction, Joe—in the right direction."

The elephant was now making some headway, and soon reached a clearing where his whole body could be seen. By his gigantic size, the doctor recognized a male of a superb species. He had two whitish tusks, beautifully curved, and about eight feet in length; and in these the shanks of the anchor had firmly caught. The animal was vainly trying with his trunk to disengage himself from the rope that attached him to the car.

"Get up—go ahead, old fellow!" shouted Joe, with delight, doing his best to urge this rather novel team. "Here is a new style of traveling! No more horses for me. An elephant, if you please!"

"But where is he taking us to?" said Kennedy, whose rifle itched in his grasp.

"He's taking us exactly to where we want to go, my dear Dick. A little patience!"

" 'Wig-a-more! Wig-a-more!' as the Scotch country folks say," shouted Joe, in high glee. "Gee-up! Gee-up there!"

The huge animal now broke into a very rapid gallop. He flung his trunk from side to side, and his monstrous bounds gave the car several rather heavy thumps. Meanwhile the doctor stood ready, hatchet in hand, to cut the rope, should need arise.

"But," said he, "we shall not give up our anchor until the last moment."

This drive, with an elephant for the team, lasted about an hour and a half; yet the animal did not seem in the least fatigued. These immense creatures can go over a great deal of ground, and, from one day to another, are found at enormous distances from there they were last seen, like the whales, whose mass and speed they rival.

"In fact," said Joe, "it's a whale that we have harpooned; and we're only doing just what whalemen do when out fishing."

But a change in the nature of the ground compelled the doctor to vary his style of locomotion. A dense grove of *calmadores* was descried on the horizon, about three miles away, on the north of the prairie. So it became necessary to detach the balloon from its draft animal at last.

Kennedy was intrusted with the job of bringing the elephant to a halt. He drew his rifle to his shoulder, but his position was not favorable to a successful shot; so that the first ball fired flattened itself on the animal's skull, as it would have done against an iron plate. The creature did not seem in the least troubled by it; but, at the sound of the discharge, he had increased his speed, and now was going as fast as a horse at full gallop.

"The deuce!" ejaculated Kennedy.

"What a solid head!" commented Joe.

"We'll try some conical balls behind the shoulder joint," said Kennedy, reloading his rifle with care. In another moment he fired.

The animal gave a terrible cry, but went on faster than ever.

"Come!" said Joe, taking aim with another gun. "I must help you, or we'll never end it." And now two balls penetrated the creature's side.

The elephant halted, lifted his trunk, and resumed his run toward the wood with all his speed; he shook his huge head, and the blood began to gush from his wounds.

"Let us keep up our fire, Mr. Kennedy."

"And a continuous fire, too," urged the doctor, "for we are close on the woods."

Ten shots more were discharged. The elephant made a fearful bound; the car and balloon cracked as though everything were going to pieces, and the shock made the doctor drop his hatchet on the ground.

The situation was thus rendered really very alarming; the anchor rope, which had securely caught, could not be disengaged, nor could it yet be cut by the knives of our aeronauts, and the balloon was rushing headlong toward the wood, when the animal received a ball in the eye just as he lifted his head. On this he halted, faltered, his knees bent under him, and he uncovered his whole flank to the assaults of his enemies in the balloon.

"A bullet in his heart!" said Kennedy, discharging one last rifle shot.

The elephant uttered a long bellow of terror and agony, then raised himself up for a moment, twirling his trunk in the air, and finally fell with all his weight upon one of his tusks, which he broke off short. He was dead.

"His tusk's broken!" exclaimed Kennedy. "Ivory too that in England would bring thirty-five guineas per hundred pounds."

"As much as that?" said Joe, scrambling down to the ground by the anchor rope.

"What's the use of sighing over it, Dick?" said the doctor. "Are we ivory merchants? Did we come hither to make money?"

Joe examined the anchor and found it solidly attached to the unbroken tusk. The doctor and Dick leaped out on the ground, while the balloon, now half emptied, hovered over the body of the huge animal.

"What a splendid beast!" said Kennedy. "What a mass of flesh! I never saw an elephant of that size in India!"

"There's nothing surprising about that, my dear Dick; the elephants of Central Africa are the finest in the world. The Andersons and the Cummings have hunted so incessantly in the neighborhood of the Cape, that these animals have migrated to the equator, where they are often met with in large herds."

"In the meanwhile, I hope," added Joe, "that we'll taste a morsel of this fellow. I'll undertake to get you a good dinner at his expense. Mr. Kennedy will go off and hunt for an hour or two; the doctor will make an inspection of the balloon, and, while they're busy in that way, I'll do the cooking."

"A good arrangement!" said the doctor. "So do as you like, Joe."

"As for me," said the hunter, "I shall avail myself of the two hours' recess that Joe has condescended to let me have."

"Go, my friend, but no imprudence! Don't wander too far away."

"Never fear, doctor!" And, so saying, Dick, shouldering his gun, plunged into the woods.

Forthwith Joe went to work at his vocation. At first he made a hole in the ground two feet deep; this he filled with the dry wood that was so abundantly scattered about, where it had been strewn by the elephants, whose tracks could be seen where they had made their way through the forest. This hole filled, he heaped a pile of fagots on it a foot in height, and set fire to it.

Then he went back to the carcass of the elephant, which had fallen only about a hundred feet from the edge of the forest; he next proceeded adroitly to cut off the trunk, which might have been two feet in diameter at the base; of this he selected the most delicate portion, and then took with it one of the animal's spongy feet. In fact, these are the finest morsels, like the hump of the bison, the paws of the bear, and the head of the wild boar.

When the pile of fagots had been thoroughly consumed, inside and outside, the hole, cleared of the cinders and hot coals, retained a very high temperature. The pieces of elephant meat, surrounded with aromatic leaves, were placed in this extempore oven and covered with hot coals. Then Joe piled up a second heap of sticks over all, and when it had burned out the meat was cooked to a turn.

Then Joe took the viands from the oven, spread the savory mess upon green leaves, and arranged his dinner upon a magnificent patch of greensward. He finally brought out some biscuit, some coffee, and some cognac, and got a can of pure, fresh water from a neighboring streamlet.

The repast thus prepared was a pleasant sight to behold, and Joe, without being too proud, thought that it would also be pleasant to eat.

"A journey without danger or fatigue," he soliloquized; "your meals when you please; a swinging hammock all the time! What more could a man ask? And there was Kennedy, who didn't want to come!"

On his part, Dr. Ferguson was engrossed in a serious and thorough examination of the balloon. The latter did not appear to have suffered from the storm; the silk and the gutta-percha had resisted wonderfully, and, upon estimating the exact height of the ground and the ascensional force of the balloon, our aeronaut saw, with satisfaction, that the hydrogen was in exactly the same quantity as before. The covering had remained completely waterproof.

It was now only five days since our travelers had quitted Zanzibar; their *pemmican* had not yet been touched; their stock of biscuit and potted meat was enough for a long trip, and there was nothing to be replenished but the water.

The pipes and spiral seemed to be in perfect condition, since, thanks to their india-rubber jointings, they had yielded to all the oscillations of the balloon. His examination ended, the doctor betook himself to setting his notes in order. He made a very accurate sketch of the surrounding landscape, with its long prairie stretching away out of sight, the forest of *calmadores*, and the balloon resting motionless over the body of the dead elephant.

At the end of his two hours, Kennedy returned with a string of fat partridges and the haunch of an *oryx*, a sort of *gemsbok* belonging to the most agile species of antelopes. Joe took upon himself to prepare this surplus stock of provisions for a later repast.

"But, dinner's ready!" he shouted in his most musical voice.

And the three travelers had only to sit down on the green turf. The trunk and feet of the elephant were declared to be exquisite. Old England was toasted, as usual, and delicious Havanas perfumed this charming country for the first time.

Kennedy ate, drank, and chatted, like four; he was perfectly delighted with his new life, and seriously proposed to the doctor to settle in this forest, to construct a cabin of boughs and foliage, and, there and then, to lay the foundation of a Robinson Crusoe dynasty in Africa.

The proposition went no further, although Joe had, at once, selected the part of Man Friday for himself.

The country seemed so quiet, so deserted, that the doctor resolved to pass the night on the ground, and Joe arranged a circle of watch fires as an indispensable barrier against wild animals, for the hyenas, cougars, and jackals, attracted by the smell of the dead elephant, were prowling about in the neighborhood. Kennedy had to fire his rifle several times at these unceremonious visitors, but the night passed without any untoward occurrence.

## CHAPTER XVIII

The Karagwah—Lake Ukéréoué—A Night on an Island—The Equator—
Crossing the Lake—The Cascades—A View of the Country—The
Sources of the Nile—The Island of Benga—The Signature of
Andrea Debono—The Flag with the Arms of England

At five o'clock in the morning, preparations for departure commenced. Joe, with the hatchet which he had fortunately recovered, broke the elephant's tusks. The balloon, restored to liberty, sped away to the northwest with our travelers, at the rate of eighteen miles per hour.

The doctor had carefully taken his position by the altitude of the stars, during the preceding night. He knew that he was in latitude two degrees forty minutes below the equator, or at a distance of one hundred and sixty geographical miles. He swept along over many villages without heeding the cries that the appearance of the balloon excited; he took note of the conformation of places with quick sights; he passed the slopes of the Rubemhe, which are nearly as abrupt as the summits of the Ousagara, and, farther on, at Tenga, encountered the first projections of the Karagwah chains, which, in his opinion, are direct spurs of the Mountains of the Moon. So, the ancient legend which made these mountains the cradle of the Nile, came near to the truth, since they really border upon Lake Ukéréoué, the conjectured reservoir of the waters of the great river.

From Kafuro, the main district of the merchants of that country, he descried, at length, on the horizon, the lake so much desired and so long sought for, of which Captain Speke caught a glimpse on the 3rd of August, 1858.

Samuel Ferguson felt real emotion: he was almost in contact with one of the principal points of his expedition, and, with his spyglass constantly raised, he kept every nook and corner of the mysterious region in sight. His gaze wandered over details that might have been thus described:

"Beneath him extended a country generally destitute of cultivation; only here and there some ravines seemed under tillage; the surface, dotted with peaks of medium height, grew flat as it approached the lake; barley fields took the place of rice plantations, and there, too, could be seen growing the species of plantain from which the wine of the country is drawn, and *mwani*, the wild plant which supplies a substitute for coffee. A collection of some fifty or more circular huts, covered with a flowering thatch, constituted the capital of the Karagwah country."

He could easily distinguish the astonished countenances of a rather fine-looking race of natives of yellowish-brown complexion. Women of incredible corpulence were dawdling about through the cultivated grounds, and the doctor greatly surprised his companions by informing them that this rotundity, which is highly esteemed in that region, was obtained by an obligatory diet of curdled milk.

At noon, the *Victoria* was in one degree forty-five minutes south latitude, and at one o'clock the wind was driving her directly toward the lake.

This sheet of water was christened *Uyanza Victoria*, or Victoria Lake, by Captain Speke. At the place now mentioned it might measure about ninety miles in breadth, and at its southern extremity the captain found a group of islets, which he named the Archipelago of Bengal. He pushed his survey as far as Muanza, on the eastern coast, where he was received by the sultan. He made a triangulation of this part of the lake, but he could not procure a boat, either to cross it or to visit the great island of Ukéréoué which is very populous, is governed by three sultans, and appears to be only a promontory at low tide.

The balloon approached the lake more to the northward, to the doctor's great regret, for it had been his wish to determine its lower outlines. Its shores seemed to be thickly set with brambles and thorny plants, growing together in wild confusion, and were literally hidden, sometimes, from the gaze, by myriads of mosquitoes of a light-brown hue. The country was evidently habitable and inhabited. Troops of hippopotami could be seen disporting themselves in the forests of reeds, or plunging beneath the whitish waters of the lake.

The latter, seen from above, presented, toward the west, so broad a horizon that it might have been called a sea; the distance between the two shores is so great that communication cannot be established, and storms are frequent and violent, for the winds sweep with fury over this elevated and unsheltered basin.

The doctor experienced some difficulty in guiding his course; he was afraid of being carried toward the east, but, fortunately, a current bore him directly toward the north, and at six o'clock in the evening the balloon alighted on a small desert island in thirty minutes south latitude, and thirty-two degrees fifty-two minutes east longitude, about twenty miles from the shore.

The travelers succeeded in making fast to a tree, and, the wind having fallen calm toward evening, they remained quietly at anchor. They dared not dream of taking the ground, since here, as on the shores of the Uyanza, legions of mosquitoes covered the soil in dense clouds. Joe even came back, from securing the anchor in the tree, speckled with bites, but he kept his temper, because he found it quite the natural thing for mosquitoes to treat him as they had done.

Nevertheless, the doctor, who was less of an optimist, let out as much rope as he could, so as to escape these pitiless insects that began to rise toward him with a threatening hum.

The doctor ascertained the height of the lake above the level of the sea, as it had been determined by Captain Speke, say three thousand seven hundred and fifty feet.

"Here we are, then, on an island!" said Joe, scratching as though he'd tear his nails out.

"We could make the tour of it in a jiffy," added Kennedy, "and, excepting these confounded mosquitoes, there's not a living being to be seen on it."

"The islands with which the lake is dotted," replied the doctor, "are nothing, after all, but the tops of submerged hills; but we are lucky to have found a retreat among them, for the shores of the lake are inhabited by ferocious tribes. Take your sleep, then, since Providence has granted us a tranquil night."

"Won't you do the same, doctor?"

"No, I could not close my eyes. My thoughts would banish sleep. Tomorrow, my friends, should the wind prove favorable, we shall go due north, and we shall, perhaps, discover the sources of the Nile, that grand secret which has so long remained impenetrable. Near as we are to the sources of the renowned river, I could not sleep."

Kennedy and Joe, whom scientific speculations failed to disturb to that extent, were not long in falling into sound slumber, while the doctor held his post.

On Wednesday, April 23rd, the balloon started at four o'clock in the morning, with a grayish sky overhead; night was slow in quitting the surface of the lake, which was enveloped in a dense fog, but presently a violent breeze scattered all the mists, and, after the balloon had been swung to and fro for a moment, in opposite directions, it at length veered in a straight line toward the north.

Dr. Ferguson fairly clapped his hands for joy.

"We are on the right track!" he exclaimed. "Today or never we shall see the Nile! Look, my friends, we are crossing the equator! We are entering our own hemisphere!"

"Ah!" said Joe. "Do you think, doctor, that the equator passes here?"

"Just here, my boy!"

"Well, then, with all respect to you, sir, it seems to me that this is the very time to moisten it."

"Good!" said the doctor, laughing. "Let us have a glass of punch. You have a way of comprehending cosmography that is anything but dull."

And thus was the passage of the *Victoria* over the equator duly celebrated.

The balloon made rapid headway. In the west could be seen a low and but slightly diversified coast, and, farther away in the background, the elevated plains of the Uganda and the Usoga. At length, the rapidity of the wind became excessive, approaching thirty miles per hour.

The waters of the Nyanza, violently agitated, were foaming like the billows of a sea. By the appearance of certain long swells that followed the sinking of the waves, the doctor was enabled to conclude that the lake must have great depth of water. Only one or two rude boats were seen during this rapid passage.

"This lake is evidently, from its elevated position, the natural reservoir of the rivers in the eastern part of Africa, and the sky gives back to it in rain what it takes in vapor from the streams that flow out of it. I am certain that the Nile must here take its rise."

"Well, we shall see!" said Kennedy.

About nine o'clock they drew nearer to the western coast. It seemed deserted, and covered with woods; the wind freshened a little toward the east, and the other shore of the lake could be seen. It bent around in such a curve as to end in a wide angle toward two degrees forty minutes north latitude. Lofty mountains uplifted their arid peaks at this extremity of Nyanza; but, between them, a deep and winding gorge gave exit to a turbulent and foaming river.

While busy managing the balloon, Dr. Ferguson never ceased reconnoitering the country with eager eyes.

"Look!" he exclaimed. "Look, my friends! The statements of the Arabs were correct! They spoke of a river by which Lake Ukéréoué discharged its waters toward the north, and this river exists, and we are descending it, and it flows with a speed analogous to our own! And this drop of water now gliding away beneath our feet is, beyond all question, rushing on, to mingle with the Mediterranean! It is the Nile!"

"It is the Nile!" re-echoed Kennedy, carried away by the enthusiasm of his friend.

"Hurrah for the Nile!" shouted Joe, glad, and always ready to cheer for something.

Enormous rocks, here and there, embarrassed the course of this mysterious river. The water foamed as it fell in rapids and cataracts, which confirmed the doctor in his preconceived ideas on the subject. From the environing mountains numerous torrents came plunging and seething down, and the eye could take them in by hundreds. There could be seen, starting from the soil, delicate jets of water scattering in all directions, crossing and recrossing each other, mingling, contending in the swiftness of their progress, and all rushing toward that nascent stream which became a river after having drunk them in.

"Here is, indeed, the Nile!" reiterated the doctor, with the tone of profound conviction. "The origin of its name, like the origin of its waters, has fired the imagination of the learned; they have sought to trace it from the Greek, the Coptic, the Sanskrit; but all that matters little now, since we have made it surrender the secret of its source!"

"But," said the Scotchman, "how are you to make sure of the identity of this river with the one recognized by the travelers from the north?"

"We shall have certain, irrefutable, convincing, and infallible proof," replied Ferguson, "should the wind hold another hour in our favor!"

The mountains drew farther apart, revealing in their place numerous villages, and fields of white Indian corn, doura, and sugarcane. The tribes inhabiting the region seemed excited and hostile; they manifested more anger than adoration, and evidently saw in the aeronauts only obtrusive strangers, and not condescending deities. It appeared as though, in approaching the sources of the Nile, these men came to rob them of something, and so the *Victoria* had to keep out of range of their muskets.

"To land here would be a ticklish matter!" said the Scot.

"Well!" said Joe. "So much the worse for these natives. They'll have to do without the pleasure of our conversation."

"Nevertheless, descend I must," said the doctor, "were it only for a quarter of an hour. Without doing so I cannot verify the results of our expedition."

"It is indispensable, then, doctor?"

"Indispensable; and we will descend, even if we have to do so with a volley of musketry."

"The thing suits me," said Kennedy, toying with his pet rifle.

"And I'm ready, master, whenever you say the word!" added Joe, preparing for the fight.

"It would not be the first time," remarked the doctor, "that science has been followed up, sword in hand. The same thing happened to a French *savant* among the mountains of Spain, when he was measuring the terrestrial meridian."

"Be easy on that score, doctor, and trust to your two bodyguards."

"Are we there, master?"

"Not yet. In fact, I shall go up a little, first, in order to get an exact idea of the configuration of the country."

The hydrogen expanded, and in less than ten minutes the balloon was soaring at a height of twenty-five hundred feet above the ground.

From that elevation could be distinguished an inextricable network of smaller streams which the river received into its bosom; others came from the west, from between numerous hills, in the midst of fertile plains.

"We are not ninety miles from Gondokoro," said the doctor, measuring off the distance on his map, "and less than five miles from the point reached by the explorers from the north. Let us descend with great care."

And, upon this, the balloon was lowered about two thousand feet.

"Now, my friends, let us be ready, come what may."

"Ready it is!" said Dick and Joe, with one voice.

"Good!"

In a few moments the balloon was advancing along the bed of the river, and scarcely one hundred feet above the ground. The Nile measured but fifty fathoms in width at this point, and the natives were in great excitement, rushing to and fro, tumultuously, in the villages that lined the banks of the stream. At the second degree it forms a perpendicular cascade of ten feet in height, and consequently impassable by boats.

"Here, then, is the cascade mentioned by Debono!" exclaimed the doctor.

The basin of the river spread out, dotted with numerous islands, which Dr. Ferguson devoured with his eyes. He seemed to be seeking for a point of reference which he had not yet found.

By this time, some blacks, having ventured in a boat just under the balloon, Kennedy saluted them with a shot from his rifle, that made them regain the bank at their utmost speed.

"A good journey to you," bawled Joe, "and if I were in your place, I wouldn't try coming back again. I should be mightily afraid of a monster that can hurl thunderbolts when he pleases."

But, all at once, the doctor snatched up his spyglass, and directed it toward an island reposing in the middle of the river.

"Four trees!" he exclaimed. "Look, down there!" Sure enough, there were four trees standing alone at one end of it.

"It is Bengal Island! It is the very same," repeated the doctor, exultingly.

"And what of that?" asked Dick.

"It is there that we shall alight, if God permits."

"But, it seems to be inhabited, doctor."

"Joe is right; and, unless I'm mistaken, there is a group of about a score of natives on it now."

"We'll make them scatter; there'll be no great trouble in that," responded Ferguson.

"So be it," chimed in the hunter.

The sun was at the zenith as the balloon approached the island.

The blacks, who were members of the Makado tribe, were howling lustily, and one of them waved his bark hat in the air. Kennedy took aim at him, fired, and his hat flew about him in pieces. Thereupon there was a general scamper. The natives plunged headlong into the river, and swam to the opposite bank. Immediately, there came a shower of balls from both banks, along with a perfect cloud of arrows, but without doing the balloon any damage, where it rested with its anchor snugly secured in the fissure of a rock. Joe lost no time in sliding to the ground.

"The ladder!" cried the doctor. "Follow me, Kennedy."

"What do you wish, sir?"

"Let us alight. I want a witness."

"Here I am!"

"Mind your post, Joe, and keep a good lookout."

"Never fear, doctor; I'll answer for all that."

"Come, Dick," said the doctor, as he touched the ground.

So saying, he drew his companion along toward a group of rocks that rose upon one point of the island; there, after searching for some time, he began to rummage among the brambles, and, in so doing, scratched his hands until they bled.

Suddenly he grasped Kennedy's arm, exclaiming: "Look! Look!"

"Letters!"

Yes; there, indeed, could be descried, with perfect precision of outline, some letters carved on the rock. It was quite easy to make them out:

A. D.

"A.D.!" repeated Dr. Ferguson. "Andrea Debono—the very signature of the traveler who farthest ascended the current of the Nile."

"No doubt of that, friend Samuel," assented Kennedy.

"Are you now convinced?"

"It is the Nile! We cannot entertain a doubt on that score now," was the reply.

The doctor, for the last time, examined those precious initials, the exact form and size of which he carefully noted.

"And now," said he, "now for the balloon!"

"Quickly, then, for I see some of the natives getting ready to recross the river."

"That matters little to us now. Let the wind but send us northward for a few hours, and we shall reach Gondokoro, and press the hands of some of our countrymen."

Ten minutes more, and the balloon was majestically ascending, while Dr. Ferguson, in token of success, waved the English flag triumphantly from his car.

## CHAPTER XIX

THE NILE—THE TREMBLING MOUNTAIN—A REMEMBRANCE OF THE
COUNTRY—THE NARRATIVES OF THE ARABS—THE NYAM-NYAMS—JOE'S
SHREWD COGITATIONS—THE BALLOON RUNS THE GANTLET—
AEROSTATIC ASCENSIONS—MADAME BLANCHARD

"Which way do we head?" asked Kennedy, as he saw his friend consulting the compass.

"North-northeast."

"The deuce! But that's not the north?"

"No, Dick; and I'm afraid that we shall have some trouble in getting to Gondokoro. I am sorry for it; but, at last, we have succeeded in connecting the explorations from the east with those from the north; and we must not complain."

The balloon was now receding gradually from the Nile.

"One last look," said the doctor, "at this impassable latitude, beyond which the most intrepid travelers could not make their way. There are those intractable tribes, of whom Petherick, Arnaud, Miuni, and the young traveler Lejean, to whom we are indebted for the best work on the Upper Nile, have spoken."

"Thus, then," added Kennedy, inquiringly, "our discoveries agree with the speculations of science."

"Absolutely so. The sources of the White Nile, of the Bahr-el-Abiad, are immersed in a lake as large as a sea; it is there that it takes its rise. Poesy, undoubtedly, loses something thereby. People were fond of ascribing a celestial origin to this king of rivers. The ancients gave it the name of an ocean, and were not far from believing that it flowed directly from the sun; but we must come down from these flights from time to time, and accept what science teaches us. There will not always be scientific men, perhaps; but there always will be poets."

"We can still see cataracts," said Joe.

"Those are the cataracts of Makedo, in the third degree of latitude. Nothing could be more accurate. Oh, if we could only have followed the course of the Nile for a few hours!"

"And down yonder, below us, I see the top of a mountain," said the hunter.

"That is Mount Longwek, the *Trembling Mountain* of the Arabs. This whole country was visited by Debono, who went through it under the name of Latif-Effendi. The tribes living near the Nile are hostile to each other, and are continually waging a war of extermination. You may form some idea, then, of the difficulties he had to encounter."

The wind was carrying the balloon toward the northwest, and, in order to avoid Mount Longwek, it was necessary to seek a more slanting current.

"My friends," said the doctor, "here is where *our* passage of the African continent really commences; up to this time we have been following the traces of our predecessors. Henceforth we are to launch ourselves upon the unknown. We shall not lack the courage, shall we?"

"Never!" said Dick and Joe together, almost in a shout.

"Onward, then, and may we have the help of Heaven!"

At ten o'clock at night, after passing over ravines, forests, and scattered villages, the aeronauts reached the side of the Trembling Mountain, along whose gentle slopes they went quietly gliding. In that memorable day, the 23rd of April, they had, in fifteen hours, impelled by a rapid breeze, traversed a distance of more than three hundred and fifteen miles.

But this latter part of the journey had left them in dull spirits, and complete silence reigned in the car. Was Dr. Ferguson absorbed in the thought of his discoveries? Were his two companions thinking of their trip through those unknown regions? There were, no doubt, mingled with these reflections, the keenest reminiscences of home and distant friends. Joe alone continued to manifest the same careless philosophy, finding it quite natural that home should not be there, from the moment that he left it; but he respected the silent mood of his friends, the doctor and Kennedy.

About ten the balloon anchored on the side of the Trembling Mountain, so called, because, in Arab tradition, it is said to tremble the instant that a Mussulman sets foot upon it. The travelers then partook of a substantial meal, and all quietly passed the night as usual, keeping the regular watches.

On awaking the next morning, they all had pleasanter feelings. The weather was fine, and the wind was blowing from the right quarter; so that a good breakfast, seasoned with Joe's merry pranks, put them in high good humor.

The region they were now crossing is very extensive. It borders on the Mountains of the Moon on one side, and those of Darfur on the other—a space about as broad as Europe.

"We are, no doubt, crossing what is supposed to be the kingdom of Usoga. Geographers have pretended that there existed, in the center of Africa, a vast depression, an immense central lake. We shall see whether there is any truth in that idea," said the doctor.

"But how did they come to think so?" asked Kennedy.

"From the recitals of the Arabs. Those fellows are great narrators—too much so, probably. Some travelers, who had got as far as Kazeh, or the great lakes, saw slaves that had been brought from this region; interrogated them concerning it, and, from their different narratives, made up a jumble of notions, and deduced systems from them. Down at the bottom of it all there is some appearance of truth; and you see that they were right about the sources of the Nile."

"Nothing could be more correct," said Kennedy. "It was by the aid of these documents that some attempts at maps were made, and so I am going to try to follow our route by one of them, rectifying it when need be."

"Is all this region inhabited?" asked Joe.

"Undoubtedly; and disagreeably inhabited, too."

"I thought so."

"These scattered tribes come, one and all, under the title of Nyam-Nyams, and this compound word is only a sort of nickname. It imitates the sound of chewing."

"That's it! Excellent!" said Joe, champing his teeth as though he were eating. "Nyam-Nyam."

"My good Joe, if you were the immediate object of this chewing, you wouldn't find it so excellent."

"Why, what's the reason, sir?"

"These tribes are considered man-eaters."

"Is that really the case?"

"Not a doubt of it! It has also been asserted that these natives had tails, like mere quadrupeds; but it was soon discovered that these appendages belonged to the skins of animals that they wore for clothing."

"More's the pity! A tail's a nice thing to chase away mosquitoes."

"That may be, Joe; but we must consign the story to the domain of fable, like the dogs' heads which the traveler, Brun-Rollet, attributed to other tribes."

"Dogs' heads, eh? Quite convenient for barking, and even for man-eating!"

"But one thing that has been, unfortunately, proven true, is, the ferocity of these tribes, who are really very fond of human flesh, and devour it with avidity."

"I only hope that they won't take such a particular fancy to mine!" said Joe, with comic solemnity.

"See that!" said Kennedy.

"Yes, indeed, sir; if I have to be eaten, in a moment of famine, I want it to be for your benefit and my master's; but the idea of feeding those black fellows—gracious! I'd die of shame!"

"Well, then, Joe," said Kennedy, "that's understood; we count upon you in case of need!"

"At your service, gentlemen!"

"Joe talks in this way so as to make us take good care of him, and fatten him up."

"Maybe so!" said Joe. "Every man for himself."

In the afternoon, the sky became covered with a warm mist that oozed from the soil; the brownish vapor scarcely allowed the beholder to distinguish objects, and so, fearing collision with some unexpected mountain peak, the doctor, about five o'clock, gave the signal to halt.

The night passed without accident, but in such profound obscurity, that it was necessary to use redoubled vigilance.

The monsoon blew with extreme violence during all the next morning. The wind buried itself in the lower cavities of the balloon and shook the appendage by which the dilating pipes entered the main apparatus. They had, at last, to be tied up with cords, Joe acquitting himself very skillfully in performing that operation.

He had occasion to observe, at the same time, that the orifice of the balloon still remained hermetically sealed.

"That is a matter of double importance for us," said the doctor; "in the first place, we avoid the escape of precious gas, and then, again, we do not leave behind us an inflammable train, which we should at last inevitably set fire to, and so be consumed."

"That would be a disagreeable traveling incident!" said Joe.

"Should we be hurled to the ground?" asked Kennedy.

"Hurled! No, not quite that. The gas would burn quietly, and we should descend little by little. A similar accident happened to a French aeronaut, Madame Blanchard. She ignited her balloon while sending off fireworks, but she did not fall, and she would not have been killed, probably, had not her car dashed against a chimney and precipitated her to the ground."

"Let us hope that nothing of the kind may happen to us," said the hunter. "Up to this time our trip has not seemed to me very dangerous, and I can see nothing to prevent us reaching our destination."

"Nor can I either, my dear Dick; accidents are generally caused by the imprudence of the aeronauts, or the defective construction of their apparatus. However, in thousands of aerial ascensions, there have not been twenty fatal accidents. Usually, the danger is in the moment of leaving the ground, or of alighting, and therefore at those junctures we should never omit the utmost precaution."

"It's breakfast time," said Joe; "we'll have to put up with preserved meat and coffee until Mr. Kennedy has had another chance to get us a good slice of venison."

## CHAPTER XX

The wind had become violent and irregular; the balloon was running the gantlet through the air. Tossed at one moment toward the north, at another toward the south, it could not find one steady current.

"We are moving very swiftly without advancing much," said Kennedy, remarking the frequent oscillations of the needle of the compass.

"The balloon is rushing at the rate of at least thirty miles an hour. Lean over, and see how the country is gliding away beneath us!" said the doctor.

"See! That forest looks as though it were precipitating itself upon us!"

"The forest has become a clearing!" added the other.

"And the clearing a village!" continued Joe, a moment or two later. "Look at the faces of those astonished darkys!"

"Oh! It's natural enough that they should be astonished," said the doctor. "The French peasants, when they first saw a balloon, fired at it, thinking that it was an aerial monster. A Soudan negro may be excused, then, for opening his eyes *very* wide!"

"Faith!" said Joe, as the *Victoria* skimmed closely along the ground, at scarcely the elevation of one hundred feet, and immediately over a village. "I'll throw them an empty bottle, with your leave, doctor, and if it reaches them safe and sound, they'll worship it; if it breaks, they'll make talismans of the pieces."

So saying, he flung out a bottle, which, of course, was broken into a thousand fragments, while the negroes scampered into their round huts, uttering shrill cries.

A little farther on, Kennedy called out: "Look at that strange tree! The upper part is of one kind and the lower part of another!"

"Well!" said Joe. "Here's a country where the trees grow on top of each other."

"It's simply the trunk of a fig tree," replied the doctor, "on which there is a little vegetating earth. Some fine day, the wind left the seed of a palm on it, and the seed has taken root and grown as though it were on the plain ground."

"A fine new style of gardening," said Joe, "and I'll import the idea to England. It would be just the thing in the London parks; without counting that it would be another way to increase the number of fruit trees. We could have gardens up in the air; and the small house owners would like that!"

At this moment, they had to raise the balloon so as to pass over a forest of trees that were more than three hundred feet in height—a kind of ancient banyan.

"What magnificent trees!" exclaimed Kennedy. "I never saw anything so fine as the appearance of these venerable forests. Look, doctor!"

"The height of these banyans is really remarkable, my dear Dick; and yet, they would be nothing astonishing in the New World."

"Why, are there still loftier trees in existence?"

"Undoubtedly; among the 'mammoth trees' of California, there is a cedar four hundred and eighty feet in height. It would overtop the Houses of Parliament, and even the Great Pyramid of Egypt. The trunk at the surface of the ground was one hundred and twenty feet in circumference, and the concentric layers of the wood disclosed an age of more than four thousand years."

"But then, sir, there was nothing wonderful in it! When one has lived four thousand years, one ought to be pretty tall!" was Joe's remark.

Meanwhile, during the doctor's recital and Joe's response, the forest had given place to a large collection of huts surrounding an open space. In the middle of this grew a solitary tree, and Joe exclaimed, as he caught sight of it:

"Well! If that tree has produced such flowers as those, for the last four thousand years, I have to offer it my compliments, anyhow," and he pointed to a gigantic sycamore, whose whole trunk was covered with human bones. The flowers of which Joe spoke were heads freshly severed from the bodies, and suspended by daggers thrust into the bark of the tree.

"The war tree of these cannibals!" said the doctor. "The Indians merely carry off the scalp, but these negroes take the whole head."

"A mere matter of fashion!" said Joe. But, already, the village and the bleeding heads were disappearing on the horizon. Another place offered a still more revolting spectacle—half-devoured corpses; skeletons moldering to dust; human limbs scattered here and there, and left to feed the jackals and hyenas.

"No doubt, these are the bodies of criminals; according to the custom in Abyssinia, these people have left them a prey to the wild beasts, who kill them with their terrible teeth and claws, and then devour them at their leisure."

"Not a whit more cruel than hanging!" said the Scot. "Filthier, that's all!"

"In the southern regions of Africa, they content themselves," resumed the doctor, "with shutting up the criminal in his own hut with his cattle, and sometimes with his family. They then set fire to the hut, and the whole party are burned together. I call that cruel; but, like friend Kennedy, I think that the gallows is quite as cruel, quite as barbarous."

Joe, by the aid of his keen sight, which he did not fail to use continually, noticed some flocks of birds of prey flitting about the horizon.

"They are eagles!" exclaimed Kennedy, after reconnoitering them through the glass. "Magnificent birds, whose flight is as rapid as ours."

"Heaven preserve us from their attacks!" said the doctor. "They are more to be feared by us than wild beasts or savage tribes."

"Bah!" said the hunter. "We can drive them off with a few rifle shots."

"Nevertheless, I would prefer, dear Dick, not having to rely upon your skill, this time, for the silk of our balloon could not resist their sharp beaks; fortunately, the huge birds will, I believe, be more frightened than attracted by our machine."

"Yes! But a new idea, and I have dozens of them," said Joe. "If we could only manage to capture a team of live eagles, we could hitch them to the balloon, and they'd haul us through the air!"

"The thing has been seriously proposed," replied the doctor, "but I think it hardly practicable with creatures naturally so restive."

"Oh! We'd tame them," said Joe. "Instead of driving them with bits, we'd do it with eye-blinkers that would cover their eyes. Half blinded in that way, they'd go to the right or to the left, as we desired; when blinded completely, they would stop."

"Allow me, Joe, to prefer a favorable wind to your team of eagles. It costs less for fodder, and is more reliable."

"Well, you may have your choice, master, but I stick to my idea."

It now was noon. The *Victoria* had been going at a more moderate speed for some time; the country merely passed below it; it no longer flew.

Suddenly, shouts and whistlings were heard by our aeronauts, and, leaning over the edge of the car, they saw on the open plain below them an exciting spectacle.

Two hostile tribes were fighting furiously, and the air was dotted with volleys of arrows. The combatants were so intent upon their murderous work that they did not notice the arrival of the balloon; there were about three hundred mingled confusedly in the deadly struggle: most of them, red with the blood of the wounded, in which they fairly wallowed, were horrible to behold.

As they at last caught sight of the balloon, there was a momentary pause; but their yells redoubled, and some arrows were shot at the *Victoria*, one of them coming close enough for Joe to catch it with his hand.

"Let us rise out of range," exclaimed the doctor; "there must be no rashness! We are forbidden any risk."

Meanwhile, the massacre continued on both sides, with battle-axes and war clubs; as quickly as one of the combatants fell, a hostile warrior ran up to cut off his head, while the women, mingling in the fray, gathered up these bloody trophies, and piled them together at either extremity of the battlefield. Often, too, they even fought for these hideous spoils.

"What a frightful scene!" said Kennedy, with profound disgust.

"They're ugly acquaintances!" added Joe. "But then, if they had uniforms they'd be just like the fighters of all the rest of the world!"

"I have a keen hankering to take a hand in at that fight," said the hunter, brandishing his rifle.

"No! No!" objected the doctor, vehemently. "No, let us not meddle with what don't concern us. Do you know which is right or which is wrong, that you would assume the part of the Almighty? Let us, rather, hurry away from this revolting spectacle. Could the great captains of the world float thus above the scenes of their exploits, they would at last, perhaps, conceive a disgust for blood and conquest."

The chieftain of one of the contending parties was remarkable for his athletic proportions, his great height, and herculean strength. With one hand he plunged his spear into the compact ranks of his enemies, and with the other mowed large spaces in them with his battle-axe. Suddenly he flung away his war club, red with blood, rushed upon a wounded warrior, and, chopping off his arm at a single stroke, carried the dissevered member to his mouth, and bit it again and again.

"Ah!" ejaculated Kennedy. "The horrible brute! I can hold back no longer." And, as he spoke, the huge savage, struck full in the forehead with a rifle ball, fell headlong to the ground.

Upon this sudden mishap of their leader, his warriors seemed struck dumb with amazement; his supernatural death awed them, while it reanimated the courage and ardor of their adversaries, and, in a twinkling, the field was abandoned by half the combatants.

"Come, let us look higher up for a current to bear us away. I am sick of this spectacle," said the doctor.

But they could not get away so rapidly as to avoid the sight of the victorious tribe rushing upon the dead and the wounded, scrambling and disputing for the still warm and reeking flesh, and eagerly devouring it.

"Faugh!" uttered Joe. "It's sickening."

The balloon rose as it expanded; the howlings of the brutal horde, in the delirium of their orgy, pursued them for a few minutes; but, at length, borne away toward the south, they were carried out of sight and hearing of this horrible spectacle of cannibalism.

The surface of the country was now greatly varied, with numerous streams of water, bearing toward the east. The latter, undoubtedly, ran into those affluents of Lake Nu, or of the River of the Gazelles, concerning which M. Guillaume Lejean has given such curious details.

At nightfall, the balloon cast anchor in twenty-seven degrees east longitude, and four degrees twenty minutes north latitude, after a day's trip of one hundred and fifty miles.

## CHAPTER XXI

STRANGE SOUNDS—A NIGHT ATTACK—KENNEDY AND JOE IN THE TREE—
TWO SHOTS—"HELP! HELP!"—REPLY IN FRENCH—THE MORNING—
THE MISSIONARY—THE PLAN OF RESCUE

The night came on very dark. The doctor had not been able to reconnoiter the country. He had made fast to a very tall tree, from which he could distinguish only a confused mass through the gloom.

As usual, he took the nine-o'clock watch, and at midnight Dick relieved him.

"Keep a sharp lookout, Dick!" was the doctor's good-night injunction.

"Is there anything new on the carpet?"

"No; but I thought that I heard vague sounds below us, and, as I don't exactly know where the wind has carried us to, even an excess of caution would do no harm."

"You've probably heard the cries of wild beasts."

"No! The sounds seemed to me something altogether different from that; at all events, on the least alarm don't fail to waken us."

"I'll do so, doctor; rest easy."

After listening attentively for a moment or two longer, the doctor, hearing nothing more, threw himself on his blankets and went asleep.

The sky was covered with dense clouds, but not a breath of air was stirring; and the balloon, kept in its place by only a single anchor, experienced not the slightest oscillation.

Kennedy, leaning his elbow on the edge of the car, so as to keep an eye on the cylinder, which was actively at work, gazed out upon the calm obscurity; he eagerly scanned the horizon, and, as often happens to minds that are uneasy or possessed with preconceived notions, he fancied that he sometimes detected vague gleams of light in the distance.

At one moment he even thought that he saw them only two hundred paces away, quite distinctly, but it was a mere flash that was gone as quickly as it came, and he noticed nothing more. It was, no doubt, one of those luminous illusions that sometimes impress the eye in the midst of very profound darkness.

Kennedy was getting over his nervousness and falling into his wandering meditations again, when a sharp whistle pierced his ear.

Was that the cry of an animal or of a night-bird, or did it come from human lips?

Kennedy, perfectly comprehending the gravity of the situation, was on the point of waking his companions, but he reflected that, in any case, men or animals, the creatures that he had heard must be out of reach. So he merely saw that his weapons were all right, and then, with his night-glass, again plunged his gaze into space.

It was not long before he thought he could perceive below him vague forms that seemed to be gliding toward the tree, and then, by the aid of a ray of moonlight that shot like an electric flash between two masses of cloud, he distinctly made out a group of human figures moving in the shadow.

The adventure with the dog-faced baboons returned to his memory, and he placed his hand on the doctor's shoulder.

The latter was awake in a moment.

"Silence!" said Dick. "Let us speak below our breath."

"Has anything happened?"

"Yes, let us waken Joe."

The instant that Joe was aroused, Kennedy told him what he had seen.

"Those confounded monkeys again!" said Joe.

"Possibly, but we must be on our guard."

"Joe and I," said Kennedy, "will climb down the tree by the ladder."

"And, in the meanwhile," added the doctor, "I will take my measures so that we can ascend rapidly at a moment's warning."

"Agreed!"

"Let us go down, then!" said Joe.

"Don't use your weapons, excepting at the last extremity! It would be a useless risk to make the natives aware of our presence in such a place as this."

Dick and Joe replied with signs of assent, and then letting themselves slide noiselessly toward the tree, took their position in a fork among the strong branches where the anchor had caught.

For some moments they listened minutely and motionlessly among the foliage, and ere long Joe seized Kennedy's hand as he heard a sort of rubbing sound against the bark of the tree.

"Don't you hear that?" he whispered.

"Yes, and it's coming nearer."

"Suppose it should be a serpent? That hissing or whistling that you heard before—"

"No! There was something human in it."

"I'd prefer the savages, for I have a horror of those snakes."

"The noise is increasing," said Kennedy, again, after a lapse of a few moments.

"Yes! Something's coming up toward us—climbing."

"Keep watch on this side, and I'll take care of the other."

"Very good!"

There they were, isolated at the top of one of the larger branches shooting out in the midst of one of those miniature forests called baobab trees. The darkness, heightened by the density of the foliage, was profound; however, Joe, leaning over to Kennedy's ear and pointing down the tree, whispered:

"The blacks! They're climbing toward us."

The two friends could even catch the sound of a few words uttered in the lowest possible tones.

Joe gently brought his rifle to his shoulder as he spoke.

"Wait!" said Kennedy.

Some of the natives had really climbed the baobab, and now they were seen rising on all sides, winding along the boughs like reptiles, and advancing slowly but surely, all the time plainly enough discernible, not merely to the eye but to the nostrils, by the horrible odors of the rancid grease with which they bedaub their bodies.

Ere long, two heads appeared to the gaze of Kennedy and Joe, on a level with the very branch to which they were clinging.

"Attention!" said Kennedy. "Fire!"

The double concussion resounded like a thunderbolt and died away into cries of rage and pain, and in a moment the whole horde had disappeared.

But, in the midst of these yells and howls, a strange, unexpected—nay, what seemed an impossible—cry had been heard! A human voice had, distinctly, called aloud in the French language—

"Help! Help!"

Kennedy and Joe, dumb with amazement, had regained the car immediately.

"Did you hear that?" the doctor asked them.

"Undoubtedly, that supernatural cry, '*À moi! À moi!*' comes from a Frenchman in the hands of these barbarians!"

"A traveler."

"A missionary, perhaps."

"Poor wretch!" said Kennedy. "They're assassinating him—making a martyr of him!"

The doctor then spoke, and it was impossible for him to conceal his emotions.

"There can be no doubt of it," he said; "some unfortunate Frenchman has fallen into the hands of these savages. We must not leave this place without doing all in our power to save him. When he heard the sound of our guns, he recognized an unhoped-for assistance, a providential interposition. We shall not disappoint his last hope. Are such your views?"

"They are, doctor, and we are ready to obey you."

"Let us, then, lay our heads together to devise some plan, and in the morning we'll try to rescue him."

"But how shall we drive off those abominable blacks?" asked Kennedy.

"It's quite clear to me, from the way in which they made off, that they are unacquainted with firearms. We must, therefore, profit by their fears; but we shall await daylight before acting, and then we can form our plans of rescue according to circumstances."

"The poor captive cannot be far off," said Joe, "because—"

"Help! Help!" repeated the voice, but much more feebly this time.

"The savage wretches!" exclaimed Joe, trembling with indignation. "Suppose they should kill him tonight!"

"Do you hear, doctor," resumed Kennedy, seizing the doctor's hand. "Suppose they should kill him tonight!"

"It is not at all likely, my friends. These savage tribes kill their captives in broad daylight; they must have the sunshine."

"Now, if I were to take advantage of the darkness to slip down to the poor fellow?" said Kennedy.

"And I'll go with you," said Joe, warmly.

"Pause, my friends—pause! The suggestion does honor to your hearts and to your courage; but you would expose us all to great peril, and do still greater harm to the unfortunate man whom you wish to aid."

"Why so?" asked Kennedy. "These savages are frightened and dispersed: they will not return."

"Dick, I implore you, heed what I say. I am acting for the common good; and if by any accident you should be taken by surprise, all would be lost."

"But, think of that poor wretch, hoping for aid, waiting there, praying, calling aloud. Is no one to go to his assistance? He must think that his senses deceived him; that he heard nothing!"

"We can reassure him, on that score," said Dr. Ferguson—and, standing erect, making a speaking-trumpet of his hands, he shouted at the top of his voice, in French: "Whoever you are, be of good cheer! Three friends are watching over you."

A terrific howl from the savages responded to these words—no doubt drowning the prisoner's reply.

"They are murdering him! They are murdering him!" exclaimed Kennedy. "Our interference will have served no other purpose than to hasten the hour of his doom. We must act!"

"But how, Dick? What do you expect to do in the midst of this darkness?"

"Oh, if it was only daylight!" sighed Joe.

"Well, and suppose it were daylight?" said the doctor, in a singular tone.

"Nothing more simple, doctor," said Kennedy. "I'd go down and scatter all these savage villains with powder and ball!"

"And you, Joe, what would you do?"

"I, master? Why, I'd act more prudently, maybe, by telling the prisoner to make his escape in a certain direction that we'd agree upon."

"And how would you get him to know that?"

"By means of this arrow that I caught flying the other day. I'd tie a note to it, or I'd just call out to him in a loud voice what you want him to do, because these black fellows don't understand the language that you'd speak in!"

"Your plans are impracticable, my dear friends. The greatest difficulty would be for this poor fellow to escape at all—even admitting that he should manage to elude the vigilance of his captors. As for you, my dear Dick, with determined daring, and profiting by their alarm at our firearms, your project might possibly succeed; but, were it to fail, you would be lost, and we should have two persons to save instead of one. No! We must put all the chances on our side, and go to work differently."

"But let us act at once!" said the hunter.

"Perhaps we may," said the doctor, throwing considerable stress upon the words.

"Why, doctor, can you light up such darkness as this?"

"Who knows, Joe?"

"Ah! If you can do that, you're the greatest learned man in the world!"

The doctor kept silent for a few moments; he was thinking. His two companions looked at him with much emotion, for they were greatly excited by the strangeness of the situation. Ferguson at last resumed:

"Here is my plan: We have two hundred pounds of ballast left, since the bags we brought with us are still untouched. I'll suppose that this prisoner, who is evidently exhausted by suffering, weighs as much as one of us; there will still remain sixty pounds of ballast to throw out, in case we should want to ascend suddenly."

"How do you expect to manage the balloon?" asked Kennedy.

"This is the idea, Dick: you will admit that if I can get to the prisoner, and throw out a quantity of ballast, equal to his weight, I shall have in nowise altered the equilibrium of the balloon. But, then, if I want to get a rapid ascension, so as to escape these savages, I must employ means more energetic than the cylinder. Well, then, in throwing out this overplus of ballast at a given moment, I am certain to rise with great rapidity."

"That's plain enough."

"Yes; but there is one drawback: it consists in the fact that, in order to descend after that, I should have to part with a quantity of gas proportionate to the surplus ballast that I had thrown out. Now, the gas is precious; but we must not haggle over it when the life of a fellow creature is at stake."

"You are right, sir; we must do everything in our power to save him."

"Let us work, then, and get these bags all arranged on the rim of the car, so that they may be thrown overboard at one movement."

"But this darkness?"

"It hides our preparations, and will be dispersed only when they are finished. Take care to have all our weapons close at hand. Perhaps we may have to fire; so we have one shot in the rifle; four for the two muskets; twelve in the two revolvers; or seventeen in all, which might be fired in a quarter of a minute. But perhaps we shall not have to resort to all this noisy work. Are you ready?"

"We're ready," responded Joe.

The sacks were placed as requested, and the arms were put in good order.

"Very good!" said the doctor. "Have an eye to everything. Joe will see to throwing out the ballast, and Dick will carry off the prisoner; but let nothing be done until I give the word. Joe will first detach the anchor, and then quickly make his way back to the car."

Joe let himself slide down by the rope; and, in a few moments, reappeared at his post; while the balloon, thus liberated, hung almost motionless in the air.

In the meantime the doctor assured himself of the presence of a sufficient quantity of gas in the mixing tank to feed the cylinder, if necessary, without there being any need of resorting for some time to the Buntzen battery. He then took out the two perfectly isolated conducting wires, which served for the decomposition of the water, and, searching in his traveling sack, brought forth two pieces of charcoal, cut down to a sharp point, and fixed one at the end of each wire.

His two friends looked on, without knowing what he was about, but they kept perfectly silent. When the doctor had finished, he stood up erect in the car, and, taking the two pieces of charcoal, one in each hand, drew their points nearly together.

In a twinkling, an intense and dazzling light was produced, with an insupportable glow between the two pointed ends of charcoal, and a huge jet of electric radiance literally broke the darkness of the night.

"Oh!" ejaculated the astonished friends.

"Not a word!" cautioned the doctor.

## *CHAPTER XXII*

Dr. Ferguson darted his powerful electric jet toward various points of space, and caused it to rest on a spot from which shouts of terror were heard. His companions fixed their gaze eagerly on the place.

The baobab, over which the balloon was hanging almost motionless, stood in the center of a clearing, where, between fields of Indian corn and sugarcane, were seen some fifty low, conical huts, around which swarmed a numerous tribe.

A hundred feet below the balloon stood a large post, or stake, and at its foot lay a human being—a young man of thirty years or more, with long black hair, half naked, wasted and wan, bleeding, covered with wounds, his head bowed over upon his breast, as Christ's was, when He hung upon the cross.

The hair, cut shorter on the top of his skull, still indicated the place of a half-effaced tonsure.

"A missionary! A priest!" exclaimed Joe.

"Poor, unfortunate man!" said Kennedy.

"We must save him, Dick!" responded the doctor. "We must save him!"

The crowd of blacks, when they saw the balloon over their heads, like a huge comet with a train of dazzling light, were seized with a terror that may be readily imagined. Upon hearing their cries, the prisoner raised his head. His eyes gleamed with sudden hope, and, without too thoroughly comprehending what was taking place, he stretched out his hands to his unexpected deliverers.

"He is alive!" exclaimed Ferguson. "God be praised! The savages have got a fine scare, and we shall save him! Are you ready, friends?"

"Ready, doctor, at the word."

"Joe, shut off the cylinder!"

The doctor's order was executed. An almost imperceptible breath of air impelled the balloon directly over the prisoner, at the same time that it gently lowered with the contraction of the gas. For about ten minutes it remained floating in the midst of luminous waves, for Ferguson continued to flash right down upon the throng his glowing sheaf of rays, which, here and there, marked out swift and vivid sheets of light. The tribe, under the influence of an indescribable terror, disappeared little by little in the huts, and there was complete solitude around the stake. The doctor had, therefore, been right in counting upon the fantastic appearance of the balloon throwing out rays, as vivid as the sun's, through this intense gloom.

The car was approaching the ground; but a few of the savages, more audacious than the rest, guessing that their victim was about to escape from their clutches, came back with loud yells, and Kennedy seized his rifle. The doctor, however, besought him not to fire.

The priest, on his knees, for he had not the strength to stand erect, was not even fastened to the stake, his weakness rendering that precaution superfluous. At the instant when the car was close to the ground, the brawny Scot, laying aside his rifle, and seizing the priest around the waist, lifted him into the car, while, at the same moment, Joe tossed over the two hundred pounds of ballast.

The doctor had expected to ascend rapidly, but, contrary to his calculations, the balloon, after going up some three or four feet, remained there perfectly motionless.

"What holds us?" he asked, with an accent of terror.

Some of the savages were running toward them, uttering ferocious cries.

"Ah, ha!" said Joe. "One of those cursed blacks is hanging to the car!"

"Dick! Dick!" cried the doctor. "The water tank!"

Kennedy caught his friend's idea on the instant, and, snatching up with desperate strength one of the water tanks weighing about one hundred pounds, he tossed it overboard. The balloon, thus suddenly lightened, made a leap of three hundred feet into the air, amid the howlings of the tribe whose prisoner thus escaped them in a blaze of dazzling light.

"Hurrah!" shouted the doctor's comrades.

Suddenly, the balloon took a fresh leap, which carried it up to an elevation of a thousand feet.

"What's that?" said Kennedy, who had nearly lost his balance.

"Oh! Nothing; only that black villain leaving us!" replied the doctor, tranquilly, and Joe, leaning over, saw the savage that had clung to the car whirling over and over, with his arms outstretched in the air, and presently dashed to pieces on the ground. The doctor then separated his electric wires, and everything was again buried in profound obscurity. It was now one o'clock in the morning.

The Frenchman, who had swooned away, at length opened his eyes.

"You are saved!" were the doctor's first words.

"Saved!" he with a sad smile replied in English. "Saved from a cruel death! My brethren, I thank you, but my days are numbered, nay, even my hours, and I have but little longer to live."

With this, the missionary, again yielding to exhaustion, relapsed into his fainting fit.

"He is dying!" said Kennedy.

"No," replied the doctor, bending over him, "but he is very weak; so let us lay him under the awning."

And they did gently deposit on their blankets that poor, wasted body, covered with scars and wounds, still bleeding where fire and steel had, in twenty places, left their agonizing marks. The doctor, taking an old handkerchief, quickly prepared a little lint, which he spread over the wounds, after having washed them. These rapid attentions were bestowed with the celerity and skill of a practiced surgeon, and, when they were complete, the doctor, taking a cordial from his medicine chest, poured a few drops upon his patient's lips.

The latter feebly pressed his kind hands, and scarcely had the strength to say, "Thank you! Thank you!"

The doctor comprehended that he must be left perfectly quiet; so he closed the folds of the awning and resumed the guidance of the balloon.

The latter, after taking into account the weight of the new passenger, had been lightened of one hundred and eighty pounds, and therefore kept aloft without the aid of the cylinder. At the first dawn of day, a current drove it gently toward the west-northwest. The doctor went in under the awning for a moment or two, to look at his still-sleeping patient.

"May Heaven spare the life of our new companion! Have you any hope?" said the Scot.

"Yes, Dick, with care, in this pure, fresh atmosphere."

"How that man has suffered!" said Joe, with feeling. "He did bolder things than we've done, in venturing all alone among those savage tribes!"

"That cannot be questioned," assented the hunter.

During the entire day the doctor would not allow the sleep of his patient to be disturbed. It was really a long stupor, broken only by an occasional murmur of pain that continued to disquiet and agitate the doctor greatly.

Toward evening the balloon remained stationary in the midst of the gloom, and during the night, while Kennedy and Joe relieved each other in carefully tending the sick man, Ferguson kept watch over the safety of all.

By the morning of the next day, the balloon had moved, but very slightly, to the westward. The dawn came up pure and magnificent. The sick man was able to call his friends with a stronger voice. They raised the curtains of the awning, and he inhaled with delight the keen morning air.

"How do you feel today?" asked the doctor.

"Better, perhaps," he replied. "But you, my friends, I have not seen you yet, excepting in a dream! I can, indeed, scarcely recall what has occurred. Who are you—that your names may not be forgotten in my dying prayers?"

"We are English travelers," replied Ferguson. "We are trying to cross Africa in a balloon, and, on our way, we have had the good fortune to rescue you."

"Science has its heroes," said the missionary.

"But religion its martyrs!" rejoined the Scot.

"Are you a missionary?" asked the doctor.

"I am a priest of the Lazarist mission. Heaven sent you to me—Heaven be praised! The sacrifice of my life had been accomplished! But you come from Europe; tell me about Europe, about France! I have been without news for the last five years!"

"Five years! Alone! And among these savages!" exclaimed Kennedy with amazement.

"They are souls to redeem! Ignorant and barbarous brethren, whom religion alone can instruct and civilize."

Dr. Ferguson, yielding to the priest's request, talked to him long and fully about France. He listened eagerly, and his eyes filled with tears. He seized Kennedy's and Joe's hands by turns in his own, which were burning with fever. The doctor prepared him some tea, and he drank it with satisfaction. After that, he had strength enough to raise himself up a little, and smiled with pleasure at seeing himself borne along through so pure a sky.

"You are daring travelers!" he said, "and you will succeed in your bold enterprise. You will again behold your relatives, your friends, your country—you—"

At this moment, the weakness of the young missionary became so extreme that they had to lay him again on the bed, where a prostration, lasting for several hours, held him like a dead man under the eye of Dr. Ferguson. The latter could not suppress his emotion, for he felt that this life now in his charge was ebbing away. Were they then so soon to lose him whom they had snatched from an agonizing death? The doctor again washed and dressed the young martyr's frightful wounds, and had to sacrifice nearly his whole stock of water to refresh his burning limbs. He surrounded him with the tenderest and most intelligent care, until, at length, the sick man revived, little by little, in his arms, and recovered his consciousness if not his strength.

The doctor was able to gather something of his history from his broken murmurs.

"Speak in your native language," he said to the sufferer; "I understand it, and it will fatigue you less."

The missionary was a poor young man from the village of Aradon, in Brittany, in the Morbihan country. His earliest instincts had drawn him toward an ecclesiastical career, but to this life of self-sacrifice he was also desirous of joining a life of danger, by entering the mission of the order of priesthood of which St. Vincent de Paul was the founder, and, at twenty, he quitted his country for the inhospitable shores of Africa. From the seacoast, overcoming obstacles, little by little, braving all privations, pushing onward, afoot, and praying, he had advanced to the very center of those tribes that dwell among the tributary streams of the Upper Nile. For two years his faith was spurned, his zeal denied recognition, his charities taken in ill part, and he remained a prisoner to one of the cruelest tribes of the Nyambarra, the object of every species of maltreatment. But still he went on teaching, instructing, and praying. The tribe having been dispersed and he left for dead, in one of those combats which are so frequent between the tribes, instead of retracing his steps, he persisted in his evangelical mission. His most tranquil time was when he was taken for a madman. Meanwhile, he had made himself familiar with the idioms of the country, and he catechized in them. At length, during two more long years, he traversed these barbarous regions, impelled by that superhuman energy that comes from God. For a year past he had been residing with that tribe of the Nyam-Nyams known as the *Barafri*, one of the wildest and most ferocious of them all. The chief having died a few days before our travelers appeared, his sudden death was attributed to the missionary, and the tribe resolved to immolate him. His sufferings had already continued for the space of forty hours, and, as the doctor had supposed, he was to have perished in the blaze of the noonday sun. When he heard the sound of firearms, nature got the best of him, and he had cried out, "Help! Help!" He then thought that he must have been dreaming, when a voice, that seemed to come from the sky, had uttered words of consolation.

"I have no regrets," he said, "for the life that is passing away from me; my life belongs to God!"

"Hope still!" said the doctor. "We are near you, and we will save you now, as we saved you from the tortures of the stake."

"I do not ask so much of Heaven," said the priest, with resignation. "Blessed be God for having vouchsafed to me the joy before I die of having pressed your friendly hands, and having heard, once more, the language of my country!"

The missionary here grew weak again, and the whole day went by between hope and fear, Kennedy deeply moved, and Joe drawing his hand over his eyes more than once when he thought that no one saw him.

The balloon made little progress, and the wind seemed as though unwilling to jostle its precious burden.

Toward evening, Joe discovered a great light in the west. Under more elevated latitudes, it might have been mistaken for an immense aurora borealis, for the sky appeared on fire. The doctor very attentively examined the phenomenon.

"It is, perhaps, only a volcano in full activity," said he.

"But the wind is carrying us directly over it," replied Kennedy.

"Very well, we shall cross it then at a safe height!" said the doctor.

Three hours later, the *Victoria* was right among the mountains. Her exact position was twenty-four degrees fifteen minutes east longitude, and four degrees forty-two minutes north latitude, and four degrees forty-two minutes north latitude. In front of her a volcanic crater was pouring forth torrents of melted lava, and hurling masses of rock to an enormous height. There were jets, too, of liquid fire that fell back in dazzling cascades—a superb but dangerous spectacle, for the wind with unswerving certainty was carrying the balloon directly toward this blazing atmosphere.

This obstacle, which could not be turned, had to be crossed, so the cylinder was put to its utmost power, and the balloon rose to the height of six thousand feet, leaving between it and the volcano a space of more than three hundred fathoms.

From his bed of suffering, the dying missionary could contemplate that fiery crater from which a thousand jets of dazzling flame were that moment escaping.

"How grand it is!" said he. "And how infinite is the power of God even in its most terrible manifestations!"

This overflow of blazing lava wrapped the sides of the mountain with a veritable drapery of flame; the lower half of the balloon glowed redly in the upper night; a torrid heat ascended to the car, and Dr. Ferguson made all possible haste to escape from this perilous situation.

By ten o'clock the volcano could be seen only as a red point on the horizon, and the balloon tranquilly pursued her course in a less elevated zone of the atmosphere.

## CHAPTER XXIII

JOE IN A FIT OF RAGE—THE DEATH OF A GOOD MAN—THE NIGHT OF
WATCHING BY THE BODY—BARRENNESS AND DROUGHT—THE BURIAL—THE
QUARTZ ROCKS—JOE'S HALLUCINATIONS—A PRECIOUS BALLAST—A SURVEY OF
THE GOLD-BEARING MOUNTAINS—THE BEGINNING OF JOE'S DESPAIR

A magnificent night overspread the earth, and the missionary lay quietly asleep in utter exhaustion.

"He'll not get over it!" sighed Joe. "Poor young fellow—scarcely thirty years of age!"

"He'll die in our arms. His breathing, which was so feeble before, is growing weaker still, and I can do nothing to save him," said the doctor, despairingly.

"The infamous scoundrels!" exclaimed Joe, grinding his teeth, in one of those fits of rage that came over him at long intervals. "And to think that, in spite of all, this good man could find words only to pity them, to excuse, to pardon them!"

"Heaven has given him a lovely night, Joe—his last on earth, perhaps! He will suffer but little more after this, and his dying will be only a peaceful falling asleep."

The dying man uttered some broken words, and the doctor at once went to him. His breathing became difficult, and he asked for air. The curtains were drawn entirely back, and he inhaled with rapture the light breezes of that clear, beautiful night. The stars sent him their trembling rays, and the moon wrapped him in the white winding-sheet of its effulgence.

"My friends," said he, in an enfeebled voice, "I am going. May God requite you, and bring you to your safe harbor! May he pay for me the debt of gratitude that I owe to you!"

"You must still hope," replied Kennedy. "This is but a passing fit of weakness. You will not die. How could anyone die on this beautiful summer night?"

"Death is at hand," replied the missionary, "I know it! Let me look it in the face! Death, the commencement of things eternal, is but the end of earthly cares. Place me upon my knees, my brethren, I beseech you!"

Kennedy lifted him up, and it was distressing to see his weakened limbs bend under him.

"My God! My God!" exclaimed the dying apostle. "Have pity on me!"

His countenance shone. Far above that earth on which he had known no joys; in the midst of that night which sent to him its softest radiance; on the way to that heaven toward which he uplifted his spirit, as though in a miraculous assumption, he seemed already to live and breathe in the new existence.

His last gesture was a supreme blessing on his new friends of only one day. Then he fell back into the arms of Kennedy, whose countenance was bathed in hot tears.

"Dead!" said the doctor, bending over him. "Dead!" And with one common accord, the three friends knelt together in silent prayer.

"Tomorrow," resumed the doctor, "we shall bury him in the African soil which he has besprinkled with his blood."

During the rest of the night the body was watched, turn by turn, by the three travelers, and not a word disturbed the solemn silence. Each of them was weeping.

The next day the wind came from the south, and the balloon moved slowly over a vast plateau of mountains: there, were extinct craters; here, barren ravines; not a drop of water on those parched crests; piles of broken rocks; huge stony masses scattered hither and thither, and, interspersed with whitish marl, all indicated the most complete sterility.

Toward noon, the doctor, for the purpose of burying the body, decided to descend into a ravine, in the midst of some plutonic rocks of primitive formation. The surrounding mountains would shelter him, and enable him to bring his car to the ground, for there was no tree in sight to which he could make it fast.

But, as he had explained to Kennedy, it was now impossible for him to descend, except by releasing a quantity of gas proportionate to his loss of ballast at the time when he had rescued the missionary. He therefore opened the valve of the outside balloon. The hydrogen escaped, and the *Victoria* quietly descended into the ravine.

As soon as the car touched the ground, the doctor shut the valve. Joe leaped out, holding on the while to the rim of the car with one hand, and with the other gathering up a quantity of stones equal to his own weight. He could then use both hands, and had soon heaped into the car more than five hundred pounds of stones, which enabled both the doctor and Kennedy, in their turn, to get out. Thus the *Victoria* found herself balanced, and her ascensional force insufficient to raise her.

Moreover, it was not necessary to gather many of these stones, for the blocks were extremely heavy, so much so, indeed, that the doctor's attention was attracted by the circumstance. The soil, in fact, was bestrewn with quartz and porphyritic rocks.

"This is a singular discovery!" said the doctor, mentally.

In the meanwhile, Kennedy and Joe had strolled away a few paces, looking up a proper spot for the grave. The heat was extreme in this ravine, shut in as it was like a sort of furnace. The noonday sun poured down its rays perpendicularly into it.

The first thing to be done was to clear the surface of the fragments of rock that encumbered it, and then a quite deep grave had to be dug, so that the wild animals should not be able to disinter the corpse.

The body of the martyred missionary was then solemnly placed in it. The earth was thrown in over his remains, and above it masses of rock were deposited, in rude resemblance to a tomb.

The doctor, however, remained motionless, and lost in his reflections. He did not even heed the call of his companions, nor did he return with them to seek a shelter from the heat of the day.

"What are you thinking about, doctor?" asked Kennedy.

"About a singular freak of Nature, a curious effect of chance. Do you know, now, in what kind of soil that man of self-denial, that poor one in spirit, has just been buried?"

"No! What do you mean, doctor?"

"That priest, who took the oath of perpetual poverty, now reposes in a gold mine!"

"A gold mine!" exclaimed Kennedy and Joe in one breath.

"Yes, a gold mine," said the doctor, quietly. "Those blocks which you are trampling underfoot, like worthless stones, contain gold ore of great purity."

"Impossible! Impossible!" repeated Joe.

"You would not have to look long among those fissures of slaty schist without finding peptites of considerable value."

Joe at once rushed like a crazy man among the scattered fragments, and Kennedy was not long in following his example.

"Keep cool, Joe," said his master.

"Why, doctor, you speak of the thing quite at your ease."

"What! A philosopher of your mettle—"

"Ah, master, no philosophy holds good in this case!"

"Come! Come! Let us reflect a little. What good would all this wealth do you? We cannot carry any of it away with us."

"We can't take any of it with us, indeed?"

"It's rather too heavy for our car! I even hesitated to tell you anything about it, for fear of exciting your regret!"

"What!" said Joe, again. "Abandon these treasures—a fortune for us!—really for us—our own—leave it behind!"

"Take care, my friend! Would you yield to the thirst for gold? Has not this dead man whom you have just helped to bury, taught you the vanity of human affairs?"

"All that is true," replied Joe, "but gold! Mr. Kennedy, won't you help to gather up a trifle of all these millions?"

"What could we do with them, Joe?" said the hunter, unable to repress a smile. "We did not come hither in search of fortune, and we cannot take one home with us."

"The millions are rather heavy, you know," resumed the doctor, "and cannot very easily be put into one's pocket."

"But, at least," said Joe, driven to his last defenses, "couldn't we take some of that ore for ballast, instead of sand?"

"Very good! I consent," said the doctor, "but you must not make too many wry faces when we come to throw some thousands of crowns' worth overboard."

"Thousands of crowns!" echoed Joe. "Is it possible that there is so much gold in them, and that all this is the same?"

"Yes, my friend, this is a reservoir in which Nature has been heaping up her wealth for centuries! There is enough here to enrich whole nations! An Australia and a California both together in the midst of the wilderness!"

"And the whole of it is to remain useless!"

"Perhaps! But at all events, here's what I'll do to console you."

"That would be rather difficult to do!" said Joe, with a contrite air.

"Listen! I will take the exact bearings of this spot, and give them to you, so that, upon your return to England, you can tell our countrymen about it, and let them have a share, if you think that so much gold would make them happy."

"Ah! Master, I give up; I see that you are right, and that there is nothing else to be done. Let us fill our car with the precious mineral, and what remains at the end of the trip will be so much made."

And Joe went to work. He did so, too, with all his might, and soon had collected more than a thousand pieces of quartz, which contained gold enclosed as though in an extremely hard crystal casket.

The doctor watched him with a smile; and, while Joe went on, he took the bearings, and found that the missionary's grave lay in twenty-two degrees twenty-three minutes east longitude, and four degrees fifty-five minutes north latitude.

Then, casting one glance at the swelling of the soil, beneath which the body of the poor Frenchman reposed, he went back to his car.

He would have erected a plain, rude cross over the tomb, left solitary thus in the midst of the African deserts, but not a tree was to be seen in the environs.

"God will recognize it!" said Kennedy.

An anxiety of another sort now began to steal over the doctor's mind. He would have given much of the gold before him for a little water—for he had to replace what had been thrown overboard when the negro was carried up into the air. But it was impossible to find it in these arid regions; and this reflection gave him great uneasiness. He had to feed his cylinder continually; and he even began to find that he had not enough to quench the thirst of his party. Therefore he determined to lose no opportunity of replenishing his supply.

Upon getting back to the car, he found it burdened with the quartz blocks that Joe's greed had heaped in it. He got in, however, without saying anything. Kennedy took his customary place, and Joe followed, but not without casting a covetous glance at the treasures in the ravine.

The doctor rekindled the light in the cylinder; the spiral became heated; the current of hydrogen came in a few minutes, and the gas dilated; but the balloon did not stir an inch.

Joe looked on uneasily, but kept silent.

"Joe!" said the doctor.

Joe made no reply.

"Joe! Don't you hear me?"

Joe made a sign that he heard; but he would not understand.

"Do me the kindness to throw out some of that quartz!"

"But, doctor, you gave me leave—"

"I gave you leave to replace the ballast; that was all!"

"But—"

"Do you want to stay forever in this desert?"

Joe cast a despairing look at Kennedy; but the hunter put on the air of a man who could do nothing in the matter.

"Well, Joe?"

"Then your cylinder don't work," said the obstinate fellow.

"My cylinder? It is lit, as you perceive. But the balloon will not rise until you have thrown off a little ballast."

Joe scratched his ear, picked up a piece of quartz, the smallest in the lot, weighed and reweighed it, and tossed it up and down in his hand. It was a fragment of about three or four pounds. At last he threw it out.

But the balloon did not budge.

"Humph!" said he. "We're not going up yet."

"Not yet," said the doctor. "Keep on throwing."

Kennedy laughed. Joe now threw out some ten pounds, but the balloon stood still. Joe got very pale.

"Poor fellow!" said the doctor. "Mr. Kennedy, you and I weigh, unless I am mistaken, about four hundred pounds—so that you'll have to get rid of at least that weight, since it was put in here to make up for us."

"Throw away four hundred pounds!" said Joe, piteously.

"And some more with it, or we can't rise. Come, courage, Joe!"

The brave fellow, heaving deep sighs, began at last to lighten the balloon; but, from time to time, he would stop, and ask:

"Are you going up?"

"No, not yet," was the invariable response.

"It moves!" said he, at last.

"Keep on!" replied the doctor.

"It's going up; I'm sure."

"Keep on yet," said Kennedy.

And Joe, picking up one more block, desperately tossed it out of the car. The balloon rose a hundred feet or so, and, aided by the cylinder, soon passed above the surrounding summits.

"Now, Joe," resumed the doctor, "there still remains a handsome fortune for you; and, if we can only keep the rest of this with us until the end of our trip, there you are—rich for the balance of your days!"

Joe made no answer, but stretched himself out luxuriously on his heap of quartz.

"See, my dear Dick!" the doctor went on. "Just see the power of this metal over the cleverest lad in the world! What passions, what greed, what crimes, the knowledge of such a mine as that would cause! It is sad to think of it!"

By evening the balloon had made ninety miles to the westward, and was, in a direct line, fourteen hundred miles from Zanzibar.

# CHAPTER XXIV

THE WIND DIES AWAY—THE VICINITY OF THE DESERT—THE MISTAKE
IN THE WATER SUPPLY—THE NIGHTS OF THE EQUATOR—DR. FERGUSON'S
ANXIETIES—THE SITUATION FLATLY STATED—ENERGETIC REPLIES OF
KENNEDY AND JOE—ONE NIGHT MORE

The balloon, having been made fast to a solitary tree, almost completely dried up by the aridity of the region in which it stood, passed the night in perfect quietness; and the travelers were enabled to enjoy a little of the repose which they so greatly needed. The emotions of the day had left sad impressions on their minds.

Toward morning, the sky had resumed its brilliant purity and its heat. The balloon ascended, and, after several ineffectual attempts, fell into a current that, although not rapid, bore them toward the northwest.

"We are not making progress," said the doctor. "If I am not mistaken, we have accomplished nearly half of our journey in ten days; but, at the rate at which we are going, it would take months to end it; and that is all the more vexatious, that we are threatened with a lack of water."

"But we'll find some," said Joe. "It is not to be thought of that we shouldn't discover some river, some stream, or pond, in all this vast extent of country."

"I hope so."

"Now don't you think that it's Joe's cargo of stone that is keeping us back?"

Kennedy asked this question only to tease Joe; and he did so the more willingly because he had, for a moment, shared the poor lad's hallucinations; but, not finding anything in them, he had fallen back into the attitude of a strong-minded looker-on, and turned the affair off with a laugh.

Joe cast a mournful glance at him; but the doctor made no reply. He was thinking, not without secret terror, probably, of the vast solitudes of Sahara—for there whole weeks sometimes pass without the caravans meeting with a single spring of water. Occupied with these thoughts, he scrutinized every depression of the soil with the closest attention.

These anxieties, and the incidents recently occurring, had not been without their effect upon the spirits of our three travelers. They conversed less, and were more wrapt in their own thoughts.

Joe, clever lad as he was, seemed no longer the same person since his gaze had plunged into that ocean of gold. He kept entirely silent, and gazed incessantly upon the stony fragments heaped up in the car—worthless today, but of inestimable value tomorrow.

The appearance of this part of Africa was, moreover, quite calculated to inspire alarm: the desert was gradually expanding around them; not another village was to be seen—not even a collection of a few huts; and vegetation also was disappearing. Barely a few dwarf plants could now be noticed, like those on the wild heaths of

Scotland; then came the first tract of grayish sand and flint, with here and there a lentisk tree and brambles. In the midst of this sterility, the rudimental carcass of the globe appeared in ridges of sharply jutting rock. These symptoms of a totally dry and barren region greatly disquieted Dr. Ferguson.

It seemed as though no caravan had ever braved this desert expanse, or it would have left visible traces of its encampments, or the whitened bones of men and animals. But nothing of the kind was to be seen, and the aeronauts felt that, ere long, an immensity of sand would cover the whole of this desolate region.

However, there was no going back; they must go forward; and, indeed, the doctor asked for nothing better; he would even have welcomed a tempest to carry him beyond this country. But, there was not a cloud in the sky. At the close of the day, the balloon had not made thirty miles.

If there had been no lack of water! But there remained only three gallons in all! The doctor put aside one gallon, destined to quench the burning thirst that a heat of ninety degrees rendered intolerable. Two gallons only then remained to supply the cylinder. Hence, they could produce no more than four hundred and eighty cubic feet of gas; yet the cylinder consumed about nine cubic feet per hour. Consequently, they could not keep on longer than fifty-four hours—and all this was a mathematical calculation!

"Fifty-four hours!" said the doctor to his companions. "Therefore, as I am determined not to travel by night, for fear of passing some stream or pool, we have but three days and a half of journeying during which we must find water, at all hazards. I have thought it my duty to make you aware of the real state of the case, as I have retained only one gallon for drinking, and we shall have to put ourselves on the shortest allowance."

"Put us on short allowance, then, doctor," responded Kennedy, "but we must not despair. We have three days left, you say?"

"Yes, my dear Dick!"

"Well, as grieving over the matter won't help us, in three days there will be time enough to decide upon what is to be done; in the meanwhile, let us redouble our vigilance!"

At their evening meal, the water was strictly measured out, and the brandy was increased in quantity in the punch they drank. But they had to be careful with the spirits, the latter being more likely to produce than to quench thirst.

The car rested, during the night, upon an immense plateau, in which there was a deep hollow; its height was scarcely eight hundred feet above the level of the sea. This circumstance gave the doctor some hope, since it recalled to his mind the conjectures of geographers concerning the existence of a vast stretch of water in the center of Africa. But, if such a lake really existed, the point was to reach it, and not a sign of change was visible in the motionless sky.

To the tranquil night and its starry magnificence succeeded the unchanging daylight and the blazing rays of the sun; and, from the earliest dawn, the temperature became scorching. At five o'clock in the morning, the doctor gave the signal for departure, and, for a considerable time, the balloon remained immovable in the leaden atmosphere.

The doctor might have escaped this intense heat by rising into a higher range, but, in order to do so, he would have had to consume a large quantity of water, a thing that had now become impossible. He contented himself, therefore, with keeping the balloon at one hundred feet from the ground, and, at that elevation, a feeble current drove it toward the western horizon.

The breakfast consisted of a little dried meat and *pemmican*. By noon, the *Victoria* had advanced only a few miles.

"We cannot go any faster," said the doctor; "we no longer command—we have to obey."

"Ah! Doctor, here is one of those occasions when a propeller would not be a thing to be despised."

"Undoubtedly so, Dick, provided it would not require an expenditure of water to put it in motion, for, in that case, the situation would be precisely the same; moreover, up to this time, nothing practical of the sort has been invented. Balloons are still at that point where ships were before the invention of steam. It took six thousand years to invent propellers and screws; so we have time enough yet."

"Confounded heat!" said Joe, wiping away the perspiration that was streaming from his forehead.

"If we had water, this heat would be of service to us, for it dilates the hydrogen in the balloon, and diminishes the amount required in the spiral, although it is true that, if we were not short of the useful liquid, we should not have to economize it. Ah! That rascally savage who cost us the tank!"*

"You don't regret, though, what you did, doctor?"

"No, Dick, since it was in our power to save that unfortunate missionary from a horrible death. But, the hundred pounds of water that we threw overboard would be very useful to us now; it would be thirteen or fourteen days more of progress secured, or quite enough to carry us over this desert."

"We've made at least half the journey, haven't we?" asked Joe.

"In distance, yes; but in duration, no, should the wind leave us; and it, even now, has a tendency to die away altogether."

"Come, sir," said Joe, again, "we must not complain; we've got along pretty well, thus far, and whatever happens to me, I can't get desperate. We'll find water; mind, I tell you so."

The soil, however, ran lower from mile to mile; the undulations of the gold-bearing mountains they had left died away into the plain, like the last throes of exhausted Nature. Scanty grass took the place of the fine trees of the east; only a few belts of half-scorched herbage still contended against the invasion of the sand, and the huge rocks that had rolled down from the distant summits, crushed in their fall, had scattered in sharp-edged pebbles which soon again became coarse sand, and finally impalpable dust.

"Here, at last, is Africa, such as you pictured it to yourself, Joe! Was I not right in saying, 'Wait a little?' eh?"

"Well, master, it's all natural, at least—heat and dust. It would be foolish to look for anything else in such a country. Do you see," he added, laughing, "I had no confidence, for my part, in your forests and your prairies; they were out of reason.

---

* The water tank had been thrown overboard when the native clung to the car.

What was the use of coming so far to find scenery just like England? Here's the first time that I believe in Africa, and I'm not sorry to get a taste of it."

Toward evening, the doctor calculated that the balloon had not made twenty miles during that whole burning day, and a heated gloom closed in upon it, as soon as the sun had disappeared behind the horizon, which was traced against the sky with all the precision of a straight line.

The next day was Thursday, the 1st of May, but the days followed each other with desperate monotony. Each morning was like the one that had preceded it; noon poured down the same exhaustless rays, and night condensed in its shadow the scattered heat which the ensuing day would again bequeath to the succeeding night. The wind, now scarcely observable, was rather a gasp than a breath, and the morning could almost be foreseen when even that gasp would cease.

The doctor reacted against the gloominess of the situation and retained all the coolness and self-possession of a disciplined heart. With his glass he scrutinized every quarter of the horizon; he saw the last rising ground gradually melting to the dead level, and the last vegetation disappearing, while, before him, stretched the immensity of the desert.

The responsibility resting upon him pressed sorely, but he did not allow his disquiet to appear. Those two men, Dick and Joe, friends of his, both of them, he had induced to come with him almost by the force alone of friendship and of duty. Had he done well in that? Was it not like attempting to tread forbidden paths? Was he not, in this trip, trying to pass the borders of the impossible? Had not the Almighty reserved for later ages the knowledge of this inhospitable continent?

All these thoughts, of the kind that arise in hours of discouragement, succeeded each other and multiplied in his mind, and, by an irresistible association of ideas, the doctor allowed himself to be carried beyond the bounds of logic and of reason. After having established in his own mind what he should not have done, the next question was, what he should do, then. Would it be impossible to retrace his steps? Were there not currents higher up that would waft him to less arid regions? Well informed with regard to the countries over which he had passed, he was utterly ignorant of those to come, and thus his conscience speaking aloud to him, he resolved, in his turn, to speak frankly to his two companions. He thereupon laid the whole state of the case plainly before them; he showed them what had been done, and what there was yet to do; at the worst, they could return, or attempt it, at least. What did they think about it?

"I have no other opinion than that of my excellent master," said Joe. "What he may have to suffer, I can suffer, and that better than he can, perhaps. Where he goes, there I'll go!"

"And you, Kennedy?"

"I, doctor, I'm not the man to despair; no one was less ignorant than I of the perils of the enterprise, but I did not want to see them, from the moment that you determined to brave them. Under present circumstances, my opinion is, that we should persevere—go clear to the end. Besides, to return looks to me quite as perilous as the other course. So onward, then! You may count upon us!"

"Thanks, my gallant friends!" replied the doctor, with much real feeling. "I expected such devotion as this; but I needed these encouraging words. Yet, once again, thank you, from the bottom of my heart!"

And, with this, the three friends warmly grasped each other by the hand.

"Now, hear me!" said the doctor. "According to my solar observations, we are not more than three hundred miles from the Gulf of Guinea; the desert, therefore, cannot extend indefinitely, since the coast is inhabited, and the country has been explored for some distance back into the interior. If needs be, we can direct our course to that quarter, and it seems out of the question that we should not come across some oasis, or some well, where we could replenish our stock of water. But, what we want now, is the wind, for without it we are held here suspended in the air at a dead calm."

"Let us wait with resignation," said the hunter.

But, each of the party, in his turn, vainly scanned the space around him during that long wearisome day. Nothing could be seen to form the basis of a hope. The very last inequalities of the soil disappeared with the setting sun, whose horizontal rays stretched in long lines of fire over the flat immensity. It was the desert!

Our aeronauts had scarcely gone a distance of fifteen miles, having expended, as on the preceding day, one hundred and thirty-five cubic feet of gas to feed the cylinder, and two pints of water out of the remaining eight had been sacrificed to the demands of intense thirst.

The night passed quietly—too quietly, indeed, but the doctor did not sleep!

## CHAPTER XXV

A Little Philosophy—A Cloud on the Horizon—In the Midst of a Fog—
The Strange Balloon—An Exact View of the *Victoria*—The Palm Trees—
Traces of a Caravan—The Well in the Midst of the Desert

On the morrow, there was the same purity of sky, the same stillness of the atmosphere. The balloon rose to an elevation of five hundred feet, but it had scarcely changed its position to the westward in any perceptible degree.

"We are right in the open desert," said the doctor. "Look at that vast reach of sand! What a strange spectacle! What a singular arrangement of nature! Why should there be, in one place, such extreme luxuriance of vegetation yonder, and here, this extreme aridity, and that in the same latitude, and under the same rays of the sun?"

"The why concerns me but little," answered Kennedy, "the reason interests me less than the fact. The thing is so; that's the important part of it!"

"Oh, it is well to philosophize a little, Dick; it does no harm."

"Let us philosophize, then, if you will; we have time enough before us; we are hardly moving; the wind is afraid to blow; it sleeps."

"That will not last forever," put in Joe. "I think I see some banks of clouds in the east."

"Joe's right!" said the doctor, after he had taken a look.

"Good!" said Kennedy. "Now for our clouds, with a fine rain, and a fresh wind to dash it into our faces!"

"Well, we'll see, Dick, we'll see!"

"But this is Friday, master, and I'm afraid of Fridays!"

"Well, I hope that this very day you'll get over those notions."

"I hope so, master, too. Whew!" he added, mopping his face. "Heat's a good thing, especially in winter, but in summer it don't do to take too much of it."

"Don't you fear the effect of the sun's heat on our balloon?" asked Kennedy, addressing the doctor.

"No! The gutta-percha coating resists much higher temperatures than even this. With my spiral I have subjected it inside to as much as one hundred and fifty-eight degrees sometimes, and the covering does not appear to have suffered."

"A cloud! A real cloud!" shouted Joe at this moment, for that piercing eyesight of his beat all the glasses.

And, in fact, a thick bank of vapor, now quite distinct, could be seen slowly emerging above the horizon. It appeared to be very deep, and, as it were, puffed out. It was, in reality, a conglomeration of smaller clouds. The latter invariably retained their original formation, and from this circumstance the doctor concluded that there was no current of air in their collected mass.

This compact body of vapor had appeared about eight o'clock in the morning, and, by eleven, it had already reached the height of the sun's disk. The latter then disappeared entirely behind the murky veil, and the lower belt of cloud, at the same moment, lifted above the line of the horizon, which was again disclosed in a full blaze of daylight.

"It's only an isolated cloud," remarked the doctor. "It won't do to count much upon that."

"Look, Dick, its shape is just the same as when we saw it this morning!"

"Then, doctor, there's to be neither rain nor wind, at least for us!"

"I fear so; the cloud keeps at a great height."

"Well, doctor, suppose we were to go in pursuit of this cloud, since it refuses to burst upon us?"

"I fancy that to do so wouldn't help us much; it would be a consumption of gas, and, consequently, of water, to little purpose; but, in our situation, we must not leave anything untried; therefore, let us ascend!"

And with this, the doctor put on a full head of flame from the cylinder, and the dilation of the hydrogen, occasioned by such sudden and intense heat, sent the balloon rapidly aloft.

About fifteen hundred feet from the ground, it encountered an opaque mass of cloud, and entered a dense fog, suspended at that elevation; but it did not meet with the least breath of wind. This fog seemed even destitute of humidity, and the articles brought in contact with it were scarcely dampened in the slightest degree. The balloon, completely enveloped in the vapor, gained a little increase of speed, perhaps, and that was all.

The doctor gloomily recognized what trifling success he had obtained from his maneuver, and was relapsing into deep meditation, when he heard Joe exclaim, in tones of most intense astonishment:

"Ah! By all that's beautiful!"

"What's the matter, Joe?"

"Doctor! Mr. Kennedy! Here's something curious!"

"What is it, then?"

"We are not alone, up here! There are rogues about! They've stolen our invention!"

"Has he gone crazy?" asked Kennedy.

Joe stood there, perfectly motionless, the very picture of amazement.

"Can the hot sun have really affected the poor fellow's brain?" said the doctor, turning toward him.

"Will you tell me?"

"Look!" said Joe, pointing to a certain quarter of the sky.

"By St. James!" exclaimed Kennedy, in turn. "Why, who would have believed it? Look, look! Doctor!"

"I see it!" said the doctor, very quietly.

"Another balloon! And other passengers, like ourselves!"

And, sure enough, there was another balloon about two hundred paces from them, floating in the air with its car and its aeronauts. It was following exactly the same route as the *Victoria*.

"Well," said the doctor, "nothing remains for us but to make signals; take the flag, Kennedy, and show them our colors."

It seemed that the travelers by the other balloon had just the same idea, at the same moment, for the same kind of flag repeated precisely the same salute with a hand that moved in just the same manner.

"What does that mean?" asked Kennedy.

"They are apes," said Joe, "imitating us."

"It means," said the doctor, laughing, "that it is you, Dick, yourself, making that signal to yourself; or, in other words, that we see ourselves in the second balloon, which is no other than the *Victoria*."

"As to that, master, with all respect to you," said Joe, "you'll never make me believe it."

"Climb up on the edge of the car, Joe; wave your arms, and then you'll see."

Joe obeyed, and all his gestures were instantaneously and exactly repeated.

"It is merely the effect of the *mirage*," said the doctor, "and nothing else—a simple optical phenomenon due to the unequal refraction of light by different layers of the atmosphere, and that is all.

"It's wonderful," said Joe, who could not make up his mind to surrender, but went on repeating his gesticulations.

"What a curious sight! Do you know," said Kennedy, "that it's a real pleasure to have a view of our noble balloon in that style? She's a beauty, isn't she? And how stately her movements as she sweeps along!"

"You may explain the matter as you like," continued Joe, "it's a strange thing, anyhow!"

But ere long this picture began to fade away; the clouds rose higher, leaving the balloon, which made no further attempt to follow them, and in about an hour they disappeared in the open sky.

The wind, which had been scarcely perceptible, seemed still to diminish, and the doctor in perfect desperation descended toward the ground, and all three of the travelers, whom the incident just recorded had, for a few moments, diverted from their anxieties, relapsed into gloomy meditation, sweltering the while beneath the scorching heat.

About four o'clock, Joe descried some object standing out against the vast background of sand, and soon was able to declare positively that there were two palm trees at no great distance.

"Palm trees!" exclaimed Ferguson. "Why, then there's a spring—a well!"

He took up his glass and satisfied himself that Joe's eyes had not been mistaken.

"At length!" he said, over and over again. "Water! Water! And we are saved; for if we do move slowly, still we move, and we shall arrive at last!"

"Good, master! But suppose we were to drink a mouthful in the meantime, for this air is stifling?"

"Let us drink then, my boy!"

No one waited to be coaxed. A whole pint was swallowed then and there, reducing the total remaining supply to three pints and a half.

"Ah! That does one good!" said Joe. "Wasn't it fine? Barclay and Perkins never turned out ale equal to that!"

"See the advantage of being put on short allowance!" moralized the doctor.

"It is not great, after all," retorted Kennedy; "and if I were never again to have the pleasure of drinking water, I should agree on condition that I should never be deprived of it."

At six o'clock the balloon was floating over the palm trees.

They were two shriveled, stunted, dried-up specimens of trees—two ghosts of palms—without foliage, and more dead than alive. Ferguson examined them with terror.

At their feet could be seen the half-worn stones of a spring, but these stones, pulverized by the baking heat of the sun, seemed to be nothing now but impalpable dust. There was not the slightest sign of moisture. The doctor's heart shrank within him, and he was about to communicate his thoughts to his companions, when their exclamations attracted his attention. As far as the eye could reach to the eastward extended a long line of whitened bones; pieces of skeletons surrounded the fountain; a caravan had evidently made its way to that point, marking its progress by its bleaching remains; the weaker had fallen one by one upon the sand; the stronger, having at length reached this spring for which they panted, had there found a horrible death.

Our travelers looked at each other and turned pale.

"Let us not alight!" said Kennedy. "Let us fly from this hideous spectacle! There's not a drop of water here!"

"No, Dick, as well pass the night here as elsewhere; let us have a clear conscience in the matter. We'll dig down to the very bottom of the well. There has been a spring here, and perhaps there's something left in it!"

The *Victoria* touched the ground; Joe and Kennedy put into the car a quantity of sand equal to their weight, and leaped out. They then hastened to the well, and penetrated to the interior by a flight of steps that was now nothing but dust. The spring appeared to have been dry for years. They dug down into a parched and powdery sand—the very dryest of all sand, indeed—there was not one trace of moisture!

The doctor saw them come up to the surface of the desert, saturated with perspiration, worn out, covered with fine dust, exhausted, discouraged and despairing.

He then comprehended that their search had been fruitless. He had expected as much, and he kept silent, for he felt that, from this moment forth, he must have courage and energy enough for three.

Joe brought up with him some pieces of a leathern bottle that had grown hard and hornlike with age, and angrily flung them away among the bleaching bones of the caravan.

At supper, not a word was spoken by our travelers, and they even ate without appetite. Yet they had not, up to this moment, endured the real agonies of thirst, and were in no desponding mood, excepting for the future.

## CHAPTER XXVI

ONE HUNDRED AND THIRTEEN DEGREES—THE DOCTOR'S REFLECTIONS—
A DESPERATE SEARCH—THE CYLINDER GOES OUT—ONE HUNDRED AND
TWENTY-TWO DEGREES—CONTEMPLATION OF THE DESERT—A NIGHT WALK—
SOLITUDE—DEBILITY—JOE'S PROSPECTS—HE GIVES HIMSELF ONE DAY MORE

The distance made by the balloon during the preceding day did not exceed ten miles, and, to keep it afloat, one hundred and sixty-two cubic feet of gas had been consumed.

On Saturday morning the doctor again gave the signal for departure.

"The cylinder can work only six hours longer; and, if in that time we shall not have found either a well or a spring of water, God alone knows what will become of us!"

"Not much wind this morning, master," said Joe; "but it will come up, perhaps," he added, suddenly remarking the doctor's ill-concealed depression.

Vain hope! The atmosphere was in a dead calm—one of those calms which hold vessels captive in tropical seas. The heat had become intolerable; and the thermometer, in the shade under the awning, indicated one hundred and thirteen degrees.

Joe and Kennedy, reclining at full length near each other, tried, if not in slumber, at least in torpor, to forget their situation, for their forced inactivity gave them periods of leisure far from pleasant. That man is to be pitied the most who cannot wean himself from gloomy reflections by actual work, or some practical pursuit. But here there was nothing to look after, nothing to undertake, and they had to submit to the situation, without having it in their power to ameliorate it.

The pangs of thirst began to be severely felt; brandy, far from appeasing this imperious necessity, augmented it, and richly merited the name of "tiger's milk" applied to it by the African natives. Scarcely two pints of water remained, and that was heated. Each of the party devoured the few precious drops with his gaze, yet neither of them dared to moisten his lips with them. Two pints of water in the midst of the desert!

Then it was that Dr. Ferguson, buried in meditation, asked himself whether he had acted with prudence. Would he not have done better to have kept the water that he had decomposed in pure loss, in order to sustain him in the air? He had gained a little distance, to be sure; but was he any nearer to his journey's end? What difference did sixty miles to the rear make in this region, when there was no water to be had where they were? The wind, should it rise, would blow there as it did here, only less strongly at this point, if it came from the east. But hope urged him onward. And yet those two gallons of water, expended in vain, would have sufficed for nine days' halt in the desert. And what changes might not have occurred in nine days! Perhaps, too, while retaining the water, he might have ascended by throwing out ballast, at the cost merely of discharging some gas, when he had again to descend. But the gas in his balloon was his blood, his very life!

A thousand and one such reflections whirled in succession through his brain; and, resting his head between his hands, he sat there for hours without raising it.

"We must make one final effort," he said, at last, about ten o'clock in the morning. "We must endeavor, just once more, to find an atmospheric current to bear us away from here, and, to that end, must risk our last resources."

Therefore, while his companions slept, the doctor raised the hydrogen in the balloon to an elevated temperature, and the huge globe, filling out by the dilation of the gas, rose straight up in the perpendicular rays of the sun. The doctor searched vainly for a breath of wind, from the height of one hundred feet to that of five miles; his starting point remained fatally right below him, and absolute calm seemed to reign, up to the extreme limits of the breathing atmosphere.

At length the feeding supply of water gave out; the cylinder was extinguished for lack of gas; the Buntzen battery ceased to work, and the balloon, shrinking together, gently descended to the sand, in the very place that the car had hollowed out there.

It was noon; and solar observations gave nineteen degrees thirty-five minutes east longitude, and six degrees fifty-one minutes north latitude, or nearly five hundred miles from Lake Tchad, and more than four hundred miles from the western coast of Africa.

On the balloon taking ground, Kennedy and Joe awoke from their stupor.

"We have halted," said the Scot.

"We had to do so," replied the doctor, gravely.

His companions understood him. The level of the soil at that point corresponded with the level of the sea, and, consequently, the balloon remained in perfect equilibrium, and absolutely motionless.

The weight of the three travelers was replaced with an equivalent quantity of sand, and they got out of the car. Each was absorbed in his own thoughts; and for many hours neither of them spoke. Joe prepared their evening meal, which consisted of biscuit and *pemmican*, and was hardly tasted by either of the party. A mouthful of scalding water from their little store completed this gloomy repast.

During the night none of them kept awake; yet none could be precisely said to have slept. On the morrow there remained only half a pint of water, and this the doctor put away, all three having resolved not to touch it until the last extremity.

It was not long, however, before Joe exclaimed:

"I'm choking, and the heat is getting worse! I'm not surprised at that, though," he added, consulting the thermometer. "One hundred and forty degrees!"

"The sand scorches me," said the hunter, "as though it had just come out of a furnace; and not a cloud in this sky of fire. It's enough to drive one mad!"

"Let us not despair," responded the doctor. "In this latitude these intense heats are invariably followed by storms, and the latter come with the suddenness of lightning. Notwithstanding this disheartening clearness of the sky, great atmospheric changes may take place in less than an hour."

"But," asked Kennedy, "is there any sign whatever of that?"

"Well," replied the doctor, "I think that there is some slight symptom of a fall in the barometer."

"May Heaven hearken to you, Samuel! For here we are pinned to the ground, like a bird with broken wings."

"With this difference, however, my dear Dick, that our wings are unhurt, and I hope that we shall be able to use them again."

"Ah! Wind! Wind!" exclaimed Joe. "Enough to carry us to a stream or a well, and we'll be all right. We have provisions enough, and, with water, we could wait a month without suffering; but thirst is a cruel thing!"

It was not thirst alone, but the unchanging sight of the desert, that fatigued the mind. There was not a variation in the surface of the soil, not a hillock of sand, not a pebble, to relieve the gaze. This unbroken level discouraged the beholder, and gave him that kind of malady called the "desert sickness." The impassible monotony of the arid blue sky, and the vast yellow expanse of the desert sand, at length produced a sensation of terror. In this inflamed atmosphere the heat appeared to vibrate as it does above a blazing hearth, while the mind grew desperate in contemplating the limitless calm, and could see no reason why the thing should ever end, since immensity is a species of eternity.

Thus, at last, our hapless travelers, deprived of water in this torrid heat, began to feel symptoms of mental disorder. Their eyes swelled in their sockets, and their gaze became confused.

When night came on, the doctor determined to combat this alarming tendency by rapid walking. His idea was to pace the sandy plain for a few hours, not in search of anything, but simply for exercise.

"Come along!" he said to his companions. "Believe me, it will do you good."

"Out of the question!" said Kennedy. "I could not walk a step."

"And I," said Joe, "would rather sleep!"

"But sleep, or even rest, would be dangerous to you, my friends; you must react against this tendency to stupor. Come with me!"

But the doctor could do nothing with them, and, therefore, set off alone, amid the starry clearness of the night. The first few steps he took were painful, for they were the steps of an enfeebled man quite out of practice in walking. However, he quickly saw that the exercise would be beneficial to him, and pushed on several miles to the westward. Once in rapid motion, he felt his spirits greatly cheered, when, suddenly, a vertigo came over him; he seemed to be poised on the edge of an abyss; his knees bent under him; the vast solitude struck terror to his heart; he found himself the minute mathematical point, the center of an infinite circumference, that is to say—a nothing! The balloon had disappeared entirely in the deepening gloom. The doctor, cool, impassible, reckless explorer that he was, felt himself at last seized with a nameless dread. He strove to retrace his steps, but in vain. He called aloud. Not even an echo replied, and his voice died out in the empty vastness of surrounding space, like a pebble cast into a bottomless gulf; then, down he sank, fainting, on the sand, alone, amid the eternal silence of the desert.

At midnight he came to, in the arms of his faithful follower, Joe. The latter, uneasy at his master's prolonged absence, had set out after him, easily tracing him by the clear imprint of his feet in the sand, and had found him lying in a swoon.

"What has been the matter, sir?" was the first inquiry.

"Nothing, Joe, nothing! Only a touch of weakness, that's all. It's over now."

"Oh! It won't amount to anything, sir, I'm sure of that; but get up on your feet, if you can. There! Lean upon me, and let us get back to the balloon."

And the doctor, leaning on Joe's arm, returned along the track by which he had come.

"You were too bold, sir; it won't do to run such risks. You might have been robbed," he added, laughing. "But, sir, come now, let us talk seriously."

"Speak! I am listening to you."

"We must positively make up our minds to do something. Our present situation cannot last more than a few days longer, and if we get no wind, we are lost."

The doctor made no reply.

"Well, then, one of us must sacrifice himself for the good of all, and it is most natural that it should fall to me to do so."

"What have you to propose? What is your plan?"

"A very simple one! It is to take provisions enough, and to walk right on until I come to some place, as I must do, sooner or later. In the meantime, if Heaven sends you a good wind, you need not wait, but can start again. For my part, if I come to a village, I'll work my way through with a few Arabic words that you can write for me on a slip of paper, and I'll bring you help or lose my hide. What do you think of my plan?"

"It is absolute folly, Joe, but worthy of your noble heart. The thing is impossible. You will not leave us."

"But, sir, we must do something, and this plan can't do you any harm, for, I say again, you need not wait; and then, after all, I may succeed."

"No, Joe, no! We will not separate. That would only be adding sorrow to trouble. It was written that matters should be as they are; and it is very probably written that it shall be quite otherwise by-and-by. Let us wait, then, with resignation."

"So be it, master; but take notice of one thing: I give you a day longer, and I'll not wait after that. Today is Sunday; we might say Monday, as it is one o'clock in the morning, and if we don't get off by Tuesday, I'll run the risk. I've made up my mind to that!"

The doctor made no answer, and in a few minutes they got back to the car, where he took his place beside Kennedy, who lay there plunged in silence so complete that it could not be considered sleep.

## CHAPTER XXVII

TERRIFIC HEAT—HALLUCINATIONS—THE LAST DROPS OF WATER—
NIGHTS OF DESPAIR—AN ATTEMPT AT SUICIDE—THE SIMOOM—
THE OASIS—THE LION AND LIONESS

The doctor's first care, on the morrow, was to consult the barometer. He found that the mercury had scarcely undergone any perceptible depression.

"Nothing!" he murmured. "Nothing!"

He got out of the car and scrutinized the weather; there was only the same heat, the same cloudless sky, the same merciless drought.

"Must we, then, give up to despair?" he exclaimed, in agony.

Joe did not open his lips. He was buried in his own thoughts, and planning the expedition he had proposed.

Kennedy got up, feeling very ill, and a prey to nervous agitation. He was suffering horribly with thirst, and his swollen tongue and lips could hardly articulate a syllable.

There still remained a few drops of water. Each of them knew this, and each was thinking of it, and felt himself drawn toward them; but neither of the three dared to take a step.

Those three men, friends and companions as they were, fixed their haggard eyes upon each other with an instinct of ferocious longing, which was most plainly revealed in the hardy Scot, whose vigorous constitution yielded the soonest to these unnatural privations.

Throughout the day he was delirious, pacing up and down, uttering hoarse cries, gnawing his clinched fists, and ready to open his veins and drink his own hot blood.

"Ah!" he cried. "Land of thirst! Well might you be called the land of despair!"

At length he sank down in utter prostration, and his friends heard no other sound from him than the hissing of his breath between his parched and swollen lips.

Toward evening, Joe had his turn of delirium. The vast expanse of sand appeared to him an immense pond, full of clear and limpid water; and, more than once, he dashed himself upon the scorching waste to drink long drafts, and rose again with his mouth clogged with hot dust.

"Curses on it!" he yelled, in his madness. "It's nothing but salt water!"

Then, while Ferguson and Kennedy lay there motionless, the resistless longing came over him to drain the last few drops of water that had been kept in reserve. The natural instinct proved too strong. He dragged himself toward the car, on his knees; he glared at the bottle containing the precious fluid; he gave one wild, eager glance, seized the treasured store, and bore it to his lips.

At that instant he heard a heartrending cry close beside him—"Water! Water!"

It was Kennedy, who had crawled up close to him, and was begging there, upon his knees, and weeping piteously.

Joe, himself in tears, gave the poor wretch the bottle, and Kennedy drained the last drop with savage haste.

"Thanks!" he murmured hoarsely, but Joe did not hear him, for both alike had dropped fainting on the sand.

What took place during that fearful night neither of them knew, but, on Tuesday morning, under those showers of heat which the sun poured down upon them, the unfortunate men felt their limbs gradually drying up, and when Joe attempted to rise he found it impossible.

He looked around him. In the car, the doctor, completely overwhelmed, sat with his arms folded on his breast, gazing with idiotic fixedness upon some imaginary point in space. Kennedy was frightful to behold. He was rolling his head from right to left like a wild beast in a cage.

All at once, his eyes rested on the butt of his rifle, which jutted above the rim of the car.

"Ah!" he screamed, raising himself with a superhuman effort.

Desperate, mad, he snatched at the weapon, and turned the barrel toward his mouth.

"Kennedy!" shouted Joe, throwing himself upon his friend.

"Let go! Hands off!" moaned the Scot, in a hoarse, grating voice—and then the two struggled desperately for the rifle.

"Let go, or I'll kill you!" repeated Kennedy. But Joe clung to him only the more fiercely, and they had been contending thus without the doctor seeing them for many seconds, when, suddenly the rifle went off. At the sound of its discharge, the doctor rose up erect, like a specter, and glared around him.

But all at once his glance grew more animated; he extended his hand toward the horizon, and in a voice no longer human shrieked:

"There! There—off there!"

There was such fearful force in the cry that Kennedy and Joe released each other, and both looked where the doctor pointed.

The plain was agitated like the sea shaken by the fury of a tempest; billows of sand went tossing over each other amid blinding clouds of dust; an immense pillar was seen whirling toward them through the air from the southeast, with terrific velocity; the sun was disappearing behind an opaque veil of cloud whose enormous barrier extended clear to the horizon, while the grains of fine sand went gliding together with all the supple ease of liquid particles, and the rising dust-tide gained more and more with every second.

Ferguson's eyes gleamed with a ray of energetic hope.

"The simoom!" he exclaimed.

"The simoom!" repeated Joe, without exactly knowing what it meant.

"So much the better!" said Kennedy, with the bitterness of despair. "So much the better—we shall die!"

"So much the better!" echoed the doctor. "For we shall live!" And, so saying, he began rapidly to throw out the sand that encumbered the car.

At length his companions understood him, and took their places at his side.

"And now, Joe," said the doctor, "throw out some fifty pounds of your ore, there!"

Joe no longer hesitated, although he still felt a fleeting pang of regret. The balloon at once began to ascend.

"It was high time!" said the doctor.

The simoom, in fact, came rushing on like a thunderbolt, and a moment later the balloon would have been crushed, torn to atoms, annihilated. The awful whirlwind was almost upon it, and it was already pelted with showers of sand driven like hail by the storm.

"Out with more ballast!" shouted the doctor.

"There!" responded Joe, tossing over a huge fragment of quartz.

With this, the *Victoria* rose swiftly above the range of the whirling column, but, caught in the vast displacement of the atmosphere thereby occasioned, it was borne along with incalculable rapidity away above this foaming sea.

The three travelers did not speak. They gazed, and hoped, and even felt refreshed by the breath of the tempest.

About three o'clock, the whirlwind ceased; the sand, falling again upon the desert, formed numberless little hillocks, and the sky resumed its former tranquility.

The balloon, which had again lost its momentum, was floating in sight of an oasis, a sort of islet studded with green trees, thrown up upon the surface of this sandy ocean.

"Water! We'll find water there!" said the doctor.

And, instantly, opening the upper valve, he let some hydrogen escape, and slowly descended, taking the ground at about two hundred feet from the edge of the oasis.

In four hours the travelers had swept over a distance of two hundred and forty miles!

The car was at once ballasted, and Kennedy, closely followed by Joe, leaped out.

"Take your guns with you!" said the doctor. "Take your guns, and be careful!"

Dick grasped his rifle, and Joe took one of the fowling-pieces. They then rapidly made for the trees, and disappeared under the fresh verdure, which announced the presence of abundant springs. As they hurried on, they had not taken notice of certain large footprints and fresh tracks of some living creature marked here and there in the damp soil.

Suddenly, a dull roar was heard not twenty paces from them.

"The roar of a lion!" said Joe.

"Good for that!" said the excited hunter. "We'll fight him. A man feels strong when only a fight's in question."

"But be careful, Mr. Kennedy; be careful! The lives of all depend upon the life of one."

But Kennedy no longer heard him; he was pushing on, his eye blazing; his rifle cocked; fearful to behold in his daring rashness. There, under a palm tree, stood an enormous black-maned lion, crouching for a spring on his antagonist. Scarcely had he caught a glimpse of the hunter, when he bounded through the air; but he had not touched the ground ere a bullet pierced his heart, and he fell to the earth dead.

"Hurrah! Hurrah!" shouted Joe, with wild exultation.

Kennedy rushed toward the well, slid down the dampened steps, and flung himself at full length by the side of a fresh spring, in which he plunged his parched lips. Joe followed suit, and for some minutes nothing was heard but the sound they made with their mouths, drinking more like maddened beasts than men.

"Take care, Mr. Kennedy," said Joe at last; "let us not overdo the thing!" and he panted for breath.

But Kennedy, without a word, drank on. He even plunged his hands, and then his head, into the delicious tide—he fairly reveled in its coolness.

"But the doctor?" said Joe. "Our friend, Dr. Ferguson?"

That one word recalled Kennedy to himself, and, hastily filling a flask that he had brought with him, he started on a run up the steps of the well.

But what was his amazement when he saw an opaque body of enormous dimensions blocking up the passage! Joe, who was close upon Kennedy's heels, recoiled with him.

"We are blocked in—entrapped!"

"Impossible! What does that mean?"

Dick had no time to finish; a terrific roar made him only too quickly aware what foe confronted him.

"Another lion!" exclaimed Joe.

"A lioness, rather," said Kennedy. "Ah! Ferocious brute!" he added, "I'll settle you in a moment more!" and swiftly reloaded his rifle.

In another instant he fired, but the animal had disappeared.

"Onward!" shouted Kennedy.

"No!" interposed the other. "That shot did not kill her; her body would have rolled down the steps; she's up there, ready to spring upon the first of us who appears, and he would be a lost man!"

"But what are we to do? We must get out of this, and the doctor is expecting us."

"Let us decoy the animal. Take my piece, and give me your rifle."

"What is your plan?"

"You'll see."

And Joe, taking off his linen jacket, hung it on the end of the rifle, and thrust it above the top of the steps. The lioness flung herself furiously upon it. Kennedy was on the alert for her, and his bullet broke her shoulder. The lioness, with a frightful howl of agony, rolled down the steps, overturning Joe in her fall. The poor fellow imagined that he could already feel the enormous paws of the savage beast in his flesh, when a second detonation resounded in the narrow passage, and Dr. Ferguson appeared at the opening above with his gun in hand, and still smoking from the discharge.

Joe leaped to his feet, clambered over the body of the dead lioness, and handed up the flask full of sparkling water to his master.

To carry it to his lips, and to half-empty it at a draft, was the work of an instant, and the three travelers offered up thanks from the depths of their hearts to that Providence who had so miraculously saved them.

# CHAPTER XXVIII

An Evening of Delight—Joe's Culinary Performance—A Dissertation
on Raw Meat—The Narrative of James Bruce—Camping Out—Joe's
Dreams—The Barometer Begins to Fall—The Barometer Rises Again—
Preparations for Departure—The Tempest

The evening was lovely, and our three friends enjoyed it in the cool shade of the mimosas, after a substantial repast, at which the tea and the punch were dealt out with no niggardly hand.

Kennedy had traversed the little domain in all directions. He had ransacked every thicket and satisfied himself that the balloon party were the only living creatures in this terrestrial paradise; so they stretched themselves upon their blankets and passed a peaceful night that brought them forgetfulness of their past sufferings.

On the morrow, May 7th, the sun shone with all his splendor, but his rays could not penetrate the dense screen of the palm-tree foliage, and as there was no lack of provisions, the doctor resolved to remain where he was while waiting for a favorable wind.

Joe had conveyed his portable kitchen to the oasis, and proceeded to indulge in any number of culinary combinations, using water all the time with the most profuse extravagance.

"What a strange succession of annoyances and enjoyments!" moralized Kennedy. "Such abundance as this after such privations; such luxury after such want! Ah! I nearly went mad!"

"My dear Dick," replied the doctor, "had it not been for Joe, you would not be sitting here, today, discoursing on the instability of human affairs."

"Whole-hearted friend!" said Kennedy, extending his hand to Joe.

"There's no occasion for all that," responded the latter; "but you can take your revenge sometime, Mr. Kennedy, always hoping though that you may never have occasion to do the same for me!"

"It's a poor constitution this of ours to succumb to so little," philosophized Dr. Ferguson.

"So little water, you mean, doctor," interposed Joe. "That element must be very necessary to life."

"Undoubtedly, and persons deprived of food hold out longer than those deprived of water."

"I believe it. Besides, when needs must, one can eat anything he comes across, even his fellow creatures, although that must be a kind of food that's pretty hard to digest."

"The savages don't boggle much about it!" said Kennedy.

"Yes; but then they are savages, and accustomed to devouring raw meat; it's something that I'd find very disgusting, for my part."

"It is disgusting enough," said the doctor, "that's a fact; and so much so, indeed, that nobody believed the narratives of the earliest travelers in Africa who brought back word that many tribes on that continent subsisted upon raw meat, and people generally refused to credit the statement. It was under such circumstances that a very singular adventure befell James Bruce."

"Tell it to us, doctor; we've time enough to hear it," said Joe, stretching himself voluptuously on the cool greensward.

"By all means—James Bruce was a Scotchman, of Stirlingshire, who, between 1768 and 1772, traversed all Abyssinia, as far as Lake Tyana, in search of the sources of the Nile. He afterward returned to England, but did not publish an account of his journeys until 1790. His statements were received with extreme incredulity, and such may be the reception accorded to our own. The manners and customs of the Abyssinians seemed so different from those of the English, that no one would credit the description of them. Among other details, Bruce had put forward the assertion that the tribes of eastern Africa fed upon raw flesh, and this set everybody against him. He might say so as much as he pleased; there was no one likely to go and see! One day, in a parlor at Edinburgh, a Scotch gentleman took up the subject in his presence, as it had become the topic of daily pleasantry, and, in reference to the eating of raw flesh, said that the thing was neither possible nor true. Bruce made no reply, but went out and returned a few minutes later with a raw steak, seasoned with pepper and salt, in the African style.

"'Sir,' said he to the Scotchman, 'in doubting my statements, you have grossly affronted me; in believing the thing to be impossible, you have been egregiously mistaken; and, in proof thereof, you will now eat this beefsteak raw, or you will give me instant satisfaction!' The Scotchman had a wholesome dread of the brawny traveler, and did eat the steak, although not without a good many wry faces. Thereupon, with the utmost coolness, James Bruce added: 'Even admitting, sir, that the thing were untrue, you will, at least, no longer maintain that it is impossible.'"

"Well put in!" said Joe. "And if the Scotchman found it lie heavy on his stomach, he got no more than he deserved. If, on our return to England, they dare to doubt what we say about our travels—"

"Well, Joe, what would you do?"

"Why, I'll make the doubters swallow the pieces of the balloon, without either salt or pepper!"

All burst out laughing at Joe's queer notions, and thus the day slipped by in pleasant chat. With returning strength, hope had revived, and with hope came the courage to do and to dare. The past was obliterated in the presence of the future with providential rapidity.

Joe would have been willing to remain forever in this enchanting asylum; it was the realm he had pictured in his dreams; he felt himself at home; his master had to give him his exact location, and it was with the gravest air imaginable that he wrote down on his tablets fifteen degrees forty-three minutes east longitude, and eight degrees thirty-two minutes north latitude.

Kennedy had but one regret, to wit, that he could not hunt in that miniature forest, because, according to his ideas, there was a slight deficiency of ferocious wild beasts in it.

"But, my dear Dick," said the doctor, "haven't you rather a short memory? How about the lion and the lioness?"

"Oh, that!" he ejaculated with the contempt of a thoroughbred sportsman for game already killed. "But the fact is, that finding them here would lead one to suppose that we can't be far from a more fertile country."

"It don't prove much, Dick, for those animals, when goaded by hunger or thirst, will travel long distances, and I think that, tonight, we had better keep a more vigilant lookout, and light fires, besides."

"What, in such heat as this?" said Joe. "Well, if it's necessary, we'll have to do it, but I do think it a real pity to burn this pretty grove that has been such a comfort to us!"

"Oh! Above all things, we must take the utmost care not to set it on fire," replied the doctor, "so that others in the same strait as ourselves may someday find shelter here in the middle of the desert."

"I'll be very careful, indeed, doctor; but do you think that this oasis is known?"

"Undoubtedly; it is a halting place for the caravans that frequent the center of Africa, and a visit from one of them might be anything but pleasant to you, Joe."

"Why, are there any more of those rascally Nyam-Nyams around here?"

"Certainly; that is the general name of all the neighboring tribes, and, under the same climates, the same races are likely to have similar manners and customs."

"Pah!" said Joe. "But, after all, it's natural enough. If savages had the ways of gentlemen, where would be the difference? By George, these fine fellows wouldn't have to be coaxed long to eat the Scotchman's raw steak, nor the Scotchman either, into the bargain!"

With this very sensible observation, Joe began to get ready his firewood for the night, making just as little of it as possible. Fortunately, these precautions were superfluous; and each of the party, in his turn, dropped off into the soundest slumber.

On the next day the weather still showed no sign of change, but kept provokingly and obstinately fair. The balloon remained motionless, without any oscillation to betray a breath of wind.

The doctor began to get uneasy again. If their stay in the desert were to be prolonged like this, their provisions would give out. After nearly perishing for want of water, they would, at last, have to starve to death!

But he took fresh courage as he saw the mercury fall considerably in the barometer, and noticed evident signs of an early change in the atmosphere. He therefore resolved to make all his preparations for a start, so as to avail himself of the first opportunity. The feeding tank and the water tank were both completely filled.

Then he had to reestablish the equilibrium of the balloon, and Joe was obliged to part with another considerable portion of his precious quartz. With restored health, his ambitious notions had come back to him, and he made more than one wry face before obeying his master; but the latter convinced him that he could not carry so considerable a weight with him through the air, and gave him his choice between the water and the gold. Joe hesitated no longer, but flung out the requisite quantity of his much-prized ore upon the sand.

"The next people who come this way," he remarked, "will be rather surprised to find a fortune in such a place."

"And suppose some learned traveler should come across these specimens, eh?" suggested Kennedy.

"You may be certain, Dick, that they would take him by surprise, and that he would publish his astonishment in several folios; so that someday we shall hear of a wonderful deposit of gold-bearing quartz in the midst of the African sands!"

"And Joe there, will be the cause of it all!"

This idea of mystifying some learned sage tickled Joe hugely, and made him laugh.

During the rest of the day the doctor vainly kept on the watch for a change of weather. The temperature rose, and, had it not been for the shade of the oasis, would have been insupportable. The thermometer marked a hundred and forty-nine degrees in the sun, and a veritable rain of fire filled the air. This was the most intense heat that they had yet noted.

Joe arranged their bivouac for that evening, as he had done for the previous night; and during the watches kept by the doctor and Kennedy there was no fresh incident.

But, toward three o'clock in the morning, while Joe was on guard, the temperature suddenly fell; the sky became overcast with clouds, and the darkness increased.

"Turn out!" cried Joe, arousing his companions. "Turn out! Here's the wind!"

"At last!" exclaimed the doctor, eying the heavens. "But it is a storm! The balloon! Let us hasten to the balloon!"

It was high time for them to reach it. The *Victoria* was bending to the force of the hurricane, and dragging along the car, the latter grazing the sand. Had any portion of the ballast been accidentally thrown out, the balloon would have been swept away, and all hope of recovering it have been forever lost.

But fleet-footed Joe put forth his utmost speed, and checked the car, while the balloon beat upon the sand, at the risk of being torn to pieces. The doctor, followed by Kennedy, leaped in, and lit his cylinder, while his companions threw out the superfluous ballast.

The travelers took one last look at the trees of the oasis bowing to the force of the hurricane, and soon, catching the wind at two hundred feet above the ground, disappeared in the gloom.

## CHAPTER XXIX

Signs of Vegetation—The Fantastic Notion of a French
Author—A Magnificent Country—The Kingdom of Adamova—
The Explorations of Speke and Burton Connected with Those of
Dr. Barth—The Atlantika Mountains—The River Benoué—
The City of Yola—The Bagélé—Mount Mendif

From the moment of their departure, the travelers moved with great velocity. They longed to leave behind them the desert, which had so nearly been fatal to them.

About a quarter past nine in the morning, they caught a glimpse of some signs of vegetation: herbage floating on that sea of sand, and announcing, as the weeds upon the ocean did to Christopher Columbus, the nearness of the shore—green shoots peeping up timidly between pebbles that were, in their turn, to be the rocks of that vast expanse.

Hills, but of trifling height, were seen in wavy lines upon the horizon. Their profile, muffled by the heavy mist, was defined but vaguely. The monotony, however, was beginning to disappear.

The doctor hailed with joy the new country thus disclosed, and, like a seaman on lookout at the masthead, he was ready to shout aloud:

"Land, ho! Land!"

An hour later the continent spread broadly before their gaze, still wild in aspect, but less flat, less denuded, and with a few trees standing out against the gray sky.

"We are in a civilized country at last!" said the hunter.

"Civilized? Well, that's one way of speaking; but there are no people to be seen yet."

"It will not be long before we see them," said Ferguson, "at our present rate of travel."

"Are we still in the negro country, doctor?"

"Yes, and on our way to the country of the Arabs."

"What! Real Arabs, sir, with their camels?"

"No, not many camels; they are scarce, if not altogether unknown, in these regions. We must go a few degrees farther north to see them."

"What a pity!"

"And why, Joe?"

"Because, if the wind fell contrary, they might be of use to us."

"How so?"

"Well, sir, it's just a notion that's got into my head: we might hitch them to the car, and make them tow us along. What do you say to that, doctor?"

"Poor Joe! Another person had that idea in advance of you. It was used by a very gifted French author—M. Méry—in a romance, it is true. He has his travelers drawn along in a balloon by a team of camels; then a lion comes up, devours the camels, swallows the tow rope, and hauls the balloon in their stead; and so on through the story. You see that the whole thing is the top-flower of fancy, but has nothing in common with our style of locomotion."

Joe, a little cut down at learning that his idea had been used already, cudgeled his wits to imagine what animal could have devoured the lion; but he could not guess it, and so quietly went on scanning the appearance of the country.

A lake of medium extent stretched away before him, surrounded by an amphitheater of hills, which yet could not be dignified with the name of mountains. There were winding valleys, numerous and fertile, with their tangled thickets of the most various trees. The African oil tree rose above the mass, with leaves fifteen feet in length upon its stalk, the latter studded with sharp thorns; the bombax, or silk-cotton tree, filled the wind, as it swept by, with the fine down of its seeds; the pungent odors of the *pendanus*, the "kenda" of the Arabs, perfumed the air up to the height where the *Victoria* was sailing; the papaw tree, with its palm-shaped leaves; the *sterculier*, which produces the Soudan-nut; the baobab, and the banana tree, completed the luxuriant flora of these intertropical regions.

"The country is superb!" said the doctor.

"Here are some animals," added Joe. "Men are not far away."

"Oh, what magnificent elephants!" exclaimed Kennedy. "Is there no way to get a little shooting?"

"How could we manage to halt in a current as strong as this? No, Dick; you must taste a little of the torture of Tantalus just now. You shall make up for it afterward."

And, in truth, there was enough to excite the fancy of a sportsman. Dick's heart fairly leaped in his breast as he grasped the butt of his Purdy.

The fauna of the region were as striking as its flora. The wild ox reveled in dense herbage that often concealed his whole body; gray, black, and yellow elephants of the most gigantic size burst headlong, like a living hurricane, through the forests, breaking, rending, tearing down, devastating everything in their path; upon the woody slopes of the hills trickled cascades and springs flowing northward; there, too, the hippopotami bathed their huge forms, splashing and snorting as they frolicked in the water, and lamantines, twelve feet long, with bodies like seals, stretched themselves along the banks, turning up toward the sun their rounded teats swollen with milk.

It was a whole menagerie of rare and curious beasts in a wondrous hothouse, where numberless birds with plumage of a thousand hues gleamed and fluttered in the sunshine.

By this prodigality of Nature, the doctor recognized the splendid kingdom of Adamova.

"We are now beginning to trench upon the realm of modern discovery. I have taken up the lost scent of preceding travelers. It is a happy chance, my friends, for we shall be enabled to link the toils of Captains Burton and Speke with the explorations of Dr. Barth. We have left the Englishmen behind us, and now have caught up with the Hamburger. It will not be long, either, before we arrive at the extreme point attained by that daring explorer."

"It seems to me that there is a vast extent of country between the two explored routes," remarked Kennedy; "at least, if I am to judge by the distance that we have made."

"It is easy to determine: take the map and see what is the longitude of the southern point of Lake Ukéréoué, reached by Speke."

"It is near the thirty-seventh degree."

"And the city of Yola, which we shall sight this evening, and to which Barth penetrated, what is its position?"

"It is about in the twelfth degree of east longitude."

"Then there are twenty-five degrees, or, counting sixty miles to each, about fifteen hundred miles in all."

"A nice little walk," said Joe, "for people who have to go on foot."

"It will be accomplished, however. Livingstone and Moffat are pushing on up this line toward the interior. Nyassa, which they have discovered, is not far from Lake Tanganayika, seen by Burton. Ere the close of the century these regions will, undoubtedly, be explored. But," added the doctor, consulting his compass, "I regret that the wind is carrying us so far to the westward. I wanted to get to the north."

After twelve hours of progress, the *Victoria* found herself on the confines of Nigritia. The first inhabitants of this region, the Chouas Arabs, were feeding their wandering flocks. The immense summits of the Atlantika Mountains seen above the horizon—mountains that no European foot had yet scaled, and whose height is computed to be ten thousand feet! Their western slope determines the flow of all the waters in this region of Africa toward the ocean. They are the Mountains of the Moon to this part of the continent.

At length a real river greeted the gaze of our travelers, and, by the enormous anthills seen in its vicinity, the doctor recognized the Benoué, one of the great tributaries of the Niger, the one which the natives have called "the Fountain of the Waters."

"This river," said the doctor to his companions, "will, one day, be the natural channel of communication with the interior of Nigritia. Under the command of one of our brave captains, the steamer *Pleiad* has already ascended as far as the town of Yola. You see that we are not in an unknown country."

Numerous slaves were engaged in the labors of the field, cultivating sorgho, a kind of millet which forms the chief basis of their diet; and the most stupid expressions of astonishment ensued as the *Victoria* sped past like a meteor. That evening the balloon halted about forty miles from Yola, and ahead of it, but in the distance, rose the two sharp cones of Mount Mendif.

The doctor threw out his anchors and made fast to the top of a high tree; but a very violent wind beat upon the balloon with such force as to throw it over on its side, thus rendering the position of the car sometimes extremely dangerous. Ferguson did not close his all night, and he was repeatedly on the point of cutting the anchor rope and scudding away before the gale. At length, however, the storm abated, and the oscillations of the balloon ceased to be alarming.

On the morrow the wind was more moderate, but it carried our travelers away from the city of Yola, which recently rebuilt by the Fouillans, excited Ferguson's curiosity. However, he had to make up his mind to being borne farther to the northward and even a little to the east.

Kennedy proposed to halt in this fine hunting country, and Joe declared that the need of fresh meat was beginning to be felt; but the savage customs of the country, the attitude of the population, and some shots fired at the *Victoria*, admonished the doctor to continue his journey. They were then crossing a region that was the scene of massacres and burnings, and where warlike conflicts between the barbarian sultans, contending for their power amid the most atrocious carnage, never cease.

Numerous and populous villages of long, low huts stretched away between broad pasture fields whose dense herbage was besprinkled with violet-colored blossoms. The huts, looking like huge beehives, were sheltered behind bristling palisades. The wild hillsides and hollows frequently reminded the beholder of the glens in the Highlands of Scotland, as Kennedy more than once remarked.

In spite of all he could do, the doctor bore directly to the northeast, toward Mount Mendif, which was lost in the midst of environing clouds. The lofty summits of these mountains separate the valley of the Niger from the basin of Lake Tchad.

Soon afterward was seen the Bagélé, with its eighteen villages clinging to its flanks like a whole brood of children to their mother's bosom—a magnificent spectacle for the beholder whose gaze commanded and took in the entire picture at one view. Even the ravines were seen to be covered with fields of rice and of arachides.

By three o'clock the *Victoria* was directly in front of Mount Mendif. It had been impossible to avoid it; the only thing to be done was to cross it. The doctor, by means of a temperature increased to one hundred and eighty degrees, gave the balloon a fresh ascensional force of nearly sixteen hundred pounds, and it went up to an elevation of more than eight thousand feet, the greatest height attained during the journey. The temperature of the atmosphere was so much cooler at that point that the aeronauts had to resort to their blankets and thick coverings.

Ferguson was in haste to descend; the covering of the balloon gave indications of bursting, but in the meanwhile he had time to satisfy himself of the volcanic origin of the mountain, whose extinct craters are now but deep abysses. Immense accumulations of bird guano gave the sides of Mount Mendif the appearance of calcareous rocks, and there was enough of the deposit there to manure all the lands in the United Kingdom.

At five o'clock the *Victoria*, sheltered from the south winds, went gently gliding along the slopes of the mountain, and stopped in a wide clearing remote from any habitation. The instant it touched the soil, all needful precautions were taken to hold it there firmly; and Kennedy, fowling-piece in hand, sallied out upon the sloping plain. Ere long, he returned with half a dozen wild ducks and a kind of snipe, which Joe served up in his best style. The meal was heartily relished, and the night was passed in undisturbed and refreshing slumber.

## CHAPTER XXX

Mosfeia—The Sheik—Denham, Clapperton, and Oudney—Vogel—The
Capital of Loggoum—Toole—Becalmed Above Kernak—The Governor
and His Court—The Attack—The Incendiary Pigeons

On the next day, May 11th, the *Victoria* resumed her adventurous journey. Her
passengers had the same confidence in her that a good seaman has in his ship.

In terrific hurricanes, in tropical heats, when making dangerous departures, and
descents still more dangerous, it had, at all times and in all places, come out safely. It
might almost have been said that Ferguson managed it with a wave of the hand; and
hence, without knowing in advance where the point of arrival would be, the doctor
had no fears concerning the successful issue of his journey. However, in this country
of barbarians and fanatics, prudence obliged him to take the strictest precautions. He
therefore counseled his companions to have their eyes wide open for everything and
at all hours.

The wind drifted a little more to the northward, and, toward nine o'clock, they
sighted the larger city of Mosfeia, built upon an eminence which was itself enclosed
between two lofty mountains. Its position was impregnable, a narrow road running
between a marsh and a thick wood being the only channel of approach to it.

At the moment of which we write, a sheik, accompanied by a mounted escort, and
clad in a garb of brilliant colors, preceded by couriers and trumpeters, who put aside
the boughs of the trees as he rode up, was making his grand entry into the place.

The doctor lowered the balloon in order to get a better look at this cavalcade of
natives; but, as the balloon grew larger to their eyes, they began to show symptoms of
intense affright, and at length made off in different directions as fast as their legs and
those of their horses could carry them.

The sheik alone did not budge an inch. He merely grasped his long musket, cocked
it, and proudly waited in silence. The doctor came on to within a hundred and fifty
feet of him, and then, with his roundest and fullest voice, saluted him courteously in
the Arabic tongue.

But, upon hearing these words falling, as it seemed, from the sky, the sheik
dismounted and prostrated himself in the dust of the highway, where the doctor had
to leave him, finding it impossible to divert him from his adoration.

"Unquestionably," Ferguson remarked, "those people take us for supernatural
beings. When Europeans came among them for the first time, they were mistaken for
creatures of a higher race. When this sheik comes to speak of today's meeting, he will
not fail to embellish the circumstance with all the resources of an Arab imagination.
You may, therefore, judge what an account their legends will give of us someday."

"Not such a desirable thing, after all," said the Scot, "in the point of view that
affects civilization; it would be better to pass for mere men. That would give these
negro races a superior idea of European power."

"Very good, my dear Dick; but what can we do about it? You might sit all day explaining the mechanism of a balloon to the savants of this country, and yet they would not comprehend you, but would persist in ascribing it to supernatural aid."

"Doctor, you spoke of the first time Europeans visited these regions. Who were the visitors?" inquired Joe.

"My dear fellow, we are now upon the very track of Major Denham. It was at this very city of Mosfeia that he was received by the sultan of Mandara; he had quitted the Bornou country; he accompanied the sheik in an expedition against the Fellatahs; he assisted in the attack on the city, which, with its arrows alone, bravely resisted the bullets of the Arabs, and put the sheik's troops to flight. All this was but a pretext for murders, raids, and pillage. The major was completely plundered and stripped, and had it not been for his horse, under whose stomach he clung with the skill of an Indian rider, and was borne with a headlong gallop from his barbarous pursuers, he never could have made his way back to Kouka, the capital of Bornou."

"Who was this Major Denham?"

"A fearless Englishman, who, between 1822 and 1824, commanded an expedition into the Bornou country, in company with Captain Clapperton and Dr. Oudney. They set out from Tripoli in the month of March, reached Mourzouk, the capital of Fez, and, following the route which at a later period Dr. Barth was to pursue on his way back to Europe, they arrived, on the 16th of February, 1823, at Kouka, near Lake Tchad. Denham made several explorations in Bornou, in Mandara, and to the eastern shores of the lake. In the meantime, on the 15th of December, 1823, Captain Clapperton and Dr. Oudney had pushed their way through the Soudan country as far as Sackatoo, and Oudney died of fatigue and exhaustion in the town of Murmur."

"This part of Africa has, therefore, paid a heavy tribute of victims to the cause of science," said Kennedy.

"Yes, this country is fatal to travelers. We are moving directly toward the kingdom of Baghirmi, which Vogel traversed in 1856, so as to reach the Wadai country, where he disappeared. This young man, at the age of twenty-three, had been sent to cooperate with Dr. Barth. They met on the 1st of December, 1854, and thereupon commenced his explorations of the country. Toward 1856, he announced, in the last letters received from him, his intention to reconnoiter the kingdom of Wadai, which no European had yet penetrated. It appears that he got as far as Wara, the capital, where, according to some accounts, he was made prisoner, and, according to others, was put to death for having attempted to ascend a sacred mountain in the environs. But, we must not too lightly admit the death of travelers, since that does away with the necessity of going in search of them. For instance, how often was the death of Dr. Barth reported, to his own great annoyance! It is, therefore, very possible that Vogel may still be held as a prisoner by the sultan of Wadai, in the hope of obtaining a good ransom for him.

"Baron de Neimans was about starting for the Wadai country when he died at Cairo, in 1855; and we now know that De Heuglin has set out on Vogel's track with the expedition sent from Leipsic, so that we shall soon be accurately informed as to the fate of that young and interesting explorer."*

---

* Since the doctor's departure, letters written from El'Obeid by Mr. Muntzinger, the newly appointed head of the expedition, unfortunately place the death of Vogel beyond a doubt.

Mosfeia had disappeared from the horizon long ere this, and the Mandara country was developing to the gaze of our aeronauts its astonishing fertility, with its forests of acacias, its locust trees covered with red flowers, and the herbaceous plants of its fields of cotton and indigo trees. The river Shari, which eighty miles farther on rolled its impetuous waters into Lake Tchad, was quite distinctly seen.

The doctor got his companions to trace its course upon the maps drawn by Dr. Barth.

"You perceive," said he, "that the labors of this savant have been conducted with great precision; we are moving directly toward the Loggoum region, and perhaps toward Kernak, its capital. It was there that poor Toole died, at the age of scarcely twenty-two. He was a young Englishman, an ensign in the 80th regiment, who, a few weeks before, had joined Major Denham in Africa, and it was not long ere he there met his death. Ah! This vast country might well be called the graveyard of European travelers."

Some boats, fifty feet long, were descending the current of the Shari. The *Victoria*, then one thousand feet above the soil, hardly attracted the attention of the natives; but the wind, which until then had been blowing with a certain degree of strength, was falling off.

"Is it possible that we are to be caught in another dead calm?" sighed the doctor.

"Well, we've no lack of water, nor the desert to fear, anyhow, master," said Joe.

"No; but there are races here still more to be dreaded."

"Why!" said Joe, again. "There's something like a town."

"That is Kernak. The last puffs of the breeze are wafting us to it, and, if we choose, we can take an exact plan of the place."

"Shall we not go nearer to it?" asked Kennedy.

"Nothing easier, Dick! We are right over it. Allow me to turn the stopcock of the cylinder, and we'll not be long in descending."

Half an hour later the balloon hung motionless about two hundred feet from the ground.

"Here we are!" said the doctor. "Nearer to Kernak than a man would be to London, if he were perched in the cupola of St. Paul's. So we can take a survey at our ease."

"What is that ticktacking sound that we hear on all sides?"

Joe looked attentively, and at length discovered that the noise they heard was produced by a number of weavers beating cloth stretched in the open air, on large trunks of trees.

The capital of Loggoum could then be seen in its entire extent, like an unrolled chart. It is really a city with straight rows of houses and quite wide streets. In the midst of a large open space there was a slave market, attended by a great crowd of customers, for the Mandara women, who have extremely small hands and feet, are in excellent request, and can be sold at lucrative rates.

At the sight of the *Victoria*, the scene so often produced occurred again. At first there were outcries, and then followed general stupefaction; business was abandoned; work was flung aside, and all noise ceased. The aeronauts remained as they were, completely motionless, and lost not a detail of the populous city. They even went down to within sixty feet of the ground.

Hereupon the governor of Loggoum came out from his residence, displaying his green standard, and accompanied by his musicians, who blew on hoarse buffalo horns, as though they would split their cheeks or anything else, excepting their own lungs. The crowd at once gathered around him. In the meanwhile Dr. Ferguson tried to make himself heard, but in vain.

This population looked like proud and intelligent people, with their high foreheads, their almost aquiline noses, and their curling hair; but the presence of the *Victoria* troubled them greatly. Horsemen could be seen galloping in all directions, and it soon became evident that the governor's troops were assembling to oppose so extraordinary a foe. Joe wore himself out waving handkerchiefs of every color and shape to them; but his exertions were all to no purpose.

However, the sheik, surrounded by his court, proclaimed silence, and pronounced a discourse, of which the doctor could not understand a word. It was Arabic, mixed with Baghirmi. He could make out enough, however, by the universal language of gestures, to be aware that he was receiving a very polite invitation to depart. Indeed, he would have asked for nothing better, but for lack of wind, the thing had become impossible. His noncompliance, therefore, exasperated the governor, whose courtiers and attendants set up a furious howl to enforce immediate obedience on the part of the aerial monster.

They were odd-looking fellows those courtiers, with their five or six shirts swathed around their bodies! They had enormous stomachs, some of which actually seemed to be artificial. The doctor surprised his companions by informing them that this was the way to pay court to the sultan. The rotundity of the stomach indicated the ambition of its possessor. These corpulent gentry gesticulated and bawled at the top of their voices—one of them particularly distinguishing himself above the rest—to such an extent, indeed, that he must have been a prime minister—at least, if the disturbance he made was any criterion of his rank. The common rabble of dusky denizens united their howlings with the uproar of the court, repeating their gesticulations like so many monkeys, and thereby producing a single and instantaneous movement of ten thousand arms at one time.

To these means of intimidation, which were presently deemed insufficient, were added others still more formidable. Soldiers, armed with bows and arrows, were drawn up in line of battle; but by this time the balloon was expanding, and rising quietly beyond their reach. Upon this the governor seized a musket and aimed it at the balloon; but, Kennedy, who was watching him, shattered the uplifted weapon in the sheik's grasp.

At this unexpected blow there was a general rout. Every mother's son of them scampered for his dwelling with the utmost celerity, and stayed there, so that the streets of the town were absolutely deserted for the remainder of that day.

Night came, and not a breath of wind was stirring. The aeronauts had to make up their minds to remain motionless at the distance of but three hundred feet above the ground. Not a fire or light shone in the deep gloom, and around reigned the silence of death; but the doctor only redoubled his vigilance, as this apparent quiet might conceal some snare.

And he had reason to be watchful. About midnight, the whole city seemed to be in a blaze. Hundreds of streaks of flame crossed each other, and shot to and fro in the air like rockets, forming a regular network of fire.

"That's really curious!" said the doctor, somewhat puzzled to make out what it meant.

"By all that's glorious!" shouted Kennedy. "It looks as if the fire were ascending and coming up toward us!"

And, sure enough, with an accompaniment of musket shots, yelling, and din of every description, the mass of fire was, indeed, mounting toward the *Victoria*. Joe got ready to throw out ballast, and Ferguson was not long at guessing the truth. Thousands of pigeons, their tails garnished with combustibles, had been set loose and driven toward the *Victoria*; and now, in their terror, they were flying high up, zigzagging the atmosphere with lines of fire. Kennedy was preparing to discharge all his batteries into the middle of the ascending multitude, but what could he have done against such a numberless army? The pigeons were already whisking around the car; they were even surrounding the balloon, the sides of which, reflecting their illumination, looked as though enveloped with a network of fire.

The doctor dared hesitate no longer; and, throwing out a fragment of quartz, he kept himself beyond the reach of these dangerous assailants; and, for two hours afterward, he could see them wandering hither and thither through the darkness of the night, until, little by little, their light diminished, and they, one by one, died out.

"Now we may sleep in quiet," said the doctor.

"Not badly got up for barbarians," mused friend Joe, speaking his thoughts aloud.

"Oh, they employ these pigeons frequently, to set fire to the thatch of hostile villages; but this time the village mounted higher than they could go."

"Why, positively, a balloon need fear no enemies!"

"Yes, indeed, it may!" objected Ferguson.

"What are they, then, doctor?"

"They are the careless people in the car! So, my friends, let us have vigilance in all places and at all times."

## CHAPTER XXXI

DEPARTURE IN THE NIGHTTIME—ALL THREE—KENNEDY'S INSTINCTS—
PRECAUTIONS— THE COURSE OF THE SHARI RIVER—LAKE TCHAD—THE
WATER OF THE LAKE—THE HIPPOPOTAMUS—ONE BULLET THROWN AWAY

About three o'clock in the morning, Joe, who was then on watch, at length saw the city move away from beneath his feet. The *Victoria* was once again in motion, and both the doctor and Kennedy awoke.

The former consulted his compass, and saw, with satisfaction, that the wind was carrying them toward the north-northeast.

"We are in luck!" said he. "Works in our favor: we shall discover Lake Tchad this very day."

"Is it a broad sheet of water?" asked Kennedy.

"Somewhat, Dick. At its greatest length and breadth, it measures about one hundred and twenty miles."

"It will spice our trip with a little variety to sail over a spacious sheet of water."

"After all, though, I don't see that we have much to complain of on that score. Our trip has been very much varied, indeed; and, moreover, we are getting on under the best possible conditions."

"Unquestionably so; excepting those privations on the desert, we have encountered no serious danger."

"It is not to be denied that our noble balloon has behaved wonderfully well. Today is May 12th, and we started on the 18th of April. That makes twenty-five days of journeying. In ten days more we shall have reached our destination."

"Where is that?"

"I do not know. But what does that signify?"

"You are right again, Samuel! Let us intrust to Providence the care of guiding us and of keeping us in good health as we are now. We don't look much as though we had been crossing the most pestilential country in the world!"

"We had an opportunity of getting up in life, and that's what we have done!"

"Hurrah for trips in the air!" cried Joe. "Here we are at the end of twenty-five days in good condition, well fed, and well rested. We've had too much rest in fact, for my legs begin to feel rusty, and I wouldn't be vexed a bit to stretch them with a run of thirty miles or so!"

"You can do that, Joe, in the streets of London, but in fine we set out three together, like Denham, Clapperton, and Overweg; like Barth, Richardson, and Vogel, and, more fortunate than our predecessors here, we are three in number still. But it is most important for us not to separate. If, while one of us was on the ground, the *Victoria* should have to ascend in order to escape some sudden danger, who knows whether we should ever see each other again? Therefore it is that I say again to Kennedy frankly that I do not like his going off alone to hunt."

"But still, Samuel, you will permit me to indulge that fancy a little. There is no harm in renewing our stock of provisions. Besides, before our departure, you held out to me the prospect of some superb hunting, and thus far I have done but little in the line of the Andersons and Cummings."

"But, my dear Dick, your memory fails you, or your modesty makes you forget your own exploits. It really seems to me that, without mentioning small game, you have already an antelope, an elephant, and two lions on your conscience."

"But what's all that to an African sportsman who sees all the animals in creation strutting along under the muzzle of his rifle? There! There! Look at that troop of giraffes!"

"Those giraffes," roared Joe; "why, they're not as big as my fist."

"Because we are a thousand feet above them; but close to them you would discover that they are three times as tall as you are!"

"And what do you say to yon herd of gazelles, and those ostriches, that run with the speed of the wind?" resumed Kennedy.

"Those ostriches?" remonstrated Joe, again; "those are chickens, and the greatest kind of chickens!"

"Come, doctor, can't we get down nearer to them?" pleaded Kennedy.

"We can get closer to them, Dick, but we must not land. And what good will it do you to strike down those poor animals when they can be of no use to you? Now, if the question were to destroy a lion, a tiger, a cat, a hyena, I could understand it; but to deprive an antelope or a gazelle of life, to no other purpose than the gratification of your instincts as a sportsman, seems hardly worth the trouble. But, after all, my friend, we are going to keep at about one hundred feet only from the soil, and, should you see any ferocious wild beast, oblige us by sending a ball through its heart!"

The *Victoria* descended gradually, but still keeping at a safe height, for, in a barbarous yet very populous country, it was necessary to keep on the watch for unexpected perils.

The travelers were then directly following the course of the Shari. The charming banks of this river were hidden beneath the foliage of trees of various dyes; lianas and climbing plants wound in and out on all sides and formed the most curious combinations of color. Crocodiles were seen basking in the broad blaze of the sun or plunging beneath the waters with the agility of lizards, and in their gambols they sported about among the many green islands that intercept the current of the stream.

It was thus, in the midst of rich and verdant landscapes that our travelers passed over the district of Maffatay, and about nine o'clock in the morning reached the southern shore of Lake Tchad.

There it was at last, outstretched before them, that Caspian Sea of Africa, the existence of which was so long consigned to the realms of fable—that interior expanse of water to which only Denham's and Barth's expeditions had been able to force their way.

The doctor strove in vain to fix its precise configuration upon paper. It had already changed greatly since 1847. In fact, the chart of Lake Tchad is very difficult to trace with exactitude, for it is surrounded by muddy and almost impassable morasses, in which Barth thought that he was doomed to perish. From year to year these marshes, covered with reeds and papyrus fifteen feet high, become the lake itself. Frequently, too, the villages on its shores are half submerged, as was the case with Ngornou in 1856, and now the hippopotamus and the alligator frisk and dive where the dwellings of Bornou once stood.

The sun shot his dazzling rays over this placid sheet of water, and toward the north the two elements merged into one and the same horizon.

The doctor was desirous of determining the character of the water, which was long believed to be salt. There was no danger in descending close to the lake, and the car was soon skimming its surface like a bird at the distance of only five feet.

Joe plunged a bottle into the lake and drew it up half filled. The water was then tasted and found to be but little fit for drinking, with a certain carbonate-of-soda flavor.

While the doctor was jotting down the result of this experiment, the loud report of a gun was heard close beside him. Kennedy had not been able to resist the temptation of firing at a huge hippopotamus. The latter, who had been basking quietly, disappeared at the sound of the explosion, but did not seem to be otherwise incommoded by Kennedy's conical bullet.

"You'd have done better if you had harpooned him," said Joe.

"But how?"

"With one of our anchors. It would have been a hook just big enough for such a rousing beast as that!"

"Humph!" ejaculated Kennedy. "Joe really has an idea this time—"

"Which I beg of you not to put into execution," interposed the doctor. "The animal would very quickly have dragged us where we could not have done much to help ourselves, and where we have no business to be."

"Especially now since we've settled the question as to what kind of water there is in Lake Tchad. Is that sort of fish good to eat, Dr. Ferguson?"

"That fish, as you call it, Joe, is really a mammiferous animal of the pachydermal species. Its flesh is said to be excellent and is an article of important trade between the tribes living along the borders of the lake."

"Then I'm sorry that Mr. Kennedy's shot didn't do more damage."

"The animal is vulnerable only in the stomach and between the thighs. Dick's ball hasn't even marked him; but should the ground strike me as favorable, we shall halt at the northern end of the lake, where Kennedy will find himself in the midst of a whole menagerie, and can make up for lost time."

"Well," said Joe, "I hope then that Mr. Kennedy will hunt the hippopotamus a little; I'd like to taste the meat of that queer-looking beast. It doesn't look exactly natural to get away into the center of Africa, to feed on snipe and partridge, just as if we were in England."

## CHAPTER XXXII

The Capital of Bornou—The Islands of the Biddiomahs—
The Condors—The Doctor's Anxieties—His Precautions—
An Attack in Midair—The Balloon Covering Torn—The Fall—
Sublime Self-Sacrifice—The Northern Coast of the Lake

Since its arrival at Lake Tchad, the balloon had struck a current that edged it farther to the westward. A few clouds tempered the heat of the day, and, besides, a little air could be felt over this vast expanse of water; but about one o'clock, the *Victoria*, having slanted across this part of the lake, again advanced over the land for a space of seven or eight miles.

The doctor, who was somewhat vexed at first at this turn of his course, no longer thought of complaining when he caught sight of the city of Kouka, the capital of Bornou. He saw it for a moment, encircled by its walls of white clay, and a few rudely constructed mosques rising clumsily above that conglomeration of houses that look like playing-dice, which form most Arab towns. In the courtyards of the private dwellings, and on the public squares, grew palms and caoutchouc trees topped with a dome of foliage more than one hundred feet in breadth. Joe called attention to the fact that these immense parasols were in proper accordance with the intense heat of the sun, and made thereon some pious reflections which it were needless to repeat.

Kouka really consists of two distinct towns, separated by the "Dendal," a large boulevard three hundred yards wide, at that hour crowded with horsemen and foot passengers. On one side, the rich quarter stands squarely with its airy and lofty houses, laid out in regular order; on the other is huddled together the poor quarter, a miserable collection of low hovels of a conical shape, in which a poverty-stricken multitude vegetate rather than live, since Kouka is neither a trading nor a commercial city.

Kennedy thought it looked something like Edinburgh, were that city extended on a plain, with its two distinct boroughs.

But our travelers had scarcely the time to catch even this glimpse of it, for, with the fickleness that characterizes the air currents of this region, a contrary wind suddenly swept them some forty miles over the surface of Lake Tchad.

Then they were regaled with a new spectacle. They could count the numerous islets of the lake, inhabited by the Biddiomahs, a race of bloodthirsty and formidable pirates who are as greatly feared when neighbors as are the Touaregs of Sahara.

These estimable people were in readiness to receive the *Victoria* bravely with stones and arrows, but the balloon quickly passed their islands, fluttering over them, from one to the other with butterfly motion, like a gigantic beetle.

At this moment, Joe, who was scanning the horizon, said to Kennedy:

"There, sir, as you are always thinking of good sport, yonder is just the thing for you!"

"What is it, Joe?"

"This time, the doctor will not disapprove of your shooting."

"But what is it?"

"Don't you see that flock of big birds making for us?"

"Birds?" exclaimed the doctor, snatching his spyglass.

"I see them," replied Kennedy; "there are at least a dozen of them."

"Fourteen, exactly!" said Joe.

"Heaven grant that they may be of a kind sufficiently noxious for the doctor to let me peg away at them!"

"I should not object, but I would much rather see those birds at a distance from us!"

"Why, are you afraid of those fowls?"

"They are condors, and of the largest size. Should they attack us—"

"Well, if they do, we'll defend ourselves. We have a whole arsenal at our disposal. I don't think those birds are so very formidable."

"Who can tell?" was the doctor's only remark.

Ten minutes later, the flock had come within gunshot, and were making the air ring with their hoarse cries. They came right toward the *Victoria*, more irritated than frightened by her presence.

"How they scream! What a noise!" said Joe.

"Perhaps they don't like to see anybody poaching in their country up in the air, or daring to fly like themselves!"

"Well, now, to tell the truth, when I take a good look at them, they are an ugly, ferocious set, and I should think them dangerous enough if they were armed with Purdy-Moore rifles," admitted Kennedy.

"They have no need of such weapons," said Ferguson, looking very grave.

The condors flew around them in wide circles, their flight growing gradually closer and closer to the balloon. They swept through the air in rapid, fantastic curves, occasionally precipitating themselves headlong with the speed of a bullet, and then breaking their line of projection by an abrupt and daring angle.

The doctor, much disquieted, resolved to ascend so as to escape this dangerous proximity. He therefore dilated the hydrogen in his balloon, and it rapidly rose.

But the condors mounted with him, apparently determined not to part company.

"They seem to mean mischief!" said the hunter, cocking his rifle.

And, in fact, they were swooping nearer, and more than one came within fifty feet of them, as if defying the firearms.

"By George, I'm itching to let them have it!" exclaimed Kennedy.

"No, Dick; not now! Don't exasperate them needlessly. That would only be exciting them to attack us!"

"But I could soon settle those fellows!"

"You may think so, Dick. But you are wrong!"

"Why, we have a bullet for each of them!"

"And suppose that they were to attack the upper part of the balloon, what would you do? How would you get at them? Just imagine yourself in the presence of a troop of lions on the plain, or a school of sharks in the open ocean! For travelers in the air, this situation is just as dangerous."

"Are you speaking seriously, doctor?"

"Very seriously, Dick."

"Let us wait, then!"

"Wait! Hold yourself in readiness in case of an attack, but do not fire without my orders."

The birds then collected at a short distance, yet to near that their naked necks, entirely bare of feathers, could be plainly seen, as they stretched them out with the effort of their cries, while their gristly crests, garnished with a comb and gills of deep violet, stood erect with rage. They were of the very largest size, their bodies being more than three feet in length, and the lower surface of their white wings glittering in the sunlight. They might well have been considered winged sharks, so striking was their resemblance to those ferocious rangers of the deep.

"They are following us!" said the doctor, as he saw them ascending with him. "And, mount as we may, they can fly still higher!"

"Well, what are we to do?" asked Kennedy.

The doctor made no answer.

"Listen, Samuel!" said the sportsman. "There are fourteen of those birds; we have seventeen shots at our disposal if we discharge all our weapons. Have we not the means, then, to destroy them or disperse them? I will give a good account of some of them!"

"I have no doubt of your skill, Dick; I look upon all as dead that may come within range of your rifle, but I repeat that, if they attack the upper part of the balloon, you could not get a sight at them. They would tear the silk covering that sustains us, and we are three thousand feet up in the air!"

At this moment, one of the ferocious birds darted right at the balloon, with outstretched beak and claws, ready to rend it with either or both.

"Fire! Fire at once!" cried the doctor.

He had scarcely ceased, ere the huge creature, stricken dead, dropped headlong, turning over and over in space as he fell.

Kennedy had already grasped one of the two-barreled fowling-pieces and Joe was taking aim with another.

Frightened by the report, the condors drew back for a moment, but they almost instantly returned to the charge with extreme fury. Kennedy severed the head of one from its body with his first shot, and Joe broke the wing of another.

"Only eleven left," said he.

Thereupon the birds changed their tactics, and by common consent soared above the balloon. Kennedy glanced at Ferguson. The latter, in spite of his imperturbability, grew pale. Then ensued a moment of terrifying silence. In the next they heard a harsh tearing noise, as of something rending the silk, and the car seemed to sink from beneath the feet of our three aeronauts.

"We are lost!" exclaimed Ferguson, glancing at the barometer, which was now swiftly rising.

"Over with the ballast!" he shouted. "Over with it!"

And in a few seconds the last lumps of quartz had disappeared.

"We are still falling! Empty the water tanks! Do you hear me, Joe? We are pitching into the lake!"

Joe obeyed. The doctor leaned over and looked out. The lake seemed to come up toward him like a rising tide. Every object around grew rapidly in size while they were looking at it. The car was not two hundred feet from the surface of Lake Tchad.

"The provisions! The provisions!" cried the doctor.

And the box containing them was launched into space.

Their descent became less rapid, but the luckless aeronauts were still falling, and into the lake.

"Throw out something—something more!" cried the doctor.

"There is nothing more to throw!" was Kennedy's despairing response.

"Yes, there is!" called Joe, and with a wave of the hand he disappeared like a flash, over the edge of the car.

"Joe! Joe!" exclaimed the doctor, horror-stricken.

The *Victoria* thus relieved resumed her ascending motion, mounted a thousand feet into the air, and the wind, burying itself in the disinflated covering, bore them away toward the northern part of the lake.

"Lost!" exclaimed the sportsman, with a gesture of despair.

"Lost to save us!" responded Ferguson.

And these men, intrepid as they were, felt the large tears streaming down their cheeks. They leaned over with the vain hope of seeing some trace of their heroic companion, but they were already far away from him.

"What course shall we pursue?" asked Kennedy.

"Alight as soon as possible, Dick, and then wait."

After a sweep of some sixty miles the *Victoria* halted on a desert shore, on the north of the lake. The anchors caught in a low tree and the sportsman fastened it securely. Night came, but neither Ferguson nor Kennedy could find one moment's sleep.

# CHAPTER XXXIII

CONJECTURES—REESTABLISHMENT OF THE *VICTORIA*'S EQUILIBRIUM—
DR. FERGUSON'S NEW CALCULATIONS—KENNEDY'S HUNT—A COMPLETE
EXPLORATION OF LAKE TCHAD—TANGALIA—THE RETURN—LARI

On the morrow, the 13th of May, our travelers, for the first time, reconnoitered the part of the coast on which they had landed. It was a sort of island of solid ground in the midst of an immense marsh. Around this fragment of terra firma grew reeds as lofty as trees are in Europe, and stretching away out of sight.

These impenetrable swamps gave security to the position of the balloon. It was necessary to watch only the borders of the lake. The vast stretch of water broadened away from the spot, especially toward the east, and nothing could be seen on the horizon, neither mainland nor islands.

The two friends had not yet ventured to speak of their recent companion. Kennedy first imparted his conjectures to the doctor.

"Perhaps Joe is not lost after all," he said. "He was a skillful lad, and had few equals as a swimmer. He would find no difficulty in swimming across the Firth of Forth at Edinburgh. We shall see him again—but how and where I know not. Let us omit nothing on our part to give him the chance of rejoining us."

"May God grant it as you say, Dick!" replied the doctor, with much emotion. "We shall do everything in the world to find our lost friend again. Let us, in the first place, see where we are. But, above all things, let us rid the *Victoria* of this outside covering, which is of no further use. That will relieve us of six hundred and fifty pounds, a weight not to be despised—and the end is worth the trouble!"

The doctor and Kennedy went to work at once, but they encountered great difficulty. They had to tear the strong silk away piece by piece, and then cut it in narrow strips so as to extricate it from the meshes of the network. The tear made by the beaks of the condors was found to be several feet in length.

This operation took at least four hours, but at length the inner balloon once completely extricated did not appear to have suffered in the least degree. The *Victoria* was thus diminished in size by one fifth, and this difference was sufficiently noticeable to excite Kennedy's surprise.

"Will it be large enough?" he asked.

"Have no fears on that score, I will reestablish the equilibrium, and should our poor Joe return we shall find a way to start off with him again on our old route."

"At the moment of our fall, unless I am mistaken, we were not far from an island."

"Yes, I recollect it," said the doctor, "but that island, like all the islands on Lake Tchad, is, no doubt, inhabited by a gang of pirates and murderers. They certainly witnessed our misfortune, and should Joe fall into their hands, what will become of him unless protected by their superstitions?"

"Oh, he's just the lad to get safely out of the scrape, I repeat. I have great confidence in his shrewdness and skill."

"I hope so. Now, Dick, you may go and hunt in the neighborhood, but don't get far away whatever you do. It has become a pressing necessity for us to renew our stock of provisions, since we had to sacrifice nearly all the old lot."

"Very good, doctor, I shall not be long absent."

Hereupon, Kennedy took a double-barreled fowling-piece, and strode through the long grass toward a thicket not far off, where the frequent sound of shooting soon let the doctor know that the sportsman was making a good use of his time.

Meanwhile Ferguson was engaged in calculating the relative weight of the articles still left in the car, and in establishing the equipoise of the second balloon. He found that there were still left some thirty pounds of *pemmican*, a supply of tea and coffee, about a gallon and a half of brandy, and one empty water tank. All the dried meat had disappeared.

The doctor was aware that, by the loss of the hydrogen in the first balloon, the ascensional force at his disposal was now reduced to about nine hundred pounds. He therefore had to count upon this difference in order to rearrange his equilibrium. The new balloon measured sixty-seven thousand cubic feet, and contained thirty-three thousand four hundred and eighty feet of gas. The dilating apparatus appeared to be in good condition, and neither the battery nor the spiral had been injured.

The ascensional force of the new balloon was then about three thousand pounds, and, in adding together the weight of the apparatus, of the passengers, of the stock of water, of the car and its accessories, and putting aboard fifty gallons of water, and one hundred pounds of fresh meat, the doctor got a total weight of twenty-eight hundred and thirty pounds. He could then take with him one hundred and seventy pounds of ballast, for unforeseen emergencies, and the balloon would be in exact balance with the surrounding atmosphere.

His arrangements were completed accordingly, and he made up for Joe's weight with a surplus of ballast. He spent the whole day in these preparations, and the latter were finished when Kennedy returned. The hunter had been successful, and brought back a regular cargo of geese, wild duck, snipe, teal, and plover. He went to work at once to draw and smoke the game. Each piece, suspended on a small, thin skewer, was hung over a fire of green wood. When they seemed in good order, Kennedy, who was perfectly at home in the business, packed them away in the car.

On the morrow, the hunter was to complete his supplies.

Evening surprised our travelers in the midst of this work. Their supper consisted of *pemmican*, biscuit, and tea; and fatigue, after having given them appetite, brought them sleep. Each of them strained eyes and ears into the gloom during his watch, sometimes fancying that they heard the voice of poor Joe; but, alas! The voice that they so longed to hear was far away.

At the first streak of day, the doctor aroused Kennedy.

"I have been long and carefully considering what should be done," said he, "to find our companion."

"Whatever your plan may be, doctor, it will suit me. Speak!"

"Above all things, it is important that Joe should hear from us in some way."

"Undoubtedly. Suppose the brave fellow should take it into his head that we have abandoned him?"

"He! He knows us too well for that. Such a thought would never come into his mind. But he must be informed as to where we are."

"How can that be managed?"

"We shall get into our car and be off again through the air."

"But, should the wind bear us away?"

"Happily, it will not. See, Dick! It is carrying us back to the lake; and this circumstance, which would have been vexatious yesterday, is fortunate now. Our efforts, then, will be limited to keeping ourselves above that vast sheet of water throughout the day. Joe cannot fail to see us, and his eyes will be constantly on the lookout in that direction. Perhaps he will even manage to let us know the place of his retreat."

"If he be alone and at liberty, he certainly will."

"And if a prisoner," resumed the doctor, "it not being the practice of the natives to confine their captives, he will see us, and comprehend the object of our researches."

"But, at last," put in Kennedy—"for we must anticipate—should we find no trace—if he should have left no mark to follow him by, what are we to do?"

"We shall endeavor to regain the northern part of the lake, keeping ourselves as much in sight as possible. There we'll wait; we'll explore the banks; we'll search the water's edge, for Joe will assuredly try to reach the shore; and we will not leave the country without having done everything to find him."

"Let us set out, then!" said the hunter.

The doctor hereupon took the exact bearings of the patch of solid land they were about to leave, and arrived at the conclusion that it lay on the north shore of Lake Tchad, between the village of Lari and the village of Ingemini, both visited by Major Denham. During this time Kennedy was completing his stock of fresh meat. Although the neighboring marshes showed traces of the rhinoceros, the lamantine (or manatee), and the hippopotamus, he had no opportunity to see a single specimen of those animals.

At seven in the morning, but not without great difficulty—which to Joe would have been nothing—the balloon's anchor was detached from its hold, the gas dilated, and the new *Victoria* rose two hundred feet into the air. It seemed to hesitate at first, and went spinning around, like a top; but at last a brisk current caught it, and it advanced over the lake, and was soon borne away at a speed of twenty miles per hour.

The doctor continued to keep at a height of from two hundred to five hundred feet. Kennedy frequently discharged his rifle; and, when passing over islands, the aeronauts approached them even imprudently, scrutinizing the thickets, the bushes, the underbrush—in fine, every spot where a mass of shade or jutting rock could have afforded a retreat to their companion. They swooped down close to the long pirogues that navigated the lake; and the wild fishermen, terrified at the sight of the balloon, would plunge into the water and regain their islands with every symptom of undisguised affright.

"We can see nothing," said Kennedy, after two hours of search.

"Let us wait a little longer, Dick, and not lose heart. We cannot be far away from the scene of our accident."

By eleven o'clock the balloon had gone ninety miles. It then fell in with a new current, which, blowing almost at right angles to the other, drove them eastward about sixty miles. It next floated over a very large and populous island, which the doctor took to be Farram, on which the capital of the Biddiomahs is situated. Ferguson expected at every moment to see Joe spring up out of some thicket, flying for his life, and calling for help. Were he free, they could pick him up without trouble; were he a prisoner, they could rescue him by repeating the maneuver they had practiced to save the missionary, and he would soon be with his friends again; but nothing was seen, not a sound was heard. The case seemed desperate.

About half-past two o'clock, the *Victoria* hove in sight of Tangalia, a village situated on the eastern shore of Lake Tchad, where it marks the extreme point attained by Denham at the period of his exploration.

The doctor became uneasy at this persistent setting of the wind in that direction, for he felt that he was being thrown back to the eastward, toward the center of Africa, and the interminable deserts of that region.

"We must absolutely come to a halt," said he, "and even alight. For Joe's sake, particularly, we ought to go back to the lake; but, to begin with, let us endeavor to find an opposite current."

During more than an hour he searched at different altitudes: the balloon always came back toward the mainland. But at length, at the height of a thousand feet, a very violent breeze swept to the northwestward.

It was out of the question that Joe should have been detained on one of the islands of the lake; for, in such case he would certainly have found means to make his presence there known. Perhaps he had been dragged to the mainland. The doctor was reasoning thus to himself, when he again came in sight of the northern shore of Lake Tchad.

As for supposing that Joe had been drowned, that was not to be believed for a moment. One horrible thought glanced across the minds of both Kennedy and the doctor: caimans swarm in these waters! But neither one nor the other had the courage to distinctly communicate this impression. However, it came up to them so forcibly at last that the doctor said, without further preface:

"Crocodiles are found only on the shores of the islands or of the lake, and Joe will have skill enough to avoid them. Besides, they are not very dangerous; and the Africans bathe with impunity, and quite fearless of their attacks."

Kennedy made no reply. He preferred keeping quiet to discussing this terrible possibility.

The doctor made out the town of Lari about five o'clock in the evening. The inhabitants were at work gathering in their cotton crop in front of their huts, constructed of woven reeds, and standing in the midst of clean and neatly kept enclosures. This collection of about fifty habitations occupied a slight depression of the soil, in a valley extending between two low mountains. The force of the wind carried the doctor farther onward than he wanted to go; but it changed a second time, and bore him back exactly to his starting point, on the sort of enclosed island where he had passed the preceding night. The anchor, instead of catching the branches of the tree, took hold in the masses of reeds mixed with the thick mud of the marshes, which offered considerable resistance.

The doctor had much difficulty in restraining the balloon; but at length the wind died away with the setting in of nightfall; and the two friends kept watch together in an almost desperate state of mind.

# CHAPTER XXXIV

THE HURRICANE—A FORCED DEPARTURE—LOSS OF AN ANCHOR—
MELANCHOLY REFLECTIONS—THE RESOLUTION ADOPTED—THE
SANDSTORM—THE BURIED CARAVAN—A CONTRARY YET FAVORABLE
WIND—THE RETURN SOUTHWARD—KENNEDY AT HIS POST

At three o'clock in the morning the wind was raging. It beat down with such violence that the *Victoria* could not stay near the ground without danger. It was thrown almost flat over upon its side, and the reeds chafed the silk so roughly that it seemed as though they would tear it.

"We must be off, Dick," said the doctor; "we cannot remain in this situation."

"But, doctor, what of Joe?"

"I am not likely to abandon him. No, indeed! And should the hurricane carry me a thousand miles to the northward, I will return! But here we are endangering the safety of all."

"Must we go without him?" asked the Scot, with an accent of profound grief.

"And do you think, then," rejoined Ferguson, "that my heart does not bleed like your own? Am I not merely obeying an imperious necessity?"

"I am entirely at your orders," replied the hunter. "Let us start!"

But their departure was surrounded with unusual difficulty. The anchor, which had caught very deeply, resisted all their efforts to disengage it; while the balloon, drawing in the opposite direction, increased its tension. Kennedy could not get it free. Besides, in his present position, the maneuver had become a very perilous one, for the *Victoria* threatened to break away before he should be able to get into the car again.

The doctor, unwilling to run such a risk, made his friend get into his place, and resigned himself to the alternative of cutting the anchor rope. The *Victoria* made one bound of three hundred feet into the air, and took her route directly northward.

Ferguson had no other choice than to scud before the storm. He folded his arms, and soon became absorbed in his own melancholy reflections.

After a few moments of profound silence, he turned to Kennedy, who sat there no less taciturn.

"We have, perhaps, been tempting Providence," said he. "It does not belong to man to undertake such a journey!" And a sigh of grief escaped him as he spoke.

"It is but a few days," replied the sportsman, "since we were congratulating ourselves upon having escaped so many dangers! All three of us were shaking hands!"

"Poor Joe! Kindly and excellent disposition! Brave and candid heart! Dazzled for a moment by his sudden discovery of wealth, he willingly sacrificed his treasures! And now, he is far from us; and the wind is carrying us still farther away with resistless speed!"

"Come, doctor, admitting that he may have found refuge among the lake tribes, can he not do as the travelers who visited them before us did—like Denham, like Barth? Both of those men got back to their own country."

"Ah! My dear Dick! Joe doesn't know one word of the language; he is alone, and without resources. The travelers of whom you speak did not attempt to go forward without sending many presents in advance of them to the chiefs, and surrounded by an escort armed and trained for these expeditions. Yet, they could not avoid sufferings of the worst description! What, then, can you expect the fate of our companion to be? It is horrible to think of, and this is one of the worst calamities that it has ever been my lot to endure!"

"But, we'll come back again, doctor!"

"Come back, Dick? Yes, if we have to abandon the balloon! If we should be forced to return to Lake Tchad on foot, and put ourselves in communication with the sultan of Bornou! The Arabs cannot have retained a disagreeable remembrance of the first Europeans."

"I will follow you, doctor," replied the hunter, with emphasis. "You may count upon me! We would rather give up the idea of prosecuting this journey than not return. Joe forgot himself for our sake; we will sacrifice ourselves for his!"

This resolve revived some hope in the hearts of these two men; they felt strong in the same inspiration. Ferguson forthwith set everything at work to get into a contrary current that might bring him back again to Lake Tchad; but this was impracticable at that moment, and even to alight was out of the question on ground completely bare of trees, and with such a hurricane blowing.

The *Victoria* thus passed over the country of the Tibbous, crossed the Belad el Djerid, a desert of briers that forms the border of the Soudan, and advanced into the desert of sand streaked with the long tracks of the many caravans that pass and repass there. The last line of vegetation was speedily lost in the dim southern horizon, not far from the principal oasis in this part of Africa, whose fifty wells are shaded by magnificent trees; but it was impossible to stop. An Arab encampment, tents of striped stuff, some camels, stretching out their viperlike heads and necks along the sand, gave life to this solitude, but the *Victoria* sped by like a shooting star, and in this way traversed a distance of sixty miles in three hours, without Ferguson being able to check or guide her course.

"We cannot halt, we cannot alight!" said the doctor. "Not a tree, not an inequality of the ground! Are we then to be driven clear across Sahara? Surely, Heaven is indeed against us!"

He was uttering these words with a sort of despairing rage, when suddenly he saw the desert sands rising aloft in the midst of a dense cloud of dust, and go whirling through the air, impelled by opposing currents.

Amid this tornado, an entire caravan, disorganized, broken, and overthrown, was disappearing beneath an avalanche of sand. The camels, flung pell-mell together, were uttering dull and pitiful groans; cries and howls of despair were heard issuing from that dusty and stifling cloud, and, from time to time, a particolored garment cut the chaos of the scene with its vivid hues, and the moaning and shrieking sounded over all, a terrible accompaniment to this spectacle of destruction.

Ere long the sand had accumulated in compact masses; and there, where so recently stretched a level plain as far as the eye could see, rose now a ridgy line of hillocks, still moving from beneath—the vast tomb of an entire caravan!

The doctor and Kennedy, pallid with emotion, sat transfixed by this fearful spectacle.

They could no longer manage their balloon, which went whirling round and round in contending currents, and refused to obey the different dilations of the gas. Caught in these eddies of the atmosphere, it spun about with a rapidity that made their heads reel, while the car oscillated and swung to and fro violently at the same time. The instruments suspended under the awning clattered together as though they would be dashed to pieces; the pipes of the spiral bent to and fro, threatening to break at every instant; and the water tanks jostled and jarred with tremendous din. Although but two feet apart, our aeronauts could not hear each other speak, but with firmly clinched hands they clung convulsively to the cordage, and endeavored to steady themselves against the fury of the tempest.

Kennedy, with his hair blown wildly about his face, looked on without speaking; but the doctor had regained all his daring in the midst of this deadly peril, and not a sign of his emotion was betrayed in his countenance, even when, after a last violent twirl, the *Victoria* stopped suddenly in the midst of a most unlooked-for calm; the north wind had abruptly got the upper hand, and now drove her back with equal rapidity over the route she had traversed in the morning.

"Whither are we going now?" cried Kennedy.

"Let us leave that to Providence, my dear Dick; I was wrong in doubting it. It knows better than we, and here we are, returning to places that we had expected never to see again!"

The surface of the country, which had looked so flat and level when they were coming, now seemed tossed and uneven, like the ocean billows after a storm; a long succession of hillocks, that had scarcely settled to their places yet, indented the desert; the wind blew furiously, and the balloon fairly flew through the atmosphere.

The direction taken by our aeronauts differed somewhat from that of the morning, and thus about nine o'clock, instead of finding themselves again near the borders of Lake Tchad, they saw the desert still stretching away before them.

Kennedy remarked the circumstance.

"It matters little," replied the doctor, "the important point is to return southward; we shall come across the towns of Bornou, Wouddie, or Kouka, and I should not hesitate to halt there."

"If you are satisfied, I am content," replied the Scot, "but Heaven grant that we may not be reduced to cross the desert, as those unfortunate Arabs had to do! What we saw was frightful!"

"It often happens, Dick; these trips across the desert are far more perilous than those across the ocean. The desert has all the dangers of the sea, including the risk of being swallowed up, and added thereto are unendurable fatigues and privations."

"I think the wind shows some symptoms of moderating; the sand dust is less dense; the undulations of the surface are diminishing, and the sky is growing clearer."

"So much the better! We must now reconnoiter attentively with our glasses, and take care not to omit a single point."

"I will look out for that, doctor, and not a tree shall be seen without my informing you of it."

And, suiting the action to the word, Kennedy took his station, spyglass in hand, at the forward part of the car.

## CHAPTER XXXV

WHAT HAPPENED TO JOE—THE ISLAND OF THE BIDDIOMAHS—
THE ADORATION SHOWN HIM—THE ISLAND THAT SANK—THE SHORES
OF THE LAKE—THE TREE OF THE SERPENTS—THE FOOT TRAMP—TERRIBLE
SUFFERING—MOSQUITOES AND ANTS—HUNGER—THE *VICTORIA* SEEN—
SHE DISAPPEARS—THE SWAMP—ONE LAST DESPAIRING CRY

What had become of Joe, while his master was thus vainly seeking for him?

When he had dashed headlong into the lake, his first movement on coming to the surface was to raise his eyes and look upward. He saw the *Victoria* already risen far above the water, still rapidly ascending and growing smaller and smaller. It was soon caught in a rapid current and disappeared to the northward. His master—both his friends were saved!

"How lucky it was," thought he, "that I had that idea to throw myself out into the lake! Mr. Kennedy would soon have jumped at it, and he would not have hesitated to do as I did, for nothing's more natural than for one man to give himself up to save two others. That's mathematics!"

Satisfied on this point, Joe began to think of himself. He was in the middle of a vast lake, surrounded by tribes unknown to him, and probably ferocious. All the greater reason why he should get out of the scrape by depending only on himself. And so he gave himself no farther concern about it.

Before the attack by the birds of prey, which, according to him, had behaved like real condors, he had noticed an island on the horizon, and determining to reach it, if possible, he put forth all his knowledge and skill in the art of swimming, after having relieved himself of the most troublesome part of his clothing. The idea of a stretch of five or six miles by no means disconcerted him; and therefore, so long as he was in the open lake, he thought only of striking out straight ahead and manfully.

In about an hour and a half the distance between him and the island had greatly diminished.

But as he approached the land, a thought, at first fleeting and then tenacious, arose in his mind. He knew that the shores of the lake were frequented by huge alligators, and was well aware of the voracity of those monsters.

Now, no matter how much he was inclined to find everything in this world quite natural, the worthy fellow was no little disturbed by this reflection. He feared greatly lest white flesh like his might be particularly acceptable to the dreaded brutes, and advanced only with extreme precaution, his eyes on the alert on both sides and all around him. At length, he was not more than one hundred yards from a bank, covered with green trees, when a puff of air strongly impregnated with a musky odor reached him.

"There!" said he to himself. "Just what I expected. The crocodile isn't far off!"

With this he dived swiftly, but not sufficiently so to avoid coming into contact with an enormous body, the scaly surface of which scratched him as he passed. He thought himself lost and swam with desperate energy. Then he rose again to the top of the water, took breath and dived once more. Thus passed a few minutes of unspeakable anguish, which all his philosophy could not overcome, for he thought, all the while, that he heard behind him the sound of those huge jaws ready to snap him up forever. In this state of mind he was striking out under the water as noiselessly as possible when he felt himself seized by the arm and then by the waist.

Poor Joe! He gave one last thought to his master; and began to struggle with all the energy of despair, feeling himself the while drawn along, but not toward the bottom of the lake, as is the habit of the crocodile when about to devour its prey, but toward the surface.

So soon as he could get breath and look around him, he saw that he was between two natives as black as ebony, who held him, with a firm grip, and uttered strange cries.

"Ha!" said Joe. "Blacks instead of crocodiles! Well, I prefer it as it is; but how in the mischief dare these fellows go in bathing in such places?"

Joe was not aware that the inhabitants of the islands of Lake Tchad, like many other negro tribes, plunge with impunity into sheets of water infested with crocodiles and caimans, and without troubling their heads about them. The amphibious denizens of this lake enjoy the well-deserved reputation of being quite inoffensive.

But had not Joe escaped one peril only to fall into another? That was a question which he left events to decide; and, since he could not do otherwise, he allowed himself to be conducted to the shore without manifesting any alarm.

"Evidently," thought he, "these chaps saw the *Victoria* skimming the waters of the lake, like a monster of the air. They were the distant witnesses of my tumble, and they can't fail to have some respect for a man that fell from the sky! Let them have their own way, then."

Joe was at this stage of his meditations, when he was landed amid a yelling crowd of both sexes, and all ages and sizes, but not of all colors. In fine, he was surrounded by a tribe of Biddiomahs as black as jet. Nor had he to blush for the scantiness of his costume, for he saw that he was in "undress" in the highest style of that country.

But before he had time to form an exact idea of the situation, there was no mistaking the agitation of which he instantly became the object, and this soon enabled him to pluck up courage, although the adventure of Kazah did come back rather vividly to his memory.

"I foresee that they are going to make a god of me again," thought he, "some son of the moon most likely. Well, one trade's as good as another when a man has no choice. The main thing is to gain time. Should the *Victoria* pass this way again, I'll take advantage of my new position to treat my worshippers here to a miracle when I go sailing up into the sky!"

While Joe's thoughts were running thus, the throng pressed around him. They prostrated themselves before him; they howled; they felt him; they became even annoyingly familiar; but at the same time they had the consideration to offer him a superb banquet consisting of sour milk and rice pounded in honey. The worthy fellow, making the best of everything, took one of the heartiest luncheons he ever ate in his life, and gave his new adorers an exalted idea of how the gods tuck away their food upon grand occasions.

When evening came, the sorcerers of the island took him respectfully by the hand, and conducted him to a sort of house surrounded with talismans; but, as he was entering it, Joe cast an uneasy look at the heaps of human bones that lay scattered around this sanctuary. But he had still more time to think about them when he found himself at last shut up in the cabin.

During the evening and through a part of the night, he heard festive chantings, the reverberations of a kind of drum, and a clatter of old iron, which were very sweet, no doubt, to African ears. Then there were howling choruses, accompanied by endless dances by gangs of natives who circled round and round the sacred hut with contortions and grimaces.

Joe could catch the sound of this deafening orchestra, through the mud and reeds of which his cabin was built; and perhaps under other circumstances he might have been amused by these strange ceremonies; but his mind was soon disturbed by quite different and less agreeable reflections. Even looking at the bright side of things, he found it both stupid and sad to be left alone in the midst of this savage country and among these wild tribes. Few travelers who had penetrated to these regions had ever again seen their native land. Moreover, could he trust to the worship of which he saw himself the object? He had good reason to believe in the vanity of human greatness; and he asked himself whether, in this country, adoration did not sometimes go to the length of eating the object adored!

But, notwithstanding this rather perplexing prospect, after some hours of meditation, fatigue got the better of his gloomy thoughts, and Joe fell into a profound slumber, which would have lasted no doubt until sunrise, had not a very unexpected sensation of dampness awakened the sleeper. Ere long this dampness became water, and that water gained so rapidly that it had soon mounted to Joe's waist.

"What can this be?" said he. "A flood! A waterspout! Or a new torture invented by these blacks? Faith, though, I'm not going to wait here till it's up to my neck!"

And, so saying, he burst through the frail wall with a jog of his powerful shoulder, and found himself—where?—in the open lake! Island there was none. It had sunk during the night. In its place, the watery immensity of Lake Tchad!

"A poor country for the landowners!" said Joe, once more vigorously resorting to his skill in the art of natation.

One of those phenomena, which are by no means unusual on Lake Tchad, had liberated our brave Joe. More than one island, that previously seemed to have the solidity of rock, has been submerged in this way; and the people living along the shores of the mainland have had to pick up the unfortunate survivors of these terrible catastrophes.

Joe knew nothing about this peculiarity of the region, but he was none the less ready to profit by it. He caught sight of a boat drifting about, without occupants, and was soon aboard of it. He found it to be but the trunk of a tree rudely hollowed out; but there were a couple of paddles in it, and Joe, availing himself of a rapid current, allowed his craft to float along.

"But let us see where we are," he said. "The polar star there, that does its work honorably in pointing out the direction due north to everybody else, will, most likely, do me that service."

He discovered, with satisfaction, that the current was taking him toward the northern shore of the lake, and he allowed himself to glide with it. About two o'clock in the morning he disembarked upon a promontory covered with prickly reeds, that proved very provoking and inconvenient even to a philosopher like him; but a tree grew there expressly to offer him a bed among its branches, and Joe climbed up into it for greater security, and there, without sleeping much, however, awaited the dawn of day.

When morning had come with that suddenness which is peculiar to the equatorial regions, Joe cast a glance at the tree which had sheltered him during the last few hours, and beheld a sight that chilled the marrow in his bones. The branches of the tree were literally covered with snakes and chameleons! The foliage actually was hidden beneath their coils, so that the beholder might have fancied that he saw before him a new kind of tree that bore reptiles for its leaves and fruit. And all this horrible living mass writhed and twisted in the first rays of the morning sun! Joe experienced a keen sensation of terror mingled with disgust, as he looked at it, and he leaped precipitately from the tree amid the hissings of these new and unwelcome bedfellows.

"Now, there's something that I would never have believed!" said he.

He was not aware that Dr. Vogel's last letters had made known this singular feature of the shores of Lake Tchad, where reptiles are more numerous than in any other part of the world. But after what he had just seen, Joe determined to be more circumspect for the future; and, taking his bearings by the sun, he set off afoot toward the northeast, avoiding with the utmost care cabins, huts, hovels, and dens of every description, that might serve in any manner as a shelter for human beings.

How often his gaze was turned upward to the sky! He hoped to catch a glimpse, each time, of the *Victoria*; and, although he looked vainly during all that long, fatiguing day of sore foot travel, his confident reliance on his master remained undiminished. Great energy of character was needed to enable him thus to sustain the situation with philosophy. Hunger conspired with fatigue to crush him, for a man's system is not greatly restored and fortified by a diet of roots, the pith of plants, such as the *mélé*, or the fruit of the *doum* palm tree; and yet, according to his own calculations, Joe was enabled to push on about twenty miles to the westward.

His body bore in scores of places the marks of the thorns with which the lake reeds, the acacias, the mimosas, and other wild shrubbery through which he had to force his way, are thickly studded; and his torn and bleeding feet rendered walking both painful and difficult. But at length he managed to react against all these sufferings; and when evening came again, he resolved to pass the night on the shores of Lake Tchad.

There he had to endure the bites of myriads of insects—gnats, mosquitoes, ants half an inch long literally covered the ground; and, in less than two hours, Joe had not a rag remaining of the garments that had covered him, the insects having devoured them! It was a terrible night that did not yield our exhausted traveler an hour of sleep. During all this time the wild boars and native buffaloes, reinforced by the *ajoub*—a very dangerous species of *lamantine*—carried on their ferocious revels in the bushes and under the waters of the lake, filling the night with a hideous concert. Joe dared scarcely breathe. Even his courage and coolness had hard work to bear up against so terrible a situation.

At length, day came again, and Joe sprang to his feet precipitately; but judge of the loathing he felt when he saw what species of creature had shared his couch—a toad!—but a toad five inches in length, a monstrous, repulsive specimen of vermin that sat there staring at him with huge round eyes. Joe felt his stomach revolt at the sight, and, regaining a little strength from the intensity of his repugnance, he rushed at the top of his speed and plunged into the lake. This sudden bath somewhat allayed the pangs of the itching that tortured his whole body; and, chewing a few leaves, he set forth resolutely, again feeling an obstinate resolution in the act, for which he could hardly account even to his own mind. He no longer seemed to have entire control of his own acts, and, nevertheless, he felt within him a strength superior to despair.

However, he began now to suffer terribly from hunger. His stomach, less resigned than he was, rebelled, and he was obliged to fasten a tendril of wild vine tightly about his waist. Fortunately, he could quench his thirst at any moment, and, in recalling the sufferings he had undergone in the desert, he experienced comparative relief in his exemption from that other distressing want.

"What can have become of the *Victoria*?" he wondered. "The wind blows from the north, and she should be carried back by it toward the lake. No doubt the doctor has gone to work to right her balance, but yesterday would have given him time enough for that, so that may be today—but I must act just as if I was never to see him again. After all, if I only get to one of the large towns on the lake, I'll find myself no worse off than the travelers my master used to talk about. Why shouldn't I work my way out of the scrape as well as they did? Some of them got back home again. Come, then! The deuce! Cheer up, my boy!"

Thus talking to himself and walking on rapidly, Joe came right upon a horde of natives in the very depths of the forest, but he halted in time and was not seen by them. The negroes were busy poisoning arrows with the juice of the euphorbium—a piece of work deemed a great affair among these savage tribes, and carried on with a sort of ceremonial solemnity.

Joe, entirely motionless and even holding his breath, was keeping himself concealed in a thicket, when, happening to raise his eyes, he saw through an opening in the foliage the welcome apparition of the balloon—the *Victoria* herself—moving toward the lake, at a height of only about one hundred feet above him. But he could not make himself heard; he dared not, could not make his friends even see him!

Tears came to his eyes, not of grief but of thankfulness; his master was then seeking him; his master had not left him to perish! He would have to wait for the departure of the blacks; then he could quit his hiding place and run toward the borders of Lake Tchad!

But by this time the *Victoria* was disappearing in the distant sky. Joe still determined to wait for her; she would come back again, undoubtedly. She did, indeed, return, but farther to the eastward. Joe ran, gesticulated, shouted—but all in vain! A strong breeze was sweeping the balloon away with a speed that deprived him of all hope.

For the first time, energy and confidence abandoned the heart of the unfortunate man. He saw that he was lost. He thought his master gone beyond all prospect of return. He dared no longer think; he would no longer reflect!

Like a crazy man, his feet bleeding, his body cut and torn, he walked on during all that day and a part of the next night. He even dragged himself along, sometimes on his knees, sometimes with his hands. He saw the moment nigh when all his strength would fail, and nothing would be left to him but to sink upon the ground and die.

Thus working his way along, he at length found himself close to a marsh, or what he knew would soon become a marsh, for night had set in some hours before, and he fell by a sudden misstep into a thick, clinging mire. In spite of all his efforts, in spite of his desperate struggles, he felt himself sinking gradually in the swampy ooze, and in a few minutes he was buried to his waist.

"Here, then, at last, is death!" he thought, in agony. "And what a death!"

He now began to struggle again, like a madman; but his efforts only served to bury him deeper in the tomb that the poor doomed lad was hollowing for himself; not a log of wood or a branch to buoy him up; not a reed to which he might cling! He felt that all was over! His eyes convulsively closed!

"Master! Master! Help!" were his last words; but his voice, despairing, unaided, half stifled already by the rising mire, died away feebly on the night.

# CHAPTER XXXVI

A Throng of People on the Horizon—A Troop of Arabs—The
Pursuit—It Is He—Fall from Horseback—The Strangled Arab—A Ball
from Kennedy—Adroit Maneuvers—Caught Up flying—Joe Saved at Last

From the moment when Kennedy resumed his post of observation in the front of the car, he had not ceased to watch the horizon with his utmost attention.

After the lapse of some time he turned toward the doctor and said:

"If I am not greatly mistaken I can see, off yonder in the distance, a throng of men or animals moving. It is impossible to make them out yet, but I observe that they are in violent motion, for they are raising a great cloud of dust."

"May it not be another contrary breeze?" said the doctor. "Another whirlwind coming to drive us back northward again?" And while speaking he stood up to examine the horizon.

"I think not, Samuel; it is a troop of gazelles or of wild oxen."

"Perhaps so, Dick; but yon throng is some nine or ten miles from us at least, and on my part, even with the glass, I can make nothing of it!"

"At all events I shall not lose sight of it. There is something remarkable about it that excites my curiosity. Sometimes it looks like a body of cavalry maneuvering. Ah! I was not mistaken. It is, indeed, a squadron of horsemen. Look—look there!"

The doctor eyed the group with great attention, and, after a moment's pause, remarked:

"I believe that you are right. It is a detachment of Arabs or Tibbous, and they are galloping in the same direction with us, as though in flight, but we are going faster than they, and we are rapidly gaining on them. In half an hour we shall be near enough to see them and know what they are."

Kennedy had again lifted his glass and was attentively scrutinizing them. Meanwhile the crowd of horsemen was becoming more distinctly visible, and a few were seen to detach themselves from the main body.

"It is some hunting maneuver, evidently," said Kennedy. "Those fellows seem to be in pursuit of something. I would like to know what they are about."

"Patience, Dick! In a little while we shall overtake them, if they continue on the same route. We are going at the rate of twenty miles per hour, and no horse can keep up with that."

Kennedy again raised his glass, and a few minutes later he exclaimed:

"They are Arabs, galloping at the top of their speed; I can make them out distinctly. They are about fifty in number. I can see their *bournouses* puffed out by the wind. It is some cavalry exercise that they are going through. Their chief is a hundred paces ahead of them and they are rushing after him at headlong speed."

"Whoever they may be, Dick, they are not to be feared, and then, if necessary, we can go higher."

"Wait, doctor—wait a little!"

"It's curious," said Kennedy again, after a brief pause, "but there's something going on that I can't exactly explain. By the efforts they make, and the irregularity of their line, I should fancy that those Arabs are pursuing someone, instead of following."

"Are you certain of that, Dick?"

"Oh! Yes, it's clear enough now. I am right! It is a pursuit—a hunt—but a manhunt! That is not their chief riding ahead of them, but a fugitive."

"A fugitive!" exclaimed the doctor, growing more and more interested.

"Yes!"

"Don't lose sight of him, and let us wait!"

Three or four miles more were quickly gained upon these horsemen, who nevertheless were dashing onward with incredible speed.

"Doctor! Doctor!" shouted Kennedy in an agitated voice.

"What is the matter, Dick?"

"Is it an illusion? Can it be possible?"

"What do you mean?"

"Wait!" And so saying, the Scot wiped the sights of his spyglass carefully, and looked through it again intently.

"Well?" questioned the doctor.

"It is he, doctor!"

"He!" exclaimed Ferguson with emotion.

"It is he! No other!" And it was needless to pronounce the name.

"Yes! It is he! On horseback, and only a hundred paces in advance of his enemies! He is pursued!"

"It is Joe—Joe himself!" cried the doctor, turning pale.

"He cannot see us in his flight!"

"He will see us, though!" said the doctor, lowering the flame of his blowpipe.

"But how?"

"In five minutes we shall be within fifty feet of the ground, and in fifteen we shall be right over him!"

"We must let him know it by firing a gun!"

"No! He can't turn back to come this way. He's headed off!"

"What shall we do, then?"

"We must wait."

"Wait? And these Arabs!"

"We shall overtake them. We'll pass them. We are not more than two miles from them, and provided that Joe's horse holds out!"

"Great God!" exclaimed Kennedy, suddenly.

"What is the matter?"

Kennedy had uttered a cry of despair as he saw Joe fling himself to the ground. His horse, evidently exhausted, had just fallen headlong.

"He sees us!" cried the doctor. "And he motions to us, as he gets upon his feet!"

"But the Arabs will overtake him! What is he waiting for? Ah! The brave lad! Huzza!" shouted the sportsman, who could no longer restrain his feelings.

Joe, who had immediately sprung up after his fall, just as one of the swiftest horsemen rushed upon him, bounded like a panther, avoided his assailant by leaping to one side, jumped up behind him on the crupper, seized the Arab by the throat, and, strangling him with his sinewy hands and fingers of steel, flung him on the sand, and continued his headlong flight.

A tremendous howl was heard from the Arabs, but, completely engrossed by the pursuit, they had not taken notice of the balloon, which was now but five hundred paces behind them, and only about thirty feet from the ground. On their part, they were not twenty lengths of their horses from the fugitive.

One of them was very perceptibly gaining on Joe, and was about to pierce him with his lance, when Kennedy, with fixed eye and steady hand, stopped him short with a ball that hurled him to the earth.

Joe did not even turn his head at the report. Some of the horsemen reined in their barbs, and fell on their faces in the dust as they caught sight of the *Victoria*; the rest continued their pursuit.

"But what is Joe about?" said Kennedy. "He don't stop!"

"He's doing better than that, Dick! I understand him! He's keeping on in the same direction as the balloon. He relies upon our intelligence. Ah! The noble fellow! We'll carry him off in the very teeth of those Arab rascals! We are not more than two hundred paces from him!"

"What are we to do?" asked Kennedy.

"Lay aside your rifle, Dick."

And the Scot obeyed the request at once.

"Do you think that you can hold one hundred and fifty pounds of ballast in your arms?"

"Ay, more than that!"

"No! That will be enough!"

And the doctor proceeded to pile up bags of sand in Kennedy's arms.

"Hold yourself in readiness in the back part of the car, and be prepared to throw out that ballast at a single effort. But, for your life, don't do so until I give the word!"

"Be easy on that point."

"Otherwise, we should miss Joe, and he would be lost."

"Count upon me!"

The *Victoria* at that moment almost commanded the troop of horsemen who were still desperately urging their steeds at Joe's heels. The doctor, standing in the front of the car, held the ladder clear, ready to throw it at any moment. Meanwhile, Joe had still maintained the distance between himself and his pursuers—say about fifty feet. The *Victoria* was now ahead of the party.

"Attention!" exclaimed the doctor to Kennedy.

"I'm ready!"

"Joe, look out for yourself!" shouted the doctor in his sonorous, ringing voice, as he flung out the ladder, the lowest ratlines of which tossed up the dust of the road.

As the doctor shouted, Joe had turned his head, but without checking his horse. The ladder dropped close to him, and at the instant he grasped it the doctor again shouted to Kennedy:

"Throw ballast!"

"It's done!"

And the *Victoria*, lightened by a weight greater than Joe's, shot up one hundred and fifty feet into the air.

Joe clung with all his strength to the ladder during the wide oscillations that it had to describe, and then making an indescribable gesture to the Arabs, and climbing with the agility of a monkey, he sprang up to his companions, who received him with open arms.

The Arabs uttered a scream of astonishment and rage. The fugitive had been snatched from them on the wing, and the *Victoria* was rapidly speeding far beyond their reach.

"Master! Kennedy!" ejaculated Joe, and overwhelmed, at last, with fatigue and emotion, the poor fellow fainted away, while Kennedy, almost beside himself, kept exclaiming:

"Saved—saved!"

"Saved indeed!" murmured the doctor, who had recovered all his phlegmatic coolness.

Joe was almost naked. His bleeding arms, his body covered with cuts and bruises, told what his sufferings had been. The doctor quietly dressed his wounds, and laid him comfortably under the awning.

Joe soon returned to consciousness, and asked for a glass of brandy, which the doctor did not see fit to refuse, as the faithful fellow had to be indulged.

After he had swallowed the stimulant, Joe grasped the hands of his two friends and announced that he was ready to relate what had happened to him.

But they would not allow him to talk at that time, and he sank back into a profound sleep, of which he seemed to have the greatest possible need.

The *Victoria* was then taking an oblique line to the westward. Driven by a tempestuous wind, it again approached the borders of the thorny desert, which the travelers descried over the tops of palm trees, bent and broken by the storm; and, after having made a run of two hundred miles since rescuing Joe, it passed the tenth degree of east longitude about nightfall.

## CHAPTER XXXVII

During the night the wind lulled as though reposing after the boisterousness of
the day, and the *Victoria* remained quietly at the top of the tall sycamore. The
doctor and Kennedy kept watch by turns, and Joe availed himself of the chance to
sleep most sturdily for twenty-four hours at a stretch.

"That's the remedy he needs," said Dr. Ferguson. "Nature will take charge of his care."

With the dawn the wind sprang up again in quite strong, and moreover capricious
gusts. It shifted abruptly from south to north, but finally the *Victoria* was carried away
by it toward the west.

The doctor, map in hand, recognized the kingdom of Damerghou, an undulating
region of great fertility, in which the huts that compose the villages are constructed of
long reeds interwoven with branches of the *asclepia*. The grain mills were seen raised
in the cultivated fields, upon small scaffoldings or platforms, to keep them out of the
reach of the mice and the huge ants of that country.

They soon passed the town of Zinder, recognized by its spacious place of execution,
in the center of which stands the "tree of death." At its foot the executioner stands
waiting, and whoever passes beneath its shadow is immediately hung!

Upon consulting his compass, Kennedy could not refrain from saying:

"Look! We are again moving northward."

"No matter; if it only takes us to Timbuctoo, we shall not complain. Never was a
finer voyage accomplished under better circumstances!"

"Nor in better health," said Joe, at that instant thrusting his jolly countenance from
between the curtains of the awning.

"There he is! There's our gallant friend—our preserver!" exclaimed Kennedy,
cordially. "How goes it, Joe?"

"Oh! Why, naturally enough, Mr. Kennedy, very naturally! I never felt better in
my life! Nothing sets a man up like a little pleasure trip with a bath in Lake Tchad to
start on—eh, doctor?"

"Brave fellow!" said Ferguson, pressing Joe's hand. "What terrible anxiety you
caused us!"

"Humph! And you, sir? Do you think that I felt easy in my mind about you,
gentlemen? You gave me a fine fright, let me tell you!"

"We shall never agree in the world, Joe, if you take things in that style."

"I see that his tumble hasn't changed him a bit," added Kennedy.

"Your devotion and self-forgetfulness were sublime, my brave lad, and they saved
us, for the *Victoria* was falling into the lake, and, once there, nobody could have
extricated her."

"But, if my devotion, as you are pleased to call my summerset, saved you, did it not save me too, for here we are, all three of us, in first-rate health? Consequently we have nothing to squabble about in the whole affair."

"Oh! We can never come to a settlement with that youth," said the sportsman.

"The best way to settle it," replied Joe, "is to say nothing more about the matter. What's done is done. Good or bad, we can't take it back."

"You obstinate fellow!" said the doctor, laughing. "You can't refuse, though, to tell us your adventures, at all events."

"Not if you think it worthwhile. But, in the first place, I'm going to cook this fat goose to a turn, for I see that Mr. Kennedy has not wasted his time."

"All right, Joe!"

"Well, let us see then how this African game will sit on a European stomach!"

The goose was soon roasted by the flame of the blowpipe, and not long afterward was comfortably stowed away. Joe took his own good share, like a man who had eaten nothing for several days. After the tea and the punch, he acquainted his friends with his recent adventures. He spoke with some emotion, even while looking at things with his usual philosophy. The doctor could not refrain from frequently pressing his hand when he saw his worthy servant more considerate of his master's safety than of his own, and, in relation to the sinking of the island of the Biddiomahs, he explained to him the frequency of this phenomenon upon Lake Tchad.

At length Joe, continuing his recital, arrived at the point where, sinking in the swamp, he had uttered a last cry of despair.

"I thought I was gone," said he, "and as you came right into my mind, I made a hard fight for it. How, I couldn't tell you—but I'd made up my mind that I wouldn't go under without knowing why. Just then, I saw—two or three feet from me—what do you think? The end of a rope that had been fresh cut; so I took leave to make another jerk, and, by hook or by crook, I got to the rope. When I pulled, it didn't give; so I pulled again and hauled away and there I was on dry ground! At the end of the rope, I found an anchor! Ah, master, I've a right to call that the anchor of safety, anyhow, if you have no objection. I knew it again! It was the anchor of the *Victoria*! You had grounded there! So I followed the direction of the rope and that gave me your direction, and, after trying hard a few times more, I got out of the swamp. I had got my strength back with my spunk, and I walked on part of the night away from the lake, until I got to the edge of a very big wood. There I saw a fenced-in place, where some horses were grazing, without thinking of any harm. Now, there are times when everybody knows how to ride a horse, are there not, doctor? So I didn't spend much time thinking about it, but jumped right on the back of one of those innocent animals and away we went galloping north as fast as our legs could carry us. I needn't tell you about the towns that I didn't see nor the villages that I took good care to go around. No! I crossed the plowed fields; I leaped the hedges; I scrambled over the fences; I dug my heels into my nag; I thrashed him; I fairly lifted the poor fellow off his feet! At last I got to the end of the tilled land. Good! There was the desert. 'That suits me!' said I, 'for I can see better ahead of me and farther too.' I was hoping all the time to see the balloon tacking about and waiting for me. But not a bit of it; and so, in about three hours, I go plump, like a fool, into a camp of Arabs! Whew! What a hunt that was! You see, Mr. Kennedy, a hunter don't know what a real hunt is until he's been hunted himself! Still I advise him not to try it if he can keep out of it! My horse was so tired, he was ready to drop off his legs; they were close on me; I threw myself to the ground; then I jumped up again behind an Arab! I didn't mean the fellow any harm, and I hope he has no grudge against me for choking him, but I saw you—and you know the rest. The *Victoria* came on at my heels, and you caught me up flying, as a circus-rider does a ring. Wasn't I right in counting on you? Now, doctor, you see how simple all that was! Nothing more natural in the world! I'm ready to begin over again, if it would be of any service to you. And besides, master, as I said a while ago, it's not worth mentioning."

"My noble, gallant Joe!" said the doctor, with great feeling. "Heart of gold! We were not astray in trusting to your intelligence and skill."

"Poh! Doctor, one has only just to follow things along as they happen, and he can always work his way out of a scrape! The safest plan, you see, is to take matters as they come."

While Joe was telling his experience, the balloon had rapidly passed over a long reach of country, and Kennedy soon pointed out on the horizon a collection of structures that looked like a town. The doctor glanced at his map and recognized the place as the large village of Tagelei, in the Damerghou country.

"Here," said he, "we come upon Dr. Barth's route. It was at this place that he parted from his companions, Richardson and Overweg; the first was to follow the Zinder route, and the second that of Maradi; and you may remember that, of these three travelers, Barth was the only one who ever returned to Europe."

"Then," said Kennedy, following out on the map the direction of the *Victoria*, "we are going due north."

"Due north, Dick."

"And don't that give you a little uneasiness?"

"Why should it?"

"Because that line leads to Tripoli, and over the Great Desert."

"Oh, we shall not go so far as that, my friend—at least, I hope not."

"But where do you expect to halt?"

"Come, Dick, don't you feel some curiosity to see Timbuctoo?"

"Timbuctoo?"

"Certainly," said Joe; "nobody nowadays can think of making the trip to Africa without going to see Timbuctoo."

"You will be only the fifth or sixth European who has ever set eyes on that mysterious city."

"Ho, then, for Timbuctoo!"

"Well, then, let us try to get as far as between the seventeenth and eighteenth degrees of north latitude, and there we will seek a favorable wind to carry us westward."

"Good!" said the hunter. "But have we still far to go to the northward?"

"One hundred and fifty miles at least."

"In that case," said Kennedy, "I'll turn in and sleep a bit."

"Sleep, sir; sleep!" urged Joe. "And you, doctor, do the same yourself: you must have need of rest, for I made you keep watch a little out of time."

The sportsman stretched himself under the awning; but Ferguson, who was not easily conquered by fatigue, remained at his post.

In about three hours the *Victoria* was crossing with extreme rapidity an expanse of stony country, with ranges of lofty, naked mountains of granitic formation at the base. A few isolated peaks attained the height of even four thousand feet. Giraffes, antelopes, and ostriches were seen running and bounding with marvelous agility in the midst of forests of acacias, mimosas, souahs, and date trees. After the barrenness of the desert, vegetation was now resuming its empire. This was the country of the Kailouas, who veil their faces with a bandage of cotton, like their dangerous neighbors, the Touaregs.

At ten o'clock in the evening, after a splendid trip of two hundred and fifty miles, the *Victoria* halted over an important town. The moonlight revealed glimpses of one district half in ruins; and some pinnacles of mosques and minarets shot up here and there, glistening in the silvery rays. The doctor took a stellar observation, and discovered that he was in the latitude of Aghades.

This city, once the seat of an immense trade, was already falling into ruin when Dr. Barth visited it.

The *Victoria*, not being seen in the obscurity of night, descended about two miles above Aghades, in a field of millet. The night was calm, and began to break into dawn about three o'clock A.M.; while a light wind coaxed the balloon westward, and even a little toward the south.

Dr. Ferguson hastened to avail himself of such good fortune, and rapidly ascending resumed his aerial journey amid a long wake of golden morning sunshine.

## *CHAPTER XXXVIII*

A RAPID PASSAGE—PRUDENT RESOLVES—CARAVANS IN SIGHT—INCESSANT RAINS— GOA—THE NIGER—GOLBERRY, GEOFFROY, AND GRAY—MUNGO PARK—LAING— RENÉ CAILLIÉ—CLAPPERTON—JOHN AND RICHARD LANDER

The 17th of May passed tranquilly, without any remarkable incident; the desert gained upon them once more; a moderate wind bore the *Victoria* toward the southwest, and she never swerved to the right or to the left, but her shadow traced a perfectly straight line on the sand.

Before starting, the doctor had prudently renewed his stock of water, having feared that he should not be able to touch ground in these regions, infested as they are by the Aouelim-Minian Touaregs. The plateau, at an elevation of eighteen hundred feet above the level of the sea, sloped down toward the south. Our travelers, having crossed the Aghades route at Murzouk—a route often pressed by the feet of camels—arrived that evening, in the sixteenth degree of north latitude, and four degrees fifty-five minutes east longitude, after having passed over one hundred and eighty miles of a long and monotonous day's journey.

During the day Joe dressed the last pieces of game, which had been only hastily prepared, and he served up for supper a mess of snipe, that were greatly relished. The wind continuing good, the doctor resolved to keep on during the night, the moon, still nearly at the full, illumining it with her radiance. The *Victoria* ascended to a height of five hundred feet, and, during her nocturnal trip of about sixty miles, the gentle slumbers of an infant would not have been disturbed by her motion.

On Sunday morning, the direction of the wind again changed, and it bore to the northwestward. A few crows were seen sweeping through the air, and, off on the horizon, a flock of vultures which, fortunately, however, kept at a distance.

The sight of these birds led Joe to compliment his master on the idea of having two balloons.

"Where would we be," said he, "with only one balloon? The second balloon is like the lifeboat to a ship; in case of wreck we could always take to it and escape."

"You are right, friend Joe," said the doctor, "only that my lifeboat gives me some uneasiness. It is not so good as the main craft."

"What do you mean by that, doctor?" asked Kennedy.

"I mean to say that the new *Victoria* is not so good as the old one. Whether it be that the stuff it is made of is too much worn, or that the heat of the spiral has melted the gutta-percha, I can observe a certain loss of gas. It don't amount to much thus far, but still it is noticeable. We have a tendency to sink, and, in order to keep our elevation, I am compelled to give greater dilation to the hydrogen."

"The deuce!" exclaimed Kennedy with concern. "I see no remedy for that."

"There is none, Dick, and that is why we must hasten our progress, and even avoid night halts."

"Are we still far from the coast?" asked Joe.

"Which coast, my boy? How are we to know whither chance will carry us? All that I can say is, that Timbuctoo is still about four hundred miles to the westward."

"And how long will it take us to get there?"

"Should the wind not carry us too far out of the way, I hope to reach that city by Tuesday evening."

"Then," remarked Joe, pointing to a long file of animals and men winding across the open desert, "we shall arrive there sooner than that caravan."

Ferguson and Kennedy leaned over and saw an immense cavalcade. There were at least one hundred and fifty camels of the kind that, for twelve mutkals of gold, or about twenty-five dollars, go from Timbuctoo to Tafilet with a load of five hundred pounds upon their backs. Each animal had dangling to its tail a bag to receive its excrement, the only fuel on which the caravans can depend when crossing the desert.

These Touareg camels are of the very best race. They can go from three to seven days without drinking, and for two without eating. Their speed surpasses that of the horse, and they obey with intelligence the voice of the *khabir*, or guide of the caravan. They are known in the country under the name of *mehari*.

Such were the details given by the doctor while his companions continued to gaze upon that multitude of men, women, and children, advancing on foot and with difficulty over a waste of sand half in motion, and scarcely kept in its place by scanty nettles, withered grass, and stunted bushes that grew upon it. The wind obliterated the marks of their feet almost instantly.

Joe inquired how the Arabs managed to guide themselves across the desert, and come to the few wells scattered far between throughout this vast solitude.

"The Arabs," replied Dr. Ferguson, "are endowed by nature with a wonderful instinct in finding their way. Where a European would be at a loss, they never hesitate for a moment. An insignificant fragment of rock, a pebble, a tuft of grass, a different shade of color in the sand, suffice to guide them with accuracy. During the night they go by the polar star. They never travel more than two miles per hour, and always rest during the noonday heat. You may judge from that how long it takes them to cross Sahara, a desert more than nine hundred miles in breadth."

But the *Victoria* had already disappeared from the astonished gaze of the Arabs, who must have envied her rapidity. That evening she passed two degrees twenty minutes east longitude, and during the night left another degree behind her.

On Monday the weather changed completely. Rain began to fall with extreme violence, and not only had the balloon to resist the power of this deluge, but also the increase of weight which it caused by wetting the whole machine, car and all. This continuous shower accounted for the swamps and marshes that formed the sole surface of the country. Vegetation reappeared, however, along with the mimosas, the baobabs, and the tamarind trees.

Such was the Sonray country, with its villages topped with roofs turned over like Armenian caps. There were few mountains, and only such hills as were enough to form the ravines and pools where the *pintadoes* and snipes went sailing and diving through. Here and there, an impetuous torrent cut the roads, and had to be crossed by the natives on long vines stretched from tree to tree. The forests gave place to jungles, which alligators, hippopotami, and the rhinoceros made their haunts.

"It will not be long before we see the Niger," said the doctor. "The face of the country always changes in the vicinity of large rivers. These moving highways, as they are sometimes correctly called, have first brought vegetation with them, as they will at last bring civilization. Thus, in its course of twenty-five hundred miles, the Niger has scattered along its banks the most important cities of Africa."

"By the way," put in Joe, "that reminds me of what was said by an admirer of the goodness of Providence, who praised the foresight with which it had generally caused rivers to flow close to large cities!"

At noon the *Victoria* was passing over a petty town, a mere assemblage of miserable huts, which once was Goa, a great capital.

"It was there," said the doctor, "that Barth crossed the Niger, on his return from Timbuctoo. This is the river so famous in antiquity, the rival of the Nile, to which pagan superstition ascribed a celestial origin. Like the Nile, it has engaged the attention of geographers in all ages; and like it, also, its exploration has cost the lives of many victims; yes, even more of them than perished on account of the other."

The Niger flowed broadly between its banks, and its waters rolled southward with some violence of current; but our travelers, borne swiftly by as they were, could scarcely catch a glimpse of its curious outline.

"I wanted to talk to you about this river," said Dr. Ferguson, "and it is already far from us. Under the names of Dhiouleba, Mayo, Egghirreou, Quorra, and other titles besides, it traverses an immense extent of country, and almost competes in length with the Nile. These appellations signify simply 'the River,' according to the dialects of the countries through which it passes."

"Did Dr. Barth follow this route?" asked Kennedy.

"No, Dick: in quitting Lake Tchad, he passed through the different towns of Bornou, and intersected the Niger at Say, four degrees below Goa; then he penetrated to the bosom of those unexplored countries which the Niger embraces in its elbow; and, after eight months of fresh fatigues, he arrived at Timbuctoo; all of which we may do in about three days with as swift a wind as this."

"Have the sources of the Niger been discovered?" asked Joe.

"Long since," replied the doctor. "The exploration of the Niger and its tributaries was the object of several expeditions, the principal of which I shall mention: Between 1749 and 1758, Adamson made a reconnoissance of the river, and visited Gorea; from 1785 to 1788, Golberry and Geoffroy traveled across the deserts of Senegambia, and ascended as far as the country of the Moors, who assassinated Saugnier, Brisson, Adam, Riley, Cochelet, and so many other unfortunate men. Then came the illustrious Mungo Park, the friend of Sir Walter Scott, and, like him, a Scotchman by birth. Sent out in 1795 by the African Society of London, he got as far as Bambarra, saw the Niger, traveled five hundred miles with a slave merchant, reconnoitered the Gambia River, and returned to England in 1797. He again set out, on the 30th of January, 1805, with his brother-in-law Anderson, Scott, the designer, and a gang of workmen; he reached Gorea, there added a detachment of thirty-five soldiers to his party, and saw the Niger again on the 19th of August. But, by that time, in consequence of fatigue, privations, ill usage, the inclemencies of the weather, and the unhealthiness of the country, only eleven persons remained alive of the forty Europeans in the party. On the 16th of November, the last letters from Mungo Park reached his wife; and, a year later a trader from that country gave information that, having got as far as Boussa, on the Niger, on the 23rd of December, the unfortunate traveler's boat was upset by the cataracts in that part of the river, and he was murdered by the natives."

"And his dreadful fate did not check the efforts of others to explore that river?"

"On the contrary, Dick. Since then, there were two objects in view: namely, to recover the lost man's papers, as well as to pursue the exploration. In 1816, an expedition was organized, in which Major Grey took part. It arrived in Senegal, penetrated to the Fonta-Jallon, visited the Foullah and Mandingo populations, and returned to England without further results. In 1822, Major Laing explored all the western part of Africa near to the British possessions; and he it was who got so far as the sources of the Niger; and, according to his documents, the spring in which that immense river takes its rise is not two feet broad.

"Easy to jump over," said Joe.

"How's that? Easy you think, eh?" retorted the doctor. "If we are to believe tradition, whoever attempts to pass that spring by leaping over it is immediately swallowed up; and whoever tries to draw water from it feels himself repulsed by an invisible hand."

"I suppose a man has a right not to believe a word of that!" persisted Joe.

"Oh, by all means! Five years later, it was Major Laing's destiny to force his way across the desert of Sahara, penetrate to Timbuctoo, and perish a few miles above it, by strangling, at the hands of the Ouelad-shiman, who wanted to compel him to turn Mussulman."

"Still another victim!" said the sportsman.

"It was then that a brave young man, with his own feeble resources, undertook and accomplished the most astonishing of modern journeys—I mean the Frenchman René Caillié, who, after sundry attempts in 1819 and 1824, set out again on the 19th of April, 1827, from Rio Nunez. On the 3rd of August he arrived at Time, so thoroughly exhausted and ill that he could not resume his journey until six months later, in January, 1828. He then joined a caravan, and, protected by his Oriental dress, reached the Niger on the 10th of March, penetrated to the city of Jenné, embarked on the river, and descended it, as far as Timbuctoo, where he arrived on the 30th of April. In 1760, another Frenchman, Imbert by name, and, in 1810, an Englishman, Robert Adams, had seen this curious place; but René Caillié was to be the first European who could bring back any authentic data concerning it. On the 4th of May he quitted this 'Queen of the desert'; on the 9th, he surveyed the very spot where Major Laing had been murdered; on the 19th, he arrived at El-Arouan, and left that commercial town to brave a thousand dangers in crossing the vast solitudes comprised between the Soudan and the northern regions of Africa. At length he entered Tangiers, and on the 28th of September sailed for Toulon. In nineteen months, notwithstanding one hundred and eighty days' sickness, he had traversed Africa from west to north. Ah! Had Callié been born in England, he would have been honored as the most intrepid traveler of modern times, as was the case with Mungo Park. But in France he was not appreciated according to his worth."

"He was a sturdy fellow!" said Kennedy. "But what became of him?"

"He died at the age of thirty-nine, from the consequences of his long fatigues. They thought they had done enough in decreeing him the prize of the Geographical Society in 1828; the highest honors would have been paid to him in England.

"While he was accomplishing this remarkable journey, an Englishman had conceived a similar enterprise and was trying to push it through with equal courage, if not with equal good fortune. This was Captain Clapperton, the companion of Denham. In 1829 he reentered Africa by the western coast of the Gulf of Benin; he then followed in the track of Mungo Park and of Laing, recovered at Boussa the documents relative to the death of the former, and arrived on the 20th of August at Sackatoo, where he was seized and held as a prisoner, until he expired in the arms of his faithful attendant Richard Lander."

"And what became of this Lander?" asked Joe, deeply interested.

"He succeeded in regaining the coast and returned to London, bringing with him the captain's papers, and an exact narrative of his own journey. He then offered his services to the government to complete the reconnoissance of the Niger. He took with him his brother John, the second child of a poor couple in Cornwall, and, together, these men, between 1829 and 1831, redescended the river from Boussa to its mouth, describing it village by village, mile by mile."

"So both the brothers escaped the common fate?" queried Kennedy.

"Yes, on this expedition, at least; but in 1833 Richard undertook a third trip to the Niger, and perished by a bullet, near the mouth of the river. You see, then, my friends, that the country over which we are now passing has witnessed some noble instances of self-sacrifice which, unfortunately, have only too often had death for their reward."

## *CHAPTER XXXIX*

THE COUNTRY IN THE ELBOW OF THE NIGER—A FANTASTIC VIEW OF THE
HOMBORI MOUNTAINS—KABRA—TIMBUCTOO—THE CHART OF DR. BARTH—
A DECAYING CITY—WHITHER HEAVEN WILLS

During this dull Monday, Dr. Ferguson diverted his thoughts by giving his companions a thousand details concerning the country they were crossing. The surface, which was quite flat, offered no impediment to their progress. The doctor's sole anxiety arose from the obstinate northeast wind which continued to blow furiously, and bore them away from the latitude of Timbuctoo.

The Niger, after running northward as far as that city, sweeps around, like an immense water jet from some fountain, and falls into the Atlantic in a broad sheaf. In the elbow thus formed the country is of varied character, sometimes luxuriantly fertile, and sometimes extremely bare; fields of maize succeeded by wide spaces covered with broom corn and uncultivated plains. All kinds of aquatic birds—pelicans, wild duck, kingfishers, and the rest—were seen in numerous flocks hovering about the borders of the pools and torrents.

From time to time there appeared an encampment of Touaregs, the men sheltered under their leather tents, while their women were busied with the domestic toil outside, milking their camels and smoking their huge-bowled pipes.

By eight o'clock in the evening the *Victoria* had advanced more than two hundred miles to the westward, and our aeronauts became the spectators of a magnificent scene.

A mass of moonbeams forcing their way through an opening in the clouds, and gliding between the long lines of falling rain, descended in a golden shower on the ridges of the Hombori Mountains. Nothing could be more weird than the appearance of these seemingly basaltic summits; they stood out in fantastic profile against the somber sky, and the beholder might have fancied them to be the legendary ruins of some vast city of the Middle Ages, such as the icebergs of the polar seas sometimes mimic them in nights of gloom.

"An admirable landscape for the *Mysteries of Udolpho*!" exclaimed the doctor. "Ann Radcliffe could not have depicted yon mountains in a more appalling aspect."

"Faith!" said Joe. "I wouldn't like to be strolling alone in the evening through this country of ghosts. Do you see now, master, if it wasn't so heavy, I'd like to carry that whole landscape home to Scotland! It would do for the borders of Loch Lomond, and tourists would rush there in crowds."

"Our balloon is hardly large enough to admit of that little experiment—but I think our direction is changing. Bravo! The elves and fairies of the place are quite obliging. See, they've sent us a nice little southeast breeze, that will put us on the right track again."

In fact, the *Victoria* was resuming a more northerly route, and on the morning of the 20th she was passing over an inextricable network of channels, torrents, and streams, in fine, the whole complicated tangle of the Niger's tributaries. Many of these channels, covered with a thick growth of herbage, resembled luxuriant meadowlands. There the doctor recognized the route followed by the explorer Barth when he launched upon the river to descend to Timbuctoo. Eight hundred fathoms broad at this point, the Niger flowed between banks richly grown with cruciferous plants and tamarind trees. Herds of agile gazelles were seen skipping about, their curling horns mingling with the tall herbage, within which the alligator, half concealed, lay silently in wait for them with watchful eyes.

Long files of camels and asses laden with merchandise from Jenné were winding in under the noble trees. Ere long, an amphitheater of low-built houses was discovered at a turn of the river, their roofs and terraces heaped up with hay and straw gathered from the neighboring districts.

"There's Kabra!" exclaimed the doctor, joyously. "There is the harbor of Timbuctoo, and the city is not five miles from here!"

"Then, sir, you are satisfied?" half queried Joe.

"Delighted, my boy!"

"Very good; then everything's for the best!"

In fact, about two o'clock, the Queen of the Desert, mysterious Timbuctoo, which once, like Athens and Rome, had her schools of learned men, and her professorships of philosophy, stretched away before the gaze of our travelers.

Ferguson followed the most minute details upon the chart traced by Barth himself, and was enabled to recognize its perfect accuracy.

The city forms an immense triangle marked out upon a vast plain of white sand, its acute angle directed toward the north and piercing a corner of the desert. In the environs there was almost nothing, hardly even a few grasses, with some dwarf mimosas and stunted bushes.

As for the appearance of Timbuctoo, the reader has but to imagine a collection of billiard balls and thimbles—such is the bird's-eye view! The streets, which are quite narrow, are lined with houses only one story in height, built of bricks dried in the sun, and huts of straw and reeds, the former square, the latter conical. Upon the terraces were seen some of the male inhabitants, carelessly lounging at full length in flowing apparel of bright colors, and lance or musket in hand; but no women were visible at that hour of the day.

"Yet they are said to be handsome," remarked the doctor. "You see the three towers of the three mosques that are the only ones left standing of a great number—the city has indeed fallen from its ancient splendor! At the top of the triangle rises the Mosque of Sankore, with its ranges of galleries resting on arcades of sufficiently pure design. Farther on, and near to the Sane-Gungu quarter, is the Mosque of Sidi-Yahia and some two-story houses. But do not look for either palaces or monuments: the sheik is a mere son of traffic, and his royal palace is a countinghouse."

"It seems to me that I can see half-ruined ramparts," said Kennedy.

"They were destroyed by the Fouillanes in 1826; the city was one-third larger then, for Timbuctoo, an object generally coveted by all the tribes, since the eleventh century, has belonged in succession to the Touaregs, the Sonrayans, the Morocco men, and the Fouillanes; and this great center of civilization, where a sage like Ahmed-Baba owned, in the sixteenth century, a library of sixteen hundred manuscripts, is now nothing but a mere halfway house for the trade of Central Africa."

The city, indeed, seemed abandoned to supreme neglect; it betrayed that indifference which seems epidemic to cities that are passing away. Huge heaps of rubbish encumbered the suburbs, and, with the hill on which the marketplace stood, formed the only inequalities of the ground.

When the *Victoria* passed, there was some slight show of movement; drums were beaten; but the last learned man still lingering in the place had hardly time to notice the new phenomenon, for our travelers, driven onward by the wind of the desert, resumed the winding course of the river, and, ere long, Timbuctoo was nothing more than one of the fleeting reminiscences of their journey.

"And now," said the doctor, "Heaven may waft us whither it pleases!"

"Provided only that we go westward," added Kennedy.

"Bah!" said Joe. "I wouldn't be afraid if it was to go back to Zanzibar by the same road, or to cross the ocean to America."

"We would first have to be able to do that, Joe!"

"And what's wanting, doctor?"

"Gas, my boy; the ascending force of the balloon is evidently growing weaker, and we shall need all our management to make it carry us to the seacoast. I shall even have to throw over some ballast. We are too heavy."

"That's what comes of doing nothing, doctor; when a man lies stretched out all day long in his hammock, he gets fat and heavy. It's a lazybones trip, this of ours, master, and when we get back everybody will find us big and stout."

"Just like Joe," said Kennedy; "just the ideas for him: but wait a bit! Can you tell what we may have to go through yet? We are still far from the end of our trip. Where do you expect to strike the African coast, doctor?"

"I should find it hard to answer you, Kennedy. We are at the mercy of very variable winds; but I should think myself fortunate were we to strike it between Sierra Leone and Portendick. There is a stretch of country in that quarter where we should meet with friends."

"And it would be a pleasure to press their hands; but, are we going in the desirable direction?"

"Not any too well, Dick; not any too well! Look at the needle of the compass; we are bearing southward, and ascending the Niger toward its sources."

"A fine chance to discover them," said Joe, "if they were not known already. Now, couldn't we just find others for it, on a pinch?"

"Not exactly, Joe; but don't be alarmed: I hardly expect to go so far as that."

At nightfall the doctor threw out the last bags of sand. The *Victoria* rose higher, and the blowpipe, although working at full blast, could scarcely keep her up. At that time she was sixty miles to the southward of Timbuctoo, and in the morning the aeronauts awoke over the banks of the Niger, not far from Lake Debo.

## CHAPTER XL

Dr. Ferguson's Anxieties—Persistent Movement Southward—
A Cloud of Grasshoppers—A View of Jenné—A View of Sego—
Change of the Wind—Joe's Regrets

The flow of the river was, at that point, divided by large islands into narrow branches, with a very rapid current. Upon one among them stood some shepherds' huts, but it had become impossible to take an exact observation of them, because the speed of the balloon was constantly increasing. Unfortunately, it turned still more toward the south, and in a few moments crossed Lake Debo.

Dr. Ferguson, forcing the dilation of his aerial craft to the utmost, sought for other currents of air at different heights, but in vain; and he soon gave up the attempt, which was only augmenting the waste of gas by pressing it against the well-worn tissue of the balloon.

He made no remark, but he began to feel very anxious. This persistence of the wind to head him off toward the southern part of Africa was defeating his calculations, and he no longer knew upon whom or upon what to depend. Should he not reach the English or French territories, what was to become of him in the midst of the barbarous tribes that infest the coasts of Guinea? How should he there get to a ship to take him back to England? And the actual direction of the wind was driving him along to the kingdom of Dahomey, among the most savage races, and into the power of a ruler who was in the habit of sacrificing thousands of human victims at his public orgies. There he would be lost!

On the other hand, the balloon was visibly wearing out, and the doctor felt it failing him. However, as the weather was clearing up a little, he hoped that the cessation of the rain would bring about a change in the atmospheric currents.

It was therefore a disagreeable reminder of the actual situation when Joe said aloud:

"There! The rain's going to pour down harder than ever; and this time it will be the deluge itself, if we're to judge by yon cloud that's coming up!"

"What! Another cloud?" asked Ferguson.

"Yes, and a famous one," replied Kennedy.

"I never saw the like of it," added Joe.

"I breathe freely again!" said the doctor, laying down his spyglass. "That's not a cloud!"

"Not a cloud?" queried Joe, with surprise.

"No; it is a swarm."

"Eh?"

"A swarm of grasshoppers!"

"That? Grasshoppers!"

"Myriads of grasshoppers, that are going to sweep over this country like a waterspout; and woe to it! For, should these insects alight, it will be laid waste."

"That would be a sight worth beholding!"

"Wait a little, Joe. In ten minutes that cloud will have arrived where we are, and you can then judge by the aid of your own eyes."

The doctor was right. The cloud, thick, opaque, and several miles in extent, came on with a deafening noise, casting its immense shadow over the fields. It was composed of numberless legions of that species of grasshopper called crickets. About a hundred paces from the balloon, they settled down upon a tract full of foliage and verdure. Fifteen minutes later, the mass resumed its flight, and our travelers could, even at a distance, see the trees and the bushes entirely stripped, and the fields as bare as though they had been swept with the scythe. One would have thought that a sudden winter had just descended upon the earth and struck the region with the most complete sterility.

"Well, Joe, what do you think of that?"

"Well, doctor, it's very curious, but quite natural. What one grasshopper does on a small scale, thousands do on a grand scale."

"It's a terrible shower," said the hunter; "more so than hail itself in the devastation it causes."

"It is impossible to prevent it," replied Ferguson. "Sometimes the inhabitants have had the idea to burn the forests, and even the standing crops, in order to arrest the progress of these insects; but the first ranks plunging into the flames would extinguish them beneath their mass, and the rest of the swarm would then pass irresistibly onward. Fortunately, in these regions, there is some sort of compensation for their ravages, since the natives gather these insects in great numbers and greedily eat them."

"They are the prawns of the air," said Joe, who added that he was sorry that he had never had the chance to taste them—just for information's sake!

The country became more marshy toward evening; the forests dwindled to isolated clumps of trees; and on the borders of the river could be seen plantations of tobacco, and swampy meadowlands fat with forage. At last the city of Jenné, on a large island, came in sight, with the two towers of its clay-built mosque, and the putrid odor of the millions of swallows' nests accumulated in its walls. The tops of some baobabs, mimosas, and date trees peeped up between the houses; and, even at night, the activity of the place seemed very great. Jenné is, in fact, quite a commercial city: it supplies all the wants of Timbuctoo. Its boats on the river, and its caravans along the shaded roads, bear thither the various products of its industry.

"Were it not that to do so would prolong our journey," said the doctor, "I should like to alight at this place. There must be more than one Arab there who has traveled in England and France, and to whom our style of locomotion is not altogether new. But it would not be prudent."

"Let us put off the visit until our next trip," said Joe, laughing.

"Besides, my friends, unless I am mistaken, the wind has a slight tendency to veer a little more to the eastward, and we must not lose such an opportunity."

The doctor threw overboard some articles that were no longer of use—some empty bottles, and a case that had contained preserved meat—and thereby managed to keep the balloon in a belt of the atmosphere more favorable to his plans. At four o'clock in the morning the first rays of the sun lighted up Sego, the capital of

Bambarra, which could be recognized at once by the four towns that compose it, by its Saracenic mosques, and by the incessant going and coming of the flat-bottomed boats that convey its inhabitants from one quarter to the other. But the travelers were not more seen than they saw. They sped rapidly and directly to the northwest, and the doctor's anxiety gradually subsided.

"Two more days in this direction, and at this rate of speed, and we'll reach the Senegal River."

"And we'll be in a friendly country?" asked the hunter.

"Not altogether; but, if the worst came to the worst, and the balloon were to fail us, we might make our way to the French settlements. But, let it hold out only for a few hundred miles, and we shall arrive without fatigue, alarm, or danger, at the western coast."

"And the thing will be over!" added Joe. "Heigh-ho! So much the worse. If it wasn't for the pleasure of telling about it, I would never want to set foot on the ground again! Do you think anybody will believe our story, doctor?"

"Who can tell, Joe? One thing, however, will be undeniable: a thousand witnesses saw us start on one side of the African Continent, and a thousand more will see us arrive on the other."

"And, in that case, it seems to me that it would be hard to say that we had not crossed it," added Kennedy.

"Ah, doctor!" said Joe again, with a deep sigh, "I'll think more than once of my lumps of solid gold-ore! There was something that would have given weight to our narrative! At a grain of gold per head, I could have got together a nice crowd to listen to me, and even to admire me!"

## CHAPTER XLI

THE APPROACHES TO SENEGAL—THE BALLOON SINKS LOWER AND LOWER—
THEY KEEP THROWING OUT, THROWING OUT—THE MARABOUT AL-HADJI—
MESSRS. PASCAL, VINCENT, AND LAMBERT—A RIVAL OF MOHAMMED—
THE DIFFICULT MOUNTAINS—KENNEDY'S WEAPONS—ONE OF JOE'S
MANEUVERS—A HALT OVER A FOREST

On the 27th of May, at nine o'clock in the morning, the country presented an entirely different aspect. The slopes, extending far away, changed to hills that gave evidence of mountains soon to follow. They would have to cross the chain which separates the basin of the Niger from the basin of the Senegal, and determines the course of the watershed, whether to the Gulf of Guinea on the one hand, or to the bay of Cape Verde on the other.

As far as Senegal, this part of Africa is marked down as dangerous. Dr. Ferguson knew it through the recitals of his predecessors. They had suffered a thousand privations and been exposed to a thousand dangers in the midst of these barbarous negro tribes. It was this fatal climate that had devoured most of the companions of Mungo Park. Ferguson, therefore, was more than ever decided not to set foot in this inhospitable region.

But he had not enjoyed one moment of repose. The *Victoria* was descending very perceptibly, so much so that he had to throw overboard a number more of useless articles, especially when there was a mountaintop to pass. Things went on thus for more than one hundred and twenty miles; they were worn out with ascending and falling again; the balloon, like another rock of Sisyphus, kept continually sinking back toward the ground. The rotundity of the covering, which was now but little inflated, was collapsing already. It assumed an elongated shape, and the wind hollowed large cavities in the silken surface.

Kennedy could not help observing this.

"Is there a crack or a tear in the balloon?" he asked.

"No, but the gutta-percha has evidently softened or melted in the heat, and the hydrogen is escaping through the silk."

"How can we prevent that?"

"It is impossible. Let us lighten her. That is the only help. So let us throw out everything we can spare."

"But what shall it be?" said the hunter, looking at the car, which was already quite bare.

"Well, let us get rid of the awning, for its weight is quite considerable."

Joe, who was interested in this order, climbed up on the circle which kept together the cordage of the network, and from that place easily managed to detach the heavy curtains of the awning and throw them overboard.

"There's something that will gladden the hearts of a whole tribe of blacks," said he. "There's enough to dress a thousand of them, for they're not very extravagant with cloth."

The balloon had risen a little, but it soon became evident that it was again approaching the ground.

"Let us alight," suggested Kennedy, "and see what can be done with the covering of the balloon."

"I tell you again, Dick, that we have no means of repairing it."

"Then what shall we do?"

"We'll have to sacrifice everything not absolutely indispensable; I am anxious, at all hazards, to avoid a detention in these regions. The forests over the tops of which we are skimming are anything but safe."

"What! Are there lions in them, or hyenas?" asked Joe, with an expression of sovereign contempt.

"Worse than that, my boy! There are men, and some of the most cruel, too, in all Africa."

"How is that known?"

"By the statements of travelers who have been here before us. Then the French settlers, who occupy the colony of Senegal, necessarily have relations with the surrounding tribes. Under the administration of Colonel Faidherbe, reconnoissances have been pushed far up into the country. Officers such as Messrs. Pascal, Vincent, and Lambert have brought back precious documents from their expeditions. They have explored these countries formed by the elbow of the Senegal in places where war and pillage have left nothing but ruins."

"What, then, took place?"

"I will tell you. In 1854 a Marabout of the Senegalese Fouta, Al-Hadji by name, declaring himself to be inspired like Mohammed, stirred up all the tribes to war against the infidels—that is to say, against the Europeans. He carried destruction and desolation over the regions between the Senegal River and its tributary, the Fatémé. Three hordes of fanatics led on by him scoured the country, sparing neither a village nor a hut in their pillaging, massacring career. He advanced in person on the town of Sego, which was a long time threatened. In 1857 he worked up farther to the northward, and invested the fortification of Medina, built by the French on the bank of the river. This stronghold was defended by Paul Holl, who, for several months, without provisions or ammunition, held out until Colonel Faidherbe came to his relief. Al-Hadji and his bands then repassed the Senegal, and reappeared in the Kaarta, continuing their rapine and murder. Well, here below us is the very country in which he has found refuge with his hordes of banditti; and I assure you that it would not be a good thing to fall into his hands."

"We shall not," said Joe, "even if we have to throw overboard our clothes to save the *Victoria*."

"We are not far from the river," said the doctor, "but I foresee that our balloon will not be able to carry us beyond it."

"Let us reach its banks, at all events," said the Scot, "and that will be so much gained."

"That is what we are trying to do," rejoined Ferguson, "only that one thing makes me feel anxious."

"What is that?"

"We shall have mountains to pass, and that will be difficult to do, since I cannot augment the ascensional force of the balloon, even with the greatest possible heat that I can produce."

"Well, wait a bit," said Kennedy, "and we shall see!"

"The poor *Victoria*!" sighed Joe. "I had got fond of her as the sailor does of his ship, and I'll not give her up so easily. She may not be what she was at the start—granted; but we shouldn't say a word against her. She has done us good service, and it would break my heart to desert her."

"Be at your ease, Joe; if we leave her, it will be in spite of ourselves. She'll serve us until she's completely worn out, and I ask of her only twenty-four hours more!"

"Ah, she's getting used up! She grows thinner and thinner," said Joe, dolefully, while he eyed her. "Poor balloon!"

"Unless I am deceived," said Kennedy, "there on the horizon are the mountains of which you were speaking, doctor."

"Yes, there they are, indeed!" exclaimed the doctor, after having examined them through his spyglass. "And they look very high. We shall have some trouble in crossing them."

"Can we not avoid them?"

"I am afraid not, Dick. See what an immense space they occupy—nearly one-half of the horizon!"

"They even seem to shut us in," added Joe. "They are gaining on both our right and our left."

"We must then pass over them."

These obstacles, which threatened such imminent peril, seemed to approach with extreme rapidity, or, to speak more accurately, the wind, which was very fresh, was hurrying the balloon toward the sharp peaks. So rise it must, or be dashed to pieces.

"Let us empty our tank of water," said the doctor, "and keep only enough for one day."

"There it goes," shouted Joe.

"Does the balloon rise at all?" asked Kennedy.

"A little—some fifty feet," replied the doctor, who kept his eyes fixed on the barometer. "But that is not enough."

In truth the lofty peaks were starting up so swiftly before the travelers that they seemed to be rushing down upon them. The balloon was far from rising above them. She lacked an elevation of more than five hundred feet more.

The stock of water for the cylinder was also thrown overboard and only a few pints were retained, but still all this was not enough.

"We must pass them though!" urged the doctor.

"Let us throw out the tanks—we have emptied them." said Kennedy.

"Over with them!"

"There they go!" panted Joe. "But it's hard to see ourselves dropping off this way by piecemeal."

"Now, for your part, Joe, make no attempt to sacrifice yourself as you did the other day! Whatever happens, swear to me that you will not leave us!"

"Have no fears, my master, we shall not be separated."

The *Victoria* had ascended some hundred and twenty feet, but the crest of the mountain still towered above it. It was an almost perpendicular ridge that ended in a regular wall rising abruptly in a straight line. It still rose more than two hundred feet over the aeronauts.

"In ten minutes," said the doctor to himself, "our car will be dashed against those rocks unless we succeed in passing them!"

"Well, doctor?" queried Joe.

"Keep nothing but our *pemmican*, and throw out all the heavy meat."

Thereupon the balloon was again lightened by some fifty pounds, and it rose very perceptibly, but that was of little consequence, unless it got above the line of the mountaintops. The situation was terrifying. The *Victoria* was rushing on with great rapidity. They could feel that she would be dashed to pieces—that the shock would be fearful.

The doctor glanced around him in the car. It was nearly empty.

"If needs be, Dick, hold yourself in readiness to throw over your firearms!"

"Sacrifice my firearms?" repeated the sportsman, with intense feeling.

"My friend, I ask it; it will be absolutely necessary!"

"Samuel! Doctor!"

"Your guns, and your stock of powder and ball might cost us our lives."

"We are close to it!" cried Joe.

Sixty feet! The mountain still overtopped the balloon by sixty feet.

Joe took the blankets and other coverings and tossed them out; then, without a word to Kennedy, he threw over several bags of bullets and lead.

The balloon went up still higher; it surmounted the dangerous ridge, and the rays of the sun shone upon its uppermost extremity; but the car was still below the level of certain broken masses of rock, against which it would inevitably be dashed.

"Kennedy! Kennedy! Throw out your firearms, or we are lost!" shouted the doctor.

"Wait, sir; wait one moment!" they heard Joe exclaim, and, looking around, they saw Joe disappear over the edge of the balloon.

"Joe! Joe!" cried Kennedy.

"Wretched man!" was the doctor's agonized expression.

The flat top of the mountain may have had about twenty feet in breadth at this point, and, on the other side, the slope presented a less declivity. The car just touched the level of this plane, which happened to be quite even, and it glided over a soil composed of sharp pebbles that grated as it passed.

"We're over it! We're over it! We're clear!" cried out an exulting voice that made Ferguson's heart leap to his throat.

The daring fellow was there, grasping the lower rim of the car, and running afoot over the top of the mountain, thus lightening the balloon of his whole weight. He had to hold on with all his strength, too, for it was likely to escape his grasp at any moment.

When he had reached the opposite declivity, and the abyss was before him, Joe, by a vigorous effort, hoisted himself from the ground, and, clambering up by the cordage, rejoined his friends.

"That was all!" he coolly ejaculated.

"My brave Joe! My friend!" said the doctor, with deep emotion.

"Oh! What I did," laughed the other, "was not for you; it was to save Mr. Kennedy's rifle. I owed him that good turn for the affair with the Arab! I like to pay my debts, and now we are even," added he, handing to the sportsman his favorite weapon. "I'd feel very badly to see you deprived of it."

Kennedy heartily shook the brave fellow's hand, without being able to utter a word.

The *Victoria* had nothing to do now but to descend. That was easy enough, so that she was soon at a height of only two hundred feet from the ground, and was then in equilibrium. The surface seemed very much broken as though by a convulsion of nature. It presented numerous inequalities, which would have been very difficult to avoid during the night with a balloon that could no longer be controlled. Evening was coming on rapidly, and, notwithstanding his repugnance, the doctor had to make up his mind to halt until morning.

"We'll now look for a favorable stopping place," said he.

"Ah!" replied Kennedy. "You have made up your mind, then, at last?"

"Yes, I have for a long time been thinking over a plan which we'll try to put into execution; it is only six o'clock in the evening, and we shall have time enough. Throw out your anchors, Joe!"

Joe immediately obeyed, and the two anchors dangled below the balloon.

"I see large forests ahead of us," said the doctor; "we are going to sweep along their tops, and we shall grapple to some tree, for nothing would make me think of passing the night below, on the ground."

"But can we not descend?" asked Kennedy.

"To what purpose? I repeat that it would be dangerous for us to separate, and, besides, I claim your help for a difficult piece of work."

The *Victoria*, which was skimming along the tops of immense forests, soon came to a sharp halt. Her anchors had caught, and, the wind falling as dusk came on, she remained motionlessly suspended above a vast field of verdure, formed by the tops of a forest of sycamores.

## CHAPTER XLII

A STRUGGLE OF GENEROSITY—THE LAST SACRIFICE—THE DILATING
APPARATUS—JOE'S ADROITNESS—MIDNIGHT—THE DOCTOR'S WATCH—
KENNEDY'S WATCH—THE LATTER FALLS ASLEEP AT HIS POST—THE FIRE—
THE HOWLINGS OF THE NATIVES—OUT OF RANGE

Doctor Ferguson's first care was to take his bearings by stellar observation, and he discovered that he was scarcely twenty-five miles from Senegal.

"All that we can manage to do, my friends," said he, after having pointed his map, "is to cross the river; but, as there is neither bridge nor boat, we must, at all hazards, cross it with the balloon, and, in order to do that, we must still lighten up."

"But I don't exactly see how we can do that," replied Kennedy, anxious about his firearms, "unless one of us makes up his mind to sacrifice himself for the rest—that is, to stay behind, and, in my turn, I claim that honor."

"You, indeed!" remonstrated Joe. "Ain't I used to—"

"The question now is, not to throw ourselves out of the car, but simply to reach the coast of Africa on foot. I am a first-rate walker, a good sportsman, and—"

"I'll never consent to it!" insisted Joe.

"Your generous rivalry is useless, my brave friends," said Ferguson. "I trust that we shall not come to any such extremity; besides, if we did, instead of separating, we should keep together, so as to make our way across the country in company."

"That's the talk," said Joe; "a little tramp won't do us any harm."

"But before we try that," resumed the doctor, "we must employ a last means of lightening the balloon."

"What will that be? I should like to see it," said Kennedy, incredulously.

"We must get rid of the cylinder chests, the spiral, and the Buntzen battery. Nine hundred pounds make a rather heavy load to carry through the air."

"But then, Samuel, how will you dilate your gas?"

"I shall not do so at all. We'll have to get along without it."

"But—"

"Listen, my friends: I have calculated very exactly the amount of ascensional force left to us, and it is sufficient to carry us every one with the few objects that remain. We shall make in all a weight of hardly five hundred pounds, including the two anchors which I desire to keep."

"Dear doctor, you know more about the matter than we do; you are the sole judge of the situation. Tell us what we ought to do, and we will do it."

"I am at your orders, master," added Joe.

"I repeat, my friends, that however serious the decision may appear, we must sacrifice our apparatus."

"Let it go, then!" said Kennedy, promptly.

"To work!" said Joe.

It was no easy job. The apparatus had to be taken down piece by piece. First, they took out the mixing reservoir, then the one belonging to the cylinder, and lastly the tank in which the decomposition of the water was effected. The united strength of all three travelers was required to detach these reservoirs from the bottom of the car in which they had been so firmly secured; but Kennedy was so strong, Joe so adroit, and the doctor so ingenious, that they finally succeeded. The different pieces were thrown out, one after the other, and they disappeared below, making huge gaps in the foliage of the sycamores.

"The black fellows will be mightily astonished," said Joe, "at finding things like those in the woods; they'll make idols of them!"

The next thing to be looked after was the displacement of the pipes that were fastened in the balloon and connected with the spiral. Joe succeeded in cutting the caoutchouc jointings above the car, but when he came to the pipes he found it more difficult to disengage them, because they were held by their upper extremity and fastened by wires to the very circlet of the valve.

Then it was that Joe showed wonderful adroitness. In his naked feet, so as not to scratch the covering, he succeeded by the aid of the network, and in spite of the oscillations of the balloon, in climbing to the upper extremity, and after a thousand difficulties, in holding on with one hand to that slippery surface, while he detached the outside screws that secured the pipes in their place. These were then easily taken out, and drawn away by the lower end, which was hermetically sealed by means of a strong ligature.

The *Victoria*, relieved of this considerable weight, rose upright in the air and tugged strongly at the anchor rope.

About midnight this work ended without accident, but at the cost of most severe exertion, and the trio partook of a luncheon of *pemmican* and cold punch, as the doctor had no more fire to place at Joe's disposal.

Besides, the latter and Kennedy were dropping off their feet with fatigue.

"Lie down, my friends, and get some rest," said the doctor. "I'll take the first watch; at two o'clock I'll waken Kennedy; at four, Kennedy will waken Joe, and at six we'll start; and may Heaven have us in its keeping for this last day of the trip!"

Without waiting to be coaxed, the doctor's two companions stretched themselves at the bottom of the car and dropped into profound slumber on the instant.

The night was calm. A few clouds broke against the last quarter of the moon, whose uncertain rays scarcely pierced the darkness. Ferguson, resting his elbows on the rim of the car, gazed attentively around him. He watched with close attention the dark screen of foliage that spread beneath him, hiding the ground from his view. The least noise aroused his suspicions, and he questioned even the slightest rustling of the leaves.

He was in that mood which solitude makes more keenly felt, and during which vague terrors mount to the brain. At the close of such a journey, after having surmounted so many obstacles, and at the moment of touching the goal, one's fears are more vivid, one's emotions keener. The point of arrival seems to fly farther from our gaze.

Moreover, the present situation had nothing very consolatory about it. They were in the midst of a barbarous country, and dependent upon a vehicle that might fail them at any moment. The doctor no longer counted implicitly on his balloon; the time had gone by when he maneuvered it boldly because he felt sure of it.

Under the influence of these impressions, the doctor, from time to time, thought that he heard vague sounds in the vast forests around him; he even fancied that he saw a swift gleam of fire shining between the trees. He looked sharply and turned his night-glass toward the spot; but there was nothing to be seen, and the profoundest silence appeared to return.

He had, no doubt, been under the dominion of a mere hallucination. He continued to listen, but without hearing the slightest noise. When his watch had expired, he woke Kennedy, and, enjoining upon him to observe the extremest vigilance, took his place beside Joe, and fell sound asleep.

Kennedy, while still rubbing his eyes, which he could scarcely keep open, calmly lit his pipe. He then ensconced himself in a corner, and began to smoke vigorously by way of keeping awake.

The most absolute silence reigned around him; a light wind shook the treetops and gently rocked the car, inviting the hunter to taste the sleep that stole over him in spite of himself. He strove hard to resist it, and repeatedly opened his eyes to plunge into the outer darkness one of those looks that see nothing; but at last, yielding to fatigue, he sank back and slumbered.

How long he had been buried in this stupor he knew not, but he was suddenly aroused from it by a strange, unexpected crackling sound.

He rubbed his eyes and sprang to his feet. An intense glare half-blinded him and heated his cheek—the forest was in flames!

"Fire! Fire!" he shouted, scarcely comprehending what had happened.

His two companions started up in alarm.

"What's the matter?" was the doctor's immediate exclamation.

"Fire!" said Joe. "But who could—"

At this moment loud yells were heard under the foliage, which was now illuminated as brightly as the day.

"Ah! The savages!" cried Joe again. "They have set fire to the forest so as to be the more certain of burning us up."

"The Talabas! Al-Hadji's marabouts, no doubt," said the doctor.

A circle of fire hemmed the *Victoria* in; the crackling of the dry wood mingled with the hissing and sputtering of the green branches; the clambering vines, the foliage, all the living part of this vegetation, writhed in the destructive element. The eye took in nothing but one vast ocean of flame; the large trees stood forth in black relief in this huge furnace, their branches covered with glowing coals, while the whole blazing mass, the entire conflagration, was reflected on the clouds, and the travelers could fancy themselves enveloped in a hollow globe of fire.

"Let us escape to the ground!" shouted Kennedy. "It is our only chance of safety!"

But Ferguson checked him with a firm grasp, and, dashing at the anchor rope, severed it with one well-directed blow of his hatchet. Meanwhile, the flames, leaping up at the balloon, already quivered on its illuminated sides; but the *Victoria*, released from her fastenings, spun upward a thousand feet into the air.

Frightful yells resounded through the forest, along with the report of firearms, while the balloon, caught in a current of air that rose with the dawn of day, was borne to the westward.

It was now four o'clock in the morning.

## CHAPTER XLIII

THE TALABAS—THE PURSUIT—A DEVASTATED COUNTRY—THE WIND
BEGINS TO FALL—THE *VICTORIA* SINKS—THE LAST OF THE PROVISIONS—
THE LEAPS OF THE BALLOON—A DEFENSE WITH FIREARMS—THE WIND
FRESHENS—THE SENEGAL RIVER—THE CATARACTS OF GOUINA—
THE HOT AIR—THE PASSAGE OF THE RIVER

"Had we not taken the precaution to lighten the balloon yesterday evening, we should have been lost beyond redemption," said the doctor, after a long silence.

"See what's gained by doing things at the right time!" replied Joe. "One gets out of scrapes then, and nothing is more natural."

"We are not out of danger yet," said the doctor.

"What do you still apprehend?" queried Kennedy. "The balloon can't descend without your permission, and even were it to do so—"

"Were it to do so, Dick? Look!"

They had just passed the borders of the forest, and the three friends could see some thirty mounted men clad in broad pantaloons and the floating bournouses. They were armed, some with lances, and others with long muskets, and they were following, on their quick, fiery little steeds, the direction of the balloon, which was moving at only moderate speed.

When they caught sight of the aeronauts, they uttered savage cries, and brandished their weapons. Anger and menace could be read upon their swarthy faces, made more ferocious by thin but bristling beards. Meanwhile they galloped along without difficulty over the low levels and gentle declivities that lead down to the Senegal.

"It is, indeed, they!" said the doctor. "The cruel Talabas! The ferocious marabouts of Al-Hadji! I would rather find myself in the middle of the forest encircled by wild beasts than fall into the hands of these banditti."

"They haven't a very obliging look!" assented Kennedy. "And they are rough, stalwart fellows."

"Happily those brutes can't fly," remarked Joe; "and that's something."

"See," said Ferguson, "those villages in ruins, those huts burned down—that is their work! Where vast stretches of cultivated land were once seen, they have brought barrenness and devastation."

"At all events, however," interposed Kennedy, "they can't overtake us; and, if we succeed in putting the river between us and them, we are safe."

"Perfectly, Dick," replied Ferguson; "but we must not fall to the ground!" And, as he said this, he glanced at the barometer.

"In any case, Joe," added Kennedy, "it would do us no harm to look to our firearms."

"No harm in the world, Mr. Dick! We are lucky that we didn't scatter them along the road."

"My rifle!" said the sportsman. "I hope that I shall never be separated from it!"

And so saying, Kennedy loaded the pet piece with the greatest care, for he had plenty of powder and ball remaining.

"At what height are we?" he asked the doctor.

"About seven hundred and fifty feet; but we no longer have the power of seeking favorable currents, either going up or coming down. We are at the mercy of the balloon!"

"That is vexatious!" rejoined Kennedy. "The wind is poor; but if we had come across a hurricane like some of those we met before, these vile brigands would have been out of sight long ago."

"The rascals follow us at their leisure," said Joe. "They're only at a short gallop. Quite a nice little ride!"

"If we were within range," sighed the sportsman, "I should amuse myself with dismounting a few of them."

"Exactly," said the doctor; "but then they would have you within range also, and our balloon would offer only too plain a target to the bullets from their long guns; and, if they were to make a hole in it, I leave you to judge what our situation would be!"

The pursuit of the Talabas continued all morning; and by eleven o'clock the aeronauts had made scarcely fifteen miles to the westward.

The doctor was anxiously watching for the least cloud on the horizon. He feared, above all things, a change in the atmosphere. Should he be thrown back toward the Niger, what would become of him? Besides, he remarked that the balloon tended to fall considerably. Since the start, he had already lost more than three hundred feet, and the Senegal must be about a dozen miles distant. At his present rate of speed, he could count upon traveling only three hours longer.

At this moment his attention was attracted by fresh cries. The Talabas appeared to be much excited, and were spurring their horses.

The doctor consulted his barometer, and at once discovered the cause of these symptoms.

"Are we descending?" asked Kennedy.

"Yes!" replied the doctor.

"The mischief!" thought Joe

In the lapse of fifteen minutes the *Victoria* was only one hundred and fifty feet above the ground; but the wind was much stronger than before.

The Talabas checked their horses, and soon a volley of musketry pealed out on the air.

"Too far, you fools!" bawled Joe. "I think it would be well to keep those scamps at a distance."

And, as he spoke, he aimed at one of the horsemen who was farthest to the front, and fired. The Talaba fell headlong, and, his companions halting for a moment, the balloon gained upon them.

"They are prudent!" said Kennedy.

"Because they think that they are certain to take us," replied the doctor; "and they will succeed if we descend much farther. We must, absolutely, get higher into the air."

"What can we throw out?" asked Joe.

"All that remains of our stock of *pemmican*; that will be thirty pounds less weight to carry."

"Out it goes, sir!" said Joe, obeying orders.

The car, which was now almost touching the ground, rose again, amid the cries of the Talabas; but, half an hour later, the balloon was again falling rapidly, because the gas was escaping through the pores of the covering.

Ere long the car was once more grazing the soil, and Al-Hadji's black riders rushed toward it; but, as frequently happens in like cases, the balloon had scarcely touched the surface ere it rebounded, and only came down again a mile away.

"So we shall not escape!" said Kennedy, between his teeth.

"Throw out our reserved store of brandy, Joe," cried the doctor; "our instruments, and everything that has any weight, even to our last anchor, because go they must!"

Joe flung out the barometers and thermometers, but all that amounted to little; and the balloon, which had risen for an instant, fell again toward the ground.

The Talabas flew toward it, and at length were not more than two hundred paces away.

"Throw out the two fowling-pieces!" shouted Ferguson.

"Not without discharging them, at least," responded the sportsman; and four shots in quick succession struck the thick of the advancing group of horsemen. Four Talabas fell, amid the frantic howls and imprecations of their comrades.

The *Victoria* ascended once more, and made some enormous leaps, like a huge gum-elastic ball, bounding and rebounding through the air. A strange sight it was to see these unfortunate men endeavoring to escape by those huge aerial strides, and seeming, like the giant Antaeus, to receive fresh strength every time they touched the earth. But this situation had to terminate. It was now nearly noon; the *Victoria* was getting empty and exhausted, and assuming a more and more elongated form every instant. Its outer covering was becoming flaccid, and floated loosely in the air, and the folds of the silk rustled and grated on each other.

"Heaven abandons us!" said Kennedy. "We have to fall!"

Joe made no answer. He kept looking intently at his master.

"No!" said the latter. "We have more than one hundred and fifty pounds yet to throw out."

"What can it be, then?" said Kennedy, thinking that the doctor must be going mad.

"The car!" was his reply. "We can cling to the network. There we can hang on in the meshes until we reach the river. Quick! Quick!"

And these daring men did not hesitate a moment to avail themselves of this last desperate means of escape. They clutched the network, as the doctor directed, and Joe, holding on by one hand, with the other cut the cords that suspended the car; and the latter dropped to the ground just as the balloon was sinking for the last time.

"Hurrah! Hurrah!" shouted the brave fellow exultingly, as the *Victoria*, once more relieved, shot up again to a height of three hundred feet.

The Talabas spurred their horses, which now came tearing on at a furious gallop; but the balloon, falling in with a much more favorable wind, shot ahead of them, and was rapidly carried toward a hill that stretched across the horizon to the westward. This was a circumstance favorable to the aeronauts, because they could rise over the hill, while Al-Hadji's horde had to diverge to the northward in order to pass this obstacle.

The three friends still clung to the network. They had been able to fasten it under their feet, where it had formed a sort of swinging pocket.

Suddenly, after they had crossed the hill, the doctor exclaimed: "The river! The river! The Senegal, my friends!"

And about two miles ahead of them, there was indeed the river rolling along its broad mass of water, while the farther bank, which was low and fertile, offered a sure refuge, and a place favorable for a descent.

"Another quarter of an hour," said Ferguson, "and we are saved!"

But it was not to happen thus; the empty balloon descended slowly upon a tract almost entirely bare of vegetation. It was made up of long slopes and stony plains, a few bushes and some coarse grass, scorched by the sun.

The *Victoria* touched the ground several times, and rose again, but her rebound was diminishing in height and length. At the last one, it caught by the upper part of the network in the lofty branches of a baobab, the only tree that stood there, solitary and alone, in the midst of the waste.

"It's all over," said Kennedy.

"And at a hundred paces only from the river!" groaned Joe.

The three hapless aeronauts descended to the ground, and the doctor drew his companions toward the Senegal.

At this point the river sent forth a prolonged roaring; and when Ferguson reached its bank, he recognized the falls of Gouina. But not a boat, not a living creature was to be seen. With a breadth of two thousand feet, the Senegal precipitates itself for a height of one hundred and fifty, with a thundering reverberation. It ran, where they saw it, from east to west, and the line of rocks that barred its course extended from north to south. In the midst of the falls, rocks of strange forms started up like huge antediluvian animals, petrified there amid the waters.

The impossibility of crossing this gulf was self-evident, and Kennedy could not restrain a gesture of despair.

But Dr. Ferguson, with an energetic accent of undaunted daring, exclaimed—

"All is not over!"

"I knew it," said Joe, with that confidence in his master which nothing could ever shake.

The sight of the dried-up grass had inspired the doctor with a bold idea. It was the last chance of escape. He led his friends quickly back to where they had left the covering of the balloon.

"We have at least an hour's start of those banditti," said he. "Let us lose no time, my friends; gather a quantity of this dried grass; I want a hundred pounds of it, at least."

"For what purpose?" asked Kennedy, surprised.

"I have no more gas; well, I'll cross the river with hot air!"

"Ah, doctor," exclaimed Kennedy, "you are, indeed, a great man!"

Joe and Kennedy at once went to work, and soon had an immense pile of dried grass heaped up near the baobab.

In the meantime, the doctor had enlarged the orifice of the balloon by cutting it open at the lower end. He then was very careful to expel the last remnant of hydrogen through the valve, after which he heaped up a quantity of grass under the balloon, and set fire to it.

It takes but a little while to inflate a balloon with hot air. A head of one hundred and eighty degrees is sufficient to diminish the weight of the air it contains to the extent of one-half, by rarefying it. Thus, the *Victoria* quickly began to assume a more rounded form. There was no lack of grass; the fire was kept in full blast by the doctor's assiduous efforts, and the balloon grew fuller every instant.

It was then a quarter to four o'clock.

At this moment the band of Talabas reappeared about two miles to the northward, and the three friends could hear their cries, and the clatter of their horses galloping at full speed.

"In twenty minutes they will be here!" said Kennedy.

"More grass! More grass, Joe! In ten minutes we shall have her full of hot air."

"Here it is, doctor!"

The *Victoria* was now two-thirds inflated.

"Come, my friends, let us take hold of the network, as we did before."

"All right!" they answered together.

In about ten minutes a few jerking motions by the balloon indicated that it was disposed to start again. The Talabas were approaching. They were hardly five hundred paces away.

"Hold on fast!" cried Ferguson.

"Have no fear, master—have no fear!"

And the doctor with his foot pushed another heap of grass upon the fire.

With this the balloon, now completely inflated by the increased temperature, moved away, sweeping the branches of the baobab in her flight.

"We're off!" shouted Joe.

A volley of musketry responded to his exclamation. A bullet even plowed his shoulder; but Kennedy, leaning over and discharging his rifle with one hand, brought another of the enemy to the ground.

Cries of fury exceeding all description hailed the departure of the balloon, which had at once ascended nearly eight hundred feet. A swift current caught and swept it along with the most alarming oscillations, while the intrepid doctor and his friends saw the gulf of the cataracts yawning below them.

Ten minutes later, and without having exchanged a word, they descended gradually toward the other bank of the river.

There, astonished, speechless, terrified, stood a group of men clad in the French uniform. Judge of their amazement when they saw the balloon rise from the right bank of the river. They had well-nigh taken it for some celestial phenomenon, but their officers, a lieutenant of marines and a naval ensign, having seen mention made of Dr. Ferguson's daring expedition in the European papers, quickly explained the real state of the case.

The balloon, losing its inflation little by little, settled with the daring travelers still clinging to its network; but it was doubtful whether it would reach the land. At once some of the brave Frenchmen rushed into the water and caught the three aeronauts in their arms just as the *Victoria* fell at the distance of a few fathoms from the left bank of the Senegal.

"Dr. Ferguson!" exclaimed the lieutenant.

"The same, sir," replied the doctor, quietly, "and his two friends."

The Frenchmen escorted our travelers from the river, while the balloon, half-empty, and borne away by a swift current, sped on, to plunge, like a huge bubble, headlong with the waters of the Senegal, into the cataracts of Gouina.

"The poor *Victoria*!" was Joe's farewell remark.

The doctor could not restrain a tear, and extending his hands his two friends wrung them silently with that deep emotion which requires no spoken words.

## CHAPTER XLIV

CONCLUSION—THE CERTIFICATE—THE FRENCH SETTLEMENTS—THE POST OF MEDINA—THE *BASILIC*—SAINT LOUIS—THE ENGLISH FRIGATE—THE RETURN TO LONDON

The expedition upon the bank of the river had been sent by the governor of Senegal. It consisted of two officers, Messrs. Dufraisse, lieutenant of marines, and Rodamel, naval ensign, and with these were a sergeant and seven soldiers. For two days they had been engaged in reconnoitering the most favorable situation for a post at Gouina, when they became witnesses of Dr. Ferguson's arrival.

The warm greetings and felicitations of which our travelers were the recipients may be imagined. The Frenchmen, and they alone, having had ocular proof of the accomplishment of the daring project, naturally became Dr. Ferguson's witnesses. Hence the doctor at once asked them to give their official testimony of his arrival at the cataracts of Gouina.

"You would have no objection to signing a certificate of the fact, would you?" he inquired of Lieutenant Dufraisse.

"At your orders!" the latter instantly replied.

The Englishmen were escorted to a provisional post established on the bank of the river, where they found the most assiduous attention, and everything to supply their wants. And there the following certificate was drawn up in the terms in which it appears today, in the archives of the Royal Geographical Society of London:

We, the undersigned, do hereby declare that, on the day herein mentioned, we witnessed the arrival of Dr. Ferguson and his two companions, Richard Kennedy and Joseph Wilson, clinging to the cordage and network of a balloon, and that the said balloon fell at a distance of a few paces from us into the river, and being swept away by the current was lost in the cataracts of Gouina. In testimony whereof, we have hereunto set our hands and seals beside those of the persons hereinabove named, for the information of all whom it may concern.

Done at the Cataracts of Gouina, on the 24th of May, 1862.

(Signed),     SAMUEL FERGUSON
            RICHARD KENNEDY
            JOSEPH WILSON
            DUFRAISSE, *Lieutenant of Marines*
            RODAMEL, *Naval Ensign*
            DUFAYS, *Sergeant*
            FLIPPEAU, MAYOR, PELISSIER, LOROIS,
            RASCAGNET, GUILLON, LEBEL, *Privates*

\* \* \*

Here ended the astonishing journey of Dr. Ferguson and his brave companions, as vouched for by undeniable testimony; and they found themselves among friends in the midst of most hospitable tribes, whose relations with the French settlements are frequent and amicable.

They had arrived at Senegal on Saturday, the 24th of May, and on the 27th of the same month they reached the post of Medina, situated a little farther to the north, but on the river.

There the French officers received them with open arms, and lavished upon them all the resources of their hospitality. Thus aided, the doctor and his friends were enabled to embark almost immediately on the small steamer called the *Basilic*, which ran down to the mouth of the river.

Two weeks later, on the 10th of June, they arrived at Saint Louis, where the governor gave them a magnificent reception, and they recovered completely from their excitement and fatigue.

Besides, Joe said to everyone who chose to listen:

"That was a stupid trip of ours, after all, and I wouldn't advise anybody who is greedy for excitement to undertake it. It gets very tiresome at the last, and if it hadn't been for the adventures on Lake Tchad and at the Senegal River, I do believe that we'd have died of yawning."

An English frigate was just about to sail, and the three travelers procured passage on board of her. On the 25th of June they arrived at Portsmouth, and on the next day at London.

We will not describe the reception they got from the Royal Geographical Society, nor the intense curiosity and consideration of which they became the objects. Kennedy set off, at once, for Edinburgh, with his famous rifle, for he was in haste to relieve the anxiety of his faithful old housekeeper.

The doctor and his devoted Joe remained the same men that we have known them, excepting that one change took place at their own suggestion.

They ceased to be master and servant, in order to become bosom friends.

The journals of all Europe were untiring in their praises of the bold explorers, and the *Daily Telegraph* struck off an edition of three hundred and seventy-seven thousand copies on the day when it published a sketch of the trip.

Dr. Ferguson, at a public meeting of the Royal Geographical Society, gave a recital of his journey through the air, and obtained for himself and his companions the golden medal set apart to reward the most remarkable exploring expedition of the year 1862.

* * *

The first result of Dr. Ferguson's expedition was to establish, in the most precise manner, the facts and geographical surveys reported by Messrs. Barth, Burton, Speke, and others. Thanks to the still more recent expeditions of Messrs. Speke and Grant, De Heuglin and Muntzinger, who have been ascending to the sources of the Nile, and penetrating to the center of Africa, we shall be enabled ere long to verify, in turn, the discoveries of Dr. Ferguson in that vast region comprised between the fourteenth and thirty-third degrees of east longitude.

# A Journey to the Center of the Earth

## CHAPTER I

### THE PROFESSOR AND HIS FAMILY

On the 24th of May, 1863, my uncle, Professor Liedenbrock, rushed into his little house, No. 19 Königstrasse, one of the oldest streets in the oldest portion of the city of Hamburg.

Martha must have concluded that she was very much behindhand, for the dinner had only just been put into the oven.

"Well, now," said I to myself, "if that most impatient of men is hungry, what a disturbance he will make!"

"M. Liedenbrock so soon!" cried poor Martha in great alarm, half opening the dining-room door.

"Yes, Martha; but very likely the dinner is not half cooked, for it is not two yet. Saint Michael's clock has only just struck half-past one."

"Then why has the master come home so soon?"

"Perhaps he will tell us that himself."

"Here he is, Monsieur Axel; I will run and hide myself while you argue with him."

And Martha retreated in safety into her own dominions.

I was left alone. But how was it possible for a man of my undecided turn of mind to argue successfully with so irascible a person as the professor? With this persuasion I was hurrying away to my own little retreat upstairs, when the street door creaked upon its hinges; heavy feet made the whole flight of stairs to shake; and the master of the house, passing rapidly through the dining room, threw himself in haste into his own sanctum.

But on his rapid way he had found time to fling his hazel stick into a corner, his rough broadbrim upon the table, and these few emphatic words at his nephew:

"Axel, follow me!"

I had scarcely had time to move when the professor was again shouting after me:

"What! Not come yet?"

And I rushed into my redoubtable master's study.

Otto Liedenbrock had no mischief in him, I willingly allow that; but unless he very considerably changes as he grows older, at the end he will be a most original character.

He was professor at the Johanneum, and was delivering a series of lectures on mineralogy, in the course of every one of which he broke into a passion once or twice at least. Not at all that he was overanxious about the improvement of his class, or about the degree of attention with which they listened to him, or the success which might eventually crown his labors. Such little matters of detail never troubled him much. His teaching was, as the German philosophy calls it, "subjective"; it was to benefit himself, not others. He was a learned egotist. He was a well of science, and the pulleys worked uneasily when you wanted to draw anything out of it. In a word, he was a learned miser.

Germany has not a few professors of this sort.

To his misfortune, my uncle was not gifted with a sufficiently rapid utterance; not, to be sure, when he was talking at home, but certainly in his public delivery; this is a want much to be deplored in a speaker. The fact is, that during the course of his lectures at the Johanneum, the professor often came to a complete standstill; he fought with willful words that refused to pass his struggling lips, such words as resist and distend the cheeks, and at last break out into the unasked-for shape of a round and most unscientific oath: then his fury would gradually abate.

Now in mineralogy there are many half-Greek and half-Latin terms, very hard to articulate, and which would be most trying to a poet's measures. I don't wish to say a word against so respectable a science, far be that from me. True, in the august presence of rhombohedral crystals, retinasphaltic resins, gehlenites, Fassaites, molybdenites, tungstates of manganese, and titanite of zirconium, why, the most facile of tongues may make a slip now and then.

It therefore happened that this venial fault of my uncle's came to be pretty well understood in time, and an unfair advantage was taken of it; the students laid wait for him in dangerous places, and when he began to stumble, loud was the laughter, which is not in good taste, not even in Germans. And if there was always a full audience to honor the Liedenbrock courses, I should be sorry to conjecture how many came to make merry at my uncle's expense.

Nevertheless my good uncle was a man of deep learning—a fact I am most anxious to assert and reassert. Sometimes he might irretrievably injure a specimen by his too great ardor in handling it; but still he united the genius of a true geologist with the keen eye of the mineralogist. Armed with his hammer, his steel pointer, his magnetic needles, his blowpipe, and his bottle of nitric acid, he was a powerful man of science. He would refer any mineral to its proper place among the six hundred elementary substances now enumerated, by its fracture, its appearance, its hardness, its fusibility, its sonorousness, its smell, and its taste.

The name of Liedenbrock was honorably mentioned in colleges and learned societies. Humphry Davy, Humboldt, Captain Sir John Franklin, General Sabine, never failed to call upon him on their way through Hamburg. Becquerel, Ebelman, Brewster, Dumas, Milne-Edwards, Saint-Claire-Deville frequently consulted him upon the most difficult problems in chemistry, a science which was indebted to him for considerable discoveries, for in 1853 there had appeared at Leipzig an imposing folio by Otto Liedenbrock, entitled *A Treatise upon Transcendental Chemistry*, with plates; a work, however, which failed to cover its expenses.

To all these titles to honor let me add that my uncle was the curator of the museum of mineralogy formed by M. Struve, the Russian ambassador; a most valuable collection, the fame of which is European.

Such was the gentleman who addressed me in that impetuous manner. Fancy a tall, spare man, of an iron constitution, and with a fair complexion which took off a good ten years from the fifty he must own to. His restless eyes were in incessant motion behind his full-sized spectacles. His long, thin nose was like a knife blade. Boys have been heard to remark that that organ was magnetized and attracted iron filings. But this was merely a mischievous report; it had no attraction except for snuff, which it seemed to draw to itself in great quantities.

When I have added, to complete my portrait, that my uncle walked by mathematical strides of a yard and a half, and that in walking he kept his fists firmly closed, a sure sign of an irritable temperament, I think I shall have said enough to disenchant anyone who should by mistake have coveted much of his company.

He lived in his own little house in Königstrasse, a structure half brick and half wood, with a gable cut into steps; it looked upon one of those winding canals which intersect each other in the middle of the ancient quarter of Hamburg, and which the great fire of 1842 had fortunately spared.

It is true that the old house stood slightly off the perpendicular, and bulged out a little toward the street; its roof sloped a little to one side, like the cap over the left ear of a Tugendbund student; its lines wanted accuracy; but after all, it stood firm, thanks to an old elm which buttressed it in front, and which often in spring sent its young sprays through the window panes.

My uncle was tolerably well off for a German professor. The house was his own, and everything in it. The living contents were his goddaughter Gräuben, a young Virlandaise of seventeen, Martha, and myself. As his nephew and an orphan, I became his laboratory assistant.

I freely confess that I was exceedingly fond of geology and all its kindred sciences; the blood of a mineralogist was in my veins, and in the midst of my specimens I was always happy.

In a word, a man might live happily enough in the little old house in the Königstrasse, in spite of the restless impatience of its master, for although he was a little too excitable—he was very fond of me. But the man had no notion how to wait; nature herself was too slow for him. In April, after he had planted in the terra-cotta pots outside his window seedling plants of mignonette and convolvulus, he would go and give them a little pull by their leaves to make them grow faster. In dealing with such a strange individual there was nothing for it but prompt obedience. I therefore rushed after him.

## CHAPTER II

### A MYSTERY TO BE SOLVED AT ANY PRICE

That study of his was a museum, and nothing else. Specimens of everything known in mineralogy lay there in their places in perfect order, and correctly named, divided into inflammable, metallic, and lithoid minerals.

How well I knew all these bits of science! Many a time, instead of enjoying the company of lads of my own age, I had preferred dusting these graphites, anthracites, coals, lignites, and peats! And there were bitumens, resins, organic salts, to be protected from the least grain of dust; and metals, from iron to gold, metals whose current value altogether disappeared in the presence of the republican equality of scientific specimens; and stones too, enough to rebuild entirely the house in Königstrasse, even with a handsome additional room, which would have suited me admirably.

But on entering this study now I thought of none of all these wonders; my uncle alone filled my thoughts. He had thrown himself into a velvet easy-chair, and was grasping between his hands a book over which he bent, pondering with intense admiration.

"Here's a remarkable book! What a wonderful book!" he was exclaiming.

These ejaculations brought to my mind the fact that my uncle was liable to occasional fits of bibliomania; but no old book had any value in his eyes unless it had the virtue of being nowhere else to be found, or, at any rate, of being illegible.

"Well, now; don't you see it yet? Why, I have got a priceless treasure, that I found his morning, in rummaging in old Hevelius's shop, the Jew."

"Magnificent!" I replied, with a good imitation of enthusiasm.

What was the good of all this fuss about an old quarto, bound in rough calf, a yellow, faded volume, with a ragged seal depending from it?

But for all that there was no lull yet in the admiring exclamations of the professor.

"See," he went on, both asking the questions and supplying the answers. "Isn't it a beauty? Yes; splendid! Did you ever see such a binding? Doesn't the book open easily? Yes; it stops open anywhere. But does it shut equally well? Yes; for the binding and the leaves are flush, all in a straight line, and no gaps or openings anywhere. And look at its back, after seven hundred years. Why, Bozerian, Closs, or Purgold might have been proud of such a binding!"

While rapidly making these comments my uncle kept opening and shutting the old tome. I really could do no less than ask a question about its contents, although I did not feel the slightest interest.

"And what is the title of this marvelous work?" I asked with an affected eagerness which he must have been very blind not to see through.

"This work," replied my uncle, firing up with renewed enthusiasm, "this work is the Heims Kringla of Snorre Turlleson, the most famous Icelandic author of the twelfth century! It is the chronicle of the Norwegian princes who ruled in Iceland."

"Indeed," I cried, keeping up wonderfully, "of course it is a German translation?"

"What!" sharply replied the professor. "A translation! What should I do with a translation? This is the Icelandic original, in the magnificent idiomatic vernacular, which is both rich and simple, and admits of an infinite variety of grammatical combinations and verbal modifications."

"Like German," I happily ventured.

"Yes," replied my uncle, shrugging his shoulders; "but, in addition to all this, the Icelandic has three numbers like the Greek, and irregular declensions of nouns proper like the Latin."

"Ah!" said I, a little moved out of my indifference. "And is the type good?"

"Type! What do you mean by talking of type, wretched Axel? Type! Do you take it for a printed book, you ignorant fool? It is a manuscript, a Runic manuscript."

"Runic?"

"Yes. Do you want me to explain what that is?"

"Of course not," I replied in the tone of an injured man. But my uncle persevered, and told me, against my will, of many things I cared nothing about.

"Runic characters were in use in Iceland in former ages. They were invented, it is said, by Odin himself. Look there, and wonder, impious young man, and admire these letters, the invention of the Scandinavian god!"

Well, well! Not knowing what to say, I was going to prostrate myself before this wonderful book, a way of answering equally pleasing to gods and kings, and which has the advantage of never giving them any embarrassment, when a little incident happened to divert conversation into another channel.

This was the appearance of a dirty slip of parchment, which slipped out of the volume and fell upon the floor.

My uncle pounced upon this shred with incredible avidity. An old document, enclosed an immemorial time within the folds of this old book, had for him an immeasurable value.

"What's this?" he cried.

And he laid out upon the table a piece of parchment, five inches by three, and along which were traced certain mysterious characters.

Here is the exact facsimile. I think it important to let these strange signs be publicly known, for they were the means of drawing on Professor Liedenbrock and his nephew to undertake the most wonderful expedition of the nineteenth century.

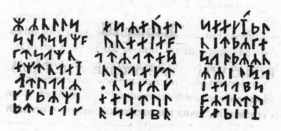

The professor mused a few moments over this series of characters; then raising his spectacles he pronounced:

"These are Runic letters; they are exactly like those of the manuscript of Snorre Turlleson. But, what on earth is their meaning?"

Runic letters appearing to my mind to be an invention of the learned to mystify this poor world, I was not sorry to see my uncle suffering the pangs of mystification. At least, so it seemed to me, judging from his fingers, which were beginning to work with terrible energy.

"It is certainly old Icelandic," he muttered between his teeth.

And Professor Liedenbrock must have known, for he was acknowledged to be quite a polyglot. Not that he could speak fluently in the two thousand languages and twelve thousand dialects which are spoken on the earth, but he knew at least his share of them.

So he was going, in the presence of this difficulty, to give way to all the impetuosity of his character, and I was preparing for a violent outbreak, when two o'clock struck by the little timepiece over the fireplace.

At that moment our good housekeeper Martha opened the study door, saying:

"Dinner is ready!"

I am afraid he sent that soup to where it would boil away to nothing, and Martha took to her heels for safety. I followed her, and hardly knowing how I got there I found myself seated in my usual place.

I waited a few minutes. No professor came. Never within my remembrance had he missed the important ceremonial of dinner. And yet what a good dinner it was! There was parsley soup, an omelette of ham garnished with spiced sorrel, a fillet of veal with compote of prunes; for dessert, crystallized fruit; the whole washed down with sweet Moselle.

All this my uncle was going to sacrifice to a bit of old parchment. As an affectionate and attentive nephew I considered it my duty to eat for him as well as for myself, which I did conscientiously.

"I have never known such a thing," said Martha. "M. Liedenbrock is not at table!"

"Who could have believed it?" I said, with my mouth full.

"Something serious is going to happen," said the servant, shaking her head.

My opinion was, that nothing more serious would happen than an awful scene when my uncle should have discovered that his dinner was devoured. I had come to the last of the fruit when a very loud voice tore me away from the pleasures of my dessert. With one spring I bounded out of the dining room into the study.

## CHAPTER III

### THE RUNIC WRITING EXERCISES THE PROFESSOR

"Undoubtedly it is Runic," said the professor, bending his brows; "but there is a secret in it, and I mean to discover the key."

A violent gesture finished the sentence.

"Sit there," he added, holding out his fist toward the table. "Sit there, and write."

I was seated in a trice.

"Now I will dictate to you every letter of our alphabet which corresponds with each of these Icelandic characters. We will see what that will give us. But, by St. Michael, if you should dare to deceive me—"

The dictation commenced. I did my best. Every letter was given me one after the other, with the following remarkable result:

| | | |
|---|---|---|
| mm.rnlls | esrevel | seecIde |
| sgtssmf | vnteief | niedrke |
| kt,samn | atrateS | saodrrn |
| emtnaeI | nvaect | rrilSa |
| Atsaar | .nvcrc | ieaabs |
| ccrmi | eevtVl | frAntv |
| dt,iac | oseibo | KediiI |

When this work was ended my uncle tore the paper from me and examined it attentively for a long time.

"What does it all mean?" he kept repeating mechanically.

Upon my honor I could not have enlightened him. Besides he did not ask me, and he went on talking to himself.

"This is what is called a cryptogram, or cipher," he said, "in which letters are purposely thrown in confusion, which if properly arranged would reveal their sense. Only think that under this jargon there may lie concealed the clue to some great discovery!"

As for me, I was of opinion that there was nothing at all in it; though, of course, I took care not to say so.

Then the professor took the book and the parchment, and diligently compared them together.

"These two writings are not by the same hand," he said; "the cipher is of later date than the book, an undoubted proof of which I see in a moment. The first letter is a double m, a letter which is not to be found in Turlleson's book, and which was only added to the alphabet in the fourteenth century. Therefore there are two hundred years between the manuscript and the document."

I admitted that this was a strictly logical conclusion.

"I am therefore led to imagine," continued my uncle, "that some possessor of this book wrote these mysterious letters. But who was that possessor? Is his name nowhere to be found in the manuscript?"

My uncle raised his spectacles, took up a strong lens, and carefully examined the blank pages of the book. On the front of the second, the title page, he noticed a sort of stain which looked like an ink blot. But in looking at it very closely he thought he could distinguish some half-effaced letters. My uncle at once fastened upon this as the center of interest, and he labored at that blot, until by the help of his microscope he ended by making out the following Runic characters which he read without difficulty.

"Arne Saknussemm!" he cried in triumph. "Why, that is the name of another Icelander, a savant of the sixteenth century, a celebrated alchemist!"

I gazed at my uncle with satisfactory admiration.

"Those alchemists," he resumed, "Avicenna, Bacon, Lully, Paracelsus, were the real and only savants of their time. They made discoveries at which we are astonished. Has not this Saknussemm concealed under his cryptogram some surprising invention? It is so; it must be so!"

The professor's imagination took fire at this hypothesis.

"No doubt," I ventured to reply, "but what interest would he have in thus hiding so marvelous a discovery?"

"Why? Why? How can I tell? Did not Galileo do the same by Saturn? We shall see. I will get at the secret of this document, and I will neither sleep nor eat until I have found it out."

My comment on this was a half-suppressed "Oh!"

"Nor you either, Axel," he added.

"The deuce!" said I to myself. "Then it is lucky I have eaten two dinners today!"

"First of all we must find out the key to this cipher; that cannot be difficult."

At these words I quickly raised my head; but my uncle went on soliloquizing.

"There's nothing easier. In this document there are a hundred and thirty-two letters, viz., seventy-seven consonants and fifty-five vowels. This is the proportion found in southern languages, while northern tongues are much richer in consonants; therefore this is in a southern language."

These were very fair conclusions, I thought.

"But what language is it?"

Here I looked for a display of learning, but I met instead with profound analysis.

"This Saknussemm," he went on, "was a very well-informed man; now since he was not writing in his own mother tongue, he would naturally select that which was currently adopted by the choice spirits of the sixteenth century; I mean Latin. If I am mistaken, I can but try Spanish, French, Italian, Greek, or Hebrew. But the savants of the sixteenth century generally wrote in Latin. I am therefore entitled to pronounce this, *à priori*, to be Latin. It is Latin."

I jumped up in my chair. My Latin memories rose in revolt against the notion that these barbarous words could belong to the sweet language of Virgil.

"Yes, it is Latin," my uncle went on; "but it is Latin confused and in disorder; *"pertubata seu inordinata,"* as Euclid has it."

"Very well," thought I, "if you can bring order out of that confusion, my dear uncle, you are a clever man."

"Let us examine carefully," said he again, taking up the leaf upon which I had written. "Here is a series of one hundred and thirty-two letters in apparent disorder. There are words consisting of consonants only, as *nrrlls*; others, on the other hand, in which vowels predominate, as for instance the fifth, *uneeief*, or the last but one, *oseibo*. Now this arrangement has evidently not been premeditated; it has arisen mathematically in obedience to the unknown law which has ruled in the succession of these letters. It appears to me a certainty that the original sentence was written in a proper manner, and afterward distorted by a law which we have yet to discover. Whoever possesses the key of this cipher will read it with fluency. What is that key? Axel, have you got it?"

I answered not a word, and for a very good reason. My eyes had fallen upon a charming picture, suspended against the wall, the portrait of Gräuben. My uncle's ward was at that time at Altona, staying with a relation, and in her absence I was very downhearted; for I may confess it to you now, the pretty Virlandaise and the professor's nephew loved each other with a patience and a calmness entirely German. We had become engaged unknown to my uncle, who was too much taken up with geology to be able to enter into such feelings as ours. Gräuben was a lovely blue-eyed blonde, rather given to gravity and seriousness; but that did not prevent her from loving me very sincerely. As for me, I adored her, if there is such a word in the German language. Thus it happened that the picture of my pretty Virlandaise threw me in a moment out of the world of realities into that of memory and fancy.

There looked down upon me the faithful companion of my labors and my recreations. Every day she helped me to arrange my uncle's precious specimens; she and I labeled them together. Mademoiselle Gräuben was an accomplished mineralogist; she could have taught a few things to a savant. She was fond of investigating abstruse scientific questions. What pleasant hours we have spent in study; and how often I envied the very stones which she handled with her charming fingers.

Then, when our leisure hours came, we used to go out together and turn into the shady avenues by the Alster, and went happily side by side up to the old windmill, which forms such an improvement to the landscape at the head of the lake. On the road we chatted hand in hand; I told her amusing tales at which she laughed heartily. Then we reached the banks of the Elbe, and after having bid good-bye to the swan, sailing gracefully amid the white water lilies, we returned to the quay by the steamer.

That is just where I was in my dream, when my uncle with a vehement thump on the table dragged me back to the realities of life.

"Come," said he, "the very first idea which would come into anyone's head to confuse the letters of a sentence would be to write the words vertically instead of horizontally."

"Indeed!" said I.

"Now we must see what would be the effect of that, Axel; put down upon this paper any sentence you like, only instead of arranging the letters in the usual way, one after the other, place them in succession in vertical columns, so as to group them together in five or six vertical lines."

I caught his meaning, and immediately produced the following literary wonder:

```
I     y     l     o     a     u
l     o     l     w     r     b
o     u     ,     n     G     e
v     w     m     d     r     n
e     e     y     e     a     !
```

"Good," said the professor, without reading them, "now set down those words in a horizontal line."

I obeyed, and with this result:

Iyloau lolwrb ou,nGe vwmdrn
eeyea!

"Excellent!" said my uncle, taking the paper hastily out of my hands. "This begins to look just like an ancient document: the vowels and the consonants are grouped together in equal disorder; there are even capitals in the middle of words, and commas too, just as in Saknussemm's parchment."

I considered these remarks very clever.

"Now," said my uncle, looking straight at me, "to read the sentence which you have just written, and with which I am wholly unacquainted, I shall only have to take the first letter of each word, then the second, the third, and so forth."

And my uncle, to his great astonishment, and my much greater, read:

"I love you well, my own dear Gräuben!"

"Hallo!" cried the professor.

Yes, indeed, without knowing what I was about, like an awkward and unlucky lover, I had compromised myself by writing this unfortunate sentence.

"Aha! You are in love with Gräuben?" he said, with the right look for a guardian.

"Yes; no!" I stammered.

"You love Gräuben," he went on once or twice dreamily. "Well, let us apply the process I have suggested to the document in question."

My uncle, falling back into his absorbing contemplations, had already forgotten my imprudent words. I merely say imprudent, for the great mind of so learned a man of course had no place for love affairs, and happily the grand business of the document gained me the victory.

Just as the moment of the supreme experiment arrived the professor's eyes flashed right through his spectacles. There was a quivering in his fingers as he grasped the old parchment. He was deeply moved. At last he gave a preliminary cough, and with profound gravity, naming in succession the first, then the second letter of each word, he dictated me the following:

```
mmessvnkaSenrA.icefdoK.segnittamvrtn
ecertserrette,rotaisadva,ednecsedsadne
lacartniiiilvIsiratracSarbmvtabiledmek
meretarcsilvcoIsleffenSnI.
```

I confess I felt considerably excited in coming to the end; these letters named, one at a time, had carried no sense to my mind; I therefore waited for the professor with great pomp to unfold the magnificent but hidden Latin of this mysterious phrase.

But who could have foretold the result? A violent thump made the furniture rattle, and spilled some ink, and my pen dropped from between my fingers.

"That's not it," cried my uncle, "there's no sense in it."

Then darting out like a shot, bowling downstairs like an avalanche, he rushed into the Königstrasse and fled.

## CHAPTER IV

## THE ENEMY TO BE STARVED INTO SUBMISSION

"He is gone!" cried Martha, running out of her kitchen at the noise of the violent slamming of doors.

"Yes," I replied, "completely gone."

"Well; and how about his dinner?" said the old servant.

"He won't have any."

"And his supper?"

"He won't have any."

"What?" cried Martha, with clasped hands.

"No, my dear Martha, he will eat no more. No one in the house is to eat anything at all. Uncle Liedenbrock is going to make us all fast until he has succeeded in deciphering an undecipherable scrawl."

"Oh, my dear! Must we then all die of hunger?"

I hardly dared to confess that, with so absolute a ruler as my uncle, this fate was inevitable.

The old servant, visibly moved, returned to the kitchen, moaning piteously.

When I was alone, I thought I would go and tell Gräuben all about it. But how should I be able to escape from the house? The professor might return at any moment. And suppose he called me? And suppose he tackled me again with this logomachy, which might vainly have been set before ancient Oedipus. And if I did not obey his call, who could answer for what might happen?

The wisest course was to remain where I was. A mineralogist at Besançon had just sent us a collection of siliceous nodules, which I had to classify: so I set to work; I sorted, labeled, and arranged in their own glass case all these hollow specimens, in the cavity of each of which was a nest of little crystals.

But this work did not succeed in absorbing all my attention. That old document kept working in my brain. My head throbbed with excitement, and I felt an undefined uneasiness. I was possessed with a presentiment of coming evil.

In an hour my nodules were all arranged upon successive shelves. Then I dropped down into the old velvet armchair, my head thrown back and my hands joined over it. I lighted my long crooked pipe, with a painting on it of an idle-looking naiad; then I amused myself watching the process of the conversion of the tobacco into carbon, which was by slow degrees making my naiad into a negress. Now and then I listened to hear whether a well-known step was on the stairs. No. Where could my uncle be at that moment? I fancied him running under the noble trees which line the road to Altona, gesticulating, making shots with his cane, thrashing the long grass, cutting the heads off the thistles, and disturbing the contemplative storks in their peaceful solitude.

Would he return in triumph or in discouragement? Which would get the upper hand, he or the secret? I was thus asking myself questions, and mechanically taking between my fingers the sheet of paper mysteriously disfigured with the incomprehensible succession of letters I had written down; and I repeated to myself, "What does it all mean?"

I sought to group the letters so as to form words. Quite impossible! When I put them together by twos, threes, fives, or sixes, nothing came of it but nonsense. To be sure the fourteenth, fifteenth, and sixteenth letters made the English word "ice"; the eighty-third and two following made "sir"; and in the midst of the document, in the second and third lines, I observed the words "rots," "mutabile," "ira," "net," "atra."

"Come now," I thought, "these words seem to justify my uncle's view about the language of the document." In the fourth line appeared the word "luco," which means a sacred wood. It is true that in the third line was the word "tabiled," which looked like Hebrew, and in the last the purely French words "mer," "arc," "mère."

All this was enough to drive a poor fellow crazy. Four different languages in this ridiculous sentence! What connection could there possibly be between such words as ice, sir, anger, cruel, sacred wood, changeable, mother, bow, and sea? The first and the last might have something to do with each other; it was not at all surprising that in a document written in Iceland there should be mention of a sea of ice; but it was quite another thing to get to the end of this cryptogram with so small a clue. So I was struggling with an insurmountable difficulty; my brain got heated, my eyes watered over that sheet of paper; its hundred and thirty-two letters seemed to flutter and fly around me like those motes of mingled light and darkness which float in the air around the head when the blood is rushing upward with undue violence. I was a prey to a kind of hallucination; I was stifling; I wanted air. Unconsciously I fanned myself with the bit of paper, the back and front of which successively came before my eyes. What was my surprise when, in one of those rapid revolutions, at the moment when the back was turned to me I thought I caught sight of the Latin words "craterem," "terrestre," and others.

A sudden light burst in upon me; these hints alone gave me the first glimpse of the truth; I had discovered the key to the cipher. To read the document, it would not even be necessary to read it through the paper. Such as it was, just such as it had been dictated to me, so it might be spelled out with ease. All those ingenious professorial combinations were coming right. He was right as to the arrangement of the letters; he was right as to the language. He had been within a hair's breadth of reading this Latin document from end to end; but that hair's breadth, chance had given it to me!

You may be sure I felt stirred up. My eyes were dim, I could scarcely see. I had laid the paper upon the table. At a glance I could tell the whole secret.

At last I became more calm. I made a wise resolve to walk twice round the room quietly and settle my nerves, and then I returned into the deep gulf of the huge armchair.

"Now I'll read it," I cried, after having well distended my lungs with air.

I leaned over the table; I laid my finger successively upon every letter; and without a pause, without one moment's hesitation, I read off the whole sentence aloud.

Stupefaction! Terror! I sat overwhelmed as if with a sudden deadly blow. What! That which I read had actually, really been done! A mortal man had had the audacity to penetrate! . . .

"Ah!" I cried, springing up. "But no! No! My uncle shall never know it. He would insist upon doing it too. He would want to know all about it. Ropes could not hold him, such a determined geologist as he is! He would start, he would, in spite of everything and everybody, and he would take me with him, and we should never get back. No, never! Never!"

My overexcitement was beyond all description.

"No! No! It shall not be," I declared energetically; "and as it is in my power to prevent the knowledge of it coming into the mind of my tyrant, I will do it. By dint of turning this document round and round, he too might discover the key. I will destroy it."

There was a little fire left on the hearth. I seized not only the paper but Saknussemm's parchment; with a feverish hand I was about to fling it all upon the coals and utterly destroy and abolish this dangerous secret, when the study door opened, and my uncle appeared.

## *CHAPTER V*

## FAMINE, THEN VICTORY, FOLLOWED BY DISMAY

I had only just time to replace the unfortunate document upon the table.
Professor Liedenbrock seemed to be greatly abstracted.

The ruling thought gave him no rest. Evidently he had gone deeply into the matter, analytically and with profound scrutiny. He had brought all the resources of his mind to bear upon it during his walk, and he had come back to apply some new combination.

He sat in his armchair, and pen in hand he began what looked very much like algebraic formula: I followed with my eyes his trembling hands, I took count of every movement. Might not some unhoped-for result come of it? I trembled, too, very unnecessarily, since the true key was in my hands, and no other would open the secret.

For three long hours my uncle worked on without a word, without lifting his head; rubbing out, beginning again, then rubbing out again, and so on a hundred times.

I knew very well that if he succeeded in setting down these letters in every possible relative position, the sentence would come out. But I knew also that twenty letters alone could form two quintillions, four hundred and thirty-two quadrillions, nine hundred and two trillions, eight billions, a hundred and seventy-six millions, six hundred and forty thousand combinations. Now, here were a hundred and thirty-two letters in this sentence, and these hundred and thirty-two letters would give a number of different sentences, each made up of at least a hundred and thirty-three figures, a number which passed far beyond all calculation or conception.

So I felt reassured as far as regarded this heroic method of solving the difficulty.

But time was passing away; night came on; the street noises ceased; my uncle, bending over his task, noticed nothing, not even Martha half opening the door; he heard not a sound, not even that excellent woman saying:

"Will not monsieur take any supper tonight?"

And poor Martha had to go away unanswered. As for me, after long resistance, I was overcome by sleep, and fell off at the end of the sofa, while uncle Liedenbrock went on calculating and rubbing out his calculations.

When I awoke next morning that indefatigable worker was still at his post. His red eyes, his pale complexion, his hair tangled between his feverish fingers, the red spots on his cheeks, revealed his desperate struggle with impossibilities, and the weariness of spirit, the mental wrestlings he must have undergone all through that unhappy night.

To tell the plain truth, I pitied him. In spite of the reproaches which I considered I had a right to lay upon him, a certain feeling of compassion was beginning to gain upon me. The poor man was so entirely taken up with his one idea that he had even forgotten how to get angry. All the strength of his feelings was concentrated upon one point alone; and as their usual vent was closed, it was to be feared lest extreme tension should give rise to an explosion sooner or later.

I might with a word have loosened the screw of the steel vice that was crushing his brain; but that word I would not speak.

Yet I was not an ill-natured fellow. Why was I dumb at such a crisis? Why so insensible to my uncle's interests?

"No, no," I repeated, "I shall not speak. He would insist upon going; nothing on earth could stop him. His imagination is a volcano, and to do that which other geologists have never done he would risk his life. I will preserve silence. I will keep the secret which mere chance has revealed to me. To discover it, would be to kill Professor Liedenbrock! Let him find it out himself if he can. I will never have it laid to my door that I led him to his destruction."

Having formed this resolution, I folded my arms and waited. But I had not reckoned upon one little incident which turned up a few hours after.

When our good Martha wanted to go to Market, she found the door locked. The big key was gone. Who could have taken it out? Assuredly, it was my uncle, when he returned the night before from his hurried walk.

Was this done on purpose? Or was it a mistake? Did he want to reduce us by famine? This seemed like going rather too far! What! should Martha and I be victims of a position of things in which we had not the smallest interest? It was a fact that a few years before this, while my uncle was working at his great classification of minerals, he was forty-eight hours without eating, and all his household were obliged to share in this scientific fast. As for me, what I remember is, that I got severe cramps in my stomach, which hardly suited the constitution of a hungry, growing lad.

Now it appeared to me as if breakfast was going to be wanting, just as supper had been the night before. Yet I resolved to be a hero, and not to be conquered by the pangs of hunger. Martha took it very seriously, and, poor woman, was very much distressed. As for me, the impossibility of leaving the house distressed me a good deal more, and for a very good reason. A caged lover's feelings may easily be imagined.

My uncle went on working, his imagination went off rambling into the ideal world of combinations; he was far away from earth, and really far away from earthly wants.

About noon hunger began to stimulate me severely. Martha had, without thinking any harm, cleared out the larder the night before, so that now there was nothing left in the house. Still I held out; I made it a point of honor.

Two o'clock struck. This was becoming ridiculous; worse than that, unbearable. I began to say to myself that I was exaggerating the importance of the document; that my uncle would surely not believe in it, that he would set it down as a mere puzzle; that if it came to the worst, we should lay violent hands on him and keep him at home if he thought on venturing on the expedition; that, after all, he might himself discover the key of the cipher, and that then I should be clear at the mere expense of my involuntary abstinence.

These reasons seemed excellent to me, though on the night before I should have rejected them with indignation; I even went so far as to condemn myself for my absurdity in having waited so long, and I finally resolved to let it all out.

I was therefore meditating a proper introduction to the matter, so as not to seem too abrupt, when the professor jumped up, clapped on his hat, and prepared to go out.

Surely he was not going out, to shut us in again! No, never!

"Uncle!" I cried.

He seemed not to hear me.

"Uncle Liedenbrock!" I cried, lifting up my voice.

"Ay," he answered like a man suddenly waking.

"Uncle, that key!"

"What key? The door key?"

"No, no!" I cried. "The key of the document."

The professor stared at me over his spectacles; no doubt he saw something unusual in the expression of my countenance; for he laid hold of my arm, and speechlessly questioned me with his eyes. Yes, never was a question more forcibly put.

I nodded my head up and down.

He shook his pityingly, as if he was dealing with a lunatic. I gave a more affirmative gesture.

His eyes glistened and sparkled with live fire, his hand was shaken threateningly.

This mute conversation at such a momentous crisis would have riveted the attention of the most indifferent. And the fact really was that I dared not speak now, so intense was the excitement for fear lest my uncle should smother me in his first joyful embraces. But he became so urgent that I was at last compelled to answer.

"Yes, that key, chance—"

"What is that you are saying?" he shouted with indescribable emotion.

"There, read that!" I said, presenting a sheet of paper on which I had written.

"But there is nothing in this," he answered, crumpling up the paper.

"No, nothing until you proceed to read from the end to the beginning."

I had not finished my sentence when the professor broke out into a cry, nay, a roar. A new revelation burst in upon him. He was transformed!

"Aha, clever Saknussemm!" he cried. "You had first written out your sentence the wrong way."

And darting upon the paper, with eyes bedimmed, and voice choked with emotion, he read the whole document from the last letter to the first.

It was conceived in the following terms:

> In Sneffels Joculis craterem quem delibat
> Umbra Scartaris Julii intra calendas descende,
> Audax viator, et terrestre centrum attinges.
> Quod feci, Arne Saknussemm.

Which bad Latin may be translated thus:

"Descend, bold traveler, into the crater of the jokul of Sneffels, which the shadow of Scartaris touches before the kalends of July, and you will attain the center of the earth; which I have done, Arne Saknussemm."

In reading this, my uncle gave a spring as if he had touched a Leyden jar. His audacity, his joy, and his convictions were magnificent to behold. He came and he went; he seized his head between both his hands; he pushed the chairs out of their places, he piled up his books; incredible as it may seem, he rattled his precious nodules of flints together; he sent a kick here, a thump there. At last his nerves calmed down, and like a man exhausted by too lavish an expenditure of vital power, he sank back exhausted into his armchair.

"What o'clock is it?" he asked after a few moments of silence.

"Three o'clock," I replied.

"Is it really? The dinner hour is past, and I did not know it. I am half dead with hunger. Come on, and after dinner—"

"Well?"

"After dinner, pack up my trunk."

"What?" I cried.

"And yours!" replied the indefatigable professor, entering the dining room.

## CHAPTER VI

## EXCITING DISCUSSIONS ABOUT AN
## UNPARALLELED ENTERPRISE

At these words a cold shiver ran through me. Yet I controlled myself; I even resolved to put a good face upon it. Scientific arguments alone could have any weight with Professor Liedenbrock. Now there were good ones against the practicability of such a journey. Penetrate to the center of the earth! What nonsense! But I kept my dialectic battery in reserve for a suitable opportunity, and I interested myself in the prospect of my dinner, which was not yet forthcoming.

It is no use to tell of the rage and imprecations of my uncle before the empty table. Explanations were given, Martha was set at liberty, ran off to the market, and did her part so well that in an hour afterward my hunger was appeased, and I was able to return to the contemplation of the gravity of the situation.

During all dinner time my uncle was almost merry; he indulged in some of those learned jokes which never do anybody any harm. Dessert over, he beckoned me into his study.

I obeyed; he sat at one end of his table, I at the other.

"Axel," said he very mildly; "you are a very ingenious young man, you have done me a splendid service, at a moment when, wearied out with the struggle, I was going to abandon the contest. Where should I have lost myself? None can tell. Never, my lad, shall I forget it; and you shall have your share in the glory to which your discovery will lead."

"Oh, come!" thought I. "He is in a good way. Now is the time for discussing that same glory."

"Before all things," my uncle resumed, "I enjoin you to preserve the most inviolable secrecy: you understand? There are not a few in the scientific world who envy my success, and many would be ready to undertake this enterprise, to whom our return should be the first news of it."

"Do you really think there are many people bold enough?" said I.

"Certainly; who would hesitate to acquire such renown? If that document were divulged, a whole army of geologists would be ready to rush into the footsteps of Arne Saknussemm."

"I don't feel so very sure of that, uncle," I replied; "for we have no proof of the authenticity of this document."

"What! Not of the book, inside which we have discovered it?"

"Granted. I admit that Saknussemm may have written these lines. But does it follow that he has really accomplished such a journey? And may it not be that this old parchment is intended to mislead?"

I almost regretted having uttered this last word, which dropped from me in an unguarded moment. The professor bent his shaggy brows, and I feared I had seriously compromised my own safety. Happily no great harm came of it. A smile flitted across the lip of my severe companion, and he answered:

"That is what we shall see."

"Ah!" said I, rather put out. "But do let me exhaust all the possible objections against this document."

"Speak, my boy, don't be afraid. You are quite at liberty to express your opinions. You are no longer my nephew only, but my colleague. Pray go on."

"Well, in the first place, I wish to ask what are this Jokul, this Sneffels, and this Scartaris, names which I have never heard before?"

"Nothing easier. I received not long ago a map from my friend, Augustus Petermann, at Liepzig. Nothing could be more apropos. Take down the third atlas in the second shelf in the large bookcase, series Z, plate 4."

I rose, and with the help of such precise instructions could not fail to find the required atlas. My uncle opened it and said:

"Here is one of the best maps of Iceland, that of Handersen, and I believe this will solve the worst of our difficulties."

I bent over the map.

"You see this volcanic island," said the professor; "observe that all the volcanoes are called jokuls, a word which means glacier in Icelandic, and under the high latitude of Iceland nearly all the active volcanoes discharge through beds of ice. Hence this term of jokul is applied to all the eruptive mountains in Iceland."

"Very good," said I; "but what of Sneffels?"

I was hoping that this question would be unanswerable; but I was mistaken. My uncle replied:

"Follow my finger along the west coast of Iceland. Do you see Reykjavik, the capital? You do. Well; ascend the innumerable fjords that indent those sea-beaten shores, and stop at the sixty-fifth degree of latitude. What do you see there?"

"I see a peninsula looking like a thigh bone with the knee bone at the end of it."

"A very fair comparison, my lad. Now do you see anything upon that knee bone?"

"Yes; a mountain rising out of the sea."

"Right. That is Snæfell."

"That Snæfell?"

"It is. It is a mountain five thousand feet high, one of the most remarkable in the world, if its crater leads down to the center of the earth."

"But that is impossible," I said shrugging my shoulders, and disgusted at such a ridiculous supposition.

"Impossible?" said the professor severely. "And why, pray?"

"Because this crater is evidently filled with lava and burning rocks, and therefore—"

"But suppose it is an extinct volcano?"

"Extinct?"

"Yes; the number of active volcanoes on the surface of the globe is at the present time only about three hundred. But there is a very much larger number of extinct ones. Now, Snæfell is one of these. Since historic times there has been but one eruption of this mountain, that of 1219; from that time it has quieted down more and more, and now it is no longer reckoned among active volcanoes."

To such positive statements I could make no reply. I therefore took refuge in other dark passages of the document.

"What is the meaning of this word Scartaris, and what have the kalends of July to do with it?"

My uncle took a few minutes to consider. For one short moment I felt a ray of hope, speedily to be extinguished. For he soon answered thus:

"What is darkness to you is light to me. This proves the ingenious care with which Saknussemm guarded and defined his discovery. Sneffels, or Snæfell, has several craters. It was therefore necessary to point out which of these leads to the center of the globe. What did the Icelandic sage do? He observed that at the approach of the kalends of July, that is to say in the last days of June, one of the peaks, called Scartaris, flung its shadow down the mouth of that particular crater, and he committed that fact to his document. Could there possibly have been a more exact guide? As soon as we have arrived at the summit of Snæfell we shall have no hesitation as to the proper road to take."

Decidedly, my uncle had answered every one of my objections. I saw that his position on the old parchment was impregnable. I therefore ceased to press him upon that part of the subject, and as above all things he must be convinced, I passed on to scientific objections, which in my opinion were far more serious.

"Well, then," I said, "I am forced to admit that Saknussemm's sentence is clear, and leaves no room for doubt. I will even allow that the document bears every mark and evidence of authenticity. That learned philosopher did get to the bottom of Sneffels, he has seen the shadow of Scartaris touch the edge of the crater before the kalends of July; he may even have heard the legendary stories told in his day about that crater reaching to the center of the world; but as for reaching it himself, as for performing the journey, and returning, if he ever went, I say no—he never, never did that."

"Now for your reason?" said my uncle ironically.

"All the theories of science demonstrate such a feat to be impracticable."

"The theories say that, do they?" replied the professor in the tone of a meek disciple. "Oh! Unpleasant theories! How the theories will hinder us, won't they?"

I saw that he was only laughing at me; but I went on all the same.

"Yes; it is perfectly well known that the internal temperature rises one degree for every 70 feet in depth; now, admitting this proportion to be constant, and the radius of the earth being fifteen hundred leagues, there must be a temperature of 360,032 degrees at the center of the earth. Therefore, all the substances that compose the body of this earth must exist there in a state of incandescent gas; for the metals that most resist the action of heat, gold, and platinum, and the hardest rocks, can never be either solid or liquid under such a temperature. I have therefore good reason for asking if it is possible to penetrate through such a medium."

"So, Axel, it is the heat that troubles you?"

"Of course it is. Were we to reach a depth of thirty miles we should have arrived at the limit of the terrestrial crust, for there the temperature will be more than 2,372 degrees."

"Are you afraid of being put into a state of fusion?"

"I will leave you to decide that question," I answered rather sullenly. "This is my decision," replied Professor Liedenbrock, putting on one of his grandest airs. "Neither you nor anybody else knows with any certainty what is going on in the interior of this globe, since not the twelve thousandth part of its radius is known; science is eminently perfectible; and every new theory is soon routed by a newer. Was it not always believed until Fourier that the temperature of the interplanetary spaces decreased perpetually? And is it not known at the present time that the greatest cold of the ethereal regions is never lower than 40 degrees below zero Fahrenheit? Why should it not be the same with the internal heat? Why should it not, at a certain depth, attain an impassable limit, instead of rising to such a point as to fuse the most infusible metals?"

As my uncle was now taking his stand upon hypotheses, of course, there was nothing to be said.

"Well, I will tell you that true savants, among them Poisson, have demonstrated that if a heat of 360,000 degrees existed in the interior of the globe, the fiery gases arising from the fused matter would acquire an elastic force which the crust of the earth would be unable to resist, and that it would explode like the plates of a bursting boiler."

"That is Poisson's opinion, my uncle, nothing more."

"Granted. But it is likewise the creed adopted by other distinguished geologists, that the interior of the globe is neither gas nor water, nor any of the heaviest minerals known, for in none of these cases would the earth weigh what it does."

"Oh, with figures you may prove anything!"

"But is it the same with facts! Is it not known that the number of volcanoes has diminished since the first days of creation? And if there is central heat may we not thence conclude that it is in process of diminution?"

"My good uncle, if you will enter into the legion of speculation, I can discuss the matter no longer."

"But I have to tell you that the highest names have come to the support of my views. Do you remember a visit paid to me by the celebrated chemist Humphry Davy in 1825?"

"Not at all, for I was not born until nineteen years afterward."

"Well, Humphry Davy did call upon me on his way through Hamburg. We were long engaged in discussing, among other problems, the hypothesis of the liquid structure of the terrestrial nucleus. We were agreed that it could not be in a liquid state, for a reason which science has never been able to confute."

"What is that reason?" I said, rather astonished.

"Because this liquid mass would be subject, like the ocean, to the lunar attraction, and therefore twice every day there would be internal tides, which, upheaving the terrestrial crust, would cause periodical earthquakes!"

"Yet it is evident that the surface of the globe has been subject to the action of fire," I replied, "and it is quite reasonable to suppose that the external crust cooled down first, while the heat took refuge down to the center."

"Quite a mistake," my uncle answered. "The earth has been heated by combustion on its surface, that is all. Its surface was composed of a great number of metals, such as potassium and sodium, which have the peculiar property of igniting at the mere contact with air and water; these metals kindled when the atmospheric vapors fell in rain upon the soil; and by and by, when the waters penetrated into the fissures of the crust of the earth, they broke out into fresh combustion with explosions and eruptions. Such was the cause of the numerous volcanoes at the origin of the earth."

"Upon my word, this is a very clever hypothesis," I exclaimed, in spite rather of myself.

"And which Humphry Davy demonstrated to me by a simple experiment. He formed a small ball of the metals which I have named, and which was a very fair representation of our globe; whenever he caused a fine dew of rain to fall upon its surface, it heaved up into little monticules, it became oxidized and formed miniature mountains; a crater broke open at one of its summits; the eruption took place, and communicated to the whole of the ball such a heat that it could not be held in the hand."

In truth, I was beginning to be shaken by the professor's arguments, besides which he gave additional weight to them by his usual ardor and fervent enthusiasm.

"You see, Axel," he added, "the condition of the terrestrial nucleus has given rise to various hypotheses among geologists; there is no proof at all for this internal heat; my opinion is that there is no such thing, it cannot be; besides we shall see for ourselves, and, like Arne Saknussemm, we shall know exactly what to hold as truth concerning this grand question."

"Very well, we *shall* see," I replied, feeling myself carried off by his contagious enthusiasm. "Yes, we shall see; that is, if it is possible to see anything there."

"And why not? May we not depend upon electric phenomena to give us light? May we not even expect light from the atmosphere, the pressure of which may render it luminous as we approach the center?"

"Yes, yes," said I; "that is possible, too."

"It is certain," exclaimed my uncle in a tone of triumph. "But silence, do you hear me? Silence upon the whole subject; and let no one get before us in this design of discovering the center of the earth."

# CHAPTER VII

## A WOMAN'S COURAGE

Thus ended this memorable séance. That conversation threw me into a fever. I came out of my uncle's study as if I had been stunned, and as if there was not air enough in all the streets of Hamburg to put me right again. I therefore made for the banks of the Elbe, where the steamer lands her passengers, which forms the communication between the city and the Hamburg railway.

Was I convinced of the truth of what I had heard? Had I not bent under the iron rule of Professor Liedenbrock? Was I to believe him in earnest in his intention to penetrate to the center of this massive globe? Had I been listening to the mad speculations of a lunatic, or to the scientific conclusions of a lofty genius? Where did truth stop? Where did error begin?

I was all adrift among a thousand contradictory hypotheses, but I could not lay hold of one.

Yet I remembered that I had been convinced, although now my enthusiasm was beginning to cool down; but I felt a desire to start at once, and not to lose time and courage by calm reflection. I had at that moment quite courage enough to strap my knapsack to my shoulders and start.

But I must confess that in another hour this unnatural excitement abated, my nerves became unstrung, and from the depths of the abysses of this earth I ascended to its surface again.

"It is quite absurd!" I cried. "There is no sense about it. No sensible young man should for a moment entertain such a proposal. The whole thing is nonexistent. I have had a bad night, I have been dreaming of horrors."

But I had followed the banks of the Elbe and passed the town. After passing the port too, I had reached the Altona road. I was led by a presentiment, soon to be realized; for shortly I espied my little Gräuben bravely returning with her light step to Hamburg.

"Gräuben!" I cried from afar off.

The young girl stopped, rather frightened perhaps to hear her name called after her on the high road. Ten yards more, and I had joined her.

"Axel!" she cried surprised. "What! Have you come to meet me? Is this why you are here, sir?"

But when she had looked upon me, Gräuben could not fail to see the uneasiness and distress of my mind.

"What is the matter?" she said, holding out her hand.

"What is the matter, Gräuben?" I cried.

In a couple of minutes my pretty Virlandaise was fully informed of the position of affairs. For a time she was silent. Did her heart palpitate as mine did? I don't know about that, but I know that her hand did not tremble in mine. We went on a hundred yards without speaking.

At last she said, "Axel!"

"My dear Gräuben."

"That will be a splendid journey!"

I gave a bound at these words.

"Yes, Axel, a journey worthy of the nephew of a savant; it is a good thing for a man to be distinguished by some great enterprise."

"What, Gräuben, won't you dissuade me from such an undertaking?"

"No, my dear Axel, and I would willingly go with you, but that a poor girl would only be in your way."

"Is that quite true?"

"It is true."

Ah! Women and young girls, how incomprehensible are your feminine hearts! When you are not the timidest, you are the bravest of creatures. Reason has nothing to do with your actions. What! Did this child encourage me in such an expedition! Would she not be afraid to join it herself? And she was driving me to it, one whom she loved!

I was disconcerted, and, if I must tell the whole truth, I was ashamed.

"Gräuben, we will see whether you will say the same thing tomorrow."

"Tomorrow, dear Axel, I will say what I say today."

Gräuben and I, hand in hand, but in silence, pursued our way. The emotions of that day were breaking my heart.

After all, I thought, the kalends of July are a long way off, and between this and then many things may take place which will cure my uncle of his desire to travel underground.

It was night when we arrived at the house in Königstrasse. I expected to find all quiet there, my uncle in bed as was his custom, and Martha giving her last touches with the feather brush.

But I had not taken into account the professor's impatience. I found him shouting— and working himself up amid a crowd of porters and messengers who were all depositing various loads in the passage. Our old servant was at her wits' end.

"Come, Axel, come, you miserable wretch," my uncle cried from as far off as he could see me. "Your boxes are not packed, and my papers are not arranged; where's the key of my carpet bag? And what have you done with my gaiters?"

I stood thunderstruck. My voice failed. Scarcely could my lips utter the words:

"Are we really going?"

"Of course, you unhappy boy! Could I have dreamed that you would have gone out for a walk instead of hurrying your preparations forward?"

"Are we to go?" I asked again, with sinking hopes.

"Yes; the day after tomorrow, early."

I could hear no more. I fled for refuge into my own little room.

All hope was now at an end. My uncle had been all the morning making purchases of a part of the tools and apparatus required for this desperate undertaking. The passage was encumbered with rope ladders, knotted cords, torches, flasks, grappling irons, alpenstocks, pickaxes, iron shod sticks, enough to load ten men.

I spent an awful night. Next morning I was called early. I had quite decided I would not open the door. But how was I to resist the sweet voice which was always music to my ears, saying, "My dear Axel?"

I came out of my room. I thought my pale countenance and my red and sleepless eyes would work upon Gräuben's sympathies and change her mind.

"Ah! My dear Axel," she said. "I see you are better. A night's rest has done you good."

"Done me good!" I exclaimed.

I rushed to the glass. Well, in fact I did look better than I had expected. I could hardly believe my own eyes.

"Axel," she said, "I have had a long talk with my guardian. He is a bold philosopher, a man of immense courage, and you must remember that his blood flows in your veins. He has confided to me his plans, his hopes, and why and how he hopes to attain his object. He will no doubt succeed. My dear Axel, it is a grand thing to devote yourself to science! What honor will fall upon Herr Liedenbrock, and so be reflected upon his companion! When you return, Axel, you will be a man, his equal, free to speak and to act independently, and free to—"

The dear girl only finished this sentence by blushing. Her words revived me. Yet I refused to believe we should start. I drew Gräuben into the professor's study.

"Uncle, is it true that we are to go?"

"Why do you doubt?"

"Well, I don't doubt," I said, not to vex him; "but, I ask, what need is there to hurry?"

"Time, time, flying with irreparable rapidity."

"But it is only the 16th May, and until the end of June—"

"What, you monument of ignorance! Do you think you can get to Iceland in a couple of days? If you had not deserted me like a fool I should have taken you to the Copenhagen office, to Liffender & Co., and you would have learned then that there is only one trip every month from Copenhagen to Reykjavik, on the 22nd."

"Well?"

"Well, if we waited for the 22nd June we should be too late to see the shadow of Scartaris touch the crater of Sneffels. Therefore we must get to Copenhagen as fast as we can to secure our passage. Go and pack up."

There was no reply to this. I went up to my room. Gräuben followed me. She undertook to pack up all things necessary for my voyage. She was no more moved than if I had been starting for a little trip to Lübeck or Heligoland. Her little hands moved without haste. She talked quietly. She supplied me with sensible reasons for our expedition. She delighted me, and yet I was angry with her. Now and then I felt I ought to break out into a passion, but she took no notice and went on her way as methodically as ever.

Finally the last strap was buckled; I came downstairs. All that day the philosophical instrument makers and the electricians kept coming and going. Martha was distracted.

"Is master mad?" she asked.

I nodded my head.

"And is he going to take you with him?"

I nodded again.

"Where to?"

I pointed with my finger downward.

"Down into the cellar?" cried the old servant.

"No," I said. "Lower down than that."

Night came. But I knew nothing about the lapse of time.

"Tomorrow morning at six precisely," my uncle decreed, "we start."

At ten o'clock I fell upon my bed, a dead lump of inert matter. All through the night terror had hold of me. I spent it dreaming of abysses. I was a prey to delirium. I felt myself grasped by the professor's sinewy hand, dragged along, hurled down, shattered into little bits. I dropped down unfathomable precipices with the accelerating velocity of bodies falling through space. My life had become an endless fall. I awoke at five with shattered nerves, trembling and weary. I came downstairs. My uncle was at table, devouring his breakfast. I stared at him with horror and disgust. But dear Gräuben was there; so I said nothing, and could eat nothing.

At half-past five there was a rattle of wheels outside. A large carriage was there to take us to the Altona railway station. It was soon piled up with my uncle's multifarious preparations.

"Where's your box?" he cried.

"It is ready," I replied, with faltering voice.

"Then make haste down, or we shall lose the train."

It was now manifestly impossible to maintain the struggle against destiny. I went up again to my room, and rolling my portmanteaus downstairs I darted after him.

At that moment my uncle was solemnly investing Gräuben with the reins of government. My pretty Virlandaise was as calm and collected as was her wont. She kissed her guardian; but could not restrain a tear in touching my cheek with her gentle lips.

"Gräuben!" I murmured.

"Go, my dear Axel, go! I am now your betrothed; and when you come back I will be your wife."

I pressed her in my arms and took my place in the carriage. Martha and the young girl, standing at the door, waved their last farewell. Then the horses, roused by the driver's whistling, darted off at a gallop on the road to Altona.

## CHAPTER VIII

### SERIOUS PREPARATIONS FOR VERTICAL DESCENT

Altona, which is but a suburb of Hamburg, is the terminus of the Kiel railway, which was to carry us to the Belts. In twenty minutes we were in Holstein.

At half-past six the carriage stopped at the station; my uncle's numerous packages, his voluminous *impedimenta*, were unloaded, removed, labeled, weighed, put into the luggage vans, and at seven we were seated face-to-face in our compartment. The whistle sounded, the engine started, we were off.

Was I resigned? No, not yet. Yet the cool morning air and the scenes on the road, rapidly changed by the swiftness of the train, drew me away somewhat from my sad reflections.

As for the professor's reflections, they went far in advance of the swiftest express. We were alone in the carriage, but we sat in silence. My uncle examined all his pockets and his traveling bag with the minutest care. I saw that he had not forgotten the smallest matter of detail.

Among other documents, a sheet of paper, carefully folded, bore the heading of the Danish consulate with the signature of W. Christiensen, consul at Hamburg and the professor's friend. With this we possessed the proper introductions to the governor of Iceland.

I also observed the famous document most carefully laid up in a secret pocket in his portfolio. I bestowed a malediction upon it, and then proceeded to examine the country.

It was a very long succession of uninteresting loamy and fertile flats, a very easy country for the construction of railways, and propitious for the laying-down of these direct level lines so dear to railway companies.

I had no time to get tired of the monotony; for in three hours we stopped at Kiel, close to the sea.

The luggage being labeled for Copenhagen, we had no occasion to look after it. Yet the professor watched every article with jealous vigilance, until all were safe on board. There they disappeared in the hold.

My uncle, notwithstanding his hurry, had so well calculated the relations between the train and the steamer that we had a whole day to spare. The steamer *Ellenora* did not start until night. Thence sprang a feverish state of excitement in which the impatient irascible traveler devoted to perdition the railway directors and the steamboat companies and the governments which allowed such intolerable slowness. I was obliged to act chorus to him when he attacked the captain of the *Ellenora* upon this subject. The captain disposed of us summarily.

At Kiel, as elsewhere, we must do something to while away the time. What with walking on the verdant shores of the bay within which nestles the little town, exploring the thick woods which make it look like a nest embowered among thick foliage, admiring the villas, each provided with a little bathing house, and moving about and grumbling, at last ten o'clock came.

The heavy coils of smoke from the *Ellenora*'s funnel unrolled in the sky, the bridge shook with the quivering of the struggling steam; we were on board, and owners for the time of two berths, one over the other, in the only saloon cabin on board.

At a quarter past the moorings were loosed and the throbbing steamer pursued her way over the dark waters of the Great Belt.

The night was dark; there was a sharp breeze and a rough sea, a few lights appeared on shore through the thick darkness; later on, I cannot tell when, a dazzling light from some lighthouse threw a bright stream of fire along the waves; and this is all I can remember of this first portion of our sail.

At seven in the morning we landed at Korsor, a small town on the west coast of Zealand. There we were transferred from the boat to another line of railway, which took us by just as flat a country as the plain of Holstein.

Three hours' traveling brought us to the capital of Denmark. My uncle had not shut his eyes all night. In his impatience I believe he was trying to accelerate the train with his feet.

At last he discerned a stretch of sea.

"The Sound!" he cried.

At our left was a huge building that looked like a hospital.

"That's a lunatic asylum," said one of or traveling companions.

Very good! thought I, just the place we want to end our days in; and great as it is, that asylum is not big enough to contain all Professor Liedenbrock's madness!

At ten in the morning, at last, we set our feet in Copenhagen; the luggage was put upon a carriage and taken with ourselves to the Phoenix Hotel in Breda Gate. This took half an hour, for the station is out of the town. Then my uncle, after a hasty toilet, dragged me after him. The porter at the hotel could speak German and English; but the professor, as a polyglot, questioned him in good Danish, and it was in the same language that that personage directed him to the Museum of Northern Antiquities.

The curator of this curious establishment, in which wonders are gathered together out of which the ancient history of the country might be reconstructed by means of its stone weapons, its cups and its jewels, was a learned savant, the friend of the Danish consul at Hamburg, Professor Thomsen.

My uncle had a cordial letter of introduction to him. As a general rule one savant greets another with coolness. But here the case was different. M. Thomsen, like a good friend, gave Professor Liedenbrock a cordial greeting, and he even vouchsafed the same kindness to his nephew. It is hardly necessary to say the secret was sacredly kept from the excellent curator; we were simply disinterested travelers visiting Iceland out of harmless curiosity.

M. Thomsen placed his services at our disposal, and we visited the quays with the object of finding out the next vessel to sail.

I was yet in hopes that there would be no means of getting to Iceland. But there was no such luck. A small Danish schooner, the *Valkyria*, was to set sail for Reykjavik on the 2nd of June. The captain, M. Bjarne, was on board. His intending passenger was so joyful that he almost squeezed his hands till they ached. That good man was rather surprised at his energy. To him it seemed a very simple thing to go to Iceland, as that was his business; but to my uncle it was sublime. The worthy captain took advantage of his enthusiasm to charge double fares; but we did not trouble ourselves about mere trifles.

"You must be on board on Tuesday, at seven in the morning," said Captain Bjarne, after having pocketed more dollars than were his due.

Then we thanked M. Thomsen for his kindness, and we returned to the Phoenix Hotel.

"It's all right, it's all right," my uncle repeated. "How fortunate we are to have found this boat ready for sailing. Now let us have some breakfast and go about the town."

We went first to Kongens-nye-Torw, an irregular square in which are two innocent-looking guns, which need not alarm anyone. Close by, at No. 5, there was a French "restaurant," kept by a cook of the name of Vincent, where we had an ample breakfast for four marks each (2s. 4d.).

Then I took a childish pleasure in exploring the city; my uncle let me take him with me, but he took notice of nothing, neither the insignificant king's palace, nor the pretty seventeenth-century bridge, which spans the canal before the museum, nor that immense cenotaph of Thorwaldsen's, adorned with horrible mural painting, and containing within it a collection of the sculptor's works, nor in a fine park the toylike chateau of Rosenberg, nor the beautiful renaissance edifice of the Exchange, nor its spire composed of the twisted tails of four bronze dragons, nor the great windmill on the ramparts, whose huge arms dilated in the sea breeze like the sails of a ship.

What delicious walks we should have had together, my pretty Virlandaise and I, along the harbor where the two-deckers and the frigate slept peaceably by the red roofing of the warehouse, by the green banks of the strait, through the deep shades of the trees among which the fort is half concealed, where the guns are thrusting out their black throats between branches of alder and willow.

But, alas! Gräuben was far away; and I never hoped to see her again.

But if my uncle felt no attraction toward these romantic scenes he was very much struck with the aspect of a certain church spire situated in the island of Amak, which forms the southwest quarter of Copenhagen.

I was ordered to direct my feet that way; I embarked on a small steamer which plies on the canals, and in a few minutes she touched the quay of the dockyard.

After crossing a few narrow streets where some convicts, in trousers half yellow and half gray, were at work under the orders of the gangers, we arrived at the Vor Frelsers Kirk. There was nothing remarkable about the church; but there was a reason why its tall spire had attracted the professor's attention. Starting from the top of the tower, an external staircase wound around the spire, the spirals circling up into the sky.

"Let us get to the top," said my uncle.

"I shall be dizzy," I said.

"The more reason why we should go up; we must get used to it."

"But—"

"Come, I tell you; don't waste our time."

I had to obey. A keeper who lived at the other end of the street handed us the key, and the ascent began.

My uncle went ahead with a light step. I followed him not without alarm, for my head was very apt to feel dizzy; I possessed neither the equilibrium of an eagle nor his fearless nature.

As long as we were protected on the inside of the winding staircase up the tower, all was well enough; but after toiling up a hundred and fifty steps the fresh air came to salute my face, and we were on the leads of the tower. There the aerial staircase began its gyrations, only guarded by a thin iron rail, and the narrowing steps seemed to ascend into infinite space!

"Never shall I be able to do it," I said.

"Don't be a coward; come up, sir," said my uncle with the coldest cruelty.

I had to follow, clutching at every step. The keen air made me giddy; I felt the spire rocking with every gust of wind; my knees began to fail; soon I was crawling on my knees, then creeping on my stomach; I closed my eyes; I seemed to be lost in space.

At last I reached the apex, with the assistance of my uncle dragging me up by the collar.

"Look down!" he cried. "Look down well! You must take a lesson in abysses."

I opened my eyes. I saw houses squashed flat as if they had all fallen down from the skies; a smoke fog seemed to drown them. Over my head ragged clouds were drifting past, and by an optical inversion they seemed stationary, while the steeple, the ball, and I were all spinning along with fantastic speed. Far away on one side was the green country, on the other the sea sparkled, bathed in sunlight. The Sound stretched away to Elsinore, dotted with a few white sails, like seagulls' wings; and in the misty east and away to the northeast lay outstretched the faintly shadowed shores of Sweden. All this immensity of space whirled and wavered, fluctuating beneath my eyes.

But I was compelled to rise, to stand up, to look. My first lesson in dizziness lasted an hour. When I got permission to come down and feel the solid street pavements, I was afflicted with severe lumbago.

"Tomorrow we will do it again," said the professor.

And it was so; for five days in succession, I was obliged to undergo this antivertiginous exercise; and whether I would or not, I made some improvement in the art of "lofty contemplations."

## CHAPTER IX

### ICELAND! BUT WHAT NEXT?

The day for our departure arrived. The day before it our kind friend M. Thomsen brought us letters of introduction to Count Trampe, the governor of Iceland, M. Picturssen, the bishop's suffragan, and M. Finsen, mayor of Reykjavik. My uncle expressed his gratitude by tremendous compressions of both his hands.

On the 2nd, at six in the evening, all our precious baggage being safely on board the *Valkyria*, the captain took us into a very narrow cabin.

"Is the wind favorable?" my uncle asked.

"Excellent," replied Captain Bjarne; "a sou'easter. We shall pass down the Sound full speed, with all sails set."

In a few minutes the schooner, under her mizzen, brigantine, topsail, and topgallant sail, loosed from her moorings and made full sail through the straits. In an hour the capital of Denmark seemed to sink below the distant waves, and the *Valkyria* was skirting the coast by Elsinore. In my nervous frame of mind I expected to see the ghost of Hamlet wandering on the legendary castle terrace.

"Sublime madman!" I said. "No doubt you would approve of our expedition. Perhaps you would keep us company to the center of the globe, to find the solution of your eternal doubts."

But there was no ghostly shape upon the ancient walls. Indeed, the castle is much younger than the heroic prince of Denmark. It now answers the purpose of a sumptuous lodge for the doorkeeper of the straits of the Sound, before which every year there pass fifteen thousand ships of all nations.

The castle of Kronsberg soon disappeared in the mist, as well as the tower of Helsingborg, built on the Swedish coast, and the schooner passed lightly on her way urged by the breezes of the Cattegat.

The *Valkyria* was a splendid sailer, but on a sailing vessel you can place no dependence. She was taking to Reykjavik coal, household goods, earthenware, woolen clothing, and a cargo of wheat. The crew consisted of five men, all Danes.

"How long will the passage take?" my uncle asked.

"Ten days," the captain replied, "if we don't meet a nor'wester in passing the Faroes."

"But are you not subject to considerable delays?"

"No, M. Liedenbrock, don't be uneasy, we shall get there in very good time."

At evening the schooner doubled the Skaw at the northern point of Denmark, in the night passed the Skager Rack, skirted Norway by Cape Lindness, and entered the North Sea.

In two days more we sighted the coast of Scotland near Peterhead, and the *Valkyria* turned her lead toward the Faroe Islands, passing between the Orkneys and Shetlands.

Soon the schooner encountered the great Atlantic swell; she had to tack against the north wind, and reached the Faroes only with some difficulty. On the 8th the captain made out Myganness, the southernmost of these islands, and from that moment took a straight course for Cape Portland, the most southerly point of Iceland.

The passage was marked by nothing unusual. I bore the troubles of the sea pretty well; my uncle, to his own intense disgust, and his greater shame, was ill all through the voyage.

He therefore was unable to converse with the captain about Snæfell, the way to get to it, the facilities for transport, he was obliged to put off these inquiries until his arrival, and spent all his time at full length in his cabin, of which the timbers creaked and shook with every pitch she took. It must be confessed he was not undeserving of his punishment.

On the 11th we reached Cape Portland. The clear open weather gave us a good view of Myrdals jokul, which overhangs it. The cape is merely a low hill with steep sides, standing lonely by the beach.

The *Valkyria* kept at some distance from the coast, taking a westerly course amid great shoals of whales and sharks. Soon we came in sight of an enormous perforated rock, through which the sea dashed furiously. The Westman islets seemed to rise out of the ocean like a group of rocks in a liquid plain. From that time the schooner took a wide berth and swept at a great distance round Cape Rejkianess, which forms the western point of Iceland.

The rough sea prevented my uncle from coming on deck to admire these shattered and surf-beaten coasts.

Forty-eight hours after, coming out of a storm which forced the schooner to scud under bare poles, we sighted east of us the beacon on Cape Skagen, where dangerous rocks extend far away seaward. An Icelandic pilot came on board, and in three hours the *Valkyria* dropped her anchor before Reykjavik, in Faxa Bay.

The professor at last emerged from his cabin, rather pale and wretched-looking, but still full of enthusiasm, and with ardent satisfaction shining in his eyes.

The population of the town, wonderfully interested in the arrival of a vessel from which everyone expected something, formed in groups upon the quay.

My uncle left in haste his floating prison, or rather hospital. But before quitting the deck of the schooner he dragged me forward, and pointing with outstretched finger north of the bay at a distant mountain terminating in a double peak, a pair of cones covered with perpetual snow, he cried:

"Snæfell! Snæfell!"

Then recommending me, by an impressive gesture, to keep silence, he went into the boat which awaited him. I followed, and presently we were treading the soil of Iceland.

The first man we saw was a good-looking fellow enough, in a general's uniform. Yet he was not a general but a magistrate, the governor of the island, M. le Baron Trampe himself. The professor was soon aware of the presence he was in. He delivered him his letters from Copenhagen, and then followed a short conversation in the Danish language, the purport of which I was quite ignorant of, and for a very good reason. But the result of this first conversation was, that Baron Trampe placed himself entirely at the service of Professor Liedenbrock.

My uncle was just as courteously received by the mayor, M. Finsen, whose appearance was as military, and disposition and office as pacific, as the governor's.

As for the bishop's suffragan, M. Picturssen, he was at that moment engaged on an episcopal visitation in the north. For the time we must be resigned to wait for the honor of being presented to him. But M. Fridrikssen, professor of natural sciences at the school of Reykjavik, was a delightful man, and his friendship became very precious to me. This modest philosopher spoke only Danish and Latin. He came to proffer me his good offices in the language of Horace, and I felt that we were made to understand each other. In fact he was the only person in Iceland with whom I could converse at all.

This good-natured gentleman made over to us two of the three rooms which his house contained, and we were soon installed in it with all our luggage, the abundance of which rather astonished the good people of Reykjavik.

"Well, Axel," said my uncle, "we are getting on, and now the worst is over."

"The worst!" I said, astonished.

"To be sure, now we have nothing to do but go down."

"Oh, if that is all, you are quite right; but after all, when we have gone down, we shall have to get up again, I suppose?"

"Oh, I don't trouble myself about that. Come, there's no time to lose; I am going to the library. Perhaps there is some manuscript of Saknussemm's there, and I should be glad to consult it."

"Well, while you are there I will go into the town. Won't you?"

"Oh, that is very uninteresting to me. It is not what is upon this island, but what is underneath, that interests me."

I went out, and wandered wherever chance took me.

It would not be easy to lose your way in Reykjavik. I was therefore under no necessity to inquire the road, which exposes one to mistakes when the only medium of intercourse is gesture.

The town extends along a low and marshy level, between two hills. An immense bed of lava bounds it on one side, and falls gently toward the sea. On the other extends the vast bay of Faxa, shut in at the north by the enormous glacier of the Snæfell, and of which the *Valkyria* was for the time the only occupant. Usually the English and French conservators of fisheries moor in this bay, but just then they were cruising about the western coasts of the island.

The longest of the only two streets that Reykjavik possesses was parallel with the beach. Here live the merchants and traders, in wooden cabins made of red planks set horizontally; the other street, running west, ends at the little lake between the house of the bishop and other noncommercial people.

I had soon explored these melancholy ways; here and there I got a glimpse of faded turf, looking like a worn-out bit of carpet, or some appearance of a kitchen garden, the sparse vegetables of which (potatoes, cabbages, and lettuces) would have figured appropriately upon a Lilliputian table. A few sickly wallflowers were trying to enjoy the air and sunshine.

About the middle of the noncommercial street I found the public cemetery, enclosed with a mud wall, and where there seemed plenty of room.

Then a few steps brought me to the governor's house, a hut compared with the town hall of Hamburg, a palace in comparison with the cabins of the Icelandic population.

Between the little lake and the town the church is built in the Protestant style, of calcined stones extracted out of the volcanoes by *their* own labor and at *their* own expense; in high westerly winds it was manifest that the red tiles of the roof would be scattered in the air, to the great danger of the faithful worshipers.

On a neighboring hill I perceived the national school, where, as I was informed later by our host, were taught Hebrew, English, French, and Danish, four languages of which, with shame I confess it, I don't know a single word; after an examination I should have had to stand last of the forty scholars educated at this little college, and I should have been held unworthy to sleep along with them in one of those little double closets, where more delicate youths would have died of suffocation the very first night.

In three hours I had seen not only the town but its environs. The general aspect was wonderfully dull. No trees, and scarcely any vegetation. Everywhere bare rocks, signs of volcanic action. The Icelandic huts are made of earth and turf, and the walls slope inward; they rather resemble roofs placed on the ground. But then these roofs are meadows of comparative fertility. Thanks to the internal heat, the grass grows on them to some degree of perfection. It is carefully mown in the hay season; if it were not, the horses would come to pasture on these green abodes.

In my excursion I met but few people. On returning to the main street I found the greater part of the population busied in drying, salting, and putting on board codfish, their chief export. The men looked like robust but heavy, blond Germans with pensive eyes, conscious of being far removed from their fellow creatures, poor exiles relegated to this land of ice, poor creatures who should have been Esquimaux, since nature had condemned them to live only just outside the Arctic Circle! In vain did I try to detect a smile upon their lips; sometimes by a spasmodic and involuntary contraction of the muscles they seemed to laugh, but they never smiled.

Their costume consisted of a coarse jacket of black woolen cloth called in Scandinavian lands a "vadmel," a hat with a very broad brim, trousers with a narrow edge of red, and a bit of leather rolled round the foot for shoes.

The women looked as sad and as resigned as the men; their faces were agreeable but expressionless, and they wore gowns and petticoats of dark "vadmel"; as maidens, they wore over their braided hair a little knitted brown cap; when married, they put around their heads a colored handkerchief, crowned with a peak of white linen.

After a good walk I returned to M. Fridrikssen's house, where I found my uncle already in his host's company.

## CHAPTER X

### INTERESTING CONVERSATIONS WITH
### ICELANDIC SAVANTS

Dinner was ready. Professor Liedenbrock devoured his portion voraciously, for his compulsory fast on board had converted his stomach into a vast unfathomable gulf. There was nothing remarkable in the meal itself; but the hospitality of our host, more Danish than Icelandic, reminded me of the heroes of old. It was evident that we were more at home than he was himself.

The conversation was carried on in the vernacular tongue, which my uncle mixed with German and M. Fridrikssen with Latin for my benefit. It turned upon scientific questions as befits philosophers; but Professor Liedenbrock was excessively reserved, and at every sentence spoke to me with his eyes, enjoining the most absolute silence upon our plans.

In the first place M. Fridrikssen wanted to know what success my uncle had had at the library.

"Your library! Why, there is nothing but a few tattered books upon almost deserted shelves."

"Indeed!" replied M. Fridrikssen. "Why, we possess eight thousand volumes, many of them valuable and scarce, works in the old Scandinavian language, and we have all the novelties that Copenhagen sends us every year."

"Where do you keep your eight thousand volumes? For my part—"

"Oh, M. Liedenbrock, they are all over the country. In this icy region we are fond of study. There is not a farmer nor a fisherman that cannot read and does not read. Our principle is that books, instead of growing moldy behind an iron grating, should be worn out under the eyes of many readers. Therefore, these volumes are passed from one to another, read over and over, referred to again and again; and it often happens that they find their way back to their shelves only after an absence of a year or two."

"And in the meantime," said my uncle rather spitefully, "strangers—"

"Well, what would you have? Foreigners have their libraries at home, and the first essential for laboring people is that they should be educated. I repeat to you the love of reading runs in Icelandic blood. In 1816 we founded a prosperous literary society; learned strangers think themselves honored in becoming members of it. It publishes books which educate our fellow countrymen, and do the country great service. If you will consent to be a corresponding member, Herr Liedenbrock, you will be giving us great pleasure."

My uncle, who had already joined about a hundred learned societies, accepted with a grace, which evidently touched M. Fridrikssen.

"Now," said he, "will you be kind enough to tell me what books you hoped to find in our library, and I may perhaps enable you to consult them?"

My uncle's eyes and mine met. He hesitated. This direct question went to the root of the matter. But after a moment's reflection he decided on speaking.

"Monsieur Fridrikssen, I wished to know if among your ancient books you possessed any of the works of Arne Saknussemm?"

"Arne Saknussemm!" replied the Reykjavik professor. "You mean that learned sixteenth-century savant, a naturalist, a chemist, and a traveler?"

"Just so!"

"One of the glories of Icelandic literature and science?"

"That's the man."

"An illustrious man anywhere!"

"Quite so."

"And whose courage was equal to his genius!"

"I see that you know him well."

My uncle was bathed in delight at hearing his hero thus described. He feasted his eyes upon M. Fridrikssen's face.

"Well," he cried, "where are his works?"

"His works, we have them not."

"What—not in Iceland?"

"They are neither in Iceland nor anywhere else."

"Why is that?"

"Because Arne Saknussemm was persecuted for heresy, and in 1573 his books were burned by the hands of the common hangman."

"Very good! Excellent!" cried my uncle, to the great scandal of the professor of natural history.

"What!" he cried.

"Yes, yes; now it is all clear, now it is all unraveled; and I see why Saknussemm, put into the Index Expurgatorius, and compelled to hide the discoveries made by his genius, was obliged to bury in an incomprehensible cryptogram the secret—"

"What secret?" asked M. Fridrikssen, starting.

"Oh, just a secret which—" my uncle stammered.

"Have you some private document in your possession?" asked our host.

"No; I was only supposing a case."

"Oh, very well," answered M. Fridrikssen, who was kind enough not to pursue the subject when he had noticed the embarrassment of his friend. "I hope you will not leave our island until you have seen some of its mineralogical wealth."

"Certainly," replied my uncle; "but I am rather late; or have not others been here before me?"

"Yes, Herr Liedenbrock; the labors of MM. Olafsen and Povelsen, pursued by order of the king, the researches of Troïl the scientific mission of MM. Gaimard and Robert on the French corvette *La Recherche*,* and lately the observations of scientific men who came in the *Reine Hortense*, have added materially to our knowledge of Iceland. But I assure you there is plenty left."

"Do you think so?" said my uncle, pretending to look very modest, and trying to hide the curiosity was flashing out of his eyes.

"Oh, yes; how many mountains, glaciers, and volcanoes there are to study, which

---

* The *Recherche* was sent out in 1835 by Admiral Duperré to learn the fate of the lost expedition of M. de Blosseville in the *Lilloise*, which has never been heard of.

are as yet but imperfectly known! Then, without going any further, that mountain in the horizon. That is Snæfell."

"Ah!" said my uncle, as coolly as he was able. "Is that Snæfell?"

"Yes; one of the most curious volcanoes, and the crater of which has scarcely ever been visited."

"Is it extinct?"

"Oh, yes; more than five hundred years."

"Well," replied my uncle, who was frantically locking his legs together to keep himself from jumping up in the air, "that is where I mean to begin my geological studies, there on that Seffel—Fessel—what do you call it?"

"Snæfell," replied the excellent M. Fridrikssen.

This part of the conversation was in Latin; I had understood every word of it, and I could hardly conceal my amusement at seeing my uncle trying to keep down the excitement and satisfaction which were brimming over in every limb and every feature. He tried hard to put on an innocent little expression of simplicity; but it looked like a diabolical grin.

"Yes," said he, "your words decide me. We will try to scale that Snæfell; perhaps even we may pursue our studies in its crater!"

"I am very sorry," said M. Fridrikssen, "that my engagements will not allow me to absent myself, or I would have accompanied you myself with both pleasure and profit."

"Oh, no, no!" replied my uncle with great animation. "We would not disturb anyone for the world, M. Fridrikssen. Still, I thank you with all my heart: the company of such a talented man would have been very serviceable, but the duties of your profession—"

I am glad to think that our host, in the innocence of his Icelandic soul, was blind to the transparent artifices of my uncle.

"I very much approve of your beginning with that volcano, M. Liedenbrock. You will gather a harvest of interesting observations. But, tell me, how do you expect to get to the peninsula of Snæfell?"

"By sea, crossing the bay. That's the most direct way."

"No doubt; but it is impossible."

"Why?"

"Because we don't possess a single boat at Reykjavik."

"You don't mean to say so?"

"You will have to go by land, following the shore. It will be longer, but more interesting."

"Very well, then; and now I shall have to see about a guide."

"I have one to offer you."

"A safe, intelligent man."

"Yes; an inhabitant of that peninsula. He is an eiderdown hunter, and very clever. He speaks Danish perfectly."

"When can I see him?"

"Tomorrow, if you like."

"Why not today?"

"Because he won't be here till tomorrow."

"Tomorrow, then," added my uncle with a sigh.

This momentous conversation ended in a few minutes with warm acknowledgments paid by the German to the Icelandic professor. At this dinner my uncle had just elicited important facts, among others, the history of Saknussemm, the reason of the mysterious document, that his host would not accompany him in his expedition, and that the very next day a guide would be waiting upon him.

## CHAPTER XI

## A GUIDE FOUND TO THE CENTER OF THE EARTH

In the evening I took a short walk on the beach and returned at night to my plank-bed, where I slept soundly all night.

When I awoke I heard my uncle talking at a great rate in the next room. I immediately dressed and joined him.

He was conversing in the Danish language with a tall man, of robust build. This fine fellow must have been possessed of great strength. His eyes, set in a large and ingenuous face, seemed to me very intelligent; they were of a dreamy sea-blue. Long hair, which would have been called red even in England, fell in long meshes upon his broad shoulders. The movements of this native were lithe and supple; but he made little use of his arms in speaking, like a man who knew nothing or cared nothing about the language of gestures. His whole appearance bespoke perfect calmness and self-possession, not indolence but tranquility. It was felt at once that he would be beholden to nobody, that he worked for his own convenience, and that nothing in this world could astonish or disturb his philosophic calmness.

I caught the shades of this Icelander's character by the way in which he listened to the impassioned flow of words which fell from the professor. He stood with arms crossed, perfectly unmoved by my uncle's incessant gesticulations. A negative was expressed by a slow movement of the head from left to right, an affirmative by a slight bend, so slight that his long hair scarcely moved. He carried economy of motion even to parsimony.

Certainly I should never have dreamed in looking at this man that he was a hunter; he did not look likely to frighten his game, nor did he seem as if he would even get near it. But the mystery was explained when M. Fridrikssen informed me that this tranquil personage was only a hunter of the eider duck, whose under plumage constitutes the chief wealth of the island. This is the celebrated eiderdown, and it requires no great rapidity of movement to get it.

Early in summer the female, a very pretty bird, goes to build her nest among the rocks of the fjords with which the coast is fringed. After building the nest she feathers it with down plucked from her own breast. Immediately the hunter, or rather the trader, comes and robs the nest, and the female recommences her work. This goes on as long as she has any down left. When she has stripped herself bare, the male takes his turn to pluck himself. But as the coarse and hard plumage of the male has no commercial value, the hunter does not take the trouble to rob the nest of this; the female therefore lays her eggs in the spoils of her mate, the young are hatched, and next year the harvest begins again.

Now, as the eider duck does not select steep cliffs for her nest, but rather the smooth terraced rocks which slope to the sea, the Icelandic hunter might exercise his calling without any inconvenient exertion. He was a farmer who was not obliged either to sow or reap his harvest, but merely to gather it in.

This grave, phlegmatic, and silent individual was called Hans Bjelke; and he came recommended by M. Fridrikssen. He was our future guide. His manners were a singular contrast with my uncle's.

Nevertheless, they soon came to understand each other. Neither looked at the amount of the payment: the one was ready to accept whatever was offered; the other was ready to give whatever was demanded. Never was bargain more readily concluded.

The result of the treaty was, that Hans engaged on his part to conduct us to the village of Stapi, on the south shore of the Snæfell peninsula, at the very foot of the volcano. By land this would be about twenty-two miles, to be done, said my uncle, in two days.

But when he learned that the Danish mile was 24,000 feet long, he was obliged to modify his calculations and allow seven or eight days for the march.

Four horses were to be placed at our disposal—two to carry him and me, two for the baggage. Hans, as was his custom, would go on foot. He knew all that part of the coast perfectly, and promised to take us the shortest way.

His engagement was not to terminate with our arrival at Stapi; he was to continue in my uncle's service for the whole period of his scientific researches, for the remuneration of three rixdales a week (about twelve shillings), but it was an express article of the covenant that his wages should be counted out to him every Saturday at six o'clock in the evening, which, according to him, was one indispensable part of the engagement.

The start was fixed for the 16th of June. My uncle wanted to pay the hunter a portion in advance, but he refused with one word:

"Efter," said he.

"After," said the professor for my edification.

The treaty concluded, Hans silently withdrew.

"A famous fellow," cried my uncle; "but he little thinks of the marvelous part he has to play in the future."

"So he is to go with us as far as—"

"As far as the center of the earth, Axel."

Forty-eight hours were left before our departure; to my great regret I had to employ them in preparations; for all our ingenuity was required to pack every article to the best advantage; instruments here, arms there, tools in this package, provisions in that: four sets of packages in all.

The instruments were:

1. An Eigel's centigrade thermometer, graduated up to 150 degrees (302 degrees Fahrenheit), which seemed to me too much or too little. Too much if the internal heat was to rise so high, for in this case we should be baked, not enough to measure the temperature of springs or any matter in a state of fusion.

2. An aneroid barometer, to indicate extreme pressures of the atmosphere. An ordinary barometer would not have answered the purpose, as the pressure would increase during our descent to a point which the mercurial barometer would not register.

3. A chronometer, made by Boissonnas, jun., of Geneva, accurately set to the meridian of Hamburg.

4. Two compasses, viz., a common compass and a dipping needle.

5. A night glass.

6. Two of Ruhmkorff's apparatus, which, by means of an electric current, supplied a safe and handy portable light.*

The arms consisted of two of Purdy's rifles and two brace of pistols. But what did we want arms for? We had neither savages nor wild beasts to fear, I supposed. But my uncle seemed to believe in his arsenal as in his instruments, and more especially in a considerable quantity of gun cotton, which is unaffected by moisture, and the explosive force of which exceeds that of gunpowder.

The tools comprised two pickaxes, two spades, a silk ropeladder, three iron-tipped sticks, a hatchet, a hammer, a dozen wedges and iron spikes, and a long knotted rope. Now this was a large load, for the ladder was 300 feet long.

And there were provisions too: this was not a large parcel, but it was comforting to know that of essence of beef and biscuits there were six months' consumption. Spirits were the only liquid, and of water we took none; but we had flasks, and my uncle depended on springs from which to fill them. Whatever objections I hazarded as to their quality, temperature, and even absence, remained ineffectual.

To complete the exact inventory of all our traveling accompaniments, I must not forget a pocket medicine chest, containing blunt scissors, splints for broken limbs, a piece of tape of unbleached linen, bandages and compresses, lint, a lancet for bleeding, all dreadful articles to take with one. Then there was a row of phials containing dextrine, alcoholic ether, liquid acetate of lead, vinegar, and ammonia drugs which afforded me no comfort. Finally, all the articles needful to supply Ruhmkorff's apparatus.

My uncle did not forget a supply of tobacco, coarse grained powder, and amadou, nor a leathern belt in which he carried a sufficient quantity of gold, silver, and paper money. Six pairs of boots and shoes, made waterproof with a composition of india rubber and naphtha, were packed among the tools.

"Clothed, shod, and equipped like this," said my uncle, "there is no telling how far we may go."

The 14th was wholly spent in arranging all our different articles. In the evening we dined with Baron Tramps; the mayor of Reykjavik and Dr. Hyaltalin, the first medical man of the place, being of the party. M. Fridrikssen was not there. I learned afterward that he and the governor disagreed upon some question of administration, and did not speak to each other. I therefore knew not a single word of all that was said at this semiofficial dinner; but I could not help noticing that my uncle talked the whole time.

On the 15th our preparations were all made. Our host gave the professor very great pleasure by presenting him with a map of Iceland far more complete than that

---

* Ruhmkorff's apparatus consists of a Bunsen pile worked with bichromate of potash, which makes no smell; an induction coil carries the electricity generated by the pile into communication with a lantern of peculiar construction; in this lantern there is a spiral glass tube from which the air has been excluded, and in which remains only a residuum of carbonic acid gas or of nitrogen. When the apparatus is put in action this gas becomes luminous, producing a white steady light. The pile and coil are placed in a leathern bag which the traveler carries over his shoulders; the lantern outside of the bag throws sufficient light into deep darkness; it enables one to venture without fear of explosions into the midst of the most inflammable gases, and is not extinguished even in the deepest waters. M. Ruhmkorff is a learned and most ingenious man of science; his great discovery is his induction coil, which produces a powerful stream of electricity. He obtained in 1864 the quinquennial prize of 50,000 francs reserved by the French government for the most ingenious application of electricity.

of Hendersen. It was the map of M. Olaf Nikolas Olsen, in the proportion of 1 to 480,000 of the actual size of the island, and published by the Icelandic Literary Society. It was a precious document for a mineralogist.

Our last evening was spent in intimate conversation with M. Fridrikssen, with whom I felt the liveliest sympathy; then, after the talk, succeeded, for me, at any rate, a disturbed and restless night.

At five in the morning I was awoke by the neighing and pawing of four horses under my window. I dressed hastily and came down into the street. Hans was finishing our packing, almost as it were without moving a limb; and yet he did his work cleverly. My uncle made more noise than execution, and the guide seemed to pay very little attention to his energetic directions.

At six o'clock our preparations were over. M. Fridrikssen shook hands with us. My uncle thanked him heartily for his extreme kindness. I constructed a few fine Latin sentences to express my cordial farewell. Then we bestrode our steeds and with his last adieu M. Fridrikssen treated me to a line of Virgil eminently applicable to such uncertain wanderers as we were likely to be:

*Et quacumque viam dedent fortuna sequamur.*

*Wherever fortune clears a way,*
*Thither our ready footsteps stray.*

# CHAPTER XII

## A BARREN LAND

We had started under a sky overcast but calm. There was no fear of heat, none of disastrous rain. It was just the weather for tourists.

The pleasure of riding on horseback over an unknown country made me easy to be pleased at our first start. I threw myself wholly into the pleasure of the trip, and enjoyed the feeling of freedom and satisfied desire. I was beginning to take a real share in the enterprise.

"Besides," I said to myself, "where's the risk? Here we are traveling all through a most interesting country! We are about to climb a very remarkable mountain; at the worst we are going to scramble down an extinct crater. It is evident that Saknussemm did nothing more than this. As for a passage leading to the center of the globe, it is mere rubbish! Perfectly impossible! Very well, then; let us get all the good we can out of this expedition, and don't let us haggle about the chances."

This reasoning having settled my mind, we got out of Reykjavik.

Hans moved steadily on, keeping ahead of us at an even, smooth, and rapid pace. The baggage horses followed him without giving any trouble. Then came my uncle and myself, looking not so very ill-mounted on our small but hardy animals.

Iceland is one of the largest islands in Europe. Its surface is 14,000 square miles, and it contains but 16,000 inhabitants. Geographers have divided it into four quarters, and we were crossing diagonally the southwest quarter, called the "Sudvester Fjordungr."

On leaving Reykjavik Hans took us by the seashore. We passed lean pastures which were trying very hard, but in vain, to look green; yellow came out best. The rugged peaks of the trachyte rocks presented faint outlines on the eastern horizon; at times a few patches of snow, concentrating the vague light, glittered upon the slopes of the distant mountains; certain peaks, boldly uprising, passed through the gray clouds, and reappeared above the moving mists, like breakers emerging in the heavens.

Often these chains of barren rocks made a dip toward the sea, and encroached upon the scanty pasturage: but there was always enough room to pass. Besides, our horses instinctively chose the easiest places without ever slackening their pace. My uncle was refused even the satisfaction of stirring up his beast with whip or voice. He had no excuse for being impatient. I could not help smiling to see so tall a man on so small a pony, and as his long legs nearly touched the ground he looked like a six-legged centaur.

"Good horse! Good horse!" he kept saying. "You will see, Axel, that there is no more sagacious animal than the Icelandic horse. He is stopped by neither snow, nor storm, nor impassable roads, nor rocks, glaciers, or anything. He is courageous, sober, and surefooted. He never makes a false step, never shies. If there is a river or fjord to cross (and we shall meet with many) you will see him plunge in at once, just as if he were amphibious, and gain the opposite bank. But we must not hurry him; we must let him have his way, and we shall get on at the rate of thirty miles a day."

"*We* may; but how about our guide?"

"Oh, never mind him. People like him get over the ground without a thought. There is so little action in this man that he will never get tired; and besides, if he wants it, he shall have my horse. I shall get cramped if I don't have a little action. The arms are all right, but the legs want exercise."

We were advancing at a rapid pace. The country was already almost a desert. Here and there was a lonely farm, called a boër built either of wood, or of sods, or of pieces of lava, looking like a poor beggar by the wayside. These ruinous huts seemed to solicit charity from passersby; and on very small provocation we should have given alms for the relief of the poor inmates. In this country there were no roads and paths, and the poor vegetation, however slow, would soon efface the rare travelers' footsteps.

Yet this part of the province, at a very small distance from the capital, is reckoned among the inhabited and cultivated portions of Iceland. What, then, must other tracts be, more desert than this desert? In the first half mile we had not seen one farmer standing before his cabin door, nor one shepherd tending a flock less wild than himself, nothing but a few cows and sheep left to themselves. What then would be those convulsed regions upon which we were advancing, regions subject to the dire phenomena of eruptions, the offspring of volcanic explosions and subterranean convulsions?

We were to know them before long, but on consulting Olsen's map, I saw that they would be avoided by winding along the seashore. In fact, the great plutonic action is confined to the central portion of the island; there, rocks of the trappean and volcanic class, including trachyte, basalt, and tuffs and agglomerates associated with streams of lava, have made this a land of supernatural horrors. I had no idea of the spectacle which was awaiting us in the peninsula of Snæfell, where these ruins of a fiery nature have formed a frightful chaos.

In two hours from Reykjavik we arrived at the burgh of Gufunes, called Aolkirkja, or principal church. There was nothing remarkable here but a few houses, scarcely enough for a German hamlet.

Hans stopped here half an hour. He shared with us our frugal breakfast; answering my uncle's questions about the road and our resting place that night with merely yes or no, except when he said "Gardär."

I consulted the map to see where Gardär was. I saw there was a small town of that name on the banks of the Hvalfjord, four miles from Reykjavik. I showed it to my uncle.

"Four miles only!" he exclaimed. "Four miles out of twenty-eight. What a nice little walk!"

He was about to make an observation to the guide, who without answering resumed his place at the head, and went on his way.

Three hours later, still treading on the colorless grass of the pasture land, we had to work round the Kolla fjord, a longer way but an easier one than across that inlet. We soon entered into a "pingstaoer," or parish, called Ejulberg, from whose steeple twelve o'clock would have struck, if Icelandic churches were rich enough to possess clocks. But they are like the parishioners who have no watches and do without.

There our horses were baited; then taking the narrow path to left between a chain of hills and the sea, they carried us to our next stage, the aolkirkja of Brantär and one mile farther on, to Saurboër "Annexia," a chapel of ease built on the south shore of the Hvalfjord.

It was now four o'clock, and we had gone four Icelandic miles, or twenty-four English miles.

In that place the fjord was at least three English miles wide; the waves rolled with a rushing din upon the sharp-pointed rocks; this inlet was confined between walls of rock, precipices crowned by sharp peaks 2,000 feet high, and remarkable for the brown strata which separated the beds of reddish tuff. However much I might respect the intelligence of our quadrupeds, I hardly cared to put it to the test by trusting myself to it on horseback across an arm of the sea.

If they are as intelligent as they are said to be, I thought, they won't try it. In any case, I will tax my intelligence to direct theirs.

But my uncle would not wait. He spurred on to the edge. His steed lowered his head to examine the nearest waves and stopped. My uncle, who had an instinct of his own, too, applied pressure, and was again refused by the animal significantly shaking his head. Then followed strong language, and the whip; but the brute answered these arguments with kicks and endeavors to throw his rider. At last the clever little pony, with a bend of his knees, started from under the professor's legs, and left him standing upon two boulders on the shore just like the colossus of Rhodes.

"Confounded brute!" cried the unhorsed horseman, suddenly degraded into a pedestrian, just as ashamed as a cavalry officer degraded to a foot soldier.

"*Färja,*" said the guide, touching his shoulder.

"What! A boat?"

"*Der,*" replied Hans, pointing to one.

"Yes," I cried; "there is a boat."

"Why did not you say so then? Well, let us go on."

"*Tidvatten,*" said the guide.

"What is he saying?"

"He says tide," said my uncle, translating the Danish word.

"No doubt we must wait for the tide."

"*Förbida,*" said my uncle.

"*Ja,*" replied Hans.

My uncle stamped with his foot, while the horses went on to the boat.

I perfectly understood the necessity of abiding a particular moment of the tide to undertake the crossing of the fjord, when, the sea having reached its greatest height, it should be slack water. Then the ebb and flow have no sensible effect, and the boat does not risk being carried either to the bottom or out to sea.

That favorable moment arrived only with six o'clock; when my uncle, myself, the guide, two other passengers, and the four horses trusted ourselves to a somewhat fragile raft. Accustomed as I was to the swift and sure steamers on the Elbe, I found the oars of the rowers rather a slow means of propulsion. It took us more than an hour to cross the fjord; but the passage was effected without any mishap.

In another half hour we had reached the aolkirkja of Gardär.

## *CHAPTER XIII*

### HOSPITALITY UNDER THE ARCTIC CIRCLE

It ought to have been nighttime, but under the 65th parallel there was nothing surprising in the nocturnal polar light. In Iceland during the months of June and July the sun does not set.

But the temperature was much lower. I was cold and more hungry than cold. Welcome was the sight of the boër, which was hospitably opened to receive us.

It was a peasant's house, but in point of hospitality it was equal to a king's. On our arrival the master came with outstretched hands, and without more ceremony he beckoned us to follow him.

To accompany him down the long, narrow, dark passage would have been impossible. Therefore, we followed, as he bid us. The building was constructed of roughly squared timbers, with rooms on both sides, four in number, all opening out into the one passage: these were the kitchen, the weaving shop, the badstofa, or family sleeping room, and the visitors' room, which was the best of all. My uncle, whose height had not been thought of in building the house, of course hit his head several times against the beams that projected from the ceilings.

We were introduced into our apartment, a large room with a floor of earth stamped hard down, and lighted by a window, the panes of which were formed of sheep's bladder, not admitting too much light. The sleeping accommodation consisted of dry litter, thrown into two wooden frames painted red, and ornamented with Icelandic sentences. I was hardly expecting so much comfort; the only discomfort proceeded from the strong odor of dried fish, hung meat, and sour milk, of which my nose made bitter complaints.

When we had laid aside our traveling wraps, the voice of the host was heard inviting us to the kitchen, the only room where a fire was lighted even in the severest cold.

My uncle lost no time in obeying the friendly call, nor was I slack in following.

The kitchen chimney was constructed on the ancient pattern; in the middle of the room was a stone for a hearth, over it in the roof a hole to let the smoke escape. The kitchen was also a dining room.

At our entrance the host, as if he had never seen us, greeted us with the word "*Sællvertu,*" which means "be happy," and came and kissed us on the cheek.

After him his wife pronounced the same words, accompanied with the same ceremonial; then the two placing their hands upon their hearts, inclined profoundly before us.

I hasten to inform the reader that this Icelandic lady was the mother of nineteen children, all, big and little, swarming in the midst of the dense wreaths of smoke with which the fire on the hearth filled the chamber. Every moment I noticed a fair-haired and rather melancholy face peeping out of the rolling volumes of smoke—they were a perfect cluster of unwashed angels.

My uncle and I treated this little tribe with kindness; and in a very short time we each had three or four of these brats on our shoulders, as many on our laps, and the rest between our knees. Those who could speak kept repeating "*Sællvertu*," in every conceivable tone; those that could not speak made up for that want by shrill cries.

This concert was brought to a close by the announcement of dinner. At that moment our hunter returned, who had been seeing his horses provided for; that is to say, he had economically let them loose in the fields, where the poor beasts had to content themselves with the scanty moss they could pull off the rocks and a few meager seaweeds, and the next day they would not fail to come of themselves and resume the labors of the previous day.

"*Sællvertu*," said Hans.

Then calmly, automatically, and dispassionately he kissed the host, the hostess, and their nineteen children.

This ceremony over, we sat at table, twenty-four in number, and therefore one upon another. The luckiest had only two urchins upon their knees.

But silence reigned in all this little world at the arrival of the soup, and the national taciturnity resumed its empire even over the children. The host served out to us a soup made of lichen and by no means unpleasant, then an immense piece of dried fish floating in butter rancid with twenty years' keeping, and, therefore, according to Icelandic gastronomy, much preferable to fresh butter. Along with this, we had "skye," a sort of clotted milk, with biscuits, and a liquid prepared from juniper berries; for beverage we had a thin milk mixed with water, called in this country "blanda." It is not for me to decide whether this diet is wholesome or not; all I can say is that I was desperately hungry, and that at dessert I swallowed to the very last gulp of a thick broth made from buckwheat.

As soon as the meal was over the children disappeared, and their elders gathered round the peat fire, which also burned such miscellaneous fuel as briars, cow dung, and fish bones. After this little pinch of warmth the different groups retired to their respective rooms. Our hostess hospitably offered us her assistance in undressing, according to Icelandic usage; but on our gracefully declining, she insisted no longer, and I was able at last to curl myself up in my mossy bed.

At five next morning we bade our host farewell, my uncle with difficulty persuading him to accept a proper remuneration; and Hans signaled the start.

At a hundred yards from Gardär the soil began to change its aspect; it became boggy and less favorable to progress. On our right the chain of mountains was indefinitely prolonged like an immense system of natural fortifications, of which we were following the counterscarp, or lesser steep; often we were met by streams, which we had to ford with great care, not to wet our packages.

The desert became wider and more hideous; yet from time to time we seemed to descry a human figure that fled at our approach, sometimes a sharp turn would bring us suddenly within a short distance of one of these specters, and I was filled with loathing at the sight of a huge deformed head, the skin shining and hairless, and repulsive sores visible through the gaps in the poor creature's wretched rags.

The unhappy being forebore to approach us and offer his misshapen hand. He fled away, but not before Hans had saluted him with the customary "*Sællvertu*."

"*Spetelsk*," said he.

"A leper!" my uncle repeated.

This word produced a repulsive effect. The horrible disease of leprosy is too common in Iceland; it is not contagious, but hereditary, and lepers are forbidden to marry.

These apparitions were not cheerful, and did not throw any charm over the less and less attractive landscapes. The last tufts of grass had disappeared from beneath our feet. Not a tree was to be seen, unless we except a few dwarf birches as low as brushwood. Not an animal but a few wandering ponies that their owners would not feed. Sometimes we could see a hawk balancing himself on his wings under the gray cloud, and then darting away south with rapid flight. I felt melancholy under this savage aspect of nature, and my thoughts went away to the cheerful scenes I had left in the far south.

We had to cross a few narrow fjords, and at last quite a wide gulf; the tide, then high, allowed us to pass over without delay, and to reach the hamlet of Alftanes, one mile beyond.

That evening, after having forded two rivers full of trout and pike, called Alfa and Heta, we were obliged to spend the night in a deserted building worthy to be haunted by all the elfins of Scandinavia. The ice king certainly held court here, and gave us all night long samples of what he could do.

No particular event marked the next day. Bogs, dead levels, melancholy desert tracks, wherever we traveled. By nightfall we had accomplished half our journey, and we lay at Krösolbt.

On the 19th of June, for about a mile, that is an Icelandic mile, we walked upon hardened lava; this ground is called in the country "hraun"; the writhen surface presented the appearance of distorted, twisted cables, sometimes stretched in length, sometimes contorted together; an immense torrent, once liquid, now solid, ran from the nearest mountains, now extinct volcanoes, but the ruins around revealed the violence of the past eruptions. Yet here and there were a few jets of steam from hot springs.

We had no time to watch these phenomena; we had to proceed on our way. Soon at the foot of the mountains the boggy land reappeared, intersected by little lakes. Our route now lay westward; we had turned the great bay of Faxa, and the twin peaks of Snæfell rose white into the cloudy sky at the distance of at least five miles.

The horses did their duty well, no difficulties stopped them in their steady career. I was getting tired; but my uncle was as firm and straight as he was at our first start. I could not help admiring his persistence, as well as the hunter's, who treated our expedition like a mere promenade.

June 20. At six p.m. we reached Büdir, a village on the seashore; and the guide there claiming his due, my uncle settled with him. It was Hans's own family, that is, his uncles and cousins, who gave us hospitality; we were kindly received, and without taxing too much the goodness of these folks, I would willingly have tarried here to recruit after my fatigues. But my uncle, who wanted no recruiting, would not hear of it, and the next morning we had to bestride our beasts again.

The soil told of the neighborhood of the mountain, whose granite foundations rose from the earth like the knotted roots of some huge oak. We were rounding the immense base of the volcano. The professor hardly took his eyes off it. He tossed up his arms and seemed to defy it, and to declare, "There stands the giant that I shall conquer." After about four hours' walking the horses stopped of their own accord at the door of the priest's house at Stapi.

## CHAPTER XIV

### BUT ARCTICS CAN BE INHOSPITABLE, TOO

Stapi is a village consisting of about thirty huts, built of lava, at the south side of the base of the volcano. It extends along the inner edge of a small fjord, enclosed between basaltic walls of the strangest construction.

Basalt is a brownish rock of igneous origin. It assumes regular forms, the arrangement of which is often very surprising. Here nature had done her work geometrically, with square and compass and plummet. Everywhere else her art consists alone in throwing down huge masses together in disorder. You see cones imperfectly formed, irregular pyramids, with a fantastic disarrangement of lines; but here, as if to exhibit an example of regularity, though in advance of the very earliest architects, she has created a severely simple order of architecture, never surpassed either by the splendors of Babylon or the wonders of Greece.

I had heard of the Giant's Causeway in Ireland, and Fingal's Cave in Staffa, one of the Hebrides; but I had never yet seen a basaltic formation.

At Stapi I beheld this phenomenon in all its beauty.

The wall that confined the fjord, like all the coast of the peninsula, was composed of a series of vertical columns thirty feet high. These straight shafts, of fair proportions, supported an architrave of horizontal slabs, the overhanging portion of which formed a semiarch over the sea. At intervals, under this natural shelter, there spread out vaulted entrances in beautiful curves, into which the waves came dashing with foam and spray. A few shafts of basalt, torn from their hold by the fury of tempests, lay along the soil like remains of an ancient temple, in ruins forever fresh, and over which centuries passed without leaving a trace of age upon them.

This was our last stage upon the earth. Hans had exhibited great intelligence, and it gave me some little comfort to think then that he was not going to leave us.

On arriving at the door of the rector's house, which was not different from the others, I saw a man shoeing a horse, hammer in hand, and with a leathern apron on.

"*Sællvertu,*" said the hunter.

"*God dag,*" said the blacksmith in good Danish.

"*Kyrkoherde,*" said Hans, turning round to my uncle.

"The rector," repeated the professor. "It seems, Axel, that this good man is the rector."

Our guide in the meanwhile was making the "kyrkoherde" aware of the position of things; when the latter, suspending his labors for a moment, uttered a sound no doubt understood between horses and farriers, and immediately a tall and ugly hag appeared from the hut. She must have been six feet at the least. I was in great alarm lest she should treat me to the Icelandic kiss; but there was no occasion to fear, nor did she do the honors at all too gracefully.

The visitors' room seemed to me the worst in the whole cabin. It was close, dirty, and evil-smelling. But we had to be content. The rector did not to go in for antique hospitality. Very far from it. Before the day was over I saw that we had to do with a blacksmith, a fisherman, a hunter, a joiner, but not at all with a minister of the Gospel. To be sure, it was a weekday; perhaps on a Sunday he made amends.

I don't mean to say anything against these poor priests, who after all are very wretched. They receive from the Danish government a ridiculously small pittance, and they get from the parish the fourth part of the tithe, which does not come to sixty marks a year (about £4). Hence the necessity to work for their livelihood; but after fishing, hunting, and shoeing horses for any length of time, one soon gets into the ways and manners of fishermen, hunters, and farriers, and other rather rude and uncultivated people; and that evening I found out that temperance was not among the virtues that distinguished my host.

My uncle soon discovered what sort of a man he had to do with; instead of a good and learned man he found a rude and coarse peasant. He therefore resolved to commence the grand expedition at once, and to leave this inhospitable parsonage. He cared nothing about fatigue, and resolved to spend some days upon the mountain.

The preparations for our departure were therefore made the very day after our arrival at Stapi. Hans hired the services of three Icelanders to do the duty of the horses in the transport of the burdens; but as soon as we had arrived at the crater these natives were to turn back and leave us to our own devices. This was to be clearly understood.

My uncle now took the opportunity to explain to Hans that it was his intention to explore the interior of the volcano to its farthest limits.

Hans merely nodded. There or elsewhere, down in the bowels of the earth, or anywhere on the surface, all was alike to him. For my own part the incidents of the journey had hitherto kept me amused, and made me forgetful of coming evils; but now my fears again were beginning to get the better of me. But what could I do? The place to resist the professor would have been Hamburg, not the foot of Snæfell.

One thought, above all others, harassed and alarmed me; it was one calculated to shake firmer nerves than mine.

Now, thought I, here we are, about to climb Snæfell. Very good. We will explore the crater. Very good, too, others have done as much without dying for it. But that is not all. If there *is* a way to penetrate into the very bowels of the island, if that ill-advised Saknussemm has told a true tale, we shall lose our way amid the deep subterranean passages of this volcano. Now, there is no proof that Snæfell is extinct. Who can assure us that an eruption is not brewing at this very moment? Does it follow that because the monster has slept since 1229 he must therefore never awake again? And if he wakes up presently, where shall we be?

It was worthwhile debating this question, and I did debate it. I could not sleep for dreaming about eruptions. Now, the part of ejected scoriae and ashes seemed to my mind a very rough one to act.

So, at last, when I could hold out no longer, I resolved to lay the case before my uncle, as prudently and as cautiously as possible, just under the form of an almost impossible hypothesis.

I went to him. I communicated my fears to him, and drew back a step to give him room for the explosion which I knew must follow. But I was mistaken.

"I was thinking of that," he replied with great simplicity.

What could those words mean? Was he actually going to listen to reason? Was he contemplating the abandonment of his plans? This was too good to be true.

After a few moments' silence, during which I dared not question him, he resumed:

"I was thinking of that. Ever since we arrived at Stapi I have been occupied with the important question you have just opened, for we must not be guilty of imprudence."

"No, indeed!" I replied with forcible emphasis.

"For six hundred years Snæfell has been dumb; but he may speak again. Now, eruptions are always preceded by certain well-known phenomena. I have therefore examined the natives, I have studied external appearances, and I can assure you, Axel, that there will be no eruption."

At this positive affirmation I stood amazed and speechless.

"You don't doubt my word?" said my uncle. "Well, follow me."

I obeyed like an automaton. Coming out from the priest's house, the professor took a straight road, which, through an opening in the basaltic wall, led away from the sea. We were soon in the open country, if one may give that name to a vast extent of mounds of volcanic products. This tract seemed crushed under a rain of enormous ejected rocks of trap, basalt, granite, and all kinds of igneous rocks.

Here and there I could see puffs and jets of steam curling up into the air, called in Icelandic "reykir," issuing from thermal springs, and indicating by their motion the volcanic energy underneath. This seemed to justify my fears: But I fell from the height of my newborn hopes when my uncle said:

"You see all these volumes of steam, Axel; well, they demonstrate that we have nothing to fear from the fury of a volcanic eruption."

"Am I to believe that?" I cried.

"Understand this clearly," added the professor. "At the approach of an eruption these jets would redouble their activity, but disappear altogether during the period of the eruption. For the elastic fluids, being no longer under pressure, go off by way of the crater instead of escaping by their usual passages through the fissures in the soil. Therefore, if these vapors remain in their usual condition, if they display no augmentation of force, and if you add to this the observation that the wind and rain are not ceasing and being replaced by a still and heavy atmosphere, then you may affirm that no eruption is preparing."

"But—"

"No more; that is sufficient. When science has uttered her voice, let babblers hold their peace."

I returned to the parsonage, very crestfallen. My uncle had beaten me with the weapons of science. Still I had one hope left, and this was that when we had reached the bottom of the crater it would be impossible, for want of a passage, to go deeper, in spite of all the Saknussemm's in Iceland.

I spent that whole night in one constant nightmare; in the heart of a volcano, and from the deepest depths of the earth I saw myself tossed up among the interplanetary spaces under the form of an eruptive rock.

The next day, June 23, Hans was awaiting us with his companions carrying provisions, tools, and instruments; two iron-pointed sticks, two rifles, and two shot belts were for my uncle and myself. Hans, as a cautious man, had added to our luggage a leathern bottle full of water, which, with that in our flasks, would ensure us a supply of water for eight days.

It was nine in the morning. The priest and his tall Megaera were awaiting us at the door. We supposed they were standing there to bid us a kind farewell. But the farewell was put in the unexpected form of a heavy bill, in which everything was charged, even to the very air we breathed in the pastoral house, infected as it was. This worthy couple were fleecing us just as a Swiss innkeeper might have done, and estimated their imperfect hospitality at the highest price.

My uncle paid without a remark: a man who is starting for the center of the earth need not be particular about a few rix dollars.

This point being settled, Hans gave the signal, and we soon left Stapi behind us.

## CHAPTER XV

### SNÆFELL AT LAST

Snæfell is 5,000 feet high. Its double cone forms the limit of a trachytic belt which stands out distinctly in the mountain system of the island. From our starting point we could see the two peaks boldly projected against the dark gray sky; I could see an enormous cap of snow coming low down upon the giant's brow.

We walked in single file, headed by the hunter, who ascended by narrow tracks, where two could not have gone abreast. There was therefore no room for conversation.

After we had passed the basaltic wall of the fjord of Stapi we passed over a vegetable fibrous peat bog, left from the ancient vegetation of this peninsula. The vast quantity of this unworked fuel would be sufficient to warm the whole population of Iceland for a century; this vast turbary measured in certain ravines had in many places a depth of seventy feet, and presented layers of carbonized remains of vegetation alternating with thinner layers of tufaceous pumice.

As a true nephew of the professor Liedenbrock, and in spite of my dismal prospects, I could not help observing with interest the mineralogical curiosities which lay about me as in a vast museum, and I constructed for myself a complete geological account of Iceland.

This most curious island has evidently been projected from the bottom of the sea at a comparatively recent date. Possibly, it may still be subject to gradual elevation. If this is the case, its origin may well be attributed to subterranean fires. Therefore, in this case, the theory of Sir Humphry Davy, Saknussemm's document, and my uncle's theories would all go off in smoke. This hypothesis led me to examine with more attention the appearance of the surface, and I soon arrived at a conclusion as to the nature of the forces which presided at its birth.

Iceland, which is entirely devoid of alluvial soil, is wholly composed of volcanic tufa, that is to say, an agglomeration of porous rocks and stones. Before the volcanoes broke out it consisted of trap rocks slowly upraised to the level of the sea by the action of central forces. The internal fires had not yet forced their way through.

But at a later period a wide chasm formed diagonally from southwest to northeast, through which was gradually forced out the trachyte which was to form a mountain chain. No violence accompanied this change; the matter thrown out was in vast quantities, and the liquid material oozing out from the abysses of the earth slowly spread in extensive plains or in hillocky masses. To this period belong the feldspar, syenites, and porphyries.

But with the help of this outflow the thickness of the crust of the island increased materially, and therefore also its powers of resistance. It may easily be conceived what vast quantities of elastic gases, what masses of molten matter accumulated beneath its solid surface while no exit was practicable after the cooling of the trachytic crust. Therefore a time would come when the elastic and explosive forces of the imprisoned gases would upheave this ponderous cover and drive out for themselves openings through tall chimneys. Hence then the volcano would distend and lift up the crust, and then burst through a crater suddenly formed at the summit or thinnest part of the volcano.

To the eruption succeeded other volcanic phenomena. Through the outlets now made first escaped the ejected basalt of which the plain we had just left presented such marvelous specimens. We were moving over gray rocks of dense and massive formation, which in cooling had formed into hexagonal prisms. Everywhere around us we saw truncated cones, formerly so many fiery mouths.

After the exhaustion of the basalt, the volcano, the power of which grew by the extinction of the lesser craters, supplied an egress to lava, ashes, and scoriae, of which I could see lengthened screes streaming down the sides of the mountain like flowing hair.

Such was the succession of phenomena which produced Iceland, all arising from the action of internal fire; and to suppose that the mass within did not still exist in a state of liquid incandescence was absurd; and nothing could surpass the absurdity of fancying that it was possible to reach the earth's center.

So I felt a little comforted as we advanced to the assault of Snæfell.

The way was growing more and more arduous, the ascent steeper and steeper; the loose fragments of rock trembled beneath us, and the utmost care was needed to avoid dangerous falls.

Hans went on as quietly as if he were on level ground; sometimes he disappeared altogether behind the huge blocks, then a shrill whistle would direct us on our way to him. Sometimes he would halt, pick up a few bits of stone, build them up into a recognizable form, and thus made landmarks to guide us in our way back. A very wise precaution in itself, but, as things turned out, quite useless.

Three hours' fatiguing march had only brought us to the base of the mountain. There Hans bid us come to a halt, and a hasty breakfast was served out. My uncle swallowed two mouthfuls at a time to get on faster. But, whether he liked it or not, this was a rest as well as a breakfast hour and he had to wait till it pleased our guide to move on, which came to pass in an hour. The three Icelanders, just as taciturn as their comrade the hunter, never spoke, and ate their breakfasts in silence.

We were now beginning to scale the steep sides of Snæfell. Its snowy summit, by an optical illusion not infrequent in mountains, seemed close to us, and yet how many weary hours it took to reach it! The stones, adhering by no soil or fibrous roots of vegetation, rolled away from under our feet, and rushed down the precipice below with the swiftness of an avalanche.

At some places the flanks of the mountain formed an angle with the horizon of at least 36 degrees; it was impossible to climb them, and these stony cliffs had to be tacked round, not without great difficulty. Then we helped each other with our sticks.

I must admit that my uncle kept as close to me as he could; he never lost sight of me, and in many straits his arm furnished me with a powerful support. He himself seemed to possess an instinct for equilibrium, for he never stumbled. The Icelanders, though burdened with our loads, climbed with the agility of mountaineers.

To judge by the distant appearance of the summit of Snæfell, it would have seemed too steep to ascend on our side. Fortunately, after an hour of fatigue and athletic exercises, in the midst of the vast surface of snow presented by the hollow between the two peaks, a kind of staircase appeared unexpectedly, which greatly facilitated our ascent. It was formed by one of those torrents of stones flung up by the eruptions, called "sting" by the Icelanders. If this torrent had not been arrested in its fall by the formation of the sides of the mountain, it would have gone on to the sea and formed more islands.

Such as it was, it did us good service. The steepness increased, but these stone steps allowed us to rise with facility, and even with such rapidity that, having rested for a moment while my companions continued their ascent, I perceived them already reduced by distance to microscopic dimensions.

At seven we had ascended the two thousand steps of this grand staircase, and we had attained a bulge in the mountain, a kind of bed on which rested the cone proper of the crater.

Three thousand two hundred feet below us stretched the sea. We had passed the limit of perpetual snow, which, on account of the moisture of the climate, is at a greater elevation in Iceland than the high latitude would give reason to suppose. The cold was excessively keen. The wind was blowing violently. I was exhausted. The professor saw that my limbs were refusing to perform their office, and in spite of his impatience he decided on stopping. He therefore spoke to the hunter, who shook his head, saying:

"*Ofvanför.*"

"It seems we must go higher," said my uncle.

Then he asked Hans for his reason.

"*Mistour,*" replied the guide.

"*Ja Mistour,*" said one of the Icelanders in a tone of alarm.

"What does that word mean?" I asked uneasily.

"Look!" said my uncle.

I looked down upon the plain. An immense column of pulverized pumice, sand, and dust was rising with a whirling circular motion like a waterspout; the wind was lashing it onto that side of Snæfell where we were holding on; this dense veil, hung across the sun, threw a deep shadow over the mountain. If that huge revolving pillar sloped down, it would involve us in its whirling eddies. This phenomenon, which is not infrequent when the wind blows from the glaciers, is called in Icelandic "mistour."

"*Hastigt! Hastigt!*" cried our guide.

Without knowing Danish I understood at once that we must follow Hans at the top of our speed. He began to circle round the cone of the crater, but in a diagonal direction so as to facilitate our progress. Presently the dust storm fell upon the mountain, which quivered under the shock; the loose stones, caught with the irresistible blasts of wind, flew about in a perfect hail as in an eruption. Happily we were on the opposite side, and sheltered from all harm. But for the precaution of our guide, our mangled bodies, torn and pounded into fragments, would have been carried afar like the ruins hurled along by some unknown meteor.

Yet Hans did not think it prudent to spend the night upon the sides of the cone. We continued our zigzag climb. The fifteen hundred remaining feet took us five hours to clear; the circuitous route, the diagonal and the counter marches, must have measured at least three leagues. I could stand it no longer. I was yielding to the effects of hunger and cold. The rarefied air scarcely gave play to the action of my lungs.

At last, at eleven in the sunlit night, the summit of Snæfell was reached, and before going in for shelter into the crater I had time to observe the midnight sun, at his lowest point, gilding with his pale rays the island that slept at my feet.

## CHAPTER XVI

### BOLDLY DOWN THE CRATER

Supper was rapidly devoured, and the little company housed themselves as best they could. The bed was hard, the shelter not very substantial, and our position an anxious one, at five thousand feet above the sea level. Yet I slept particularly well; it was one of the best nights I had ever had, and I did not even dream.

Next morning we awoke half frozen by the sharp keen air, but with the light of a splendid sun. I rose from my granite bed and went out to enjoy the magnificent spectacle that lay unrolled before me.

I stood on the very summit of the southernmost of Snæfell's peaks. The range of the eye extended over the whole island. By an optical law which obtains at all great heights, the shores seemed raised and the center depressed. It seemed as if one of Helbesmer's raised maps lay at my feet. I could see deep valleys intersecting each other in every direction, precipices like low walls, lakes reduced to ponds, rivers abbreviated into streams. On my right were numberless glaciers and innumerable peaks, some plumed with feathery clouds of smoke. The undulating surface of these endless mountains, crested with sheets of snow, reminded one of a stormy sea. If I looked westward, there the ocean lay spread out in all its magnificence, like a mere continuation of those flocklike summits. The eye could hardly tell where the snowy ridges ended and the foaming waves began.

I was thus steeped in the marvelous ecstasy which all high summits develop in the mind; and now without giddiness, for I was beginning to be accustomed to these sublime aspects of nature. My dazzled eyes were bathed in the bright flood of the solar rays. I was forgetting where and who I was, to live the life of elves and sylphs, the fanciful creation of Scandinavian superstitions. I felt intoxicated with the sublime pleasure of lofty elevations without thinking of the profound abysses into which I was shortly to be plunged. But I was brought back to the realities of things by the arrival of Hans and the professor, who joined me on the summit.

My uncle pointed out to me in the far west a light steam or mist, a semblance of land, which bounded the distant horizon of waters.

"Greenland!" said he.

"Greenland?" I cried.

"Yes; we are only thirty-five leagues from it; and during thaws the white bears, borne by the ice fields from the north, are carried even into Iceland. But never mind that. Here we are at the top of Snæfell and here are two peaks, one north and one south. Hans will tell us the name of that on which we are now standing."

The question being put, Hans replied:

"Scartaris."

My uncle shot a triumphant glance at me.

"Now for the crater!" he cried.

The crater of Snæfell resembled an inverted cone, the opening of which might be half a league in diameter. Its depth appeared to be about two thousand feet. Imagine the aspect of such a reservoir, brim full and running over with liquid fire amid the rolling thunder. The bottom of the funnel was about 250 feet in circuit, so that the gentle slope allowed its lower brim to be reached without much difficulty. Involuntarily I compared the whole crater to an enormous erected mortar, and the comparison put me in a terrible fright.

"What madness," I thought, "to go down into a mortar, perhaps a loaded mortar, to be shot up into the air at a moment's notice!"

But I did not try to back out of it. Hans with perfect coolness resumed the lead, and I followed him without a word.

In order to facilitate the descent, Hans wound his way down the cone by a spiral path. Our route lay amid eruptive rocks, some of which, shaken out of their loosened beds, rushed bounding down the abyss, and in their fall awoke echoes remarkable for their loud and well-defined sharpness.

In certain parts of the cone there were glaciers. Here Hans advanced only with extreme precaution, sounding his way with his iron-pointed pole, to discover any crevasses in it. At particularly dubious passages we were obliged to connect ourselves with each other by a long cord, in order that any man who missed his footing might be held up by his companions. This solid formation was prudent, but did not remove all danger.

Yet, notwithstanding the difficulties of the descent, down steeps unknown to the guide, the journey was accomplished without accidents, except the loss of a coil of rope, which escaped from the hands of an Icelander, and took the shortest way to the bottom of the abyss.

At midday we arrived. I raised my head and saw straight above me the upper aperture of the cone, framing a bit of sky of very small circumference, but almost perfectly round. Just upon the edge appeared the snowy peak of Saris, standing out sharp and clear against endless space.

At the bottom of the crater were three chimneys, through which, in its eruptions, Snæfell had driven forth fire and lava from its central furnace. Each of these chimneys was a hundred feet in diameter. They gaped before us right in our path. I had not the courage to look down either of them. But Professor Liedenbrock had hastily surveyed all three; he was panting, running from one to the other, gesticulating, and uttering incoherent expressions. Hans and his comrades, seated upon loose lava rocks, looked at him with as much wonder as they knew how to express, and perhaps taking him for an escaped lunatic.

Suddenly my uncle uttered a cry. I thought his foot must have slipped and that he had fallen down one of the holes. But, no; I saw him, with arms outstretched and legs straddling wide apart, erect before a granite rock that stood in the center of the crater, just like a pedestal made ready to receive a statue of Pluto. He stood like a man stupefied, but the stupefaction soon gave way to delirious rapture.

"Axel, Axel," he cried. "Come, come!"

I ran. Hans and the Icelanders never stirred.

"Look!" cried the professor.

And, sharing his astonishment, but I think not his joy, I read on the western face of the block, in Runic characters, half moldered away with lapse of ages, this thrice-accursed name:

"Arne Saknussemm!" replied my uncle. "Do you yet doubt?"

I made no answer; and I returned in silence to my lava seat in a state of utter speechless consternation. Here was crushing evidence.

How long I remained plunged in agonizing reflections I cannot tell; all that I know is, that on raising my head again, I saw only my uncle and Hans at the bottom of the crater. The Icelanders had been dismissed, and they were now descending the outer slopes of Snæfell to return to Stapi.

Hans slept peaceably at the foot of a rock, in a lava bed, where he had found a suitable couch for himself; but my uncle was pacing around the bottom of the crater like a wild beast in a cage. I had neither the wish nor the strength to rise, and following the guide's example I went off into an unhappy slumber, fancying I could hear ominous noises or feel tremblings within the recesses of the mountain.

Thus the first night in the crater passed away.

The next morning, a gray, heavy, cloudy sky seemed to droop over the summit of the cone. I did not know this first from the appearances of nature, but I found it out by my uncle's impetuous wrath.

I soon found out the cause, and hope dawned again in my heart. For this reason.

Of the three ways open before us, one had been taken by Saknussemm. The indications of the learned Icelander hinted at in the cryptogram, pointed to this fact that the shadow of Scartaris came to touch that particular way during the latter days of the month of June.

That sharp peak might hence be considered as the gnomon of a vast sundial, the shadow projected from which on a certain day would point out the road to the center of the earth.

Now, no sun no shadow, and therefore no guide. Here was June 25. If the sun was clouded for six days we must postpone our visit till next year.

My limited powers of description would fail, were I to attempt a picture of the professor's angry impatience. The day wore on, and no shadow came to lay itself along the bottom of the crater. Hans did not move from the spot he had selected; yet he must be asking himself what were we waiting for, if he asked himself anything at all. My uncle spoke not a word to me. His gaze, ever directed upward, was lost in the gray and misty space beyond.

On the 26th nothing yet. Rain mingled with snow was falling all day long. Hans built a hut of pieces of lava. I felt a malicious pleasure in watching the thousand rills and cascades that came tumbling down the sides of the cone, and the deafening continuous din awaked by every stone against which they bounded.

My uncle's rage knew no bounds. It was enough to irritate a meeker man than he; for it was foundering almost within the port.

But Heaven never sends unmixed grief, and for Professor Liedenbrock there was a satisfaction in store proportioned to his desperate anxieties.

The next day the sky was again overcast; but on the 29th of June, the last day but one of the month, with the change of the moon came a change of weather. The sun poured a flood of light down the crater. Every hillock, every rock and stone, every projecting surface had its share of the beaming torrent, and threw its shadow on the ground. Among them all, Scartaris laid down his sharp-pointed angular shadow, which began to move slowly in the opposite direction to that of the radiant orb.

My uncle turned too, and followed it.

At noon, being at its least extent, it came and softly fell upon the edge of the middle chimney.

"There it is! There it is!" shouted the professor.

"Now for the center of the globe!" he added in Danish.

I looked at Hans, to hear what he would say.

"*Forüt!*" was his tranquil answer.

"Forward!" replied my uncle.

It was thirteen minutes past one.

## CHAPTER XVII

### VERTICAL DESCENT

Now began our real journey. Hitherto our toil had overcome all difficulties, now difficulties would spring up at every step.

I had not yet ventured to look down the bottomless pit into which I was about to take a plunge. The supreme hour had come. I might now either share in the enterprise or refuse to move forward. But I was ashamed to recoil in the presence of the hunter. Hans accepted the enterprise with such calmness, such indifference, such perfect disregard of any possible danger that I blushed at the idea of being less brave than he. If I had been alone I might have once more tried the effect of argument; but in the presence of the guide I held my peace; my heart flew back to my sweet Virlandaise, and I approached the central chimney.

I have already mentioned that it was a hundred feet in diameter, and three hundred feet round. I bent over a projecting rock and gazed down. My hair stood on end with terror. The bewildering feeling of vacuity laid hold upon me. I felt my center of gravity shifting its place, and giddiness mounting into my brain like drunkenness. There is nothing more treacherous than this attraction down deep abysses. I was just about to drop down, when a hand laid hold of me. It was that of Hans. I suppose I had not taken as many lessons on gulf exploration as I ought to have done in the Frelsers Kirk at Copenhagen.

But, however short was my examination of this well, I had taken some account of its conformation. Its almost perpendicular walls were bristling with innumerable projections which would facilitate the descent. But if there was no want of steps, still there was no rail. A rope fastened to the edge of the aperture might have helped us down. But how were we to unfasten it, when arrived at the other end?

My uncle employed a very simple expedient to obviate this difficulty. He uncoiled a cord of the thickness of a finger, and four hundred feet long; first he dropped half of it down, then he passed it round a lava block that projected conveniently, and threw the other half down the chimney. Each of us could then descend by holding with the hand both halves of the rope, which would not be able to unroll itself from its hold; when two hundred feet down, it would be easy to get possession of the whole of the rope by letting one end go and pulling down by the other. Then the exercise would go on again ad infinitum.

"Now," said my uncle, after having completed these preparations, "now let us look to our loads. I will divide them into three lots; each of us will strap one upon his back. I mean only fragile articles."

Of course, we were not included under that head.

"Hans," said he, "will take charge of the tools and a portion of the provisions; you, Axel, will take another third of the provisions, and the arms; and I will take the rest of the provisions and the delicate instruments."

"But," said I, "the clothes, and that mass of ladders and ropes, what is to become of them?"

"They will go down by themselves."

"How so?" I asked.

"You will see presently."

My uncle was always willing to employ magnificent resources. Obeying orders, Hans tied all the nonfragile articles in one bundle, corded them firmly, and sent them bodily down the gulf before us.

I listened to the dull thuds of the descending bale. My uncle, leaning over the abyss, followed the descent of the luggage with a satisfied nod, and only rose erect when he had quite lost sight of it.

"Very well, now it is our turn."

Now I ask any sensible man if it was possible to hear those words without a shudder.

The professor fastened his package of instruments upon his shoulders; Hans took the tools; I took the arms: and the descent commenced in the following order; Hans, my uncle, and myself. It was effected in profound silence, broken only by the descent of loosened stones down the dark gulf.

I dropped as it were, frantically clutching the double cord with one hand and buttressing myself from the wall with the other by means of my stick. One idea overpowered me almost, fear lest the rock should give way from which I was hanging. This cord seemed a fragile thing for three persons to be suspended from. I made as little use of it as possible, performing wonderful feats of equilibrium upon the lava projections which my foot seemed to catch hold of like a hand.

When one of these slippery steps shook under the heavier form of Hans, he said in his tranquil voice:

*"Gif akt!"*

"Attention!" repeated my uncle.

In half an hour we were standing upon the surface of a rock jammed in across the chimney from one side to the other.

Hans pulled the rope by one of its ends, the other rose in the air; after passing the higher rock it came down again, bringing with it a rather dangerous shower of bits of stone and lava.

Leaning over the edge of our narrow standing ground, I observed that the bottom of the hole was still invisible.

The same maneuver was repeated with the cord, and half an hour after we had descended another two hundred feet.

I don't suppose the maddest geologist under such circumstances would have studied the nature of the rocks that we were passing. I am sure I did trouble my head about them. Pliocene, Miocene, Eocene, Cretaceous, Jurassic, Triassic, Permian, Carboniferous, Devonian, Silurian, or primitive was all one to me. But the professor, no doubt, was pursuing his observations or taking notes, for in one of our halts he said to me:

"The farther I go the more confidence I feel. The order of these volcanic formations affords the strongest confirmation to the theories of Davy. We are now among the primitive rocks, upon which the chemical operations took place which are produced by the contact of elementary bases of metals with water. I repudiate the notion of central heat altogether. We shall see further proof of that very soon."

No variation, always the same conclusion. Of course, I was not inclined to argue. My silence was taken for consent and the descent went on.

Another three hours, and I saw no bottom to the chimney yet. When I lifted my head I perceived the gradual contraction of its aperture. Its walls, by a gentle incline, were drawing closer to each other, and it was beginning to grow darker.

Still we kept descending. It seemed to me that the falling stones were meeting with an earlier resistance, and that the concussion gave a more abrupt and deadened sound.

As I had taken care to keep an exact account of our maneuvers with the rope, which I knew that we had repeated fourteen times, each descent occupying half an hour, the conclusion was easy that we had been seven hours, plus fourteen quarters of rest, making ten hours and a half. We had started at one, it must therefore now be eleven o'clock; and the depth to which we had descended was fourteen times 200 feet, or 2,800 feet.

At this moment I heard the voice of Hans.

"Halt!" he cried.

I stopped short just as I was going to place my feet upon my uncle's head.

"We are there," he cried.

"Where?" said I, stepping near to him.

"At the bottom of the perpendicular chimney," he answered.

"Is there no way farther?"

"Yes; there is a sort of passage which inclines to the right. We will see about that tomorrow. Let us have our supper, and go to sleep."

The darkness was not yet complete. The provision case was opened; we refreshed ourselves, and went to sleep as well as we could upon a bed of stones and lava fragments.

When lying on my back, I opened my eyes and saw a bright sparkling point of light at the extremity of the gigantic tube 3,000 feet long, now a vast telescope.

It was a star which, seen from this depth, had lost all scintillation, and which by my computation should be 3 Ursa minor. Then I fell fast asleep.

## CHAPTER XVIII

### THE WONDERS OF TERRESTRIAL DEPTHS

At eight in the morning a ray of daylight came to wake us up. The thousand shining surfaces of lava on the walls received it on its passage, and scattered it like a shower of sparks.

There was light enough to distinguish surrounding objects.

"Well, Axel, what do you say to it?" cried my uncle, rubbing his hands. "Did you ever spend a quieter night in our little house at Königsberg? No noise of cart wheels, no cries of basket women, no boatmen shouting!"

"No doubt it is very quiet at the bottom of this well, but there is something alarming in the quietness itself."

"Now, come!" my uncle cried. "If you are frightened already, what will you be by and by? We have not gone a single inch yet into the bowels of the earth."

"What do you mean?"

"I mean that we have only reached the level of the island, long vertical tube, which terminates at the mouth of the crater, has its lower end only at the level of the sea."

"Are you sure of that?"

"Quite sure. Consult the barometer."

In fact, the mercury, which had risen in the instrument as fast as we descended, had stopped at twenty-nine inches.

"You see," said the professor, "we have now only the pressure of our atmosphere, and I shall be glad when the aneroid takes the place of the barometer."

And in truth this instrument would become useless as soon as the weight of the atmosphere should exceed the pressure ascertained at the level of the sea.

"But," I said, "is there not reason to fear that this ever-increasing pressure will become at last very painful to bear?"

"No; we shall descend at a slow rate, and our lungs will become inured to a denser atmosphere. Aeronauts find the want of air as they rise to high elevations, but we shall perhaps have too much: of the two, this is what I should prefer. Don't let us lose a moment. Where is the bundle we sent down before us?"

I then remembered that we had searched for it in vain the evening before. My uncle questioned Hans, who, after having examined attentively with the eye of a huntsman, replied:

"*Der huppe!*"

"Up there."

And so it was. The bundle had been caught by a projection a hundred feet above us. Immediately the Icelander climbed up like a cat, and in a few minutes the package was in our possession.

"Now," said my uncle, "let us breakfast; but we must lay in a good stock, for we don't know how long we may have to go on."

The biscuit and extract of meat were washed down with a draft of water mingled with a little gin.

Breakfast over, my uncle drew from his pocket a small notebook, intended for scientific observations. He consulted his instruments, and recorded:

"Monday, July 1.

"Chronometer, 8.17 a.m.; barometer, 297 in.; thermometer, 6° (43°F). Direction, E.S.E."

This last observation applied to the dark gallery, and was indicated by the compass.

"Now, Axel," cried the professor with enthusiasm, "now we are really going into the interior of the earth. At this precise moment the journey commences."

So saying, my uncle took in one hand Ruhmkorff's apparatus, which was hanging from his neck; and with the other he formed an electric communication with the coil in the lantern, and a sufficiently bright light dispersed the darkness of the passage.

Hans carried the other apparatus, which was also put into action. This ingenious application of electricity would enable us to go on for a long time by creating an artificial light even in the midst of the most inflammable gases.

"Now, march!" cried my uncle.

Each shouldered his package. Hans drove before him the load of cords and clothes; and, myself walking last, we entered the gallery.

At the moment of becoming engulfed in this dark gallery, I raised my head, and saw for the last time through the length of that vast tube the sky of Iceland, which I was never to behold again.

The lava, in the last eruption of 1229, had forced a passage through this tunnel. It still lined the walls with a thick and glistening coat. The electric light was here intensified a hundredfold by reflection.

The only difficulty in proceeding lay in not sliding too fast down an incline of about forty-five degrees; happily certain asperities and a few blisterings here and there formed steps, and we descended, letting our baggage slip before us from the end of a long rope.

But that which formed steps under our feet became stalactites overhead. The lava, which was porous in many places, had formed a surface covered with small rounded blisters; crystals of opaque quartz, set with limpid tears of glass, and hanging like clustered chandeliers from the vaulted roof, seemed as it were to kindle and form a sudden illumination as we passed on our way. It seemed as if the genii of the depths were lighting up their palace to receive their terrestrial guests.

"It is magnificent!" I cried spontaneously. "My uncle, what a sight! Don't you admire those blending hues of lava, passing from reddish-brown to bright yellow by imperceptible shades? And these crystals are just like globes of light."

"Ah, you think so, do you, Axel, my boy? Well, you will see greater splendors than these, I hope. Now let us march: march!"

He had better have said slide, for we did nothing but drop down the steep inclines. It was the *facifs descensus Averni* of Virgil. The compass, which I consulted frequently, gave our direction as southeast with inflexible steadiness. This lava stream deviated neither to the right nor to the left.

Yet there was no sensible increase of temperature. This justified Davy's theory, and more than once I consulted the thermometer with surprise. Two hours after our departure it only marked 10° (50°F), an increase of only 4°. This gave reason for believing that our descent was more horizontal than vertical. As for the exact depth reached, it was very easy to ascertain that; the professor measured accurately the angles of deviation and inclination on the road, but he kept the results to himself.

About eight in the evening he signaled to stop. Hans sat down at once. The lamps were hung upon a projection in the lava; we were in a sort of cavern where there was plenty of air. Certain puffs of air reached us. What atmospheric disturbance was the cause of them? I could not answer that question at the moment. Hunger and fatigue made me incapable of reasoning. A descent of seven hours consecutively is not made without considerable expenditure of strength. I was exhausted. The order to "halt" therefore gave me pleasure. Hans laid our provisions upon a block of lava, and we ate with a good appetite. But one thing troubled me, our supply of water was half consumed. My uncle reckoned upon a fresh supply from subterranean sources, but hitherto we had met with none. I could not help drawing his attention to this circumstance.

"Are you surprised at this want of springs?" he said.

"More than that, I am anxious about it; we have only water enough for five days."

"Don't be uneasy, Axel, we shall find more than we want."

"When?"

"When we have left this bed of lava behind us. How could springs break through such walls as these?"

"But perhaps this passage runs to a very great depth. It seems to me that we have made no great progress vertically."

"Why do you suppose that?"

"Because if we had gone deep into the crust of earth, we should have encountered greater heat."

"According to your system," said my uncle. "But what does the thermometer say?"

"Hardly fifteen degrees (59°F), nine degrees only since our departure."

"Well, what is your conclusion?"

"This is my conclusion. According to exact observations, the increase of temperature in the interior of the globe advances at the rate of one degree (1.8°F) for every hundred feet. But certain local conditions may modify this rate. Thus at Yakoutsk in Siberia the increase of a degree is ascertained to be reached every 36 feet. This difference depends upon the heat-conducting power of the rocks. Moreover, in the neighborhood of an extinct volcano, through gneiss, it has been observed that the increase of a degree is only attained at every 125 feet. Let us therefore assume this last hypothesis as the most suitable to our situation, and calculate."

"Well, do calculate, my boy."

"Nothing is easier," said I, putting down figures in my notebook. "Nine times a hundred and twenty-five feet gives a depth of eleven hundred and twenty-five feet."

"Very accurate indeed."

"Well?"

"By my observation we are at 10,000 feet below the level of the sea."

"Is that possible?"

"Yes, or figures are of no use."

The professor's calculations were quite correct. We had already attained a depth of six thousand feet beyond that hitherto reached by the foot of man, such as the mines of Kitz Bahl in Tyrol, and those of Wuttembourg in Bohemia.

The temperature, which ought to have been 81° (178°F) was scarcely 15° (59°F). Here was cause for reflection.

## CHAPTER XIX

### GEOLOGICAL STUDIES IN SITU

Next day, Tuesday, June 30, at 6 a.m., the descent began again. We were still following the gallery of lava, a real natural staircase, and as gently sloping as those inclined planes which in some old houses are still found instead of flights of steps. And so we went on until 12:17, the precise moment when we overtook Hans, who had stopped.

"Ah! Here we are," exclaimed my uncle, "at the very end of the chimney."

I looked around me. We were standing at the intersection of two roads, both dark and narrow. Which were we to take? This was a difficulty.

Still my uncle refused to admit an appearance of hesitation, either before me or the guide; he pointed out the eastern tunnel, and we were soon all three in it.

Besides there would have been interminable hesitation before this choice of roads; for since there was no indication whatever to guide our choice, we were obliged to trust to chance.

The slope of this gallery was scarcely perceptible, and its sections very unequal. Sometimes we passed a series of arches succeeding each other like the majestic arcades of a Gothic cathedral. Here the architects of the Middle Ages might have found studies for every form of the sacred art which sprang from the development of the pointed arch. A mile farther we had to bow our heads under corniced elliptic arches in the Romanesque style; and massive pillars standing out from the wall bent under the spring of the vault that rested heavily upon them. In other places this magnificence gave way to narrow channels between low structures which looked like beaver's huts, and we had to creep along through extremely narrow passages.

The heat was perfectly bearable. Involuntarily I began to think of its heat when the lava thrown out by Snæfell was boiling and working through this now-silent road. I imagined the torrents of fire hurled back at every angle in the gallery, and the accumulation of intensely heated vapors in the midst of this confined channel.

I only hope, thought I, that this so-called extinct volcano won't take a fancy in his old age to begin his sports again!

I abstained from communicating these fears to Professor Liedenbrock. He would never have understood them at all. He had but one idea—forward! He walked, he slid, he scrambled, he tumbled, with a persistence which one could not but admire.

By six in the evening, after a not very fatiguing walk, we had gone two leagues south, but scarcely a quarter of a mile down.

My uncle said it was time to go to sleep. We ate without talking, and went to sleep without reflection.

Our arrangements for the night were very simple; a railway rug each, into which we rolled ourselves, was our sole covering. We had neither cold nor intrusive visits to fear. Travelers who penetrate into the wilds of central Africa, and into the pathless forests of the New World, are obliged to watch over each other by night. But we enjoyed absolute safety and utter seclusion; no savages or wild beasts infested these silent depths.

Next morning, we awoke fresh and in good spirits. The road was resumed. As the day before, we followed the path of the lava. It was impossible to tell what rocks we were passing: the tunnel, instead of tending lower, approached more and more nearly to a horizontal direction, I even fancied a slight rise. But about ten this upward tendency became so evident, and therefore so fatiguing, that I was obliged to slacken my pace.

"Well, Axel?" demanded the professor impatiently.

"Well, I cannot stand it any longer," I replied.

"What! After three hours' walk over such easy ground."

"It may be easy, but it is tiring all the same."

"What, when we have nothing to do but keep going down!"

"Going up, if you please."

"Going up!" said my uncle, with a shrug.

"No doubt, for the last half-hour the inclines have gone the other way, and at this rate we shall soon arrive upon the level soil of Iceland."

The professor nodded slowly and uneasily like a man that declines to be convinced. I tried to resume the conversation. He answered not a word, and gave the signal for a start. I saw that his silence was nothing but ill humor.

Still I had courageously shouldered my burden again, and was rapidly following Hans, whom my uncle preceded. I was anxious not to be left behind. My greatest care was not to lose sight of my companions. I shuddered at the thought of being lost in the mazes of this vast subterranean labyrinth.

Besides, if the ascending road did become steeper, I was comforted with the thought that it was bringing us nearer to the surface. There was hope in this. Every step confirmed me in it, and I was rejoicing at the thought of meeting my little Gräuben again.

By midday there was a change in the appearance of this wall of the gallery. I noticed it by a diminution of the amount of light reflected from the sides; solid rock was appearing in the place of the lava coating. The mass was composed of inclined and sometimes vertical strata. We were passing through rocks of the transition or Silurian system.

"It is evident," I cried, "the marine deposits formed in the second period, these shales, limestones, and sandstones. We are turning away from the primary granite. We are just as if we were people of Hamburg going to Lübeck by way of Hanover!"

I had better have kept my observations to myself. But my geological instinct was stronger than my prudence, and Uncle Liedenbrock heard my exclamation.

"What's that you are saying?" he asked.

"See," I said, pointing to the varied series of sandstones and limestones, and the first indication of slate.

"Well?"

"We are at the period when the first plants and animals appeared."

"Do you think so?"

"Look close, and examine."

I obliged the professor to move his lamp over the walls of the gallery. I expected some signs of astonishment; but he spoke not a word, and went on.

Had he understood me or not? Did he refuse to admit, out of self-love as an uncle and a philosopher, that he had mistaken his way when he chose the eastern tunnel? Or was he determined to examine this passage to its farthest extremity? It was evident that we had left the lava path, and that this road could not possibly lead to the extinct furnace of Snæfell.

Yet I asked myself if I was not depending too much on this change in the rock. Might I not myself be mistaken? Were we really crossing the layers of rock which overlie the granite foundation?

If I am right, I thought, I must soon find some fossil remains of primitive life; and then we must yield to evidence. I will look.

I had not gone a hundred paces before incontestable proofs presented themselves. It could not be otherwise, for in the Silurian age the seas contained at least fifteen hundred vegetable and animal species. My feet, which had become accustomed to the indurated lava floor, suddenly rested upon a dust composed of the debris of plants and shells. In the walls were distinct impressions of fucoids and lycopodites.

Professor Liedenbrock could not be mistaken, I thought, and yet he pushed on, with, I suppose, his eyes resolutely shut.

This was only invincible obstinacy. I could hold out no longer. I picked up a perfectly formed shell, which had belonged to an animal not unlike the woodlouse: then, joining my uncle, I said:

"Look at this!"

"Very well," said he quietly, "it is the shell of a crustacean, of an extinct species called a trilobite. Nothing more."

"But don't you conclude—?"

"Just what you conclude yourself. Yes; I do, perfectly. We have left the granite and the lava. It is possible that I may be mistaken. But I cannot be sure of that until I have reached the very end of this gallery."

"You are right in doing this, my uncle, and I should quite approve of your determination, if there were not a danger threatening us nearer and nearer."

"What danger?"

"The want of water."

"Well, Axel, we will put ourselves upon rations."

## CHAPTER XX

## THE FIRST SIGNS OF DISTRESS

In fact, we had to ration ourselves. Our provision of water could not last more than three days. I found that out for certain when supper time came. And, to our sorrow, we had little reason to expect to find a spring in these transition beds.

The whole of the next day the gallery opened before us its endless arcades. We moved on almost without a word. Hans's silence seemed to be infecting us.

The road was now not ascending, at least not perceptibly. Sometimes, even, it seemed to have a slight fall. But this tendency, which was very trifling, could not do anything to reassure the professor; for there was no change in the beds, and the transitional characteristics became more and more decided.

The electric light was reflected in sparkling splendor from the schist, limestone, and old red sandstone of the walls. It might have been thought that we were passing through a section of Wales, of which an ancient people gave its name to this system. Specimens of magnificent marbles clothed the walls, some of a grayish agate fantastically veined with white, others of rich crimson or yellow dashed with splotches of red; then came dark cherry-colored marbles relieved by the lighter tints of limestone.

The greater part of these bore impressions of primitive organisms. Creation had evidently advanced since the day before. Instead of rudimentary trilobites, I noticed remains of a more perfect order of beings, among others ganoid fishes and some of those sauroids in which paleontologists have discovered the earliest reptile forms. The Devonian seas were peopled by animals of these species, and deposited them by thousands in the rocks of the newer formation.

It was evident that we were ascending that scale of animal life in which man fills the highest place. But Professor Liedenbrock seemed not to notice it.

He was awaiting one of two events, either the appearance of a vertical well opening before his feet, down which our descent might be resumed, or that of some obstacle which should effectually turn us back on our own footsteps. But evening came and neither wish was gratified.

On Friday, after a night during which I felt pangs of thirst, our little troop again plunged into the winding passages of the gallery.

After ten hours' walking I observed a singular deadening of the reflection of our lamps from the side walls. The marble, the schist, the limestone, and the sandstone were giving way to a dark and lusterless lining. At one moment, the tunnel becoming very narrow, I leaned against the wall.

When I removed my hand it was black. I looked nearer, and found we were in a coal formation.

"A coal mine!" I cried.

"A mine without miners," my uncle replied.

"Who knows?" I asked.

"I know," the professor pronounced decidedly, "I am certain that this gallery driven through beds of coal was never pierced by the hand of man. But whether it be the hand of nature or not does not matter. Supper time is come; let us sup."

Hans prepared some food. I scarcely ate, and I swallowed down the few drops of water rationed out to me. One flask half full was all we had left to slake the thirst of three men.

After their meal my two companions laid themselves down upon their rugs, and found in sleep a solace for their fatigue. But I could not sleep, and I counted every hour until morning.

On Saturday, at six, we started afresh. In twenty minutes we reached a vast open space; I then knew that the hand of man had not hollowed out this mine; the vaults would have been shored up, and, as it was, they seemed to be held up by a miracle of equilibrium.

This cavern was about a hundred feet wide and a hundred and fifty in height. A large mass had been rent asunder by a subterranean disturbance. Yielding to some vast power from below it had broken asunder, leaving this great hollow into which human beings were now penetrating for the first time.

The whole history of the Carboniferous period was written upon these gloomy walls, and a geologist might with ease trace all its diverse phases. The beds of coal were separated by strata of sandstone or compact clays, and appeared crushed under the weight of overlying strata.

At the age of the world which preceded the secondary period, the earth was clothed with immense vegetable forms, the product of the double influence of tropical heat and constant moisture; a vapory atmosphere surrounded the earth, still veiling the direct rays of the sun.

Thence arises the conclusion that the high temperature then existing was due to some other source than the heat of the sun. Perhaps even the orb of day may not have been ready yet to play the splendid part he now acts. There were no "climates" as yet, and a torrid heat, equal from pole to equator, was spread over the whole surface of the globe. Whence this heat? Was it from the interior of the earth?

Notwithstanding the theories of Professor Liedenbrock, a violent heat did at that time brood within the body of the spheroid. Its action was felt to the very last coats of the terrestrial crust; the plants, unacquainted with the beneficent influences of the sun, yielded neither flowers nor scent. But their roots drew vigorous life from the burning soil of the early days of this planet.

There were but few trees. Herbaceous plants alone existed. There were tall grasses, ferns, lycopods, besides sigillaria, asterophyllites, now scarce plants, but then the species might be counted by thousands.

The coal measures owe their origin to this period of profuse vegetation. The yet elastic and yielding crust of the earth obeyed the fluid forces beneath. Thence innumerable fissures and depressions. The plants, sunk underneath the waters, formed by degrees into vast accumulated masses.

Then came the chemical action of nature; in the depths of the seas the vegetable accumulations first became peat; then, acted upon by generated gases and the heat of fermentation, they underwent a process of complete mineralization.

Thus were formed those immense coalfields, which nevertheless are not inexhaustible, and which three centuries at the present accelerated rate of consumption will exhaust unless the industrial world will devise a remedy.

These reflections came into my mind while I was contemplating the mineral wealth stored up in this portion of the globe. These no doubt, I thought, will never be discovered; the working of such deep mines would involve too large an outlay, and where would be the use as long as coal is yet spread far and wide near the surface? Such as my eyes behold these virgin stores, such they will be when this world comes to an end.

But still we marched on, and I alone was forgetting the length of the way by losing myself in the midst of geological contemplations. The temperature remained what it had been during our passage through the lava and schists. Only my sense of smell was forcibly affected by an odor of protocarburet of hydrogen. I immediately recognized in this gallery the presence of a considerable quantity of the dangerous gas called by miners firedamp, the explosion of which has often occasioned such dreadful catastrophes.

Happily, our light was from Ruhmkorff's ingenious apparatus. If unfortunately we had explored this gallery with torches, a terrible explosion would have put an end to traveling and travelers at one stroke.

This excursion through the coal mine lasted till night. My uncle scarcely could restrain his impatience at the horizontal road. The darkness, always deep twenty yards before us, prevented us from estimating the length of the gallery; and I was beginning to think it must be endless, when suddenly at six o'clock a wall very unexpectedly stood before us. Right or left, top or bottom, there was no road farther; we were at the end of a blind alley. "Very well, it's all right!" cried my uncle. "Now, at any rate, we shall know what we are about. We are not in Saknussemm's road, and all we have to do is to go back. Let us take a night's rest, and in three days we shall get to the fork in the road."

"Yes," said I, "if we have any strength left."

"Why not?"

"Because tomorrow we shall have no water."

"Nor courage either?" asked my uncle severely.

I dared make no answer.

## CHAPTER XXI

### COMPASSION FUSES THE PROFESSOR'S HEART

Next day we started early. We had to hasten forward. It was a three days' march to the crossroads.

I will not speak of the sufferings we endured in our return. My uncle bore them with the angry impatience of a man obliged to own his weakness; Hans with the resignation of his passive nature; I, I confess, with complaints and expressions of despair. I had no spirit to oppose this ill fortune.

As I had foretold, the water failed entirely by the end of the first day's retrograde march. Our fluid aliment was now nothing but gin; but this infernal fluid burned my throat, and I could not even endure the sight of it. I found the temperature and the air stifling. Fatigue paralyzed my limbs. More than once I dropped down motionless. Then there was a halt; and my uncle and the Icelander did their best to restore me. But I saw that the former was struggling painfully against excessive fatigue and the tortures of thirst.

At last, on Tuesday, July 8, we arrived on our hands and knees, and half dead, at the junction of the two roads. There I dropped like a lifeless lump, extended on the lava soil. It was ten in the morning.

Hans and my uncle, clinging to the wall, tried to nibble a few bits of biscuit. Long moans escaped from my swollen lips.

After some time my uncle approached me and raised me in his arms.

"Poor boy!" said he, in genuine tones of compassion.

I was touched with these words, not being accustomed to see the excitable professor in a softened mood. I grasped his trembling hands in mine. He let me hold them and looked at me. His eyes were moistened.

Then I saw him take the flask that was hanging at his side. To my amazement he placed it on my lips.

"Drink!" said he.

Had I heard him? Was my uncle beside himself? I stared at, him stupidly, and felt as if I could not understand him.

"Drink!" he said again.

And raising his flask he emptied it every drop between my lips.

Oh! Infinite pleasure! A slender sip of water came to moisten my burning mouth. It was but one sip, but it was enough to recall my ebbing life.

I thanked my uncle with clasped hands.

"Yes," he said, "a draft of water; but it is the very last—you hear!—the last. I had kept it as a precious treasure at the bottom of my flask. Twenty times, nay, a hundred times, have I fought against a frightful impulse to drink it off. But no, Axel, I kept it for you."

"My dear uncle," I said, while hot tears trickled down my face.

"Yes, my poor boy, I knew that as soon as you arrived at these crossroads you would drop half dead, and I kept my last drop of water to reanimate you."

"Thank you, thank you," I said. Although my thirst was only partially quenched, yet some strength had returned. The muscles of my throat, until then contracted, now relaxed again; and the inflammation of my lips abated somewhat; and I was now able to speak.

"Let us see," I said, "we have now but one thing to do. We have no water; we must go back."

While I spoke my uncle avoided looking at me; he hung his head down; his eyes avoided mine.

"We must return," I exclaimed vehemently; "we must go back on our way to Snæfell. May God give us strength to climb up the crater again!"

"Return!" said my uncle, as if he was rather answering himself than me.

"Yes, return, without the loss of a minute."

A long silence followed.

"So then, Axel," replied the professor ironically, "you have found no courage or energy in these few drops of water?"

"Courage?"

"I see you just as feeble-minded as you were before, and still expressing only despair!"

What sort of a man was this I had to do with, and what schemes was he now revolving in his fearless mind?

"What! You won't go back?"

"Should I renounce this expedition just when we have the fairest chance of success! Never!"

"Then must we resign ourselves to destruction?"

"No, Axel, no; go back. Hans will go with you. Leave me to myself!"

"Leave you here!"

"Leave me, I tell you. I have undertaken this expedition. I will carry it out to the end, and I will not return. Go, Axel, go!"

My uncle was in high state of excitement. His voice, which had for a moment been tender and gentle, had now become hard and threatening. He was struggling with gloomy resolutions against impossibilities. I would not leave him in this bottomless abyss, and on the other hand the instinct of self-preservation prompted me to fly.

The guide watched this scene with his usual phlegmatic unconcern. Yet he understood perfectly well what was going on between his two companions. The gestures themselves were sufficient to show that we were each bent on taking a different road; but Hans seemed to take no part in a question upon which depended his life. He was ready to start at a given signal, or to stay, if his master so willed it.

How I wished at this moment I could have made him understand me. My words, my complaints, my sorrow would have had some influence over that frigid nature. Those dangers which our guide could not understand I could have demonstrated and proved to him. Together we might have overruled the obstinate professor; if it were needed, we might perhaps have compelled him to regain the heights of Snæfell.

I drew near to Hans. I placed my hand upon his. He made no movement. My parted lips sufficiently revealed my sufferings. The Icelander slowly moved his head, and calmly pointing to my uncle said:

"Master."

"Master!" I shouted. "You madman! No, he is not the master of our life; we must fly, we must drag him. Do you hear me? Do you understand?"

I had seized Hans by the arm. I wished to oblige him to rise. I strove with him. My uncle interposed.

"Be calm, Axel! You will get nothing from that immovable servant. Therefore, listen to my proposal."

I crossed my arms, and confronted my uncle boldly.

"The want of water," he said, "is the only obstacle in our way. In this eastern gallery made up of lavas, schists, and coal, we have not met with a single particle of moisture. Perhaps we shall be more fortunate if we follow the western tunnel."

I shook my head incredulously.

"Hear me to the end," the professor went on with a firm voice. "While you were lying there motionless, I went to examine the conformation of that gallery. It penetrates directly downward, and in a few hours it will bring us to the granite rocks. There we must meet with abundant springs. The nature of the rock assures me of this, and instinct agrees with logic to support my conviction. Now, this is my proposal. When Columbus asked of his ships' crews for three days more to discover a new world, those crews, disheartened and sick as they were, recognized the justice of the claim, and he discovered America. I am the Columbus of this netherworld, and I only ask for one more day. If in a single day I have not met with the water that we want, I swear to you we will return to the surface of the earth."

In spite of my irritation I was moved with these words, as well as with the violence my uncle was doing to his own wishes in making so hazardous a proposal.

"Well," I said, "do as you will, and God reward your superhuman energy. You have now but a few hours to tempt fortune. Let us start!"

## CHAPTER XXII

### TOTAL FAILURE OF WATER

This time the descent commenced by the new gallery. Hans walked first as was his custom.

We had not gone a hundred yards when the professor, moving his lantern along the walls, cried:

"Here are primitive rocks. Now we are in the right way. Forward!"

When in its early stages the earth was slowly cooling, its contraction gave rise in its crust to disruptions, distortions, fissures, and chasms. The passage through which we were moving was such a fissure, through which at one time granite poured out in a molten state. Its thousands of windings formed an inextricable labyrinth through the primeval mass.

As fast as we descended, the succession of beds forming the primitive foundation came out with increasing distinctness. Geologists consider this primitive matter to be the base of the mineral crust of the earth, and have ascertained it to be composed of three different formations, schist, gneiss, and mica schist, resting upon that unchangeable foundation, the granite.

Never had mineralogists found themselves in so marvelous a situation to study nature in situ. What the boring machine, an insensible, inert instrument, was unable to bring to the surface of the inner structure of the globe, we were able to peruse with our own eyes and handle with our own hands.

Through the beds of schist, colored with delicate shades of green, ran in winding course threads of copper and manganese, with traces of platinum and gold. I thought, what riches are here buried at an unapproachable depth in the earth, hidden forever from the covetous eyes of the human race! These treasures have been buried at such a profound depth by the convulsions of primeval times that they run no chance of ever being molested by the pickaxe or the spade.

To the schists succeeded gneiss, partially stratified, remarkable for the parallelism and regularity of its lamina, then mica schists, laid in large plates or flakes, revealing their lamellated structure by the sparkle of the white shining mica.

The light from our apparatus, reflected from the small facets of quartz, shot sparkling rays at every angle, and I seemed to be moving through a diamond, within which the quickly darting rays broke across each other in a thousand flashing coruscations.

About six o'clock this brilliant fete of illuminations underwent a sensible abatement of splendor, then almost ceased. The walls assumed a crystallized though somber appearance; mica was more closely mingled with the feldspar and quartz to form the proper rocky foundations of the earth, which bears without distortion or crushing the weight of the four terrestrial systems. We were immured within prison walls of granite.

It was eight in the evening. No signs of water had yet appeared. I was suffering horribly. My uncle strode on. He refused to stop. He was listening anxiously for the murmur of distant springs. But, no, there was dead silence.

And now my limbs were failing beneath me. I resisted pain and torture, that I might not stop my uncle, which would have driven him to despair, for the day was drawing near to its end, and it was his last.

At last I failed utterly; I uttered a cry and fell.

"Come to me, I am dying."

My uncle retraced his steps. He gazed upon me with his arms crossed; then these muttered words passed his lips:

"It's all over!"

The last thing I saw was a fearful gesture of rage, and my eyes closed.

When I reopened them I saw my two companions motionless and rolled up in their coverings. Were they asleep? As for me, I could not get one moment's sleep. I was suffering too keenly, and what embittered my thoughts was that there was no remedy. My uncle's last words echoed painfully in my ears: "It's all over!" For in such a fearful state of debility, it was madness to think of ever reaching the upper world again.

We had above us a league and a half of terrestrial crust. The weight of it seemed to be crushing down upon my shoulders. I felt weighed down, and I exhausted myself with imaginary violent exertions to turn round upon my granite couch.

A few hours passed away. A deep silence reigned around us, the silence of the grave. No sound could reach us through walls, the thinnest of which were five miles thick.

Yet in the midst of my stupefaction I seemed to be aware of a noise. It was dark down the tunnel, but I seemed to see the Icelander vanishing from our sight with the lamp in his hand.

Why was he leaving us? Was Hans going to forsake us? My uncle was fast asleep. I wanted to shout, but my voice died upon my parched and swollen lips. The darkness became deeper, and the last sound died away in the far distance.

"Hans has abandoned us," I cried. "Hans! Hans!"

But these words were only spoken within me. They went no farther. Yet after the first moment of terror I felt ashamed of suspecting a man of such extraordinary faithfulness. Instead of ascending he was descending the gallery. An evil design would have taken him up, not down. This reflection restored me to calmness, and I turned to other thoughts. None but some weighty motive could have induced so quiet a man to forfeit his sleep. Was he on a journey of discovery? Had he during the silence of the night caught a sound, a murmuring of something in the distance, which had failed to affect my hearing?

## CHAPTER XXIII

### WATER DISCOVERED

For a whole hour I was trying to work out in my delirious brain the reasons which might have influenced this seemingly tranquil huntsman. The absurdest notions ran in utter confusion through my mind. I thought madness was coming on!

But at last a noise of footsteps was heard in the dark abyss. Hans was approaching. A flickering light was beginning to glimmer on the wall of our darksome prison; then it came out full at the mouth of the gallery. Hans appeared.

He drew close to my uncle, laid his hand upon his shoulder, and gently woke him. My uncle rose up.

"What is the matter?" he asked.

"*Watten!*" replied the huntsman.

No doubt under the inspiration of intense pain everybody becomes endowed with the gift of divers tongues. I did not know a word of Danish, yet instinctively I understood the word he had uttered.

"Water! Water!" I cried, clapping my hands and gesticulating like a madman.

"Water!" repeated my uncle. "*Hvar?*" he asked, in Icelandic.

"*Nedat,*" replied Hans.

"Where? Down below!" I understood it all. I seized the hunter's hands, and pressed them while he looked on me without moving a muscle of his countenance.

The preparations for our departure were not long in making, and we were soon on our way down a passage inclining two feet in seven. In an hour we had gone a mile and a quarter, and descended two thousand feet.

Then I began to hear distinctly quite a new sound of something running within the thickness of the granite wall, a kind of dull, dead rumbling, like distant thunder. During the first part of our walk, not meeting with the promised spring, I felt my agony returning; but then my uncle acquainted me with the cause of the strange noise.

"Hans was not mistaken," he said. "What you hear is the rushing of a torrent."

"A torrent?" I exclaimed.

"There can be no doubt; a subterranean river is flowing around us."

We hurried forward in the greatest excitement. I was no longer sensible of my fatigue. This murmuring of waters close at hand was already refreshing me. It was audibly increasing. The torrent, after having for some time flowed over our heads, was now running within the left wall, roaring and rushing. Frequently I touched the wall, hoping to feel some indications of moisture: But there was no hope here.

Yet another half hour, another half league was passed.

Then it became clear that the hunter had gone no farther. Guided by an instinct peculiar to mountaineers, he had as it were felt this torrent through the rock; but he had certainly seen none of the precious liquid; he had drunk nothing himself.

Soon it became evident that if we continued our walk we should widen the distance between ourselves and the stream, the noise of which was becoming fainter.

We returned. Hans stopped where the torrent seemed closest. I sat near the wall, while the waters were flowing past me at a distance of two feet with extreme violence. But there was a thick granite wall between us and the object of our desires.

Without reflection, without asking if there were any means of procuring the water, I gave way to a movement of despair.

Hans glanced at me with, I thought, a smile of compassion.

He rose and took the lamp. I followed him. He moved toward the wall. I looked on. He applied his ear against the dry stone, and moved it slowly to and fro, listening intently. I perceived at once that he was examining to find the exact place where the torrent could be heard the loudest. He met with that point on the left side of the tunnel, at three feet from the ground.

I was stirred up with excitement. I hardly dared guess what the hunter was about to do. But I could not but understand, and applaud and cheer him on, when I saw him lay hold of the pickaxe to make an attack upon the rock.

"We are saved!" I cried.

"Yes," cried my uncle, almost frantic with excitement. "Hans is right. Capital fellow! Who but he would have thought of it?"

Yes; who but he? Such an expedient, however simple, would never have entered into our minds. True, it seemed most hazardous to strike a blow of the hammer in this part of the earth's structure. Suppose some displacement should occur and crush us all! Suppose the torrent, bursting through, should drown us in a sudden flood! There was nothing vain in these fancies. But still no fears of falling rocks or rushing floods could stay us now; and our thirst was so intense that, to satisfy it, we would have dared the waves of the North Atlantic.

Hans set about the task which my uncle and I together could not have accomplished. If our impatience had armed our hands with power, we should have shattered the rock into a thousand fragments. Not so Hans. Full of self-possession, he calmly wore his way through the rock with a steady succession of light and skillful strokes, working through an aperture six inches wide at the outside. I could hear a louder noise of flowing waters, and I fancied I could feel the delicious fluid refreshing my parched lips.

The pick had soon penetrated two feet into the granite partition, and our man had worked for above an hour. I was in an agony of impatience. My uncle wanted to employ stronger measures, and I had some difficulty in dissuading him; still he had just taken a pickaxe in his hand, when a sudden hissing was heard, and a jet of water spurted out with violence against the opposite wall.

Hans, almost thrown off his feet by the violence of the shock, uttered a cry of grief and disappointment, of which I soon understood the cause, when plunging my hands into the spouting torrent, I withdrew them in haste, for the water was scalding hot.

"The water is at the boiling point," I cried.

"Well, never mind, let it cool," my uncle replied.

The tunnel was filling with steam, while a stream was forming, which by degrees wandered away into subterranean windings, and soon we had the satisfaction of swallowing our first draft.

Could anything be more delicious than the sensation that our burning, intolerable thirst was passing away, and leaving us to enjoy comfort and pleasure? But where was this water from? No matter. It was water; and though still warm, it brought life back to the dying. I kept drinking without stopping, and almost without tasting.

At last after a most delightful time of reviving energy, I cried, "Why, this is a chalybeate spring!"

"Nothing could be better for the digestion," said my uncle. "It is highly impregnated with iron. It will be as good for us as going to the spa, or to Töplitz."

"Well, it is delicious!"

"Of course it is, water should be, found six miles underground. It has an inky flavor, which is not at all unpleasant. What a capital source of strength Hans has found for us here. We will call it after his name."

"Agreed," I cried.

And Hansbach it was from that moment.

Hans was none the prouder. After a moderate draft, he went quietly into a corner to rest.

"Now," I said, "we must not lose this water."

"What is the use of troubling ourselves?" my uncle replied. "I fancy it will never fail."

"Never mind, we cannot be sure; let us fill the water bottle and our flasks, and then stop up the opening."

My advice was followed so far as getting in a supply; but the stopping up of the hole was not so easy to accomplish. It was in vain that we took up fragments of granite, and stuffed them in with tow, we only scalded our hands without succeeding. The pressure was too great, and our efforts were fruitless.

"It is quite plain," said I, "that the higher body of this water is at a considerable elevation. The force of the jet shows that."

"No doubt," answered my uncle. "If this column of water is 32,000 feet high—that is, from the surface of the earth, it is equal to the weight of a thousand atmospheres. But I have got an idea."

"Well?"

"Why should we trouble ourselves to stop the stream from coming out at all?"

"Because—" Well, I could not assign a reason.

"When our flasks are empty, where shall we fill them again? Can we tell that?"

No; there was no certainty.

"Well, let us allow the water to run on. It will flow down, and will both guide and refresh us."

"That is well planned," I cried. "With this stream for our guide, there is no reason why we should not succeed in our undertaking."

"Ah, my boy! You agree with me now," cried the professor, laughing.

"I agree with you most heartily."

"Well, let us rest awhile; and then we will start again."

I was forgetting that it was night. The chronometer soon informed me of that fact; and in a very short time, refreshed and thankful, we all three fell into a sound sleep.

## CHAPTER XXIV

### WELL SAID, OLD MOLE! CANST THOU WORK I' THE GROUND SO FAST?

By the next day we had forgotten all our sufferings. At first, I was wondering that I was no longer thirsty, and I was for asking for the reason. The answer came in the murmuring of the stream at my feet.

We breakfasted, and drank of this excellent chalybeate water. I felt wonderfully stronger, and quite decided upon pushing on. Why should not so firmly convinced a man as my uncle, furnished with so industrious a guide as Hans, and accompanied by so determined a nephew as myself, go on to final success? Such were the magnificent plans which struggled for mastery within me. If it had been proposed to me to return to the summit of Snæfell, I should have indignantly declined.

Most fortunately, all we had to do was to descend.

"Let us start!" I cried, awakening by my shouts the echoes of the vaulted hollows of the earth.

On Thursday, at 8 a.m., we started afresh. The granite tunnel winding from side to side, earned us past unexpected turns, and seemed almost to form a labyrinth; but, on the whole, its direction seemed to be southeasterly. My uncle never ceased to consult his compass, to keep account of the ground gone over.

The gallery dipped down a very little way from the horizontal, scarcely more than two inches in a fathom, and the stream ran gently murmuring at our feet. I compared it to a friendly genius guiding us underground, and caressed with my hand the soft naiad, whose comforting voice accompanied our steps. With my reviving spirits these mythological notions seemed to come unbidden.

As for my uncle, he was beginning to storm against the horizontal road. He loved nothing better than a vertical path; but this way seemed indefinitely prolonged, and instead of sliding along the hypotenuse as we were now doing, he would willingly have dropped down the terrestrial radius. But there was no help for it, and as long as we were approaching the center at all we felt that we must not complain.

From time to time, a steeper path appeared; our naiad then began to tumble before us with a hoarser murmur, and we went down with her to a greater depth.

On the whole, that day and the next we made considerable way horizontally, very little vertically.

On Friday evening, the 10th of July, according to our calculations, we were thirty leagues southeast of Reykjavik, and at a depth of two leagues and a half.

At our feet there now opened a frightful abyss. My uncle, however, was not to be daunted, and he clapped his hands at the steepness of the descent.

"This will take us a long way," he cried, "and without much difficulty; for the projections in the rock form quite a staircase."

The ropes were so fastened by Hans as to guard against accident, and the descent commenced. I can hardly call it perilous, for I was beginning to be familiar with this kind of exercise.

This well, or abyss, was a narrow cleft in the mass of the granite, called by geologists a "fault," and caused by the unequal cooling of the globe of the earth. If it had at one time been a passage for eruptive matter thrown out by Snæfell, I still could not understand why no trace was left of its passage. We kept going down a kind of winding staircase, which seemed almost to have been made by the hand of man.

Every quarter of an hour we were obliged to halt, to take a little necessary repose and restore the action of our limbs. We then sat down upon a fragment of rock, and we talked as we ate and drank from the stream.

Of course, down this fault the Hansbach fell in a cascade, and lost some of its volume; but there was enough and to spare to slake our thirst. Besides, when the incline became more gentle, it would of course resume its peaceable course. At this moment it reminded me of my worthy uncle, in his frequent fits of impatience and anger, while below it ran with the calmness of the Icelandic hunter.

On the 6th and 7th of July we kept following the spiral curves of this singular well, penetrating in actual distance no more than two leagues; but being carried to a depth of five leagues below the level of the sea. But on the 8th, about noon, the fault took, toward the southeast, a much gentler slope, one of about forty-five degrees.

Then the road became monotonously easy. It could not be otherwise, for there was no landscape to vary the stages of our journey.

On Wednesday, the 15th, we were seven leagues underground, and had traveled fifty leagues away from Snæfell. Although we were tired, our health was perfect, and the medicine chest had not yet had occasion to be opened.

My uncle noted every hour the indications of the compass, the chronometer, the aneroid, and the thermometer the very same which he has published in his scientific report of our journey. It was therefore not difficult to know exactly our whereabouts. When he told me that we had gone fifty leagues horizontally, I could not repress an exclamation of astonishment, at the thought that we had now long left Iceland behind us.

"What is the matter?" he cried.

"I was reflecting that if your calculations are correct we are no longer under Iceland."

"Do you think so?"

"I am not mistaken," I said, and examining the map, I added, "We have passed Cape Portland, and those fifty leagues bring us under the wide expanse of ocean."

"Under the sea," my uncle repeated, rubbing his hands with delight.

"Can it be?" I said. "Is the ocean spread above our heads?"

"Of course, Axel. What can be more natural? At Newcastle are there not coal mines extending far under the sea?"

It was all very well for the professor to call this so simple, but I could not feel quite easy at the thought that the boundless ocean was rolling over my head. And yet it really mattered very little whether it was the plains and mountains that covered our heads, or the Atlantic waves, as long as we were arched over by solid granite. And, besides, I was getting used to this idea; for the tunnel, now running straight, now winding as capriciously in its inclines as in its turnings, but constantly preserving its southeasterly direction, and always running deeper, was gradually carrying us to very great depths indeed.

Four days later, Saturday, the 18th of July, in the evening, we arrived at a kind of vast grotto; and here my uncle paid Hans his weekly wages, and it was settled that the next day, Sunday, should be a day of rest.

# CHAPTER XXV

## DE PROFUNDIS

I therefore awoke next day relieved from the preoccupation of an immediate start. Although we were in the very deepest of known depths, there was something not unpleasant about it. And, besides, we were beginning to get accustomed to this troglodyte* life. I no longer thought of sun, moon, and stars, trees, houses, and towns, nor of any of those terrestrial superfluities which are necessaries of men who live upon the earth's surface. Being fossils, we looked upon all those things as mere jokes.

The grotto was an immense apartment. Along its granite floor ran our faithful stream. At this distance from its spring the water was scarcely tepid, and we drank of it with pleasure.

After breakfast the professor gave a few hours to the arrangement of his daily notes.

"First," said he, "I will make a calculation to ascertain our exact position. I hope, after our return, to draw a map of our journey, which will be in reality a vertical section of the globe, containing the track of our expedition."

"That will be curious, uncle; but are your observations sufficiently accurate to enable you to do this correctly?"

"Yes; I have everywhere observed the angles and the inclines. I am sure there is no error. Let us see where we are now. Take your compass, and note the direction."

I looked, and replied carefully:

"Southeast by east."

"Well," answered the professor, after a rapid calculation, "I infer that we have gone eighty-five leagues since we started."

"Therefore we are under mid-Atlantic?"

"To be sure we are."

"And perhaps at this very moment there is a storm above, and ships over our heads are being rudely tossed by the tempest."

"Quite probable."

"And whales are lashing the roof of our prison with their tails?"

"It may be, Axel, but they won't shake us here. But let us go back to our calculation. Here we are eighty-five leagues southeast of Snæfell, and I reckon that we are at a depth of sixteen leagues."

"Sixteen leagues?" I cried.

"No doubt."

"Why, this is the very limit assigned by science to the thickness of the crust of the earth."

"I don't deny it."

"And here, according to the law of increasing temperature, there ought to be a heat of 2,732°F!"

---

* τρωγλη, a hole; δύω, to creep into. The name of an Ethiopian tribe who lived in caves and holes.

"So there should, my lad."

"And all this solid granite ought to be running in fusion."

"You see that it is not so, and that, as so often happens, facts come to overthrow theories."

"I am obliged to agree; but, after all, it is surprising."

"What does the thermometer say?"

"Twenty-seven, six tenths (82°F)."

"Therefore the savants are wrong by 2,705°, and the proportional increase is a mistake. Therefore Humphry Davy was right, and I am not wrong in following him. What do you say now?"

"Nothing."

In truth, I had a good deal to say. I gave way in no respect to Davy's theory. I still held to the central heat, although I did not feel its effects. I preferred to admit in truth, that this chimney of an extinct volcano, lined with lavas, which are nonconductors of heat, did not suffer the heat to pass through its walls.

But without stopping to look up new arguments, I simply took up our situation such as it was.

"Well, admitting all your calculations to be quite correct, you must allow me to draw one rigid result therefrom."

"What is it? Speak freely."

"At the latitude of Iceland, where we now are, the radius of the earth, the distance from the center to the surface is about 1,583 leagues; let us say in round numbers 1,600 leagues, or 4,800 miles. Out of 1,600 leagues we have gone twelve!"

"So you say."

"And these twelve at a cost of 85 leagues diagonally?"

"Exactly so."

"In twenty days?"

"Yes."

"Now, sixteen leagues are the hundredth part of the earth's radius. At this rate we shall be two thousand days, or nearly five years and a half, in getting to the center."

No answer was vouchsafed to this rational conclusion. "Without reckoning, too, that if a vertical depth of sixteen leagues can be attained only by a diagonal descent of eighty-four, it follows that we must go eight thousand miles in a southeasterly direction; so that we shall emerge from some point in the earth's circumference instead of getting to the center!"

"Confusion to all your figures, and all your hypotheses besides," shouted my uncle in a sudden rage. "What is the basis of them all? How do you know that this passage does not run straight to our destination? Besides, there is a precedent. What one man has done, another may do."

"I hope so; but, still, I may be permitted—"

"You shall have my leave to hold your tongue, Axel, but not to talk in that irrational way."

I could see the awful professor bursting through my uncle's skin, and I took timely warning.

"Now look at your aneroid. What does that say?"

"It says we are under considerable pressure."

"Very good; so you see that by going gradually down, and getting accustomed to the density of the atmosphere, we don't suffer at all."

"Nothing, except a little pain in the ears."

"That's nothing, and you may get rid of even that by quick breathing whenever you feel the pain."

"Exactly so," I said, determined not to say a word that might cross my uncle's prejudices. "There is even positive pleasure in living in this dense atmosphere. Have you observed how intense sound is down here?"

"No doubt it is. A deaf man would soon learn to hear perfectly."

"But won't this density augment?"

"Yes; according to a rather obscure law. It is well known that the weight of bodies diminishes as fast as we descend. You know that it is at the surface of the globe that weight is most sensibly felt, and that at the center there is no weight at all."

"I am aware of that; but, tell me, will not air at last acquire the density of water?"

"Of course, under a pressure of seven hundred and ten atmospheres."

"And how, lower down still?"

"Lower down the density will still increase."

"But how shall we go down then?"

"Why, we must fill our pockets with stones."

"Well, indeed, my worthy uncle, you are never at a loss for an answer."

I dared venture no farther into the region of probabilities, for I might presently have stumbled upon an impossibility, which would have brought the professor on the scene when he was not wanted.

Still, it was evident that the air, under a pressure which might reach that of thousands of atmospheres, would at last reach the solid state, and then, even if our bodies could resist the strain, we should be stopped, and no reasonings would be able to get us on any farther.

But I did not advance this argument. My uncle would have met it with his inevitable Saknussemm, a precedent which possessed no weight with me; for even if the journey of the learned Icelander were really attested, there was one very simple answer, that in the sixteenth century there was neither barometer or aneroid and therefore Saknussemm could not tell how far he had gone.

But I kept this objection to myself, and waited the course of events.

The rest of the day was passed in calculations and in conversations. I remained a steadfast adherent of the opinions of Professor Liedenbrock, and I envied the stolid indifference of Hans, who, without going into causes and effects, went on with his eyes shut wherever his destiny guided him.

## CHAPTER XXVI

## THE WORST PERIL OF ALL

It must be confessed that hitherto things had not gone on so badly, and that I had small reason to complain. If our difficulties became no worse, we might hope to reach our end. And to what a height of scientific glory we should then attain! I had become quite a Liedenbrock in my reasonings; seriously I had. But would this state of things last in the strange place we had come to? Perhaps it might.

For several days steeper inclines, some even frightfully near to the perpendicular, brought us deeper and deeper into the mass of the interior of the earth. Some days we advanced nearer to the center by a league and a half, or nearly two leagues. These were perilous descents, in which the skill and marvelous coolness of Hans were invaluable to us. That unimpassioned Icelander devoted himself with incomprehensible deliberation; and, thanks to him, we crossed many a dangerous spot which we should never have cleared alone.

But his habit of silence gained upon him day by day, and was infecting us. External objects produce decided effects upon the brain. A man shut up between four walls soon loses the power to associate words and ideas together. How many prisoners in solitary confinement become idiots, if not mad, for want of exercise for the thinking faculty!

During the fortnight following our last conversation, no incident occurred worthy of being recorded. But I have good reason for remembering one very serious event which took place at this time, and of which I could scarcely now forget the smallest details.

By the 7th of August our successive descents had brought us to a depth of thirty leagues; that is, that for a space of thirty leagues there were over our heads solid beds of rock, ocean, continents, and towns. We must have been two hundred leagues from Iceland.

On that day the tunnel went down a gentle slope. I was ahead of the others. My uncle was carrying one of Ruhmkorff's lamps and I the other. I was examining the beds of granite.

Suddenly turning round I observed that I was alone.

Well, well, I thought; I have been going too fast, or Hans and my uncle have stopped on the way. Come, this won't do; I must join them. Fortunately there is not much of an ascent.

I retraced my steps. I walked for a quarter of an hour. I gazed into the darkness. I shouted. No reply: my voice was lost in the midst of the cavernous echoes which alone replied to my call.

I began to feel uneasy. A shudder ran through me.

"Calmly!" I said aloud to myself. "I am sure to find my companions again. There are not two roads. I was too far ahead. I will return!"

For half an hour I climbed up. I listened for a call, and in that dense atmosphere a voice could reach very far. But there was a dreary silence in all that long gallery. I stopped. I could not believe that I was lost. I was only bewildered for a time, not lost. I was sure I should find my way again.

"Come," I repeated, "since there is but one road, and they are on it, I must find them again. I have but to ascend still. Unless, indeed, missing me, and supposing me to be behind, they too should have gone back. But even in this case I have only to make the greater haste. I shall find them, I am sure."

I repeated these words in the fainter tones of a half-convinced man. Besides, to associate even such simple ideas with words, and reason with them, was a work of time.

A doubt then seized upon me. Was I indeed in advance when we became separated? Yes, to be sure I was. Hans was after me, preceding my uncle. He had even stopped for a while to strap his baggage better over his shoulders. I could remember this little incident. It was at that very moment that I must have gone on.

Besides, I thought, have not I a guarantee that I shall not lose my way, a clue in the labyrinth, that cannot be broken, my faithful stream? I have but to trace it back, and I must come upon them.

This conclusion revived my spirits, and I resolved to resume my march without loss of time.

How I then blessed my uncle's foresight in preventing the hunter from stopping up the hole in the granite. This beneficent spring, after having satisfied our thirst on the road, would now be my guide among the windings of the terrestrial crust.

Before starting afresh I thought a wash would do me good. I stooped to bathe my face in the Hansbach.

To my stupefaction and utter dismay my feet trod only—the rough dry granite. The stream was no longer at my feet.

## CHAPTER XXVII

### LOST IN THE BOWELS OF THE EARTH

To describe my despair would be impossible. No words could tell it. I was buried alive, with the prospect before me of dying of hunger and thirst.

Mechanically I swept the ground with my hands. How dry and hard the rock seemed to me!

But how had I left the course of the stream? For it was a terrible fact that it no longer ran at my side. Then I understood the reason of that fearful silence, when for the last time I listened to hear if any sound from my companions could reach my ears. At the moment when I left the right road I had not noticed the absence of the stream. It is evident that at that moment a deviation had presented itself before me, while the Hansbach, following the caprice of another incline, had gone with my companions away into unknown depths.

How was I to return? There was not a trace of their footsteps or of my own, for the foot left no mark upon the granite floor. I racked my brain for a solution of this impracticable problem. One word described my position. Lost!

Lost at an immeasurable depth! Thirty leagues of rock seemed to weigh upon my shoulders with a dreadful pressure. I felt crushed.

I tried to carry back my ideas to things on the surface of the earth. I could scarcely succeed. Hamburg, the house in the Königstrasse, my poor Gräuben, all that busy world underneath which I was wandering about, was passing in rapid confusion before my terrified memory. I could revive with vivid reality all the incidents of our voyage, Iceland, M. Fridriksssen, Snæfell. I said to myself that if, in such a position as I was now in, I was fool enough to cling to one glimpse of hope, it would be madness, and that the best thing I could do was to despair.

What human power could restore me to the light of the sun by rending asunder the huge arches of rock which united over my head, buttressing each other with impregnable strength? Who could place my feet on the right path, and bring me back to my company?

"Oh, my uncle!" burst from my lips in the tone of despair.

It was my only word of reproach, for I knew how much he must be suffering in seeking me, wherever he might be.

When I saw myself thus far removed from all earthly help, I had recourse to heavenly succour. The remembrance of my childhood, the recollection of my mother, whom I had only known in my tender early years, came back to me, and I knelt in prayer imploring for the divine help of which I was so little worthy.

This return of trust in God's providence allayed the turbulence of my fears, and I was enabled to concentrate upon my situation all the force of my intelligence.

I had three days' provisions with me and my flask was full. But I could not remain alone for long. Should I go up or down?

Up, of course; up continually.

I must thus arrive at the point where I had left the stream, that fatal turn in the road. With the stream at my feet, I might hope to regain the summit of Snæfell.

Why had I not thought of that sooner? Here was evidently a chance of safety. The most pressing duty was to find out again the course of the Hansbach. I rose, and leaning upon my iron-pointed stick I ascended the gallery. The slope was rather steep. I walked on without hope but without indecision, like a man who has made up his mind.

For half an hour I met with no obstacle. I tried to recognize my way by the form of the tunnel, by the projections of certain rocks, by the disposition of the fractures. But no particular sign appeared, and I soon saw that this gallery could not bring me back to the turning point. It came to an abrupt end. I struck against an impenetrable wall, and fell down upon the rock.

Unspeakable despair then seized upon me. I lay overwhelmed, aghast! My last hope was shattered against this granite wall.

Lost in this labyrinth, whose windings crossed each other in all directions, it was no use to think of flight any longer. Here I must die the most dreadful of deaths. And, strange to say, the thought came across me that when someday my petrified remains should be found thirty leagues below the surface in the bowels of the earth, the discovery might lead to grave scientific discussions.

I tried to speak aloud, but hoarse sounds alone passed my dry lips. I panted for breath.

In the midst of my agony a new terror laid hold of me. In falling my lamp had got wrong. I could not set it right, and its light was paling and would soon disappear altogether.

I gazed painfully upon the luminous current growing weaker and weaker in the wire coil. A dim procession of moving shadows seemed slowly unfolding down the darkening walls. I scarcely dared to shut my eyes for one moment, for fear of losing the least glimmer of this precious light. Every instant it seemed about to vanish and the dense blackness to come rolling in palpably upon me.

One last trembling glimmer shot feebly up. I watched it in trembling and anxiety; I drank it in as if I could preserve it, concentrating upon it the full power of my eyes, as upon the very last sensation of light which they were ever to experience, and the next moment I lay in the heavy gloom of deep, thick, unfathomable darkness.

A terrible cry of anguish burst from me. Upon earth, in the midst of the darkest night, light never abdicates its functions altogether. It is still subtle and diffusive, but whatever little there may be, the eye still catches that little. Here there was not an atom; the total darkness made me totally blind.

Then I began to lose my head. I arose with my arms stretched out before me, attempting painfully to feel my way. I began to run wildly, hurrying through the inextricable maze, still descending, still running through the substance of the earth's thick crust, a struggling denizen of geological "faults," crying, shouting, yelling, soon bruised by contact with the jagged rock, falling and rising again bleeding, trying to drink the blood which covered my face, and even waiting for some rock to shatter my skull against.

I shall never know whither my mad career took me. After the lapse of some hours, no doubt exhausted, I fell like a lifeless lump at the foot of the wall, and lost all consciousness.

## CHAPTER XXVIII

## THE RESCUE IN THE WHISPERING GALLERY

When I returned to partial life my face was wet with tears. How long that state of insensibility had lasted I cannot say. I had no means now of taking account of time. Never was solitude equal to this, never had any living being been so utterly forsaken.

After my fall I had lost a good deal of blood. I felt it flowing over me. Ah! How happy I should have been could I have died, and if death were not yet to be gone through. I would think no longer. I drove away every idea, and, conquered by my grief, I rolled myself to the foot of the opposite wall.

Already I was feeling the approach of another faint, and was hoping for complete annihilation, when a loud noise reached me. It was like the distant rumble of continuous thunder, and I could hear its sounding undulations rolling far away into the remote recesses of the abyss.

Whence could this noise proceed? It must be from some phenomenon proceeding in the great depths amid which I lay helpless. Was it an explosion of gas? Was it the fall of some mighty pillar of the globe?

I listened still. I wanted to know if the noise would be repeated. A quarter of an hour passed away. Silence reigned in this gallery. I could not hear even the beating of my heart.

Suddenly my ear, resting by chance against the wall, caught, or seemed to catch, certain vague, indescribable, distant, articulate sounds, as of words.

"This is a delusion," I thought.

But it was not. Listening more attentively, I heard in reality a murmuring of voices. But my weakness prevented me from understanding what the voices said. Yet it was language, I was sure of it.

For a moment I feared the words might be my own, brought back by the echo. Perhaps I had been crying out unknown to myself. I closed my lips firmly, and laid my ear against the wall again.

"Yes, truly, someone is speaking; those are words!"

Even a few feet from the wall I could hear distinctly. I succeeded in catching uncertain, strange, indistinguishable words. They came as if pronounced in low murmured whispers. The word "*forlorad*" was several times repeated in a tone of sympathy and sorrow.

"Help!" I cried with all my might. "Help!"

I listened, I watched in the darkness for an answer, a cry, a mere breath of sound, but nothing came. Some minutes passed. A whole world of ideas had opened in my mind. I thought that my weakened voice could never penetrate to my companions.

"It is they," I repeated. "What other men can be thirty leagues underground?"

I again began to listen. Passing my ear over the wall from one place to another, I found the point where the voices seemed to be best heard. The word "*forlorad*" again returned; then the rolling of thunder which had roused me from my lethargy.

"No," I said, "no; it is not through such a mass that a voice can be heard. I am surrounded by granite walls, and the loudest explosion could never be heard here! This noise comes along the gallery. There must be here some remarkable exercise of acoustic laws!"

I listened again, and this time, yes this time, I did distinctly hear my name pronounced across the wide interval.

It was my uncle's own voice! He was talking to the guide. And "*forlorad*" is a Danish word.

Then I understood it all. To make myself heard, I must speak along this wall, which would conduct the sound of my voice just as wire conducts electricity.

But there was no time to lose. If my companions moved but a few steps away, the acoustic phenomenon would cease. I therefore approached the wall, and pronounced these words as clearly as possible:

"Uncle Liedenbrock!"

I waited with the deepest anxiety. Sound does not travel with great velocity. Even increased density air has no effect upon its rate of traveling; it merely augments its intensity. Seconds, which seemed ages, passed away, and at last these words reached me:

"Axel! Axel! Is it you?"

. . .

"Yes, yes," I replied.

. . .

"My boy, where are you?"

. . .

"Lost, in the deepest darkness."

. . .

"Where is your lamp?"

. . .

"It is out."

. . .

"And the stream?"

. . .

"Disappeared."

. . .

"Axel, Axel, take courage!"

. . .

"Wait! I am exhausted! I can't answer. Speak to me!"

. . .

"Courage," resumed my uncle. "Don't speak. Listen to me. We have looked for you up the gallery and down the gallery. Could not find you. I wept for you, my poor boy. At last, supposing you were still on the Hansbach, we fired our guns. Our voices are audible to each other, but our hands cannot touch. But don't despair, Axel! It is a great thing that we can hear each other."

. . .

During this time I had been reflecting. A vague hope was returning to my heart. There was one thing I must know to begin with. I placed my lips close to the wall, saying:

"My uncle!"

. . .

"My boy!" came to me after a few seconds.

. . .

"We must know how far we are apart."

. . .

"That is easy."

. . .

"You have your chronometer?"

. . .

"Yes."

. . .

"Well, take it. Pronounce my name, noting exactly the second when you speak. I will repeat it as soon as it shall come to me, and you will observe the exact moment when you get my answer."

"Yes; and half the time between my call and your answer will exactly indicate that which my voice will take in coming to you."

. . .

"Just so, my uncle."

. . .

"Are you ready?"

. . .

"Yes."

. . .

"Now, attention. I am going to call your name."

. . .

I put my ear to the wall, and as soon as the name "Axel" came I immediately replied "Axel," then waited.

. . .

"Forty seconds," said my uncle. "Forty seconds between the two words; so the sound takes twenty seconds in coming. Now, at the rate of 1,120 feet in a second, this is 22,400 feet, or four miles and a quarter, nearly."

. . .

"Four miles and a quarter!" I murmured.

. . .

"It will soon be over, Axel."

. . .

"Must I go up or down?"

. . .

"Down—for this reason: We are in a vast chamber, with endless galleries. Yours must lead into it, for it seems as if all the clefts and fractures of the globe radiated round this vast cavern. So get up, and begin walking. Walk on, drag yourself along, if necessary slide down the steep places, and at the end you will find us ready to receive you. Now begin moving."

. . .

These words cheered me up.

"Good-bye, uncle." I cried. "I am going. There will be no more voices heard when once I have started. So good-bye!"

. . .

"Good-bye, Axel, *au revoir!*"

. . .

These were the last words I heard.

This wonderful underground conversation, carried on with a distance of four miles and a quarter between us, concluded with these words of hope. I thanked God from my heart, for it was He who had conducted me through those vast solitudes to the point where, alone of all others perhaps, the voices of my companions could have reached me.

This acoustic effect is easily explained on scientific grounds. It arose from the concave form of the gallery and the conducting power of the rock. There are many examples of this propagation of sounds which remain unheard in the intermediate space. I remember that a similar phenomenon has been observed in many places; among others, on the internal surface of the gallery of the dome of St. Paul's in London, and especially in the midst of the curious caverns among the quarries near Syracuse, the most wonderful of which is called Dionysus's Ear.

These remembrances came into my mind, and I clearly saw that since my uncle's voice really reached me, there could be no obstacle between us. Following the direction by which the sound came, of course I should arrive in his presence, if my strength did not fail me.

I therefore rose; I rather dragged myself than walked. The slope was rapid, and I slid down.

Soon the swiftness of the descent increased horribly, and threatened to become a fall. I no longer had the strength to stop myself.

Suddenly there was no ground under me. I felt myself revolving in air, striking and rebounding against the craggy projections of a vertical gallery, quite a well; my head struck against a sharp corner of the rock, and I became unconscious.

## *CHAPTER XXIX*

### THALATTA! THALATTA!

When I came to myself, I was stretched in half darkness, covered with thick coats and blankets. My uncle was watching over me, to discover the least sign of life. At my first sigh he took my hand; when I opened my eyes he uttered a cry of joy.

"He lives! He lives!" he cried.

"Yes, I am still alive," I answered feebly.

"My dear nephew," said my uncle, pressing me to his breast, "you are saved."

I was deeply touched with the tenderness of his manner as he uttered these words, and still more with the care with which he watched over me. But such trials were wanted to bring out the professor's tenderer qualities.

At this moment Hans came, he saw my hand in my uncle's, and I may safely say that there was joy in his countenance.

"*God dag*," said he.

"How do you do, Hans? How are you? And now, uncle, tell me where we are at the present moment."

"Tomorrow, Axel, tomorrow. Now you are too faint and weak. I have bandaged your head with compresses which must not be disturbed. Sleep now, and tomorrow I will tell you all."

"But do tell me what time it is, and what day."

"It is Sunday, the 8th of August, and it is ten at night. You must ask me no more questions until the 10th."

In truth I was very weak, and my eyes involuntarily closed. I wanted a good night's rest; and I therefore went off to sleep, with the knowledge that I had been four long days alone in the heart of the earth.

Next morning, on awakening, I looked round me. My couch, made up of all our traveling gear, was in a charming grotto, adorned with splendid stalactites, and the soil of which was a fine sand. It was half light. There was no torch, no lamp, yet certain mysterious glimpses of light came from without through a narrow opening in the grotto. I heard too a vague and indistinct noise, something like the murmuring of waves breaking upon a shingly shore, and at times I seemed to hear the whistling of wind.

I wondered whether I was awake, whether I was dreaming, whether my brain, crazed by my fall, was not affected by imaginary noises. Yet neither eyes nor ears could be so utterly deceived.

It is a ray of daylight, I thought, sliding in through this cleft in the rock! That is indeed the murmuring of waves! That is the rustling noise of wind. Am I quite mistaken, or have we returned to the surface of the earth? Has my uncle given up the expedition, or is it happily terminated?

I was asking myself these unanswerable questions when the professor entered.

"Good morning, Axel," he cried cheerily. "I feel sure you are better."

"Yes, I am indeed," said I, sitting up on my couch.

"You can hardly fail to be better, for you have slept quietly. Hans and I watched you by turns, and we have noticed you were evidently recovering."

"Indeed, I do feel a great deal better, and I will give you a proof of that presently if you will let me have my breakfast."

"You shall eat, lad. The fever has left you. Hans rubbed your wounds with some ointment or other of which the Icelanders keep the secret, and they have healed marvelously. Our hunter is a splendid fellow!"

While he went on talking, my uncle prepared a few provisions, which I devoured eagerly, notwithstanding his advice to the contrary. All the while I was overwhelming him with questions which he answered readily.

I then learned that my providential fall had brought me exactly to the extremity of an almost perpendicular shaft; and as I had landed in the midst of an accompanying torrent of stones, the least of which would have been enough to crush me, the conclusion was that a loose portion of the rock had come down with me. This frightful conveyance had thus carried me into the arms of my uncle, where I fell bruised, bleeding, and insensible.

"Truly it is wonderful that you have not been killed a hundred times over. But, for the love of God, don't let us ever separate again, or we many never see each other more."

"Not separate! Is the journey not over, then?" I opened a pair of astonished eyes, which immediately called for the question:

"What is the matter, Axel?"

"I have a question to ask you. You say that I am safe and sound?"

"No doubt you are."

"And all my limbs unbroken?"

"Certainly."

"And my head?"

"Your head, except for a few bruises, is all right; and it is on your shoulders, where it ought to be."

"Well, I am afraid my brain is affected."

"Your mind affected!"

"Yes, I fear so. Are we again on the surface of the globe?"

"No, certainly not."

"Then I must be mad; for don't I see the light of day, and don't I hear the wind blowing, and the sea breaking on the shore?"

"Ah! Is that all?"

"Do tell me all about it."

"I can't explain the inexplicable, but you will soon see and understand that geology has not yet learned all it has to learn."

"Then let us go," I answered quickly.

"No, Axel; the open air might be bad for you."

"Open air?"

"Yes; the wind is rather strong. You must not expose yourself."

"But I assure you I am perfectly well."

"A little patience, my nephew. A relapse might get us into trouble, and we have no time to lose, for the voyage may be a long one."

"The voyage!"

"Yes, rest today, and tomorrow we will set sail."

"Set sail!"—and I almost leaped up.

What did it all mean? Had we a river, a lake, a sea to depend upon? Was there a ship at our disposal in some underground harbor?

My curiosity was highly excited, my uncle vainly tried to restrain me. When he saw that my impatience was doing me harm, he yielded.

I dressed in haste. For greater safety I wrapped myself in a blanket, and came out of the grotto.

## *CHAPTER XXX*

### A NEW MARE INTERNUM

At first I could hardly see anything. My eyes, unaccustomed to the light, quickly closed. When I was able to reopen them, I stood more stupefied even than surprised.

"The sea!" I cried.

"Yes," my uncle replied, "the Liedenbrock Sea; and I don't suppose any other discoverer will ever dispute my claim to name it after myself as its first discoverer."

A vast sheet of water, the commencement of a lake or an ocean, spread far away beyond the range of the eye, reminding me forcibly of that open sea which drew from Xenophon's ten thousand Greeks, after their long retreat, the simultaneous cry, "Thalatta! Thalatta!" The sea! The sea! The deeply indented shore was lined with a breadth of fine shining sand, softly lapped by the waves, and strewn with the small shells which had been inhabited by the first of created beings. The waves broke on this shore with the hollow echoing murmur peculiar to vast enclosed spaces. A light foam flew over the waves before the breath of a moderate breeze, and some of the spray fell upon my face. On this slightly inclining shore, about a hundred fathoms from the limit of the waves, came down the foot of a huge wall of vast cliffs, which rose majestically to an enormous height. Some of these, dividing the beach with their sharp spurs, formed capes and promontories, worn away by the ceaseless action of the surf. Farther on, the eye discerned their massive outline sharply defined against the hazy distant horizon.

It was quite an ocean, with the irregular shores of earth, but desert and frightfully wild in appearance.

If my eyes were able to range afar over this great sea, it was because a peculiar light brought to view every detail of it. It was not the light of the sun, with his dazzling shafts of brightness and the splendor of his rays; nor was it the pale and uncertain shimmer of the moonbeams, the dim reflection of a nobler body of light. No; the illuminating power of this light, its trembling diffusiveness, its bright, clear whiteness, and its low temperature, showed that it must be of electric origin. It was like an aurora borealis, a continuous cosmical phenomenon, filling a cavern of sufficient extent to contain an ocean.

The vault that spanned the space above, the sky, if it could be called so, seemed composed of vast plains of cloud, shifting and variable vapors, which by their condensation must at certain times fall in torrents of rain. I should have thought that under so powerful a pressure of the atmosphere there could be no evaporation; and yet, under a law unknown to me, there were broad tracts of vapor suspended in the air. But then "the weather was fine." The play of the electric light produced singular effects upon the upper strata of cloud. Deep shadows reposed upon their lower wreaths; and often, between two separated fields of cloud, there glided down a ray of unspeakable luster. But it was not solar light, and there was no heat. The general effect was sad, supremely melancholy. Instead of the shining firmament, spangled with its innumerable stars, shining singly or in clusters, I felt that all these subdued and shaded lights were ribbed in by vast walls of granite, which seemed to overpower me with their weight, and that all this space, great as it was, would not be enough for the march of the humblest of satellites.

Then I remembered the theory of an English captain who likened the earth to a vast hollow sphere, in the interior of which the air became luminous because of the vast pressure that weighed upon it; while two stars, Pluto and Proserpine, rolled within upon the circuit of their mysterious orbits.

We were in reality shut up inside an immeasurable excavation. Its width could not be estimated, since the shore ran widening as far as eye could reach, nor could its length, for the dim horizon bounded the new. As for its height, it must have been several leagues. Where this vault rested upon its granite base no eye could tell; but there was a cloud hanging far above, the height of which we estimated at 12,000 feet, a greater height than that of any terrestrial vapor, and no doubt due to the great density of the air.

The word cavern does not convey any idea of this immense space; words of human tongue are inadequate to describe the discoveries of him who ventures into the deep abysses of earth.

Besides, I could not tell upon what geological theory to account for the existence of such an excavation. Had the cooling of the globe produced it? I knew of celebrated caverns from the descriptions of travelers, but had never heard of any of such dimensions as this.

If the grotto of Guachara, in Colombia, visited by Humboldt, had not given up the whole of the secret of its depth to the philosopher, who investigated it to the depth of 2,500 feet, it probably did not extend much farther. The immense mammoth cave in Kentucky is of gigantic proportions, since its vaulted roof rises five hundred feet above the level of an unfathomable lake and travelers have explored its ramifications to the extent of forty miles. But what were these cavities compared to that in which I stood with wonder and admiration, with its sky of luminous vapors, its bursts of electric light, and a vast sea filling its bed? My imagination fell powerless before such immensity.

I gazed upon these wonders in silence. Words failed me to express my feelings. I felt as if I was in some distant planet Uranus or Neptune—and in the presence of phenomena of which my terrestrial experience gave me no cognizance. For such novel sensations, new words were wanted; and my imagination failed to supply them. I gazed, I thought, I admired, with a stupefaction mingled with a certain amount of fear.

The unforeseen nature of this spectacle brought back the color to my cheeks. I was under a new course of treatment with the aid of astonishment, and my convalescence was promoted by this novel system of therapeutics; besides, the dense and breezy air invigorated me, supplying more oxygen to my lungs.

It will be easily conceived that after an imprisonment of forty-seven days in a narrow gallery, it was the height of physical enjoyment to breathe a moist air impregnated with saline particles.

I was delighted to leave my dark grotto. My uncle, already familiar with these wonders, had ceased to feel surprise.

"You feel strong enough to walk a little way now?" he asked.

"Yes, certainly; and nothing could be more delightful."

"Well, take my arm, Axel, and let us follow the windings of the shore."

I eagerly accepted, and we began to coast along this new sea. On the left huge pyramids of rock, piled one upon another, produced a prodigious titanic effect. Down their sides flowed numberless waterfalls, which went on their way in brawling but pellucid streams. A few light vapors, leaping from rock to rock, denoted the place of hot springs; and streams flowed softly down to the common basin, gliding down the gentle slopes with a softer murmur.

Among these streams I recognized our faithful traveling companion, the Hansbach, coming to lose its little volume quietly in the mighty sea, just as if it had done nothing else since the beginning of the world.

"We shall see it no more," I said, with a sigh.

"What matters," replied the philosopher, "whether this or another serves to guide us?"

I thought him rather ungrateful.

But at that moment my attention was drawn to an unexpected sight. At a distance of five hundred paces, at the turn of a high promontory, appeared a high, tufted, dense forest. It was composed of trees of moderate height, formed like umbrellas, with exact geometrical outlines. The currents of wind seemed to have had no effect upon their shape, and in the midst of the windy blasts they stood unmoved and firm, just like a clump of petrified cedars.

I hastened forward. I could not give any name to these singular creations. Were they some of the two hundred thousand species of vegetables known hitherto, and did they claim a place of their own in the lacustrine flora? No; when we arrived under their shade my surprise turned into admiration. There stood before me productions of earth, but of gigantic stature, which my uncle immediately named.

"It is only a forest of mushrooms," said he.

And he was right. Imagine the large development attained by these plants, which prefer a warm, moist climate. I knew that the *Lycopodon giganteum* attains, according to Bulliard, a circumference of eight or nine feet; but here were pale mushrooms, thirty to forty feet high, and crowned with a cap of equal diameter. There they stood in thousands. No light could penetrate between their huge cones, and complete darkness reigned beneath those giants; they formed settlements of domes placed in close array like the round, thatched roofs of a central African city.

Yet I wanted to penetrate farther underneath, though a chill fell upon me as soon as I came under those cellular vaults. For half an hour we wandered from side to side in the damp shades, and it was a comfortable and pleasant change to arrive once more upon the seashore.

But the subterranean vegetation was not confined to these fungi. Farther on rose groups of tall trees of colorless foliage and easy to recognize. They were lowly shrubs of earth, here attaining gigantic size; lycopodiums, a hundred feet high; the huge sigillaria, found in our coal mines; tree ferns, as tall as our fir trees in northern latitudes; lepidodendra, with cylindrical forked stems, terminated by long leaves, and bristling with rough hairs like those of the cactus.

"Wonderful, magnificent, splendid!" cried my uncle. "Here is the entire flora of the second period of the world—the transition period. These, humble garden plants with us, were tall trees in the early ages. Look, Axel, and admire it all. Never had botanist such a feast as this!"

"You are right, my uncle. Providence seems to have preserved in this immense conservatory the antediluvian plants which the wisdom of philosophers has so sagaciously put together again."

"It is a conservatory, Axel; but is it not also a menagerie?"

"Surely not a menagerie!"

"Yes; no doubt of it. Look at that dust under your feet; see the bones scattered on the ground."

"So there are!" I cried. "Bones of extinct animals."

I had rushed upon these remains, formed of indestructible phosphates of lime, and without hesitation I named these monstrous bones, which lay scattered about like decayed trunks of trees.

"Here is the lower jaw of a mastodon," I said. "These are the molar teeth of the deinotherium; this femur must have belonged to the greatest of those beasts, the megatherium. It certainly is a menagerie, for these remains were not brought here by a deluge. The animals to which they belonged roamed on the shores of this subterranean sea, under the shade of those arborescent trees. Here are entire skeletons. And yet I cannot understand the appearance of these quadrupeds in a granite cavern."

"Why?"

"Because animal life existed upon the earth only in the secondary period, when a sediment of soil had been deposited by the rivers, and taken the place of the incandescent rocks of the primitive period."

"Well, Axel, there is a very simple answer to your objection that this soil is alluvial."

"What! At such a depth below the surface of the earth?"

"No doubt; and there is a geological explanation of the fact. At a certain period the earth consisted only of an elastic crust or bark, alternately acted on by forces from above or below, according to the laws of attraction and gravitation. Probably there were subsidences of the outer crust, when a portion of the sedimentary deposits was carried down sudden openings."

"That may be," I replied; "but if there have been creatures now extinct in these underground regions, why may not some of those monsters be now roaming through these gloomy forests, or hidden behind the steep crags?"

And as this unpleasant notion got hold of me, I surveyed with anxious scrutiny the open spaces before me; but no living creature appeared upon the barren strand.

I felt rather tired, and went to sit down at the end of a promontory, at the foot of which the waves came and beat themselves into spray. Thence my eye could sweep every part of the bay; within its extremity a little harbor was formed between the pyramidal cliffs, where the still waters slept untouched by the boisterous winds. A brig and two or three schooners might have moored within it in safety. I almost fancied I should presently see some ship issue from it, full sail, and take to the open sea under the southern breeze.

But this illusion lasted a very short time. We were the only living creatures in this subterranean world. When the wind lulled, a deeper silence than that of the deserts fell upon the arid, naked rocks, and weighed upon the surface of the ocean. I then desired to pierce the distant haze, and to rend asunder the mysterious curtain that hung across the horizon. Anxious queries arose to my lips. Where did that sea terminate? Where did it lead to? Should we ever know anything about its opposite shores?

My uncle made no doubt about it at all; I both desired and feared.

After spending an hour in the contemplation of this marvelous spectacle, we returned to the shore to regain the grotto, and I fell asleep in the midst of the strangest thoughts.

## CHAPTER XXXI

### PREPARATIONS FOR A VOYAGE OF DISCOVERY

The next morning I awoke feeling perfectly well. I thought a bath would do me good, and I went to plunge for a few minutes into the waters of this Mediterranean Sea, for assuredly it better deserved this name than any other sea.

I came back to breakfast with a good appetite. Hans was a good caterer for our little household; he had water and fire at his disposal, so that he was able to vary our bill of fare now and then. For dessert he gave us a few cups of coffee, and never was coffee so delicious.

"Now," said my uncle, "now is the time for high tide, and we must not lose the opportunity to study this phenomenon."

"What! The tide!" I cried. "Can the influence of the sun and moon be felt down here?"

"Why not? Are not all bodies subject throughout their mass to the power of universal attraction? This mass of water cannot escape the general law. And in spite of the heavy atmospheric pressure on the surface, you will see it rise like the Atlantic itself."

At the same moment we reached the sand on the shore, and the waves were by slow degrees encroaching on the shore.

"Here is the tide rising," I cried.

"Yes, Axel; and judging by these ridges of foam, you may observe that the sea will rise about twelve feet."

"This is wonderful," I said.

"No; it is quite natural."

"You may say so, uncle; but to me it is most extraordinary, and I can hardly believe my eyes. Who would ever have imagined, under this terrestrial crust, an ocean with ebbing and flowing tides, with winds and storms?"

"Well," replied my uncle, "is there any scientific reason against it?"

"No; I see none, as soon as the theory of central heat is given up."

"So then, thus far," he answered, "the theory of Sir Humphry Davy is confirmed."

"Evidently it is; and now there is no reason why there should not be seas and continents in the interior of the earth."

"No doubt," said my uncle; "and inhabited too."

"To be sure," said I; "and why should not these waters yield to us fishes of unknown species?"

"At any rate," he replied, "we have not seen any yet."

"Well, let us make some lines, and see if the bait will draw here as it does in sublunary regions."

"We will try, Axel, for we must penetrate all secrets of these newly discovered regions."

"But where are we, uncle? For I have not yet asked you that question, and your instruments must be able to furnish the answer."

"Horizontally, three hundred and fifty leagues from Iceland."

"So much as that?"

"I am sure of not being a mile out of my reckoning."

"And does the compass still show southeast?"

"Yes; with a westerly deviation of nineteen degrees forty-five minutes, just as aboveground. As for its dip, a curious fact is coming to light, which I have observed carefully: that the needle, instead of dipping toward the pole as in the Northern Hemisphere, on the contrary, rises from it."

"Would you then conclude," I said, "that the magnetic pole is somewhere between the surface of the globe and the point where we are?"

"Exactly so; and it is likely enough that if we were to reach the spot beneath the polar regions, about that seventy-first degree where Sir James Ross has discovered the magnetic pole to be situated, we should see the needle point straight up. Therefore that mysterious center of attraction is at no great depth."

I remarked: "It is so; and here is a fact which science has scarcely suspected."

"Science, my lad, has been built upon many errors; but they are errors which it was good to fall into, for they led to the truth."

"What depth have we now reached?"

"We are thirty-five leagues below the surface."

"So," I said, examining the map, "the Highlands of Scotland are over our heads, and the Grampians are raising their rugged summits above us."

"Yes," answered the professor laughing. "It is rather a heavy weight to bear, but a solid arch spans over our heads. The great Architect has built it of the best materials; and never could man have given it so wide a stretch. What are the finest arches of bridges and the arcades of cathedrals, compared with this far-reaching vault, with a radius of three leagues, beneath which a wide and tempest-tossed ocean may flow at its ease?"

"Oh, I am not afraid that it will fall down upon my head. But now what are your plans? Are you not thinking of returning to the surface now?"

"Return! No, indeed! We will continue our journey, everything having gone on well so far."

"But how are we to get down below this liquid surface?"

"Oh, I am not going to dive head foremost. But if all oceans are properly speaking but lakes, since they are encompassed by land, of course this internal sea will be surrounded by a coast of granite, and on the opposite shores we shall find fresh passages opening."

"How long do you suppose this sea to be?"

"Thirty or forty leagues; so that we have no time to lose, and we shall set sail tomorrow."

I looked about for a ship.

"Set sail, shall we? But I should like to see my boat first."

"It will not be a boat at all, but a good, well-made raft."

"Why," I said, "a raft would be just as hard to make as a boat, and I don't see——"

"I know you don't see; but you might hear if you would listen. Don't you hear the hammer at work? Hans is already busy at it."

"What, has he already felled the trees?"

"Oh, the trees were already down. Come, and you will see for yourself."

After half an hour's walking, on the other side of the promontory which formed the little natural harbor, I perceived Hans at work. In a few more steps I was at his side. To my great surprise a half-finished raft was already lying on the sand, made of a peculiar kind of wood, and a great number of planks, straight and bent, and of frames, were covering the ground, enough almost for a little fleet.

"Uncle, what wood is this?" I cried.

"It is fir, pine, or birch, and other northern coniferae, mineralized by the action of the sea. It is called surturbrand, a variety of brown coal or lignite, found chiefly in Iceland."

"But surely, then, like other fossil wood, it must be as hard as stone, and cannot float?"

"Sometimes that may happen; some of these woods become true anthracites; but others, such as this, have only gone through the first stage of fossil transformation. Just look," added my uncle, throwing into the sea one of those precious waifs.

The bit of wood, after disappearing, returned to the surface and oscillated to and fro with the waves.

"Are you convinced?" said my uncle.

"I am quite convinced, although it is incredible!"

By next evening, thanks to the industry and skill of our guide, the raft was made. It was ten feet by five; the planks of surturbrand, braced strongly together with cords, presented an even surface, and when launched this improvised vessel floated easily upon the waves of the Liedenbrock Sea.

## CHAPTER XXXII

### WONDERS OF THE DEEP

On the 13th of August we awoke early. We were now to begin to adopt a mode of traveling both more expeditious and less fatiguing than hitherto.

A mast was made of two poles spliced together, a yard was made of a third, a blanket borrowed from our coverings made a tolerable sail. There was no want of cordage for the rigging, and everything was well and firmly made.

The provisions, the baggage, the instruments, the guns, and a good quantity of fresh water from the rocks around, all found their proper places on board; and at six the professor gave the signal to embark. Hans had fitted up a rudder to steer his vessel. He took the tiller, and unmoored; the sail was set, and we were soon afloat. At the moment of leaving the harbor, my uncle, who was tenaciously fond of naming his new discoveries, wanted to give it a name, and proposed mine among others.

"But I have a better to propose," I said: "Gräuben. Let it be called Port Gräuben; it will look very well upon the map."

"Port Gräuben let it be then."

And so the cherished remembrance of my Virlandaise became associated with our adventurous expedition.

The wind was from the northwest. We went with it at a high rate of speed. The dense atmosphere acted with great force and impelled us swiftly on.

In an hour my uncle had been able to estimate our progress. At this rate, he said, we shall make thirty leagues in twenty-four hours, and we shall soon come in sight of the opposite shore.

I made no answer, but went and sat forward. The northern shore was already beginning to dip under the horizon. The eastern and western strands spread wide as if to bid us farewell. Before our eyes lay far and wide a vast sea; shadows of great clouds swept heavily over its silver-gray surface; the glistening bluish rays of electric light, here and there reflected by the dancing drops of spray, shot out little sheaves of light from the track we left in our rear. Soon we entirely lost sight of land; no object was left for the eye to judge by, and but for the frothy track of the raft, I might have thought we were standing still.

About twelve, immense shoals of seaweeds came in sight. I was aware of the great powers of vegetation that characterize these plants, which grow at a depth of twelve thousand feet, reproduce themselves under a pressure of four hundred atmospheres, and sometimes form barriers strong enough to impede the course of a ship. But never, I think, were such seaweeds as those which we saw floating in immense waving lines upon the sea of Liedenbrock.

Our raft skirted the whole length of the fuci, three or four thousand feet long, undulating like vast serpents beyond the reach of sight; I found some amusement in tracing these endless waves, always thinking I should come to the end of them, and for hours my patience was vying with my surprise.

What natural force could have produced such plants, and what must have been the appearance of the earth in the first ages of its formation, when, under the action of heat and moisture, the vegetable kingdom alone was developing on its surface?

Evening came, and, as on the previous day, I perceived no change in the luminous condition of the air. It was a constant condition, the permanency of which might be relied upon.

After supper I laid myself down at the foot of the mast, and fell asleep in the midst of fantastic reveries.

Hans, keeping fast by the helm, let the raft run on, which, after all, needed no steering, the wind blowing directly aft.

Since our departure from Port Gräuben, Professor Liedenbrock had entrusted the log to my care; I was to register every observation, make entries of interesting phenomena, the direction of the wind, the rate of sailing, the way we made—in a word, every particular of our singular voyage.

I shall therefore reproduce here these daily notes, written, so to speak, as the course of events directed, in order to furnish an exact narrative of our passage.

Friday, August 14. Wind steady, N.W. The raft makes rapid way in a direct line. Coast thirty leagues to leeward. Nothing in sight before us. Intensity of light the same. Weather fine; that is to say, that the clouds are flying high, are light, and bathed in a white atmosphere resembling silver in a state of fusion. Therm. 89°F.

At noon Hans prepared a hook at the end of a line. He baited it with a small piece of meat and flung it into the sea. For two hours nothing was caught. Are these waters, then, bare of inhabitants? No, there's a pull at the line. Hans draws it in and brings out a struggling fish.

"A sturgeon," I cried; "a small sturgeon."

The professor eyes the creature attentively, and his opinion differs from mine.

The head of this fish was flat, but rounded in front, and the anterior part of its body was plated with bony, angular scales; it had no teeth, its pectoral fins were large, and of tail there was none. The animal belonged to the same order as the sturgeon, but differed from that fish in many essential particulars. After a short examination my uncle pronounced his opinion.

"This fish belongs to an extinct family, of which only fossil traces are found in the Devonian formations."

"What!" I cried. "Have we taken alive an inhabitant of the seas of primitive ages?"

"Yes; and you will observe that these fossil fishes have no identity with any living species. To have in one's possession a living specimen is a happy event for a naturalist."

"But to what family does it belong?"

"It is of the order of ganoids, of the family of the cephalaspidae; and a species of pterichthys. But this one displays a peculiarity confined to all fishes that inhabit subterranean waters. It is blind, and not only blind, but actually has no eyes at all."

I looked: nothing could be more certain. But supposing it might be a solitary case, we baited afresh, and threw out our line. Surely this ocean is well peopled with fish, for in another couple of hours we took a large quantity of pterichthydes, as well as of others belonging to the extinct family of the dipterides, but of which my uncle could not tell the species; none had organs of sight. This unhoped-for catch recruited our stock of provisions.

Thus it is evident that this sea contains none but species known to us in their fossil state, in which fishes as well as reptiles are the less perfectly and completely organized the farther back their date of creation.

Perhaps we may yet meet with some of those saurians which science has reconstructed out of a bit of bone or cartilage. I took up the telescope and scanned the whole horizon, and found it everywhere a desert sea. We are far away removed from the shores.

I gaze upward in the air. Why should not some of the strange birds restored by the immortal Cuvier again flap their "sail-broad vans" in this dense and heavy atmosphere? There are sufficient fish for their support. I survey the whole space that stretches overhead; it is as desert as the shore was.

Still my imagination carried me away among the wonderful speculations of paleontology. Though awake I fell into a dream. I thought I could see floating on the surface of the waters enormous chelonia, pre-Adamite tortoises, resembling floating islands. Over the dimly lighted strand there trod the huge mammals of the first ages of the world, the leptotherium (slender beast), found in the caverns of Brazil; the merycotherium (ruminating beast), found in the "drift" of ice-clad Siberia. Farther on, the pachydermatous lophiodon (crested toothed), a gigantic tapir, hides behind the rocks to dispute its prey with the anoplotherium (unarmed beast), a strange creature, which seemed a compound of horse, rhinoceros, camel, and hippopotamus. The colossal mastodon (nipple-toothed) twists and untwists his trunk, and brays and pounds with his huge tusks the fragments of rock that cover the shore; while the megatherium (huge beast), buttressed upon his enormous hinder paws, grubs in the soil, awaking the sonorous echoes of the granite rocks with his tremendous roarings. Higher up, the protopitheca—the first monkey that appeared on the globe—is climbing up the steep ascents. Higher yet, the pterodactyle (wing-fingered) darts in irregular zigzags to and fro in the heavy air. In the uppermost regions of the air immense birds, more powerful than the cassowary, and larger than the ostrich, spread their vast breadth of wings and strike with their heads the granite vault that bounds the sky.

All this fossil world rises to life again in my vivid imagination. I return to the scriptural periods or ages of the world, conventionally called "days," long before the appearance of man, when the unfinished world was as yet unfitted for his support. Then my dream backed even farther still into the ages before the creation of living beings. The mammals disappear, then the birds vanish, then the reptiles of the secondary period, and finally the fish, the crustaceans, mollusks, and articulated beings. Then the zoophytes of the transition period also return to nothing. I am the only living thing in the world: all life is concentrated in my beating heart alone. There are no more seasons; climates are no more; the heat of the globe continually increases and neutralizes that of the sun. Vegetation becomes accelerated. I glide like a shade among arborescent ferns, treading with unsteady feet the colored marls and the particolored clays; I lean for support against the trunks of immense conifers; I lie in the shade of sphenophylla (wedge-leaved), asterophylla (star-leaved), and lycopods, a hundred feet high.

Ages seem no more than days! I am passed, against my will, in retrograde order, through the long series of terrestrial changes. Plants disappear; granite rocks soften; intense heat converts solid bodies into thick fluids; the waters again cover the face of the earth; they boil, they rise in whirling eddies of steam; white and ghastly mists wrap round the shifting forms of the earth, which by imperceptible degrees dissolves into a gaseous mass, glowing fiery red and white, as large and as shining as the sun.

And I myself am floating with wild caprice in the midst of this nebulous mass of fourteen hundred thousand times the volume of the earth into which it will one day be condensed, and carried forward among the planetary bodies. My body is no longer firm and terrestrial; it is resolved into its constituent atoms, subtilized, volatilized. Sublimed into imponderable vapor, I mingle and am lost in the endless foods of those vast globular volumes of vaporous mists, which roll upon their flaming orbits through infinite space.

But is it not a dream? Whither is it carrying me? My feverish hand has vainly attempted to describe upon paper its strange and wonderful details. I have forgotten everything that surrounds me. The professor, the guide, the raft—are all gone out of my ken. An illusion has laid hold upon me.

"What is the matter?" my uncle breaks in.

My staring eyes are fixed vacantly upon him.

"Take care, Axel, or you will fall overboard."

At that moment I felt the sinewy hand of Hans seizing me vigorously. But for him, carried away by my dream, I should have thrown myself into the sea.

"Is he mad?" cried the professor.

"What is it all about?" at last I cried, returning to myself.

"Do you feel ill?" my uncle asked.

"No; but I have had a strange hallucination; it is over now. Is all going on right?"

"Yes, it is a fair wind and a fine sea; we are sailing rapidly along, and if I am not out in my reckoning, we shall soon land."

At these words I rose and gazed round upon the horizon, still everywhere bounded by clouds alone.

## *CHAPTER XXXIII*

### A BATTLE OF MONSTERS

Saturday, August 15. The sea unbroken all round. No land in sight. The horizon seems extremely distant.

My head is still stupefied with the vivid reality of my dream.

My uncle has had no dreams, but he is out of temper. He examines the horizon all round with his glass, and folds his arms with the air of an injured man.

I remark that Professor Liedenbrock has a tendency to relapse into an impatient mood, and I make a note of it in my log. All my danger and sufferings were needed to strike a spark of human feeling out of him; but now that I am well his nature has resumed its sway. And yet, what cause was there for anger? Is not the voyage prospering as favorably as possible under the circumstances? Is not the raft spinning along with marvelous speed?

"You seem anxious, my uncle," I said, seeing him continually with his glass to his eye.

"Anxious! No, not at all."

"Impatient, then?"

"One might be, with less reason than now."

"Yet we are going very fast."

"What does that signify? I am not complaining that the rate is slow, but that the sea is so wide."

I then remembered that the professor, before starting, had estimated the length of this underground sea at thirty leagues. Now we had made three times the distance, yet still the southern coast was not in sight.

"We are not descending as we ought to be," the professor declares. "We are losing time, and the fact is, I have not come all this way to take a little sail upon a pond on a raft."

He called this sea a pond, and our long voyage, taking a little sail!

"But," I remarked, "since we have followed the road that Saknussemm has shown us—"

"That is just the question. Have we followed that road? Did Saknussemm meet this sheet of water? Did he cross it? Has not the stream that we followed led us altogether astray?"

"At any rate we cannot feel sorry to have come so far. This prospect is magnificent, and—"

"But I don't care for prospects. I came with an object, and I mean to attain it. Therefore don't talk to me about views and prospects."

I take this as my answer, and I leave the professor to bite his lips with impatience. At six in the evening Hans asks for his wages, and his three rix dollars are counted out to him.

Sunday, August 16. Nothing new. Weather unchanged. The wind freshens. On awaking, my first thought was to observe the intensity of the light. I was possessed with an apprehension lest the electric light should grow dim, or fail altogether. But there seemed no reason to fear. The shadow of the raft was clearly outlined upon the surface of the waves.

Truly this sea is of infinite width. It must be as wide as the Mediterranean or the Atlantic—and why not?

My uncle took soundings several times. He tied the heaviest of our pickaxes to a long rope which he let down two hundred fathoms. No bottom yet; and we had some difficulty in hauling up our plummet.

But when the pick was shipped again, Hans pointed out on its surface deep prints as if it had been violently compressed between two hard bodies.

I looked at the hunter.

"*Tänder*," said he.

I could not understand him, and turned to my uncle who was entirely absorbed in his calculations. I had rather not disturb him while he is quiet. I return to the Icelander. He by a snapping motion of his jaws conveys his ideas to me.

"Teeth!" I cried, considering the iron bar with more attention.

Yes, indeed, those are the marks of teeth imprinted upon the metal! The jaws which they arm must be possessed of amazing strength. Is there some monster beneath us belonging to the extinct races, more voracious than the shark, more fearful in vastness than the whale? I could not take my eyes off this indented iron bar. Surely will my last night's dream be realized?

These thoughts agitated me all day, and my imagination scarcely calmed down after several hours' sleep.

Monday, August 17. I am trying to recall the peculiar instincts of the monsters of the pre-Adamite world, who, coming next in succession after the mollusks, the crustaceans, and the fishes, preceded the animals of mammalian race upon the earth. The world then belonged to reptiles. Those monsters held the mastery in the seas of the secondary period. They possessed a perfect organization, gigantic proportions, prodigious strength. The saurians of our day, the alligators and the crocodiles, are but feeble reproductions of their forefathers of primitive ages.

I shudder as I recall these monsters to my remembrance. No human eye has ever beheld them living. They burdened this earth a thousand ages before man appeared, but their fossil remains, found in the argillaceous limestone called by the English the lias, have enabled their colossal structure to be perfectly built up again and anatomically ascertained.

I saw at the Hamburg museum the skeleton of one of these creatures thirty feet in length. Am I then fated—I, a denizen of earth—to be placed face-to-face with these representatives of long-extinct families? No; surely it cannot be! Yet the deep marks of conical teeth upon the iron pick are certainly those of the crocodile.

My eyes are fearfully bent upon the sea. I dread to see one of these monsters darting forth from its submarine caverns. I suppose Professor Liedenbrock was of my opinion too, and even shared my fears, for after having examined the pick, his eyes traversed the ocean from side to side. What a very bad notion that was of his,

I thought to myself, to take soundings just here! He has disturbed some monstrous beast in its remote den, and if we are not attacked on our voyage—

I look at our guns and see that they are all right. My uncle notices it, and looks on approvingly.

Already widely disturbed regions on the surface of the water indicate some commotion below. The danger is approaching. We must be on the lookout.

Tuesday, August 18. Evening came, or rather the time came when sleep weighs down the weary eyelids, for there is no night here, and the ceaseless light wearies the eyes with its persistence just as if we were sailing under an arctic sun. Hans was at the helm. During his watch I slept.

Two hours afterward a terrible shock awoke me. The raft was heaved up on a watery mountain and pitched down again, at a distance of twenty fathoms.

"What is the matter?" shouted my uncle. "Have we struck land?"

Hans pointed with his finger at a dark mass six hundred yards away, rising and falling alternately with heavy plunges. I looked and cried:

"It is an enormous porpoise."

"Yes," replied my uncle, "and there is a sea lizard of vast size."

"And farther on a monstrous crocodile. Look at its vast jaws and its rows of teeth! It is diving down!"

"There's a whale, a whale!" cried the professor. "I can see its great fins. See how he is throwing out air and water through his blowers."

And in fact two liquid columns were rising to a considerable height above the sea. We stood amazed, thunderstruck, at the presence of such a herd of marine monsters. They were of supernatural dimensions; the smallest of them would have crunched our raft, crew and all, at one snap of its huge jaws.

Hans wants to tack to get away from this dangerous neighborhood; but he sees on the other hand enemies not less terrible; a tortoise forty feet long, and a serpent of thirty, lifting its fearful head and gleaming eyes above the flood.

Flight was out of the question now. The reptiles rose; they wheeled around our little raft with a rapidity greater than that of express trains. They described around us gradually narrowing circles. I took up my rifle. But what could a ball do against the scaly armor with which these enormous beasts were clad?

We stood dumb with fear. They approach us close: on one side the crocodile, on the other the serpent. The remainder of the sea monsters have disappeared. I prepare to fire. Hans stops me by a gesture. The two monsters pass within a hundred and fifty yards of the raft, and hurl themselves the one upon the other, with a fury which prevents them from seeing us.

At three hundred yards from us the battle was fought. We could distinctly observe the two monsters engaged in deadly conflict. But it now seems to me as if the other animals were taking part in the fray—the porpoise, the whale, the lizard, the tortoise. Every moment I seem to see one or other of them. I point them to the Icelander. He shakes his head negatively.

"*Tva*," says he.

"What two? Does he mean that there are only two animals?"

"He is right," said my uncle, whose glass has never left his eye.

"Surely you must be mistaken," I cried.

"No: the first of those monsters has a porpoise's snout, a lizard's head, a crocodile's teeth; and hence our mistake. It is the ichthyosaurus (the fish lizard), the most terrible of the ancient monsters of the deep."

"And the other?"

"The other is a plesiosaurus (almost lizard), a serpent, armored with the carapace and the paddles of a turtle; he is the dreadful enemy of the other."

Hans had spoken truly. Two monsters only were creating all this commotion; and before my eyes are two reptiles of the primitive world. I can distinguish the eye of the ichthyosaurus glowing like a red-hot coal, and as large as a man's head. Nature has endowed it with an optical apparatus of extreme power, and capable of resisting the pressure of the great volume of water in the depths it inhabits. It has been appropriately called the saurian whale, for it has both the swiftness and the rapid movements of this monster of our own day. This one is not less than a hundred feet long, and I can judge of its size when it sweeps over the waters the vertical coils of its tail. Its jaw is enormous, and according to naturalists it is armed with no less than one hundred and eighty-two teeth.

The plesiosaurus, a serpent with a cylindrical body and a short tail, has four flappers or paddles to act like oars. Its body is entirely covered with a thick armor of scales, and its neck, as flexible as a swan's, rises thirty feet above the waves.

Those huge creatures attacked each other with the greatest animosity. They heaved around them liquid mountains, which rolled even to our raft and rocked it perilously. Twenty times we were near capsizing. Hissings of prodigious force are heard. The two beasts are fast locked together; I cannot distinguish the one from the other. The probable rage of the conqueror inspires us with intense fear.

One hour, two hours pass away. The struggle continues with unabated ferocity. The combatants alternately approach and recede from our raft. We remain motionless, ready to fire. Suddenly the ichthyosaurus and the plesiosaurus disappear below, leaving a whirlpool eddying in the water. Several minutes pass by while the fight goes on underwater.

All at once an enormous head is darted up, the head of the plesiosaurus. The monster is wounded to death. I no longer see his scaly armor. Only his long neck shoots up, drops again, coils and uncoils, droops, lashes the waters like a gigantic whip, and writhes like a worm that you tread on. The water is splashed for a long way around. The spray almost blinds us. But soon the reptile's agony draws to an end; its movements become fainter, its contortions cease to be so violent, and the long serpentine form lies a lifeless log on the laboring deep.

As for the ichthyosaurus—has he returned to his submarine cavern? Or will he reappear on the surface of the sea?

## CHAPTER XXXIV

### THE GREAT GEYSER

Wednesday, August 19. Fortunately the wind blows violently, and has enabled us to flee from the scene of the late terrible struggle. Hans keeps at his post at the helm. My uncle, whom the absorbing incidents of the combat had drawn away from his contemplations, began again to look impatiently around him.

The voyage resumes its uniform tenor, which I don't care to break with a repetition of such events as yesterday's.

Thursday, Aug. 20. Wind N.N.E., unsteady and fitful. Temperature high. Rate three and a half leagues an hour.

About noon a distant noise is heard. I note the fact without being able to explain it. It is a continuous roar.

"In the distance," says the professor, "there is a rock or islet, against which the sea is breaking."

Hans climbs up the mast, but sees no breakers. The ocean is smooth and unbroken to its farthest limit.

Three hours pass away. The roarings seem to proceed from a very distant waterfall. I remark upon this to my uncle, who replies doubtfully: "Yes, I am convinced that I am right." Are we, then, speeding forward to some cataract which will cast us down an abyss? This method of getting on may please the professor, because it is vertical; but for my part I prefer the more ordinary modes of horizontal progression.

At any rate, some leagues to the windward there must be some noisy phenomenon, for now the roarings are heard with increasing loudness. Do they proceed from the sky or the ocean?

I look up to the atmospheric vapors, and try to fathom their depths. The sky is calm and motionless. The clouds have reached the utmost limit of the lofty vault, and there lie still bathed in the bright glare of the electric light. It is not there that we must seek for the cause of this phenomenon. Then I examine the horizon, which is unbroken and clear of all mist. There is no change in its aspect. But if this noise arises from a fall, a cataract, if all this ocean flows away headlong into a lower basin yet, if that deafening roar is produced by a mass of falling water, the current must needs accelerate, and its increasing speed will give me the measure of the peril that threatens us. I consult the current: there is none. I throw an empty bottle into the sea: it lies still.

About four Hans rises, lays hold of the mast, climbs to its top. Thence his eye sweeps a large area of sea, and it is fixed upon a point. His countenance exhibits no surprise, but his eye is immovably steady.

"He sees something," says my uncle.

"I believe he does."

Hans comes down, then stretches his arm to the south, saying:

*"Dere nere!"*

"Down there?" repeated my uncle.

Then, seizing his glass, he gazes attentively for a minute, which seems to me an age. "Yes, yes!" he cried. "I see a vast inverted cone rising from the surface."

"Is it another sea beast?"

"Perhaps it is."

"Then let us steer farther westward, for we know something of the danger of coming across monsters of that sort."

"Let us go straight on," replied my uncle.

I appealed to Hans. He maintained his course inflexibly.

Yet, if at our present distance from the animal, a distance of twelve leagues at the least, the column of water driven through its blowers may be distinctly seen, it must needs be of vast size. The commonest prudence would counsel immediate flight; but we did not come so far to be prudent.

Imprudently, therefore, we pursue our way. The nearer we approach, the higher mounts the jet of water. What monster can possibly fill itself with such a quantity of water, and spurt it up so continuously?

At eight in the evening we are not two leagues distant from it. Its body—dusky, enormous, hillocky—lies spread upon the sea like an islet. Is it illusion or fear? Its length seems to me a couple of thousand yards. What can be this cetacean, which neither Cuvier nor Blumenbach knew anything about? It lies motionless, as if asleep; the sea seems unable to move it in the least; it is the waves that undulate upon its sides. The column of water thrown up to a height of five hundred feet falls in rain with a deafening uproar. And here are we scudding like lunatics before the wind, to get near to a monster that a hundred whales a day would not satisfy!

Terror seizes upon me. I refuse to go further. I will cut the halyards if necessary! I am in open mutiny against the professor, who vouchsafes no answer.

Suddenly Hans rises, and pointing with his finger at the menacing object, he says: "*Holm.*"

"An island!" cries my uncle.

"That's not an island!" I cried skeptically.

"It's nothing else," shouted the professor, with a loud laugh.

"But that column of water?"

"*Geyser*," said Hans.

"No doubt it is a geyser, like those in Iceland."

At first I protest against being so widely mistaken as to have taken an island for a marine monster. But the evidence is against me, and I have to confess my error. It is nothing worse than a natural phenomenon.

As we approach nearer, the dimensions of the liquid column become magnificent. The islet resembles, with a most deceiving likeness, an enormous cetacean, whose head dominates the waves at a height of twenty yards. The geyser, a word meaning "fury," rises majestically from its extremity. Deep and heavy explosions are heard from time to time, when the enormous jet, possessed with more furious violence, shakes its plumy crest, and springs with a bound till it reaches the lowest stratum of the clouds. It stands alone. No steam vents, no hot springs surround it, and all the volcanic power of the region is concentrated here. Sparks of electric fire mingle with the dazzling sheaf of lighted fluid, every drop of which refracts the prismatic colors.

"Let us land," said the professor.

"But we must carefully avoid this waterspout, which would sink our raft in a moment."

Hans, steering with his usual skill, brought us to the other extremity of the islet.

I leaped up on the rock; my uncle lightly followed, while our hunter remained at his post, like a man too wise ever to be astonished.

We walked upon granite mingled with siliceous tufa. The soil shivers and shakes under our feet, like the sides of an overheated boiler filled with steam struggling to get loose. We come in sight of a small central basin, out of which the geyser springs. I plunge a register thermometer into the boiling water. It marks an intense heat of 325°, which is far above the boiling point; therefore this water issues from an ardent furnace, which is not at all in harmony with Professor Liedenbrock's theories. I cannot help making the remark.

"Well," he replied, "how does that make against my doctrine?"

"Oh, nothing at all," I said, seeing that I was going in opposition to immovable obstinacy.

Still I am constrained to confess that hitherto we have been wonderfully favored, and that for some reason unknown to myself we have accomplished our journey under singularly favorable conditions of temperature. But it seems manifest to me that someday we shall reach a region where the central heat attains its highest limits, and goes beyond a point that can be registered by our thermometers.

"That is what we shall see." So says the professor, who, having named this volcanic islet after his nephew, gives the signal to embark again.

For some minutes I am still contemplating the geyser. I notice that it throws up its column of water with variable force: sometimes sending it to a great height, then again to a lower, which I attribute to the variable pressure of the steam accumulated in its reservoir.

At last we leave the island, rounding away past the low rocks on its southern shore. Hans has taken advantage of the halt to refit his rudder.

But before going any farther I make a few observations, to calculate the distance we have gone over, and note them in my journal. We have crossed two hundred and seventy leagues of sea since leaving Port Gräuben; and we are six hundred and twenty leagues from Iceland, under England.

## CHAPTER XXXV

### AN ELECTRIC STORM

Friday, August 21. On the morrow the magnificent geyser has disappeared. The wind has risen, and has rapidly carried us away from Axel Island. The roarings become lost in the distance.

The weather—if we may use that term—will change before long. The atmosphere is charged with vapors, pervaded with the electricity generated by the evaporation of saline waters. The clouds are sinking lower, and assume an olive hue. The electric light can scarcely penetrate through the dense curtain which has dropped over the theater on which the battle of the elements is about to be waged.

I feel peculiar sensations, like many creatures on earth at the approach of violent atmospheric changes. The heavily voluted cumulus clouds lower gloomily and threateningly; they wear that implacable look which I have sometimes noticed at the outbreak of a great storm. The air is heavy; the sea is calm.

In the distance the clouds resemble great bales of cotton, piled up in picturesque disorder. By degrees they dilate, and gain in huge size what they lose in number. Such is their ponderous weight that they cannot rise from the horizon; but, obeying an impulse from higher currents, their dense consistency slowly yields. The gloom upon them deepens; and they soon present to our view a ponderous mass of almost level surface. From time to time a fleecy tuft of mist, with yet some gleaming light left upon it, drops down upon the dense floor of gray, and loses itself in the opaque and impenetrable mass.

The atmosphere is evidently charged and surcharged with electricity. My whole body is saturated; my hair bristles just as when you stand upon an insulated stool under the action of an electrical machine. It seems to me as if my companions, the moment they touched me, would receive a severe shock like that from an electric eel.

At ten in the morning the symptoms of storm become aggravated. The wind never lulls but to acquire increased strength; the vast bank of heavy clouds is a huge reservoir of fearful windy gusts and rushing storms.

I am loath to believe these atmospheric menaces, and yet I cannot help muttering: "Here's some very bad weather coming on."

The professor made no answer. His temper is awful, to judge from the working of his features, as he sees this vast length of ocean unrolling before him to an indefinite extent. He can only spare time to shrug his shoulders viciously.

"There's a heavy storm coming on," I cried, pointing toward the horizon. "Those clouds seem as if they were going to crush the sea."

A deep silence falls on all around. The lately roaring winds are hushed into a dead calm; nature seems to breathe no more, and to be sinking into the stillness of death. On the mast already I see the light play of a lambent St. Elmo's fire; the outstretched sail catches not a breath of wind, and hangs like a sheet of lead. The rudder stands motionless in a sluggish, waveless sea. But if we have now ceased to advance why do we yet leave that sail loose, which at the first shock of the tempest may capsize us in a moment?

"Let us reef the sail and cut the mast down!" I cried. "That will be safest."

"No, no! Never!" shouted my impetuous uncle. "Never! Let the wind catch us if it will! What I want is to get the least glimpse of rock or shore, even if our raft should be smashed into shivers!"

The words were hardly out of his mouth when a sudden change took place in the southern sky. The piled-up vapors condense into water; and the air, put into violent action to supply the vacuum left by the condensation of the mists, rouses itself into a whirlwind. It rushes on from the farthest recesses of the vast cavern. The darkness deepens; scarcely can I jot down a few hurried notes. The helm makes a bound. My uncle falls full length; I creep close to him. He has laid a firm hold upon a rope, and appears to watch with grim satisfaction this awful display of elemental strife.

Hans stirs not. His long hair blown by the pelting storm, and laid flat across his immovable countenance, makes him a strange figure; for the end of each lock of loose flowing hair is tipped with little luminous radiations. This frightful mask of electric sparks suggests to me, even in this dizzy excitement, a comparison with pre-Adamite man, the contemporary of the ichthyosaurus and the megatherium.

The mast yet holds firm. The sail stretches tight like a bubble ready to burst. The raft flies at a rate that I cannot reckon, but not so fast as the foaming clouds of spray which it dashes from side to side in its headlong speed.

"The sail! The sail!" I cry, motioning to lower it.

"No!" replies my uncle.

"*Nej!*" repeats Hans, leisurely shaking his head.

But now the rain forms a rushing cataract in front of that horizon toward which we are running with such maddening speed. But before it has reached us the rain cloud parts asunder, the sea boils, and the electric fires are brought into violent action by a mighty chemical power that descends from the higher regions. The most vivid flashes of lightning are mingled with the violent crash of continuous thunder. Ceaseless fiery arrows dart in and out among the flying thunderclouds; the vaporous mass soon glows with incandescent heat; hailstones rattle fiercely down, and as they dash upon our iron tools they too emit gleams and flashes of lurid light. The heaving waves resemble fiery volcanic hills, each belching forth its own interior flames, and every crest is plumed with dancing fire. My eyes fail under the dazzling light, my ears are stunned with the incessant crash of thunder. I must be bound to the mast, which bows like a reed before the mighty strength of the storm.

(Here my notes become vague and indistinct. I have only been able to find a few which I seem to have jotted down almost unconsciously. But their very brevity and their obscurity reveal the intensity of the excitement which dominated me, and describe the actual position even better than my memory could do.)

Sunday, August 23. Where are we? Driven forward with a swiftness that cannot be measured.

The night was fearful; no abatement of the storm. The din and uproar are incessant; our ears are bleeding; to exchange a word is impossible.

The lightning flashes with intense brilliancy, and never seems to cease for a moment. Zigzag streams of bluish-white fire dash down upon the sea and rebound, and then take an upward flight till they strike the granite vault that overarches our heads. Suppose that solid roof should crumble down upon our heads! Other flashes with incessant play cross their vivid fires, while others again roll themselves into balls of living fire which explode like bombshells, but the music of which scarcely adds to the din of the battle strife that almost deprives us of our senses of hearing and sight; the limit of intense loudness has been passed within which the human ear can distinguish one sound from another. If all the powder magazines in the world were to explode at once, we should hear no more than we do now.

From the undersurface of the clouds there are continual emissions of lurid light; electric matter is in continual evolution from their component molecules; the gaseous elements of the air need to be slaked with moisture; for innumerable columns of water rush upward into the air and fall back again in white foam.

Whither are we flying? My uncle lies full length across the raft.

The heat increases. I refer to the thermometer; it indicates . . . (the figure is obliterated).

Monday, August 24. Will there be an end to it? Is the atmospheric condition, having once reached this density, to become final?

We are prostrated and worn out with fatigue. But Hans is as usual. The raft bears on still to the southeast. We have made two hundred leagues since we left Axel Island.

At noon the violence of the storm redoubles. We are obliged to secure as fast as possible every article that belongs to our cargo. Each of us is lashed to some part of the raft. The waves rise above our heads.

For three days we have never been able to make each other hear a word. Our mouths open, our lips move, but not a word can be heard. We cannot even make ourselves heard by approaching our mouth close to the ear.

My uncle has drawn nearer to me. He has uttered a few words. They seem to be "We are lost"; but I am not sure.

At last I write down the words: "Let us lower the sail."

He nods his consent.

Scarcely has he lifted his head again before a ball of fire has bounded over the waves and lighted on board our raft. Mast and sail flew up in an instant together, and I saw them carried up to prodigious height, resembling in appearance a pterodactyl, one of those strong birds of the infant world.

We lay there, our blood running cold with unspeakable terror. The fireball, half of it white, half azure blue, and the size of a ten-inch shell, moved slowly about the raft, but revolving on its own axis with astonishing velocity, as if whipped round by the force of the whirlwind. Here it comes, there it glides, now it is up the ragged stump of the mast, thence it lightly leaps on the provision bag, descends with a light bound, and just skims the powder magazine. Horrible! We shall be blown up; but no, the dazzling disk of mysterious light nimbly leaps aside; it approaches Hans, who fixes his blue eye upon it steadily; it threatens the head of my uncle, who falls upon his knees with his head down to avoid it. And now my turn comes; pale and trembling under the blinding splendor and the melting heat, it drops at my feet, spinning silently round upon the deck; I try to move my foot away, but cannot.

A suffocating smell of nitrogen fills the air, it enters the throat, it fills the lungs. We suffer stifling pains.

Why am I unable to move my foot? Is it riveted to the planks? Alas! The fall upon our fated raft of this electric globe has magnetized every iron article on board. The instruments, the tools, our guns are clashing and clanking violently in their collisions with each other; the nails of my boots cling tenaciously to a plate of iron let into the timbers, and I cannot draw my foot away from the spot. At last by a violent effort I release myself at the instant when the ball in its gyrations was about to seize upon it, and carry me off my feet . . .

Ah! What a flood of intense and dazzling light! The globe has burst, and we are deluged with tongues of fire!

Then all the light disappears. I could just see my uncle at full length on the raft, and Hans still at his helm and spitting fire under the action of the electricity which has saturated him.

But where are we going to? Where?

\* \* \*

Tuesday, August 25. I recover from a long swoon. The storm continues to roar and rage; the lightnings dash hither and thither, like broods of fiery serpents filling all the air. Are we still under the sea? Yes, we are borne at incalculable speed. We have been carried under England, under the Channel, under France, perhaps under the whole of Europe.

\* \* \*

A fresh noise is heard! Surely it is the sea breaking upon the rocks! But then . . .

# CHAPTER XXXVI

## CALM PHILOSOPHIC DISCUSSIONS

Here I end what I may call my log, happily saved from the wreck, and I resume my narrative as before.

What happened when the raft was dashed upon the rocks is more than I can tell. I felt myself hurled into the waves; and if I escaped from death, and if my body was not torn over the sharp edges of the rocks, it was because the powerful arm of Hans came to my rescue.

The brave Icelander carried me out of the reach of the waves, over a burning sand where I found myself by the side of my uncle.

Then he returned to the rocks, against which the furious waves were beating, to save what he could. I was unable to speak. I was shattered with fatigue and excitement; I wanted a whole hour to recover even a little.

But a deluge of rain was still falling, though with that violence which generally denotes the near cessation of a storm. A few overhanging rocks afforded us some shelter from the storm. Hans prepared some food, which I could not touch; and each of us, exhausted with three sleepless nights, fell into a broken and painful sleep.

The next day the weather was splendid. The sky and the sea had sunk into sudden repose. Every trace of the awful storm had disappeared. The exhilarating voice of the professor fell upon my ears as I awoke; he was ominously cheerful.

"Well, my boy," he cried, "have you slept well?"

Would not anyone have thought that we were still in our cheerful little house on the Königsstrasse and that I was only just coming down to breakfast, and that I was to be married to Gräuben that day?

Alas! If the tempest had but sent the raft a little more east, we should have passed under Germany, under my beloved town of Hamburg, under the very street where dwelt all that I loved most in the world. Then only forty leagues would have separated us! But they were forty leagues perpendicular of solid granite wall, and in reality we were a thousand leagues asunder!

All these painful reflections rapidly crossed my mind before I could answer my uncle's question.

"Well, now," he repeated, "won't you tell me how you have slept?"

"Oh, very well," I said. "I am only a little knocked up, but I shall soon be better."

"Oh," says my uncle, "that's nothing to signify. You are only a little bit tired."

"But you, uncle, you seem in very good spirits this morning."

"Delighted, my boy, delighted. We have got there."

"To our journey's end?"

"No; but we have got to the end of that endless sea. Now we shall go by land, and really begin to go down! Down! Down!"

"But, my dear uncle, do let me ask you one question."

"Of course, Axel."

"How about returning?"

"Returning? Why, you are talking about the return before the arrival."

"No, I only want to know how that is to be managed."

"In the simplest way possible. When we have reached the center of the globe, either we shall find some new way to get back, or we shall come back like decent folks the way we came. I feel pleased at the thought that it is sure not to be shut against us."

"But then we shall have to refit the raft."

"Of course."

"Then, as to provisions, have we enough to last?"

"Yes; to be sure we have. Hans is a clever fellow, and I am sure he must have saved a large part of our cargo. But still let us go and make sure."

We left this grotto which lay open to every wind. At the same time I cherished a trembling hope which was a fear as well. It seemed to me impossible that the terrible wreck of the raft should not have destroyed everything on board. On my arrival on the shore I found Hans surrounded by an assemblage of articles all arranged in good order. My uncle shook hands with him with a lively gratitude. This man, with almost superhuman devotion, had been at work all the while that we were asleep, and had saved the most precious of the articles at the risk of his life.

Not that we had suffered no losses. For instance, our firearms; but we might do without them. Our stock of powder had remained uninjured after having risked blowing up during the storm.

"Well," cried the professor, "as we have no guns we cannot hunt, that's all."

"Yes, but how about the instruments?"

"Here is the aneroid, the most useful of all, and for which I would have given all the others. By means of it I can calculate the depth and know when we have reached the center; without it we might very likely go beyond, and come out at the antipodes!"

Such high spirits as these were rather too strong.

"But where is the compass? I asked.

"Here it is, upon this rock, in perfect condition, as well as the thermometers and the chronometer. The hunter is a splendid fellow."

There was no denying it. We had all our instruments. As for tools and appliances, there they all lay on the ground—ladders, ropes, picks, spades, etc.

Still there was the question of provisions to be settled, and I asked, "How are we off for provisions?"

The boxes containing these were in a line upon the shore, in a perfect state of preservation; for the most part the sea had spared them, and what with biscuits, salt meat, spirits, and salt fish, we might reckon on four months' supply.

"Four months!" cried the professor. "We have time to go and to return; and with what is left I will give a grand dinner to my friends at the Johannæum."

I ought by this time to have been quite accustomed to my uncle's ways; yet there was always something fresh about him to astonish me.

"Now," said he, "we will replenish our supply of water with the rain which the storm has left in all these granite basins; therefore we shall have no reason to fear anything from thirst. As for the raft, I will recommend Hans to do his best to repair it, although I don't expect it will be of any further use to us."

"How so?" I cried.

"An idea of my own, my lad. I don't think we shall come out by the way that we went in."

I stared at the professor with a good deal of mistrust. I asked, was he not touched in the brain? And yet there was method in his madness.

"And now let us go to breakfast," said he.

I followed him to a headland, after he had given his instructions to the hunter. There preserved meat, biscuit, and tea made us an excellent meal, one of the best I ever remember. Hunger, the fresh air, the calm quiet weather, after the commotions we had gone through, all contributed to give me a good appetite.

While breakfasting I took the opportunity to put to my uncle the question where we were now.

"That seems to me," I said, "rather difficult to make out."

"Yes, it is difficult," he said, "to calculate exactly; perhaps even impossible, since during these three stormy days I have been unable to keep any account of the rate or direction of the raft; but still we may get an approximation."

"The last observation," I remarked, "was made on the island, when the geyser was—"

"You mean Axel Island. Don't decline the honor of having given your name to the first island ever discovered in the central parts of the globe."

"Well," said I, "let it be Axel Island. Then we had cleared two hundred and seventy leagues of sea, and we were six hundred leagues from Iceland."

"Very well," answered my uncle; "let us start from that point and count four days' storm, during which our rate cannot have been less than eighty leagues in the twenty-four hours."

"That is right; and this would make three hundred leagues more."

"Yes, and the Liedenbrock Sea would be six hundred leagues from shore to shore. Surely, Axel, it may vie in size with the Mediterranean itself."

"Especially," I replied, "if it happens that we have only crossed it in its narrowest part. And it is a curious circumstance," I added, "that if my computations are right, and we are nine hundred leagues from Reykjavik, we have now the Mediterranean above our head."

"That is a good long way, my friend. But whether we are under Turkey or the Atlantic depends very much upon the question in what direction we have been moving. Perhaps we have deviated."

"No, I think not. Our course has been the same all along, and I believe this shore is southeast of Port Gräuben."

"Well," replied my uncle, "we may easily ascertain this by consulting the compass. Let us go and see what it says."

The professor moved toward the rock upon which Hans had laid down the instruments. He was gay and full of spirits; he rubbed his hands, he studied his attitudes. I followed him, curious to know if I was right in my estimate. As soon as we had arrived at the rock my uncle took the compass, laid it horizontally, and questioned the needle, which, after a few oscillations, presently assumed a fixed position. My uncle looked, and looked, and looked again. He rubbed his eyes, and then turned to me thunderstruck with some unexpected discovery.

"What is the matter?" I asked.

He motioned to me to look. An exclamation of astonishment burst from me. The north pole of the needle was turned to what we supposed to be the south. It pointed to the shore instead of to the open sea! I shook the box, examined it again, it was in perfect condition. In whatever position I placed the box the needle pertinaciously returned to this unexpected quarter. Therefore there seemed no reason to doubt that during the storm there had been a sudden change of wind unperceived by us, which had brought our raft back to the shore which we thought we had left so long a distance behind us.

## CHAPTER XXXVII

### THE LIEDENBROCK MUSEUM OF GEOLOGY

How shall I describe the strange series of passions which in succession shook the breast of Professor Liedenbrock? First stupefaction, then incredulity, lastly a downright burst of rage. Never had I seen the man so put out of countenance and so disturbed. The fatigues of our passage across, the dangers met, had all to be begun over again. We had gone backward instead of forward!

But my uncle rapidly recovered himself.

"Aha! Will fate play tricks upon me? Will the elements lay plots against me? Shall fire, air, and water make a combined attack against me? Well, they shall know what a determined man can do. I will not yield. I will not stir a single foot backward, and it will be seen whether man or nature is to have the upper hand!"

Erect upon the rock, angry and threatening, Otto Liedenbrock was a rather grotesque fierce parody upon the fierce Achilles defying the lightning. But I thought it my duty to interpose and attempt to lay some restraint upon this unmeasured fanaticism.

"Just listen to me," I said firmly. "Ambition must have a limit somewhere; we cannot perform impossibilities; we are not at all fit for another sea voyage; who would dream of undertaking a voyage of five hundred leagues upon a heap of rotten planks, with a blanket in rags for a sail, a stick for a mast, and fierce winds in our teeth? We cannot steer; we shall be buffeted by the tempests, and we should be fools and madmen to attempt to cross a second time."

I was able to develop this series of unanswerable reasons for ten minutes without interruption; not that the professor was paying any respectful attention to his nephew's arguments, but because he was deaf to all my eloquence.

"To the raft!" he shouted.

Such was his only reply. It was no use for me to entreat, supplicate, get angry, or do anything else in the way of opposition; it would only have been opposing a will harder than the granite rock.

Hans was finishing the repairs of the raft. One would have thought that this strange being was guessing at my uncle's intentions. With a few more pieces of surturbrand he had refitted our vessel. A sail already hung from the new mast, and the wind was playing in its waving folds.

The professor said a few words to the guide, and immediately he put everything on board and arranged every necessary for our departure. The air was clear—and the northwest wind blew steadily.

What could I do? Could I stand against the two? It was impossible? If Hans had but taken my side! But no, it was not to be. The Icelander seemed to have renounced all will of his own and made a vow to forget and deny himself. I could get nothing out of a servant so feudalized, as it were, to his master. My only course was to proceed.

I was therefore going with as much resignation as I could find to resume my accustomed place on the raft, when my uncle laid his hand upon my shoulder.

"We shall not sail until tomorrow," he said.

I made a movement intended to express resignation.

"I must neglect nothing," he said; "and since my fate has driven me on this part of the coast, I will not leave it until I have examined it."

To understand what followed, it must be borne in mind that, through circumstances hereafter to be explained, we were not really where the professor supposed we were. In fact we were not upon the north shore of the sea.

"Now let us start upon fresh discoveries," I said.

And leaving Hans to his work, we started off together. The space between the water and the foot of the cliffs was considerable. It took half an hour to bring us to the wall of rock. We trampled under our feet numberless shells of all the forms and sizes which existed in the earliest ages of the world. I also saw immense carapaces more than fifteen feet in diameter. They had been the coverings of those gigantic glyptodons or armadillos of the Pleiocene period, of which the modern tortoise is but a miniature representative. The soil was besides this scattered with stony fragments, boulders rounded by water action, and ridged up in successive lines. I was therefore led to the conclusion that at one time the sea must have covered the ground on which we were treading. On the loose and scattered rocks, now out of the reach of the highest tides, the waves had left manifest traces of their power to wear their way in the hardest stone.

This might up to a certain point explain the existence of an ocean forty leagues beneath the surface of the globe. But in my opinion this liquid mass would be lost by degrees farther and farther within the interior of the earth, and it certainly had its origin in the waters of the ocean overhead, which had made their way hither through some fissure. Yet it must be believed that that fissure is now closed, and that all this cavern or immense reservoir was filled in a very short time. Perhaps even this water, subjected to the fierce action of central heat, had partly been resolved into vapor. This would explain the existence of those clouds suspended over our heads and the development of that electricity which raised such tempests within the bowels of the earth.

This theory of the phenomena we had witnessed seemed satisfactory to me; for however great and stupendous the phenomena of nature, fixed physical laws will or may always explain them.

We were therefore walking upon sedimentary soil, the deposits of the waters of former ages. The professor was carefully examining every little fissure in the rocks. Wherever he saw a hole he always wanted to know the depth of it. To him this was important.

We had traversed the shores of the Liedenbrock sea for a mile when we observed a sudden change in the appearance of the soil. It seemed upset, contorted, and convulsed by a violent upheaval of the lower strata. In many places depressions or elevations gave witness to some tremendous power effecting the dislocation of strata.

We moved with difficulty across these granite fissures and chasms mingled with silex, crystals of quartz, and alluvial deposits, when a field, nay, more than a field, a vast plain, of bleached bones lay spread before us. It seemed like an immense cemetery, where the remains of twenty ages mingled their dust together. Huge mounds of bony fragments rose stage after stage in the distance. They undulated away to the limits of the horizon, and melted in the distance in a faint haze. There within three square miles were accumulated the materials for a complete history of the animal life of ages, a history scarcely outlined in the too recent strata of the inhabited world.

But an impatient curiosity impelled our steps; crackling and rattling, our feet were trampling on the remains of prehistoric animals and interesting fossils, the possession of which is a matter of rivalry and contention between the museums of great cities. A thousand Cuviers could never have reconstructed the organic remains deposited in this magnificent and unparalleled collection.

I stood amazed. My uncle had uplifted his long arms to the vault which was our sky; his mouth gaping wide, his eyes flashing behind his shining spectacles, his head balancing with an up-and-down motion, his whole attitude denoted unlimited astonishment. Here he stood facing an immense collection of scattered leptotheria, mericotheria, lophiodia, anoplotheria, megatheria, mastodons, protopithecae, pterodactyls, and all sorts of extinct monsters here assembled together for his special satisfaction. Fancy an enthusiastic bibliomaniac suddenly brought into the midst of the famous Alexandrian library burned by Omar and restored by a miracle from its ashes! Just such a crazed enthusiast was my uncle, Professor Liedenbrock.

But more was to come, when, with a rush through clouds of bone dust, he laid his hand upon a bare skull, and cried with a voice trembling with excitement:

"Axel! Axel! A human head!"

"A human skull?" I cried, no less astonished.

"Yes, nephew. Aha! M. Milne-Edwards! Ah! M. de Quatrefages, how I wish you were standing here at the side of Otto Liedenbrock!"

## CHAPTER XXXVIII

### THE PROFESSOR IN HIS CHAIR AGAIN

To understand this apostrophe of my uncle's, made to absent French savants, it will be necessary to allude to an event of high importance in a paleontological point of view, which had occurred a little while before our departure.

On the 28th of March, 1863, some excavators working under the direction of M. Boucher de Perthes, in the stone quarries of Moulin Quignon, near Abbeville, in the department of Somme, found a human jawbone fourteen feet beneath the surface. It was the first fossil of this nature that had ever been brought to light. Not far distant were found stone hatchets and flint arrowheads stained and encased by lapse of time with a uniform coat of rust.

The noise of this discovery was very great, not in France alone, but in England and in Germany. Several savants of the French Institute, and among them MM. Milne-Edwards and de Quatrefages, saw at once the importance of this discovery, proved to demonstration the genuineness of the bone in question, and became the most ardent defendants in what the English called this "trial of a jawbone." To the geologists of the United Kingdom, who believed in the certainty of the fact—Messrs. Falconer, Busk, Carpenter, and others—scientific Germans were soon joined, and among them the forwardest, the most fiery, and the most enthusiastic, was my Uncle Liedenbrock.

Therefore the genuineness of a fossil human relic of the Quaternary period seemed to be incontestably proved and admitted.

It is true that this theory met with a most obstinate opponent in M. Elie de Beaumont. This high authority maintained that the soil of Moulin Quignon was not diluvial at all, but was of much more recent formation; and, agreeing in that with Cuvier, he refused to admit that the human species could be contemporary with the animals of the Quaternary period. My Uncle Liedenbrock, along with the great body of the geologists, had maintained his ground, disputed, and argued, until M. Elie de Beaumont stood almost alone in his opinion.

We knew all these details, but we were not aware that since our departure the question had advanced to farther stages. Other, similar maxillaries, though belonging to individuals of various types and different nations, were found in the loose gray soil of certain grottoes in France, Switzerland, and Belgium, as well as weapons, tools, earthen utensils, bones of children and adults. The existence therefore of man in the Quaternary period seemed to become daily more certain.

Nor was this all. Fresh discoveries of remains in the Pleiocene formation had emboldened other geologists to refer back the human species to a higher antiquity still. It is true that these remains were not human bones, but objects bearing the traces of his handiwork, such as fossil leg bones of animals, sculptured and carved evidently by the hand of man.

Thus, at one bound, the record of the existence of man receded far back into the history of the ages past; he was a predecessor of the mastodon; he was a contemporary of the southern elephant; he lived a hundred thousand years ago, when, according to geologists, the Pleiocene formation was in progress.

Such then was the state of paleontological science, and what we knew of it was sufficient to explain our behavior in the presence of this stupendous Golgotha. Anyone may now understand the frenzied excitement of my uncle, when, twenty yards farther on, he found himself face-to-face with a primitive man!

It was a perfectly recognizable human body. Had some particular soil, like that of the cemetery St. Michel, at Bordeaux, preserved it thus for so many ages? It might be so. But this dried corpse, with its parchmentlike skin drawn tightly over the bony frame, the limbs still preserving their shape, sound teeth, abundant hair, and finger- and toenails of frightful length, this desiccated mummy startled us by appearing just as it had lived countless ages ago. I stood mute before this apparition of remote antiquity. My uncle, usually so garrulous, was struck dumb likewise. We raised the body. We stood it up against a rock. It seemed to stare at us out of its empty orbits. We sounded with our knuckles his hollow frame.

After some moments' silence the professor was himself again. Otto Liedenbrock, yielding to his nature, forgot all the circumstances of our eventful journey, forgot where we were standing, forgot the vaulted cavern which contained us. No doubt he was in mind back again in his Johanneum, holding forth to his pupils, for he assumed his learned air; and addressing himself to an imaginary audience, he proceeded thus:

"Gentlemen, I have the honor to introduce to you a man of the Quaternary or post-Tertiary system. Eminent geologists have denied his existence, others no less eminent have affirmed it. The St. Thomases of paleontology, if they were here, might now touch him with their fingers, and would be obliged to acknowledge their error. I am quite aware that science has to be on its guard with discoveries of this kind. I know what capital enterprising individuals like Barnum have made out of fossil men. I have heard the tale of the kneepan of Ajax, the pretended body of Orestes claimed to have been found by the Spartans, and of the body of Asterius, ten cubits long, of which Pausanias speaks. I have read the reports of the skeleton of Trapani, found in the fourteenth century, and which was at the time identified as that of Polyphemus; and the history of the giant unearthed in the sixteenth century near Palermo. You know as well as I do, gentlemen, the analysis made at Lucerne in 1577 of those huge bones which the celebrated Dr. Felix Plater affirmed to be those of a giant nineteen feet high. I have gone through the treatises of Cassanion, and all those memoirs, pamphlets, answers, and rejoinders published respecting the skeleton of Teutobochus, the invader of Gaul, dug out of a sandpit in the Dauphiné, in 1613. In the eighteenth century I would have stood up for Scheuchzer's pre-Adamite man against Peter Campet. I have perused a writing, entitled Gigan—"

Here my uncle's unfortunate infirmity met him—that of being unable in public to pronounce hard words.

"The pamphlet entitled Gigan—"

He could get no further.

"Giganteo—"

It was not to be done. The unlucky word would not come out. At the Johanneum there would have been a laugh.

"Gigantostéologie," at last the professor burst out, between two words which I shall not record here.

Then rushing on with renewed vigor, and with great animation:

"Yes, gentlemen, I know all these things, and more. I know that Cuvier and Blumenbach have recognized in these bones nothing more remarkable than the bones of the mammoth and other mammals of the post-Tertiary period. But in the presence of this specimen, to doubt would be to insult science. There stands the body! You may see it, touch it. It is not a mere skeleton; it is an entire body, preserved for a purely anthropological end and purpose."

I was good enough not to contradict this startling assertion.

"If I could only wash it in a solution of sulfuric acid," pursued my uncle, "I should be able to clear it from all the earthy particles and the shells which are encrusted about it. But I do not possess that valuable solvent. Yet, such as it is, the body shall tell us its own wonderful story."

Here the professor laid hold of the fossil skeleton, and handled it with the skill of a dexterous showman.

"You see," he said, "that it is not six feet long, and that we are still separated by a long interval from the pretended race of giants. As for the family to which it belongs, it is evidently Caucasian. It is the white race, our own. The skull of this fossil is a regular oval, or rather ovoid. It exhibits no prominent cheekbones, no projecting jaws. It presents no appearance of that prognathism which diminishes the facial angle.* Measure that angle. It is nearly ninety degrees. But I will go further in my deductions, and I will affirm that this specimen of the human family is of the Japhetic race, which has since spread from the Indies to the Atlantic. Don't smile, gentlemen."

Nobody was smiling; but the learned professor was frequently disturbed by the broad smiles provoked by his learned eccentricities.

"Yes," he pursued with animation, "this is a fossil man, the contemporary of the mastodons whose remains fill this amphitheater. But if you ask me how he came there, how those strata on which he lay slipped down into this enormous hollow in the globe, I confess I cannot answer that question. No doubt in the post-Tertiary period considerable commotions were still disturbing the crust of the earth. The long-continued cooling of the globe produced chasms, fissures, clefts, and faults, into which, very probably, portions of the upper earth may have fallen. I make no rash assertions; but there is the man surrounded by his own works, by hatchets, by flint arrowheads, which are the characteristics of the Stone Age. And unless he came here, like myself, as a tourist on a visit and as a pioneer of science, I can entertain no doubt of the authenticity of his remote origin."

The professor ceased to speak, and the audience broke out into loud and unanimous applause. For of course my uncle was right, and wiser men than his nephew would have had some trouble to refute his statements.

---

* The facial angle is formed by two lines; one touching the brow and the front teeth, the other from the orifice of the ear to the lower line of the nostrils. The greater this angle, the higher intelligence denoted by the formation of the skull. Prognathism is that projection of the jawbones which sharpens or lessens this angle, and which is illustrated in the Negro countenance and in the lowest savages.

Another remarkable thing. This fossil body was not the only one in this immense catacomb. We came upon other bodies at every step among this mortal dust, and my uncle might select the most curious of these specimens to demolish the incredulity of skeptics.

In fact it was a wonderful spectacle, that of these generations of men and animals commingled in a common cemetery. Then one very serious question arose presently which we scarcely dared to suggest. Had all those creatures slid through a great fissure in the crust of the earth, down to the shores of the Liedenbrock Sea, when they were dead and turning to dust, or had they lived and grown and died here in this subterranean world under a false sky, just like inhabitants of the upper earth? Until the present time we had seen alive only marine monsters and fishes. Might not some living man, some native of the abyss, be yet a wanderer below on this desert strand?

## CHAPTER XXXIX

### FOREST SCENERY ILLUMINATED BY ELECTRICITY

For another half hour we trod upon a pavement of bones. We pushed on, impelled by our burning curiosity. What other marvels did this cavern contain? What new treasures lay here for science to unfold? I was prepared for any surprise, my imagination was ready for any astonishment however astounding.

We had long lost sight of the seashore behind the hills of bones. The rash professor, careless of losing his way, hurried me forward. We advanced in silence, bathed in luminous electric fluid. By some phenomenon which I am unable to explain, it lighted up all sides of every object equally. Such was its diffusiveness, there being no central point from which the light emanated, that shadows no longer existed. You might have thought yourself under the rays of a vertical sun in a tropical region at noonday and the height of summer. No vapor was visible. The rocks, the distant mountains, a few isolated clumps of forest trees in the distance, presented a weird and wonderful aspect under these totally new conditions of a universal diffusion of light. We were like Hoffmann's shadowless man.

After walking a mile we reached the outskirts of a vast forest, but not one of those forests of fungi which bordered Port Gräuben.

Here was the vegetation of the tertiary period in its fullest blaze of magnificence. Tall palms, belonging to species no longer living, splendid palmacites, firs, yews, cypress trees, thujas, representatives of the conifers, were linked together by a tangled network of long climbing plants. A soft carpet of moss and hepaticas luxuriously clothed the soil. A few sparkling streams ran almost in silence under what would have been the shade of the trees, but that there was no shadow. On their banks grew tree ferns similar to those we grow in hothouses. But a remarkable feature was the total absence of color in all those trees, shrubs, and plants, growing without the life-giving heat and light of the sun. Everything seemed mixed-up and confounded in one uniform silver gray or light brown tint like that of fading and faded leaves. Not a green leaf anywhere, and the flowers—which were abundant enough in the Tertiary period, which first gave birth to flowers—looked like brown-paper flowers, without color or scent.

My Uncle Liedenbrock ventured to penetrate under this colossal grove. I followed him, not without fear. Since nature had here provided vegetable nourishment, why should not the terrible mammals be there too? I perceived in the broad clearings left by fallen trees, decayed with age, leguminose plants, acerineae, rubiceae, and many other eatable shrubs, dear to ruminant animals at every period. Then I observed, mingled together in confusion, trees of countries far apart on the surface of the globe. The oak and the palm were growing side by side, the Australian eucalyptus leaned against the Norwegian pine, the birch tree of the north mingled its foliage with New Zealand kauris. It was enough to distract the most ingenious classifier of terrestrial botany.

Suddenly I halted. I drew back my uncle.

The diffused light revealed the smallest object in the dense and distant thickets. I had thought I saw—no! I did see, with my own eyes, vast colossal forms moving among the trees. They were gigantic animals; it was a herd of mastodons—not fossil remains, but living and resembling those the bones of which were found in the marshes of Ohio in 1801. I saw those huge elephants whose long, flexible trunks were grouting and turning up the soil under the trees like a legion of serpents. I could hear the crashing noise of their long ivory tusks boring into the old decaying trunks. The boughs cracked, and the leaves torn away by cartloads went down the cavernous throats of the vast brutes.

So, then, the dream in which I had had a vision of the prehistoric world, of the Tertiary and post-Tertiary periods, was now realized. And there we were alone, in the bowels of the earth, at the mercy of its wild inhabitants!

My uncle was gazing with intense and eager interest.

"Come on!" said he, seizing my arm. "Forward! Forward!"

"No, I will not!" I cried. "We have no firearms. What could we do in the midst of a herd of these four-footed giants? Come away, uncle—come! No human being may with safety dare the anger of these monstrous beasts."

"No human creature?" replied my uncle in a lower voice. "You are wrong, Axel. Look, look down there! I fancy I see a living creature similar to ourselves: it is a man!"

I looked, shaking my head incredulously. But though at first I was unbelieving, I had to yield to the evidence of my senses.

In fact, at a distance of a quarter of a mile, leaning against the trunk of a gigantic kauri, stood a human being, the Proteus of those subterranean regions, a new son of Neptune, watching this countless herd of mastodons.

*Immanis pecoris custos, immanior ipse.**

Yes, truly, huger still himself. It was no longer a fossil being like him whose dried remains we had easily lifted up in the field of bones; it was a giant, able to control those monsters. In stature he was at least twelve feet high. His head, huge and unshapely as a buffalo's, was half hidden in the thick and tangled growth of his unkempt hair. It most resembled the mane of the primitive elephant. In his hand he wielded with ease an enormous bough, a staff worthy of this shepherd of the geologic period.

We stood petrified and speechless with amazement. But he might see us! We must fly!

"Come, do come!" I said to my uncle, who for once allowed himself to be persuaded.

In another quarter of an hour our nimble heels had carried us beyond the reach of this horrible monster.

And yet, now that I can reflect quietly, now that my spirit has grown calm again, now that months have slipped by since this strange and supernatural meeting, what am I to think? What am I to believe? I must conclude that it was impossible that our senses had been deceived, that our eyes did not see what we supposed they saw. No human being lives in this subterranean world; no generation of men dwells in those inferior caverns of the globe, unknown to and unconnected with the inhabitants of its surface. It is absurd to believe it!

---

* "The shepherd of gigantic herds, and huger still himself."

I had rather admit that it may have been some animal whose structure resembled the human, some ape or baboon of the early geological ages, some protopitheca, or some mesopitheca, some early or middle ape like that discovered by Mr. Lartet in the bone cave of Sansau. But this creature surpassed in stature all the measurements known in modern paleontology. But that a man, a living man, and therefore whole generations doubtless besides, should be buried there in the bowels of the earth, is impossible.

However, we had left behind us the luminous forest, dumb with astonishment, overwhelmed and struck down with a terror which amounted to stupefaction. We kept running on for fear the horrible monster might be on our track. It was a flight, a fall, like that fearful pulling and dragging which is peculiar to nightmare. Instinctively we got back to the Liedenbrock Sea, and I cannot say into what vagaries my mind would not have carried me but for a circumstance which brought me back to practical matters.

Although I was certain that we were now treading upon a soil not hitherto touched by our feet, I often perceived groups of rocks which reminded me of those about Port Gräuben. Besides, this seemed to confirm the indications of the needle, and to show that we had against our will returned to the north of the Liedenbrock Sea. Occasionally we felt quite convinced. Brooks and waterfalls were tumbling everywhere from the projections in the rocks. I thought I recognized the bed of surturbrand, our faithful Hansbach, and the grotto in which I had recovered life and consciousness. Then a few paces farther on, the arrangement of the cliffs, the appearance of an unrecognized stream, or the strange outline of a rock, came to throw me again into doubt.

I communicated my doubts to my uncle. Like myself, he hesitated; he could recognize nothing again amid this monotonous scene.

"Evidently," said I, "we have not landed again at our original starting point, but the storm has carried us a little higher, and if we follow the shore we shall find Port Gräuben."

"If that is the case it will be useless to continue our exploration, and we had better return to our raft. But, Axel, are you not mistaken?"

"It is difficult to speak decidedly, uncle, for all these rocks are so very much alike. Yet I think I recognize the promontory at the foot of which Hans constructed our launch. We must be very near the little port, if indeed this is not it," I added, examining a creek which I thought I recognized.

"No, Axel, we should at least find our own traces and I see nothing—"

"But I do see," I cried, darting upon an object lying on the sand.

And I showed my uncle a rusty dagger which I had just picked up.

"Come," said he, "had you this weapon with you?"

"I! No, certainly! But you, perhaps—"

"Not that I am aware," said the professor. "I have never had this object in my possession."

"Well, this is strange!"

"No, Axel, it is very simple. The Icelanders often wear arms of this kind. This must have belonged to Hans, and he has lost it."

I shook my head. Hans had never had an object like this in his possession.

"Did it not belong to some pre-Adamite warrior?" I cried, "to some living man, contemporary with the huge cattle-driver? But no. This is not a relic of the Stone Age. It is not even of the Iron Age. This blade is steel—"

My uncle stopped me abruptly on my way to a dissertation which would have taken me a long way, and said coolly:

"Be calm, Axel, and reasonable. This dagger belongs to the sixteenth century; it is a poniard, such as gentlemen carried in their belts to give the coup de grace. Its origin is Spanish. It was never either yours, or mine, or the hunter's, nor did it belong to any of those human beings who may or may not inhabit this inner world. See, it was never jagged like this by cutting men's throats; its blade is coated with a rust neither a day, nor a year, nor a hundred years old."

The professor was getting excited according to his wont, and was allowing his imagination to run away with him.

"Axel, we are on the way toward the grand discovery. This blade has been left on the strand for from one to three hundred years, and has blunted its edge upon the rocks that fringe this subterranean sea!"

"But it has not come alone. It has not twisted itself out of shape; some one has been here before us!

"Yes—a man has."

"And who was that man?"

"A man who has engraved his name somewhere with that dagger. That man wanted once more to mark the way to the center of the earth. Let us look about: look about!"

And, wonderfully interested, we peered all along the high wall, peeping into every fissure which might open out into a gallery.

And so we arrived at a place where the shore was much narrowed. Here the sea came to lap the foot of the steep cliff, leaving a passage no wider than a couple of yards. Between two boldly projecting rocks appeared the mouth of a dark tunnel.

There, upon a granite slab, appeared two mysterious graven letters, half eaten away by time. They were the initials of the bold and daring traveler:

$$\cdot \, \textbf{1} \cdot \textbf{h} \cdot$$

"A. S.," shouted my uncle. "Arne Saknussemm! Arne Saknussemm everywhere!"

## *CHAPTER XL*

### PREPARATIONS FOR BLASTING A PASSAGE TO THE CENTER OF THE EARTH

Since the start upon this marvelous pilgrimage I had been through so many astonishments that I might well be excused for thinking myself well hardened against any further surprise. Yet at the sight of these two letters, engraved on this spot three hundred years ago, I stood aghast in dumb amazement. Not only were the initials of the learned alchemist visible upon the living rock, but there lay the iron point with which the letters had been engraved. I could no longer doubt of the existence of that wonderful traveler and of the fact of his unparalleled journey, without the most glaring incredulity.

While these reflections were occupying me, Professor Liedenbrock had launched into a somewhat rhapsodical eulogium, of which Arne Saknussemm was, of course, the hero.

"Thou marvelous genius!" he cried. "Thou hast not forgotten one indication which might serve to lay open to mortals the road through the terrestrial crust; and thy fellow creatures may even now, after the lapse of three centuries, again trace thy footsteps through these deep and darksome ways. You reserved the contemplation of these wonders for other eyes besides your own. Your name, graven from stage to stage, leads the bold follower of your footsteps to the very center of our planet's core, and there again we shall find your own name written with your own hand. I too will inscribe my name upon this dark granite page. But forever henceforth let this cape that advances into the sea discovered by yourself be known by your own illustrious name—Cape Saknussemm."

Such were the glowing words of panegyric which fell upon my attentive ear, and I could not resist the sentiment of enthusiasm with which I too was infected. The fire of zeal kindled afresh in me. I forgot everything. I dismissed from my mind the past perils of the journey, the future danger of our return. That which another had done I supposed we might also do, and nothing that was not superhuman appeared impossible to me.

"Forward! Forward!" I cried.

I was already darting down the gloomy tunnel when the professor stopped me; he, the man of impulse, counseled patience and coolness.

"Let us first return to Hans," he said, "and bring the raft to this spot."

I obeyed, not without dissatisfaction, and passed out rapidly among the rocks on the shore.

I said, "Uncle, do you know it seems to me that circumstances have wonderfully befriended us hitherto?"

"You think so, Axel?"

"No doubt; even the tempest has put us on the right way. Blessings on that storm! It has brought us back to this coast from which fine weather would have carried us far away. Suppose we had touched with our prow (the prow of a rudder!) the southern shore of the Liedenbrock Sea, what would have become of us? We should never have seen the name of Saknussemm, and we should at this moment be imprisoned on a rockbound, impassable coast."

"Yes, Axel, it is providential that while supposing we were steering south we should have just got back north at Cape Saknussemm. I must say that this is astonishing, and that I feel I have no way to explain it."

"What does that signify, uncle? Our business is not to explain facts, but to use them!"

"Certainly; but—"

"Well, uncle, we are going to resume the northern route, and to pass under the north countries of Europe—under Sweden, Russia, Siberia: who knows where?—instead of burrowing under the deserts of Africa, or perhaps the waves of the Atlantic; and that is all I want to know."

"Yes, Axel, you are right. It is all for the best, since we have left that weary, horizontal sea, which led us nowhere. Now we shall go down, down, down! Do you know that it is now only 1,500 leagues to the center of the globe?"

"Is that all?" I cried. "Why, that's nothing. Let us start: march!"

All this crazy talk was going on still when we met the hunter. Everything was made ready for our instant departure. Every bit of cordage was put on board. We took our places, and with our sail set, Hans steered us along the coast to Cape Saknussemm.

The wind was unfavorable to a species of launch not calculated for shallow water. In many places we were obliged to push ourselves along with iron-pointed sticks. Often the sunken rocks just beneath the surface obliged us to deviate from our straight course. At last, after three hours' sailing, about six in the evening we reached a place suitable for our landing. I jumped ashore, followed by my uncle and the Icelander. This short passage had not served to cool my ardor. On the contrary, I even proposed to burn "our ship," to prevent the possibility of return; but my uncle would not consent to that. I thought him singularly lukewarm.

"At least," I said, "don't let us lose a minute."

"Yes, yes, lad," he replied; "but first let us examine this new gallery, to see if we shall require our ladders."

My uncle put his Ruhmkorff's apparatus in action; the raft moored to the shore was left alone; the mouth of the tunnel was not twenty yards from us; and our party, with myself at the head, made for it without a moment's delay.

The aperture, which was almost round, was about five feet in diameter; the dark passage was cut out in the live rock and lined with a coat of the eruptive matter which formerly issued from it; the interior was level with the ground outside, so that we were able to enter without difficulty. We were following a horizontal plane, when, only six paces in, our progress was interrupted by an enormous block just across our way.

"Accursed rock!" I cried in a passion, finding myself suddenly confronted by an impassable obstacle.

Right and left we searched in vain for a way, up and down, side to side; there was no getting any farther. I felt fearfully disappointed, and I would not admit that the obstacle was final. I stopped, I looked underneath the block: no opening. Above:

granite still. Hans passed his lamp over every portion of the barrier in vain. We must give up all hope of passing it.

I sat down in despair. My uncle strode from side to side in the narrow passage.

"But how was it with Saknussemm?" I cried.

"Yes," said my uncle, "was he stopped by this stone barrier?"

"No, no," I replied with animation. "This fragment of rock has been shaken down by some shock or convulsion, or by one of those magnetic storms which agitate these regions, and has blocked up the passage which lay open to him. Many years have elapsed since the return of Saknussemm to the surface and the fall of this huge fragment. Is it not evident that this gallery was once the way open to the course of the lava, and that at that time there must have been a free passage? See here are recent fissures grooving and channeling the granite roof. This roof itself is formed of fragments of rock carried down, of enormous stones, as if by some giant's hand; but at one time the expulsive force was greater than usual, and this block, like the falling keystone of a ruined arch, has slipped down to the ground and blocked up the way. It is only an accidental obstruction, not met by Saknussemm, and if we don't destroy it we shall be unworthy to reach the center of the earth."

Such was my sentence! The soul of the professor had passed into me. The genius of discovery possessed me wholly. I forgot the past, I scorned the future. I gave not a thought to the things of the surface of this globe into which I had dived; its cities and its sunny plains, Hamburg and the Königstrasse, even poor Gräuben, who must have given us up for lost, all were for the time dismissed from the pages of my memory.

"Well," cried my uncle, "let us make a way with our pickaxes."

"Too hard for the pickaxe."

"Well, then, the spade."

"That would take us too long."

"What, then?"

"Why gunpowder, to be sure! Let us mine the obstacle and blow it up."

"Oh, yes, it is only a bit of rock to blast!"

"Hans, to work!" cried my uncle.

The Icelander returned to the raft and soon came back with an iron bar which he made use of to bore a hole for the charge. This was no easy work. A hole was to be made large enough to hold fifty pounds of guncotton, whose expansive force is four times that of gunpowder.

I was terribly excited. While Hans was at work I was actively helping my uncle to prepare a slow match of wetted powder encased in linen.

"This will do it," I said.

"It will," replied my uncle.

By midnight our mining preparations were over; the charge was rammed into the hole, and the slow match uncoiled along the gallery showed its end outside the opening.

A spark would now develop the whole of our preparations into activity.

"Tomorrow," said the professor.

I had to be resigned and to wait six long hours.

## CHAPTER XLI

### THE GREAT EXPLOSION AND THE RUSH DOWN BELOW

The next day, Thursday, August 27, is a well-remembered date in our subterranean journey. It never returns to my memory without sending through me a shudder of horror and a palpitation of the heart. From that hour we had no further occasion for the exercise of reason, or judgment, or skill, or contrivance. We were henceforth to be hurled along, the playthings of the fierce elements of the deep.

At six we were afoot. The moment drew near to clear a way by blasting through the opposing mass of granite.

I begged for the honor of lighting the fuse. This duty done, I was to join my companions on the raft, which had not yet been unloaded; we should then push off as far as we could and avoid the dangers arising from the explosion, the effects of which were not likely to be confined to the rock itself.

The fuse was calculated to burn ten minutes before setting fire to the mine. I therefore had sufficient time to get away to the raft.

I prepared to fulfill my task with some anxiety.

After a hasty meal, my uncle and the hunter embarked while I remained on shore. I was supplied with a lighted lantern to set fire to the fuse. "Now go," said my uncle, "and return immediately to us."

"Don't be uneasy," I replied. "I will not play by the way."

I immediately proceeded to the mouth of the tunnel. I opened my lantern. I laid hold of the end of the match.

The professor stood, chronometer in hand.

"Ready?" he cried.

"Ay."

"Fire!"

I instantly plunged the end of the fuse into the lantern. It spluttered and flamed, and I ran at the top of my speed to the raft.

"Come on board quickly, and let us push off."

Hans, with a vigorous thrust, sent us from the shore. The raft shot twenty fathoms out to sea.

It was a moment of intense excitement. The professor was watching the hand of the chronometer.

"Five minutes more!" he said. "Four! Three!"

My pulse beat half-seconds.

"Two! One! Down, granite rocks; down with you."

What took place at that moment? I believe I did not hear the dull roar of the explosion. But the rocks suddenly assumed a new arrangement: they rent asunder like a curtain. I saw a bottomless pit open on the shore. The sea, lashed into sudden fury, rose up in an enormous billow, on the ridge of which the unhappy raft was uplifted bodily in the air with all its crew and cargo.

We all three fell down flat. In less than a second we were in deep, unfathomable darkness. Then I felt as if not only myself but the raft also had no support beneath. I thought it was sinking; but it was not so. I wanted to speak to my uncle, but the roaring of the waves prevented him from hearing even the sound of my voice.

In spite of darkness, noise, astonishment, and terror, I then understood what had taken place.

On the other side of the blown-up rock was an abyss. The explosion had caused a kind of earthquake in this fissured and abysmal region; a great gulf had opened; and the sea, now changed into a torrent, was hurrying us along into it.

I gave myself up for lost.

An hour passed away—two hours, perhaps—I cannot tell. We clutched each other fast, to save ourselves from being thrown off the raft. We felt violent shocks whenever we were borne heavily against the craggy projections. Yet these shocks were not very frequent, from which I concluded that the gully was widening. It was no doubt the same road that Saknussemm had taken; but instead of walking peaceably down it, as he had done, we were carrying a whole sea along with us.

These ideas, it will be understood, presented themselves to my mind in a vague and undetermined form. I had difficulty in associating any ideas together during this headlong race, which seemed like a vertical descent. To judge by the air which was whistling past me and made a whizzing in my ears, we were moving faster than the fastest express trains. To light a torch under these conditions would have been impossible; and our last electric apparatus had been shattered by the force of the explosion.

I was therefore much surprised to see a clear light shining near me. It lighted up the calm and unmoved countenance of Hans. The skillful huntsman had succeeded in lighting the lantern; and although it flickered so much as to threaten to go out, it threw a fitful light across the awful darkness.

I was right in my supposition. It was a wide gallery. The dim light could not show us both its walls at once. The fall of the waters which were carrying us away exceeded that of the swiftest rapids in American rivers. Its surface seemed composed of a sheaf of arrows hurled with inconceivable force; I cannot convey my impressions by a better comparison. The raft, occasionally seized by an eddy, spun round as it still flew along. When it approached the walls of the gallery I threw on them the light of the lantern, and I could judge somewhat of the velocity of our speed by noticing how the jagged projections of the rocks spun into endless ribbons and bands, so that we seemed confined within a network of shifting lines. I supposed we were running at the rate of thirty leagues an hour.

My uncle and I gazed on each other with haggard eyes, clinging to the stump of the mast, which had snapped asunder at the first shock of our great catastrophe. We kept our backs to the wind, not to be stifled by the rapidity of a movement which no human power could check.

Hours passed away. No change in our situation; but a discovery came to complicate matters and make them worse.

In seeking to put our cargo into somewhat better order, I found that the greater part of the articles embarked had disappeared at the moment of the explosion, when the sea broke in upon us with such violence. I wanted to know exactly what we had saved, and with the lantern in my hand I began my examination. Of our instruments none were saved but the compass and the chronometer; our stock of ropes and ladders was reduced to the bit of cord rolled round the stump of the mast! Not a spade, not a pickaxe, not a hammer was left us; and, irreparable disaster! We had only one day's provisions left.

I searched every nook and corner, every crack and cranny in the raft. There was nothing. Our provisions were reduced to one bit of salt meat and a few biscuits.

I stared at our failing supplies stupidly. I refused to take in the gravity of our loss. And yet what was the use of troubling myself. If we had had provisions enough for months, how could we get out of the abyss into which we were being hurled by an irresistible torrent? Why should we fear the horrors of famine, when death was swooping down upon us in a multitude of other forms? Would there be time left to die of starvation?

Yet by an inexplicable play of the imagination I forgot my present dangers, to contemplate the threatening future. Was there any chance of escaping from the fury of this impetuous torrent, and of returning to the surface of the globe? I could not form the slightest conjecture how or when. But one chance in a thousand, or ten thousand, is still a chance; while death from starvation would leave us not the smallest hope in the world.

The thought came into my mind to declare the whole truth to my uncle, to show him the dreadful straits to which we were reduced, and to calculate how long we might yet expect to live. But I had the courage to preserve silence. I wished to leave him cool and self-possessed.

At that moment the light from our lantern began to sink by little and little, and then went out entirely. The wick had burned itself out. Black night reigned again; and there was no hope left of being able to dissipate the palpable darkness. We had yet a torch left, but we could not have kept it alight. Then, like a child, I closed my eyes firmly, not to see the darkness.

After a considerable lapse of time our speed redoubled. I could perceive it by the sharpness of the currents that blew past my face. The descent became steeper. I believe we were no longer sliding, but falling down. I had an impression that we were dropping vertically. My uncle's hand, and the vigorous arm of Hans, held me fast.

Suddenly, after a space of time that I could not measure, I felt a shock. The raft had not struck against any hard resistance, but had suddenly been checked in its fall. A waterspout, an immense liquid column, was beating upon the surface of the waters. I was suffocating! I was drowning!

But this sudden flood was not of long duration. In a few seconds I found myself in the air again, which I inhaled with all the force of my lungs. My uncle and Hans were still holding me fast by the arms; and the raft was still carrying us.

## CHAPTER XLII

### HEADLONG SPEED UPWARD THROUGH THE HORRORS OF DARKNESS

It might have been, as I guessed, about ten at night. The first of my senses which came into play after this last bout was that of hearing. All at once I could hear; and it was a real exercise of the sense of hearing. I could hear the silence in the gallery after the din which for hours had stunned me. At last these words of my uncle's came to me like a vague murmuring:

"We are going up."

"What do you mean?" I cried.

"Yes, we are going up—up!"

I stretched out my arm. I touched the wall, and drew back my hand bleeding. We were ascending with extreme rapidity.

"The torch! The torch!" cried the professor.

Not without difficulty Hans succeeded in lighting the torch; and the flame, preserving its upward tendency, threw enough light to show us what kind of a place we were in.

"Just as I thought," said the professor. "We are in a tunnel not four-and-twenty feet in diameter. The water had reached the bottom of the gulf. It is now rising to its level, and carrying us with it."

"Where to?"

"I cannot tell; but we must be ready for anything. We are mounting at a speed which seems to me of fourteen feet in a second, or ten miles an hour. At this rate we shall get on."

"Yes, if nothing stops us; if this well has an aperture. But suppose it to be stopped. If the air is condensed by the pressure of this column of water we shall be crushed."

"Axel," replied the professor with perfect coolness, "our situation is almost desperate; but there are some chances of deliverance, and it is these that I am considering. If at every instant we may perish, so at every instant we may be saved. Let us then be prepared to seize upon the smallest advantage."

"But what shall we do now?"

"Recruit our strength by eating."

At these words I fixed a haggard eye upon my uncle. That which I had been so unwilling to confess at last had to be told.

"Eat, did you say?"

"Yes, at once."

The professor added a few words in Danish, but Hans shook his head mournfully.

"What!" cried my uncle. "Have we lost our provisions?"

"Yes; here is all we have left; one bit of salt meat for the three."

My uncle stared at me as if he could not understand.

"Well," said I, "do you think we have any chance of being saved?"

My question was unanswered.

An hour passed away. I began to feel the pangs of a violent hunger. My companions were suffering too, and not one of us dared touch this wretched remnant of our goodly store.

But now we were mounting up with excessive speed. Sometimes the air would cut our breath short, as is experienced by aeronauts ascending too rapidly. But while they suffer from cold in proportion to their rise, we were beginning to feel a contrary effect. The heat was increasing in a manner to cause us the most fearful anxiety, and certainly the temperature was at this moment at the height of 100°F.

What could be the meaning of such a change? Up to this time facts had supported the theories of Davy and of Liedenbrock; until now particular conditions of nonconducting rocks, electricity, and magnetism had tempered the laws of nature, giving us only a moderately warm climate, for the theory of a central fire remained in my estimation the only one that was true and explicable. Were we then turning back to where the phenomena of central heat ruled in all their rigor and would reduce the most refractory rocks to the state of a molten liquid? I feared this, and said to the professor:

"If we are neither drowned, nor shattered to pieces, nor starved to death, there is still the chance that we may be burned alive and reduced to ashes."

At this he shrugged his shoulders and returned to his thoughts.

Another hour passed, and, except some slight increase in the temperature, nothing new had happened.

"Come," said he, "we must determine upon something."

"Determine on what?" said I.

"Yes, we must recruit our strength by carefully rationing ourselves, and so prolong our existence by a few hours. But we shall be reduced to very great weakness at last."

"And our last hour is not far off."

"Well, if there is a chance of safety, if a moment for active exertion presents itself, where should we find the required strength if we allowed ourselves to be enfeebled by hunger?"

"Well, uncle, when this bit of meat has been devoured, what shall we have left?"

"Nothing, Axel, nothing at all. But will it do you any more good to devour it with your eyes than with your teeth? Your reasoning has in it neither sense nor energy."

"Then don't you despair?" I cried irritably.

"No, certainly not," was the professor's firm reply.

"What! Do you think there is any chance of safety left?"

"Yes, I do; as long as the heart beats, as long as body and soul keep together, I cannot admit that any creature endowed with a will has need to despair of life."

Resolute words these! The man who could speak so, under such circumstances, was of no ordinary type.

"Finally, what do you mean to do?" I asked.

"Eat what is left to the last crumb, and recruit our fading strength. This meal will be our last, perhaps: so let it be! But at any rate we shall once more be men, and not exhausted, empty bags."

"Well, let us consume it then," I cried.

My uncle took the piece of meat and the few biscuits which had escaped from the general destruction. He divided them into three equal portions and gave one to each. This made about a pound of nourishment for each. The professor ate his greedily, with a kind of feverish rage. I ate without pleasure, almost with disgust; Hans quietly, moderately, masticating his small mouthfuls without any noise, and relishing them with the calmness of a man above all anxiety about the future. By diligent search he had found a flask of Hollands; he offered it to us each in turn, and this generous beverage cheered us up slightly.

"*Forträfflig*," said Hans, drinking in his turn.

"Excellent," replied my uncle.

A glimpse of hope had returned, although without cause. But our last meal was over, and it was now five in the morning.

Man is so constituted that health is a purely negative state. Hunger once satisfied, it is difficult for a man to imagine the horrors of starvation; they cannot be understood without being felt.

Therefore it was that after our long fast these few mouthfuls of meat and biscuit made us triumph over our past agonies.

But as soon as the meal was done, we each of us fell deep into thought. What was Hans thinking of—that man of the far West, but who seemed ruled by the fatalist doctrines of the East?

As for me, my thoughts were made up of remembrances, and they carried me up to the surface of the globe of which I ought never to have taken leave. The house in the Königstrasse, my poor dear Gräuben, that kind soul Martha, flitted like visions before my eyes, and in the dismal moanings which from time to time reached my ears I thought I could distinguish the roar of the traffic of the great cities upon earth.

My uncle still had his eye upon his work. Torch in hand, he tried to gather some idea of our situation from the observation of the strata. This calculation could, at best, be but a vague approximation; but a learned man is always a philosopher when he succeeds in remaining cool, and assuredly Professor Liedenbrock possessed this quality to a surprising degree.

I could hear him murmuring geological terms. I could understand them, and in spite of myself I felt interested in this last geological study.

"Eruptive granite," he was saying. "We are still in the primitive period. But we are going up, up, higher still. Who can tell?"

Ah! Who can tell? With his hand he was examining the perpendicular wall, and in a few more minutes he continued:

"This is gneiss! Here is mica schist! Ah! Presently we shall come to the transition period, and then—"

What did the professor mean? Could he be trying to measure the thickness of the crust of the earth that lay between us and the world above? Had he any means of making this calculation? No, he had not the aneroid, and no guessing could supply its place.

Still the temperature kept rising, and I felt myself steeped in a broiling atmosphere. I could only compare it to the heat of a furnace at the moment when the molten metal is running into the mold. Gradually we had been obliged to throw aside our coats and waistcoats, the lightest covering became uncomfortable and even painful.

"Are we rising into a fiery furnace?" I cried at one moment when the heat was redoubling.

"No," replied my uncle, "that is impossible—quite impossible!"

"Yet," I answered, feeling the wall, "this well is burning hot."

At the same moment, touching the water, I had to withdraw my hand in haste.

"The water is scalding," I cried.

This time the professor's only answer was an angry gesture.

Then an unconquerable terror seized upon me, from which I could no longer get free. I felt that a catastrophe was approaching before which the boldest spirit must quail. A dim, vague notion laid hold of my mind, but which was fast hardening into certainty. I tried to repel it, but it would return. I dared not express it in plain terms. Yet a few involuntary observations confirmed me in my view. By the flickering light of the torch I could distinguish contortions in the granite beds; a phenomenon was unfolding in which electricity would play the principal part; then this unbearable heat, this boiling water! I consulted the compass.

The compass had lost its properties! It had ceased to act properly!

## CHAPTER XLIII

### SHOT OUT OF A VOLCANO AT LAST!

Yes: our compass was no longer a guide; the needle flew from pole to pole with a kind of frenzied impulse; it ran round the dial, and spun hither and thither as if it were giddy or intoxicated.

I knew quite well that according to the best received theories the mineral covering of the globe is never at absolute rest; the changes brought about by the chemical decomposition of its component parts, the agitation caused by great liquid torrents, and the magnetic currents, are continually tending to disturb it—even when living beings upon its surface may fancy that all is quiet below. A phenomenon of this kind would not have greatly alarmed me, or at any rate it would not have given rise to dreadful apprehensions.

But other facts, other circumstances, of a peculiar nature, came to reveal to me by degrees the true state of the case. There came incessant and continuous explosions. I could only compare them to the loud rattle of a long train of chariots driven at full speed over the stones, or a roar of uninterminitting thunder.

Then the disordered compass, thrown out of gear by the electric currents, confirmed me in a growing conviction. The mineral crust of the globe threatened to burst up, the granite foundations to come together with a crash, the fissure through which we were helplessly driven would be filled up, the void would be full of crushed fragments of rock, and we poor wretched mortals were to be buried and annihilated in this dreadful consummation.

"My uncle," I cried, "we are lost now, utterly lost!"

"What are you in a fright about now?" was the calm rejoinder. "What is the matter with you?"

"The matter? Look at those quaking walls! Look at those shivering rocks. Don't you feel the burning heat? Don't you see how the water boils and bubbles? Are you blind to the dense vapors and steam growing thicker and denser every minute? See this agitated compass needle. It is an earthquake that is threatening us."

My undaunted uncle calmly shook his head.

"Do you think," said he, "an earthquake is coming?"

"I do."

"Well, I think you are mistaken."

"What! Don't you recognize the symptoms?"

"Of an earthquake? No! I am looking out for something better."

"What can you mean? Explain?"

"It is an eruption, Axel."

"An eruption! Do you mean to affirm that we are running up the shaft of a volcano?"

"I believe we are," said the indomitable professor with an air of perfect self-possession; "and it is the best thing that could possibly happen to us under our circumstances."

The best thing! Was my uncle stark mad? What did the man mean? And what was the use of saying facetious things at a time like this?

"What!" I shouted. "Are we being taken up in an eruption? Our fate has flung us here among burning lavas, molten rocks, boiling waters, and all kinds of volcanic matter; we are going to be pitched out, expelled, tossed up, vomited, spit out high into the air, along with fragments of rock, showers of ashes and scoria, in the midst of a towering rush of smoke and flames; and it is the best thing that could happen to us!"

"Yes," replied the professor, eyeing me over his spectacles, "I don't see any other way of reaching the surface of the earth."

I pass rapidly over the thousand ideas which passed through my mind. My uncle was right, undoubtedly right; and never had he seemed to me more daring and more confirmed in his notions than at this moment when he was calmly contemplating the chances of being shot out of a volcano!

In the meantime up we went; the night passed away in continual ascent; the din and uproar around us became more and more intensified; I was stifled and stunned; I thought my last hour was approaching; and yet imagination is such a strong thing that even in this supreme hour I was occupied with strange and almost childish speculations. But I was the victim, not the master, of my own thoughts.

It was very evident that we were being hurried upward upon the crest of a wave of eruption; beneath our raft were boiling waters, and under these the more sluggish lava was working its way up in a heated mass, together with shoals of fragments of rock which, when they arrived at the crater, would be dispersed in all directions high and low. We were imprisoned in the shaft or chimney of some volcano. There was no room to doubt of that.

But this time, instead of Snæfell, an extinct volcano, we were inside one in full activity. I wondered, therefore, where could this mountain be, and in what part of the world we were to be shot out.

I made no doubt but that it would be in some northern region. Before its disorders set in, the needle had never deviated from that direction. From Cape Saknussemm we had been carried due north for hundreds of leagues. Were we under Iceland again? Were we destined to be thrown up out of Hecla, or by which of the seven other fiery craters in that island? Within a radius of five hundred leagues to the west I remembered under this parallel of latitude only the imperfectly known volcanoes of the northeast coast of America. To the east there was only one in the 80th degree of north latitude, the Esk in Jan Mayen Island, not far from Spitzbergen! Certainly there was no lack of craters, and there were some capacious enough to throw out a whole army! But I wanted to know which of them was to serve us for an exit from the inner world.

Toward morning the ascending movement became accelerated. If the heat increased, instead of diminishing, as we approached nearer to the surface of the globe, this effect was due to local causes alone, and those volcanic. The manner of our locomotion left no doubt in my mind. An enormous force, a force of hundreds of atmospheres, generated by the extreme pressure of confined vapors, was driving us irresistibly forward. But to what numberless dangers it exposed us!

Soon lurid lights began to penetrate the vertical gallery which widened as we went up. Right and left I could see deep channels, like huge tunnels, out of which escaped dense volumes of smoke; tongues of fire lapped the walls, which crackled and sputtered under the intense heat.

"See, see, my uncle!" I cried.

"Well, those are only sulfurous flames and vapors, which one must expect to see in an eruption. They are quite natural."

"But suppose they should wrap us round."

"But they won't wrap us round."

"But we shall be stifled."

"We shall not be stifled at all. The gallery is widening, and if it becomes necessary, we shall abandon the raft, and creep into a crevice."

"But the water—the rising water?"

"There is no more water, Axel; only a lava paste, which is bearing us up on its surface to the top of the crater."

The liquid column had indeed disappeared, to give place to dense and still boiling eruptive matter of all kinds. The temperature was becoming unbearable. A thermometer exposed to this atmosphere would have marked 150°. The perspiration streamed from my body. But for the rapidity of our ascent we should have been suffocated.

But the professor gave up his idea of abandoning the raft, and it was well he did. However roughly joined together, those planks afforded us a firmer support than we could have found anywhere else.

About eight in the morning a new incident occurred. The upward movement ceased. The raft lay motionless.

"What is this?" I asked, shaken by this sudden stoppage as if by a shock.

"It is a halt," replied my uncle.

"Is the eruption checked?" I asked.

"I hope not."

I rose, and tried to look around me. Perhaps the raft itself, stopped in its course by a projection, was staying the volcanic torrent. If this were the case, we should have to release it as soon as possible.

But it was not so. The blast of ashes, scorix, and rubbish had ceased to rise.

"Has the eruption stopped?" I cried.

"Ah!" said my uncle between his clenched teeth. "You are afraid. But don't alarm yourself—this lull cannot last long. It has lasted now five minutes, and in a short time we shall resume our journey to the mouth of the crater."

As he spoke, the professor continued to consult his chronometer, and he was again right in his prognostications. The raft was soon hurried and driven forward with a rapid but irregular movement, which lasted about ten minutes, and then stopped again.

"Very good," said my uncle; "in ten minutes more we shall be off again, for our present business lies with an intermittent volcano. It gives us time now and then to take breath."

This was perfectly true. When the ten minutes were over we started off again with renewed and increased speed. We were obliged to lay fast hold of the planks of the raft, not to be thrown off. Then again the paroxysm was over.

I have since reflected upon this singular phenomenon without being able to explain it. At any rate it was clear that we were not in the main shaft of the volcano, but in a lateral gallery where there were felt recurrent tunes of reaction.

How often this operation was repeated I cannot say. All I know is, that at each fresh impulse we were hurled forward with a greatly increased force, and we seemed as if we were mere projectiles. During the short halts we were stifled with the heat; while we were being projected forward the hot air almost stopped my breath. I thought for a moment how delightful it would be to find myself carried suddenly into the arctic regions, with a cold 30° below the freezing point. My overheated brain conjured up visions of white plains of cool snow, where I might roll and allay my feverish heat. Little by little my brain, weakened by so many constantly repeated shocks, seemed to be giving way altogether. But for the strong arm of Hans I should more than once have had my head broken against the granite roof of our burning dungeon.

I have therefore no exact recollection of what took place during the following hours. I have a confused impression left of continuous explosions, loud detonations, a general shaking of the rocks all around us, and of a spinning movement with which our raft was once whirled helplessly round. It rocked upon the lava torrent, amid a dense fall of ashes. Snorting flames darted their fiery tongues at us. There were wild, fierce puffs of stormy wind from below, resembling the blasts of vast iron furnaces blowing all at one time; and I caught a glimpse of the figure of Hans lighted up by the fire; and all the feeling I had left was just what I imagine must be the feeling of an unhappy criminal doomed to be blown away alive from the mouth of a cannon, just before the trigger is pulled, and the flying limbs and rags of flesh and skin fill the quivering air and spatter the bloodstained ground.

## CHAPTER XLIV

### SUNNY LANDS IN THE BLUE MEDITERRANEAN

When I opened my eyes again I felt myself grasped by the belt with the strong hand of our guide. With the other arm he supported my uncle. I was not seriously hurt, but I was shaken and bruised and battered all over. I found myself lying on the sloping side of a mountain only two yards from a gaping gulf, which would have swallowed me up had I leaned at all that way. Hans had saved me from death while I lay rolling on the edge of the crater.

"Where are we?" asked my uncle irascibly, as if he felt much injured by being landed upon the earth again.

The hunter shook his head in token of complete ignorance.

"Is it Iceland?" I asked.

"*Nej*," replied Hans.

"What! Not Iceland?" cried the professor.

"Hans must be mistaken," I said, raising myself up.

This was our final surprise after all the astonishing events of our wonderful journey. I expected to see a white cone covered with the eternal snow of ages rising from the midst of the barren deserts of the icy north, faintly lighted with the pale rays of the arctic sun, far away in the highest latitudes known; but contrary to all our expectations, my uncle, the Icelander, and myself were sitting halfway down a mountain baked under the burning rays of a southern sun, which was blistering us with the heat, and blinding us with the fierce light of his nearly vertical rays.

I could not believe my own eyes; but the heated air and the sensation of burning left me no room for doubt. We had come out of the crater half naked, and the radiant orb to which we had been strangers for two months was lavishing upon us out of his blazing splendors more of his light and heat than we were able to receive with comfort.

When my eyes had become accustomed to the bright light to which they had been so long strangers, I began to use them to set my imagination right. At least I would have it to be Spitzbergen, and I was in no humor to give up this notion.

The professor was the first to speak, and said:

"Well, this is not much like Iceland."

"But is it Jan Mayen?" I asked.

"Nor that either," he answered. "This is no northern mountain; here are no granite peaks capped with snow. Look, Axel, look!"

Above our heads, at a height of five hundred feet or more, we saw the crater of a volcano, through which, at intervals of fifteen minutes or so, there issued with loud explosions lofty columns of fire, mingled with pumice stones, ashes, and flowing lava. I could feel the heaving of the mountain, which seemed to breathe like a huge whale, and puff out fire and wind from its vast blowholes. Beneath, down a pretty steep declivity, ran streams of lava for eight or nine hundred feet, giving the mountain a height of about 1,300 or 1,400 feet. But the base of the mountain was hidden in a perfect bower of rich verdure, among which I was able to distinguish the olive, the fig, and vines, covered with their luscious purple bunches.

I was forced to confess that there was nothing arctic here.

When the eye passed beyond these green surroundings it rested on a wide, blue expanse of sea or lake, which appeared to enclose this enchanting island, within a compass of only a few leagues. Eastward lay a pretty little white seaport town or village, with a few houses scattered around it, and in the harbor of which a few vessels of peculiar rig were gently swayed by the softly swelling waves. Beyond it, groups of islets rose from the smooth, blue waters, but in such numbers that they seemed to dot the sea like a shoal. To the west distant coasts lined the dim horizon, on some rose blue mountains of smooth, undulating forms; on a more distant coast arose a prodigious cone crowned on its summit with a snowy plume of white cloud. To the northward lay spread a vast sheet of water, sparkling and dancing under the hot, bright rays, the uniformity broken here and there by the topmast of a gallant ship appearing above the horizon, or a swelling sail moving slowly before the wind.

This unforeseen spectacle was most charming to eyes long used to underground darkness.

"Where are we? Where are we?" I asked faintly.

Hans closed his eyes with lazy indifference. What did it matter to him? My uncle looked round with dumb surprise.

"Well, whatever mountain this may be," he said at last, "it is very hot here. The explosions are going on still, and I don't think it would look well to have come out by an eruption, and then to get our heads broken by bits of falling rock. Let us get down. Then we shall know better what we are about. Besides, I am starving, and parching with thirst."

Decidedly the professor was not given to contemplation. For my part, I could for another hour or two have forgotten my hunger and my fatigue to enjoy the lovely scene before me; but I had to follow my companions.

The slope of the volcano was in many places of great steepness. We slid down screes of ashes, carefully avoiding the lava streams which glided sluggishly by us like fiery serpents. As we went I chattered and asked all sorts of questions as to our whereabouts, for I was too much excited not to talk a great deal.

"We are in Asia," I cried, "on the coasts of India, in the Malay Islands, or in Oceania. We have passed through half the globe, and come out nearly at the antipodes."

"But the compass?" said my uncle.

"Ay, the compass!" I said, greatly puzzled. "According to the compass we have gone northward."

"Has it lied?"

"Surely not. Could it lie?"

"Unless, indeed, this is the North Pole!"

"Oh, no, it is not the pole; but—"

Well, here was something that baffled us completely. I could not tell what to say.

But now we were coming into that delightful greenery, and I was suffering greatly from hunger and thirst. Happily, after two hours' walking, a charming country lay open before us, covered with olive trees, pomegranate trees, and delicious vines, all of which seemed to belong to anybody who pleased to claim them. Besides, in our state of destitution and famine we were not likely to be particular. Oh, the inexpressible pleasure of pressing those cool, sweet fruits to our lips, and eating grapes by mouthfuls off the rich, full bunches! Not far off, in the grass, under the delicious shade of the trees, I discovered a spring of fresh, cool water, in which we luxuriously bathed our faces, hands, and feet.

While we were thus enjoying the sweets of repose a child appeared out of a grove of olive trees.

"Ah!" I cried. "Here is an inhabitant of this happy land!"

It was but a poor boy, miserably ill-clad, a sufferer from poverty, and our aspect seemed to alarm him a great deal; in fact, only half clothed, with ragged hair and beards, we were a suspicious-looking party; and if the people of the country knew anything about thieves, we were very likely to frighten them.

Just as the poor little wretch was going to take to his heels, Hans caught hold of him, and brought him to us, kicking and struggling.

My uncle began to encourage him as well as he could, and said to him in good German:

"*Was heiszt diesen Berg, mein Knablein? Sage mir geschwind!*" ("What is this mountain called, my little friend?")

The child made no answer.

"Very well," said my uncle. "I infer that we are not in Germany."

He put the same question in English.

We got no forwarder. I was a good deal puzzled.

"Is the child dumb?" cried the professor, who, proud of his knowledge of many languages, now tried French: "*Comment appellet-on cette montagne, mon enfant?*"

Silence still.

"Now let us try Italian," said my uncle; and he said: "*Dove noi siamo?*"

"Yes, where are we?" I impatiently repeated.

But there was no answer still.

"Will you speak when you are told?" exclaimed my uncle, shaking the urchin by the ears. "*Come si noma questa isola?*"

"Stromboli," replied the little herdboy, slipping out of Hans' hands and scudding into the plain across the olive trees.

We were hardly thinking of that. Stromboli! What an effect this unexpected name produced upon my mind! We were in the midst of the Mediterranean Sea, on an island of the Aeolian archipelago, in the ancient Strongyle, where Aeolus kept the winds and the storms chained up, to be let loose at his will. And those distant blue mountains in the east were the mountains of Calabria. And that threatening volcano far away in the south was the fierce Etna.

"Stromboli, Stromboli!" I repeated.

My uncle kept time to my exclamations with hands and feet, as well as with words. We seemed to be chanting in chorus!

What a journey we had accomplished! How marvelous! Having entered by one volcano, we had issued out of another more than two thousand miles from Snæfell and from that barren, faraway Iceland! The strange chances of our expedition had carried us into the heart of the fairest region in the world. We had exchanged the bleak regions of perpetual snow and of impenetrable barriers of ice for those of brightness and "the rich hues of all glorious things." We had left over our heads the murky sky and cold fogs of the frigid zone to revel under the azure sky of Italy!

After our delicious repast of fruits and cold, clear water we set off again to reach the port of Stromboli. It would not have been wise to tell how we came there. The superstitious Italians would have set us down for fire-devils vomited out of hell; so we presented ourselves in the humble guise of shipwrecked mariners. It was not so glorious, but it was safer.

On my way I could hear my uncle murmuring: "But the compass! That compass! It pointed due north. How are we to explain that fact?"

"My opinion is," I replied disdainfully, "that it is best not to explain it. That is the easiest way to shelve the difficulty."

"Indeed, sir! The occupant of a professorial chair at the Johanneum unable to explain the reason of a cosmical phenomenon! Why, it would be simply disgraceful!"

And as he spoke, my uncle, half undressed, in rags, a perfect scarecrow, with his leathern belt around him, settling his spectacles upon his nose and looking learned and imposing, was himself again, the terrible German professor of mineralogy.

One hour after we had left the grove of olives, we arrived at the little port of San Vicenzo, where Hans claimed his thirteen week's wages, which was counted out to him with a hearty shaking of hands all round.

At that moment, if he did not share our natural emotion, at least his countenance expanded in a manner very unusual with him, and while with the ends of his fingers he lightly pressed our hands, I believe he smiled.

# CHAPTER XLV

## ALL'S WELL THAT ENDS WELL

Such is the conclusion of a history which I cannot expect everybody to believe, for some people will believe nothing against the testimony of their own experience. However, I am indifferent to their incredulity, and they may believe as much or as little as they please.

The Stromboliotes received us kindly as shipwrecked mariners. They gave us food and clothing. After waiting forty-eight hours, on the 31st of August a small craft took us to Messina, where a few days' rest completely removed the effect of our fatigues.

On Friday, September the 4th, we embarked on the steamer Volturno, employed by the French Messageries Imperiales, and in three days more we were at Marseilles, having no care on our minds except that abominable deceitful compass, which we had mislaid somewhere and could not now examine; but its inexplicable behavior exercised my mind fearfully. On the 9th of September, in the evening, we arrived at Hamburg.

I cannot describe to you the astonishment of Martha or the joy of Gräuben.

"Now you are a hero, Axel," said to me my blushing fiancée, my betrothed, "you will not leave me again!"

I looked tenderly upon her, and she smiled through her tears.

How can I describe the extraordinary sensation produced by the return of Professor Liedenbrock? Thanks to Martha's ineradicable tattling, the news that the professor had gone to discover a way to the center of the earth had spread over the whole civilized world. People refused to believe it, and when they saw him they would not believe him any the more. Still, the appearance of Hans, and sundry pieces of intelligence derived from Iceland, tended to shake the confidence of the unbelievers.

Then my uncle became a great man, and I was now the nephew of a great man— which is not a privilege to be despised.

Hamburg gave a grand fete in our honor. A public audience was given to the professor at the Johanneum, at which he told all about our expedition, with only one omission, the unexplained and inexplicable behavior of our compass. On the same day, with much state, he deposited in the archives of the city the now-famous document of Saknussemm, and expressed his regret that circumstances over which he had no control had prevented him from following to the very center of the earth the track of the learned Icelander. He was modest notwithstanding his glory, and he was all the more famous for his humility.

So much honor could not but excite envy. There were those who envied him his fame; and as his theories, resting upon known facts, were in opposition to the systems of science upon the question of the central fire, he sustained with his pen and by his voice remarkable discussions with the learned of every country.

For my part I cannot agree with his theory of gradual cooling: in spite of what I have seen and felt, I believe, and always shall believe, in the central heat. But I admit that certain circumstances not yet sufficiently understood may tend to modify in places the action of natural phenomena.

While these questions were being debated with great animation, my uncle met with a real sorrow. Our faithful Hans, in spite of our entreaties, had left Hamburg; the man to whom we owed all our success and our lives too would not suffer us to reward him as we could have wished. He was seized with the mal de pays, a complaint for which we have not even a name in English.

"*Farval*," said he one day; and with that simple word he left us and sailed for Reykjavik, which he reached in safety.

We were strongly attached to our brave eiderdown hunter; though far away in the remotest north, he will never be forgotten by those whose lives he protected, and certainly I shall not fail to endeavor to see him once more before I die.

To conclude, I have to add that this "Journey into the Interior of the Earth" created a wonderful sensation in the world. It was translated into all civilized languages. The leading newspapers extracted the most interesting passages, which were commented upon, picked to pieces, discussed, attacked, and defended with equal enthusiasm and determination, both by believers and skeptics. Rare privilege! My uncle enjoyed during his lifetime the glory he had deservedly won; and he may even boast the distinguished honor of an offer from Mr. Barnum, to exhibit him on most advantageous terms in all the principal cities in the United States!

But there was one "dead fly" amid all this glory and honor; one fact, one incident, of the journey remained a mystery. Now to a man eminent for his learning, an unexplained phenomenon is an unbearable hardship. Well! It was yet reserved for my uncle to be completely happy.

One day, while arranging a collection of minerals in his cabinet, I noticed in a corner this unhappy compass, which we had long lost sight of; I opened it, and began to watch it.

It had been in that corner for six months, little mindful of the trouble it was giving.

Suddenly, to my intense astonishment, I noticed a strange fact, and I uttered a cry of surprise.

"What is the matter?" my uncle asked.

"That compass!"

"Well?"

"See, its poles are reversed!"

"Reversed?"

"Yes, they point the wrong way."

My uncle looked, he compared, and the house shook with his triumphant leap of exultation.

A light broke in upon his spirit and mine.

"See there," he cried, as soon as he was able to speak. "After our arrival at Cape Saknussemm the north pole of the needle of this confounded compass began to point south instead of north."

"Evidently!"

"Here, then, is the explanation of our mistake. But what phenomenon could have caused this reversal of the poles?"

"The reason is evident, uncle."

"Tell me, then, Axel."

"During the electric storm on the Liedenbrock Sea, that ball of fire, which magnetized all the iron on board, reversed the poles of our magnet!"

"Aha! Aha!" shouted the professor with a loud laugh. "So it was just an electric joke!"

From that day forth the professor was the most glorious of savants, and I was the happiest of men; for my pretty Virlandaise, resigning her place as ward, took her position in the old house on the Königstrasse in the double capacity of niece to my uncle and wife to a certain happy youth. What is the need of adding that the illustrious Otto Liedenbrock, corresponding member of all the scientific, geographical, and mineralogical societies of all the civilized world, was now her uncle and mine?

# Twenty Thousand Leagues Under the Sea

## PART ONE

### CHAPTER I

#### A SHIFTING REEF

The year 1866 was signalized by a remarkable incident, a mysterious and puzzling phenomenon, which doubtless no one has yet forgotten. Not to mention rumors which agitated the maritime population and excited the public mind, even in the interior of continents, seafaring men were particularly excited. Merchants, common sailors, captains of vessels, skippers, both of Europe and America, naval officers of all countries, and the governments of several states on the two continents, were deeply interested in the matter.

For some time past vessels had been met by "an enormous thing," a long object, spindle-shaped, occasionally phosphorescent, and infinitely larger and more rapid in its movements than a whale.

The facts relating to this apparition (entered in various log-books) agreed in most respects as to the shape of the object or creature in question, the untiring rapidity of its movements, its surprising power of locomotion, and the peculiar life with which it seemed endowed. If it was a whale, it surpassed in size all those hitherto classified in science. Taking into consideration the mean of observations made at divers times—rejecting the timid estimate of those who assigned to this object a length of two hundred feet, equally with the exaggerated opinions which set it down as a mile in width and three in length—we might fairly conclude that this mysterious being surpassed greatly all dimensions admitted by the learned ones of the day, if it existed at all. And that it did exist was an undeniable fact; and, with that tendency which disposes the human mind in favor of the marvelous, we can understand the excitement produced in the entire world by this supernatural apparition. As to classing it in the list of fables, the idea was out of the question.

On July 20, 1866, the steamer *Governor Higginson*, of the Calcutta and Burnach Steam Navigation Company, had met this moving mass five miles off the east coast of Australia. Captain Baker thought at first that he was in the presence of an unknown sandbank; he even prepared to determine its exact position when two columns of water, projected by the mysterious object, shot with a hissing noise a hundred and fifty feet up into the air. Now, unless the sandbank had been submitted to the intermittent eruption of a geyser, the *Governor Higginson* had to do neither more nor less than with an aquatic mammal, unknown till then, which threw up from its blowholes columns of water mixed with air and vapor.

Similar facts were observed on July 23 in the same year, in the Pacific Ocean, by the *Columbus*, of the West India and Pacific Steam Navigation Company. But this extraordinary creature could transport itself from one place to another with surprising velocity; as, in an interval of three days, the *Governor Higginson* and the *Columbus* had observed it at two different points of the chart, separated by a distance of more than seven hundred nautical leagues.

Fifteen days later, two thousand miles farther off, the *Helvetia*, of the Compagnie-Nationale, and the *Shannon*, of the Royal Mail Steamship Company, sailing to windward in that portion of the Atlantic lying between the United States and Europe, respectively signaled the monster to each other in 42° 15' north latitude and 60° 35' west longitude. In these simultaneous observations they thought themselves justified in estimating the minimum length of the mammal at more than three hundred and fifty feet, as the *Shannon* and *Helvetia* were of smaller dimensions than it, though they measured three hundred feet overall.

Now the largest whales, those which frequent those parts of the sea around the Aleutian, Kulammak, and Umgullich Islands, have never exceeded the length of sixty yards, if they attain that.

In every place of great resort the monster was the fashion. They sang of it in the cafés, ridiculed it in the papers, and represented it on the stage. All kinds of stories were circulated regarding it. There appeared in the papers caricatures of every gigantic and imaginary creature, from the white whale, the terrible "Moby Dick" of sub-arctic regions, to the immense kraken, whose tentacles could entangle a ship of five hundred tons and hurry it into the abyss of the ocean. The legends of ancient times were even revived.

Then burst forth the unending argument between the believers and the nonbelievers in the societies of the wise and the scientific journals. "The question of the monster" inflamed all minds. Editors of scientific journals, quarreling with believers in the supernatural, spilled seas of ink during this memorable campaign, some even drawing blood; for from the sea serpent they came to direct personalities.

For six months war was waged with various fortune in the leading articles of the Geographical Institution of Brazil, the Royal Academy of Science in Berlin, the British Association, the Smithsonian Institution of Washington, in the discussions of the "Indian Archipelago," of the Cosmos of the Abbé Moigno, in the Mittheilungen of Petermann, in the scientific chronicles of the great journals of France and other countries. The cheaper journals replied keenly and with inexhaustible zest. These satirical writers parodied a remark of Linnaeus, quoted by the adversaries of the monster, maintaining that "nature did not make fools," and adjured their contemporaries not to give the lie to nature, by admitting the existence of krakens, sea-serpents, "Moby Dicks," and other lubrications of delirious sailors. At length an article in a well-known satirical journal by a favorite contributor, the chief of staff, settled the monster, like Hippolytus, giving it the death-blow amid a universal burst of laughter. Wit had conquered science.

During the first months of the year 1867 the question seemed buried, never to revive, when new facts were brought before the public. It was then no longer a scientific problem to be solved, but a real danger seriously to be avoided. The question took quite another shape. The monster became a small island, a rock, a reef, but a reef of indefinite and shifting proportions.

On March 5, 1867, the *Moravian*, of the Montreal Ocean Company, finding herself during the night in 27° 30' latitude and 72° 15' longitude, struck on her starboard quarter a rock, marked in no chart for that part of the sea. Under the combined efforts of the wind and its four hundred horsepower, it was going at the rate of thirteen knots. Had it not been for the superior strength of the hull of the *Moravian*, she would have been broken by the shock and gone down with the 237 passengers she was bringing home from Canada.

The accident happened about five o'clock in the morning, as the day was breaking. The officers of the quarter-deck hurried to the after-part of the vessel. They examined the sea with the most careful attention. They saw nothing but a strong eddy about three cables' length distant, as if the surface had been violently agitated. The bearings of the place were taken exactly, and the *Moravian* continued its route without apparent damage. Had it struck on a submerged rock, or on an enormous wreck? They could not tell; but, on examination of the ship's bottom when undergoing repairs, it was found that part of her keel was broken.

This fact, so grave in itself, might perhaps have been forgotten like many others if, three weeks after, it had not been reenacted under similar circumstances. But, thanks to the nationality of the victim of the shock, thanks to the reputation of the company to which the vessel belonged, the circumstance became extensively circulated.

On April 13, 1867, the sea being beautiful, the breeze favorable, the *Scotia*, of the Cunard Company's line, found herself in 15° 12' longitude and 45° 37' latitude. She was going at the speed of thirteen knots and a half.

At seventeen minutes past four in the afternoon, while the passengers were assembled at lunch in the great saloon, a slight shock was felt on the hull of the *Scotia*, on her quarter, a little aft of the port-paddle.

The *Scotia* had not struck, but she had been struck, and seemingly by something rather sharp and penetrating than blunt. The shock had been so slight that no one had been alarmed, had it not been for the shouts of the carpenter's watch, who rushed on to the bridge, exclaiming, "We are sinking! We are sinking!" At first the passengers were much frightened, but Captain Anderson hastened to reassure them. The danger could not be imminent. The *Scotia*, divided into seven compartments by strong partitions, could brave with impunity any leak. Captain Anderson went down immediately into the hold. He found that the sea was pouring into the fifth compartment; and the rapidity of the influx proved that the force of the water was considerable. Fortunately this compartment did not hold the boilers, or the fires would have been immediately extinguished. Captain Anderson ordered the engines to be stopped at once, and one of the men went down to ascertain the extent of the injury. Some minutes afterward they discovered the existence of a large hole, two yards in diameter, in the ship's bottom. Such a leak could not be stopped; and the *Scotia*, her paddles half submerged, was obliged to continue her course. She was then three hundred miles from Cape

Clear, and, after three days' delay, which caused great uneasiness in Liverpool, she entered the basin of the company.

The engineers visited the *Scotia*, which was put in dry dock. They could scarcely believe it possible; at two yards and a half below watermark was a regular rent, in the form of an isosceles triangle. The broken place in the iron plates was so perfectly defined that it could not have been more neatly done by a punch. It was clear, then, that the instrument producing the perforation was not of a common stamp and, after having been driven with prodigious strength, and piercing an iron plate one and three-eighth inches thick, had withdrawn itself by a backward motion.

Such was the last fact, which resulted in exciting once more the torrent of public opinion. From this moment all unlucky casualties which could not be otherwise accounted for were put down to the monster.

Upon this imaginary creature rested the responsibility of all these shipwrecks, which unfortunately were considerable; for of three thousand ships whose loss was annually recorded at Lloyd's, the number of sailing and steamships supposed to be totally lost, from the absence of all news, amounted to not less than two hundred!

Now, it was the "monster" who, justly or unjustly, was accused of their disappearance, and, thanks to it, communication between the different continents became more and more dangerous. The public demanded sharply that the seas should at any price be relieved from this formidable cetacean.

## CHAPTER II

### PRO AND CON

At the period when these events took place, I had just returned from a scientific research in the disagreeable territory of Nebraska, in the United States. In virtue of my office as Assistant Professor in the Museum of Natural History in Paris, the French government had attached me to that expedition. After six months in Nebraska, I arrived in New York toward the end of March, laden with a precious collection. My departure for France was fixed for the first days in May. Meanwhile I was occupying myself in classifying my mineralogical, botanical, and zoological riches, when the accident happened to the *Scotia*.

I was perfectly up in the subject which was the question of the day. How could I be otherwise? I had read and reread all the American and European papers without being any nearer a conclusion. This mystery puzzled me. Under the impossibility of forming an opinion, I jumped from one extreme to the other. That there really was something could not be doubted, and the incredulous were invited to put their finger on the wound of the *Scotia*.

On my arrival at New York the question was at its height. The theory of the floating island, and the unapproachable sandbank, supported by minds little competent to form a judgment, was abandoned. And, indeed, unless this shoal had a machine in its stomach, how could it change its position with such astonishing rapidity?

From the same cause, the idea of a floating hull of an enormous wreck was given up.

There remained, then, only two possible solutions of the question, which created two distinct parties: on one side, those who were for a monster of colossal strength; on the other, those who were for a submarine vessel of enormous motive power.

But this last theory, plausible as it was, could not stand against inquiries made in both worlds. That a private gentleman should have such a machine at his command was not likely. Where, when, and how was it built? And how could its construction have been kept secret? Certainly a government might possess such a destructive machine. And in these disastrous times, when the ingenuity of man has multiplied the power of weapons of war, it was possible that, without the knowledge of others, a state might try to work such a formidable engine. After the chassepots came the torpedoes, after the torpedoes the submarine rams, then—the reaction. At least, I hope so.

But the idea of a war machine fell before the declaration of governments. As public interest was in question, and transatlantic communications suffered, their veracity could not be doubted. But how admit that the construction of this submarine boat had escaped the public eye? For a private gentleman to keep the secret under such circumstances would be very difficult, and for a state whose every act is persistently watched by powerful rivals, certainly impossible.

Upon my arrival in New York several persons did me the honor of consulting me on the phenomenon in question. I had published in France a work in quarto, in two volumes, entitled *Mysteries of the Great Submarine Grounds*. This book, highly approved of in the learned world, gained for me a special reputation in this rather obscure branch of Natural History. My advice was asked. As long as I could deny the reality of the fact, I confined myself to a decided negative. But soon, finding myself driven into a corner, I was obliged to explain myself point by point. And even "the Honorable Pierre Aronnax, Professor in the Museum of Paris," was called upon by the *New York Herald* to express a definite opinion of some sort. I did something. I spoke for want of power to hold my tongue. I discussed the question in all its forms, politically and scientifically; and I give here an extract from a carefully studied article which I published in the issue of April 30. It ran as follows:

"After examining one by one the different theories, rejecting all other suggestions, it becomes necessary to admit the existence of a marine animal of enormous power.

"The great depths of the ocean are entirely unknown to us. Soundings cannot reach them. What passes in those remote depths—what beings live, or can live, twelve or fifteen miles beneath the surface of the waters—what is the organization of these animals, we can scarcely conjecture. However, the solution of the problem submitted to me may modify the form of the dilemma. Either we do know all the varieties of beings which people our planet, or we do not. If we do not know them all—if Nature has still secrets in the deeps for us, nothing is more conformable to reason than to admit the existence of fish, or cetaceans of other kinds, or even of new species, of an organization formed to inhabit the strata inaccessible to soundings, and which an accident of some sort, either fantastical or capricious, has brought at long intervals to the upper level of the ocean.

"If, on the contrary, we do know all living kinds, we must necessarily seek for the animal in question among those marine beings already classed; and, in that case, I should be disposed to admit the existence of a gigantic narwhal.

"The common narwhal, or unicorn of the sea, often attains a length of sixty feet. Increase its size fivefold or tenfold, give it strength proportionate to its size, lengthen its destructive weapons, and you obtain the animal required. It will have the proportions determined by the officers of the *Shannon*, the instrument required by the perforation of the *Scotia*, and the power necessary to pierce the hull of the steamer.

"Indeed, the narwhal is armed with a sort of ivory sword, a halberd, according to the expression of certain naturalists. The principal tusk has the hardness of steel. Some of these tusks have been found buried in the bodies of whales, which the unicorn always attacks with success. Others have been drawn out, not without trouble, from the bottoms of ships, which they had pierced through and through, as a gimlet pierces a barrel. The Museum of the Faculty of Medicine of Paris possesses one of these defensive weapons, two yards and a quarter in length, and fifteen inches in diameter at the base.

"Very well! Suppose this weapon to be six times stronger and the animal ten times more powerful; launch it at the rate of twenty miles an hour, and you obtain a shock capable of producing the catastrophe required. Until further information, therefore, I shall maintain it to be a sea unicorn of colossal dimensions, armed not with a halberd, but with a real spur, as the armored frigates, or the 'rams' of war, whose massiveness and motive power it would possess at the same time. Thus may this puzzling phenomenon be explained, unless there be something over and above all that one has ever conjectured, seen, perceived, or experienced; which is just within the bounds of possibility."

These last words were cowardly on my part; but, up to a certain point, I wished to shelter my dignity as professor, and not give too much cause for laughter to the Americans, who laugh well when they do laugh. I reserved for myself a way of escape. In effect, however, I admitted the existence of the "monster." My article was warmly discussed, which procured it a high reputation. It rallied around it a certain number of partisans. The solution it proposed gave, at least, full liberty to the imagination. The human mind delights in grand conceptions of supernatural beings. And the sea is precisely their best vehicle, the only medium through which these giants (against which terrestrial animals, such as elephants or rhinoceroses, are as nothing) can be produced or developed.

The industrial and commercial papers treated the question chiefly from this point of view. The *Shipping and Mercantile Gazette*, the *Lloyd's List*, the *Packet-Boat*, and the *Maritime and Colonial Review*, all papers devoted to insurance companies which threatened to raise their rates of premium, were unanimous on this point. Public opinion had been pronounced. The United States were the first in the field; and in New York they made preparations for an expedition destined to pursue this narwhal. A frigate of great speed, the *Abraham Lincoln*, was put in commission as soon as possible. The arsenals were opened to Commander Farragut, who hastened the arming of his frigate; but, as it always happens, the moment it was decided to pursue the monster, the monster did not appear. For two months no one heard it spoken of. No ship met with it. It seemed as if this unicorn knew of the plots weaving around it. It had been so much talked of, even through the Atlantic cable, that jesters pretended that this slender fly had stopped a telegram on its passage and was making the most of it.

So when the frigate had been armed for a long campaign, and provided with formidable fishing apparatus, no one could tell what course to pursue. Impatience grew apace, when, on June 2, they learned that a steamer of the line of San Francisco, from California to Shanghai, had seen the animal three weeks before in the North Pacific Ocean. The excitement caused by this news was extreme. The ship was revictualed and well stocked with coal.

Three hours before the *Abraham Lincoln* left Brooklyn pier, I received a letter worded as follows:

> *To M. Aronnax, Professor in the Museum of Paris,*
> *Fifth Avenue Hotel, New York.*
> Sir: If you will consent to join the *Abraham Lincoln* in this expedition, the government of the United States will with pleasure see France represented in the enterprise. Commander Farragut has a cabin at your disposal.
>
> Very cordially yours,<br>J. B. Hobson, Secretary of Marine.

## *CHAPTER III*

## I FORM MY RESOLUTION

Three seconds before the arrival of J. B. Hobson's letter I no more thought of pursuing the unicorn than of attempting the passage of the North Sea. Three seconds after reading the letter of the honorable Secretary of Marine, I felt that my true vocation, the sole end of my life, was to chase this disturbing monster and purge it from the world.

But I had just returned from a fatiguing journey, weary and longing for repose. I aspired to nothing more than again seeing my country, my friends, my little lodging by the Jardin des Plantes, my dear and precious collections—but nothing could keep me back! I forgot all—fatigue, friends and collections—and accepted without hesitation the offer of the American government.

"Besides," thought I, "all roads lead back to Europe; and the unicorn may be amiable enough to hurry me toward the coast of France. This worthy animal may allow itself to be caught in the seas of Europe (for my particular benefit), and I will not bring back less than half a yard of his ivory halberd to the Museum of Natural History." But in the meanwhile I must seek this narwhal in the North Pacific Ocean, which, to return to France, was taking the road to the antipodes.

"Conseil," I called in an impatient voice.

Conseil was my servant, a true, devoted Flemish boy, who had accompanied me in all my travels. I liked him, and he returned the liking well. He was quiet by nature, regular from principle, zealous from habit, evincing little disturbance at the different surprises of life, very quick with his hands, and apt at any service required of him; and, despite his name, never giving advice—even when asked for it.

Conseil had followed me for the last ten years wherever science led. Never once did he complain of the length or fatigue of a journey, never make an objection to pack his portmanteau for whatever country it might be, or however far away, whether China or Congo. Besides all this, he had good health, which defied all sickness, and solid muscles, but no nerves; good morals are understood. This boy was thirty years old, and his age to that of his master as fifteen to twenty. May I be excused for saying that I was forty years old?

But Conseil had one fault: he was ceremonious to a degree, and would never speak to me but in the third person, which was sometimes provoking.

"Conseil," said I again, beginning with feverish hands to make preparations for my departure.

Certainly I was sure of this devoted boy. As a rule, I never asked him if it were convenient for him or not to follow me in my travels; but this time the expedition in question might be prolonged, and the enterprise might be hazardous in pursuit of an animal capable of sinking a frigate as easily as a nutshell. Here there was matter for reflection even to the most impassive man in the world. What would Conseil say?

"Conseil," I called a third time.

Conseil appeared.

"Did you call, sir?" said he, entering.

"Yes, my boy; make preparations for me and yourself too. We leave in two hours."

"As you please, sir," replied Conseil, quietly.

"Not an instant to lose; lock in my trunk all traveling utensils, coats, shirts, and stockings—without counting, as many as you can, and make haste."

"And your collections, sir?" observed Conseil.

"We will think of them by and by."

"What! The archiotherium, the hyracotherium, the oreodons, the cheropotamus, and the other skins?"

"They will keep them at the hotel."

"We are not returning to Paris, then?" said Conseil.

"Oh! Certainly," I answered, evasively, "by making a curve."

"Will the curve please you, sir?"

"Oh! It will be nothing; not quite so direct a road, that is all. We take our passage in the *Abraham Lincoln*."

"As you think proper, sir," coolly replied Conseil.

"You see, my friend, it has to do with the monster—the famous narwhal. We are going to purge it from the seas. The author of a work in quarto, in two volumes, on the *Mysteries of the Great Submarine Grounds* cannot forbear embarking with Commander Farragut. A glorious mission, but a dangerous one! We cannot tell where we may go; these animals can be very capricious. But we will go whether or no; we have got a captain who is pretty wide-awake."

I opened a credit account for Babiroussa, and, Conseil following, I jumped into a cab. Our luggage was transported to the deck of the frigate immediately. I hastened on board and asked for Commander Farragut. One of the sailors conducted me to the poop, where I found myself in the presence of a good-looking officer, who held out his hand to me.

"Monsieur Pierre Aronnax?" said he.

"Himself," replied I. "Commander Farragut?"

"You are welcome, Professor; your cabin is ready for you."

I bowed, and desired to be conducted to the cabin destined for me.

The *Abraham Lincoln* had been well chosen and equipped for her new destination. She was a frigate of great speed, fitted with high-pressure engines which admitted a pressure of seven atmospheres. Under this the *Abraham Lincoln* attained the mean speed of nearly eighteen knots and a third an hour—a considerable speed, but, nevertheless, insufficient to grapple with this gigantic cetacean.

The interior arrangements of the frigate corresponded to its nautical qualities. I was well satisfied with my cabin, which was in the after part, opening upon the gunroom.

"We shall be well off here," said I to Conseil.

"As well, by your honor's leave, as a hermit-crab in the shell of a whelk," said Conseil.

I left Conseil to stow our trunks conveniently away, and remounted the poop in order to survey the preparations for departure.

At that moment Commander Farragut was ordering the last moorings to be cast loose which held the *Abraham Lincoln* to the pier of Brooklyn. So in a quarter of an hour, perhaps less, the frigate would have sailed without me. I should have missed this extraordinary, supernatural, and incredible expedition, the recital of which may well meet with some suspicion.

But Commander Farragut would not lose a day nor an hour in scouring the seas in which the animal had been sighted. He sent for the engineer.

"Is the steam full on?" asked he.

"Yes, sir," replied the engineer.

"Go ahead," cried Commander Farragut.

The quay of Brooklyn, and all that part of New York bordering on the East River, was crowded with spectators. Three cheers burst successively from five hundred thousand throats; thousands of handkerchiefs were waved above the heads of the compact mass, saluting the *Abraham Lincoln*, until she reached the waters of the Hudson, at the point of that elongated peninsula which forms the town of New York. Then the frigate, following the coast of New Jersey along the right bank of the beautiful river, covered with villas, passed between the forts, which saluted her with their heaviest guns. The *Abraham Lincoln* answered by hoisting the American colors three times, whose thirty-nine stars shone resplendent from the mizzen-peak; then modifying its speed to take the narrow channel marked by buoys placed in the inner bay formed by Sandy Hook Point, it coasted the long sandy beach, where some thousands of spectators gave it one final cheer. The escort of boats and tenders still followed the frigate, and did not leave her until they came abreast of the light-ship whose two lights marked the entrance of New York Channel.

Six bells struck, the pilot got into his boat, and rejoined the little schooner which was waiting under our lee, the fires were made up, the screw beat the waves more rapidly, the frigate skirted the low yellow coast of Long Island; and at eight bells, after having lost sight in the northwest of the lights of Fire Island, she ran at full steam on to the dark waters of the Atlantic.

## CHAPTER IV

### NED LAND

Captain Farragut was a good seaman, worthy of the frigate he commanded. His vessel and he were one. He was the soul of it. On the question of the monster there was no doubt in his mind, and he would not allow the existence of the animal to be disputed on board. He believed in it, as certain good women believe in the leviathan—by faith, not by reason. The monster did exist, and he had sworn to rid the seas of it. Either Captain Farragut would kill the narwhal, or the narwhal would kill the captain. There was no third course.

The officers on board shared the opinion of their chief. They were ever chatting, discussing, and calculating the various chances of a meeting, watching narrowly the vast surface of the ocean. More than one took up his quarters voluntarily in the cross-trees, who would have cursed such a berth under any other circumstances. As long as the sun described its daily course, the rigging was crowded with sailors, whose feet were burned to such an extent by the heat of the deck as to render it unbearable; still the *Abraham Lincoln* had not yet breasted the suspected waters of the Pacific. As to the ship's company, they desired nothing better than to meet the unicorn, to harpoon it, hoist it on board, and despatch it. They watched the sea with eager attention.

Besides, Captain Farragut had spoken of a certain sum of two thousand dollars, set apart for whoever should first sight the monster, were he cabin-boy, common seaman, or officer.

I leave you to judge how eyes were used on board the *Abraham Lincoln*.

For my own part I was not behind the others, and, left to no one my share of daily observations. The frigate might have been called the *Argus*, for a hundred reasons. Only one among us, Conseil, seemed to protest by his indifference against the question which so interested us all, and seemed to be out of keeping with the general enthusiasm on board.

I have said that Captain Farragut had carefully provided his ship with every apparatus for catching the gigantic cetacean. No whaler had ever been better armed. We possessed every known engine, from the harpoon thrown by the hand to the barbed arrows of the blunderbuss, and the explosive balls of the duck-gun. On the forecastle lay the perfection of a breech-loading gun, very thick at the breech, and very narrow in the bore, the model of which had been in the Exhibition of 1867. This precious weapon of American origin could throw with ease a conical projectile of nine pounds to a mean distance of ten miles.

Thus the *Abraham Lincoln* wanted for no means of destruction; and, what was better still she had on board Ned Land, the prince of harpooners.

Ned Land was a Canadian, with an uncommon quickness of hand, and who knew no equal in his dangerous occupation. Skill, coolness, audacity, and cunning he possessed in a superior degree, and it must be a cunning whale or a singularly "cute" cachalot to escape the stroke of his harpoon.

Ned Land was about forty years of age; he was a tall man (more than six feet high), strongly built, grave and taciturn, occasionally violent, and very passionate when contradicted. His person attracted attention, but above all the boldness of his look, which gave a singular expression to his face.

Who calls himself Canadian calls himself French; and, little communicative as Ned Land was, I must admit that he took a certain liking for me. My nationality drew him to me, no doubt. It was an opportunity for him to talk, and for me to hear, that old language of Rabelais, which is still in use in some Canadian provinces. The harpooner's family was originally from Quebec, and was already a tribe of hardy fishermen when this town belonged to France.

Little by little, Ned Land acquired a taste for chatting, and I loved to hear the recital of his adventures in the polar seas. He related his fishing, and his combats, with natural poetry of expression; his recital took the form of an epic poem, and I seemed to be listening to a Canadian Homer singing the *Iliad* of the regions of the North.

I am portraying this hardy companion as I really knew him. We are old friends now, united in that unchangeable friendship which is born and cemented amid extreme dangers. Ah, brave Ned! I ask no more than to live a hundred years longer, that I may have more time to dwell the longer on your memory.

Now, what was Ned Land's opinion upon the question of the marine monster? I must admit that he did not believe in the unicorn, and was the only one on board who did not share that universal conviction. He even avoided the subject, which I one day thought it my duty to press upon him. One magnificent evening, July 30 (that is to say, three weeks after our departure), the frigate was abreast of Cape Blanc, thirty miles to leeward of the coast of Patagonia. We had crossed the Tropic of Capricorn, and the Straits of Magellan opened less than seven hundred miles to the south. Before eight days were over the *Abraham Lincoln* would be plowing the waters of the Pacific.

Seated on the poop, Ned Land and I were chatting of one thing and another as we looked at this mysterious sea, whose great depths had up to this time been inaccessible to the eye of man. I naturally led up the conversation to the giant unicorn, and examined the various chances of success or failure of the expedition. But, seeing that Ned Land let me speak without saying too much himself, I pressed him more closely.

"Well, Ned," said I, "is it possible that you are not convinced of the existence of this cetacean that we are following? Have you any particular reason for being so incredulous?"

The harpooner looked at me fixedly for some moments before answering, struck his broad forehead with his hand (a habit of his), as if to collect himself, and said at last, "Perhaps I have, Mr. Aronnax."

"But, Ned, you, a whaler by profession, familiarized with all the great marine mammalia—you ought to be the last to doubt under such circumstances!"

"That is just what deceives you, Professor," replied Ned. "As a whaler I have followed many a cetacean, harpooned a great number, and killed several; but, however strong or well-armed they may have been, neither their tails nor their weapons would have been able even to scratch the iron plates of a steamer."

"But, Ned, they tell of ships which the teeth of the narwhal have pierced through and through."

"Wooden ships—that is possible," replied the Canadian, "but I have never seen it done; and, until further proof, I deny that whales, cetaceans, or sea unicorns could ever produce the effect you describe."

"Well, Ned, I repeat it with a conviction resting on the logic of facts. I believe in the existence of a mammal power fully organized, belonging to the branch of vertebrata, like the whales, the cachalots, or the dolphins, and furnished with a horn of defense of great penetrating power."

"Hum!" said the harpooner, shaking his head with the air of a man who would not be convinced.

"Notice one thing, my worthy Canadian," I resumed. "If such an animal is in existence, if it inhabits the depths of the ocean, if it frequents the strata lying miles below the surface of the water, it must necessarily possess an organization the strength of which would defy all comparison."

"And why this powerful organization?" demanded Ned.

"Because it requires incalculable strength to keep one's self in these strata and resist their pressure. Listen to me. Let us admit that the pressure of the atmosphere is represented by the weight of a column of water thirty-two feet high. In reality the column of water would be shorter, as we are speaking of seawater, the density of which is greater than that of freshwater. Very well, when you dive, Ned, as many times 32 feet of water as there are above you, so many times does your body bear a pressure equal to that of the atmosphere, that is to say, 15 pounds for each square inch of its surface. It follows, then, that at 320 feet this pressure equals that of 10 atmospheres, of 100 atmospheres at 3,200 feet, and of 1,000 atmospheres at 32,000 feet, that is, about 6 miles; which is equivalent to saying that if you could attain this depth in the ocean, each square three-eighths of an inch of the surface of your body would bear a pressure of 5,600 pounds. Ah! My brave Ned, do you know how many square inches you carry on the surface of your body?"

"I have no idea, Mr. Aronnax."

"About 6,500; and as in reality the atmospheric pressure is about 15 pounds to the square inch, your 6,500 square inches bear at this moment a pressure of 97,500 pounds."

"Without my perceiving it?"

"Without your perceiving it. And if you are not crushed by such a pressure, it is because the air penetrates the interior of your body with equal pressure. Hence perfect equilibrium between the interior and exterior pressure, which thus neutralize each other, and which allows you to bear it without inconvenience. But in the water it is another thing."

"Yes, I understand," replied Ned, becoming more attentive; "because the water surrounds me, but does not penetrate."

"Precisely, Ned: so that at 32 feet beneath the surface of the sea you would undergo a pressure of 97,500 pounds; at 320 feet, ten times that pressure; at 3,200 feet, a hundred times that pressure; lastly, at 32,000 feet, a thousand times that pressure would be 97,500,000 pounds—that is to say, that you would be flattened as if you had been drawn from the plates of a hydraulic machine!"

"The devil!" exclaimed Ned.

"Very well, my worthy harpooner, if some vertebrate, several hundred yards long, and large in proportion, can maintain itself in such depths—of those whose surface is represented by millions of square inches, that is by tens of millions of pounds, we must estimate the pressure they undergo. Consider, then, what must be the resistance of their bony structure, and the strength of their organization to withstand such pressure!"

"Why!" exclaimed Ned Land. "They must be made of iron plates eight inches thick, like the armored frigates."

"As you say, Ned. And think what destruction such a mass would cause, if hurled with the speed of an express train against the hull of a vessel."

"Yes—certainly—perhaps," replied the Canadian, shaken by these figures, but not yet willing to give in.

"Well, have I convinced you?"

"You have convinced me of one thing, sir, which is that, if such animals do exist at the bottom of the seas, they must necessarily be as strong as you say."

"But if they do not exist, mine obstinate harpooner, how explain the accident to the *Scotia?*"

# CHAPTER V

## AT A VENTURE

The voyage of the *Abraham Lincoln* was for a long time marked by no special incident. But one circumstance happened which showed the wonderful dexterity of Ned Land, and proved what confidence we might place in him.

On June 30, the frigate spoke with some American whalers, from whom we learned that they knew nothing about the narwhal. But one of them, the captain of the *Monroe*, knowing that Ned Land had shipped on board the *Abraham Lincoln*, begged for his help in chasing a whale they had in sight. Commander Farragut, desirous of seeing Ned Land at work, gave him permission to go on board the *Monroe*. And fate served our Canadian so well that, instead of one whale, he harpooned two with a double blow, striking one straight to the heart, and catching the other after some minutes' pursuit.

Decidedly, if the monster ever had to do with Ned Land's harpoon, I would not bet in its favor.

The frigate skirted the southeast coast of America with great rapidity. On July 3 we were at the opening of the Straits of Magellan, level with Cape Vierges. But Commander Farragut would not take a tortuous passage, but doubled Cape Horn.

The ship's crew agreed with him. And certainly it was possible that they might meet the narwhal in this narrow pass. Many of the sailors affirmed that the monster could not pass there, "that he was too big for that!"

On July 6, about three o'clock in the afternoon, the *Abraham Lincoln*, at fifteen miles to the south, doubled the solitary island, this lost rock at the extremity of the American continent, to which some Dutch sailors gave the name of their native town, Cape Horn. The course was taken toward the northwest, and the next day the screw of the frigate was at last beating the waters of the Pacific.

"Keep your eyes open!" called out the sailors.

And they were opened widely. Both eyes and glasses, a little dazzled, it is true, by the prospect of two thousand dollars, had not an instant's repose. Day and night they watched the surface of the ocean, and even nyctalopes, whose faculty of seeing in the darkness multiplies their chances a hundredfold, would have had enough to do to gain the prize.

I myself, for whom money had no charms, was not the least attentive on board. Giving but few minutes to my meals, but a few hours to sleep, indifferent to either rain or sunshine, I did not leave the poop of the vessel. Now leaning on the netting of the forecastle, now on the taffrail, I devoured with eagerness the soft foam which whitened the sea as far as the eye could reach; and how often have I shared the emotion of the majority of the crew, when some capricious whale raised its black back above the waves! The poop of the vessel was crowded on a moment. The cabins poured forth a torrent of sailors and officers, each with heaving breast and troubled eye watching the course of the cetacean. I looked and looked till I was nearly blind, while Conseil kept repeating in a calm voice:

"If, sir, you would not squint so much, you would see better!"

But vain excitement! The *Abraham Lincoln* checked its speed and made for the animal signaled, a simple whale, or common cachalot, which soon disappeared amid a storm of abuse.

But the weather was good. The voyage was being accomplished under the most favorable auspices. It was then the bad season in Australia, the July of that zone corresponding to our January in Europe, but the sea was beautiful and easily scanned around a vast circumference.

On July 20, the Tropic of Capricorn was cut by 105° of longitude, and the 27th of the same month we crossed the Equator on the 110th meridian. This passed, the frigate took a more decided westerly direction, and scoured the central waters of the Pacific. Commander Farragut thought, and with reason, that it was better to remain in deep water, and keep clear of continents or islands, which the beast itself seemed to shun (perhaps because there was not enough water for him! suggested the greater part of the crew). The frigate passed at some distance from the Marquesas and the Sandwich Islands, crossed the Tropic of Cancer, and made for the China Seas. We were on the theater of the last diversions of the monster: and, to say truth, we no longer lived on board. The entire ship's crew were undergoing a nervous excitement, of which I can give no idea: they could not eat, they could not sleep—twenty times a day, a misconception or an optical illusion of some sailor seated on the taffrail, would cause dreadful perspirations, and these emotions, twenty times repeated, kept us in a state of excitement so violent that a reaction was unavoidable.

And truly, reaction soon showed itself. For three months, during which a day seemed an age, the *Abraham Lincoln* furrowed all the waters of the Northern Pacific, running at whales, making sharp deviations from her course, veering suddenly from one tack to another, stopping suddenly, putting on steam, and backing ever and anon at the risk of deranging her machinery, and not one point of the Japanese or American coast was left unexplored.

The warmest partisans of the enterprise now became its most ardent detractors. Reaction mounted from the crew to the captain himself, and certainly, had it not been for the resolute determination on the part of Captain Farragut, the frigate would have headed due southward. This useless search could not last much longer. The *Abraham Lincoln* had nothing to reproach herself with, she had done her best to succeed. Never had an American ship's crew shown more zeal or patience; its failure could not be placed to their charge—there remained nothing but to return.

This was represented to the commander. The sailors could not hide their discontent, and the service suffered. I will not say there was a mutiny on board, but after a reasonable period of obstinacy, Captain Farragut (as Columbus did) asked for three days' patience. If in three days the monster did not appear, the man at the helm should give three turns of the wheel, and the *Abraham Lincoln* would make for the European seas.

This promise was made on November 2. It had the effect of rallying the ship's crew. The ocean was watched with renewed attention. Each one wished for a last glance in which to sum up his remembrance. Glasses were used with feverish activity. It was a grand defiance given to the giant narwhal, and he could scarcely fail to answer the summons and "appear."

Two days passed, the steam was at half pressure; a thousand schemes were tried to attract the attention and stimulate the apathy of the animal in case it should be met in those parts. Large quantities of bacon were trailed in the wake of the ship, to the great satisfaction (I must say) of the sharks. Small craft radiated in all directions around the *Abraham Lincoln* as she lay to, and did not leave a spot of the sea unexplored. But the night of November 4 arrived without the unveiling of this submarine mystery.

The next day, November 5, at twelve, the delay would (morally speaking) expire; after that time, Commander Farragut, faithful to his promise, was to turn the course to the southeast and abandon forever the northern regions of the Pacific.

The frigate was then in 31° 15' north latitude and 136° 42' east longitude. The coast of Japan still remained less than two hundred miles to leeward. Night was approaching. They had just struck eight bells; large clouds veiled the face of the moon, then in its first quarter. The sea undulated peaceably under the stern of the vessel.

At that moment I was leaning forward on the starboard netting. Conseil, standing near me, was looking straight before him. The crew, perched in the ratlines, examined the horizon which contracted and darkened by degrees. Officers with their night glasses scoured the growing darkness: sometimes the ocean sparkled under the rays of the moon, which darted between two clouds, then all trace of light was lost in the darkness.

In looking at Conseil, I could see he was undergoing a little of the general influence. At least I thought so. Perhaps for the first time his nerves vibrated to a sentiment of curiosity.

"Come, Conseil," said I, "this is the last chance of pocketing the two thousand dollars."

"May I be permitted to say, sir," replied Conseil, "that I never reckoned on getting the prize; and, had the government of the Union offered a hundred thousand dollars, it would have been none the poorer."

"You are right, Conseil. It is a foolish affair after all, and one upon which we entered too lightly. What time lost, what useless emotions! We should have been back in France six months ago."

"In your little room, sir," replied Conseil, "and in your museum, sir; and I should have already classed all your fossils, sir. And the Babiroussa would have been installed in its cage in the Jardin des Plantes, and have drawn all the curious people of the capital!"

"As you say, Conseil. I fancy we shall run a fair chance of being laughed at for our pains."

"That's tolerably certain," replied Conseil, quietly; "I think they will make fun of you, sir. And, must I say it—?"

"Go on, my good friend."

"Well, sir, you will only get your deserts."

"Indeed!"

"When one has the honor of being a savant as you are, sir, one should not expose one's self to—"

Conseil had not time to finish his compliment. In the midst of general silence a voice had just been heard. It was the voice of Ned Land shouting:

"Look out there! The very thing we are looking for—on our weather beam!"

# CHAPTER VI

## AT FULL STEAM

At this cry the whole ship's crew hurried toward the harpooner—commander, officers, masters, sailors, cabin boys; even the engineers left their engines, and the stokers their furnaces.

The order to stop her had been given, and the frigate now simply went on by her own momentum. The darkness was then profound, and, however good the Canadian's eyes were, I asked myself how he had managed to see, and what he had been able to see. My heart beat as if it would break. But Ned Land was not mistaken, and we all perceived the object he pointed to. At two cables' length from the *Abraham Lincoln*, on the starboard quarter, the sea seemed to be illuminated all over. It was not a mere phosphoric phenomenon. The monster emerged some fathoms from the water, and then threw out that very intense but mysterious light mentioned in the report of several captains. This magnificent irradiation must have been produced by an agent of great shining power. The luminous part traced on the sea an immense oval, much elongated, the center of which condensed a burning heat, whose overpowering brilliancy died out by successive gradations.

"It is only a massing of phosphoric particles," cried one of the officers.

"No, sir, certainly not," I replied. "That brightness is of an essentially electrical nature. Besides, see, see! It moves; it is moving forward, backward; it is darting toward us!"

A general cry arose from the frigate.

"Silence!" said the captain. "Up with the helm, reverse the engines."

The steam was shut off, and the *Abraham Lincoln*, beating to port, described a semicircle.

"Right the helm, go ahead," cried the captain.

These orders were executed, and the frigate moved rapidly from the burning light.

I was mistaken. She tried to sheer off, but the supernatural animal approached with a velocity double her own.

We gasped for breath. Stupefaction more than fear made us dumb and motionless. The animal gained on us, sporting with the waves. It made the round of the frigate, which was then making fourteen knots, and enveloped it with its electric rings like luminous dust.

Then it moved away two or three miles, leaving a phosphorescent track, like those volumes of steam that the express trains leave behind. All at once from the dark line of the horizon whither it retired to gain its momentum, the monster rushed suddenly toward the *Abraham Lincoln* with alarming rapidity, stopped suddenly about twenty feet from the hull, and died out—not diving under the water, for its brilliancy did not abate—but suddenly, and as if the source of this brilliant emanation was exhausted. Then it reappeared on the other side of the vessel, as if it had turned and slid under the hull. Any moment a collision might have occurred which would have been fatal to us. However, I was astonished at the maneuvers of the frigate. She fled and did not attack.

On the captain's face, generally so impassive, was an expression of unaccountable astonishment.

"Mr. Aronnax," he said, "I do not know with what formidable being I have to deal, and I will not imprudently risk my frigate in the midst of this darkness. Besides, how attack this unknown thing, how defend one's self from it? Wait for daylight, and the scene will change."

"You have no further doubt, captain, of the nature of the animal?"

"No, sir; it is evidently a gigantic narwhal, and an electric one."

"Perhaps," added I, "one can only approach it with a torpedo."

"Undoubtedly," replied the captain, "if it possesses such dreadful power, it is the most terrible animal that ever was created. That is why, sir, I must be on my guard."

The crew were on their feet all night. No one thought of sleep. The *Abraham Lincoln*, not being able to struggle with such velocity, had moderated its pace, and sailed at half speed. For its part, the narwhal, imitating the frigate, let the waves rock it at will, and seemed decided not to leave the scene of the struggle. Toward midnight, however, it disappeared, or, to use a more appropriate term, it "died out" like a large glowworm. Had it fled? One could only fear, not hope it. But at seven minutes to one o'clock in the morning a deafening whistling was heard, like that produced by a body of water rushing with great violence.

The captain, Ned Land, and I were then on the poop, eagerly peering through the profound darkness.

"Ned Land," asked the commander, "you have often heard the roaring of whales?"

"Often, sir; but never such whales the sight of which brought me in two thousand dollars. If I can only approach within four harpoons' length of it!"

"But to approach it," said the commander, "I ought to put a whaler at your disposal?"

"Certainly, sir."

"That will be trifling with the lives of my men."

"And mine too," simply said the harpooner.

Toward two o'clock in the morning, the burning light reappeared, not less intense, about five miles to windward of the *Abraham Lincoln*. Notwithstanding the distance, and the noise of the wind and sea, one heard distinctly the loud strokes of the animal's tail, and even its panting breath. It seemed that, at the moment that the enormous narwhal had come to take breath at the surface of the water, the air was engulfed in its lungs, like the steam in the vast cylinders of a machine of two thousand horsepower.

"Hum!" thought I, "a whale with the strength of a cavalry regiment would be a pretty whale!"

We were on the *qui vive* till daylight, and prepared for the combat. The fishing implements were laid along the hammock nettings. The second lieutenant loaded the blunderbusses, which could throw harpoons to the distance of a mile, and long duck-guns, with explosive bullets, which inflicted mortal wounds even to the most terrible animals. Ned Land contented himself with sharpening his harpoon—a terrible weapon in his hands.

At six o'clock day began to break; and, with the first glimmer of light, the electric light of the narwhal disappeared. At seven o'clock the day was sufficiently advanced, but a very thick sea fog obscured our view, and the best spyglasses could not pierce it. That caused disappointment and anger.

I climbed the mizzenmast. Some officers were already perched on the mastheads. At eight o'clock the fog lay heavily on the waves, and its thick scrolls rose little by little. The horizon grew wider and clearer at the same time. Suddenly, just as on the day before, Ned Land's voice was heard:

"The thing itself on the port quarter!" cried the harpooner.

Every eye was turned toward the point indicated. There, a mile and a half from the frigate, a long blackish body emerged a yard above the waves. Its tail, violently agitated, produced a considerable eddy. Never did a tail beat the sea with such violence. An immense track, of dazzling whiteness, marked the passage of the animal, and described a long curve.

The frigate approached the cetacean. I examined it thoroughly.

The reports of the *Shannon* and of the *Helvetia* had rather exaggerated its size, and I estimated its length at only two hundred and fifty feet. As to its dimensions, I could only conjecture them to be admirably proportioned. While I watched this phenomenon, two jets of steam and water were ejected from its vents, and rose to the height of 120 feet; thus I ascertained its way of breathing. I concluded definitely that it belonged to the vertebrate branch, class mammalia.

The crew waited impatiently for their chief's orders. The latter, after having observed the animal attentively, called the engineer. The engineer ran to him.

"Sir," said the commander, "you have steam up?"

"Yes, sir," answered the engineer.

"Well, make up your fires and put on all steam."

Three hurrahs greeted this order. The time for the struggle had arrived. Some moments after, the two funnels of the frigate vomited torrents of black smoke, and the bridge quaked under the trembling of the boilers.

The *Abraham Lincoln*, propelled by her wonderful screw, went straight at the animal. The latter allowed it to come within half a cable's length; then, as if disdaining to dive, it took a little turn, and stopped a short distance off.

This pursuit lasted nearly three-quarters of an hour, without the frigate gaining two yards on the cetacean. It was quite evident that at that rate we should never come up with it.

"Well, Mr. Land," asked the captain, "do you advise me to put the boats out to sea?"

"No, sir," replied Ned Land; "because we shall not take that beast easily."

"What shall we do then?"

"Put on more steam if you can, sir. With your leave, I mean to post myself under the bowsprit, and, if we get within harpooning distance, I shall throw my harpoon."

"Go, Ned," said the captain. "Engineer, put on more pressure."

Ned Land went to his post. The fires were increased, the screw revolved forty-three times a minute, and the steam poured out of the valves. We heaved the log, and calculated that the *Abraham Lincoln* was going at the rate of eighteen and a half miles an hour.

But the accursed animal swam at the same speed.

For a whole hour the frigate kept up this pace, without gaining six feet. It was humiliating for one of the swiftest sailers in the American navy. A stubborn anger seized the crew; the sailors abused the monster, who, as before, disdained to answer them; the captain no longer contented himself with twisting his beard—he gnawed it.

The engineer was called again.

"You have turned full steam on?"

"Yes, sir," replied the engineer.

The speed of the *Abraham Lincoln* increased. Its masts trembled down to their stepping holes, and the clouds of smoke could hardly find way out of the narrow funnels.

They heaved the log a second time.

"Well?" asked the captain of the man at the wheel.

"Nineteen miles and three-tenths, sir."

"Clap on more steam."

The engineer obeyed. The manometer showed ten degrees. But the cetacean grew warm itself, no doubt; for without straining itself, it made nineteen and three-tenths miles.

What a pursuit! No, I cannot describe the emotion that vibrated through me. Ned Land kept his post, harpoon in hand. Several times the animal let us gain upon it. "We shall catch it! We shall catch it!" cried the Canadian. But just as he was going to strike, the cetacean stole away with a rapidity that could not be estimated at less than thirty miles an hour, and even during our maximum of speed, it bullied the frigate, going around and around it. A cry of fury broke from everyone!

At noon we were no further advanced than at eight o'clock in the morning.

The captain then decided to take more direct means.

"Ah!" said he. "That animal goes quicker than the *Abraham Lincoln*. Very well! We will see whether it will escape these conical bullets. Send your men to the forecastle, sir."

The forecastle gun was immediately loaded and slewed around. But the shot passed some feet above the cetacean, which was half a mile off.

"Another, more to the right," cried the commander, "and five dollars to whoever will hit that infernal beast."

An old gunner with a gray beard—that I can see now—with steady eye and grave face, went up to the gun and took a long aim. A loud report was heard, with which were mingled the cheers of the crew.

The bullet did its work; it hit the animal, and, sliding off the rounded surface, was lost in two miles' depth of sea.

The chase began again, and the captain, leaning toward me, said:

"I will pursue that beast till my frigate bursts up."

"Yes," answered I; "and you will be quite right to do it."

I wished the beast would exhaust itself, and not be insensible to fatigue like a steam engine. But it was of no use. Hours passed, without its showing any signs of exhaustion.

However, it must be said in praise of the *Abraham Lincoln* that she struggled on indefatigably. I cannot reckon the distance she made under three hundred miles during this unlucky day, November 6. But night came on, and overshadowed the rough ocean.

Now I thought our expedition was at an end, and that we should never again see the extraordinary animal. I was mistaken. At ten minutes to eleven in the evening, the electric light reappeared three miles to windward of the frigate, as pure, as intense as during the preceding night.

The narwhal seemed motionless; perhaps, tired with its day's work, it slept, letting itself float with the undulation of the waves. Now was a chance of which the captain resolved to take advantage.

He gave his orders. The *Abraham Lincoln* kept up half steam, and advanced cautiously so as not to awake its adversary. It is no rare thing to meet in the middle of the ocean whales so sound asleep that they can be successfully attacked, and Ned Land had harpooned more than one during its sleep. The Canadian went to take his place again under the bowsprit.

The frigate approached noiselessly, stopped at two cables' lengths from the animal, and following its track. No one breathed; a deep silence reigned on the bridge. We were not a hundred feet from the burning focus, the light of which increased and dazzled our eyes.

At this moment, leaning on the forecastle bulwark, I saw below me Ned Land grappling the martingale in one hand, brandishing his terrible harpoon in the other, scarcely twenty feet from the motionless animal. Suddenly his arm straightened, and the harpoon was thrown; I heard the sonorous stroke of the weapon, which seemed to have struck a hard body. The electric light went out suddenly, and two enormous waterspouts broke over the bridge of the frigate, rushing like a torrent from stem to stern, overthrowing men, and breaking the lashings of the spars. A fearful shock followed, and, thrown over the rail without having time to stop myself, I fell into the sea.

## CHAPTER VII

### AN UNKNOWN SPECIES OF WHALE

This unexpected fall so stunned me that I have no clear recollection of my sensations at the time. I was at first drawn down to a depth of about twenty feet. I am a good swimmer (though without pretending to rival Byron or Edgar Poe, who were masters of the art), and in that plunge I did not lose my presence of mind. Two vigorous strokes brought me to the surface of the water. My first care was to look for the frigate. Had the crew seen me disappear? Had the *Abraham Lincoln* veered around? Would the captain put out a boat? Might I hope to be saved?

The darkness was intense. I caught a glimpse of a black mass disappearing in the east, its beacon lights dying out in the distance. It was the frigate! I was lost.

"Help, help!" I shouted, swimming toward the *Abraham Lincoln* in desperation.

My clothes encumbered me; they seemed glued to my body, and paralyzed my movements.

I was sinking! I was suffocating!

"Help!"

This was my last cry. My mouth filled with water; I struggled against being drawn down the abyss. Suddenly my clothes were seized by a strong hand, and I felt myself quickly drawn up to the surface of the sea; and I heard, yes, I heard these words pronounced in my ear:

"If master would be so good as to lean on my shoulder, master would swim with much greater ease."

I seized with one hand my faithful Conseil's arm.

"Is it you?" said I. "You?"

"Myself," answered Conseil; "and waiting master's orders."

"That shock threw you as well as me into the sea?"

"No; but, being in my master's service, I followed him."

The worthy fellow thought that was but natural.

"And the frigate?" I asked.

"The frigate?" replied Conseil, turning on his back. "I think that master had better not count too much on her."

"You think so?"

"I say that, at the time I threw myself into the sea, I heard the men at the wheel say, 'The screw and the rudder are broken.'"

"Broken?"

"Yes, broken by the monster's teeth. It is the only injury the *Abraham Lincoln* has sustained. But it is a bad look-out for us—she no longer answers her helm."

"Then we are lost!"

"Perhaps so," calmly answered Conseil. "However, we have still several hours before us, and one can do a good deal in some hours."

Conseil's imperturbable coolness set me up again. I swam more vigorously; but, cramped by my clothes, which stuck to me like a leaden weight, I felt great difficulty in bearing up. Conseil saw this.

"Will master let me make a slit?" said he; and, slipping an open knife under my clothes, he ripped them up from top to bottom very rapidly. Then he cleverly slipped them off me, while I swam for both of us.

Then I did the same for Conseil, and we continued to swim near to each other.

Nevertheless, our situation was no less terrible. Perhaps our disappearance had not been noticed; and, if it had been, the frigate could not tack, being without its helm. Conseil argued on this supposition, and laid his plans accordingly. This quiet boy was perfectly self-possessed. We then decided that, as our only chance of safety was being picked up by the *Abraham Lincoln*'s boats, we ought to manage so as to wait for them as long as possible. I resolved then to husband our strength, so that both should not be exhausted at the same time; and this is how we managed: while one of us lay on our back, quite still, with arms crossed, and legs stretched out, the other would swim and push the other on in front. This towing business did not last more than ten minutes each; and relieving each other thus, we could swim on for some hours, perhaps till daybreak. Poor chance! But hope is so firmly rooted in the heart of man! Moreover, there were two of us. Indeed I declare (though it may seem improbable) if I sought to destroy all hope—if I wished to despair, I could not.

The collision of the frigate with the cetacean had occurred about eleven o'clock in the evening before. I reckoned then we should have eight hours to swim before sunrise, an operation quite practicable if we relieved each other. The sea, very calm, was in our favor. Sometimes I tried to pierce the intense darkness that was only dispelled by the phosphorescence caused by our movements. I watched the luminous waves that broke over my hand, whose mirrorlike surface was spotted with silvery rings. One might have said that we were in a bath of quicksilver.

Near one o'clock in the morning, I was seized with dreadful fatigue. My limbs stiffened under the strain of violent cramp. Conseil was obliged to keep me up, and our preservation devolved on him alone. I heard the poor boy pant; his breathing became short and hurried. I found that he could not keep up much longer.

"Leave me! Leave me!" I said to him.

"Leave my master? Never!" replied he. "I would drown first."

Just then the moon appeared through the fringes of a thick cloud that the wind was driving to the east. The surface of the sea glittered with its rays. This kindly light reanimated us. My head got better again. I looked at all points of the horizon. I saw the frigate! She was five miles from us, and looked like a dark mass, hardly discernible. But no boats!

I would have cried out. But what good would it have been at such a distance! My swollen lips could utter no sounds. Conseil could articulate some words, and I heard him repeat at intervals, "Help! Help!"

Our movements were suspended for an instant; we listened. It might be only a singing in the ear, but it seemed to me as if a cry answered the cry from Conseil.

"Did you hear?" I murmured.

"Yes! Yes!"

And Conseil gave one more despairing cry.

This time there was no mistake! A human voice responded to ours! Was it the voice of another unfortunate creature, abandoned in the middle of the ocean, some other victim of the shock sustained by the vessel? Or rather was it a boat from the frigate, that was hailing us in the darkness?

Conseil made a last effort, and, leaning on my shoulder, while I struck out in a desperate effort, he raised himself half out of the water, then fell back exhausted.

"What did you see?"

"I saw——" murmured he; "I saw——but do not talk——reserve all your strength!"

What had he seen? Then, I know not why, the thought of the monster came into my head for the first time! But that voice! The time is past for Jonahs to take refuge in whales' bellies! However, Conseil was towing me again. He raised his head sometimes, looked before us, and uttered a cry of recognition, which was responded to by a voice that came nearer and nearer. I scarcely heard it. My strength was exhausted; my fingers stiffened; my hand afforded me support no longer; my mouth, convulsively opening, filled with salt water. Cold crept over me. I raised my head for the last time, then I sank.

At this moment a hard body struck me. I clung to it: then I felt that I was being drawn up, that I was brought to the surface of the water, that my chest collapsed—I fainted.

It is certain that I soon came to, thanks to the vigorous rubbings that I received. I half opened my eyes.

"Conseil!" I murmured.

"Does master call me?" asked Conseil.

Just then, by the waning light of the moon which was sinking down to the horizon, I saw a face which was not Conseil's and which I immediately recognized.

"Ned!" I cried.

"The same, sir, who is seeking his prize!" replied the Canadian.

"Were you thrown into the sea by the shock to the frigate?"

"Yes, Professor; but more fortunate than you, I was able to find a footing almost directly upon a floating island."

"An island?"

"Or, more correctly speaking, on our gigantic narwhal."

"Explain yourself, Ned!"

"Only I soon found out why my harpoon had not entered its skin and was blunted."

"Why, Ned, why?"

"Because, Professor, that beast is made of sheet iron."

The Canadian's last words produced a sudden revolution in my brain. I wriggled myself quickly to the top of the being, or object, half out of the water, which served us for a refuge. I kicked it. It was evidently a hard, impenetrable body, and not the soft substance that forms the bodies of the great marine mammalia. But this hard body might be a bony covering, like that of the antediluvian animals; and I should be free to class this monster among amphibious reptiles, such as tortoises or alligators.

Well, no! The blackish back that supported me was smooth, polished, without scales. The blow produced a metallic sound; and, incredible though it may be, it seemed, I might say, as if it was made of riveted plates.

There was no doubt about it! This monster, this natural phenomenon that had puzzled the learned world, and over thrown and misled the imagination of seamen of both hemispheres, it must be owned was a still more astonishing phenomenon, inasmuch as it was a simply human construction.

We had no time to lose, however. We were lying upon the back of a sort of submarine boat, which appeared (as far as I could judge) like a huge fish of steel. Ned Land's mind was made up on this point. Conseil and I could only agree with him.

Just then a bubbling began at the back of this strange thing (which was evidently propelled by a screw), and it began to move. We had only just time to seize hold of the upper part, which rose about seven feet out of the water, and happily its speed was not great.

"As long as it sails horizontally," muttered Ned Land, "I do not mind; but, if it takes a fancy to dive, I would not give two straws for my life."

The Canadian might have said still less. It became really necessary to communicate with the beings, whatever they were, shut up inside the machine. I searched all over the outside for an aperture, a panel, or a manhole, to use a technical expression; but the lines of the iron rivets, solidly driven into the joints of the iron plates, were clear and uniform. Besides, the moon disappeared then, and left us in total darkness.

At last this long night passed. My indistinct remembrance prevents my describing all the impressions it made. I can only recall one circumstance. During some lulls of the wind and sea, I fancied I heard several times vague sounds, a sort of fugitive harmony produced by words of command. What was, then, the mystery of this submarine craft, of which the whole world vainly sought an explanation? What kind of beings existed in this strange boat? What mechanical agent caused its prodigious speed?

Daybreak appeared. The morning mists surrounded us, but they soon cleared off. I was about to examine the hull, which formed on deck a kind of horizontal platform, when I felt it gradually sinking.

"Oh! Confound it!" cried Ned Land, kicking the resounding plate. "Open, you inhospitable rascals!"

Happily the sinking movement ceased. Suddenly a noise, like iron works violently pushed aside, came from the interior of the boat. One iron plate was moved, a man appeared, uttered an odd cry, and disappeared immediately.

Some moments after, eight strong men, with masked faces, appeared noiselessly, and drew us down into their formidable machine.

# CHAPTER VIII

## MOBILIS IN MOBILI

This forcible abduction, so roughly carried out, was accomplished with the rapidity of lightning. I shivered all over. Whom had we to deal with? No doubt some new sort of pirates, who explored the sea in their own way. Hardly had the narrow panel closed upon me, when I was enveloped in darkness. My eyes, dazzled with the outer light, could distinguish nothing. I felt my naked feet cling to the rungs of an iron ladder. Ned Land and Conseil, firmly seized, followed me. At the bottom of the ladder, a door opened, and shut after us immediately with a bang.

We were alone. Where, I could not say, hardly imagine. All was black, and such a dense black that, after some minutes, my eyes had not been able to discern even the faintest glimmer.

Meanwhile, Ned Land, furious at these proceedings, gave free vent to his indignation.

"Confound it!" cried he. "Here are people who come up to the Scotch for hospitality. They only just miss being cannibals. I should not be surprised at it, but I declare that they shall not eat me without my protesting."

"Calm yourself, friend Ned, calm yourself," replied Conseil, quietly. "Do not cry out before you are hurt. We are not quite done for yet."

"Not quite," sharply replied the Canadian, "but pretty near, at all events. Things look black. Happily, my bowie knife I have still, and I can always see well enough to use it. The first of these pirates who lays a hand on me—"

"Do not excite yourself, Ned," I said to the harpooner, "and do not compromise us by useless violence. Who knows that they will not listen to us? Let us rather try to find out where we are."

I groped about. In five steps I came to an iron wall, made of plates bolted together. Then turning back I struck against a wooden table, near which were ranged several stools. The boards of this prison were concealed under a thick mat, which deadened the noise of the feet. The bare walls revealed no trace of window or door. Conseil, going around the reverse way, met me, and we went back to the middle of the cabin, which measured about twenty feet by ten. As to its height, Ned Land, in spite of his own great height, could not measure it.

Half an hour had already passed without our situation being bettered, when the dense darkness suddenly gave way to extreme light. Our prison was suddenly lighted, that is to say, it became filled with a luminous matter, so strong that I could not bear it at first. In its whiteness and intensity I recognized that electric light which played around the submarine boat like a magnificent phenomenon of phosphorescence. After shutting my eyes involuntarily, I opened them, and saw that this luminous agent came from a half globe, unpolished, placed in the roof of the cabin.

"At last one can see," cried Ned Land, who, knife in hand, stood on the defensive.

"Yes," said I; "but we are still in the dark about ourselves."

"Let master have patience," said the imperturbable Conseil.

The sudden lighting of the cabin enabled me to examine it minutely. It only contained a table and five stools. The invisible door might be hermetically sealed. No noise was heard. All seemed dead in the interior of this boat. Did it move, did it float on the surface of the ocean, or did it dive into its depths? I could not guess.

A noise of bolts was now heard, the door opened, and two men appeared.

One was short, very muscular, broad-shouldered, with robust limbs, strong head, an abundance of black hair, thick moustache, a quick penetrating look, and the vivacity which characterizes the population of southern France.

The second stranger merits a more detailed description. I made out his prevailing qualities directly: self-confidence—because his head was well set on his shoulders, and his black eyes looked around with cold assurance; calmness—for his skin, rather pale, showed his coolness of blood; energy—evinced by the rapid contraction of his lofty brows; and courage—because his deep breathing denoted great power of lungs.

Whether this person was thirty-five or fifty years of age, I could not say. He was tall, had a large forehead, straight nose, a clearly cut mouth, beautiful teeth, with fine taper hands, indicative of a highly nervous temperament. This man was certainly the most admirable specimen I had ever met. One particular feature was his eyes, rather far from each other, and which could take in nearly a quarter of the horizon at once.

This faculty—I verified it later—gave him a range of vision far superior to Ned Land's. When this stranger fixed upon an object, his eyebrows met, his large eyelids closed around so as to contract the range of his vision, and he looked as if he magnified the objects lessened by distance, as if he pierced those sheets of water so opaque to our eyes, and as if he read the very depths of the seas.

The two strangers, with caps made from the fur of the sea otter, and shod with sea boots of seal's skin, were dressed in clothes of a particular texture, which allowed free movement of the limbs. The taller of the two, evidently the chief on board, examined us with great attention, without saying a word; then, turning to his companion, talked with him in an unknown tongue. It was a sonorous, harmonious, and flexible dialect, the vowels seeming to admit of very varied accentuation.

The other replied by a shake of the head, and added two or three perfectly incomprehensible words. Then he seemed to question me by a look.

I replied in good French that I did not know his language; but he seemed not to understand me, and my situation became more embarrassing.

"If master were to tell our story," said Conseil, "perhaps these gentlemen may understand some words."

I began to tell our adventures, articulating each syllable clearly, and without omitting one single detail. I announced our names and rank, introducing in person Professor Aronnax, his servant Conseil, and master Ned Land, the harpooner.

The man with the soft calm eyes listened to me quietly, even politely, and with extreme attention; but nothing in his countenance indicated that he had understood my story. When I finished, he said not a word.

There remained one resource, to speak English. Perhaps they would know this almost universal language. I knew it—as well as the German language—well enough to read it fluently, but not to speak it correctly. But, anyhow, we must make ourselves understood.

"Go on in your turn," I said to the harpooner; "speak your best Anglo-Saxon, and try to do better than I."

Ned did not beg off, and recommenced our story.

To his great disgust, the harpooner did not seem to have made himself more intelligible than I had. Our visitors did not stir. They evidently understood neither the language of England nor of France.

Very much embarrassed, after having vainly exhausted our speaking resources, I knew not what part to take, when Conseil said:

"If master will permit me, I will relate it in German."

But in spite of the elegant terms and good accent of the narrator, the German language had no success. At last, nonplussed, I tried to remember my first lessons, and to narrate our adventures in Latin, but with no better success. This last attempt being of no avail, the two strangers exchanged some words in their unknown language, and retired.

The door shut.

"It is an infamous shame," cried Ned Land, who broke out for the twentieth time. "We speak to those rogues in French, English, German, and Latin, and not one of them has the politeness to answer!"

"Calm yourself," I said to the impetuous Ned; "anger will do no good."

"But do you see, Professor," replied our irascible companion, "that we shall absolutely die of hunger in this iron cage?"

"Bah!" said Conseil, philosophically. "We can hold out some time yet."

"My friends," I said, "we must not despair. We have been worse off than this. Do me the favor to wait a little before forming an opinion upon the commander and crew of this boat."

"My opinion is formed," replied Ned Land, sharply. "They are rascals."

"Good! And from what country?"

"From the land of rogues!"

"My brave Ned, that country is not clearly indicated on the map of the world; but I admit that the nationality of the two strangers is hard to determine. Neither English, French, nor German, that is quite certain. However, I am inclined to think that the commander and his companion were born in low latitudes. There is southern blood in them. But I cannot decide by their appearance whether they are Spaniards, Turks, Arabians, or Indians. As to their language, it is quite incomprehensible."

"There is the disadvantage of not knowing all languages," said Conseil, "or the disadvantage of not having one universal language."

As he said these words, the door opened. A steward entered. He brought us clothes, coats and trousers, made of a stuff I did not know. I hastened to dress myself, and my companions followed my example. During that time, the steward—dumb, perhaps deaf—had arranged the table, and laid three plates.

"This is something like!" said Conseil.

"Bah!" said the angry harpooner. "What do you suppose they eat here? Tortoise liver, filleted shark, and beef steaks from seadogs."

"We shall see," said Conseil.

The dishes, of bell metal, were placed on the table, and we took our places. Undoubtedly we had to do with civilized people, and, had it not been for the electric light which flooded us, I could have fancied I was in the dining room of the Adelphi Hotel at Liverpool, or at the Grand Hotel in Paris. I must say, however, that there was neither bread nor wine. The water was fresh and clear, but it was water and did not suit Ned Land's taste. Among the dishes which were brought to us, I recognized several fish delicately dressed; but of some, although excellent, I could give no opinion, neither could I tell to what kingdom they belonged, whether animal or vegetable. As to the dinner-service, it was elegant, and in perfect taste. Each utensil—spoon, fork, knife, plate—had a letter engraved on it, with a motto above it, of which this is an exact facsimile:

MOBILIS IN MOBILI

N.

The letter *N* was no doubt the initial of the name of the enigmatical person who commanded at the bottom of the seas.

Ned and Conseil did not reflect much. They devoured the food, and I did likewise. I was, besides, reassured as to our fate; and it seemed evident that our hosts would not let us die of want.

However, everything has an end, everything passes away, even the hunger of people who have not eaten for fifteen hours. Our appetites satisfied, we felt overcome with sleep.

"Faith! I shall sleep well," said Conseil.

"So shall I," replied Ned Land.

My two companions stretched themselves on the cabin carpet, and were soon sound asleep. For my own part, too many thoughts crowded my brain, too many insoluble questions pressed upon me, too many fancies kept my eyes half open. Where were we? What strange power carried us on? I felt—or rather fancied I felt—the machine sinking down to the lowest beds of the sea. Dreadful nightmares beset me; I saw in these mysterious asylums a world of unknown animals, among which this submarine boat seemed to be of the same kind, living, moving, and formidable as they. Then my brain grew calmer, my imagination wandered into vague unconsciousness, and I soon fell into a deep sleep.

## CHAPTER IX

### NED LAND'S TEMPERS

How long we slept I do not know; but our sleep must have lasted long, for it rested us completely from our fatigues. I woke first. My companions had not moved, and were still stretched in their corner.

Hardly roused from my somewhat hard couch, I felt my brain freed, my mind clear. I then began an attentive examination of our cell. Nothing was changed inside. The prison was still a prison—the prisoners, prisoners. However, the steward, during our sleep, had cleared the table. I breathed with difficulty. The heavy air seemed to oppress my lungs. Although the cell was large, we had evidently consumed a great part of the oxygen that it contained. Indeed, each man consumes, in one hour, the oxygen contained in more than 176 pints of air, and this air, charged (as then) with a nearly equal quantity of carbonic acid, becomes unbreathable.

It became necessary to renew the atmosphere of our prison, and no doubt the whole in the submarine boat. That gave rise to a question in my mind. How would the commander of this floating dwelling-place proceed? Would he obtain air by chemical means, in getting by heat the oxygen contained in chlorate of potash, and in absorbing carbonic acid by caustic potash? Or—a more convenient, economical, and consequently more probable alternative—would he be satisfied to rise and take breath at the surface of the water, like a whale, and so renew for twenty-four hours the atmospheric provision?

In fact, I was already obliged to increase my respirations to eke out of this cell the little oxygen it contained, when suddenly I was refreshed by a current of pure air, and perfumed with saline emanations. It was an invigorating sea breeze, charged with iodine. I opened my mouth wide, and my lungs saturated themselves with fresh particles.

At the same time I felt the boat rolling. The iron-plated monster had evidently just risen to the surface of the ocean to breathe, after the fashion of whales. I found out from that the mode of ventilating the boat.

When I had inhaled this air freely, I sought the conduit pipe, which conveyed to us the beneficial whiff, and I was not long in finding it. Above the door was a ventilator, through which volumes of fresh air renewed the impoverished atmosphere of the cell.

I was making my observations, when Ned and Conseil awoke almost at the same time, under the influence of this reviving air. They rubbed their eyes, stretched themselves, and were on their feet in an instant.

"Did master sleep well?" asked Conseil, with his usual politeness.

"Very well, my brave boy. And you, Mr. Land?"

"Soundly, Professor. But, I don't know if I am right or not, there seems to be a sea breeze!"

A seaman could not be mistaken, and I told the Canadian all that had passed during his sleep.

"Good!" said he. "That accounts for those roarings we heard, when the supposed narwhal sighted the *Abraham Lincoln*."

"Quite so, Master Land; it was taking breath."

"Only, Mr. Aronnax, I have no idea what o'clock it is, unless it is dinnertime."

"Dinnertime! My good fellow? Say rather breakfast time, for we certainly have begun another day."

"So," said Conseil, "we have slept twenty-four hours?"

"That is my opinion."

"I will not contradict you," replied Ned Land. "But, dinner or breakfast, the steward will be welcome, whichever he brings."

"Master Land, we must conform to the rules on board, and I suppose our appetites are in advance of the dinner hour."

"That is just like you, friend Conseil," said Ned, impatiently. "You are never out of temper, always calm; you would return thanks before grace, and die of hunger rather than complain!"

Time was getting on, and we were fearfully hungry; and this time the steward did not appear. It was rather too long to leave us, if they really had good intentions toward us. Ned Land, tormented by the cravings of hunger, got still more angry; and, notwithstanding his promise, I dreaded an explosion when he found himself with one of the crew.

For two hours more Ned Land's temper increased; he cried, he shouted, but in vain. The walls were deaf. There was no sound to be heard in the boat; all was still as death. It did not move, for I should have felt the trembling motion of the hull under the influence of the screw. Plunged in the depths of the waters, it belonged no longer to earth: this silence was dreadful.

I felt terrified, Conseil was calm, Ned Land roared.

Just then a noise was heard outside. Steps sounded on the metal flags. The locks were turned, the door opened, and the steward appeared.

Before I could rush forward to stop him, the Canadian had thrown him down, and held him by the throat. The steward was choking under the grip of his powerful hand.

Conseil was already trying to unclasp the harpooner's hand from his half-suffocated victim, and I was going to fly to the rescue, when suddenly I was nailed to the spot by hearing these words in French:

"Be quiet, Master Land; and you, Professor, will you be so good as to listen to me?"

## CHAPTER X

### THE MAN OF THE SEAS

It was the commander of the vessel who thus spoke.

At these words, Ned Land rose suddenly. The steward, nearly strangled, tottered out on a sign from his master. But such was the power of the commander on board, that not a gesture betrayed the resentment which this man must have felt toward the Canadian. Conseil interested in spite of himself, I stupefied, awaited in silence the result of this scene.

The commander, leaning against the corner of a table with his arms folded, scanned us with profound attention. Did he hesitate to speak? Did he regret the words which he had just spoken in French? One might almost think so.

After some moments of silence, which not one of us dreamed of breaking, "Gentlemen," said he, in a calm and penetrating voice, "I speak French, English, German, and Latin equally well. I could, therefore, have answered you at our first interview, but I wished to know you first, then to reflect. The story told by each one, entirely agreeing in the main points, convinced me of your identity. I know now that chance has brought before me M. Pierre Aronnax, Professor of Natural History at the Museum of Paris, entrusted with a scientific mission abroad; Conseil, his servant; and Ned Land, of Canadian origin, harpooner on board the frigate *Abraham Lincoln* of the navy of the United States of America."

I bowed assent. It was not a question that the commander put to me. Therefore there was no answer to be made. This man expressed himself with perfect ease, without any accent. His sentences were well turned, his words clear, and his fluency of speech remarkable. Yet, I did not recognize in him a fellow countryman.

He continued the conversation in these terms:

"You have doubtless thought, sir, that I have delayed long in paying you this second visit. The reason is that, your identity recognized, I wished to weigh maturely what part to act toward you. I have hesitated much. Most annoying circumstances have brought you into the presence of a man who has broken all the ties of humanity. You have come to trouble my existence."

"Unintentionally!" said I.

"Unintentionally?" replied the stranger, raising his voice a little. "Was it unintentionally that the *Abraham Lincoln* pursued me all over the seas? Was it unintentionally that you took passage in this frigate? Was it unintentionally that your cannonballs rebounded off the plating of my vessel? Was it unintentionally that Mr. Ned Land struck me with his harpoon?"

I detected a restrained irritation in these words. But to these recriminations I had a very natural answer to make, and I made it.

"Sir," said I, "no doubt you are ignorant of the discussions which have taken place concerning you in America and Europe. You do not know that divers accidents, caused by collisions with your submarine machine, have excited public feeling in the two continents. I omit the theories without number by which it was sought to explain that of which you alone possess the secret. But you must understand that, in pursuing you over the high seas of the Pacific, the *Abraham Lincoln* believed itself to be chasing some powerful sea monster, of which it was necessary to rid the ocean at any price."

A half-smile curled the lips of the commander; then, in a calmer tone:

"M. Aronnax," he replied, "dare you affirm that your frigate would not as soon have pursued and cannonaded a submarine boat as a monster?"

This question embarrassed me, for certainly Captain Farragut might not have hesitated. He might have thought it his duty to destroy a contrivance of this kind, as he would a gigantic narwhal.

"You understand then, sir," continued the stranger, "that I have the right to treat you as enemies?"

I answered nothing, purposely. For what good would it be to discuss such a proposition, when force could destroy the best arguments?

"I have hesitated some time," continued the commander; "nothing obliged me to show you hospitality. If I chose to separate myself from you, I should have no interest in seeing you again; I could place you upon the deck of this vessel which has served you as a refuge, I could sink beneath the waters, and forget that you had ever existed. Would not that be my right?"

"It might be the right of a savage," I answered, "but not that of a civilized man."

"Professor," replied the commander, quickly, "I am not what you call a civilized man! I have done with society entirely, for reasons which I alone have the right of appreciating. I do not, therefore, obey its laws, and I desire you never to allude to them before me again!"

This was said plainly. A flash of anger and disdain kindled in the eyes of the Unknown, and I had a glimpse of a terrible past in the life of this man. Not only had he put himself beyond the pale of human laws, but he had made himself independent of them, free in the strictest acceptation of the word, quite beyond their reach! Who then would dare to pursue him at the bottom of the sea, when, on its surface, he defied all attempts made against him?

What vessel could resist the shock of his submarine monitor? What cuirass, however thick, could withstand the blows of his spur? No man could demand from him an account of his actions; God, if he believed in one—his conscience, if he had one—were the sole judges to whom he was answerable.

These reflections crossed my mind rapidly, while the stranger personage was silent, absorbed, and as if wrapped up in himself. I regarded him with fear mingled with interest, as, doubtless, Oedipus regarded the Sphinx.

After rather a long silence, the commander resumed the conversation.

"I have hesitated," said he, "but I have thought that my interest might be reconciled with that pity to which every human being has a right. You will remain on board my vessel, since fate has cast you there. You will be free; and, in exchange for this liberty, I shall only impose one single condition. Your word of honor to submit to it will suffice."

"Speak, sir," I answered. "I suppose this condition is one which a man of honor may accept?"

"Yes, sir; it is this: It is possible that certain events, unforeseen, may oblige me to consign you to your cabins for some hours or some days, as the case may be. As I desire never to use violence, I expect from you, more than all the others, a passive obedience. In thus acting, I take all the responsibility: I acquit you entirely, for I make it an impossibility for you to see what ought not to be seen. Do you accept this condition?"

Then things took place on board which, to say the least, were singular, and which ought not to be seen by people who were not placed beyond the pale of social laws. Among the surprises which the future was preparing for me, this might not be the least.

"We accept," I answered; "only I will ask your permission, sir, to address one question to you—one only."

"Speak, sir."

"You said that we should be free on board."

"Entirely."

"I ask you, then, what you mean by this liberty?"

"Just the liberty to go, to come, to see, to observe even all that passes here save under rare circumstances—the liberty, in short, which we enjoy ourselves, my companions and I."

It was evident that we did not understand one another.

"Pardon me, sir," I resumed, "but this liberty is only what every prisoner has of pacing his prison. It cannot suffice us."

"It must suffice you, however."

"What! We must renounce forever seeing our country, our friends, our relations again?"

"Yes, sir. But to renounce that unendurable worldly yoke which men believe to be liberty is not perhaps so painful as you think."

"Well," exclaimed Ned Land, "never will I give my word of honor not to try to escape."

"I did not ask you for your word of honor, Master Land," answered the commander, coldly.

"Sir," I replied, beginning to get angry in spite of myself, "you abuse your situation toward us; it is cruelty."

"No, sir, it is clemency. You are my prisoners of war. I keep you, when I could, by a word, plunge you into the depths of the ocean. You attacked me. You came to surprise a secret which no man in the world must penetrate—the secret of my whole existence. And you think that I am going to send you back to that world which must know me no more? Never! In retaining you, it is not you whom I guard—it is myself."

These words indicated a resolution taken on the part of the commander, against which no arguments would prevail.

"So, sir," I rejoined, "you give us simply the choice between life and death?"

"Simply."

"My friends," said I, "to a question thus put, there is nothing to answer. But no word of honor binds us to the master of this vessel."

"None, sir," answered the Unknown.

Then, in a gentler tone, he continued:

"Now, permit me to finish what I have to say to you. I know you, M. Aronnax. You and your companions will not, perhaps, have so much to complain of in the chance which has bound you to my fate. You will find among the books which are my favorite study the work which you have published on 'the depths of the sea.' I have often read it. You have carried out your work as far as terrestrial science permitted you. But you do not know all—you have not seen all. Let me tell you then, Professor, that you will not regret the time passed on board my vessel. You are going to visit the land of marvels."

These words of the commander had a great effect upon me. I cannot deny it. My weak point was touched; and I forgot, for a moment, that the contemplation of these sublime subjects was not worth the loss of liberty. Besides, I trusted to the future to decide this grave question. So I contented myself with saying:

"By what name ought I to address you?"

"Sir," replied the commander, "I am nothing to you but Captain Nemo; and you and your companions are nothing to me but the passengers of the *Nautilus*."

Captain Nemo called. A steward appeared. The captain gave him his orders in that strange language which I did not understand. Then, turning toward the Canadian and Conseil:

"A repast awaits you in your cabin," said he. "Be so good as to follow this man."

"And now, M. Aronnax, our breakfast is ready. Permit me to lead the way."

"I am at your service, Captain."

I followed Captain Nemo; and as soon as I had passed through the door, I found myself in a kind of passage lighted by electricity, similar to the waist of a ship. After we had proceeded a dozen yards, a second door opened before me.

I then entered a dining room, decorated and furnished in severe taste. High oaken sideboards, inlaid with ebony, stood at the two extremities of the room, and upon their shelves glittered china, porcelain, and glass of inestimable value. The plate on the table sparkled in the rays which the luminous ceiling shed around, while the light was tempered and softened by exquisite paintings.

In the center of the room was a table richly laid out. Captain Nemo indicated the place I was to occupy.

The breakfast consisted of a certain number of dishes, the contents of which were furnished by the sea alone; and I was ignorant of the nature and mode of preparation of some of them. I acknowledged that they were good, but they had a peculiar flavor, which I easily became accustomed to. These different aliments appeared to me to be rich in phosphorus, and I thought they must have a marine origin.

Captain Nemo looked at me. I asked him no questions, but he guessed my thoughts, and answered of his own accord the questions which I was burning to address to him.

"The greater part of these dishes are unknown to you," he said to me. "However, you may partake of them without fear. They are wholesome and nourishing. For a long time I have renounced the food of the earth, and I am never ill now. My crew, who are healthy, are fed on the same food."

"So," said I, "all these eatables are the produce of the sea?"

"Yes, Professor, the sea supplies all my wants. Sometimes I cast my nets in tow, and I draw them in ready to break. Sometimes I hunt in the midst of this element, which appears to be inaccessible to man, and quarry the game which dwells in my submarine forests. My flocks, like those of Neptune's old shepherds, graze fearlessly in the immense prairies of the ocean. I have a vast property there, which I cultivate myself, and which is always sown by the hand of the Creator of all things."

"I can understand perfectly, sir, that your nets furnish excellent fish for your table; I can understand also that you hunt aquatic game in your submarine forests; but I cannot understand at all how a particle of meat, no matter how small, can figure in your bill of fare."

"This, which you believe to be meat, Professor, is nothing else than fillet of turtle. Here are also some dolphins' livers, which you take to be ragout of pork. My cook is a clever fellow, who excels in dressing these various products of the ocean. Taste all these dishes. Here is a preserve of sea cucumber, which a Malay would declare to be unrivaled in the world; here is a cream, of which the milk has been furnished by the cetacea, and the sugar by the great fucus of the North Sea; and, lastly, permit me to offer you some preserve of anemones, which is equal to that of the most delicious fruits."

I tasted, more from curiosity than as a connoisseur, while Captain Nemo enchanted me with his extraordinary stories.

"You like the sea, Captain?"

"Yes; I love it! The sea is everything. It covers seven tenths of the terrestrial globe. Its breath is pure and healthy. It is an immense desert, where man is never lonely, for he feels life stirring on all sides. The sea is only the embodiment of a supernatural and wonderful existence. It is nothing but love and emotion; it is the 'Living Infinite,' as one of your poets has said. In fact, Professor, nature manifests herself in it by her three kingdoms—mineral, vegetable, and animal. The sea is the vast reservoir of nature. The globe began with sea, so to speak; and who knows if it will not end with it? In it is supreme tranquility. The sea does not belong to despots. Upon its surface men can still exercise unjust laws, fight, tear one another to pieces, and be carried away with terrestrial horrors. But at thirty feet below its level, their reign ceases, their influence is quenched, and their power disappears. Ah! Sir, live—live in the bosom of the waters! There only is independence! There I recognize no masters! There I am free!"

Captain Nemo suddenly became silent in the midst of this enthusiasm, by which he was quite carried away. For a few moments he paced up and down, much agitated. Then he became more calm, regained his accustomed coldness of expression, and turning toward me:

"Now, Professor," said he, "if you wish to go over the *Nautilus*, I am at your service."

Captain Nemo rose. I followed him. A double door, contrived at the back of the dining room, opened, and I entered a room equal in dimensions to that which I had just quitted.

It was a library. High pieces of furniture, of black violet ebony inlaid with brass, supported upon their wide shelves a great number of books uniformly bound. They followed the shape of the room, terminating at the lower part in huge divans, covered with brown leather, which were curved, to afford the greatest comfort.

Light movable desks, made to slide in and out at will, allowed one to rest one's book while reading. In the center stood an immense table, covered with pamphlets, among which were some newspapers, already of old date. The electric light flooded everything; it was shed from four unpolished globes half sunk in the volutes of the ceiling. I looked with real admiration at this room, so ingeniously fitted up, and I could scarcely believe my eyes.

"Captain Nemo," said I to my host, who had just thrown himself on one of the divans, "this is a library which would do honor to more than one of the continental palaces, and I am absolutely astounded when I consider that it can follow you to the bottom of the seas."

"Where could one find greater solitude or silence, Professor?" replied Captain Nemo. "Did your study in the Museum afford you such perfect quiet?"

"No, sir; and I must confess that it is a very poor one after yours. You must have six or seven thousand volumes here."

"Twelve thousand, M. Aronnax. These are the only ties which bind me to the earth. But I had done with the world on the day when my *Nautilus* plunged for the first time beneath the waters. That day I bought my last volumes, my last pamphlets, my last papers, and from that time I wish to think that men no longer think or write. These books, Professor, are at your service besides, and you can make use of them freely."

I thanked Captain Nemo, and went up to the shelves of the library. Works on science, morals, and literature abounded in every language; but I did not see one single work on political economy; that subject appeared to be strictly proscribed. Strange to say, all these books were irregularly arranged, in whatever language they were written; and this medley proved that the captain of the *Nautilus* must have read indiscriminately the books which he took up by chance.

"Sir," said I to the captain, "I thank you for having placed this library at my disposal. It contains treasures of science, and I shall profit by them."

"This room is not only a library," said Captain Nemo, "it is also a smoking room."

"A smoking room!" I cried. "Then one may smoke on board?"

"Certainly."

"Then, sir, I am forced to believe that you have kept up a communication with Havana."

"Not any," answered the captain. "Accept this cigar, M. Aronnax; and, though it does not come from Havana, you will be pleased with it, if you are a connoisseur."

I took the cigar which was offered me; its shape recalled the London ones, but it seemed to be made of leaves of gold. I lighted it at a little brazier, which was supported upon an elegant bronze stem, and drew the first whiffs with the delight of a lover of smoking who has not smoked for two days.

"It is excellent, but it is not tobacco."

"No!" answered the captain. "This tobacco comes neither from Havana nor from the East. It is a kind of seaweed, rich in nicotine, with which the sea provides me, but somewhat sparingly."

At that moment Captain Nemo opened a door which stood opposite to that by which I had entered the library, and I passed into an immense drawing room splendidly lighted.

It was a vast, four-sided room, thirty feet long, eighteen wide, and fifteen high. A luminous ceiling, decorated with light arabesques, shed a soft clear light over all the marvels accumulated in this museum. For it was in fact a museum, in which an intelligent and prodigal hand had gathered all the treasures of nature and art, with the artistic confusion which distinguishes a painter's studio.

Thirty first-rate pictures, uniformly framed, separated by bright drapery, ornamented the walls, which were hung with tapestry of severe design. I saw works of great value, the greater part of which I had admired in the special collections of Europe, and in the exhibitions of paintings. The several schools of the old masters were represented by a Madonna of Raphael, a Virgin of Leonardo da Vinci, a nymph of Corregio, a woman of Titian, an Adoration of Veronese, an Assumption of Murillo, a portrait of Holbein, a monk of Velasquez, a martyr of Ribera, a fair of Rubens, two Flemish landscapes of Teniers, three little "genre" pictures of Gerard Dow, Metsu, and Paul Potter, two specimens of Gericault and Prudhon, and some sea pieces of Backhuysen and Vernet. Among the works of modern painters were pictures with the signatures of Delacroix, Ingres, Decamps, Troyon, Meissonier, Daubigny, etc.; and some admirable statues in marble and bronze, after the finest antique models, stood upon pedestals in the corners of this magnificent museum. Amazement, as the captain of the *Nautilus* had predicted, had already begun to take possession of me.

"Professor," said this strange man, "you must excuse the unceremonious way in which I receive you, and the disorder of this room."

"Sir," I answered, "without seeking to know who you are, I recognize in you an artist."

"An amateur, nothing more, sir. Formerly I loved to collect these beautiful works created by the hand of man. I sought them greedily, and ferreted them out indefatigably, and I have been able to bring together some objects of great value. These are my last souvenirs of that world which is dead to me. In my eyes, your modern artists are already old; they have two or three thousand years of existence; I confound them in my own mind. Masters have no age."

"And these musicians?" said I, pointing out some works of Weber, Rossini, Mozart, Beethoven, Haydn, Meyerbeer, Herold, Wagner, Auber, Gounod, and a number of others, scattered over a large model piano-organ which occupied one of the panels of the drawing room.

"These musicians," replied Captain Nemo, "are the contemporaries of Orpheus; for in the memory of the dead all chronological differences are effaced; and I am dead, Professor; as much dead as those of your friends who are sleeping six feet under the earth!"

Captain Nemo was silent, and seemed lost in a profound reverie. I contemplated him with deep interest, analyzing in silence the strange expression of his countenance. Leaning on his elbow against an angle of a costly mosaic table, he no longer saw me— he had forgotten my presence.

I did not disturb this reverie, and continued my observation of the curiosities which enriched this drawing room.

Under elegant glass cases, fixed by copper rivets, were classed and labeled the most precious productions of the sea which had ever been presented to the eye of a naturalist. My delight as a professor may be conceived.

The division containing the zoophytes presented the most curious specimens of the two groups of polypi and echinodermes. In the first group, the tubipores, were gorgones arranged like a fan, soft sponges of Syria, ises of the Moluccas, pennatules, an admirable virgularia of the Norwegian seas, variegated unbellulairae, alcyonariae, a whole series of madrepores, which my master Milne Edwards has so cleverly classified, among which I remarked some wonderful flabellinae oculinae of the island of Bourbon, the "Neptune's car" of the Antilles, superb varieties of corals—in short, every species of those curious polypi of which entire islands are formed, which will one day become continents. Of the echinodermes, remarkable for their coating of spines, asteri, sea stars, pantacrinae, comatules, asterophons, echini, holothuri, etc., represented individually a complete collection of this group.

A somewhat nervous conchyliologist would certainly have fainted before other more numerous cases, in which were classified the specimens of mollusks. It was a collection of inestimable value, which time fails me to describe minutely. Among these specimens I will quote from memory only the elegant royal hammer-fish of the Indian Ocean, whose regular white spots stood out brightly on a red and brown ground, an imperial spondyle, bright-colored, bristling with spines, a rare specimen in the European museums (I estimated its value at not less than £1000); a common hammer-fish of the seas of New Holland, which is only procured with difficulty; exotic buccardia of Senegal; fragile white bivalve shells, which a breath might shatter like a soap-bubble; several varieties of the aspirgillum of Java, a kind of calcareous tube, edged with leafy folds, and much debated by amateurs; a whole series of trochi, some a greenish-yellow, found in the American seas, others a reddish-brown, natives of Australian waters; others from the Gulf of Mexico, remarkable for their imbricated shell; stellari found in the Southern Seas; and last, the rarest of all, the magnificent spur of New Zealand; and every description of delicate and fragile shells to which science has given appropriate names.

Apart, in separate compartments, were spread out chaplets of pearls of the greatest beauty, which reflected the electric light in little sparks of fire; pink pearls, torn from the pinna-marina of the Red Sea; green pearls of the haliotyde iris; yellow, blue and black pearls, the curious productions of the divers mollusks of every ocean, and certain mussels of the water-courses of the North; lastly, several specimens of inestimable value which had been gathered from the rarest pintadines. Some of these pearls were larger than a pigeon's egg, and were worth as much, and more than that which the traveler Tavernier sold to the Shah of Persia for three millions, and surpassed the one in the possession of the Imaum of Muscat, which I had believed to be unrivaled in the world.

Therefore, to estimate the value of this collection was simply impossible. Captain Nemo must have expended millions in the acquirement of these various specimens, and I was thinking what source he could have drawn from, to have been able thus to gratify his fancy for collecting, when I was interrupted by these words:

"You are examining my shells, Professor? Unquestionably they must be interesting to a naturalist; but for me they have a far greater charm, for I have collected them all with my own hand, and there is not a sea on the face of the globe which has escaped my researches."

"I can understand, Captain, the delight of wandering about in the midst of such riches. You are one of those who have collected their treasures themselves. No museum in Europe possesses such a collection of the produce of the ocean. But if I exhaust all my admiration upon it, I shall have none left for the vessel which carries it. I do not wish to pry into your secrets: but I must confess that this *Nautilus*, with the motive power which is confined in it, the contrivances which enable it to be worked, the powerful agent which propels it, all excite my curiosity to the highest pitch. I see suspended on the walls of this room instruments of whose use I am ignorant."

"You will find these same instruments in my own room, Professor, where I shall have much pleasure in explaining their use to you. But first come and inspect the cabin which is set apart for your own use. You must see how you will be accommodated on board the *Nautilus*."

I followed Captain Nemo who, by one of the doors opening from each panel of the drawing room, regained the waist. He conducted me toward the bow, and there I found, not a cabin, but an elegant room, with a bed, dressing table, and several other pieces of excellent furniture.

I could only thank my host.

"Your room adjoins mine," said he, opening a door, "and mine opens into the drawing room that we have just quitted."

I entered the captain's room: it had a severe, almost a monkish aspect. A small iron bedstead, a table, some articles for the toilet; the whole lighted by a skylight. No comforts, the strictest necessaries only.

Captain Nemo pointed to a seat.

"Be so good as to sit down," he said. I seated myself, and he began thus:

## CHAPTER XI

### ALL BY ELECTRICITY

**66** Sir," said Captain Nemo, showing me the instruments hanging on the walls of his room, "here are the contrivances required for the navigation of the *Nautilus*. Here, as in the drawing room, I have them always under my eyes, and they indicate my position and exact direction in the middle of the ocean. Some are known to you, such as the thermometer, which gives the internal temperature of the *Nautilus*; the barometer, which indicates the weight of the air and foretells the changes of the weather; the hygrometer, which marks the dryness of the atmosphere; the storm-glass, the contents of which, by decomposing, announce the approach of tempests; the compass, which guides my course; the sextant, which shows the latitude by the altitude of the sun; chronometers, by which I calculate the longitude; and glasses for day and night, which I use to examine the points of the horizon, when the *Nautilus* rises to the surface of the waves."

"These are the usual nautical instruments," I replied, "and I know the use of them. But these others, no doubt, answer to the particular requirements of the *Nautilus*. This dial with movable needle is a manometer, is it not?"

"It is actually a manometer. But by communication with the water, whose external pressure it indicates, it gives our depth at the same time."

"And these other instruments, the use of which I cannot guess?"

"Here, Professor, I ought to give you some explanations. Will you be kind enough to listen to me?"

He was silent for a few moments, then he said:

"There is a powerful agent, obedient, rapid, easy, which conforms to every use, and reigns supreme on board my vessel. Everything is done by means of it. It lights, warms it, and is the soul of my mechanical apparatus. This agent is electricity."

"Electricity?" I cried in surprise.

"Yes, sir."

"Nevertheless, Captain, you possess an extreme rapidity of movement, which does not agree well with the power of electricity. Until now, its dynamic force has remained under restraint, and has only been able to produce a small amount of power."

"Professor," said Captain Nemo, "my electricity is not everybody's. You know what seawater is composed of. In a thousand grams are found ninety-six and a half percent of water, and about two and two-thirds percent of chloride of sodium; then, in a smaller quantity, chlorides of magnesium and of potassium, bromide of magnesium, sulfate of magnesia, sulfate and carbonate of lime. You see, then, that chloride of sodium forms a large part of it. So it is this sodium that I extract from the seawater, and of which I compose my ingredients. I owe all to the ocean; it produces electricity, and electricity gives heat, light, motion, and, in a word, life to the *Nautilus*."

"But not the air you breathe?"

"Oh! I could manufacture the air necessary for my consumption, but it is useless, because I go up to the surface of the water when I please. However, if electricity does not furnish me with air to breathe, it works at least the powerful pumps that are stored in spacious reservoirs, and which enable me to prolong at need, and as long as I will, my stay in the depths of the sea. It gives a uniform and unintermittent light, which the sun does not. Now look at this clock; it is electrical, and goes with a regularity that defies the best chronometers. I have divided it into twenty-four hours, like the Italian clocks, because for me there is neither night nor day, sun nor moon, but only that factitious light that I take with me to the bottom of the sea. Look! Just now, it is ten o'clock in the morning."

"Exactly."

"Another application of electricity. This dial hanging in front of us indicates the speed of the *Nautilus*. An electric thread puts it in communication with the screw, and the needle indicates the real speed. Look! Now we are spinning along with a uniform speed of fifteen miles an hour."

"It is marvelous! And I see, Captain, you were right to make use of this agent that takes the place of wind, water, and steam."

"We have not finished, M. Aronnax," said Captain Nemo, rising. "If you will allow me, we will examine the stern of the *Nautilus*."

Really, I knew already the anterior part of this submarine boat, of which this is the exact division, starting from the ship's head: the dining room, five yards long, separated from the library by a watertight partition; the library, five yards long; the large drawing room, ten yards long, separated from the captain's room by a second watertight partition; the said room, five yards in length; mine, two and a half yards; and, lastly a reservoir of air, seven and a half yards, that extended to the bows. Total length thirty-five yards, or one hundred and five feet. The partitions had doors that were shut hermetically by means of India rubber instruments, and they ensured the safety of the *Nautilus* in case of a leak.

I followed Captain Nemo through the waist, and arrived at the center of the boat. There was a sort of well that opened between two partitions. An iron ladder, fastened with an iron hook to the partition, led to the upper end. I asked the captain what the ladder was used for.

"It leads to the small boat," he said.

"What! Have you a boat?" I exclaimed, in surprise.

"Of course; an excellent vessel, light and insubmersible, that serves either as a fishing or as a pleasure boat."

"But then, when you wish to embark, you are obliged to come to the surface of the water?"

"Not at all. This boat is attached to the upper part of the hull of the *Nautilus*, and occupies a cavity made for it. It is decked, quite watertight, and held together by solid bolts. This ladder leads to a man-hole made in the hull of the *Nautilus*, that corresponds with a similar hole made in the side of the boat. By this double opening I get into the small vessel. They shut the one belonging to the *Nautilus*; I shut the other by means of screw pressure. I undo the bolts, and the little boat goes up to the surface of the sea with prodigious rapidity. I then open the panel of the bridge, carefully shut till then; I mast it, hoist my sail, take my oars, and I'm off."

"But how do you get back on board?"

"I do not come back, M. Aronnax; the *Nautilus* comes to me."

"By your orders?"

"By my orders. An electric thread connects us. I telegraph to it, and that is enough."

"Really," I said, astonished at these marvels, "nothing can be more simple."

After having passed by the cage of the staircase that led to the platform, I saw a cabin six feet long, in which Conseil and Ned Land, enchanted with their repast, were devouring it with avidity. Then a door opened into a kitchen nine feet long, situated between the large storerooms. There electricity, better than gas itself, did all the cooking. The streams under the furnaces gave out to the sponges of platina a heat which was regularly kept up and distributed. They also heated a distilling apparatus, which, by evaporation, furnished excellent drinkable water. Near this kitchen was a bathroom comfortably furnished, with hot and cold water taps.

Next to the kitchen was the berth room of the vessel, sixteen feet long. But the door was shut, and I could not see the management of it, which might have given me an idea of the number of men employed on board the *Nautilus*.

At the bottom was a fourth partition that separated this office from the engine room. A door opened, and I found myself in the compartment where Captain Nemo—certainly an engineer of a very high order—had arranged his locomotive machinery. This engine room, clearly lighted, did not measure less than sixty-five feet in length. It was divided into two parts; the first contained the materials for producing electricity, and the second the machinery that connected it with the screw. I examined it with great interest, in order to understand the machinery of the *Nautilus*.

"You see," said the captain, "I use Bunsen's contrivances, not Ruhmkorff's. Those would not have been powerful enough. Bunsen's are fewer in number, but strong and large, which experience proves to be the best. The electricity produced passes forward, where it works, by electromagnets of great size, on a system of levers and cogwheels that transmit the movement to the axle of the screw. This one, the diameter of which is nineteen feet, and the thread twenty-three feet, performs about 120 revolutions in a second."

"And you get then?"

"A speed of fifty miles an hour."

"I have seen the *Nautilus* maneuver before the *Abraham Lincoln*, and I have my own ideas as to its speed. But this is not enough. We must see where we go. We must be able to direct it to the right, to the left, above, below. How do you get to the great depths, where you find an increasing resistance, which is rated by hundreds of atmospheres? How do you return to the surface of the ocean? And how do you maintain yourselves in the requisite medium? Am I asking too much?"

"Not at all, Professor," replied the captain, with some hesitation; "since you may never leave this submarine boat. Come into the saloon, it is our usual study, and there you will learn all you want to know about the *Nautilus*."

# CHAPTER XII

## SOME FIGURES

A moment after we were seated on a divan in the saloon smoking. The captain showed me a sketch that gave the plan, section, and elevation of the *Nautilus*. Then he began his description in these words:

"Here, M. Aronnax, are the several dimensions of the boat you are in. It is an elongated cylinder with conical ends. It is very like a cigar in shape, a shape already adopted in London in several constructions of the same sort. The length of this cylinder, from stem to stern, is exactly 232 feet, and its maximum breadth is twenty-six feet. It is not built quite like your long-voyage steamers, but its lines are sufficiently long, and its curves prolonged enough, to allow the water to slide off easily, and oppose no obstacle to its passage. These two dimensions enable you to obtain by a simple calculation the surface and cubic contents of the *Nautilus*. Its area measures 6,032 feet; and its contents about 1,500 cubic yards; that is to say, when completely immersed it displaces 50,000 feet of water, or weighs 1,500 tons.

"When I made the plans for this submarine vessel, I meant that nine-tenths should be submerged: consequently it ought only to displace nine-tenths of its bulk, that is to say, only to weigh that number of tons. I ought not, therefore, to have exceeded that weight, constructing it on the aforesaid dimensions.

"The *Nautilus* is composed of two hulls, one inside, the other outside, joined by T-shaped irons, which render it very strong. Indeed, owing to this cellular arrangement it resists like a block, as if it were solid. Its sides cannot yield; it coheres spontaneously, and not by the closeness of its rivets; and its perfect union of the materials enables it to defy the roughest seas.

"These two hulls are composed of steel plates, whose density is from 0.7 to 0.8 that of water. The first is not less than two inches and a half thick and weighs 394 tons. The second envelope, the keel, twenty inches high and ten thick, weighs only sixty-two tons. The engine, the ballast, the several accessories and apparatus appendages, the partitions and bulkheads, weigh 961.62 tons. Do you follow all this?"

"I do."

"Then, when the *Nautilus* is afloat under these circumstances, one-tenth is out of the water. Now, if I have made reservoirs of a size equal to this tenth, or capable of holding 150 tons, and if I fill them with water, the boat, weighing then 1,507 tons, will be completely immersed. That would happen, Professor. These reservoirs are in the lower part of the *Nautilus*. I turn on taps and they fill, and the vessel sinks that had just been level with the surface."

"Well, Captain, but now we come to the real difficulty. I can understand your rising to the surface; but, diving below the surface, does not your submarine contrivance encounter a pressure, and consequently undergo an upward thrust of one atmosphere for every thirty feet of water, just about fifteen pounds per square inch?"

"Just so, sir."

"Then, unless you quite fill the *Nautilus*, I do not see how you can draw it down to those depths."

"Professor, you must not confound statics with dynamics or you will be exposed to grave errors. There is very little labor spent in attaining the lower regions of the ocean, for all bodies have a tendency to sink. When I wanted to find out the necessary increase of weight required to sink the *Nautilus*, I had only to calculate the reduction of volume that seawater acquires according to the depth."

"That is evident."

"Now, if water is not absolutely incompressible, it is at least capable of very slight compression. Indeed, after the most recent calculations this reduction is only 0.000436 of an atmosphere for each thirty feet of depth. If we want to sink 3,000 feet, I should keep account of the reduction of bulk under a pressure equal to that of a column of water of a thousand feet. The calculation is easily verified. Now, I have supplementary reservoirs capable of holding a hundred tons. Therefore I can sink to a considerable depth. When I wish to rise to the level of the sea, I only let off the water, and empty all the reservoirs if I want the *Nautilus* to emerge from the tenth part of her total capacity."

I had nothing to object to these reasonings.

"I admit your calculations, Captain," I replied; "I should be wrong to dispute them since daily experience confirms them; but I foresee a real difficulty in the way."

"What, sir?"

"When you are about 1,000 feet deep, the walls of the *Nautilus* bear a pressure of 100 atmospheres. If, then, just now you were to empty the supplementary reservoirs, to lighten the vessel, and to go up to the surface, the pumps must overcome the pressure of 100 atmospheres, which is 1,500 pounds per square inch. From that a power—"

"That electricity alone can give," said the captain, hastily. "I repeat, sir, that the dynamic power of my engines is almost infinite. The pumps of the *Nautilus* have an enormous power, as you must have observed when their jets of water burst like a torrent upon the *Abraham Lincoln*. Besides, I use subsidiary reservoirs only to attain a mean depth of 750 to 1,000 fathoms, and that with a view of managing my machines. Also, when I have a mind to visit the depths of the ocean five or six miles below the surface, I make use of slower but not less infallible means."

"What are they, Captain?"

"That involves my telling you how the *Nautilus* is worked."

"I am impatient to learn."

"To steer this boat to starboard or port, to turn, in a word, following a horizontal plan, I use an ordinary rudder fixed on the back of the stern-post, and with one wheel and some tackle to steer by. But I can also make the *Nautilus* rise and sink, and sink and rise, by a vertical movement by means of two inclined planes fastened to its sides, opposite the center of flotation, planes that move in every direction, and that are worked by powerful levers from the interior. If the planes are kept parallel with the boat, it moves horizontally. If slanted, the *Nautilus*, according to this inclination, and under the influence of the screw, either sinks diagonally or rises diagonally as it suits me. And even if I wish to rise more quickly to the surface, I ship the screw, and the pressure of the water causes the *Nautilus* to rise vertically like a balloon filled with hydrogen."

"Bravo, Captain! But how can the steersman follow the route in the middle of the waters?"

"The steersman is placed in a glazed box, that is raised about the hull of the *Nautilus*, and furnished with lenses."

"Are these lenses capable of resisting such pressure?"

"Perfectly. Glass, which breaks at a blow, is, nevertheless, capable of offering considerable resistance. During some experiments of fishing by electric light in 1864 in the Northern Seas, we saw plates less than a third of an inch thick resist a pressure of sixteen atmospheres. Now, the glass that I use is not less than thirty times thicker."

"Granted. But, after all, in order to see, the light must exceed the darkness, and in the midst of the darkness in the water, how can you see?"

"Behind the steersman's cage is placed a powerful electric reflector, the rays from which light up the sea for half a mile in front."

"Ah! Bravo, bravo, Captain! Now I can account for this phosphorescence in the supposed narwhal that puzzled us so. I now ask you if the boarding of the *Nautilus* and of the *Scotia*, that has made such a noise, has been the result of a chance rencontre?"

"Quite accidental, sir. I was sailing only one fathom below the surface of the water when the shock came. It had no bad result."

"None, sir. But now, about your rencontre with the *Abraham Lincoln*?"

"Professor, I am sorry for one of the best vessels in the American navy; but they attacked me, and I was bound to defend myself. I contented myself, however, with putting the frigate *hors de combat*; she will not have any difficulty in getting repaired at the next port."

"Ah, Commander! Your *Nautilus* is certainly a marvelous boat."

"Yes, Professor; and I love it as if it were part of myself. If danger threatens one of your vessels on the ocean, the first impression is the feeling of an abyss above and below. On the *Nautilus* men's hearts never fail them. No defects to be afraid of, for the double shell is as firm as iron; no rigging to attend to; no sails for the wind to carry away; no boilers to burst; no fire to fear, for the vessel is made of iron, not of wood; no coal to run short, for electricity is the only mechanical agent; no collision to fear, for it alone swims in deep water; no tempest to brave, for when it dives below the water it reaches absolute tranquility. There, sir! That is the perfection of vessels! And if it is true that the engineer has more confidence in the vessel than the builder, and the builder than the captain himself, you understand the trust I repose in my *Nautilus*; for I am at once captain, builder, and engineer."

"But how could you construct this wonderful *Nautilus* in secret?"

"Each separate portion, M. Aronnax, was brought from different parts of the globe."

"But these parts had to be put together and arranged?"

"Professor, I had set up my workshops upon a desert island in the ocean. There my workmen, that is to say, the brave men that I instructed and educated, and myself have put together our *Nautilus*. Then, when the work was finished, fire destroyed all trace of our proceedings on this island, that I could have jumped over if I had liked."

"Then the cost of this vessel is great?"

"M. Aronnax, an iron vessel costs £145 per ton. Now the *Nautilus* weighed 1,500. It came therefore to £67,500, and £80,000 more for fitting it up, and about £200,000, with the works of art and the collections it contains."

"One last question, Captain Nemo."

"Ask it, Professor."

"You are rich?"

"Immensely rich, sir; and I could, without missing it, pay the national debt of France."

I stared at the singular person who spoke thus. Was he playing upon my credulity? The future would decide that.

# CHAPTER XIII

## THE BLACK RIVER

The portion of the terrestrial globe which is covered by water is estimated at upward of eighty millions of acres. This fluid mass comprises two billions two hundred and fifty millions of cubic miles, forming a spherical body of a diameter of sixty leagues, the weight of which would be three quintillions of tons. To comprehend the meaning of these figures, it is necessary to observe that a quintillion is to a billion as a billion is to unity; in other words, there are as many billions in a quintillion as there are units in a billion. This mass of fluid is equal to about the quantity of water which would be discharged by all the rivers of the earth in forty thousand years.

During the geological epochs the ocean originally prevailed everywhere. Then by degrees, in the Silurian period, the tops of the mountains began to appear, the islands emerged, then disappeared in partial deluges, reappeared, became settled, formed continents, till at length the earth became geographically arranged, as we see in the present day. The solid had wrested from the liquid thirty-seven million six hundred and fifty-seven square miles, equal to twelve billions nine hundred and sixty millions of acres.

The shape of continents allows us to divide the waters into five great portions: the Arctic or Frozen Ocean, the Antarctic, or Frozen Ocean, the Indian, the Atlantic, and the Pacific Oceans.

The Pacific Ocean extends from north to south between the two Polar Circles, and from east to west between Asia and America, over an extent of 145 degrees of longitude. It is the quietest of seas; its currents are broad and slow, it has medium tides, and abundant rain. Such was the ocean that my fate destined me first to travel over under these strange conditions.

"Sir," said Captain Nemo, "we will, if you please, take our bearings and fix the starting point of this voyage. It is a quarter to twelve; I will go up again to the surface."

The captain pressed an electric clock three times. The pumps began to drive the water from the tanks; the needle of the manometer marked by a different pressure the ascent of the *Nautilus*, then it stopped.

"We have arrived," said the captain.

I went to the central staircase which opened on to the platform, clambered up the iron steps, and found myself on the upper part of the *Nautilus*.

The platform was only three feet out of water. The front and back of the *Nautilus* was of that spindle-shape which caused it justly to be compared to a cigar. I noticed that its iron plates, slightly overlaying each other, resembled the shell which clothes the bodies of our large terrestrial reptiles. It explained to me how natural it was, in spite of all glasses, that this boat should have been taken for a marine animal.

Toward the middle of the platform the longboat, half buried in the hull of the vessel, formed a slight excrescence. Fore and aft rose two cages of medium height with inclined sides, and partly closed by thick lenticular glasses; one destined for the steersman who directed the *Nautilus*, the other containing a brilliant lantern to give light on the road.

The sea was beautiful, the sky pure. Scarcely could the long vehicle feel the broad undulations of the ocean. A light breeze from the east rippled the surface of the waters. The horizon, free from fog, made observation easy. Nothing was in sight. Not a quicksand, not an island. A vast desert.

Captain Nemo, by the help of his sextant, took the altitude of the sun, which ought also to give the latitude. He waited for some moments till its disk touched the horizon. While taking observations not a muscle moved, the instrument could not have been more motionless in a hand of marble.

"Twelve o'clock, sir," said he. "When you like——"

I cast a last look upon the sea, slightly yellowed by the Japanese coast, and descended to the saloon.

"And now, sir, I leave you to your studies," added the captain; "our course is E.N.E., our depth is twenty-six fathoms. Here are maps on a large scale by which you may follow it. The saloon is at your disposal, and, with your permission, I will retire." Captain Nemo bowed, and I remained alone, lost in thoughts all bearing on the commander of the *Nautilus*.

For a whole hour was I deep in these reflections, seeking to pierce this mystery so interesting to me. Then my eyes fell upon the vast planisphere spread upon the table, and I placed my finger on the very spot where the given latitude and longitude crossed.

The sea has its large rivers like the continents. They are special currents known by their temperature and their color. The most remarkable of these is known by the name of the Gulf Stream. Science has decided on the globe the direction of five principal currents: one in the North Atlantic, a second in the South, a third in the North Pacific, a fourth in the South, and a fifth in the southern Indian Ocean. It is even probable that a sixth current existed at one time or another in the northern Indian Ocean, when the Caspian and Aral Seas formed but one vast sheet of water.

At this point indicated on the planisphere one of these currents was rolling, the Kuro-Scivo of the Japanese, the Black River, which, leaving the Gulf of Bengal, where it is warmed by the perpendicular rays of a tropical sun, crosses the Straits of Malacca along the coast of Asia, turns into the North Pacific to the Aleutian Islands, carrying with it trunks of camphor trees and other indigenous productions, and edging the waves of the ocean with the pure indigo of its warm water. It was this current that the *Nautilus* was to follow. I followed it with my eye; saw it lose itself in the vastness of the Pacific, and felt myself drawn with it, when Ned Land and Conseil appeared at the door of the saloon.

My two brave companions remained petrified at the sight of the wonders spread before them.

"Where are we, where are we?" exclaimed the Canadian. "In the museum at Quebec?"

"My friends," I answered, making a sign for them to enter, "you are not in Canada, but on board the *Nautilus*, fifty yards below the level of the sea."

"But, M. Aronnax," said Ned Land, "can you tell me how many men there are on board? Ten, twenty, fifty, a hundred?"

"I cannot answer you, Mr. Land; it is better to abandon for a time all idea of seizing the *Nautilus* or escaping from it. This ship is a masterpiece of modern industry, and I should be sorry not to have seen it. Many people would accept the situation forced upon us, if only to move among such wonders. So be quiet and let us try and see what passes around us."

"See!" exclaimed the harpooner. "But we can see nothing in this iron prison! We are walking—we are sailing—blindly."

Ned Land had scarcely pronounced these words when all was suddenly darkness. The luminous ceiling was gone, and so rapidly that my eyes received a painful impression.

We remained mute, not stirring, and not knowing what surprise awaited us, whether agreeable or disagreeable. A sliding noise was heard: one would have said that panels were working at the sides of the *Nautilus*.

"It is the end of the end!" said Ned Land.

Suddenly light broke at each side of the saloon, through two oblong openings. The liquid mass appeared vividly lit up by the electric gleam. Two crystal plates separated us from the sea. At first I trembled at the thought that this frail partition might break, but strong bands of copper bound them, giving an almost infinite power of resistance.

The sea was distinctly visible for a mile all around the *Nautilus*. What a spectacle! What pen can describe it? Who could paint the effects of the light through those transparent sheets of water, and the softness of the successive gradations from the lower to the superior strata of the ocean?

We know the transparency of the sea and that its clearness is far beyond that of rock-water. The mineral and organic substances which it holds in suspension heightens its transparency. In certain parts of the ocean at the Antilles, under seventy-five fathoms of water, can be seen with surprising clearness a bed of sand. The penetrating power of the solar rays does not seem to cease for a depth of one hundred and fifty fathoms. But in this middle fluid traveled over by the *Nautilus*, the electric brightness was produced even in the bosom of the waves. It was no longer luminous water, but liquid light.

On each side a window opened into this unexplored abyss. The obscurity of the saloon showed to advantage the brightness outside, and we looked out as if this pure crystal had been the glass of an immense aquarium.

"You wished to see, friend Ned; well, you see now."

"Curious! Curious!" muttered the Canadian, who, forgetting his ill temper, seemed to submit to some irresistible attraction. "And one would come farther than this to admire such a sight!"

"Ah!" thought I to myself. "I understand the life of this man; he has made a world apart for himself, in which he treasures all his greatest wonders."

For two whole hours an aquatic army escorted the *Nautilus*. During their games, their bounds, while rivaling each other in beauty, brightness, and velocity, I distinguished the green labre; the banded mullet, marked by a double line of black; the round-tailed goby, of a white color, with violet spots on the back; the Japanese scombrus, a beautiful mackerel of these seas, with a blue body and silvery head; the brilliant azurors, whose name alone defies description; some banded spares, with variegated fins of blue and yellow; the woodcocks of the seas, some specimens of which attain a yard in length; Japanese salamanders, spider lampreys, serpents six feet long, with eyes small and lively, and a huge mouth bristling with teeth; with many other species.

Our imagination was kept at its height, interjections followed quickly on each other. Ned named the fish, and Conseil classed them. I was in ecstasies with the vivacity of their movements and the beauty of their forms. Never had it been given to me to surprise these animals, alive and at liberty, in their natural element. I will not mention all the varieties which passed before my dazzled eyes, all the collection of the seas of China and Japan. These fish, more numerous than the birds of the air, came, attracted, no doubt, by the brilliant focus of the electric light.

Suddenly there was daylight in the saloon, the iron panels closed again, and the enchanting vision disappeared. But for a long time I dreamt on, till my eyes fell on the instruments hanging on the partition. The compass still showed the course to be E.N.E., the manometer indicated a pressure of five atmospheres, equivalent to a depth of twenty-five fathoms, and the electric log gave a speed of fifteen miles an hour. I expected Captain Nemo, but he did not appear. The clock marked the hour of five.

Ned Land and Conseil returned to their cabin, and I retired to my chamber. My dinner was ready. It was composed of turtle soup made of the most delicate hawksbills, of a surmullet served with puff paste (the liver of which, prepared by itself, was most delicious), and fillets of the emperor-holocanthus, the savor of which seemed to me superior even to salmon.

I passed the evening reading, writing, and thinking. Then sleep overpowered me, and I stretched myself on my couch of zostera, and slept profoundly, while the *Nautilus* was gliding rapidly through the current of the Black River.

## CHAPTER XIV

### A NOTE OF INVITATION

The next day was November 9. I awoke after a long sleep of twelve hours. Conseil came, according to custom, to know "how I passed the night," and to offer his services. He had left his friend the Canadian sleeping like a man who had never done anything else all his life. I let the worthy fellow chatter as he pleased, without caring to answer him. I was preoccupied by the absence of the captain during our sitting of the day before, and hoping to see him today.

As soon as I was dressed I went into the saloon. It was deserted. I plunged into the study of the shell treasures hidden behind the glasses.

The whole day passed without my being honored by a visit from Captain Nemo. The panels of the saloon did not open. Perhaps they did not wish us to tire of these beautiful things.

The course of the *Nautilus* was E.N.E., her speed twelve knots, the depth below the surface between twenty-five and thirty fathoms.

The next day, November 10, the same desertion, the same solitude. I did not see one of the ship's crew: Ned and Conseil spent the greater part of the day with me. They were astonished at the puzzling absence of the captain. Was this singular man ill? Had he altered his intentions with regard to us?

After all, as Conseil said, we enjoyed perfect liberty, we were delicately and abundantly fed. Our host kept to his terms of the treaty. We could not complain, and, indeed, the singularity of our fate reserved such wonderful compensation for us that we had no right to accuse it as yet.

That day I commenced the journal of these adventures which has enabled me to relate them with more scrupulous exactitude and minute detail.

November 11, early in the morning. The fresh air spreading over the interior of the *Nautilus* told me that we had come to the surface of the ocean to renew our supply of oxygen. I directed my steps to the central staircase, and mounted the platform.

It was six o'clock, the weather was cloudy, the sea gray, but calm. Scarcely a billow. Captain Nemo, whom I hoped to meet, would he be there? I saw no one but the steersman imprisoned in his glass cage. Seated upon the projection formed by the hull of the pinnace, I inhaled the salt breeze with delight.

By degrees the fog disappeared under the action of the sun's rays, the radiant orb rose from behind the eastern horizon. The sea flamed under its glance like a train of gunpowder. The clouds scattered in the heights were colored with lively tints of beautiful shades, and numerous "mare's tails," which betokened wind for that day. But what was wind to this *Nautilus*, which tempests could not frighten!

I was admiring this joyous rising of the sun, so gay, and so life-giving, when I heard steps approaching the platform. I was prepared to salute Captain Nemo, but it was his second (whom I had already seen on the captain's first visit) who appeared. He advanced on the platform, not seeming to see me. With his powerful glass to his eye, he scanned every point of the horizon with great attention. This examination over, he approached the panel and pronounced a sentence in exactly these terms. I have remembered it, for every morning it was repeated under exactly the same conditions. It was thus worded:

"*Nautron respoc lorni virch.*"

What it meant I could not say.

These words pronounced, the second descended. I thought that the *Nautilus* was about to return to its submarine navigation. I regained the panel and returned to my chamber.

Five days sped thus, without any change in our situation. Every morning I mounted the platform. The same phrase was pronounced by the same individual. But Captain Nemo did not appear.

I had made up my mind that I should never see him again, when, on November 16, on returning to my room with Ned and Conseil, I found upon my table a note addressed to me. I opened it impatiently. It was written in a bold, clear hand, the characters rather pointed, recalling the German type. The note was worded as follows:

November 16, 1867

To Professor Arronax, on board the *Nautilus*:
    Captain Nemo invites Professor Aronnax to a hunting-party, which will take place tomorrow morning in the forests of the island of Crespo. He hopes that nothing will prevent the Professor from being present, and he will with pleasure see him joined by his companions.

Captain Nemo, Commander of the *Nautilus*

"A hunt!" exclaimed Ned.

"And in the forests of the island of Crespo!" added Conseil.

"Oh! Then the gentleman is going on *terra firma*?" replied Ned Land.

"That seems to me to be clearly indicated," said I, reading the letter once more.

"Well, we must accept," said the Canadian. "But once more on dry ground, we shall know what to do. Indeed, I shall not be sorry to eat a piece of fresh venison."

Without seeking to reconcile what was contradictory between Captain Nemo's manifest aversion to islands and continents, and his invitation to hunt in a forest, I contented myself with replying:

"Let us first see where the island of Crespo is."

I consulted the planisphere, and in 32° 40' north latitude and 157° 50' west longitude, I found a small island, recognized in 1801 by Captain Crespo, and marked in the ancient Spanish maps as Rocca de la Plata, the meaning of which is "the Silver Rock." We were then about eighteen hundred miles from our starting point, and the course of the *Nautilus*, a little changed, was bringing it back toward the southeast.

I showed this little rock, lost in the midst of the North Pacific, to my companions.

"If Captain Nemo does sometimes go on dry ground," said I, "he at least chooses desert islands."

Ned Land shrugged his shoulders without speaking, and Conseil and he left me.

After supper, which was served by the steward, mute and impassive, I went to bed, not without some anxiety.

The next morning, November 17, on awakening, I felt that the *Nautilus* was perfectly still. I dressed quickly and entered the saloon.

Captain Nemo was there, waiting for me. He rose, bowed, and asked me if it was convenient for me to accompany him. As he made no allusion to his absence during the last eight days, I did not mention it, and simply answered that my companions and myself were ready to follow him.

We entered the dining room, where breakfast was served.

"M. Aronnax," said the captain, "pray, share my breakfast without ceremony; we will chat as we eat. For, though I promised you a walk in the forest, I did not undertake to find hotels there. So breakfast as a man who will most likely not have his dinner till very late."

I did honor to the repast. It was composed of several kinds of fish, and slices of sea cucumber, and different sorts of seaweed. Our drink consisted of pure water, to which the captain added some drops of a fermented liquor, extracted by the Kamschatcha method from a seaweed known under the name of Rhodomenia palmata. Captain Nemo ate at first without saying a word. Then he began:

"Sir, when I proposed to you to hunt in my submarine forest of Crespo, you evidently thought me mad. Sir, you should never judge lightly of any man."

"But Captain, believe me—"

"Be kind enough to listen, and you will then see whether you have any cause to accuse me of folly and contradiction."

"I listen."

"You know as well as I do, Professor, that man can live underwater, providing he carries with him a sufficient supply of breathable air. In submarine works, the workman, clad in an impervious dress, with his head in a metal helmet, receives air from above by means of forcing pumps and regulators."

"That is a diving apparatus," said I.

"Just so, but under these conditions the man is not at liberty; he is attached to the pump which sends him air through an India rubber tube, and if we were obliged to be thus held to the *Nautilus*, we could not go far."

"And the means of getting free?" I asked.

"It is to use the Rouquayrol apparatus, invented by two of your own countrymen, which I have brought to perfection for my own use, and which will allow you to risk yourself under these new physiological conditions without any organ whatever suffering. It consists of a reservoir of thick iron plates, in which I store the air under a pressure of fifty atmospheres. This reservoir is fixed on the back by means of braces, like a soldier's knapsack. Its upper part forms a box in which the air is kept by means of a bellows, and therefore cannot escape unless at its normal tension. In the Rouquayrol apparatus such as we use, two India rubber pipes leave this box and join a sort of tent which holds the nose and mouth; one is to introduce fresh air, the other to let out the foul, and the tongue closes one or the other according to the wants of the respirator. But I, in encountering great pressures at the bottom of the sea, was obliged to shut my head, like that of a diver in a ball of copper; and it is to this ball of copper that the two pipes, the inspirator and the expirator, open."

"Perfectly, Captain Nemo; but the air that you carry with you must soon be used; when it only contains fifteen percent of oxygen it is no longer fit to breathe."

"Right! But I told you, M. Aronnax, that the pumps of the *Nautilus* allow me to store the air under considerable pressure, and on those conditions the reservoir of the apparatus can furnish breathable air for nine or ten hours."

"I have no further objections to make," I answered. "I will only ask you one thing, Captain—how can you light your road at the bottom of the sea?"

"With the Ruhmkorff apparatus, M. Aronnax; one is carried on the back, the other is fastened to the waist. It is composed of a Bunsen pile, which I do not work with bichromate of potash, but with sodium. A wire is introduced which collects the electricity produced, and directs it toward a particularly made lantern. In this lantern is a spiral glass which contains a small quantity of carbonic gas. When the apparatus is at work this gas becomes luminous, giving out a white and continuous light. Thus provided, I can breathe and I can see."

"Captain Nemo, to all my objections you make such crushing answers that I dare no longer doubt. But, if I am forced to admit the Rouquayrol and Ruhmkorff apparatus, I must be allowed some reservations with regard to the gun I am to carry."

"But it is not a gun for powder," answered the captain.

"Then it is an air-gun."

"Doubtless! How would you have me manufacture gunpowder on board, without either saltpeter, sulfur, or charcoal?"

"Besides," I added, "to fire underwater in a medium eight hundred and fifty-five times denser than the air, we must conquer very considerable resistance."

"That would be no difficulty. There exist guns, according to Fulton, perfected in England by Philip Coles and Burley, in France by Furcy, and in Italy by Landi, which are furnished with a peculiar system of closing, which can fire under these conditions. But I repeat, having no powder, I use air under great pressure, which the pumps of the *Nautilus* furnish abundantly."

"But this air must be rapidly used?"

"Well, have I not my Rouquayrol reservoir, which can furnish it at need? A tap is all that is required. Besides, M. Aronnax, you must see yourself that, during our submarine hunt, we can spend but little air and but few balls."

"But it seems to me that in this twilight, and in the midst of this fluid, which is very dense compared with the atmosphere, shots could not go far, nor easily prove mortal."

"Sir, on the contrary, with this gun every blow is mortal; and, however lightly the animal is touched, it falls as if struck by a thunderbolt."

"Why?"

"Because the balls sent by this gun are not ordinary balls, but little cases of glass. These glass cases are covered with a case of steel, and weighted with a pellet of lead; they are real Leyden bottles, into which the electricity is forced to a very high tension. With the slightest shock they are discharged, and the animal, however strong it may be, falls dead. I must tell you that these cases are size number four, and that the charge for an ordinary gun would be ten."

"I will argue no longer," I replied, rising from the table. "I have nothing left me but to take my gun. At all events, I will go where you go."

Captain Nemo then led me aft; and in passing before Ned's and Conseil's cabin, I called my two companions, who followed promptly. We then came to a cell near the machinery room, in which we put on our walking dress.

# CHAPTER XV

## A WALK ON THE BOTTOM OF THE SEA

This cell was, to speak correctly, the arsenal and wardrobe of the *Nautilus*. A dozen diving apparatuses hung from the partition waiting our use.

Ned Land, on seeing them, showed evident repugnance to dress himself in one.

"But, my worthy Ned, the forests of the island of Crespo are nothing but submarine forests."

"Good!" said the disappointed harpooner, who saw his dreams of fresh meat fade away. "And you, M. Aronnax, are you going to dress yourself in those clothes?"

"There is no alternative, Master Ned."

"As you please, sir," replied the harpooner, shrugging his shoulders; "but, as for me, unless I am forced, I will never get into one."

"No one will force you, Master Ned," said Captain Nemo.

"Is Conseil going to risk it?" asked Ned.

"I follow my master wherever he goes," replied Conseil.

At the captain's call two of the ship's crew came to help us dress in these heavy and impervious clothes, made of India rubber without seam, and constructed expressly to resist considerable pressure. One would have thought it a suit of armor, both supple and resisting. This suit formed trousers and waistcoat. The trousers were finished off with thick boots, weighted with heavy leaden soles. The texture of the waistcoat was held together by bands of copper, which crossed the chest, protecting it from the great pressure of the water, and leaving the lungs free to act; the sleeves ended in gloves, which in no way restrained the movement of the hands. There was a vast difference noticeable between these consummate apparatuses and the old cork breastplates, jackets, and other contrivances in vogue during the eighteenth century.

Captain Nemo and one of his companions (a sort of Hercules, who must have possessed great strength), Conseil, and myself were soon enveloped in the dresses. There remained nothing more to be done but to enclose our heads in the metal box. But, before proceeding to this operation, I asked the captain's permission to examine the guns.

One of the *Nautilus* men gave me a simple gun, the butt end of which, made of steel, hollow in the center, was rather large. It served as a reservoir for compressed air, which a valve, worked by a spring, allowed to escape into a metal tube. A box of projectiles in a groove in the thickness of the butt end contained about twenty of these electric balls, which, by means of a spring, were forced into the barrel of the gun. As soon as one shot was fired, another was ready.

"Captain Nemo," said I, "this arm is perfect, and easily handled: I only ask to be allowed to try it. But how shall we gain the bottom of the sea?"

"At this moment, Professor, the *Nautilus* is stranded in five fathoms, and we have nothing to do but to start."

"But how shall we get off?"

"You shall see."

Captain Nemo thrust his head into the helmet, Conseil and I did the same, not without hearing an ironical "Good sport!" from the Canadian. The upper part of our dress terminated in a copper collar upon which was screwed the metal helmet. Three holes, protected by thick glass, allowed us to see in all directions, by simply turning our head in the interior of the headdress. As soon as it was in position, the Rouquayrol apparatus on our backs began to act; and, for my part, I could breathe with ease.

With the Ruhmkorff lamp hanging from my belt, and the gun in my hand, I was ready to set out. But to speak the truth, imprisoned in these heavy garments, and glued to the deck by my leaden soles, it was impossible for me to take a step.

But this state of things was provided for. I felt myself being pushed into a little room contiguous to the wardrobe room. My companions followed, towed along in the same way. I heard a watertight door, furnished with stopper plates, close upon us, and we were wrapped in profound darkness.

After some minutes, a loud hissing was heard. I felt the cold mount from my feet to my chest. Evidently from some part of the vessel they had, by means of a tap, given entrance to the water, which was invading us, and with which the room was soon filled. A second door cut in the side of the *Nautilus* then opened. We saw a faint light. In another instant our feet trod the bottom of the sea.

And now, how can I retrace the impression left upon me by that walk under the waters? Words are impotent to relate such wonders! Captain Nemo walked in front, his companion followed some steps behind. Conseil and I remained near each other, as if an exchange of words had been possible through our metallic cases. I no longer felt the weight of my clothing, or of my shoes, of my reservoir of air, or my thick helmet, in the midst of which my head rattled like an almond in its shell.

The light, which lit the soil thirty feet below the surface of the ocean, astonished me by its power. The solar rays shone through the watery mass easily, and dissipated all color, and I clearly distinguished objects at a distance of a hundred and fifty yards. Beyond that the tints darkened into fine gradations of ultramarine, and faded into vague obscurity. Truly this water which surrounded me was but another air denser than the terrestrial atmosphere, but almost as transparent. Above me was the calm surface of the sea. We were walking on fine, even sand, not wrinkled, as on a flat shore, which retains the impression of the billows. This dazzling carpet, really a reflector, repelled the rays of the sun with wonderful intensity, which accounted for the vibration which penetrated every atom of liquid. Shall I be believed when I say that, at the depth of thirty feet, I could see as if I was in broad daylight?

For a quarter of an hour I trod on this sand, sown with the impalpable dust of shells. The hull of the *Nautilus*, resembling a long shoal, disappeared by degrees; but its lantern, when darkness should overtake us in the waters, would help to guide us on board by its distinct rays.

Soon forms of objects outlined in the distance were discernible. I recognized magnificent rocks, hung with a tapestry of zoophytes of the most beautiful kind, and I was at first struck by the peculiar effect of this medium.

It was then ten in the morning; the rays of the sun struck the surface of the waves at rather an oblique angle, and at the touch of their light, decomposed by refraction as through a prism, flowers, rocks, plants, shells, and polypi were shaded at the edges by the seven solar colors. It was marvelous, a feast for the eyes, this complication of colored tints, a perfect kaleidoscope of green, yellow, orange, violet, indigo, and blue; in one word, the whole palette of an enthusiastic colorist! Why could I not communicate to Conseil the lively sensations which were mounting to my brain, and rival him in expressions of admiration? For aught I knew, Captain Nemo and his companion might be able to exchange thoughts by means of signs previously agreed upon. So, for want of better, I talked to myself; I declaimed in the copper box which covered my head, thereby expending more air in vain words than was perhaps wise.

Various kinds of isis, clusters of pure tuft-coral, prickly fungi, and anemones formed a brilliant garden of flowers, decked with their collarettes of blue tentacles, sea stars studding the sandy bottom. It was a real grief to me to crush under my feet the brilliant specimens of mollusks which strewed the ground by thousands, of hammerheads, donaciae (veritable bounding shells), of staircases, and red helmet-shells, angel-wings, and many others produced by this inexhaustible ocean. But we were bound to walk, so we went on, while above our heads waved medusae whose umbrellas of opal or rose-pink, escalloped with a band of blue, sheltered us from the rays of the sun and fiery pelagiae, which, in the darkness, would have strewn our path with phosphorescent light.

All these wonders I saw in the space of a quarter of a mile, scarcely stopping, and following Captain Nemo, who beckoned me on by signs. Soon the nature of the soil changed; to the sandy plain succeeded an extent of slimy mud which the Americans call "ooze," composed of equal parts of silicious and calcareous shells. We then traveled over a plain of seaweed of wild and luxuriant vegetation. This sward was of close texture, and soft to the feet, and rivaled the softest carpet woven by the hand of man. But while verdure was spread at our feet, it did not abandon our heads. A light network of marine plants, of that inexhaustible family of seaweeds of which more than two thousand kinds are known, grew on the surface of the water.

I noticed that the green plants kept nearer the top of the sea, while the red were at a greater depth, leaving to the black or brown the care of forming gardens and parterres in the remote beds of the ocean.

We had quitted the *Nautilus* about an hour and a half. It was near noon; I knew by the perpendicularity of the sun's rays, which were no longer refracted. The magical colors disappeared by degrees, and the shades of emerald and sapphire were effaced. We walked with a regular step, which rang upon the ground with astonishing intensity; the slightest noise was transmitted with a quickness to which the ear is unaccustomed on the earth; indeed, water is a better conductor of sound than air, in the ratio of four to one. At this period the earth sloped downward; the light took a uniform tint. We were at a depth of a hundred and five yards and twenty inches, undergoing a pressure of six atmospheres.

At this depth I could still see the rays of the sun, though feebly; to their intense brilliancy had succeeded a reddish twilight, the lowest state between day and night; but we could still see well enough; it was not necessary to resort to the Ruhmkorff apparatus as yet. At this moment Captain Nemo stopped; he waited till I joined him, and then pointed to an obscure mass, looming in the shadow, at a short distance.

"It is the forest of the island of Crespo," thought I; and I was not mistaken.

# CHAPTER XVI

## A SUBMARINE FOREST

We had at last arrived on the borders of this forest, doubtless one of the finest of Captain Nemo's immense domains. He looked upon it as his own, and considered he had the same right over it that the first men had in the first days of the world. And, indeed, who would have disputed with him the possession of this submarine property? What other hardier pioneer would come, hatchet in hand, to cut down the dark copses?

This forest was composed of large tree-plants; and the moment we penetrated under its vast arcades, I was struck by the singular position of their branches—a position I had not yet observed.

Not an herb which carpeted the ground, not a branch which clothed the trees, was either broken or bent, nor did they extend horizontally; all stretched up to the surface of the ocean. Not a filament, not a ribbon, however thin they might be, but kept as straight as a rod of iron. The fuci and lianas grew in rigid perpendicular lines, due to the density of the element which had produced them. Motionless yet, when bent to one side by the hand, they directly resumed their former position. Truly it was the region of perpendicularity!

I soon accustomed myself to this fantastic position, as well as to the comparative darkness which surrounded us. The soil of the forest seemed covered with sharp blocks, difficult to avoid. The submarine flora struck me as being very perfect, and richer even than it would have been in the arctic or tropical zones, where these productions are not so plentiful. But for some minutes I involuntarily confounded the genera, taking animals for plants; and who would not have been mistaken? The fauna and the flora are too closely allied in this submarine world.

These plants are self-propagated, and the principle of their existence is in the water, which upholds and nourishes them. The greater number, instead of leaves, shoot forth blades of capricious shapes, comprised within a scale of colors pink, carmine, green, olive, fawn, and brown.

"Curious anomaly, fantastic element!" said an ingenious naturalist, "In which the animal kingdom blossoms, and the vegetable does not!"

In about an hour Captain Nemo gave the signal to halt; I, for my part, was not sorry, and we stretched ourselves under an arbor of alariae, the long thin blades of which stood up like arrows.

This short rest seemed delicious to me; there was nothing wanting but the charm of conversation; but, impossible to speak, impossible to answer, I only put my great copper head to Conseil's. I saw the worthy fellow's eyes glistening with delight, and, to show his satisfaction, he shook himself in his breastplate of air, in the most comical way in the world.

After four hours of this walking, I was surprised not to find myself dreadfully hungry. How to account for this state of the stomach I could not tell. But instead I felt an insurmountable desire to sleep, which happens to all divers. And my eyes soon closed behind the thick glasses, and I fell into a heavy slumber, which the movement alone had prevented before. Captain Nemo and his robust companion, stretched in the clear crystal, set us the example.

How long I remained buried in this drowsiness I cannot judge, but, when I woke, the sun seemed sinking toward the horizon. Captain Nemo had already risen, and I was beginning to stretch my limbs, when an unexpected apparition brought me briskly to my feet.

A few steps off, a monstrous sea spider, about thirty-eight inches high, was watching me with squinting eyes, ready to spring upon me. Though my diver's dress was thick enough to defend me from the bite of this animal, I could not help shuddering with horror. Conseil and the sailor of the *Nautilus* awoke at this moment. Captain Nemo pointed out the hideous crustacean, which a blow from the butt end of the gun knocked over, and I saw the horrible claws of the monster writhe in terrible convulsions. This incident reminded me that other animals more to be feared might haunt these obscure depths, against whose attacks my diving dress would not protect me. I had never thought of it before, but I now resolved to be upon my guard. Indeed, I thought that this halt would mark the termination of our walk; but I was mistaken, for, instead of returning to the *Nautilus*, Captain Nemo continued his bold excursion. The ground was still on the incline, its declivity seemed to be getting greater, and to be leading us to greater depths. It must have been about three o'clock when we reached a narrow valley, between high perpendicular walls, situated about seventy-five fathoms deep. Thanks to the perfection of our apparatus, we were forty-five fathoms below the limit which nature seems to have imposed on man as to his submarine excursions.

I say seventy-five fathoms, though I had no instrument by which to judge the distance. But I knew that even in the clearest waters the solar rays could not penetrate further. And accordingly the darkness deepened. At ten paces not an object was visible. I was groping my way, when I suddenly saw a brilliant white light. Captain Nemo had just put his electric apparatus into use; his companion did the same, and Conseil and I followed their example. By turning a screw I established a communication between the wire and the spiral glass, and the sea, lit by our four lanterns, was illuminated for a circle of thirty-six yards.

As we walked I thought the light of our Ruhmkorff apparatus could not fail to draw some inhabitant from its dark couch. But if they did approach us, they at least kept at a respectful distance from the hunters. Several times I saw Captain Nemo stop, put his gun to his shoulder, and after some moments drop it and walk on. At last, after about four hours, this marvelous excursion came to an end. A wall of superb rocks, in an imposing mass, rose before us, a heap of gigantic blocks, an enormous, steep granite shore, forming dark grottos, but which presented no practicable slope; it was the prop of the island of Crespo. It was the earth! Captain Nemo stopped suddenly. A gesture of his brought us all to a halt; and, however desirous I might be to scale the wall, I was obliged to stop. Here ended Captain Nemo's domains. And he would not go beyond them. Further on was a portion of the globe he might not trample upon.

The return began. Captain Nemo had returned to the head of his little band, directing their course without hesitation. I thought we were not following the same road to return to the *Nautilus*. The new road was very steep, and consequently very painful. We approached the surface of the sea rapidly. But this return to the upper strata was not so sudden as to cause relief from the pressure too rapidly, which might have produced serious disorder in our organization, and brought on internal lesions, so fatal to divers. Very soon light reappeared and grew, and, the sun being low on the horizon, the refraction edged the different objects with a spectral ring. At ten yards and a half deep, we walked amid a shoal of little fish of all kinds, more numerous than the birds of the air, and also more agile; but no aquatic game worthy of a shot had as yet met our gaze, when at that moment I saw the captain shoulder his gun quickly, and follow a moving object into the shrubs. He fired; I heard a slight hissing, and a creature fell stunned at some distance from us. It was a magnificent sea otter, an enhydrus, the only exclusively marine quadruped. This otter was five feet long, and must have been very valuable. Its skin, chestnut-brown above and silvery underneath, would have made one of those beautiful furs so sought after in the Russian and Chinese markets: the fineness and the luster of its coat would certainly fetch £80. I admired this curious mammal, with its rounded head ornamented with short ears, its round eyes, and white whiskers like those of a cat, with webbed feet and nails, and tufted tail. This precious animal, hunted and tracked by fishermen, has now become very rare, and taken refuge chiefly in the northern parts of the Pacific, or probably its race would soon become extinct.

Captain Nemo's companion took the beast, threw it over his shoulder, and we continued our journey. For one hour a plain of sand lay stretched before us. Sometimes it rose to within two yards and some inches of the surface of the water. I then saw our image clearly reflected, drawn inversely, and above us appeared an identical group reflecting our movements and our actions; in a word, like us in every point, except that they walked with their heads downward and their feet in the air.

Another effect I noticed, which was the passage of thick clouds which formed and vanished rapidly; but on reflection I understood that these seeming clouds were due to the varying thickness of the reeds at the bottom, and I could even see the fleecy foam which their broken tops multiplied on the water, and the shadows of large birds passing above our heads, whose rapid flight I could discern on the surface of the sea.

On this occasion I was witness to one of the finest gun shots which ever made the nerves of a hunter thrill. A large bird of great breadth of wing, clearly visible, approached, hovering over us. Captain Nemo's companion shouldered his gun and fired, when it was only a few yards above the waves. The creature fell stunned, and the force of its fall brought it within the reach of dexterous hunter's grasp. It was an albatross of the finest kind.

Our march had not been interrupted by this incident. For two hours we followed these sandy plains, then fields of algae very disagreeable to cross. Candidly, I could do no more when I saw a glimmer of light, which, for a half mile, broke the darkness of the waters. It was the lantern of the *Nautilus*. Before twenty minutes were over we should be on board, and I should be able to breathe with ease, for it seemed that my reservoir supplied air very deficient in oxygen. But I did not reckon on an accidental meeting which delayed our arrival for some time.

I had remained some steps behind, when I presently saw Captain Nemo coming hurriedly toward me. With his strong hand he bent me to the ground, his companion doing the same to Conseil. At first I knew not what to think of this sudden attack, but I was soon reassured by seeing the captain lie down beside me, and remain immovable.

I was stretched on the ground, just under the shelter of a bush of algae, when, raising my head, I saw some enormous mass, casting phosphorescent gleams, pass blusteringly by.

My blood froze in my veins as I recognized two formidable sharks which threatened us. It was a couple of tintoreas, terrible creatures, with enormous tails and a dull glassy stare, the phosphorescent matter ejected from holes pierced around the muzzle. Monstrous brutes, which would crush a whole man in their iron jaws! I did not know whether Conseil stopped to classify them; for my part, I noticed their silver bellies, and their huge mouths bristling with teeth, from a very unscientific point of view, and more as a possible victim than as a naturalist.

Happily the voracious creatures do not see well. They passed without seeing us, brushing us with their brownish fins, and we escaped by a miracle from a danger certainly greater than meeting a tiger full-face in the forest. Half an hour after, guided by the electric light we reached the *Nautilus*. The outside door had been left open, and Captain Nemo closed it as soon as we had entered the first cell. He then pressed a knob. I heard the pumps working in the midst of the vessel, I felt the water sinking from around me, and in a few moments the cell was entirely empty. The inside door then opened, and we entered the vestry.

There our diving dress was taken off, not without some trouble, and, fairly worn out from want of food and sleep, I returned to my room, in great wonder at this surprising excursion at the bottom of the sea.

# CHAPTER XVII

## FOUR THOUSAND LEAGUES UNDER THE PACIFIC

The next morning, November 18, I had quite recovered from my fatigues of the day before, and I went up onto the platform, just as the second lieutenant was uttering his daily phrase.

I was admiring the magnificent aspect of the ocean when Captain Nemo appeared. He did not seem to be aware of my presence, and began a series of astronomical observations. Then, when he had finished, he went and leaned on the cage of the watch-light, and gazed abstractedly on the ocean. In the meantime, a number of the sailors of the *Nautilus*, all strong and healthy men, had come up onto the platform. They came to draw up the nets that had been laid all night. These sailors were evidently of different nations, although the European type was visible in all of them. I recognized some unmistakable Irishmen, Frenchmen, some Slavs, and a Greek or a Candiote. They were civil, and only used that odd language among themselves, the origin of which I could not guess, neither could I question them.

The nets were hauled in. They were a large kind of "chaluts," like those on the Normandy coasts, great pockets that the waves and a chain fixed in the smaller meshes kept open. These pockets, drawn by iron poles, swept through the water, and gathered in everything in their way. That day they brought up curious specimens from those productive coasts—fishing-frogs, that, from their comical movements, have acquired the name of buffoons; black commersons, furnished with antennae; trigger-fish, encircled with red bands; orthragorisci, with very subtle venom; some olive-colored lampreys; macrorhynci, covered with silvery scales; trichiuri, the electric power of which is equal to that of the gymnotus and cramp-fish; scaly notopteri with transverse brown bands; greenish cod; several varieties of gobies, etc.; also some larger fish; a caranx with a prominent head a yard long; several fine bonitos, streaked with blue and silver; and three splendid tunnies, which in spite of the swiftness of their motion, had not escaped the net.

I reckoned that the haul had brought in more than nine hundredweight of fish. It was a fine haul, but not to be wondered at. Indeed, the nets are let down for several hours, and enclose in their meshes an infinite variety. We had no lack of excellent food, and the rapidity of the *Nautilus* and the attraction of the electric light could always renew our supply. These several productions of the sea were immediately lowered through the panel to the steward's room, some to be eaten fresh, and others pickled.

The fishing ended, the provision of air renewed, I thought that the *Nautilus* was about to continue its submarine excursion, and was preparing to return to my room, when, without further preamble, the captain turned to me, saying:

"Professor, is not this ocean gifted with real life? It has its tempers and its gentle moods. Yesterday it slept as we did, and now it has woke after a quiet night. Look!" he continued, "it wakes under the caresses of the sun. It is going to renew its diurnal existence. It is an interesting study to watch the play of its organization. It has a pulse, arteries, spasms; and I agree with the learned Maury, who discovered in it a circulation as real as the circulation of blood in animals.

"Yes, the ocean has indeed circulation, and to promote it, the Creator has caused things to multiply in it—caloric, salt, and animalculae."

When Captain Nemo spoke thus, he seemed altogether changed, and aroused an extraordinary emotion in me.

"Also," he added, "true existence is there; and I can imagine the foundations of nautical towns, clusters of submarine houses, which, like the *Nautilus*, would ascend every morning to breathe at the surface of the water, free towns, independent cities. Yet who knows whether some despot—"

Captain Nemo finished his sentence with a violent gesture. Then, addressing me as if to chase away some sorrowful thought:

"M. Aronnax," he asked, "do you know the depth of the ocean?"

"I only know, Captain, what the principal soundings have taught us."

"Could you tell me them, so that I can suit them to my purpose?"

"These are some," I replied, "that I remember. If I am not mistaken, a depth of 8,000 yards has been found in the North Atlantic, and 2,500 yards in the Mediterranean. The most remarkable soundings have been made in the South Atlantic, near the thirty-fifth parallel, and they gave 12,000 yards, 14,000 yards, and 15,000 yards. To sum up all, it is reckoned that if the bottom of the sea were leveled, its mean depth would be about one and three-quarter leagues."

"Well, Professor," replied the captain, "we shall show you better than that I hope. As to the mean depth of this part of the Pacific, I tell you it is only 4,000 yards."

Having said this, Captain Nemo went toward the panel, and disappeared down the ladder. I followed him, and went into the large drawing room. The screw was immediately put in motion, and the log gave twenty miles an hour.

During the days and weeks that passed, Captain Nemo was very sparing of his visits. I seldom saw him. The lieutenant pricked the ship's course regularly on the chart, so I could always tell exactly the route of the *Nautilus*.

Nearly every day, for some time, the panels of the drawing room were opened, and we were never tired of penetrating the mysteries of the submarine world.

The general direction of the *Nautilus* was southeast, and it kept between 100 and 150 yards of depth. One day, however, I do not know why, being drawn diagonally by means of the inclined planes, it touched the bed of the sea. The thermometer indicated a temperature of 4.25 degrees centigrade: a temperature that at this depth seemed common to all latitudes.

At three o'clock in the morning of November 26 the *Nautilus* crossed the Tropic of Cancer at 172° longitude. On the 27th instant it sighted the Sandwich Islands, where Cook died, February 14, 1779. We had then gone 4,860 leagues from our starting point. In the morning, when I went on the platform, I saw two miles to windward, Hawaii, the largest of the seven islands that form the group. I saw clearly the cultivated ranges, and the several mountain chains that run parallel with the side, and the volcanoes that overtop Mouna-Rea, which rise 5,000 yards above the level of the sea. Besides other things the nets brought up, were several flabellariae and graceful polypi, that are peculiar to that part of the ocean. The direction of the *Nautilus* was still to the southeast. It crossed the equator on December 1, in 142° longitude; and on the 4th of the same month, after crossing rapidly and without anything in particular occurring, we sighted the Marquesas group. I saw, three miles off, Martin's peak in Nouka-Hiva, the largest of the group that belongs to France. I only saw the woody mountains against the horizon, because Captain Nemo did not wish to bring the ship to the wind. There the nets brought up beautiful specimens of fish: some with azure fins and tails like gold, the flesh of which is unrivaled; some nearly destitute of scales, but of exquisite flavor; others, with bony jaws, and yellow-tinged gills, as good as bonitos; all fish that would be of use to us. After leaving these charming islands protected by the French flag, from December 4 to 11, the *Nautilus* sailed over about 2,000 miles. This navigation was remarkable for the meeting with an immense shoal of calmars, near neighbors to the cuttle. The French fishermen call them *hornets*; they belong to the cephalopod class, and to the dibranchial family, that comprehends the cuttles and the argonauts. These animals were particularly studied by students of antiquity, and they furnished numerous metaphors to the popular orators, as well as excellent dishes for the tables of the rich citizens, if one can believe Athenaeus, a Greek doctor, who lived before Galen. It was during the night of December 9 or 10 that the *Nautilus* came across this shoal of mollusks that are peculiarly nocturnal. One could count them by millions. They emigrate from the temperate to the warmer zones, following the track of herrings and sardines. We watched them through the thick crystal panes, swimming down the wind with great rapidity, moving by means of their locomotive tube, pursuing fish and mollusks, eating the little ones, eaten by the big ones, and tossing about in indescribable confusion the ten arms that nature has placed on their heads like a crest of pneumatic serpents. The *Nautilus*, in spite of its speed, sailed for several hours in the midst of these animals, and its nets brought in an enormous quantity, among which I recognized the nine species that D'Orbigny classed for the Pacific. One saw, while crossing, that the sea displays the most wonderful sights. They were in endless variety. The scene changed continually, and we were called upon not only to contemplate the works of the Creator in the midst of the liquid element, but to penetrate the awful mysteries of the ocean.

During the daytime of December 11, I was busy reading in the large drawing room. Ned Land and Conseil watched the luminous water through the half-open panels. The *Nautilus* was immovable. While its reservoirs were filled, it kept at a depth of 1,000 yards, a region rarely visited in the ocean, and in which large fish were seldom seen.

I was then reading a charming book by Jean Mace, *The Slaves of the Stomach*, and I was learning some valuable lessons from it, when Conseil interrupted me.

"Will master come here a moment?" he said, in a curious voice.

"What is the matter, Conseil?"

"I want master to look."

I rose, went, and leaned on my elbows before the panes and watched.

In a full electric light, an enormous black mass, quite immovable, was suspended in the midst of the waters. I watched it attentively, seeking to find out the nature of this gigantic cetacean. But a sudden thought crossed my mind. "A vessel!" I said, half aloud.

"Yes," replied the Canadian, "a disabled ship that has sunk perpendicularly."

Ned Land was right; we were close to a vessel of which the tattered shrouds still hung from their chains. The keel seemed to be in good order, and it had been wrecked at most some few hours. Three stumps of masts, broken off about two feet above the bridge, showed that the vessel had had to sacrifice its masts. But, lying on its side, it had filled, and it was heeling over to port. This skeleton of what it had once been was a sad spectacle as it lay lost under the waves, but sadder still was the sight of the bridge, where some corpses, bound with ropes, were still lying. I counted five—four men, one of whom was standing at the helm, and a woman standing by the poop, holding an infant in her arms. She was quite young. I could distinguish her features, which the water had not decomposed, by the brilliant light from the *Nautilus*. In one despairing effort, she had raised her infant above her head—poor little thing!—whose arms encircled its mother's neck. The attitude of the four sailors was frightful, distorted as they were by their convulsive movements, while making a last effort to free themselves from the cords that bound them to the vessel. The steersman alone, calm, with a grave, clear face, his gray hair glued to his forehead, and his hand clutching the wheel of the helm, seemed even then to be guiding the three broken masts through the depths of the ocean.

What a scene! We were dumb; our hearts beat fast before this shipwreck, taken as it were from life and photographed in its last moments. And I saw already, coming toward it with hungry eyes, enormous sharks, attracted by the human flesh.

However, the *Nautilus*, turning, went around the submerged vessel, and in one instant I read on the stern: *The Florida, Sunderland.*

## CHAPTER XVIII

### VANIKORO

This terrible spectacle was the forerunner of the series of maritime catastrophes that the *Nautilus* was destined to meet with in its route. As long as it went through more frequented waters, we often saw the hulls of shipwrecked vessels that were rotting in the depths, and deeper down cannons, bullets, anchors, chains, and a thousand other iron materials eaten up by rust. However, on December 11 we sighted the Pomotou Islands, the old "dangerous group" of Bougainville, that extend over a space of 500 leagues at E.S.E. to W.N.W., from the Island Ducie to that of Lazareff. This group covers an area of 370 square leagues, and it is formed of sixty groups of islands, among which the Gambier group is remarkable, over which France exercises sway. These are coral islands, slowly raised, but continuous, created by the daily work of polypi. Then this new island will be joined later on to the neighboring groups, and a fifth continent will stretch from New Zealand and New Caledonia, and from thence to the Marquesas.

One day, when I was suggesting this theory to Captain Nemo, he replied coldly: "The earth does not want new continents, but new men."

Chance had conducted the *Nautilus* toward the island of Clermont-Tonnere, one of the most curious of the group, that was discovered in 1822 by Captain Bell of the *Minerva*. I could study now the madreporal system, to which are due the islands in this ocean.

Madrepores (which must not be mistaken for corals) have a tissue lined with a calcareous crust, and the modifications of its structure have induced M. Milne Edwards, my worthy master, to class them into five sections. The animalcule that the marine polypus secretes live by millions at the bottom of their cells. Their calcareous deposits become rocks, reefs, and large and small islands. Here they form a ring, surrounding a little inland lake, that communicates with the sea by means of gaps. There they make barriers of reefs like those on the coasts of New Caledonia and the various Pomoton islands. In other places, like those at Reunion and at Maurice, they raise fringed reefs, high, straight walls, near which the depth of the ocean is considerable.

Some cable-lengths off the shores of the island of Clermont I admired the gigantic work accomplished by these microscopical workers. These walls are specially the work of those madrepores known as milleporas, porites, madrepores, and astraeas. These polypi are found particularly in the rough beds of the sea, near the surface; and consequently it is from the upper part that they begin their operations, in which they bury themselves by degrees with the debris of the secretions that support them. Such is, at least, Darwin's theory, who thus explains the formation of the atolls, a superior theory (to my mind) to that given of the foundation of the madreporical works, summits of mountains or volcanoes, that are submerged some feet below the level of the sea.

I could observe closely these curious walls, for perpendicularly they were more than 300 yards deep, and our electric sheets lighted up this calcareous matter brilliantly. Replying to a question Conseil asked me as to the time these colossal barriers took to be raised, I astonished him much by telling him that learned men reckoned it about the eighth of an inch in a hundred years.

Toward evening Clermont-Tonnerre was lost in the distance, and the route of the *Nautilus* was sensibly changed. After having crossed the Tropic of Capricorn in 135° longitude, it sailed W.N.W., making again for the tropical zone. Although the summer sun was very strong, we did not suffer from heat, for at fifteen or twenty fathoms below the surface, the temperature did not rise above from ten to twelve degrees.

On December 15, we left to the east the bewitching group of the Societies and the graceful Tahiti, queen of the Pacific. I saw in the morning, some miles to the windward, the elevated summits of the island. These waters furnished our table with excellent fish, mackerel, bonitos, and some varieties of a sea serpent.

On December 25 the *Nautilus* sailed into the midst of the New Hebrides, discovered by Quiros in 1606, and that Bougainville explored in 1768, and to which Cook gave its present name in 1773. This group is composed principally of nine large islands, that form a band of 120 leagues N.N.S. to S.S.W., between 15° and 2° south latitude, and 164° and 168° longitude. We passed tolerably near to the island of Aurou, that at noon looked like a mass of green woods, surmounted by a peak of great height.

That day being Christmas Day, Ned Land seemed to regret sorely the noncelebration of "Christmas," the family fete of which Protestants are so fond. I had not seen Captain Nemo for a week, when, on the morning of the 27th, he came into the large drawing room, always seeming as if he had seen you five minutes before. I was busily tracing the route of the *Nautilus* on the planisphere. The captain came up to me, put his finger on one spot on the chart, and said this single word.

"Vanikoro."

The effect was magical! It was the name of the islands on which La Perouse had been lost! I rose suddenly.

"The *Nautilus* has brought us to Vanikoro?" I asked.

"Yes, Professor," said the captain.

"And I can visit the celebrated islands where the *Boussole* and the *Astrolabe* struck?"

"If you like, Professor."

"When shall we be there?"

"We are there now."

Followed by Captain Nemo, I went up on to the platform, and greedily scanned the horizon.

To the northeast two volcanic islands emerged of unequal size, surrounded by a coral reef that measured forty miles in circumference. We were close to Vanikoro, really the one to which Dumont d'Urville gave the name of Isle de la Recherche, and exactly facing the little harbor of Vanou, situated in 16° 4' south latitude, and 164° 32' east longitude. The earth seemed covered with verdure from the shore to the summits in the interior, that were crowned by Mount Kapogo, 476 feet high. The *Nautilus*, having passed the outer belt of rocks by a narrow strait, found itself among breakers where the sea was from thirty to forty fathoms deep. Under the verdant shade of some mangroves I perceived some savages, who appeared greatly surprised at our approach. In the long black body, moving between wind and water, did they not see some formidable cetacean that they regarded with suspicion?

Just then Captain Nemo asked me what I knew about the wreck of La Perouse.

"Only what everyone knows, Captain," I replied.

"And could you tell me what everyone knows about it?" he inquired, ironically.

"Easily."

I related to him all that the last works of Dumont d'Urville had made known—works from which the following is a brief account.

La Perouse and his second, Captain de Langle, were sent by Louis XVI, in 1785, on a voyage of circumnavigation. They embarked in the corvettes *Boussole* and the *Astrolabe*, neither of which were again heard of. In 1791, the French government, justly uneasy as to the fate of these two sloops, manned two large merchantmen, the *Récherché* and the *Esperance*, which left Brest on September 28 under the command of Bruni d'Entrecasteaux.

Two months after, they learned from Bowen, commander of the *Albemarle*, that the debris of shipwrecked vessels had been seen on the coasts of New Georgia. But D'Entrecasteaux, ignoring this communication—rather uncertain, besides—directed his course toward the Admiralty Islands, mentioned in a report of Captain Hunter's as being the place where La Perouse was wrecked.

They sought in vain. The *Esperance* and the *Récherché* passed before Vanikoro without stopping there, and, in fact, this voyage was most disastrous, as it cost D'Entrecasteaux his life, and those of two of his lieutenants, besides several of his crew.

Captain Dillon, a shrewd old Pacific sailor, was the first to find unmistakable traces of the wrecks. On the May 15, 1824, his vessel, the *St. Patrick*, passed close to Tikopia, one of the New Hebrides. There a Lascar came alongside in a canoe, sold him the handle of a sword in silver that bore the print of characters engraved on the hilt. The Lascar pretended that six years before, during a stay at Vanikoro, he had seen two Europeans that belonged to some vessels that had run aground on the reefs some years ago.

Dillon guessed that he meant La Perouse, whose disappearance had troubled the whole world. He tried to get on to Vanikoro, where, according to the Lascar, he would find numerous debris of the wreck, but winds and tides prevented him.

Dillon returned to Calcutta. There he interested the Asiatic Society and the Indian Company in his discovery. A vessel, to which was given the name of the *Récherché*, was put at his disposal, and he set out, January 23, 1827, accompanied by a French agent.

The *Récherché*, after touching at several points in the Pacific, cast anchor before Vanikoro, July 7, 1827, in that same harbor of Vanou where the *Nautilus* was at this time.

There it collected numerous relics of the wreck—iron utensils, anchors, pulley-strops, swivel-guns, an 18-pound shot, fragments of astronomical instruments, a piece of crown work, and a bronze clock, bearing this inscription—"*Bazin m'a fait,*" the mark of the foundry of the arsenal at Brest about 1785. There could be no further doubt.

Dillon, having made all inquiries, stayed in the unlucky place till October. Then he quitted Vanikoro, and directed his course toward New Zealand; put into Calcutta, April 7, 1828, and returned to France, where he was warmly welcomed by Charles X.

But at the same time, without knowing Dillon's movements, Dumont d'Urville had already set out to find the scene of the wreck. And they had learned from a whaler that some medals and a cross of St. Louis had been found in the hands of some savages of Louisiade and New Caledonia. Dumont d'Urville, commander of the *Astrolabe*, had then sailed, and two months after Dillon had left Vanikoro he put into Hobart Town. There he learned the results of Dillon's inquiries, and found that a certain James Hobbs, second lieutenant of the Union of Calcutta, after landing on an island situated 8° 18' south latitude, and 156° 30' east longitude, had seen some iron bars and red stuffs used by the natives of these parts. Dumont d'Urville, much perplexed, and not knowing how to credit the reports of low-class journals, decided to follow Dillon's track.

On February 10, 1828, the *Astrolabe* appeared off Tikopia, and took as guide and interpreter a deserter found on the island; made his way to Vanikoro, sighted it on the 12th inst., lay among the reefs until the 14th, and not until the 20th did he cast anchor within the barrier in the harbor of Vanou.

On the 23rd, several officers went around the island and brought back some unimportant trifles. The natives, adopting a system of denials and evasions, refused to take them to the unlucky place. This ambiguous conduct led them to believe that the natives had ill-treated the castaways, and indeed they seemed to fear that Dumont d'Urville had come to avenge La Perouse and his unfortunate crew.

However, on the 26th, appeased by some presents, and understanding that they had no reprisals to fear, they led M. Jacquireot to the scene of the wreck.

There, in three or four fathoms of water, between the reefs of Pacou and Vanou, lay anchors, cannons, pigs of lead and iron, embedded in the limy concretions. The large boat and the whaler belonging to the *Astrolabe* were sent to this place, and, not without some difficulty, their crews hauled up an anchor weighing 1,800 pounds, a brass gun, some pigs of iron, and two copper swivel-guns.

Dumont d'Urville, questioning the natives, learned too that La Perouse, after losing both his vessels on the reefs of this island, had constructed a smaller boat, only to be lost a second time. Where, no one knew.

But the French government, fearing that Dumont d'Urville was not acquainted with Dillon's movements, had sent the sloop *Bayonnaise*, commanded by Legoarant de Tromelin, to Vanikoro, which had been stationed on the west coast of America. The *Bayonnaise* cast her anchor before Vanikoro some months after the departure of the *Astrolabe*, but found no new document; but stated that the savages had respected the monument to La Perouse. That is the substance of what I told Captain Nemo.

"So," he said, "no one knows now where the third vessel perished that was constructed by the castaways on the island of Vanikoro?"

"No one knows."

Captain Nemo said nothing, but signed to me to follow him into the large saloon. The *Nautilus* sank several yards below the waves, and the panels were opened.

I hastened to the aperture, and under the crustaceans of coral, covered with fungi, syphonules, alcyons, madrepores, through myriads of charming fish—girelles, glyphisidri, pompherides, diacopes, and holocentres—I recognized certain debris that the drags had not been able to tear up—iron stirrups, anchors, cannons, bullets, capstan fittings, the stem of a ship, all objects clearly proving the wreck of some vessel, and now carpeted with living flowers. While I was looking on this desolate scene, Captain Nemo said, in a sad voice:

"Commander La Perouse set out December 7, 1785, with his vessels the *Boussole* and the *Astrolabe*. He first cast anchor at Botany Bay, visited the Friendly Isles, New Caledonia, then directed his course toward Santa Cruz, and put into Namouka, one of the Hapai group. Then his vessels struck on the unknown reefs of Vanikoro. The *Boussole*, which went first, ran aground on the southerly coast. The *Astrolabe* went to its help, and ran aground too. The first vessel was destroyed almost immediately. The second, stranded under the wind, resisted some days. The natives made the castaways welcome. They installed themselves in the island, and constructed a smaller boat with the debris of the two large ones. Some sailors stayed willingly at Vanikoro; the others, weak and ill, set out with La Perouse. They directed their course toward the Solomon Islands, and there perished, with everything, on the westerly coast of the chief island of the group, between Capes Deception and Satisfaction."

"How do you know that?"

"By this, that I found on the spot where was the last wreck."

Captain Nemo showed me a tin-plate box, stamped with the French arms, and corroded by the salt water. He opened it, and I saw a bundle of papers, yellow but still readable.

They were the instructions of the naval minister to Commander La Perouse, annotated in the margin in Louis XVI's handwriting.

"Ah! It is a fine death for a sailor!" said Captain Nemo, at last. "A coral tomb makes a quiet grave; and I trust that I and my comrades will find no other."

## CHAPTER XIX

### TORRES STRAITS

During the night of December 27 or 28, the *Nautilus* left the shores of Vanikoro with great speed. Her course was southwesterly, and in three days she had gone over the 750 leagues that separated it from La Perouse's group and the southeast point of Papua.

Early on January 1, 1863, Conseil joined me on the platform.

"Master, will you permit me to wish you a happy New Year?"

"What! Conseil; exactly as if I was at Paris in my study at the Jardin des Plantes? Well, I accept your good wishes, and thank you for them. Only, I will ask you what you mean by a 'Happy New Year' under our circumstances? Do you mean the year that will bring us to the end of our imprisonment, or the year that sees us continue this strange voyage?"

"Really, I do not know how to answer, master. We are sure to see curious things, and for the last two months we have not had time for dullness. The last marvel is always the most astonishing; and, if we continue this progression, I do not know how it will end. It is my opinion that we shall never again see the like. I think then, with no offense to master, that a happy year would be one in which we could see everything."

On January 2 we had made 11,340 miles, or 5,250 French leagues, since our starting point in the Japan Seas. Before the ship's head stretched the dangerous shores of the Coral Sea, on the northeast coast of Australia. Our boat lay along some miles from the redoubtable bank on which Cook's vessel was lost, June 10, 1770. The boat in which Cook was struck on a rock, and, if it did not sink, it was owing to a piece of coral that was broken by the shock, and fixed itself in the broken keel.

I had wished to visit the reef, 360 leagues long, against which the sea, always rough, broke with great violence, with a noise like thunder. But just then the inclined planes drew the *Nautilus* down to a great depth, and I could see nothing of the high coral walls. I had to content myself with the different specimens of fish brought up by the nets. I remarked, among others, some germons, a species of mackerel as large as a tunny, with bluish sides, and striped with transverse bands, that disappear with the animal's life.

These fish followed us in shoals, and furnished us with very delicate food. We took also a large number of gilt-heads, about one and a half inches long, tasting like dorys; and flying pyrapeds like submarine swallows, which, in dark nights, light alternately the air and water with their phosphorescent light. Among the mollusks and zoophytes, I found in the meshes of the net several species of alcyonarians, echini, hammers, spurs, dials, cerites, and hyalleae. The flora was represented by beautiful floating seaweeds, laminariae, and macrocystes, impregnated with the mucilage that transudes through their pores; and among which I gathered an admirable *Nemastoma geliniarois*, that was classed among the natural curiosities of the museum.

Two days after crossing the coral sea, January 4, we sighted the Papuan coasts. On this occasion, Captain Nemo informed me that his intention was to get into the Indian Ocean by the Strait of Torres. His communication ended there.

The Torres Straits are nearly thirty-four leagues wide; but they are obstructed by an innumerable quantity of islands, islets, breakers, and rocks, that make its navigation almost impracticable; so that Captain Nemo took all needful precautions to cross them. The *Nautilus*, floating betwixt wind and water, went at a moderate pace. Her screw, like a cetacean's tail, beat the waves slowly.

Profiting by this, I and my two companions went up on to the deserted platform. Before us was the steersman's cage, and I expected that Captain Nemo was there directing the course of the *Nautilus*. I had before me the excellent charts of the Straits of Torres, and I consulted them attentively. Around the *Nautilus* the sea dashed furiously. The course of the waves, that went from southeast to northwest at the rate of two and a half miles, broke on the coral that showed itself here and there.

"This is a bad sea!" remarked Ned Land.

"Detestable indeed, and one that does not suit a boat like the *Nautilus*."

"The captain must be very sure of his route, for I see there pieces of coral that would do for its keel if it only touched them slightly."

Indeed the situation was dangerous, but the *Nautilus* seemed to slide like magic off these rocks. It did not follow the routes of the *Astrolabe* and the *Boussole* exactly, for they proved fatal to Dumont d'Urville. It bore more northward, coasted the Islands of Murray, and came back to the southwest toward Cumberland Passage. I thought it was going to pass it by, when, going back to northwest, it went through a large quantity of islands and islets little known, toward the Island Sound and Canal Mauvais.

I wondered if Captain Nemo, foolishly imprudent, would steer his vessel into that pass where Dumont d'Urville's two corvettes touched; when, swerving again, and cutting straight through to the west, he steered for the island of Gilboa.

It was then three in the afternoon. The tide began to recede, being quite full. The *Nautilus* approached the island, that I still saw, with its remarkable border of screw-pines. He stood off it at about two miles distant. Suddenly a shock overthrew me. The *Nautilus* just touched a rock, and stayed immovable, laying lightly to port side.

When I rose, I perceived Captain Nemo and his lieutenant on the platform. They were examining the situation of the vessel, and exchanging words in their incomprehensible dialect.

She was situated thus: Two miles, on the starboard side, appeared Gilboa, stretching from north to west like an immense arm. Toward the south and east some coral showed itself, left by the ebb. We had run aground, and in one of those seas where the tides are middling—a sorry matter for the floating of the *Nautilus*. However, the vessel had not suffered, for her keel was solidly joined. But, if she could neither glide off nor move, she ran the risk of being forever fastened to these rocks, and then Captain Nemo's submarine vessel would be done for.

I was reflecting thus, when the captain, cool and calm, always master of himself, approached me.

"An accident?" I asked.

"No; an incident."

"But an incident that will oblige you perhaps to become an inhabitant of this land from which you flee?"

Captain Nemo looked at me curiously, and made a negative gesture, as much as to say that nothing would force him to set foot on terra firma again. Then he said:

"Besides, M. Aronnax, the *Nautilus* is not lost; it will carry you yet into the midst of the marvels of the ocean. Our voyage is only begun, and I do not wish to be deprived so soon of the honor of your company."

"However, Captain Nemo," I replied, without noticing the ironical turn of his phrase, "the *Nautilus* ran aground in open sea. Now the tides are not strong in the Pacific; and, if you cannot lighten the *Nautilus*, I do not see how it will be reinflated."

"The tides are not strong in the Pacific: you are right there, Professor; but in Torres Straits one finds still a difference of a yard and a half between the level of high and low seas. Today is January 4, and in five days the moon will be full. Now, I shall be very much astonished if that satellite does not raise these masses of water sufficiently, and render me a service that I should be indebted to her for."

Having said this, Captain Nemo, followed by his lieutenant, redescended to the interior of the *Nautilus*. As to the vessel, it moved not, and was immovable, as if the coralline polypi had already walled it up with their in destructible cement.

"Well, sir?" said Ned Land, who came up to me after the departure of the captain.

"Well, friend Ned, we will wait patiently for the tide on the 9th instant; for it appears that the moon will have the goodness to put it off again."

"Really?"

"Really."

"And this Captain is not going to cast anchor at all since the tide will suffice?" said Conseil, simply.

The Canadian looked at Conseil, then shrugged his shoulders.

"Sir, you may believe me when I tell you that this piece of iron will navigate neither on nor under the sea again; it is only fit to be sold for its weight. I think, therefore, that the time has come to part company with Captain Nemo."

"Friend Ned, I do not despair of this stout *Nautilus*, as you do; and in four days we shall know what to hold to on the Pacific tides. Besides, flight might be possible if we were in sight of the English or Provencal coast; but on the Papuan shores, it is another thing; and it will be time enough to come to that extremity if the *Nautilus* does not recover itself again, which I look upon as a grave event."

"But do they know, at least, how to act circumspectly? There is an island; on that island there are trees; under those trees, terrestrial animals, bearers of cutlets and roast beef, to which I would willingly give a trial."

"In this, friend Ned is right," said Conseil, "and I agree with him. Could not master obtain permission from his friend Captain Nemo to put us on land, if only so as not to lose the habit of treading on the solid parts of our planet?"

"I can ask him, but he will refuse."

"Will master risk it?" asked Conseil, "and we shall know how to rely upon the captain's amiability."

To my great surprise, Captain Nemo gave me the permission I asked for, and he gave it very agreeably, without even exacting from me a promise to return to the vessel; but flight across New Guinea might be very perilous, and I should not have counseled Ned Land to attempt it. Better to be a prisoner on board the *Nautilus* than to fall into the hands of the natives.

At eight o'clock, armed with guns and hatchets, we got off the *Nautilus*. The sea was pretty calm; a slight breeze blew on land. Conseil and I rowing, we sped along quickly, and Ned steered in the straight passage that the breakers left between them. The boat was well handled, and moved rapidly.

Ned Land could not restrain his joy. He was like a prisoner that had escaped from prison, and knew not that it was necessary to reenter it.

"Meat! We are going to eat some meat; and what meat!" he replied. "Real game! No, bread, indeed."

"I do not say that fish is not good; we must not abuse it; but a piece of fresh venison, grilled on live coals, will agreeably vary our ordinary course."

"Glutton!" said Conseil. "He makes my mouth water."

"It remains to be seen," I said, "if these forests are full of game, and if the game is not such as will hunt the hunter himself."

"Well said, M. Aronnax," replied the Canadian, whose teeth seemed sharpened like the edge of a hatchet; "but I will eat tiger—loin of tiger—if there is no other quadruped on this island."

"Friend Ned is uneasy about it," said Conseil.

"Whatever it may be," continued Ned Land, "every animal with four paws without feathers, or with two paws without feathers, will be saluted by my first shot."

"Very well! Master Land's imprudences are beginning."

"Never fear, M. Aronnax," replied the Canadian; "I do not want twenty-five minutes to offer you a dish, of my sort."

At half-past eight the *Nautilus* boat ran softly aground on a heavy sand, after having happily passed the coral reef that surrounds the island of Gilboa.

## CHAPTER XX

### A FEW DAYS ON LAND

I was much impressed on touching land. Ned Land tried the soil with his feet, as if to take possession of it. However, it was only two months before that we had become, according to Captain Nemo, "passengers on board the *Nautilus*," but, in reality, prisoners of its commander.

In a few minutes we were within musket-shot of the coast. The whole horizon was hidden behind a beautiful curtain of forests. Enormous trees, the trunks of which attained a height of 200 feet, were tied to each other by garlands of bindweed, real natural hammocks, which a light breeze rocked. They were mimosas, figs, hibisci, and palm trees, mingled together in profusion; and under the shelter of their verdant vault grew orchids, leguminous plants, and ferns.

But, without noticing all these beautiful specimens of Papuan flora, the Canadian abandoned the agreeable for the useful. He discovered a coconut tree, beat down some of the fruit, broke them, and we drunk the milk and ate the nut with a satisfaction that protested against the ordinary food on the *Nautilus*.

"Excellent!" said Ned Land.

"Exquisite!" replied Conseil.

"And I do not think," said the Canadian, "that he would object to our introducing a cargo of coconuts on board."

"I do not think he would, but he would not taste them."

"So much the worse for him," said Conseil.

"And so much the better for us," replied Ned Land. "There will be more for us."

"One word only, Master Land," I said to the harpooner, who was beginning to ravage another coconut tree. "Coconuts are good things, but before filling the canoe with them it would be wise to reconnoiter and see if the island does not produce some substance not less useful. Fresh vegetables would be welcome on board the *Nautilus*."

"Master is right," replied Conseil; "and I propose to reserve three places in our vessel, one for fruits, the other for vegetables, and the third for the venison, of which I have not yet seen the smallest specimen."

"Conseil, we must not despair," said the Canadian.

"Let us continue," I returned, "and lie in wait. Although the island seems uninhabited, it might still contain some individuals that would be less hard than we on the nature of game."

"Ho! Ho!" said Ned Land, moving his jaws significantly.

"Well, Ned!" said Conseil.

"My word!" returned the Canadian. "I begin to understand the charms of anthropophagy."

"Ned! Ned! What are you saying? You, a man-eater? I should not feel safe with you, especially as I share your cabin. I might perhaps wake one day to find myself half devoured."

"Friend Conseil, I like you much, but not enough to eat you unnecessarily."

"I would not trust you," replied Conseil. "But enough. We must absolutely bring down some game to satisfy this cannibal, or else one of these fine mornings, master will find only pieces of his servant to serve him."

While we were talking thus, we were penetrating the somber arches of the forest, and for two hours we surveyed it in all directions.

Chance rewarded our search for eatable vegetables, and one of the most useful products of the tropical zones furnished us with precious food that we missed on board. I would speak of the breadfruit tree, very abundant in the island of Gilboa; and I remarked chiefly the variety destitute of seeds, which bears in Malaya the name of "rima."

Ned Land knew these fruits well. He had already eaten many during his numerous voyages, and he knew how to prepare the eatable substance. Moreover, the sight of them excited him, and he could contain himself no longer.

"Master," he said, "I shall die if I do not taste a little of this breadfruit pie."

"Taste it, friend Ned—taste it as you want. We are here to make experiments—make them."

"It won't take long," said the Canadian.

And, provided with a lentil, he lighted a fire of dead wood that crackled joyously. During this time, Conseil and I chose the best fruits of the breadfruit. Some had not then attained a sufficient degree of maturity; and their thick skin covered a white but rather fibrous pulp. Others, the greater number yellow and gelatinous, waited only to be picked.

These fruits enclosed no kernel. Conseil brought a dozen to Ned Land, who placed them on a coal fire, after having cut them in thick slices, and while doing this repeating:

"You will see, master, how good this bread is. More so when one has been deprived of it so long. It is not even bread," added he, "but a delicate pastry. You have eaten none, master?"

"No, Ned."

"Very well, prepare yourself for a juicy thing. If you do not come for more, I am no longer the king of harpooners."

After some minutes, the part of the fruits that was exposed to the fire was completely roasted. The interior looked like a white pasty, a sort of soft crumb, the flavor of which was like that of an artichoke.

It must be confessed this bread was excellent, and I ate of it with great relish.

"What time is it now?" asked the Canadian.

"Two o'clock at least," replied Conseil.

"How time flies on firm ground!" sighed Ned Land.

"Let us be off," replied Conseil.

We returned through the forest, and completed our collection by a raid upon the cabbage-palms, that we gathered from the tops of the trees, little beans that I recognized as the "abrou" of the Malays, and yams of a superior quality.

We were loaded when we reached the boat. But Ned Land did not find his provisions sufficient. Fate, however, favored us. Just as we were pushing off, he perceived several trees, from twenty-five to thirty feet high, a species of palm tree.

At last, at five o'clock in the evening, loaded with our riches, we quitted the shore, and half an hour after we hailed the *Nautilus*. No one appeared on our arrival. The enormous iron-plated cylinder seemed deserted. The provisions embarked, I descended to my chamber, and after supper slept soundly.

The next day, January 6, nothing new on board. Not a sound inside, not a sign of life. The boat rested along the edge, in the same place in which we had left it. We resolved to return to the island. Ned Land hoped to be more fortunate than on the day before with regard to the hunt, and wished to visit another part of the forest.

At dawn we set off. The boat, carried on by the waves that flowed to shore, reached the island in a few minutes.

We landed, and, thinking that it was better to give in to the Canadian, we followed Ned Land, whose long limbs threatened to distance us. He wound up the coast toward the west: then, fording some torrents, he gained the high plain that was bordered with admirable forests. Some kingfishers were rambling along the watercourses, but they would not let themselves be approached. Their circumspection proved to me that these birds knew what to expect from bipeds of our species, and I concluded that, if the island was not inhabited, at least human beings occasionally frequented it.

After crossing a rather large prairie, we arrived at the skirts of a little wood that was enlivened by the songs and flight of a large number of birds.

"There are only birds," said Conseil.

"But they are eatable," replied the harpooner.

"I do not agree with you, friend Ned, for I see only parrots there."

"Friend Conseil," said Ned, gravely, "the parrot is like pheasant to those who have nothing else."

"And," I added, "this bird, suitably prepared, is worth knife and fork."

Indeed, under the thick foliage of this wood, a world of parrots were flying from branch to branch, only needing a careful education to speak the human language. For the moment, they were chattering with parrots of all colors, and grave cockatoos, who seemed to meditate upon some philosophical problem, while brilliant red lories passed like a piece of bunting carried away by the breeze, papuans, with the finest azure colors, and in all a variety of winged things most charming to behold, but few eatable.

However, a bird peculiar to these lands, and which has never passed the limits of the Arrow and Papuan islands, was wanting in this collection. But fortune reserved it for me before long.

After passing through a moderately thick copse, we found a plain obstructed with bushes. I saw then those magnificent birds, the disposition of whose long feathers obliges them to fly against the wind. Their undulating flight, graceful aerial curves, and the shading of their colors, attracted and charmed one's looks. I had no trouble in recognizing them.

"Birds of paradise!" I exclaimed.

The Malays, who carry on a great trade in these birds with the Chinese, have several means that we could not employ for taking them. Sometimes they put snares on the top of high trees that the birds of paradise prefer to frequent. Sometimes they catch them with a viscous birdlime that paralyzes their movements. They even go so far as to poison the fountains that the birds generally drink from. But we were obliged to fire at them during flight, which gave us few chances to bring them down; and, indeed, we vainly exhausted one half our ammunition.

About eleven o'clock in the morning, the first range of mountains that form the center of the island was traversed, and we had killed nothing. Hunger drove us on. The hunters had relied on the products of the chase, and they were wrong. Happily Conseil, to his great surprise, made a double shot and secured breakfast. He brought down a white pigeon and a wood-pigeon, which, cleverly plucked and suspended from a skewer, was roasted before a red fire of dead wood. While these interesting birds were cooking, Ned prepared the fruit of the bread-tree. Then the wood-pigeons were devoured to the bones, and declared excellent. The nutmeg, with which they are in the habit of stuffing their crops, flavors their flesh and renders it delicious eating.

"Now, Ned, what do you miss now?"

"Some four-footed game, M. Aronnax. All these pigeons are only side dishes and trifles; and until I have killed an animal with cutlets I shall not be content."

"Nor I, Ned, if I do not catch a bird of paradise."

"Let us continue hunting," replied Conseil. "Let us go toward the sea. We have arrived at the first declivities of the mountains, and I think we had better regain the region of forests."

That was sensible advice, and was followed out. After walking for one hour we had attained a forest of sago trees. Some inoffensive serpents glided away from us. The birds of paradise fled at our approach, and truly I despaired of getting near one when Conseil, who was walking in front, suddenly bent down, uttered a triumphal cry, and came back to me bringing a magnificent specimen.

"Ah! Bravo, Conseil!"

"Master is very good."

"No, my boy; you have made an excellent stroke. Take one of these living birds, and carry it in your hand."

"If master will examine it, he will see that I have not deserved great merit."

"Why, Conseil?"

"Because this bird is as drunk as a quail."

"Drunk!"

"Yes, sir; drunk with the nutmegs that it devoured under the nutmeg-tree, under which I found it. See, friend Ned, see the monstrous effects of intemperance!"

"By Jove!" exclaimed the Canadian. "Because I have drunk gin for two months, you must needs reproach me!"

However, I examined the curious bird. Conseil was right. The bird, drunk with the juice, was quite powerless. It could not fly; it could hardly walk.

This bird belonged to the most beautiful of the eight species that are found in Papua and in the neighboring islands. It was the "large emerald bird, the most rare kind." It measured three feet in length. Its head was comparatively small, its eyes placed near the opening of the beak, and also small. But the shades of color were beautiful, having a yellow beak, brown feet and claws, nut-colored wings with purple tips, pale yellow at the back of the neck and head, and emerald color at the throat, chestnut on the breast and belly. Two horned, downy nets rose from below the tail, that prolonged the long light feathers of admirable fineness, and they completed the whole of this marvelous bird, that the natives have poetically named the "bird of the sun."

But if my wishes were satisfied by the possession of the bird of paradise, the Canadian's were not yet. Happily, about two o'clock, Ned Land brought down a magnificent hog; from the brood of those the natives call "bari-outang." The animal came in time for us to procure real quadruped meat, and he was well received. Ned Land was very proud of his shot. The hog, hit by the electric ball, fell stone dead. The Canadian skinned and cleaned it properly, after having taken half a dozen cutlets, destined to furnish us with a grilled repast in the evening. Then the hunt was resumed, which was still more marked by Ned and Conseil's exploits.

Indeed, the two friends, beating the bushes, roused a herd of kangaroos that fled and bounded along on their elastic paws. But these animals did not take to flight so rapidly but what the electric capsule could stop their course.

"Ah, Professor!" cried Ned Land, who was carried away by the delights of the chase. "What excellent game, and stewed, too! What a supply for the *Nautilus*! Two! Three! Five down! And to think that we shall eat that flesh, and that the idiots on board shall not have a crumb!"

I think that, in the excess of his joy, the Canadian, if he had not talked so much, would have killed them all. But he contented himself with a single dozen of these interesting marsupians. These animals were small. They were a species of those "kangaroo rabbits" that live habitually in the hollows of trees, and whose speed is extreme; but they are moderately fat, and furnish, at least, estimable food. We were very satisfied with the results of the hunt. Happy Ned proposed to return to this enchanting island the next day, for he wished to depopulate it of all the eatable quadrupeds. But he had reckoned without his host.

At six o'clock in the evening we had regained the shore; our boat was moored to the usual place. The *Nautilus*, like a long rock, emerged from the waves two miles from the beach. Ned Land, without waiting, occupied himself about the important dinner business. He understood all about cooking well. The "bari-outang," grilled on the coals, soon scented the air with a delicious odor.

Indeed, the dinner was excellent. Two wood-pigeons completed this extraordinary menu. The sago pasty, the artocarpus bread, some mangoes, half a dozen pineapples, and the liquor fermented from some coconuts overjoyed us. I even think that my worthy companions' ideas had not all the plainness desirable.

"Suppose we do not return to the *Nautilus* this evening?" said Conseil.

"Suppose we never return?" added Ned Land.

Just then a stone fell at our feet and cut short the harpooner's proposition.

## CHAPTER XXI

### CAPTAIN NEMO'S THUNDERBOLT

We looked at the edge of the forest without rising, my hand stopping in the action of putting it to my mouth, Ned Land's completing its office.

"Stones do not fall from the sky," remarked Conseil, "or they would merit the name aerolites."

A second stone, carefully aimed, that made a savory pigeon's leg fall from Conseil's hand, gave still more weight to his observation. We all three arose, shouldered our guns, and were ready to reply to any attack.

"Are they apes?" cried Ned Land.

"Very nearly—they are savages."

"To the boat!" I said, hurrying to the sea.

It was indeed necessary to beat a retreat, for about twenty natives armed with bows and slings appeared on the skirts of a copse that masked the horizon to the right, hardly a hundred steps from us.

Our boat was moored about sixty feet from us. The savages approached us, not running, but making hostile demonstrations. Stones and arrows fell thickly.

Ned Land had not wished to leave his provisions; and, in spite of his imminent danger, his pig on one side and kangaroos on the other, he went tolerably fast. In two minutes we were on the shore. To load the boat with provisions and arms, to push it out to sea, and ship the oars, was the work of an instant. We had not gone two cable-lengths, when a hundred savages, howling and gesticulating, entered the water up to their waists. I watched to see if their apparition would attract some men from the *Nautilus* on to the platform. But no. The enormous machine, lying off, was absolutely deserted.

Twenty minutes later we were on board. The panels were open. After making the boat fast, we entered into the interior of the *Nautilus*.

I descended to the drawing room, from whence I heard some chords. Captain Nemo was there, bending over his organ, and plunged in a musical ecstasy.

"Captain!"

He did not hear me.

"Captain!" I said, touching his hand.

He shuddered, and, turning around, said, "Ah! It is you, Professor? Well, have you had a good hunt, have you botanized successfully?"

"Yes, Captain; but we have unfortunately brought a troop of bipeds, whose vicinity troubles me."

"What bipeds?"

"Savages."

"Savages!" he echoed, ironically. "So you are astonished, Professor, at having set foot on a strange land and finding savages? Savages! Where are there not any? Besides, are they worse than others, these whom you call savages?"

"But, Captain—"

"How many have you counted?"

"A hundred at least."

"M. Aronnax," replied Captain Nemo, placing his fingers on the organ stops, "when all the natives of Papua are assembled on this shore, the *Nautilus* will have nothing to fear from their attacks."

The captain's fingers were then running over the keys of the instrument, and I remarked that he touched only the black keys, which gave his melodies an essentially Scotch character. Soon he had forgotten my presence, and had plunged into a reverie that I did not disturb. I went up again on to the platform: night had already fallen; for, in this low latitude, the sun sets rapidly and without twilight. I could only see the island indistinctly; but the numerous fires, lighted on the beach, showed that the natives did not think of leaving it. I was alone for several hours, sometimes thinking of the natives—but without any dread of them, for the imperturbable confidence of the captain was catching—sometimes forgetting them to admire the splendors of the night in the tropics. My remembrances went to France in the train of those zodiacal stars that would shine in some hours' time. The moon shone in the midst of the constellations of the zenith.

The night slipped away without any mischance, the islanders frightened no doubt at the sight of a monster aground in the bay. The panels were open, and would have offered an easy access to the interior of the *Nautilus*.

At six o'clock in the morning of January 8, I went up on to the platform. The dawn was breaking. The island soon showed itself through the dissipating fogs, first the shore, then the summits.

The natives were there, more numerous than on the day before—five or six hundred perhaps—some of them, profiting by the low water, had come on to the coral, at less than two cable-lengths from the *Nautilus*. I distinguished them easily; they were true Papuans, with athletic figures, men of good race, large high foreheads, large, but not broad and flat, and white teeth. Their woolly hair, with a reddish tinge, showed off on their black shining bodies like those of the Nubians. From the lobes of their ears, cut and distended, hung chaplets of bones. Most of these savages were naked. Among them, I remarked some women, dressed from the hips to knees in quite a crinoline of herbs, that sustained a vegetable waistband. Some chiefs had ornamented their necks with a crescent and collars of glass beads, red and white; nearly all were armed with bows, arrows, and shields and carried on their shoulders a sort of net containing those round stones which they cast from their slings with great skill. One of these chiefs, rather near to the *Nautilus*, examined it attentively. He was, perhaps, a "mado" of high rank, for he was draped in a mat of banana leaves, notched around the edges, and set off with brilliant colors.

I could easily have knocked down this native, who was within a short length; but I thought that it was better to wait for real hostile demonstrations. Between Europeans and savages, it is proper for the Europeans to parry sharply, not to attack.

During low water the natives roamed about near the *Nautilus*, but were not troublesome; I heard them frequently repeat the word "Assai," and by their gestures I understood that they invited me to go on land, an invitation that I declined.

So that, on that day, the boat did not push off, to the great displeasure of Master Land, who could not complete his provisions.

This adroit Canadian employed his time in preparing the viands and meat that he had brought off the island. As for the savages, they returned to the shore about eleven o'clock in the morning, as soon as the coral tops began to disappear under the rising tide; but I saw their numbers had increased considerably on the shore. Probably they came from the neighboring islands, or very likely from Papua. However, I had not seen a single native canoe. Having nothing better to do, I thought of dragging these beautiful limpid waters, under which I saw a profusion of shells, zoophytes, and marine plants. Moreover, it was the last day that the *Nautilus* would pass in these parts, if it float in open sea the next day, according to Captain Nemo's promise.

I therefore called Conseil, who brought me a little light drag, very like those for the oyster fishery. Now to work! For two hours we fished unceasingly, but without bringing up any rarities. The drag was filled with midas-ears, harps, melames, and particularly the most beautiful hammers I have ever seen. We also brought up some sea slugs, pearl oysters, and a dozen little turtles that were reserved for the pantry on board.

But just when I expected it least, I put my hand on a wonder, I might say a natural deformity, very rarely met with. Conseil was just dragging, and his net came up filled with divers ordinary shells, when, all at once, he saw me plunge my arm quickly into the net, to draw out a shell, and heard me utter a cry.

"What is the matter, sir?" he asked in surprise. "Has master been bitten?"

"No, my boy; but I would willingly have given a finger for my discovery."

"What discovery?"

"This shell," I said, holding up the object of my triumph.

"It is simply an olive porphyry, genus olive, order of the pectinibranchidae, class of gasteropods, subclass mollusca."

"Yes, Conseil; but, instead of being rolled from right to left, this olive turns from left to right."

"Is it possible?"

"Yes, my boy; it is a left shell."

Shells are all right-handed, with rare exceptions; and, when by chance their spiral is left, amateurs are ready to pay their weight in gold.

Conseil and I were absorbed in the contemplation of our treasure, and I was promising myself to enrich the museum with it, when a stone unfortunately thrown by a native struck against, and broke, the precious object in Conseil's hand. I uttered a cry of despair! Conseil took up his gun, and aimed at a savage who was poising his sling at ten yards from him. I would have stopped him, but his blow took effect and broke the bracelet of amulets which encircled the arm of the savage.

"Conseil!" cried I. "Conseil!"

"Well, sir! Do you not see that the cannibal has commenced the attack?"

"A shell is not worth the life of a man," said I.

"Ah! The scoundrel!" cried Conseil. "I would rather he had broken my shoulder!"

Conseil was in earnest, but I was not of his opinion. However, the situation had changed some minutes before, and we had not perceived. A score of canoes surrounded the *Nautilus*. These canoes, scooped out of the trunk of a tree, long, narrow, well adapted for speed, were balanced by means of a long bamboo pole, which floated on the water. They were managed by skillful, half-naked paddlers, and I watched their advance with some uneasiness. It was evident that these Papuans had already had dealings with the Europeans and knew their ships. But this long iron cylinder anchored in the bay, without masts or chimneys, what could they think of it? Nothing good, for at first they kept at a respectful distance. However, seeing it motionless, by degrees they took courage, and sought to familiarize themselves with it. Now this familiarity was precisely what it was necessary to avoid. Our arms, which were noiseless, could only produce a moderate effect on the savages, who have little respect for aught but blustering things. The thunderbolt without the reverberations of thunder would frighten man but little, though the danger lies in the lightning, not in the noise.

At this moment the canoes approached the *Nautilus*, and a shower of arrows alighted on her.

I went down to the saloon, but found no one there. I ventured to knock at the door that opened into the captain's room. "Come in," was the answer.

I entered, and found Captain Nemo deep in algebraical calculations of $x$ and other quantities.

"I am disturbing you," said I, for courtesy's sake.

"That is true, M. Aronnax," replied the captain; "but I think you have serious reasons for wishing to see me?"

"Very grave ones; the natives are surrounding us in their canoes, and in a few minutes we shall certainly be attacked by many hundreds of savages."

"Ah!" said Captain Nemo quietly. "They are come with their canoes?"

"Yes, sir."

"Well, sir, we must close the hatches."

"Exactly, and I came to say to you—"

"Nothing can be more simple," said Captain Nemo. And, pressing an electric button, he transmitted an order to the ship's crew.

"It is all done, sir," said he, after some moments. "The pinnace is ready, and the hatches are closed. You do not fear, I imagine, that these gentlemen could stave in walls on which the balls of your frigate have had no effect?"

"No, Captain; but a danger still exists."

"What is that, sir?"

"It is that tomorrow, at about this hour, we must open the hatches to renew the air of the *Nautilus*. Now, if, at this moment, the Papuans should occupy the platform, I do not see how you could prevent them from entering."

"Then, sir, you suppose that they will board us?"

"I am certain of it."

"Well, sir, let them come. I see no reason for hindering them. After all, these Papuans are poor creatures, and I am unwilling that my visit to the island should cost the life of a single one of these wretches."

Upon that I was going away; but Captain Nemo detained me, and asked me to sit down by him. He questioned me with interest about our excursions on shore, and our hunting; and seemed not to understand the craving for meat that possessed the

Canadian. Then the conversation turned on various subjects, and, without being more communicative, Captain Nemo showed himself more amiable.

Among other things, we happened to speak of the situation of the *Nautilus*, run aground in exactly the same spot in this strait where Dumont d'Urville was nearly lost. Apropos of this:

"This D'Urville was one of your great sailors," said the captain to me, "one of your most intelligent navigators. He is the Captain Cook of you Frenchmen. Unfortunate man of science, after having braved the icebergs of the South Pole, the coral reefs of Oceania, the cannibals of the Pacific, to perish miserably in a railway train! If this energetic man could have reflected during the last moments of his life, what must have been uppermost in his last thoughts, do you suppose?"

So speaking, Captain Nemo seemed moved, and his emotion gave me a better opinion of him. Then, chart in hand, we reviewed the travels of the French navigator, his voyages of circumnavigation, his double detention at the South Pole, which led to the discovery of Adelaide and Louis Philippe, and fixing the hydrographical bearings of the principal islands of Oceania.

"That which your D'Urville has done on the surface of the seas," said Captain Nemo, "that have I done under them, and more easily, more completely than he. The *Astrolabe* and the *Boussole*, incessantly tossed about by the hurricane, could not be worth the *Nautilus*, quiet repository of labor that she is, truly motionless in the midst of the waters.

"Tomorrow," added the captain, rising, "tomorrow, at twenty minutes to three p.m., the *Nautilus* shall float, and leave the Strait of Torres uninjured."

Having curtly pronounced these words, Captain Nemo bowed slightly. This was to dismiss me, and I went back to my room.

There I found Conseil, who wished to know the result of my interview with the captain.

"My boy," said I, "when I feigned to believe that his *Nautilus* was threatened by the natives of Papua, the captain answered me very sarcastically. I have but one thing to say to you: Have confidence in him, and go to sleep in peace."

"Have you no need of my services, sir?"

"No, my friend. What is Ned Land doing?"

"If you will excuse me, sir," answered Conseil, "friend Ned is busy making a kangaroo-pie which will be a marvel."

I remained alone and went to bed, but slept indifferently. I heard the noise of the savages, who stamped on the platform, uttering deafening cries. The night passed thus, without disturbing the ordinary repose of the crew. The presence of these cannibals affected them no more than the soldiers of a masked battery care for the ants that crawl over its front.

At six in the morning I rose. The hatches had not been opened. The inner air was not renewed, but the reservoirs, filled ready for any emergency, were now resorted to, and discharged several cubic feet of oxygen into the exhausted atmosphere of the *Nautilus*.

I worked in my room till noon, without having seen Captain Nemo, even for an instant. On board no preparations for departure were visible.

I waited still some time, then went into the large saloon. The clock marked half-past two. In ten minutes it would be high tide; and, if Captain Nemo had not made a rash promise, the *Nautilus* would be immediately detached. If not, many months would pass ere she could leave her bed of coral.

However, some warning vibrations began to be felt in the vessel. I heard the keel grating against the rough calcareous bottom of the coral reef.

At five-and-twenty minutes to three, Captain Nemo appeared in the saloon.

"We are going to start," said he.

"Ah!" replied I.

"I have given the order to open the hatches."

"And the Papuans?"

"The Papuans?" answered Captain Nemo, slightly shrugging his shoulders.

"Will they not come inside the *Nautilus*?"

"How?"

"Only by leaping over the hatches you have opened."

"M. Aronnax," quietly answered Captain Nemo, "they will not enter the hatches of the *Nautilus* in that way, even if they were open."

I looked at the captain.

"You do not understand?" said he.

"Hardly."

"Well, come and you will see."

I directed my steps toward the central staircase. There Ned Land and Conseil were slyly watching some of the ship's crew, who were opening the hatches, while cries of rage and fearful vociferations resounded outside.

The port lids were pulled down outside. Twenty horrible faces appeared. But the first native who placed his hand on the stair rail, struck from behind by some invisible force, I know not what, fled, uttering the most fearful cries and making the wildest contortions.

Ten of his companions followed him. They met with the same fate.

Conseil was in ecstasy. Ned Land, carried away by his violent instincts, rushed on to the staircase. But the moment he seized the rail with both hands, he, in his turn, was overthrown.

"I am struck by a thunderbolt," cried he, with an oath.

This explained all. It was no rail; but a metallic cable charged with electricity from the deck communicating with the platform. Whoever touched it felt a powerful shock—and this shock would have been mortal if Captain Nemo had discharged into the conductor the whole force of the current. It might truly be said that between his assailants and himself he had stretched a network of electricity which none could pass with impunity.

Meanwhile, the exasperated Papuans had beaten a retreat paralyzed with terror. As for us, half laughing, we consoled and rubbed the unfortunate Ned Land, who swore like one possessed.

But at this moment the *Nautilus*, raised by the last waves of the tide, quitted her coral bed exactly at the fortieth minute fixed by the captain. Her screw swept the waters slowly and majestically. Her speed increased gradually, and, sailing on the surface of the ocean, she quitted safe and sound the dangerous passes of the Straits of Torres.

## CHAPTER XXII

### "AEGRI SOMNIA"

The following day, January 10, the *Nautilus* continued her course between two seas, but with such remarkable speed that I could not estimate it at less than thirty-five miles an hour. The rapidity of her screw was such that I could neither follow nor count its revolutions. When I reflected that this marvelous electric agent, after having afforded motion, heat, and light to the *Nautilus*, still protected her from outward attack, and transformed her into an ark of safety which no profane hand might touch without being thunderstricken, my admiration was unbounded, and from the structure it extended to the engineer who had called it into existence.

Our course was directed to the west, and on January 11 we doubled Cape Wessel, situated in 135° longitude and 10° south latitude, which forms the east point of the Gulf of Carpentaria. The reefs were still numerous, but more equalized, and marked on the chart with extreme precision. The *Nautilus* easily avoided the breakers of Money to port and the Victoria reefs to starboard, placed at 130° longitude and on the 10th parallel, which we strictly followed.

On January 13, Captain Nemo arrived in the Sea of Timor, and recognized the island of that name in 122° longitude.

From this point the direction of the *Nautilus* inclined toward the southwest. Her head was set for the Indian Ocean. Where would the fancy of Captain Nemo carry us next? Would he return to the coast of Asia or would he approach again the shores of Europe? Improbable conjectures both, to a man who fled from inhabited continents. Then would he descend to the south? Was he going to double the Cape of Good Hope, then Cape Horn, and finally go as far as the Antarctic pole? Would he come back at last to the Pacific, where his *Nautilus* could sail free and independently? Time would show.

After having skirted the sands of Cartier, of Hibernia, Seringapatam, and Scott, last efforts of the solid against the liquid element, on January 14 we lost sight of land altogether. The speed of the *Nautilus* was considerably abated, and with irregular course she sometimes swam in the bosom of the waters, sometimes floated on their surface.

During this period of the voyage, Captain Nemo made some interesting experiments on the varied temperature of the sea, in different beds. Under ordinary conditions these observations are made by means of rather complicated instruments, and with somewhat doubtful results, by means of thermometrical sounding-leads, the glasses often breaking under the pressure of the water, or an apparatus grounded on the variations of the resistance of metals to the electric currents. Results so obtained could not be correctly calculated. On the contrary, Captain Nemo went himself to test the temperature in the depths of the sea, and his thermometer, placed in communication with the different sheets of water, gave him the required degree immediately and accurately.

It was thus that, either by overloading her reservoirs or by descending obliquely by means of her inclined planes, the *Nautilus* successively attained the depth of three, four, five, seven, nine, and ten thousand yards, and the definite result of this experience was that the sea preserved an average temperature of four degrees and a half at a depth of five thousand fathoms under all latitudes.

On January 16, the *Nautilus* seemed becalmed only a few yards beneath the surface of the waves. Her electric apparatus remained inactive and her motionless screw left her to drift at the mercy of the currents. I supposed that the crew was occupied with interior repairs, rendered necessary by the violence of the mechanical movements of the machine.

My companions and I then witnessed a curious spectacle. The hatches of the saloon were open, and, as the beacon light of the *Nautilus* was not in action, a dim obscurity reigned in the midst of the waters. I observed the state of the sea, under these conditions, and the largest fish appeared to me no more than scarcely defined shadows, when the *Nautilus* found herself suddenly transported into full light. I thought at first that the beacon had been lighted, and was casting its electric radiance into the liquid mass. I was mistaken, and after a rapid survey perceived my error.

The *Nautilus* floated in the midst of a phosphorescent bed which, in this obscurity, became quite dazzling. It was produced by myriads of luminous animalculae, whose brilliancy was increased as they glided over the metallic hull of the vessel. I was surprised by lightning in the midst of these luminous sheets, as though they had been rivulets of lead melted in an ardent furnace or metallic masses brought to a white heat, so that, by force of contrast, certain portions of light appeared to cast a shade in the midst of the general ignition, from which all shade seemed banished. No; this was not the calm irradiation of our ordinary lightning. There was unusual life and vigor: this was truly living light!

In reality, it was an infinite agglomeration of colored infusoria, of veritable globules of jelly, provided with a threadlike tentacle, and of which as many as twenty-five thousand have been counted in less than two cubic half-inches of water; and their light was increased by the glimmering peculiar to the medusae, starfish, aurelia, and other phosphorescent zoophytes, impregnated by the grease of the organic matter decomposed by the sea, and, perhaps, the mucus secreted by the fish.

During several hours the *Nautilus* floated in these brilliant waves, and our admiration increased as we watched the marine monsters disporting themselves like salamanders. I saw there in the midst of this fire that burns not the swift and elegant porpoise (the indefatigable clown of the ocean), and some swordfish ten feet long, those prophetic heralds of the hurricane whose formidable sword would now and then strike the glass of the saloon. Then appeared the smaller fish, the balista, the leaping mackerel, wolf-thorn-tails, and a hundred others which striped the luminous atmosphere as they swam. This dazzling spectacle was enchanting! Perhaps some atmospheric condition increased the intensity of this phenomenon. Perhaps some storm agitated the surface of the waves. But at this depth of some yards, the *Nautilus* was unmoved by its fury and reposed peacefully in still water.

So we progressed, incessantly charmed by some new marvel. Conseil arranged and classed his zoophytes, his ariculata, his mollusks, his fishes. The days passed rapidly away, and I took no account of them. Ned, according to habit, tried to vary the diet on board. Like snails, we were fixed to our shells, and I declare it is easy to lead a snail's life.

Thus this life seemed easy and natural, and we thought no longer of the life we led on land; but something happened to recall us to the strangeness of our situation.

On January 18, the *Nautilus* was in 105° longitude and 15° south latitude. The weather was threatening, the sea rough and rolling. There was a strong east wind. The barometer, which had been going down for some days, foreboded a coming storm. I went up on to the platform just as the second lieutenant was taking the measure of the horary angles, and waited, according to habit till the daily phrase was said. But on this day it was exchanged for another phrase not less incomprehensible. Almost directly, I saw Captain Nemo appear with a glass, looking toward the horizon.

For some minutes he was immovable, without taking his eye off the point of observation. Then he lowered his glass and exchanged a few words with his lieutenant. The latter seemed to be a victim to some emotion that he tried in vain to repress. Captain Nemo, having more command over himself, was cool. He seemed, too, to be making some objections to which the lieutenant replied by formal assurances. At least I concluded so by the difference of their tones and gestures. For myself, I had looked carefully in the direction indicated without seeing anything. The sky and water were lost in the clear line of the horizon.

However, Captain Nemo walked from one end of the platform to the other, without looking at me, perhaps without seeing me. His step was firm, but less regular than usual. He stopped sometimes, crossed his arms, and observed the sea. What could he be looking for on that immense expanse?

The *Nautilus* was then some hundreds of miles from the nearest coast.

The lieutenant had taken up the glass and examined the horizon steadfastly, going and coming, stamping his foot and showing more nervous agitation than his superior officer. Besides, this mystery must necessarily be solved, and before long; for, upon an order from Captain Nemo, the engine, increasing its propelling power, made the screw turn more rapidly.

Just then the lieutenant drew the captain's attention again. The latter stopped walking and directed his glass toward the place indicated. He looked long. I felt very much puzzled, and descended to the drawing room, and took out an excellent telescope that I generally used. Then, leaning on the cage of the watch-light that jutted out from the front of the platform, set myself to look over all the line of the sky and sea.

But my eye was no sooner applied to the glass than it was quickly snatched out of my hands.

I turned around. Captain Nemo was before me, but I did not know him. His face was transfigured. His eyes flashed sullenly; his teeth were set; his stiff body, clenched fists, and head shrunk between his shoulders, betrayed the violent agitation that pervaded his whole frame. He did not move. My glass, fallen from his hands, had rolled at his feet.

Had I unwittingly provoked this fit of anger? Did this incomprehensible person imagine that I had discovered some forbidden secret? No; I was not the object of this hatred, for he was not looking at me; his eye was steadily fixed upon the impenetrable point of the horizon. At last Captain Nemo recovered himself. His agitation subsided. He addressed some words in a foreign language to his lieutenant, then turned to me. "M. Aronnax," he said, in rather an imperious tone, "I require you to keep one of the conditions that bind you to me."

"What is it, Captain?"

"You must be confined, with your companions, until I think fit to release you."

"You are the master," I replied, looking steadily at him. "But may I ask you one question?"

"None, sir."

There was no resisting this imperious command, it would have been useless. I went down to the cabin occupied by Ned Land and Conseil, and told them the captain's determination. You may judge how this communication was received by the Canadian.

But there was not time for altercation. Four of the crew waited at the door, and conducted us to that cell where we had passed our first night on board the *Nautilus*.

Ned Land would have remonstrated, but the door was shut upon him.

"Will master tell me what this means?" asked Conseil.

I told my companions what had passed. They were as much astonished as I, and equally at a loss how to account for it.

Meanwhile, I was absorbed in my own reflections, and could think of nothing but the strange fear depicted in the captain's countenance. I was utterly at a loss to account for it, when my cogitations were disturbed by these words from Ned Land:

"Hallo! Breakfast is ready."

And indeed the table was laid. Evidently Captain Nemo had given this order at the same time that he had hastened the speed of the *Nautilus*.

"Will master permit me to make a recommendation?" asked Conseil.

"Yes, my boy."

"Well, it is that master breakfasts. It is prudent, for we do not know what may happen."

"You are right, Conseil."

"Unfortunately," said Ned Land, "they have only given us the ship's fare."

"Friend Ned," asked Conseil, "what would you have said if the breakfast had been entirely forgotten?"

This argument cut short the harpooner's recriminations.

We sat down to table. The meal was eaten in silence.

Just then the luminous globe that lighted the cell went out, and left us in total darkness. Ned Land was soon asleep, and what astonished me was that Conseil went off into a heavy slumber. I was thinking what could have caused his irresistible drowsiness, when I felt my brain becoming stupefied. In spite of my efforts to keep my eyes open, they would close. A painful suspicion seized me. Evidently soporific substances had been mixed with the food we had just taken. Imprisonment was not enough to conceal Captain Nemo's projects from us, sleep was more necessary. I then heard the panels shut. The undulations of the sea, which caused a slight rolling motion, ceased. Had the *Nautilus* quitted the surface of the ocean? Had it gone back to the motionless bed of water? I tried to resist sleep. It was impossible. My breathing grew weak. I felt a mortal cold freeze my stiffened and half-paralyzed limbs. My eyelids, like leaden caps, fell over my eyes. I could not raise them; a morbid sleep, full of hallucinations, bereft me of my being. Then the visions disappeared, and left me in complete insensibility.

## CHAPTER XXIII

### THE CORAL KINGDOM

The next day I woke with my head singularly clear. To my great surprise, I was in my own room. My companions, no doubt, had been reinstated in their cabin, without having perceived it any more than I. Of what had passed during the night they were as ignorant as I was, and to penetrate this mystery I only reckoned upon the chances of the future.

I then thought of quitting my room. Was I free again or a prisoner? Quite free. I opened the door, went to the half-deck, went up the central stairs. The panels, shut the evening before, were open. I went on to the platform.

Ned Land and Conseil waited there for me. I questioned them; they knew nothing. Lost in a heavy sleep in which they had been totally unconscious, they had been astonished at finding themselves in their cabin.

As for the *Nautilus*, it seemed quiet and mysterious as ever. It floated on the surface of the waves at a moderate pace. Nothing seemed changed on board.

The second lieutenant then came on to the platform, and gave the usual order below.

As for Captain Nemo, he did not appear.

Of the people on board, I only saw the impassive steward, who served me with his usual dumb regularity.

About two o'clock, I was in the drawing room, busied in arranging my notes, when the captain opened the door and appeared. I bowed. He made a slight inclination in return, without speaking. I resumed my work, hoping that he would perhaps give me some explanation of the events of the preceding night. He made none. I looked at him. He seemed fatigued; his heavy eyes had not been refreshed by sleep; his face looked very sorrowful. He walked to and fro, sat down and got up again, took a chance book, put it down, consulted his instruments without taking his habitual notes, and seemed restless and uneasy. At last, he came up to me, and said:

"Are you a doctor, M. Aronnax?"

I so little expected such a question that I stared some time at him without answering.

"Are you a doctor?" he repeated. "Several of your colleagues have studied medicine."

"Well," said I, "I am a doctor and resident surgeon to the hospital. I practiced several years before entering the museum."

"Very well, sir."

My answer had evidently satisfied the captain. But, not knowing what he would say next, I waited for other questions, reserving my answers according to circumstances.

"M. Aronnax, will you consent to prescribe for one of my men?" he asked.

"Is he ill?"

"Yes."

"I am ready to follow you."

"Come, then."

I own my heartbeat, I do not know why. I saw a certain connection between the illness of one of the crew and the events of the day before; and this mystery interested me at least as much as the sick man.

Captain Nemo conducted me to the poop of the *Nautilus*, and took me into a cabin situated near the sailors' quarters.

There, on a bed, lay a man about forty years of age, with a resolute expression of countenance, a true type of an Anglo-Saxon.

I leaned over him. He was not only ill, he was wounded. His head, swathed in bandages covered with blood, lay on a pillow. I undid the bandages, and the wounded man looked at me with his large eyes and gave no sign of pain as I did it. It was a horrible wound. The skull, shattered by some deadly weapon, left the brain exposed, which was much injured. Clots of blood had formed in the bruised and broken mass, in color like the dregs of wine.

There was both contusion and suffusion of the brain. His breathing was slow, and some spasmodic movements of the muscles agitated his face. I felt his pulse. It was intermittent. The extremities of the body were growing cold already, and I saw death must inevitably ensue. After dressing the unfortunate man's wounds, I readjusted the bandages on his head, and turned to Captain Nemo.

"What caused this wound?" I asked.

"What does it signify?" he replied, evasively. "A shock has broken one of the levers of the engine, which struck myself. But your opinion as to his state?"

I hesitated before giving it.

"You may speak," said the captain. "This man does not understand French."

I gave a last look at the wounded man.

"He will be dead in two hours."

"Can nothing save him?"

"Nothing."

Captain Nemo's hand contracted, and some tears glistened in his eyes, which I thought incapable of shedding any.

For some moments I still watched the dying man, whose life ebbed slowly. His pallor increased under the electric light that was shed over his deathbed. I looked at his intelligent forehead, furrowed with premature wrinkles, produced probably by misfortune and sorrow. I tried to learn the secret of his life from the last words that escaped his lips.

"You can go now, M. Aronnax," said the captain.

I left him in the dying man's cabin, and returned to my room much affected by this scene. During the whole day, I was haunted by uncomfortable suspicions, and at night I slept badly, and between my broken dreams I fancied I heard distant sighs like the notes of a funeral psalm. Were they the prayers of the dead, murmured in that language that I could not understand?

The next morning I went on to the bridge. Captain Nemo was there before me. As soon as he perceived me he came to me.

"Professor, will it be convenient to you to make a submarine excursion today?"

"With my companions?" I asked.

"If they like."

"We obey your orders, Captain."

"Will you be so good then as to put on your cork jackets?"

It was not a question of dead or dying. I rejoined Ned Land and Conseil, and told them of Captain Nemo's proposition. Conseil hastened to accept it, and this time the Canadian seemed quite willing to follow our example.

It was eight o'clock in the morning. At half-past eight we were equipped for this new excursion, and provided with two contrivances for light and breathing. The double door was open; and, accompanied by Captain Nemo, who was followed by a dozen of the crew, we set foot, at a depth of about thirty feet, on the solid bottom on which the *Nautilus* rested.

A slight declivity ended in an uneven bottom, at fifteen fathoms depth. This bottom differed entirely from the one I had visited on my first excursion under the waters of the Pacific Ocean. Here, there was no fine sand, no submarine prairies, no sea forest. I immediately recognized that marvelous region in which, on that day, the captain did the honors to us. It was the coral kingdom. In the zoophyte branch and in the alcyon class I noticed the gorgoneae, the isidiae, and the corollariae.

The light produced a thousand charming varieties, playing in the midst of the branches that were so vividly colored. I seemed to see the membraneous and cylindrical tubes tremble beneath the undulation of the waters. I was tempted to gather their fresh petals, ornamented with delicate tentacles, some just blown, the others budding, while a small fish, swimming swiftly, touched them slightly, like flights of birds. But if my hand approached these living flowers, these animated, sensitive plants, the whole colony took alarm. The white petals reentered their red cases, the flowers faded as I looked, and the bush changed into a block of stony knobs.

Chance had thrown me just by the most precious specimens of the zoophyte. This coral was more valuable than that found in the Mediterranean, on the coasts of France, Italy and Barbary. Its tints justified the poetical names of "Flower of Blood," and "Froth of Blood," that trade has given to its most beautiful productions. Coral is sold for £20 per ounce; and in this place the watery beds would make the fortunes of a company of coral-divers. This precious matter, often confused with other polypi, formed then the inextricable plots called "macciota," and on which I noticed several beautiful specimens of pink coral.

But soon the bushes contract, and the arborizations increase. Real petrified thickets, long joints of fantastic architecture, were disclosed before us. Captain Nemo placed himself under a dark gallery, where by a slight declivity we reached a depth of a hundred yards. The light from our lamps produced sometimes magical effects, following the rough outlines of the natural arches and pendants disposed like lusters, that were tipped with points of fire. Between the coralline shrubs I noticed other polypi not less curious—melites, and irises with articulated ramifactions; also some tufts of coral, some green, others red, like seaweed encrusted in their calcareous salts, that naturalists, after long discussion, have definitely classed in the vegetable kingdom. But following the remark of a thinking man, "there is perhaps the real point where life rises obscurely from the sleep of a stone, without detaching itself from the rough point of departure."

At last, after walking two hours, we had attained a depth of about three hundred yards, that is to say, the extreme limit on which coral begins to form. But there was no isolated bush, nor modest brushwood, at the bottom of lofty trees. It was an immense forest of large mineral vegetations, enormous petrified trees, united by garlands of elegant sea bindweed, all adorned with clouds and reflections. We passed freely under their high branches, lost in the shade of the waves.

Captain Nemo had stopped. I and my companions halted, and, turning around, I saw his men were forming a semicircle around their chief. Watching attentively, I observed that four of them carried on their shoulders an object of an oblong shape.

We occupied, in this place, the center of a vast glade surrounded by the lofty foliage of the submarine forest. Our lamps threw over this place a sort of clear twilight that singularly elongated the shadows on the ground. At the end of the glade the darkness increased, and was only relieved by little sparks reflected by the points of coral.

Ned Land and Conseil were near me. We watched, and I thought I was going to witness a strange scene. On observing the ground, I saw that it was raised in certain places by slight excrescences encrusted with limy deposits, and disposed with a regularity that betrayed the hand of man.

In the midst of the glade, on a pedestal of rocks roughly piled up, stood a cross of coral that extended its long arms that one might have thought were made of petrified blood. Upon a sign from Captain Nemo one of the men advanced; and at some feet from the cross he began to dig a hole with a pickaxe that he took from his belt. I understood all! This glade was a cemetery, this hole a tomb, this oblong object the body of the man who had died in the night! The captain and his men had come to bury their companion in this general resting-place, at the bottom of this inaccessible ocean!

The grave was being dug slowly; the fish fled on all sides while their retreat was being thus disturbed; I heard the strokes of the pickaxe, which sparkled when it hit upon some flint lost at the bottom of the waters. The hole was soon large and deep enough to receive the body. Then the bearers approached; the body, enveloped in a tissue of white linen, was lowered into the damp grave. Captain Nemo, with his arms crossed on his breast, and all the friends of him who had loved them, knelt in prayer.

The grave was then filled in with the rubbish taken from the ground, which formed a slight mound. When this was done, Captain Nemo and his men rose; then, approaching the grave, they knelt again, and all extended their hands in sign of a last adieu. Then the funeral procession returned to the *Nautilus*, passing under the arches of the forest, in the midst of thickets, along the coral bushes, and still on the ascent. At last the light of the ship appeared, and its luminous track guided us to the *Nautilus*. At one o'clock we had returned.

As soon as I had changed my clothes I went up on to the platform, and, a prey to conflicting emotions, I sat down near the binnacle. Captain Nemo joined me. I rose and said to him:

"So, as I said he would, this man died in the night?"

"Yes, M. Aronnax."

"And he rests now, near his companions, in the coral cemetery?"

"Yes, forgotten by all else, but not by us. We dug the grave, and the polypi undertake to seal our dead for eternity." And, burying his face quickly in his hands, he tried in vain to suppress a sob. Then he added: "Our peaceful cemetery is there, some hundred feet below the surface of the waves."

"Your dead sleep quietly, at least, Captain, out of the reach of sharks."

"Yes, sir, of sharks and men," gravely replied the captain.

# PART TWO

## CHAPTER I

### THE INDIAN OCEAN

We now come to the second part of our journey under the sea. The first ended with the moving scene in the coral cemetery which left such a deep impression on my mind. Thus, in the midst of this great sea, Captain Nemo's life was passing, even to his grave, which he had prepared in one of its deepest abysses. There, not one of the ocean's monsters could trouble the last sleep of the crew of the *Nautilus*, of those friends riveted to each other in death as in life. "Nor any man, either," had added the captain. Still the same fierce, implacable defiance toward human society!

I could no longer content myself with the theory which satisfied Conseil.

That worthy fellow persisted in seeing in the commander of the *Nautilus* one of those unknown servants who return mankind contempt for indifference. For him, he was a misunderstood genius who, tired of earth's deceptions, had taken refuge in this inaccessible medium, where he might follow his instincts freely. To my mind, this explains but one side of Captain Nemo's character. Indeed, the mystery of that last night during which we had been chained in prison, the sleep, and the precaution so violently taken by the captain of snatching from my eyes the glass I had raised to sweep the horizon, the mortal wound of the man, due to an unaccountable shock of the *Nautilus*, all put me on a new track. No; Captain Nemo was not satisfied with shunning man. His formidable apparatus not only suited his instinct of freedom, but perhaps also the design of some terrible retaliation.

At this moment nothing is clear to me; I catch but a glimpse of light amid all the darkness, and I must confine myself to writing as events shall dictate.

That day, January 24, 1868, at noon, the second officer came to take the altitude of the sun. I mounted the platform, lit a cigar, and watched the operation. It seemed to me that the man did not understand French; for several times I made remarks in a loud voice, which must have drawn from him some involuntary sign of attention, if he had understood them; but he remained undisturbed and dumb.

As he was taking observations with the sextant, one of the sailors of the *Nautilus* (the strong man who had accompanied us on our first submarine excursion to the island of Crespo) came to clean the glasses of the lantern. I examined the fittings of the apparatus, the strength of which was increased a hundredfold by lenticular rings, placed similar to those in a lighthouse, and which projected their brilliance in a horizontal plane. The electric lamp was combined in such a way as to give its most powerful light. Indeed, it was produced in *vacuo*, which ensured both its steadiness and its intensity. This vacuum economized the graphite points between which the luminous arc was developed—an important point of economy for Captain Nemo, who could not easily have replaced them; and under these conditions their waste was imperceptible. When the *Nautilus* was ready to continue its submarine journey, I went down to the saloon. The panel was closed, and the course marked direct west.

We were furrowing the waters of the Indian Ocean, a vast liquid plain, with a surface of 1,200,000,000 acres, and whose waters are so clear and transparent that anyone leaning over them would turn giddy. The *Nautilus* usually floated between fifty and a hundred fathoms deep. We went on so for some days. To anyone but myself, who had a great love for the sea, the hours would have seemed long and monotonous; but the daily walks on the platform, when I steeped myself in the reviving air of the ocean, the sight of the rich waters through the windows of the saloon, the books in the library, the compiling of my memoirs, took up all my time, and left me not a moment of ennui or weariness.

For some days we saw a great number of aquatic birds, sea mews or gulls. Some were cleverly killed and, prepared in a certain way, made very acceptable water-game. Among large-winged birds, carried a long distance from all lands and resting upon the waves from the fatigue of their flight, I saw some magnificent albatrosses, uttering discordant cries like the braying of an ass, and birds belonging to the family of the longipennates. The family of the totipalmates was represented by the sea-swallows, which caught the fish from the surface, and by numerous phaetons, or lepturi; among others, the phaeton with red lines, as large as a pigeon, whose white plumage, tinted with pink, shows off to advantage the blackness of its wings.

As to the fish, they always provoked our admiration when we surprised the secrets of their aquatic life through the open panels. I saw many kinds which I never before had a chance of observing.

I shall notice chiefly ostracions peculiar to the Red Sea, the Indian Ocean, and that part which washes the coast of tropical America. These fish, like the tortoise, the armadillo, the sea hedgehog, and the Crustacea, are protected by a breastplate which is neither chalky nor stony, but real bone. In some it takes the form of a solid triangle, in others of a solid quadrangle. Among the triangular I saw some an inch and a half in length, with wholesome flesh and a delicious flavor; they are brown at the tail, and yellow at the fins, and I recommend their introduction into freshwater, to which a certain number of sea fish easily accustom themselves. I would also mention quadrangular ostracions, having on the back four large tubercles; some dotted over with white spots on the lower part of the body, and which may be tamed like birds; trigons provided with spikes formed by the lengthening of their bony shell, and which, from their strange gruntings, are called "sea pigs"; also dromedaries with large humps in the shape of a cone, whose flesh is very tough and leathery.

I now borrow from the daily notes of Master Conseil. "Certain fish of the genus petrodon peculiar to those seas, with red backs and white chests, which are distinguished by three rows of longitudinal filaments; and some electrical, seven inches long, decked in the liveliest colors. Then, as specimens of other kinds, some ovoides, resembling an egg of a dark brown color, marked with white bands, and without tails; diodons, real sea porcupines, furnished with spikes, and capable of swelling in such a way as to look like cushions bristling with darts; hippocampi, common to every ocean; some pegasi with lengthened snouts, which their pectoral fins, being much elongated and formed in the shape of wings, allow, if not to fly, at least to shoot into the air; pigeon spatulae, with tails covered with many rings of shell; macrognathi with long jaws, an excellent fish, nine inches long, and bright with most agreeable colors; pale-colored calliomores, with rugged heads; and plenty of chaetpdons, with long and tubular muzzles, which kill insects by shooting them, as from an air-gun, with a single drop of water. These we may call the flycatchers of the seas.

"In the eighty-ninth genus of fish, classed by Lacepede, belonging to the second lower class of bony, characterized by opercules and bronchial membranes, I remarked the scorpaena, the head of which is furnished with spikes, and which has but one dorsal fin; these creatures are covered, or not, with little shells, according to the subclass to which they belong. The second subclass gives us specimens of didactyles fourteen or fifteen inches in length, with yellow rays, and heads of a most fantastic appearance. As to the first sub-class, it gives several specimens of that singular looking fish appropriately called a 'sea frog,' with large head, sometimes pierced with holes, sometimes swollen with protuberances, bristling with spikes, and covered with tubercles; it has irregular and hideous horns; its body and tail are covered with callosities; its sting makes a dangerous wound; it is both repugnant and horrible to look at."

From January 21 to 23, the *Nautilus* went at the rate of two hundred and fifty leagues in twenty-four hours, being five hundred and forty miles, or twenty-two miles an hour. If we recognized so many different varieties of fish, it was because, attracted by the electric light, they tried to follow us; the greater part, however, were soon distanced by our speed, though some kept their place in the waters of the *Nautilus* for a time. The morning of the 24th, in 12° 5' south latitude, and 94° 33' longitude, we observed Keeling Island, a coral formation, planted with magnificent cocos, and which had been visited by Mr. Darwin and Captain Fitzroy. The *Nautilus* skirted the shores of this desert island for a little distance. Its nets brought up numerous specimens of polypi and curious shells of mollusca. Some precious productions of the species of delphinulae enriched the treasures of Captain Nemo, to which I added an astraea punctifera, a kind of parasite polypus often found fixed to a shell.

Soon Keeling Island disappeared from the horizon, and our course was directed to the northwest in the direction of the Indian Peninsula.

From Keeling Island our course was slower and more variable, often taking us into great depths. Several times they made use of the inclined planes, which certain internal levers placed obliquely to the waterline. In that way we went about two miles, but without ever obtaining the greatest depths of the Indian Sea, which soundings of seven thousand fathoms have never reached. As to the temperature of the lower strata, the thermometer invariably indicated 4° above zero. I only observed that in the upper regions the water was always colder in the high levels than at the surface of the sea.

On January 25, the ocean was entirely deserted; the *Nautilus* passed the day on the surface, beating the waves with its powerful screw and making them rebound to a great height. Who under such circumstances would not have taken it for a gigantic cetacean? Three parts of this day I spent on the platform. I watched the sea. Nothing on the horizon, till about four o'clock a steamer running west on our counter. Her masts were visible for an instant, but she could not see the *Nautilus*, being too low in the water. I fancied this steamboat belonged to the P.O. Company, which runs from Ceylon to Sydney, touching at King George's Point and Melbourne.

At five o'clock in the evening, before that fleeting twilight which binds night to day in tropical zones, Conseil and I were astonished by a curious spectacle.

It was a shoal of argonauts traveling along on the surface of the ocean. We could count several hundreds. They belonged to the tubercle kind which are peculiar to the Indian seas.

These graceful mollusks moved backward by means of their locomotive tube, through which they propelled the water already drawn in. Of their eight tentacles, six were elongated, and stretched out floating on the water, while the other two, rolled up flat, were spread to the wing like a light sail. I saw their spiral-shaped and fluted shells, which Cuvier justly compares to an elegant skiff. A boat indeed! It bears the creature which secretes it without its adhering to it.

For nearly an hour the *Nautilus* floated in the midst of this shoal of mollusks. Then I know not what sudden fright they took. But as if at a signal every sail was furled, the arms folded, the body drawn in, the shells turned over, changing their center of gravity, and the whole fleet disappeared under the waves. Never did the ships of a squadron maneuver with more unity.

At that moment night fell suddenly, and the reeds, scarcely raised by the breeze, lay peaceably under the sides of the *Nautilus*.

The next day, January 26, we cut the equator at the eighty-second meridian and entered the northern hemisphere. During the day a formidable troop of sharks accompanied us, terrible creatures, which multiply in these seas and make them very dangerous. They were "cestracio philippi" sharks, with brown backs and whitish bellies, armed with eleven rows of teeth—eyed sharks—their throat being marked with a large black spot surrounded with white like an eye. There were also some Isabella sharks, with rounded snouts marked with dark spots. These powerful creatures often hurled themselves at the windows of the saloon with such violence as to make us feel very insecure. At such times Ned Land was no longer master of himself. He wanted to go to the surface and harpoon the monsters, particularly certain smooth hound sharks, whose mouth is studded with teeth like a mosaic; and large tiger sharks nearly six yards long, the last named of which seemed to excite him more particularly. But the *Nautilus*, accelerating her speed, easily left the most rapid of them behind.

On January 27, at the entrance of the vast Bay of Bengal, we met repeatedly a forbidding spectacle, dead bodies floating on the surface of the water. They were the dead of the Indian villages, carried by the Ganges to the level of the sea, and which the vultures, the only undertakers of the country, had not been able to devour. But the sharks did not fail to help them at their funeral work.

About seven o'clock in the evening, the *Nautilus*, half-immersed, was sailing in a sea of milk. At first sight the ocean seemed lactified. Was it the effect of the lunar rays? No; for the moon, scarcely two days old, was still lying hidden under the horizon in the rays of the sun. The whole sky, though lit by the sidereal rays, seemed black by contrast with the whiteness of the waters.

Conseil could not believe his eyes, and questioned me as to the cause of this strange phenomenon. Happily I was able to answer him.

"It is called a milk sea," I explained. "A large extent of white wavelets often to be seen on the coasts of Amboyna, and in these parts of the sea."

"But, sir," said Conseil, "can you tell me what causes such an effect? For I suppose the water is not really turned into milk."

"No, my boy; and the whiteness which surprises you is caused only by the presence of myriads of infusoria, a sort of luminous little worm, gelatinous and without color, of the thickness of a hair, and whose length is not more than seven-thousandths of an inch. These insects adhere to one another sometimes for several leagues."

"Several leagues!" exclaimed Conseil.

"Yes, my boy; and you need not try to compute the number of these infusoria. You will not be able, for, if I am not mistaken, ships have floated on these milk seas for more than forty miles."

Toward midnight the sea suddenly resumed its usual color; but behind us, even to the limits of the horizon, the sky reflected the whitened waves, and for a long time seemed impregnated with the vague glimmerings of an aurora borealis.

## CHAPTER II

### A NOVEL PROPOSAL OF CAPTAIN NEMO'S

On February 28, when at noon the *Nautilus* came to the surface of the sea, in 9° 4' north latitude, there was land in sight about eight miles to westward. The first thing I noticed was a range of mountains about two thousand feet high, the shapes of which were most capricious. On taking the bearings, I knew that we were nearing the island of Ceylon, the pearl which hangs from the lobe of the Indian Peninsula.

Captain Nemo and his second appeared at this moment. The captain glanced at the map. Then turning to me, said:

"The island of Ceylon, noted for its pearl fisheries. Would you like to visit one of them, M. Aronnax?"

"Certainly, Captain."

"Well, the thing is easy. Though, if we see the fisheries, we shall not see the fishermen. The annual exportation has not yet begun. Never mind, I will give orders to make for the Gulf of Manaar, where we shall arrive in the night."

The captain said something to his second, who immediately went out. Soon the *Nautilus* returned to her native element, and the manometer showed that she was about thirty feet deep.

"Well, sir," said Captain Nemo, "you and your companions shall visit the Bank of Manaar, and if by chance some fisherman should be there, we shall see him at work."

"Agreed, Captain!"

"By the by, M. Aronnax, you are not afraid of sharks?"

"Sharks!" exclaimed I.

This question seemed a very hard one.

"Well?" continued Captain Nemo.

"I admit, Captain, that I am not yet very familiar with that kind of fish."

"We are accustomed to them," replied Captain Nemo, "and in time you will be too. However, we shall be armed, and on the road we may be able to hunt some of the tribe. It is interesting. So, till tomorrow, sir, and early."

This said in a careless tone, Captain Nemo left the saloon. Now, if you were invited to hunt the bear in the mountains of Switzerland, what would you say? "Very well! Tomorrow we will go and hunt the bear." If you were asked to hunt the lion in the plains of Atlas, or the tiger in the Indian jungles, what would you say? "Ha! Ha! It seems we are going to hunt the tiger or the lion!" But when you are invited to hunt the shark in its natural element, you would perhaps reflect before accepting the invitation. As for myself, I passed my hand over my forehead, on which stood large drops of cold perspiration. "Let us reflect," said I, "and take our time. Hunting otters in submarine forests, as we did in the island of Crespo, will pass; but going up and down at the bottom of the sea, where one is almost certain to meet sharks, is quite another thing! I know well that in certain countries, particularly in the Andaman

Islands, the negroes never hesitate to attack them with a dagger in one hand and a running noose in the other; but I also know that few who affront those creatures ever return alive. However, I am not a negro, and if I were I think a little hesitation in this case would not be ill-timed."

At this moment Conseil and the Canadian entered, quite composed, and even joyous. They knew not what awaited them.

"Faith, sir," said Ned Land, "your Captain Nemo—the devil take him!—has just made us a very pleasant offer."

"Ah!" said I. "You know?"

"If agreeable to you, sir," interrupted Conseil, "the commander of the *Nautilus* has invited us to visit the magnificent Ceylon fisheries tomorrow, in your company; he did it kindly, and behaved like a real gentleman."

"He said nothing more?"

"Nothing more, sir, except that he had already spoken to you of this little walk."

"Sir," said Conseil, "would you give us some details of the pearl fishery?"

"As to the fishing itself," I asked, "or the incidents, which?"

"On the fishing," replied the Canadian; "before entering upon the ground, it is as well to know something about it."

"Very well; sit down, my friends, and I will teach you."

Ned and Conseil seated themselves on an ottoman, and the first thing the Canadian asked was:

"Sir, what is a pearl?"

"My worthy Ned," I answered, "to the poet, a pearl is a tear of the sea; to the Orientals, it is a drop of dew solidified; to the ladies, it is a jewel of an oblong shape, of a brilliancy of mother-of-pearl substance, which they wear on their fingers, their necks, or their ears; for the chemist it is a mixture of phosphate and carbonate of lime, with a little gelatine; and lastly, for naturalists, it is simply a morbid secretion of the organ that produces the mother-of-pearl among certain bivalves."

"Branch of mollusks," said Conseil.

"Precisely so, my learned Conseil; and, among these testacea the earshell, the tridacnae, the turbots, in a word, all those which secrete mother-of-pearl, that is, the blue, bluish, violet, or white substance which lines the interior of their shells, are capable of producing pearls."

"Mussels too?" asked the Canadian.

"Yes, mussels of certain waters in Scotland, Wales, Ireland, Saxony, Bohemia, and France."

"Good! For the future I shall pay attention," replied the Canadian.

"But," I continued, "the particular mollusk which secretes the pearl is the pearl oyster, the meleagrina margaritiferct, that precious pintadine. The pearl is nothing but a nacreous formation, deposited in a globular form, either adhering to the oyster shell, or buried in the folds of the creature. On the shell it is fast; in the flesh it is loose; but always has for a kernel a small hard substance, maybe a barren egg, maybe a grain of sand, around which the pearly matter deposits itself year after year successively, and by thin concentric layers."

"Are many pearls found in the same oyster?" asked Conseil.

"Yes, my boy. Some are a perfect casket. One oyster has been mentioned, though I allow myself to doubt it, as having contained no less than a hundred and fifty sharks."

"A hundred and fifty sharks!" exclaimed Ned Land.

"Did I say sharks?" said I hurriedly. "I meant to say a hundred and fifty pearls. Sharks would not be sense."

"Certainly not," said Conseil; "but will you tell us now by what means they extract these pearls?"

"They proceed in various ways. When they adhere to the shell, the fishermen often pull them off with pincers; but the most common way is to lay the oysters on mats of the seaweed which covers the banks. Thus they die in the open air; and at the end of ten days they are in a forward state of decomposition. They are then plunged into large reservoirs of seawater; then they are opened and washed. Now begins the double work of the sorters. First they separate the layers of pearls, known in commerce by the name of bastard whites and bastard blacks, which are delivered in boxes of two hundred and fifty and three hundred pounds each. Then they take the parenchyma of the oyster, boil it, and pass it through a sieve in order to extract the very smallest pearls."

"The price of these pearls varies according to their size?" asked Conseil.

"Not only according to their size," I answered, "but also according to their shape, their water (that is, their color), and their luster: that is, that bright and diapered sparkle which makes them so charming to the eye. The most beautiful are called virgin pearls, or paragons. They are formed alone in the tissue of the mollusk, are white, often opaque, and sometimes have the transparency of an opal; they are generally round or oval. The round are made into bracelets, the oval into pendants, and, being more precious, are sold singly. Those adhering to the shell of the oyster are more irregular in shape, and are sold by weight. Lastly, in a lower order are classed those small pearls known under the name of seed pearls; they are sold by measure, and are especially used in embroidery for church ornaments."

"But," said Conseil, "is this pearl fishery dangerous?"

"No," I answered, quickly; "particularly if certain precautions are taken."

"What does one risk in such a calling?" said Ned Land. "The swallowing of some mouthfuls of seawater?"

"As you say, Ned. By the by," said I, trying to take Captain Nemo's careless tone, "are you afraid of sharks, brave Ned?"

"I!" replied the Canadian. "A harpooner by profession? It is my trade to make light of them."

"But," said I, "it is not a question of fishing for them with an iron-swivel, hoisting them into the vessel, cutting off their tails with a blow of a chopper, ripping them up, and throwing their heart into the sea!"

"Then, it is a question of—"

"Precisely."

"In the water?"

"In the water."

"Faith, with a good harpoon! You know, sir, these sharks are ill-fashioned beasts. They turn on their bellies to seize you, and in that time—"

Ned Land had a way of saying "seize" which made my blood run cold.

"Well, and you, Conseil, what do you think of sharks?"

"Me!" said Conseil. "I will be frank, sir."

"So much the better," thought I.

"If you, sir, mean to face the sharks, I do not see why your faithful servant should not face them with you."

## CHAPTER III

### A PEARL OF TEN MILLIONS

The next morning at four o'clock I was awakened by the steward whom Captain Nemo had placed at my service. I rose hurriedly, dressed, and went into the saloon.

Captain Nemo was awaiting me.

"M. Aronnax," said he, "are you ready to start?"

"I am ready."

"Then please to follow me."

"And my companions, Captain?"

"They have been told and are waiting."

"Are we not to put on our diver's dresses?" asked I.

"Not yet. I have not allowed the *Nautilus* to come too near this coast, and we are some distance from the Manaar Bank; but the boat is ready, and will take us to the exact point of disembarking, which will save us a long way. It carries our diving apparatus, which we will put on when we begin our submarine journey."

Captain Nemo conducted me to the central staircase, which led on the platform. Ned and Conseil were already there, delighted at the idea of the "pleasure party" which was preparing. Five sailors from the *Nautilus*, with their oars, waited in the boat, which had been made fast against the side.

The night was still dark. Layers of clouds covered the sky, allowing but few stars to be seen. I looked on the side where the land lay, and saw nothing but a dark line enclosing three parts of the horizon, from southwest to northwest. The *Nautilus*, having returned during the night up the western coast of Ceylon, was now west of the bay, or rather gulf, formed by the mainland and the island of Manaar. There, under the dark waters, stretched the pintadine bank, an inexhaustible field of pearls, the length of which is more than twenty miles.

Captain Nemo, Ned Land, Conseil, and I took our places in the stern of the boat. The master went to the tiller; his four companions leaned on their oars, the painter was cast off, and we sheered off.

The boat went toward the south; the oarsmen did not hurry. I noticed that their strokes, strong in the water, only followed each other every ten seconds, according to the method generally adopted in the navy. While the craft was running by its own velocity, the liquid drops struck the dark depths of the waves crisply like spats of melted lead. A little billow, spreading wide, gave a slight roll to the boat, and some samphire reeds flapped before it.

We were silent. What was Captain Nemo thinking of? Perhaps of the land he was approaching, and which he found too near to him, contrary to the Canadian's opinion, who thought it too far off. As to Conseil, he was merely there from curiosity.

About half-past five the first tints on the horizon showed the upper line of coast more distinctly. Flat enough in the east, it rose a little to the south. Five miles still lay between us, and it was indistinct owing to the mist on the water. At six o'clock it became suddenly daylight, with that rapidity peculiar to tropical regions, which know neither dawn nor twilight. The solar rays pierced the curtain of clouds, piled up on the eastern horizon, and the radiant orb rose rapidly. I saw land distinctly, with a few trees scattered here and there. The boat neared Manaar Island, which was rounded to the south. Captain Nemo rose from his seat and watched the sea.

At a sign from him the anchor was dropped, but the chain scarcely ran, for it was little more than a yard deep, and this spot was one of the highest points of the bank of pintadines.

"Here we are, M. Aronnax," said Captain Nemo. "You see that enclosed bay? Here, in a month will be assembled the numerous fishing boats of the exporters, and these are the waters their divers will ransack so boldly. Happily, this bay is well situated for that kind of fishing. It is sheltered from the strongest winds; the sea is never very rough here, which makes it favorable for the diver's work. We will now put on our dresses, and begin our walk."

I did not answer, and, while watching the suspected waves, began with the help of the sailors to put on my heavy sea dress. Captain Nemo and my companions were also dressing. None of the *Nautilus* men were to accompany us on this new excursion.

Soon we were enveloped to the throat in India rubber clothing; the air apparatus fixed to our backs by braces. As to the Ruhmkorff apparatus, there was no necessity for it. Before putting my head into the copper cap, I had asked the question of the captain.

"They would be useless," he replied. "We are going to no great depth, and the solar rays will be enough to light our walk. Besides, it would not be prudent to carry the electric light in these waters; its brilliancy might attract some of the dangerous inhabitants of the coast most inopportunely."

As Captain Nemo pronounced these words, I turned to Conseil and Ned Land. But my two friends had already encased their heads in the metal cap, and they could neither hear nor answer.

One last question remained to ask of Captain Nemo.

"And our arms?" asked I. "Our guns?"

"Guns! What for? Do not mountaineers attack the bear with a dagger in their hand, and is not steel surer than lead? Here is a strong blade; put it in your belt, and we start."

I looked at my companions; they were armed like us, and, more than that, Ned Land was brandishing an enormous harpoon, which he had placed in the boat before leaving the *Nautilus*.

Then, following the captain's example, I allowed myself to be dressed in the heavy copper helmet, and our reservoirs of air were at once in activity. An instant after we were landed, one after the other, in about two yards of water upon an even sand. Captain Nemo made a sign with his hand, and we followed him by a gentle declivity till we disappeared under the waves.

Over our feet, like coveys of snipe in a bog, rose shoals of fish, of the genus monoptera, which have no other fins but their tail. I recognized the Javanese, a real serpent two and a half feet long, of a livid color underneath, and which might easily be mistaken for a conger eel if it were not for the golden stripes on its side. In the genus stromateus, whose bodies are very flat and oval, I saw some of the most brilliant colors, carrying their dorsal fin like a scythe; an excellent eating fish, which, dried and pickled, is known by the name of Karawade; then some tranquebars, belonging to the genus apsiphoroides, whose body is covered with a shell cuirass of eight longitudinal plates.

The heightening sun lit the mass of waters more and more. The soil changed by degrees. To the fine sand succeeded a perfect causeway of boulders, covered with a carpet of mollusks and zoophytes. Among the specimens of these branches I noticed some placenae, with thin unequal shells, a kind of ostracion peculiar to the Red Sea and the Indian Ocean; some orange lucinae with rounded shells; rockfish three feet and a half long, which raised themselves under the waves like hands ready to seize one. There were also some panopyres, slightly luminous; and lastly, some oculines, like magnificent fans, forming one of the richest vegetations of these seas.

In the midst of these living plants, and under the arbors of the hydrophytes, were layers of clumsy articulates, particularly some raninae, whose carapace formed a slightly rounded triangle; and some horrible looking parthenopes.

At about seven o'clock we found ourselves at last surveying the oyster banks on which the pearl oysters are reproduced by millions.

Captain Nemo pointed with his hand to the enormous heap of oysters; and I could well understand that this mine was inexhaustible, for nature's creative power is far beyond man's instinct of destruction. Ned Land, faithful to his instinct, hastened to fill a net which he carried by his side with some of the finest specimens. But we could not stop. We must follow the captain, who seemed to guide himself by paths known only to himself. The ground was sensibly rising, and sometimes, on holding up my arm, it was above the surface of the sea. Then the level of the bank would sink capriciously. Often we rounded high rocks scarped into pyramids. In their dark fractures huge crustacea, perched upon their high claws like some war machine, watched us with fixed eyes, and under our feet crawled various kinds of annelids.

At this moment there opened before us a large grotto dug in a picturesque heap of rocks and carpeted with all the thick warp of the submarine flora. At first it seemed very dark to me. The solar rays seemed to be extinguished by successive gradations, until its vague transparency became nothing more than drowned light. Captain Nemo entered; we followed. My eyes soon accustomed themselves to this relative state of darkness. I could distinguish the arches springing capriciously from natural pillars, standing broad upon their granite base, like the heavy columns of Tuscan architecture. Why had our incomprehensible guide led us to the bottom of this submarine crypt? I was soon to know. After descending a rather sharp declivity, our feet trod the bottom of a kind of circular pit. There Captain Nemo stopped, and with his hand indicated an object I had not yet perceived. It was an oyster of extraordinary dimensions, a gigantic tridacne, a goblet which could have contained a whole lake of holy water, a basin the breadth of which was more than two yards and a half, and consequently larger than that ornamenting the saloon of the *Nautilus*. I approached this extraordinary mollusk. It adhered by its filaments to a table of granite, and there, isolated, it developed itself in the calm waters of the grotto. I estimated the weight of this tridacne at 600 pounds. Such an oyster would contain 30 pounds of meat; and one must have the stomach of a Gargantua to demolish some dozens of them.

Captain Nemo was evidently acquainted with the existence of this bivalve, and seemed to have a particular motive in verifying the actual state of this tridacne. The shells were a little open; the captain came near and put his dagger between to prevent them from closing; then with his hand he raised the membrane with its fringed edges, which formed a cloak for the creature. There, between the folded plaits, I saw a loose pearl, whose size equaled that of a coconut. Its globular shape, perfect clearness, and admirable luster made it altogether a jewel of inestimable value. Carried away by my curiosity, I stretched out my hand to seize it, weigh it, and touch it; but the captain stopped me, made a sign of refusal, and quickly withdrew his dagger, and the two shells closed suddenly. I then understood Captain Nemo's intention. In leaving this pearl hidden in the mantle of the tridacne he was allowing it to grow slowly. Each year the secretions of the mollusk would add new concentric circles. I estimated its value at £500,000 at least.

After ten minutes Captain Nemo stopped suddenly. I thought he had halted previously to returning. No; by a gesture he bade us crouch beside him in a deep fracture of the rock, his hand pointed to one part of the liquid mass, which I watched attentively.

About five yards from me a shadow appeared, and sank to the ground. The disquieting idea of sharks shot through my mind, but I was mistaken; and once again it was not a monster of the ocean that we had anything to do with.

It was a man, a living man, an Indian, a fisherman, a poor devil who, I suppose, had come to glean before the harvest. I could see the bottom of his canoe anchored some feet above his head. He dived and went up successively. A stone held between his feet, cut in the shape of a sugar loaf, while a rope fastened him to his boat, helped him to descend more rapidly. This was all his apparatus. Reaching the bottom, about five yards deep, he went on his knees and filled his bag with oysters picked up at random. Then he went up, emptied it, pulled up his stone, and began the operation once more, which lasted thirty seconds.

The diver did not see us. The shadow of the rock hid us from sight. And how should this poor Indian ever dream that men, beings like himself, should be there under the water watching his movements and losing no detail of the fishing? Several times he went up in this way, and dived again. He did not carry away more than ten at each plunge, for he was obliged to pull them from the bank to which they adhered by means of their strong byssus. And how many of those oysters for which he risked his life had no pearl in them! I watched him closely; his maneuvers were regular; and for the space of half an hour no danger appeared to threaten him.

I was beginning to accustom myself to the sight of this interesting fishing, when suddenly, as the Indian was on the ground, I saw him make a gesture of terror, rise, and make a spring to return to the surface of the sea.

I understood his dread. A gigantic shadow appeared just above the unfortunate diver. It was a shark of enormous size advancing diagonally, his eyes on fire, and his jaws open. I was mute with horror and unable to move.

The voracious creature shot toward the Indian, who threw himself on one side to avoid the shark's fins; but not its tail, for it struck his chest and stretched him on the ground.

This scene lasted but a few seconds: the shark returned, and, turning on his back, prepared himself for cutting the Indian in two, when I saw Captain Nemo rise suddenly, and then, dagger in hand, walk straight to the monster, ready to fight face-to-face with him. The very moment the shark was going to snap the unhappy fisherman in two, he perceived his new adversary, and, turning over, made straight toward him.

I can still see Captain Nemo's position. Holding himself well together, he waited for the shark with admirable coolness; and, when it rushed at him, threw himself on one side with wonderful quickness, avoiding the shock, and burying his dagger deep into its side. But it was not all over. A terrible combat ensued.

The shark had seemed to roar, if I might say so. The blood rushed in torrents from its wound. The sea was dyed red, and through the opaque liquid I could distinguish nothing more. Nothing more until the moment when, like lightning, I saw the undaunted Captain hanging on to one of the creature's fins, struggling, as it were, hand to hand with the monster, and dealing successive blows at his enemy, yet still unable to give a decisive one.

The shark's struggles agitated the water with such fury that the rocking threatened to upset me.

I wanted to go to the captain's assistance, but, nailed to the spot with horror, I could not stir.

I saw the haggard eye; I saw the different phases of the fight. The captain fell to the earth, upset by the enormous mass which leaned upon him. The shark's jaws opened wide, like a pair of factory shears, and it would have been all over with the captain; but, quick as thought, harpoon in hand, Ned Land rushed toward the shark and struck it with its sharp point.

The waves were impregnated with a mass of blood. They rocked under the shark's movements, which beat them with indescribable fury. Ned Land had not missed his aim. It was the monster's death rattle. Struck to the heart, it struggled in dreadful convulsions, the shock of which overthrew Conseil.

But Ned Land had disentangled the captain, who, getting up without any wound, went straight to the Indian, quickly cut the cord which held him to his stone, took him in his arms, and, with a sharp blow of his heel, mounted to the surface.

We all three followed in a few seconds, saved by a miracle, and reached the fisherman's boat.

Captain Nemo's first care was to recall the unfortunate man to life again. I did not think he could succeed. I hoped so, for the poor creature's immersion was not long; but the blow from the shark's tail might have been his deathblow.

Happily, with the captain's and Conseil's sharp friction, I saw consciousness return by degrees. He opened his eyes. What was his surprise, his terror even, at seeing four great copper heads leaning over him! And, above all, what must he have thought when Captain Nemo, drawing from the pocket of his dress a bag of pearls, placed it in his hand! This munificent charity from the man of the waters to the poor Cingalese was accepted with a trembling hand. His wondering eyes showed that he knew not to what superhuman beings he owed both fortune and life.

At a sign from the captain we regained the bank, and, following the road already traversed, came in about half an hour to the anchor which held the canoe of the *Nautilus* to the earth.

Once on board, we each, with the help of the sailors, got rid of the heavy copper helmet.

Captain Nemo's first word was to the Canadian.

"Thank you, Master Land," said he.

"It was in revenge, Captain," replied Ned Land. "I owed you that."

A ghastly smile passed across the captain's lips, and that was all.

"To the *Nautilus*," said he.

The boat flew over the waves. Some minutes after we met the shark's dead body floating. By the black marking of the extremity of its fins, I recognized the terrible melanopteron of the Indian Seas, of the species of shark so properly called. It was more than twenty-five feet long; its enormous mouth occupied one-third of its body. It was an adult, as was known by its six rows of teeth placed in an isosceles triangle in the upper jaw.

While I was contemplating this inert mass, a dozen of these voracious beasts appeared around the boat; and, without noticing us, threw themselves upon the dead body and fought with one another for the pieces.

At half-past eight we were again on board the *Nautilus*. There I reflected on the incidents which had taken place in our excursion to the Manaar Bank.

Two conclusions I must inevitably draw from it—one bearing upon the unparalleled courage of Captain Nemo, the other upon his devotion to a human being, a representative of that race from which he fled beneath the sea. Whatever he might say, this strange man had not yet succeeded in entirely crushing his heart.

When I made this observation to him, he answered in a slightly moved tone:

"That Indian, sir, is an inhabitant of an oppressed country; and I am still, and shall be, to my last breath, one of them!"

## CHAPTER IV

### THE RED SEA

In the course of the day of January 29, the island of Ceylon disappeared under the horizon, and the *Nautilus*, at a speed of twenty miles an hour, slid into the labyrinth of canals which separate the Maldives from the Laccadives. It coasted even the island of Kiltan, a land originally coraline, discovered by Vasco da Gama in 1499, and one of the nineteen principal islands of the Laccadive Archipelago, situated between 10° and 14° 30' north latitude, and 69° 50' 72" east longitude.

We had made 16,220 miles, or 7,500 (French) leagues from our starting point in the Japanese Seas.

The next day (January 30), when the *Nautilus* went to the surface of the ocean there was no land in sight. Its course was N.N.E., in the direction of the Sea of Oman, between Arabia and the Indian Peninsula, which serves as an outlet to the Persian Gulf. It was evidently a block without any possible egress. Where was Captain Nemo taking us to? I could not say. This, however, did not satisfy the Canadian, who that day came to me asking where we were going.

"We are going where our captain's fancy takes us, Master Ned."

"His fancy cannot take us far, then," said the Canadian. "The Persian Gulf has no outlet; and, if we do go in, it will not be long before we are out again."

"Very well, then, we will come out again, Master Land; and if, after the Persian Gulf, the *Nautilus* would like to visit the Red Sea, the Straits of Bab-el-mandeb are there to give us entrance."

"I need not tell you, sir," said Ned Land, "that the Red Sea is as much closed as the gulf, as the Isthmus of Suez is not yet cut; and, if it was, a boat as mysterious as ours would not risk itself in a canal cut with sluices. And again, the Red Sea is not the road to take us back to Europe."

"But I never said we were going back to Europe."

"What do you suppose, then?"

"I suppose that, after visiting the curious coasts of Arabia and Egypt, the *Nautilus* will go down the Indian Ocean again, perhaps cross the Channel of Mozambique, perhaps off the Mascarenhas, so as to gain the Cape of Good Hope."

"And once at the Cape of Good Hope?" asked the Canadian, with peculiar emphasis.

"Well, we shall penetrate into that Atlantic which we do not yet know. Ah! Friend Ned, you are getting tired of this journey under the sea; you are surfeited with the incessantly varying spectacle of submarine wonders. For my part, I shall be sorry to see the end of a voyage which it is given to so few men to make."

For four days, till February 3, the *Nautilus* scoured the Sea of Oman, at various speeds and at various depths. It seemed to go at random, as if hesitating as to which road it should follow, but we never passed the Tropic of Cancer.

In quitting this sea we sighted Muscat for an instant, one of the most important towns of the country of Oman. I admired its strange aspect, surrounded by black rocks upon which its white houses and forts stood in relief. I saw the rounded domes of its mosques, the elegant points of its minarets, its fresh and verdant terraces. But it was only a vision! The *Nautilus* soon sank under the waves of that part of the sea.

We passed along the Arabian coast of Mahrah and Hadramaut, for a distance of six miles, its undulating line of mountains being occasionally relieved by some ancient ruin. On February 5 we at last entered the Gulf of Aden, a perfect funnel introduced into the neck of Bab-el-mandeb, through which the Indian waters entered the Red Sea.

On February 6, the *Nautilus* floated in sight of Aden, perched upon a promontory which a narrow isthmus joins to the mainland, a kind of inaccessible Gibraltar, the fortifications of which were rebuilt by the English after taking possession in 1839. I caught a glimpse of the octagon minarets of this town, which was at one time the richest commercial magazine on the coast.

I certainly thought that Captain Nemo, arrived at this point, would back out again; but I was mistaken, for he did no such thing, much to my surprise.

The next day, February 7, we entered the Straits of Bab-el-mandeb, the name of which, in the Arab tongue, means "the Gate of Tears."

To twenty miles in breadth, it is only thirty-two in length. And for the *Nautilus*, starting at full speed, the crossing was scarcely the work of an hour. But I saw nothing, not even the island of Perim, with which the British government has fortified the position of Aden. There were too many English or French steamers of the line of Suez to Bombay, Calcutta to Melbourne, and from Bourbon to the Mauritius, furrowing this narrow passage, for the *Nautilus* to venture to show itself. So it remained prudently below. At last about noon, we were in the waters of the Red Sea.

I would not even seek to understand the caprice which had decided Captain Nemo upon entering the gulf. But I quite approved of the *Nautilus* entering it. Its speed was lessened: sometimes it kept on the surface, sometimes it dived to avoid a vessel, and thus I was able to observe the upper and lower parts of this curious sea.

On February 8, from the first dawn of day, Mocha came in sight, now a ruined town, whose walls would fall at a gunshot, yet which shelters here and there some verdant date trees; once an important city, containing six public markets, and twenty-six mosques, and whose walls, defended by fourteen forts, formed a girdle of two miles in circumference.

The *Nautilus* then approached the African shore, where the depth of the sea was greater. There, between two waters clear as crystal, through the open panels we were allowed to contemplate the beautiful bushes of brilliant coral and large blocks of rock clothed with a splendid fur of green variety of sites and landscapes along these sandbanks and algae and fuci. What an indescribable spectacle, and what variety of sites and landscapes along these sandbanks and volcanic islands which bound the Libyan coast! But where these shrubs appeared in all their beauty was on the eastern coast, which the *Nautilus* soon gained. It was on the coast of Tehama, for there not only did this display of zoophytes flourish beneath the level of the sea, but they also formed picturesque interlacings which unfolded themselves about sixty feet above the surface, more capricious but less highly colored than those whose freshness was kept up by the vital power of the waters.

What charming hours I passed thus at the window of the saloon! What new specimens of submarine flora and fauna did I admire under the brightness of our electric lantern!

On February 9, the *Nautilus* floated in the broadest part of the Red Sea, which is comprised between Souakin, on the west coast, and Komfidah, on the east coast, with a diameter of ninety miles.

That day at noon, after the bearings were taken, Captain Nemo mounted the platform, where I happened to be, and I was determined not to let him go down again without at least pressing him regarding his ulterior projects. As soon as he saw me he approached and graciously offered me a cigar.

"Well, sir, does this Red Sea please you? Have you sufficiently observed the wonders it covers, its fish, its zoophytes, its parterres of sponges, and its forests of coral? Did you catch a glimpse of the towns on its borders?"

"Yes, Captain Nemo," I replied; "and the *Nautilus* is wonderfully fitted for such a study. Ah! It is an intelligent boat!"

"Yes, sir, intelligent and invulnerable. It fears neither the terrible tempests of the Red Sea, nor its currents, nor its sandbanks."

"Certainly," said I, "this sea is quoted as one of the worst, and in the time of the ancients, if I am not mistaken, its reputation was detestable."

"Detestable, M. Aronnax. The Greek and Latin historians do not speak favorably of it, and Strabo says it is very dangerous during the Etesian winds and in the rainy season. The Arabian Edrisi portrays it under the name of the Gulf of Colzoum, and relates that vessels perished there in great numbers on the sandbanks and that no one would risk sailing in the night. It is, he pretends, a sea subject to fearful hurricanes, strewn with inhospitable islands, and 'which offers nothing good either on its surface or in its depths.' Such, too, is the opinion of Arrian, Agatharcides, and Artemidorus."

"One may see," I replied, "that these historians never sailed on board the *Nautilus*."

"Just so," replied the captain, smiling; "and in that respect moderns are not more advanced than the ancients. It required many ages to find out the mechanical power of steam. Who knows if, in another hundred years, we may not see a second *Nautilus*? Progress is slow, M. Aronnax."

"It is true," I answered; "your boat is at least a century before its time, perhaps an era. What a misfortune that the secret of such an invention should die with its inventor!"

Captain Nemo did not reply. After some minutes' silence he continued:

"You were speaking of the opinions of ancient historians upon the dangerous navigation of the Red Sea."

"It is true," said I; "but were not their fears exaggerated?"

"Yes and no, M. Aronnax," replied Captain Nemo, who seemed to know the Red Sea by heart. "That which is no longer dangerous for a modern vessel, well rigged, strongly built, and master of its own course, thanks to obedient steam, offered all sorts of perils to the ships of the ancients. Picture to yourself those first navigators venturing in ships made of planks sewn with the cords of the palm tree, saturated with the grease of the sea dog, and covered with powdered resin! They had not even instruments wherewith to take their bearings, and they went by guess among currents of which they scarcely knew anything. Under such conditions shipwrecks were, and must have been, numerous. But in our time, steamers running between Suez and the South Seas have nothing more to fear from the fury of this gulf, in spite of contrary trade winds. The captain and passengers do not prepare for their departure by offering propitiatory sacrifices; and, on their return, they no longer go ornamented with wreaths and gilt fillets to thank the gods in the neighboring temple."

"I agree with you," said I; "and steam seems to have killed all gratitude in the hearts of sailors. But, Captain, since you seem to have especially studied this sea, can you tell me the origin of its name?"

"There exist several explanations on the subject, M. Aronnax. Would you like to know the opinion of a chronicler of the fourteenth century?"

"Willingly."

"This fanciful writer pretends that its name was given to it after the passage of the Israelites, when Pharaoh perished in the waves which closed at the voice of Moses."

"A poet's explanation, Captain Nemo," I replied; "but I cannot content myself with that. I ask you for your personal opinion."

"Here it is, M. Aronnax. According to my idea, we must see in this appellation of the Red Sea a translation of the Hebrew word 'Edom'; and if the ancients gave it that name, it was on account of the particular color of its waters."

"But up to this time I have seen nothing but transparent waves and without any particular color."

"Very likely; but as we advance to the bottom of the gulf, you will see this singular appearance. I remember seeing the Bay of Tor entirely red, like a sea of blood."

"And you attribute this color to the presence of a microscopic seaweed?"

"Yes."

"So, Captain Nemo, it is not the first time you have overrun the Red Sea on board the *Nautilus?*"

"No, sir."

"As you spoke a while ago of the passage of the Israelites and of the catastrophe to the Egyptians, I will ask whether you have met with the traces under the water of this great historical fact?"

"No, sir; and for a good reason."

"What is it?"

"It is that the spot where Moses and his people passed is now so blocked up with sand that the camels can barely bathe their legs there. You can well understand that there would not be water enough for my *Nautilus*."

"And the spot?" I asked.

"The spot is situated a little above the Isthmus of Suez, in the arm which formerly made a deep estuary, when the Red Sea extended to the Salt Lakes. Now, whether this passage were miraculous or not, the Israelites, nevertheless, crossed there to reach the Promised Land, and Pharaoh's army perished precisely on that spot; and I think that excavations made in the middle of the sand would bring to light a large number of arms and instruments of Egyptian origin."

"That is evident," I replied; "and for the sake of archaeologists let us hope that these excavations will be made sooner or later, when new towns are established on the isthmus, after the construction of the Suez Canal; a canal, however, very useless to a vessel like the *Nautilus*."

"Very likely; but useful to the whole world," said Captain Nemo. "The ancients well understood the utility of a communication between the Red Sea and the Mediterranean for their commercial affairs: but they did not think of digging a canal direct, and took the Nile as an intermediate. Very probably the canal which united the Nile to the Red Sea was begun by Sesostris, if we may believe tradition. One thing is certain, that in the year 615 before Jesus Christ, Necos undertook the works of an alimentary canal to the waters of the Nile across the plain of Egypt, looking toward Arabia. It took four days to go up this canal, and it was so wide that two triremes could go abreast. It was carried on by Darius, the son of Hystaspes, and probably finished by Ptolemy II. Strabo saw it navigated: but its decline from the point of departure, near Bubastes, to the Red Sea was so slight that it was only navigable for a few months in the year. This canal answered all commercial purposes to the age of Antonius, when it was abandoned and blocked up with sand. Restored by order of the Caliph Omar, it was definitely destroyed in 761 or 762 by Caliph Al-Mansor, who wished to prevent the arrival of provisions to Mohammed-ben-Abdallah, who had revolted against him. During the expedition into Egypt, your General Bonaparte discovered traces of the works in the Desert of Suez; and, surprised by the tide, he nearly perished before regaining Hadjaroth, at the very place where Moses had encamped three thousand years before him."

"Well, Captain, what the ancients dared not undertake, this junction between the two seas, which will shorten the road from Cadiz to India, M. Lesseps has succeeded in doing; and before long he will have changed Africa into an immense island."

"Yes, M. Aronnax; you have the right to be proud of your countryman. Such a man brings more honor to a nation than great captains. He began, like so many others, with disgust and rebuffs; but he has triumphed, for he has the genius of will. And it is sad to think that a work like that, which ought to have been an international work and which would have sufficed to make a reign illustrious, should have succeeded by the energy of one man. All honor to M. Lesseps!"

"Yes! Honor to the great citizen," I replied, surprised by the manner in which Captain Nemo had just spoken.

"Unfortunately," he continued, "I cannot take you through the Suez Canal; but you will be able to see the long jetty of Port Said after tomorrow, when we shall be in the Mediterranean."

"The Mediterranean!" I exclaimed.

"Yes, sir; does that astonish you?"

"What astonishes me is to think that we shall be there the day after tomorrow."

"Indeed?"

"Yes, Captain, although by this time I ought to have accustomed myself to be surprised at nothing since I have been on board your boat."

"But the cause of this surprise?"

"Well! It is the fearful speed you will have to put on the *Nautilus*, if the day after tomorrow she is to be in the Mediterranean, having made the round of Africa, and doubled the Cape of Good Hope!"

"Who told you that she would make the round of Africa and double the Cape of Good Hope, sir?"

"Well, unless the *Nautilus* sails on dry land, and passes above the isthmus—"

"Or beneath it, M. Aronnax."

"Beneath it?"

"Certainly," replied Captain Nemo quietly. "A long time ago nature made under this tongue of land what man has this day made on its surface."

"What! Such a passage exists?"

"Yes; a subterranean passage, which I have named the Arabian Tunnel. It takes us beneath Suez and opens into the Gulf of Pelusium."

"But this isthmus is composed of nothing but quick sands?"

"To a certain depth. But at fifty-five yards only there is a solid layer of rock."

"Did you discover this passage by chance?" I asked, more and more surprised.

"Chance and reasoning, sir; and by reasoning even more than by chance. Not only does this passage exist, but I have profited by it several times. Without that I should not have ventured this day into the impassable Red Sea. I noticed that in the Red Sea and in the Mediterranean there existed a certain number of fish of a kind perfectly identical. Certain of the fact, I asked myself was it possible that there was no communication between the two seas? If there was, the subterranean current must necessarily run from the Red Sea to the Mediterranean, from the sole cause of difference of level. I caught a large number of fish in the neighborhood of Suez. I passed a copper ring through their tails, and threw them back into the sea. Some months later, on the coast of Syria, I caught some of my fish ornamented with the ring. Thus the communication between the two was proved. I then sought for it with my *Nautilus*; I discovered it, ventured into it, and before long, sir, you too will have passed through my Arabian Tunnel!"

## CHAPTER V

### THE ARABIAN TUNNEL

That same evening, in 21° 30' north latitude, the *Nautilus* floated on the surface of the sea, approaching the Arabian coast. I saw Djeddah, the most important countinghouse of Egypt, Syria, Turkey, and India. I distinguished clearly enough its buildings, the vessels anchored at the quays, and those whose draft of water obliged them to anchor in the roads. The sun, rather low on the horizon, struck full on the houses of the town, bringing out their whiteness. Outside, some wooden cabins, and some made of reeds, showed the quarter inhabited by the Bedouins. Soon Djeddah was shut out from view by the shadows of night, and the *Nautilus* found herself under water slightly phosphorescent.

The next day, February 10, we sighted several ships running to windward. The *Nautilus* returned to its submarine navigation; but at noon, when her bearings were taken, the sea being deserted, she rose again to her waterline.

Accompanied by Ned and Conseil, I seated myself on the platform. The coast on the eastern side looked like a mass faintly printed upon a damp fog.

We were leaning on the sides of the pinnace, talking of one thing and another, when Ned Land, stretching out his hand toward a spot on the sea, said:

"Do you see anything there, sir?"

"No, Ned," I replied; "but I have not your eyes, you know."

"Look well," said Ned, "there, on the starboard beam, about the height of the lantern! Do you not see a mass which seems to move?"

"Certainly," said I, after close attention; "I see something like a long black body on the top of the water."

And certainly before long the black object was not more than a mile from us. It looked like a great sandbank deposited in the open sea. It was a gigantic dugong!

Ned Land looked eagerly. His eyes shone with covetousness at the sight of the animal. His hand seemed ready to harpoon it. One would have thought he was awaiting the moment to throw himself into the sea and attack it in its element.

At this instant Captain Nemo appeared on the platform. He saw the dugong, understood the Canadian's attitude, and, addressing him, said:

"If you held a harpoon just now, Master Land, would it not burn your hand?"

"Just so, sir."

"And you would not be sorry to go back, for one day, to your trade of a fisherman and to add this cetacean to the list of those you have already killed?"

"I should not, sir."

"Well, you can try."

"Thank you, sir," said Ned Land, his eyes flaming.

"Only," continued the captain, "I advise you for your own sake not to miss the creature."

"Is the dugong dangerous to attack?" I asked, in spite of the Canadian's shrug of the shoulders.

"Yes," replied the captain; "sometimes the animal turns upon its assailants and overturns their boat. But for Master Land this danger is not to be feared. His eye is prompt, his arm sure."

At this moment seven men of the crew, mute and immovable as ever, mounted the platform. One carried a harpoon and a line similar to those employed in catching whales. The pinnace was lifted from the bridge, pulled from its socket, and let down into the sea. Six oarsmen took their seats, and the coxswain went to the tiller. Ned, Conseil, and I went to the back of the boat.

"You are not coming, Captain?" I asked.

"No, sir; but I wish you good sport."

The boat put off, and, lifted by the six rowers, drew rapidly toward the dugong, which floated about two miles from the *Nautilus*.

Arrived some cable-lengths from the cetacean, the speed slackened, and the oars dipped noiselessly into the quiet waters. Ned Land, harpoon in hand, stood in the forepart of the boat. The harpoon used for striking the whale is generally attached to a very long cord which runs out rapidly as the wounded creature draws it after him. But here the cord was not more than ten fathoms long, and the extremity was attached to a small barrel which, by floating, was to show the course the dugong took under the water.

I stood and carefully watched the Canadian's adversary. This dugong, which also bears the name of the halicore, closely resembles the manatee; its oblong body terminated in a lengthened tail, and its lateral fins in perfect fingers. Its difference from the manatee consisted in its upper jaw, which was armed with two long and pointed teeth which formed on each side diverging tusks.

This dugong which Ned Land was preparing to attack was of colossal dimensions; it was more than seven yards long. It did not move, and seemed to be sleeping on the waves, which circumstance made it easier to capture.

The boat approached within six yards of the animal. The oars rested on the rowlocks. I half rose. Ned Land, his body thrown a little back, brandished the harpoon in his experienced hand.

Suddenly a hissing noise was heard, and the dugong disappeared. The harpoon, although thrown with great force; had apparently only struck the water.

"Curse it!" exclaimed the Canadian furiously. "I have missed it!"

"No," said I; "the creature is wounded—look at the blood; but your weapon has not stuck in his body."

"My harpoon! My harpoon!" cried Ned Land.

The sailors rowed on, and the coxswain made for the floating barrel. The harpoon regained, we followed in pursuit of the animal.

The latter came now and then to the surface to breathe. Its wound had not weakened it, for it shot onward with great rapidity.

The boat, rowed by strong arms, flew on its track. Several times it approached within some few yards, and the Canadian was ready to strike, but the dugong made off with a sudden plunge, and it was impossible to reach it.

Imagine the passion which excited impatient Ned Land! He hurled at the unfortunate creature the most energetic expletives in the English tongue. For my part, I was only vexed to see the dugong escape all our attacks.

We pursued it without relaxation for an hour, and I began to think it would prove difficult to capture, when the animal, possessed with the perverse idea of vengeance of which he had cause to repent, turned upon the pinnace and assailed us in its turn.

This maneuver did not escape the Canadian.

"Look out!" he cried.

The coxswain said some words in his outlandish tongue, doubtless warning the men to keep on their guard.

The dugong came within twenty feet of the boat, stopped, sniffed the air briskly with its large nostrils (not pierced at the extremity, but in the upper part of its muzzle). Then, taking a spring, he threw himself upon us.

The pinnace could not avoid the shock, and half upset, shipped at least two tons of water, which had to be emptied; but, thanks to the coxswain, we caught it sideways, not full front, so we were not quite overturned. While Ned Land, clinging to the bows, belabored the gigantic animal with blows from his harpoon, the creature's teeth were buried in the gunwale, and it lifted the whole thing out of the water, as a lion does a roebuck. We were upset over one another, and I know not how the adventure would have ended, if the Canadian, still enraged with the beast, had not struck it to the heart.

I heard its teeth grind on the iron plate, and the dugong disappeared, carrying the harpoon with him. But the barrel soon returned to the surface, and shortly after the body of the animal, turned on its back. The boat came up with it, took it in tow, and made straight for the *Nautilus*.

It required tackle of enormous strength to hoist the dugong on to the platform. It weighed 10,000 pounds.

The next day, February 11, the larder of the *Nautilus* was enriched by some more delicate game. A flight of sea swallows rested on the *Nautilus*. It was a species of the *Sterna nilotica*, peculiar to Egypt; its beak is black, head gray and pointed, the eye surrounded by white spots, the back, wings, and tail of a grayish color, the belly and throat white, and claws red. They also took some dozen of Nile ducks, a wild bird of high flavor, its throat and upper part of the head white with black spots.

About five o'clock in the evening we sighted to the north the Cape of Ras-Mohammed. This cape forms the extremity of Arabia Petraea, comprised between the Gulf of Suez and the Gulf of Acabah.

The *Nautilus* penetrated into the Straits of Jubal, which leads to the Gulf of Suez. I distinctly saw a high mountain, towering between the two gulfs of Ras-Mohammed. It was Mount Horeb, that Sinai at the top of which Moses saw God face-to-face.

At six o'clock the *Nautilus*, sometimes floating, sometimes immersed, passed some distance from Tor, situated at the end of the bay, the waters of which seemed tinted with red, an observation already made by Captain Nemo. Then night fell in the midst of a heavy silence, sometimes broken by the cries of the pelican and other night birds, and the noise of the waves breaking upon the shore, chafing against the rocks, or the panting of some far-off steamer beating the waters of the gulf with its noisy paddles.

From eight to nine o'clock the *Nautilus* remained some fathoms under the water.

According to my calculation we must have been very near Suez. Through the panel of the saloon I saw the bottom of the rocks brilliantly lit up by our electric lamp. We seemed to be leaving the straits behind us more and more.

At a quarter past nine, the vessel having returned to the surface, I mounted the platform. Most impatient to pass through Captain Nemo's tunnel, I could not stay in one place, so came to breathe the fresh night air.

Soon in the shadow I saw a pale light, half discolored by the fog, shining about a mile from us.

"A floating lighthouse!" said someone near me.

I turned, and saw the captain.

"It is the floating light of Suez," he continued. "It will not be long before we gain the entrance of the tunnel."

"The entrance cannot be easy?"

"No, sir; for that reason I am accustomed to go into the steersman's cage and myself direct our course. And now, if you will go down, M. Aronnax, the *Nautilus* is going under the waves, and will not return to the surface until we have passed through the Arabian Tunnel."

Captain Nemo led me toward the central staircase; halfway down he opened a door, traversed the upper deck, and landed in the pilot's cage, which it may be remembered rose at the extremity of the platform. It was a cabin measuring six feet square, very much like that occupied by the pilot on the steamboats of the Mississippi or Hudson. In the midst worked a wheel, placed vertically, and caught to the tiller rope, which ran to the back of the *Nautilus*. Four light ports with lenticular glasses, let in a groove in the partition of the cabin, allowed the man at the wheel to see in all directions.

This cabin was dark; but soon my eyes accustomed themselves to the obscurity, and I perceived the pilot, a strong man, with his hands resting on the spokes of the wheel. Outside, the sea appeared vividly lit up by the lantern, which shed its rays from the back of the cabin to the other extremity of the platform.

"Now," said Captain Nemo, "let us try to make our passage."

Electric wires connected the pilot's cage with the machinery room, and from there the captain could communicate simultaneously to his *Nautilus* the direction and the speed. He pressed a metal knob, and at once the speed of the screw diminished.

I looked in silence at the high straight wall we were running by at this moment, the immovable base of a massive sandy coast. We followed it thus for an hour only some few yards off.

Captain Nemo did not take his eye from the knob, suspended by its two concentric circles in the cabin. At a simple gesture, the pilot modified the course of the *Nautilus* every instant.

I had placed myself at the port scuttle, and saw some magnificent substructures of coral, zoophytes, seaweed, and fucus, agitating their enormous claws, which stretched out from the fissures of the rock.

At a quarter past ten, the captain himself took the helm. A large gallery, black and deep, opened before us. The *Nautilus* went boldly into it. A strange roaring was heard around its sides. It was the waters of the Red Sea, which the incline of the tunnel precipitated violently toward the Mediterranean. The *Nautilus* went with the torrent, rapid as an arrow, in spite of the efforts of the machinery, which, in order to offer more effective resistance, beat the waves with reversed screw.

On the walls of the narrow passage I could see nothing but brilliant rays, straight lines, furrows of fire, traced by the great speed, under the brilliant electric light. My heart beat fast.

At thirty-five minutes past ten, Captain Nemo quitted the helm, and, turning to me, said:

"The Mediterranean!"

In less than twenty minutes, the *Nautilus*, carried along by the torrent, had passed through the Isthmus of Suez.

# CHAPTER VI

## THE GRECIAN ARCHIPELAGO

The next day, February 12, at the dawn of day, the *Nautilus* rose to the surface. I hastened on to the platform. Three miles to the south the dim outline of Pelusium was to be seen. A torrent had carried us from one sea to another. About seven o'clock Ned and Conseil joined me.

"Well, Sir Naturalist," said the Canadian, in a slightly jovial tone, "and the Mediterranean?"

"We are floating on its surface, friend Ned."

"What!" said Conseil. "This very night."

"Yes, this very night; in a few minutes we have passed this impassable isthmus."

"I do not believe it," replied the Canadian.

"Then you are wrong, Master Land," I continued; "this low coast which rounds off to the south is the Egyptian coast. And you who have such good eyes, Ned, you can see the jetty of Port Said stretching into the sea."

The Canadian looked attentively.

"Certainly you are right, sir, and your captain is a first-rate man. We are in the Mediterranean. Good! Now, if you please, let us talk of our own little affair, but so that no one hears us."

I saw what the Canadian wanted, and, in any case, I thought it better to let him talk, as he wished it; so we all three went and sat down near the lantern, where we were less exposed to the spray of the blades.

"Now, Ned, we listen; what have you to tell us?"

"What I have to tell you is very simple. We are in Europe; and before Captain Nemo's caprices drag us once more to the bottom of the Polar Seas, or lead us into Oceania, I ask to leave the *Nautilus*."

I wished in no way to shackle the liberty of my companions, but I certainly felt no desire to leave Captain Nemo.

Thanks to him, and thanks to his apparatus, I was each day nearer the completion of my submarine studies; and I was rewriting my book of submarine depths in its very element. Should I ever again have such an opportunity of observing the wonders of the ocean? No, certainly not! And I could not bring myself to the idea of abandoning the *Nautilus* before the cycle of investigation was accomplished.

"Friend Ned, answer me frankly, are you tired of being on board? Are you sorry that destiny has thrown us into Captain Nemo's hands?"

The Canadian remained some moments without answering. Then, crossing his arms, he said:

"Frankly, I do not regret this journey under the seas. I shall be glad to have made it; but, now that it is made, let us have done with it. That is my idea."

"It will come to an end, Ned."

"Where and when?"

"Where I do not know—when I cannot say; or, rather, I suppose it will end when these seas have nothing more to teach us."

"Then what do you hope for?" demanded the Canadian.

"That circumstances may occur as well six months hence as now by which we may and ought to profit."

"Oh!" said Ned Land. "And where shall we be in six months, if you please, Sir Naturalist?"

"Perhaps in China; you know the *Nautilus* is a rapid traveler. It goes through water as swallows through the air, or as an express on the land. It does not fear frequented seas; who can say that it may not beat the coasts of France, England, or America, on which flight may be attempted as advantageously as here."

"M. Aronnax," replied the Canadian, "your arguments are rotten at the foundation. You speak in the future, 'We shall be there! We shall be here!' I speak in the present, 'We are here, and we must profit by it.'"

Ned Land's logic pressed me hard, and I felt myself beaten on that ground. I knew not what argument would now tell in my favor.

"Sir," continued Ned, "let us suppose an impossibility: if Captain Nemo should this day offer you your liberty, would you accept it?"

"I do not know," I answered.

"And if," he added, "the offer made you this day was never to be renewed, would you accept it?"

"Friend Ned, this is my answer. Your reasoning is against me. We must not rely on Captain Nemo's goodwill. Common prudence forbids him to set us at liberty. On the other side, prudence bids us profit by the first opportunity to leave the *Nautilus*."

"Well, M. Aronnax, that is wisely said."

"Only one observation—just one. The occasion must be serious, and our first attempt must succeed; if it fails, we shall never find another, and Captain Nemo will never forgive us."

"All that is true," replied the Canadian. "But your observation applies equally to all attempts at flight, whether in two years' time, or in two days'. But the question is still this: If a favorable opportunity presents itself, it must be seized."

"Agreed! And now, Ned, will you tell me what you mean by a favorable opportunity?"

"It will be that which, on a dark night, will bring the *Nautilus* a short distance from some European coast."

"And you will try and save yourself by swimming?"

"Yes, if we were near enough to the bank, and if the vessel was floating at the time. Not if the bank was far away, and the boat was under the water."

"And in that case?"

"In that case, I should seek to make myself master of the pinnace. I know how it is worked. We must get inside, and the bolts once drawn, we shall come to the surface of the water, without even the pilot, who is in the bows, perceiving our flight."

"Well, Ned, watch for the opportunity; but do not forget that a hitch will ruin us."

"I will not forget, sir."

"And now, Ned, would you like to know what I think of your project?"

"Certainly, M. Aronnax."

"Well, I think—I do not say I hope—I think that this favorable opportunity will never present itself."

"Why not?"

"Because Captain Nemo cannot hide from himself that we have not given up all hope of regaining our liberty, and he will be on his guard, above all, in the seas and in the sight of European coasts."

"We shall see," replied Ned Land, shaking his head determinedly.

"And now, Ned Land," I added, "let us stop here. Not another word on the subject. The day that you are ready, come and let us know, and we will follow you. I rely entirely upon you."

Thus ended a conversation which, at no very distant time, led to such grave results. I must say here that facts seemed to confirm my foresight, to the Canadian's great despair. Did Captain Nemo distrust us in these frequented seas? Or did he only wish to hide himself from the numerous vessels, of all nations, which plowed the Mediterranean? I could not tell; but we were oftener between waters and far from the coast. Or, if the *Nautilus* did emerge, nothing was to be seen but the pilot's cage; and sometimes it went to great depths, for, between the Grecian Archipelago and Asia Minor we could not touch the bottom by more than a thousand fathoms.

Thus I only knew we were near the island of Carpathos, one of the Sporades, by Captain Nemo reciting these lines from Virgil:

> *Est Carpathio Neptuni gurgite vates,*
> *Caeruleus Proteus,*

as he pointed to a spot on the planisphere.

It was indeed the ancient abode of Proteus, the old shepherd of Neptune's flocks, now the island of Scarpanto, situated between Rhodes and Crete. I saw nothing but the granite base through the glass panels of the saloon.

The next day, February 14, I resolved to employ some hours in studying the fish of the archipelago; but for some reason or other the panels remained hermetically sealed. Upon taking the course of the *Nautilus*, I found that we were going toward Candia, the ancient Isle of Crete. At the time I embarked on the *Abraham Lincoln*, the whole of this island had risen in insurrection against the despotism of the Turks. But how the insurgents had fared since that time I was absolutely ignorant, and it was not Captain Nemo, deprived of all land communications, who could tell me.

I made no allusion to this event when that night I found myself alone with him in the saloon. Besides, he seemed to be taciturn and preoccupied. Then, contrary to his custom, he ordered both panels to be opened, and, going from one to the other, observed the mass of waters attentively. To what end I could not guess; so, on my side, I employed my time in studying the fish passing before my eyes.

Among others, I remarked some gobies, mentioned by Aristotle, and commonly known by the name of sea-braches which are more particularly met with in the salt waters lying near the Delta of the Nile. Near them rolled some sea-bream, half-phosphorescent, a kind of sparus, which the Egyptians ranked among their sacred animals, whose arrival in the waters of the river announced a fertile overflow, and was celebrated by religious ceremonies. I also noticed some cheilines about nine inches long, a bony fish with transparent shell, whose livid color is mixed with red spots; they are great eaters of marine vegetation, which gives them an exquisite flavor. These cheilines were much sought after by the epicures of ancient Rome; the inside, dressed with the soft roe of the lamprey, peacocks' brains, and tongues of the phenicoptera, composed that divine dish of which Vitellius was so enamored.

Another inhabitant of these seas drew my attention, and led my mind back to recollections of antiquity. It was the remora, that fastens on to the shark's belly. This little fish, according to the ancients, hooking on to the ship's bottom, could stop its movements; and one of them, by keeping back Antony's ship during the battle of Actium, helped Augustus to gain the victory. On how little hangs the destiny of nations! I observed some fine anthiae, which belong to the order of lutjans, a fish held sacred by the Greeks, who attributed to them the power of hunting the marine monsters from waters they frequented. Their name signifies *flower*, and they justify their appellation by their shaded colors, their shades compromising the whole gamut of reds, from the paleness of the rose to the brightness of the ruby, and the fugitive tints that clouded their dorsal fin. My eyes could not leave the wonders of the sea, when they were suddenly struck by an unexpected apparition.

In the midst of the waters a man appeared, a diver, carrying at his belt a leathern purse. It was not a body abandoned to the waves; it was a living man, swimming with a strong hand, disappearing occasionally to take breath at the surface.

I turned toward Captain Nemo, and in an agitated voice exclaimed:

"A man shipwrecked! He must be saved at any price!"

The captain did not answer me, but came and leaned against the panel.

The man had approached, and, with his face flattened against the glass, was looking at us.

To my great amazement, Captain Nemo signed to him. The diver answered with his hand, mounted immediately to the surface of the water, and did not appear again.

"Do not be uncomfortable," said Captain Nemo. "It is Nicholas of Cape Matapan, surnamed Pesca. He is well known in all the Cyclades. A bold diver! Water is his element, and he lives more in it than on land, going continually from one island to another, even as far as Crete."

"You know him, Captain?"

"Why not, M. Aronnax?"

Saying which, Captain Nemo went toward a piece of furniture standing near the left panel of the saloon. Near this piece of furniture, I saw a chest bound with iron, on the cover of which was a copper plate, bearing the cypher of the *Nautilus* with its device.

At that moment, the captain, without noticing my presence, opened the piece of furniture, a sort of strongbox, which held a great many ingots.

They were ingots of gold. From whence came this precious metal, which represented an enormous sum? Where did the captain gather this gold from? And what was he going to do with it?

I did not say one word. I looked. Captain Nemo took the ingots one by one, and arranged them methodically in the chest, which he filled entirely. I estimated the contents at more than 4,000 pounds weight of gold, that is to say, nearly £200,000.

The chest was securely fastened, and the captain wrote an address on the lid, in characters which must have belonged to modern Greece.

This done, Captain Nemo pressed a knob, the wire of which communicated with the quarters of the crew. Four men appeared, and, not without some trouble, pushed the chest out of the saloon. Then I heard them hoisting it up the iron staircase by means of pulleys.

At that moment, Captain Nemo turned to me.

"And you were saying, sir?" said he.

"I was saying nothing, Captain."

"Then, sir, if you will allow me, I will wish you good night."

Whereupon he turned and left the saloon.

I returned to my room much troubled, as one may believe. I vainly tried to sleep—I sought the connecting link between the apparition of the diver and the chest filled with gold. Soon, I felt by certain movements of pitching and tossing that the *Nautilus* was leaving the depths and returning to the surface.

Then I heard steps upon the platform; and I knew they were unfastening the pinnace and launching it upon the waves. For one instant it struck the side of the *Nautilus*, then all noise ceased.

Two hours after, the same noise, the same going and coming was renewed; the boat was hoisted on board, replaced in its socket, and the *Nautilus* again plunged under the waves.

So these millions had been transported to their address. To what point of the continent? Who was Captain Nemo's correspondent?

The next day I related to Conseil and the Canadian the events of the night, which had excited my curiosity to the highest degree. My companions were not less surprised than myself.

"But where does he take his millions to?" asked Ned Land.

To that there was no possible answer. I returned to the saloon after having breakfast and set to work. Till five o'clock in the evening I employed myself in arranging my notes. At that moment (ought I to attribute it to some peculiar idiosyncrasy?) I felt so great a heat that I was obliged to take off my coat. It was strange, for we were under low latitudes; and even then the *Nautilus*, submerged as it was, ought to experience no change of temperature. I looked at the manometer; it showed a depth of sixty feet, to which atmospheric heat could never attain.

I continued my work, but the temperature rose to such a pitch as to be intolerable.

"Could there be fire on board?" I asked myself.

I was leaving the saloon, when Captain Nemo entered; he approached the thermometer, consulted it, and, turning to me, said:

"Forty-two degrees."

"I have noticed it, Captain," I replied; "and if it gets much hotter we cannot bear it."

"Oh, sir, it will not get better if we do not wish it."

"You can reduce it as you please, then?"

"No; but I can go farther from the stove which produces it."

"It is outward, then!"

"Certainly; we are floating in a current of boiling water."

"Is it possible!" I exclaimed.

"Look."

The panels opened, and I saw the sea entirely white all around. A sulfurous smoke was curling amid the waves, which boiled like water in a copper. I placed my hand on one of the panes of glass, but the heat was so great that I quickly took it off again.

"Where are we?" I asked.

"Near the island of Santorin, sir," replied the captain. "I wished to give you a sight of the curious spectacle of a submarine eruption."

"I thought," said I, "that the formation of these new islands was ended."

"Nothing is ever ended in the volcanic parts of the sea," replied Captain Nemo; "and the globe is always being worked by subterranean fires. Already, in the nineteenth year of our era, according to Cassiodorus and Pliny, a new island, Theia (the divine), appeared in the very place where these islets have recently been formed. Then they sank under the waves, to rise again in the year 69, when they again subsided. Since that time to our days the Plutonian work has been suspended. But on February 3, 1866, a new island, which they named George Island, emerged from the midst of the sulfurous vapor near Nea Kamenni, and settled again the 6th of the same month. Seven days after, on February 13, the island of Aphroessa appeared, leaving between Nea Kamenni and itself a canal ten yards broad. I was in these seas when the phenomenon occurred, and I was able therefore to observe all the different phases. The island of Aphroessa, of round form, measured 300 feet in diameter, and 30 feet in height. It was composed of black and vitreous lava, mixed with fragments of feldspar. And lastly, on March 10, a smaller island, called Reka, showed itself near Nea Kamenni, and since then these three have joined together, forming but one and the same island."

"And the canal in which we are at this moment?" I asked.

"Here it is," replied Captain Nemo, showing me a map of the archipelago. "You see, I have marked the new islands."

I returned to the glass. The *Nautilus* was no longer moving, the heat was becoming unbearable. The sea, which till now had been white, was red, owing to the presence of salts of iron. In spite of the ship's being hermetically sealed, an insupportable smell of sulfur filled the saloon, and the brilliancy of the electricity was entirely extinguished by bright scarlet flames. I was in a bath, I was choking, I was broiled.

"We can remain no longer in this boiling water," said I to the captain.

"It would not be prudent," replied the impassive Captain Nemo.

An order was given; the *Nautilus* tacked about and left the furnace it could not brave with impunity. A quarter of an hour after we were breathing fresh air on the surface. The thought then struck me that, if Ned Land had chosen this part of the sea for our flight, we should never have come alive out of this sea of fire.

The next day, February 16, we left the basin which, between Rhodes and Alexandria, is reckoned about 1,500 fathoms in depth, and the *Nautilus*, passing some distance from Cerigo, quitted the Grecian Archipelago after having doubled Cape Matapan.

# CHAPTER VII

## THE MEDITERRANEAN IN FORTY-EIGHT HOURS

The Mediterranean, the blue sea par excellence, "the great sea" of the Hebrews, "the sea" of the Greeks, the "mare nostrum" of the Romans, bordered by orange trees, aloes, cacti, and sea pines; embalmed with the perfume of the myrtle, surrounded by rude mountains, saturated with pure and transparent air, but incessantly worked by underground fires; a perfect battlefield in which Neptune and Pluto still dispute the empire of the world!

It is upon these banks, and on these waters, says Michelet, that man is renewed in one of the most powerful climates of the globe. But, beautiful as it was, I could only take a rapid glance at the basin whose superficial area is two million of square yards. Even Captain Nemo's knowledge was lost to me, for this puzzling person did not appear once during our passage at full speed. I estimated the course which the *Nautilus* took under the waves of the sea at about six hundred leagues, and it was accomplished in forty-eight hours. Starting on the morning of February 16 from the shores of Greece, we had crossed the Straits of Gibraltar by sunrise on the 18th.

It was plain to me that this Mediterranean, enclosed in the midst of those countries which he wished to avoid, was distasteful to Captain Nemo. Those waves and those breezes brought back too many remembrances, if not too many regrets. Here he had no longer that independence and that liberty of gait which he had when in the open seas, and his *Nautilus* felt itself cramped between the close shores of Africa and Europe.

Our speed was now twenty-five miles an hour. It may be well understood that Ned Land, to his great disgust, was obliged to renounce his intended flight. He could not launch the pinnace, going at the rate of twelve or thirteen yards every second. To quit the *Nautilus* under such conditions would be as bad as jumping from a train going at full speed—an imprudent thing, to say the least of it. Besides, our vessel only mounted to the surface of the waves at night to renew its stock of air; it was steered entirely by the compass and the log.

I saw no more of the interior of this Mediterranean than a traveler by express train perceives of the landscape which flies before his eyes; that is to say, the distant horizon, and not the nearer objects which pass like a flash of lightning.

In the midst of the mass of waters brightly lit up by the electric light gilded some of those lampreys, more than a yard long, common to almost every climate. Some of the oxyrhynchi, a kind of ray five feet broad, with white belly and gray spotted back, spread out like a large shawl carried along by the current. Other rays passed so quickly that I could not see if they deserved the name of eagles which was given to them by the ancient Greeks, or the qualification of rats, toads, and bats, with which modern fishermen have loaded them. A few milander sharks, twelve feet long, endowed with wonderful fineness of scent, appeared like large blue shadows. Some dorades of the shark kind, some of which measured seven feet and a half, showed themselves in their dress of blue and silver, encircled by small bands which struck sharply against the somber tints of their fins, a fish consecrated to Venus, the eyes of which are encased in a socket of gold, a precious species, friend of all waters, fresh or salt, an inhabitant of rivers, lakes, and oceans, living in all climates, and bearing all temperatures; a race belonging to the geological era of the earth, and which has preserved all the beauty of its first days. Magnificent sturgeons, nine or ten yards long, creatures of great speed, striking the panes of glass with their strong tails, displayed their bluish backs with small brown spots; they resemble the sharks, but are not equal to them in strength, and are to be met with in all seas. But of all the diverse inhabitants of the Mediterranean, those I observed to the greatest advantage, when the *Nautilus* approached the surface, belonged to the sixty-third genus of bony fish. They were a kind of tunny, with bluish-black backs, and silvery breastplates, whose dorsal fins threw out sparkles of gold. They are said to follow in the wake of vessels whose refreshing shade they seek from the fire of the tropical sky, and they did not belie the saying, for they accompanied the *Nautilus* as they did in former times the vessel of La Perouse. For many a long hour they struggled to keep up with our vessel. I was never tired of admiring these creatures really built for speed—their small heads, their bodies lithe and cigar-shaped, which in some were more than three yards long, their pectoral fins and forked tail endowed with remarkable strength. They swam in a triangle, like certain flocks of birds, whose rapidity they equaled, and of which the ancients used to say that they understood geomertry and strategy. But still they do not escape the pursuit of the Provencals, who esteem them as highly as the inhabitants of the Propontis and of Italy used to do; and these precious, but blind and foolhardy creatures, perish by millions in the nets of the Marseillaise.

With regard to the species of fish common to the Atlantic and the Mediterranean, the giddy speed of the *Nautilus* prevented me from observing them with any degree of accuracy.

As to marine mammals, I thought, in passing the entrance of the Adriatic, that I saw two or three cachalots, furnished with one dorsal fin, of the genus physetera, some dolphins of the genus globicephala, peculiar to the Mediterranean, the back part of the head being marked like a zebra with small lines; also, a dozen of seals, with white bellies and black hair, known by the name of *monks*, and which really have the air of a Dominican; they are about three yards in length.

As to zoophytes, for some instants I was able to admire a beautiful orange galeolaria, which had fastened itself to the port panel; it held on by a long filament, and was divided into an infinity of branches, terminated by the finest lace which could ever have been woven by the rivals of Arachne herself. Unfortunately, I could not take this admirable specimen; and doubtless no other Mediterranean zoophyte would have offered itself to my observation, if, on the night of the 16th, the *Nautilus* had not, singularly enough, slackened its speed, under the following circumstances.

We were then passing between Sicily and the coast of Tunis. In the narrow space between Cape Bon and the Straits of Messina the bottom of the sea rose almost suddenly. There was a perfect bank, on which there was not more than nine fathoms of water, while on either side the depth was ninety fathoms.

The *Nautilus* had to maneuver very carefully so as not to strike against this submarine barrier.

I showed Conseil, on the map of the Mediterranean, the spot occupied by this reef.

"But if you please, sir," observed Conseil, "it is like a real isthmus joining Europe to Africa."

"Yes, my boy, it forms a perfect bar to the Straits of Lybia, and the soundings of Smith have proved that in former times the continents between Cape Boco and Cape Furina were joined."

"I can well believe it," said Conseil.

"I will add," I continued, "that a similar barrier exists between Gibraltar and Ceuta, which in geological times formed the entire Mediterranean."

"What if some volcanic burst should one day raise these two barriers above the waves?"

"It is not probable, Conseil."

"Well, but allow me to finish, please, sir; if this phenomenon should take place, it will be troublesome for M. Lesseps, who has taken so much pains to pierce the isthmus."

"I agree with you; but I repeat, Conseil, this phenomenon will never happen. The violence of subterranean force is ever diminishing. Volcanoes, so plentiful in the first days of the world, are being extinguished by degrees; the internal heat is weakened, the temperature of the lower strata of the globe is lowered by a perceptible quantity every century to the detriment of our globe, for its heat is its life."

"But the sun?"

"The sun is not sufficient, Conseil. Can it give heat to a dead body?"

"Not that I know of."

"Well, my friend, this earth will one day be that cold corpse; it will become uninhabitable and uninhabited like the moon, which has long since lost all its vital heat."

"In how many centuries?"

"In some hundreds of thousands of years, my boy."

"Then," said Conseil, "we shall have time to finish our journey—that is, if Ned Land does not interfere with it."

And Conseil, reassured, returned to the study of the bank, which the *Nautilus* was skirting at a moderate speed.

There, beneath the rocky and volcanic bottom, lay outspread a living flora of sponges and reddish cydippes, which emitted a slight phosphorescent light, commonly known by the name of sea cucumbers; and walking comatulae more than a yard long, the purple of which completely colored the water around.

The *Nautilus* having now passed the high bank on the Libyan Straits, returned to the deep waters and its accustomed speed.

From that time on no more mollusks, no more articulates, no more zoophytes; barely a few large fish passing like shadows.

During the night of February 16 and 17, we had entered the second Mediterranean basin, the greatest depth of which was 1,450 fathoms. The *Nautilus*, by the action of its crew, slid down the inclined planes and buried itself in the lowest depths of the sea.

On February 18, about three o'clock in the morning, we were at the entrance of the Straits of Gibraltar. There once existed two currents: an upper one, long since recognized, which conveys the waters of the ocean into the basin of the Mediterranean; and a lower countercurrent, which reasoning has now shown to exist. Indeed, the volume of water in the Mediterranean, incessantly added to by the waves of the Atlantic and by rivers falling into it, would each year raise the level of this sea, for its evaporation is not sufficient to restore the equilibrium. As it is not so, we must necessarily admit the existence of an undercurrent, which empties into the basin of the Atlantic through the Straits of Gibraltar the surplus waters of the Mediterranean. A fact indeed; and it was this countercurrent by which the *Nautilus* profited. It advanced rapidly by the narrow pass. For one instant I caught a glimpse of the beautiful ruins of the temple of Hercules, buried in the ground, according to Pliny, and with the low island which supports it; and a few minutes later we were floating on the Atlantic.

# CHAPTER VIII

## VIGO BAY

The Atlantic! A vast sheet of water whose superficial area covers twenty-five millions of square miles, the length of which is nine thousand miles, with a mean breadth of two thousand seven hundred—an ocean whose parallel winding shores embrace an immense circumference, watered by the largest rivers of the world, the St. Lawrence, the Mississippi, the Amazon, the Plata, the Orinoco, the Niger, the Senegal, the Elbe, the Loire, and the Rhine, which carry water from the most civilized, as well as from the most savage, countries! Magnificent field of water, incessantly plowed by vessels of every nation, sheltered by the flags of every nation, and which terminates in those two terrible points so dreaded by mariners, Cape Horn and the Cape of Tempests.

The *Nautilus* was piercing the water with its sharp spur, after having accomplished nearly ten thousand leagues in three months and a half, a distance greater than the great circle of the earth. Where were we going now, and what was reserved for the future? The *Nautilus*, leaving the Straits of Gibraltar, had gone far out. It returned to the surface of the waves, and our daily walks on the platform were restored to us.

I mounted at once, accompanied by Ned Land and Conseil. At a distance of about twelve miles, Cape St. Vincent was dimly to be seen, forming the southwestern point of the Spanish peninsula. A strong southerly gale was blowing. The sea was swollen and billowy; it made the *Nautilus* rock violently. It was almost impossible to keep one's foot on the platform, which the heavy rolls of the sea beat over every instant. So we descended after inhaling some mouthfuls of fresh air.

I returned to my room, Conseil to his cabin; but the Canadian, with a preoccupied air, followed me. Our rapid passage across the Mediterranean had not allowed him to put his project into execution, and he could not help showing his disappointment. When the door of my room was shut, he sat down and looked at me silently.

"Friend Ned," said I, "I understand you; but you cannot reproach yourself. To have attempted to leave the *Nautilus* under the circumstances would have been folly."

Ned Land did not answer; his compressed lips and frowning brow showed with him the violent possession this fixed idea had taken of his mind.

"Let us see," I continued; "we need not despair yet. We are going up the coast of Portugal again; France and England are not far off, where we can easily find refuge. Now if the *Nautilus*, on leaving the Straits of Gibraltar, had gone to the south, if it had carried us toward regions where there were no continents, I should share your uneasiness. But we know now that Captain Nemo does not fly from civilized seas, and in some days I think you can act with security."

Ned Land still looked at me fixedly; at length his fixed lips parted, and he said, "It is for tonight."

I drew myself up suddenly. I was, I admit, little prepared for this communication. I wanted to answer the Canadian, but words would not come.

"We agreed to wait for an opportunity," continued Ned Land, "and the opportunity has arrived. This night we shall be but a few miles from the Spanish coast. It is cloudy. The wind blows freely. I have your word, M. Aronnax, and I rely upon you."

As I was silent, the Canadian approached me.

"Tonight, at nine o'clock," said he. "I have warned Conseil. At that moment Captain Nemo will be shut up in his room, probably in bed. Neither the engineers nor the ship's crew can see us. Conseil and I will gain the central staircase, and you, M. Aronnax, will remain in the library, two steps from us, waiting my signal. The oars, the mast, and the sail are in the canoe. I have even succeeded in getting some provisions. I have procured an English wrench, to unfasten the bolts which attach it to the shell of the *Nautilus*. So all is ready, till tonight."

"The sea is bad."

"That I allow," replied the Canadian; "but we must risk that. Liberty is worth paying for; besides, the boat is strong, and a few miles with a fair wind to carry us is no great thing. Who knows but by tomorrow we may be a hundred leagues away? Let circumstances only favor us, and by ten or eleven o'clock we shall have landed on some spot of terra firma, alive or dead. But adieu now, till tonight."

With these words the Canadian withdrew, leaving me almost dumb. I had imagined that, the chance gone, I should have time to reflect and discuss the matter. My obstinate companion had given me no time; and, after all, what could I have said to him? Ned Land was perfectly right. There was almost the opportunity to profit by. Could I retract my word, and take upon myself the responsibility of compromising the future of my companions? Tomorrow Captain Nemo might take us far from all land.

At that moment a rather loud hissing noise told me that the reservoirs were filling, and that the *Nautilus* was sinking under the waves of the Atlantic.

A sad day I passed, between the desire of regaining my liberty of action and of abandoning the wonderful *Nautilus*, and leaving my submarine studies incomplete.

What dreadful hours I passed thus! Sometimes seeing myself and companions safely landed, sometimes wishing, in spite of my reason, that some unforeseen circumstance would prevent the realization of Ned Land's project.

Twice I went to the saloon. I wished to consult the compass. I wished to see if the direction the *Nautilus* was taking was bringing us nearer or taking us farther from the coast. But no; the *Nautilus* kept in Portuguese waters.

I must therefore take my part and prepare for flight. My luggage was not heavy; my notes, nothing more.

As to Captain Nemo, I asked myself what he would think of our escape; what trouble, what wrong it might cause him and what he might do in case of its discovery or failure. Certainly I had no cause to complain of him; on the contrary, never was hospitality freer than his. In leaving him I could not be taxed with ingratitude. No oath bound us to him. It was on the strength of circumstances he relied, and not upon our word, to fix us forever.

I had not seen the captain since our visit to the island of Santorin. Would chance bring me to his presence before our departure? I wished it, and I feared it at the same time. I listened if I could hear him walking the room contiguous to mine. No sound reached my ear. I felt an unbearable uneasiness. This day of waiting seemed eternal. Hours struck too slowly to keep pace with my impatience.

My dinner was served in my room as usual. I ate but little; I was too preoccupied. I left the table at seven o'clock. A hundred and twenty minutes (I counted them) still separated me from the moment in which I was to join Ned Land. My agitation redoubled. My pulse beat violently. I could not remain quiet. I went and came, hoping to calm my troubled spirit by constant movement. The idea of failure in our bold enterprise was the least painful of my anxieties; but the thought of seeing our project discovered before leaving the *Nautilus*, of being brought before Captain Nemo, irritated, or (what was worse) saddened, at my desertion, made my heart beat.

I wanted to see the saloon for the last time. I descended the stairs and arrived in the museum, where I had passed so many useful and agreeable hours. I looked at all its riches, all its treasures, like a man on the eve of an eternal exile, who was leaving never to return.

These wonders of nature, these masterpieces of art, among which for so many days my life had been concentrated, I was going to abandon them forever! I should like to have taken a last look through the windows of the saloon into the waters of the Atlantic: but the panels were hermetically closed, and a cloak of steel separated me from that ocean which I had not yet explored.

In passing through the saloon, I came near the door let into the angle which opened into the captain's room. To my great surprise, this door was ajar. I drew back involuntarily. If Captain Nemo should be in his room, he could see me. But, hearing no sound, I drew nearer. The room was deserted. I pushed open the door and took some steps forward. Still the same monklike severity of aspect.

Suddenly the clock struck eight. The first beat of the hammer on the bell awoke me from my dreams. I trembled as if an invisible eye had plunged into my most secret thoughts, and I hurried from the room.

There my eye fell upon the compass. Our course was still north. The log indicated moderate speed, the manometer a depth of about sixty feet.

I returned to my room, clothed myself warmly—sea boots, an otterskin cap, a great coat of byssus, lined with sealskin; I was ready, I was waiting. The vibration of the screw alone broke the deep silence which reigned on board. I listened attentively. Would no loud voice suddenly inform me that Ned Land had been surprised in his projected flight? A mortal dread hung over me, and I vainly tried to regain my accustomed coolness.

At a few minutes to nine, I put my ear to the captain's door. No noise. I left my room and returned to the saloon, which was half in obscurity, but deserted.

I opened the door communicating with the library. The same insufficient light, the same solitude. I placed myself near the door leading to the central staircase, and there waited for Ned Land's signal.

At that moment the trembling of the screw sensibly diminished, then it stopped entirely. The silence was now only disturbed by the beatings of my own heart. Suddenly a slight shock was felt; and I knew that the *Nautilus* had stopped at the bottom of the ocean. My uneasiness increased. The Canadian's signal did not come. I felt inclined to join Ned Land and beg of him to put off his attempt. I felt that we were not sailing under our usual conditions.

At this moment the door of the large saloon opened, and Captain Nemo appeared. He saw me, and without further preamble began in an amiable tone of voice:

"Ah, sir! I have been looking for you. Do you know the history of Spain?"

Now, one might know the history of one's own country by heart; but in the condition I was at the time, with troubled mind and head quite lost, I could not have said a word of it.

"Well," continued Captain Nemo, "you heard my question! Do you know the history of Spain?"

"Very slightly," I answered.

"Well, here are learned men having to learn," said the captain. "Come, sit down, and I will tell you a curious episode in this history. Sir, listen well," said he; "this history will interest you on one side, for it will answer a question which doubtless you have not been able to solve."

"I listen, Captain," said I, not knowing what my interlocutor was driving at, and asking myself if this incident was bearing on our projected flight.

"Sir, if you have no objection, we will go back to 1702. You cannot be ignorant that your king, Louis XIV, thinking that the gesture of a potentate was sufficient to bring the Pyrenees under his yoke, had imposed the Duke of Anjou, his grandson, on the Spaniards. This prince reigned more or less badly under the name of Philip V, and had a strong party against him abroad. Indeed, the preceding year, the royal houses of Holland, Austria, and England had concluded a treaty of alliance at the Hague, with the intention of plucking the crown of Spain from the head of Philip V, and placing it on that of an archduke to whom they prematurely gave the title of Charles III.

"Spain must resist this coalition; but she was almost entirely unprovided with either soldiers or sailors. However, money would not fail them, provided that their galleons, laden with gold and silver from America, once entered their ports. And about the end of 1702 they expected a rich convoy which France was escorting with a fleet of twenty-three vessels, commanded by Admiral Château-Renaud, for the ships of the coalition were already beating the Atlantic. This convoy was to go to Cadiz, but the admiral, hearing that an English fleet was cruising in those waters, resolved to make for a French port.

"The Spanish commanders of the convoy objected to this decision. They wanted to be taken to a Spanish port, and, if not to Cadiz, into Vigo Bay, situated on the northwest coast of Spain, and which was not blocked.

"Admiral Château-Renaud had the rashness to obey this injunction, and the galleons entered Vigo Bay.

"Unfortunately, it formed an open road which could not be defended in any way. They must therefore hasten to unload the galleons before the arrival of the combined fleet; and time would not have failed them had not a miserable question of rivalry suddenly arisen.

"You are following the chain of events?" asked Captain Nemo.

"Perfectly," said I, not knowing the end proposed by this historical lesson.

"I will continue. This is what passed. The merchants of Cadiz had a privilege by which they had the right of receiving all merchandise coming from the West Indies. Now, to disembark these ingots at the port of Vigo was depriving them of their rights. They complained at Madrid, and obtained the consent of the weak-minded Philip that the convoy, without discharging its cargo, should remain sequestered in the roads of Vigo until the enemy had disappeared.

"But while coming to this decision, on October 22, 1702, the English vessels arrived in Vigo Bay, when Admiral Château-Renaud, in spite of inferior forces, fought bravely. But, seeing that the treasure must fall into the enemy's hands, he burned and scuttled every galleon, which went to the bottom with their immense riches."

Captain Nemo stopped. I admit I could not see yet why this history should interest me.

"Well?" I asked.

"Well, M. Aronnax," replied Captain Nemo, "we are in that Vigo Bay; and it rests with yourself whether you will penetrate its mysteries."

The captain rose, telling me to follow him. I had had time to recover. I obeyed. The saloon was dark, but through the transparent glass the waves were sparkling. I looked.

For half a mile around the *Nautilus*, the waters seemed bathed in electric light. The sandy bottom was clean and bright. Some of the ship's crew in their diving dresses were clearing away half-rotten barrels and empty cases from the midst of the blackened wrecks. From these cases and from these barrels escaped ingots of gold and silver, cascades of piastres and jewels. The sand was heaped up with them. Laden with their precious booty, the men returned to the *Nautilus*, disposed of their burden, and went back to this inexhaustible fishery of gold and silver.

I understood now. This was the scene of the battle of October 22, 1702. Here on this very spot the galleons laden for the Spanish government had sunk. Here Captain Nemo came, according to his wants, to pack up those millions with which he burdened the *Nautilus*. It was for him and him alone America had given up her precious metals. He was heir direct, without anyone to share, in those treasures torn from the Incas and from the conquered of Ferdinand Cortez.

"Did you know, sir," he asked, smiling, "that the sea contained such riches?"

"I knew," I answered, "that they value money held in suspension in these waters at two millions."

"Doubtless; but to extract this money the expense would be greater than the profit. Here, on the contrary, I have but to pick up what man has lost—and not only in Vigo Bay, but in a thousand other ports where shipwrecks have happened, and which are marked on my submarine map. Can you understand now the source of the millions I am worth?"

"I understand, Captain. But allow me to tell you that in exploring Vigo Bay you have only been beforehand with a rival society."

"And which?"

"A society which has received from the Spanish government the privilege of seeking those buried galleons. The shareholders are led on by the allurement of an enormous bounty, for they value these rich shipwrecks at five hundred millions."

"Five hundred millions they were," answered Captain Nemo, "but they are so no longer."

"Just so," said I; "and a warning to those shareholders would be an act of charity. But who knows if it would be well received? What gamblers usually regret above all is less the loss of their money than of their foolish hopes. After all, I pity them less than the thousands of unfortunates to whom so much riches well-distributed would have been profitable, while for them they will be forever barren."

I had no sooner expressed this regret than I felt that it must have wounded Captain Nemo.

"Barren!" he exclaimed, with animation. "Do you think then, sir, that these riches are lost because I gather them? Is it for myself alone, according to your idea, that I take the trouble to collect these treasures? Who told you that I did not make a good use of it? Do you think I am ignorant that there are suffering beings and oppressed races on this earth, miserable creatures to console, victims to avenge? Do you not understand?"

Captain Nemo stopped at these last words, regretting perhaps that he had spoken so much. But I had guessed that, whatever the motive which had forced him to seek independence under the sea, it had left him still a man, that his heart still beat for the sufferings of humanity, and that his immense charity was for oppressed races as well as individuals. And I then understood for whom those millions were destined which were forwarded by Captain Nemo when the *Nautilus* was cruising in the waters of Crete.

# CHAPTER IX

## A VANISHED CONTINENT

The next morning, February 19, I saw the Canadian enter my room. I expected this visit. He looked very disappointed.

"Well, sir?" said he.

"Well, Ned, fortune was against us yesterday."

"Yes; that captain must needs stop exactly at the hour we intended leaving his vessel."

"Yes, Ned, he had business at his banker's."

"His banker's!"

"Or rather his banking house; by that I mean the ocean, where his riches are safer than in the chests of the state."

I then related to the Canadian the incidents of the preceding night, hoping to bring him back to the idea of not abandoning the captain; but my recital had no other result than an energetically expressed regret from Ned that he had not been able to take a walk on the battlefield of Vigo on his own account.

"However," said he, "all is not ended. It is only a blow of the harpoon lost. Another time we must succeed; and tonight, if necessary—"

"In what direction is the *Nautilus* going?" I asked.

"I do not know," replied Ned.

"Well, at noon we shall see the point."

The Canadian returned to Conseil. As soon as I was dressed, I went into the saloon. The compass was not reassuring. The course of the *Nautilus* was S.S.W. We were turning our backs on Europe.

I waited with some impatience till the ship's place was pricked on the chart. At about half-past eleven the reservoirs were emptied, and our vessel rose to the surface of the ocean. I rushed toward the platform. Ned Land had preceded me. No more land in sight. Nothing but an immense sea. Some sails on the horizon, doubtless those going to San Roque in search of favorable winds for doubling the Cape of Good Hope. The weather was cloudy. A gale of wind was preparing. Ned raved, and tried to pierce the cloudy horizon. He still hoped that behind all that fog stretched the land he so longed for.

At noon the sun showed itself for an instant. The second profited by this brightness to take its height. Then, the sea becoming more billowy, we descended, and the panel closed.

An hour after, upon consulting the chart, I saw the position of the *Nautilus* was marked at 16° 17' longitude, and 33° 22' latitude, at 150 leagues from the nearest coast. There was no means of flight, and I leave you to imagine the rage of the Canadian when I informed him of our situation.

For myself, I was not particularly sorry. I felt lightened of the load which had oppressed me, and was able to return with some degree of calmness to my accustomed work.

That night, about eleven o'clock, I received a most unexpected visit from Captain Nemo. He asked me very graciously if I felt fatigued from my watch of the preceding night. I answered in the negative.

"Then, M. Aronnax, I propose a curious excursion."

"Propose, Captain?"

"You have hitherto only visited the submarine depths by daylight, under the brightness of the sun. Would it suit you to see them in the darkness of the night?"

"Most willingly."

"I warn you, the way will be tiring. We shall have far to walk, and must climb a mountain. The roads are not well kept."

"What you say, Captain, only heightens my curiosity; I am ready to follow you."

"Come then, sir, we will put on our diving dresses."

Arrived at the robing room, I saw that neither of my companions nor any of the ship's crew were to follow us on this excursion. Captain Nemo had not even proposed my taking with me either Ned or Conseil.

In a few moments we had put on our diving dresses; they placed on our backs the reservoirs, abundantly filled with air, but no electric lamps were prepared. I called the captain's attention to the fact.

"They will be useless," he replied.

I thought I had not heard aright, but I could not repeat my observation, for the captain's head had already disappeared in its metal case. I finished harnessing myself. I felt them put an iron-pointed stick into my hand, and some minutes later, after going through the usual form, we set foot on the bottom of the Atlantic at a depth of 150 fathoms. Midnight was near. The waters were profoundly dark, but Captain Nemo pointed out in the distance a reddish spot, a sort of large light shining brilliantly about two miles from the *Nautilus*. What this fire might be, what could feed it, why and how it lit up the liquid mass, I could not say. In any case, it did light our way, vaguely, it is true, but I soon accustomed myself to the peculiar darkness, and I understood, under such circumstances, the uselessness of the Ruhmkorff apparatus.

As we advanced, I heard a kind of pattering above my head. The noise redoubling, sometimes producing a continual shower, I soon understood the cause. It was rain falling violently, and crisping the surface of the waves. Instinctively the thought flashed across my mind that I should be wet through! By the water! In the midst of the water! I could not help laughing at the odd idea. But, indeed, in the thick diving dress, the liquid element is no longer felt, and one only seems to be in an atmosphere somewhat denser than the terrestrial atmosphere. Nothing more.

After half an hour's walk the soil became stony. Medusae, microscopic crustacea, and pennatules lit it slightly with their phosphorescent gleam. I caught a glimpse of pieces of stone covered with millions of zoophytes and masses of seaweed. My feet often slipped upon this sticky carpet of seaweed, and without my iron-tipped stick I should have fallen more than once. In turning around, I could still see the whitish lantern of the *Nautilus* beginning to pale in the distance.

But the rosy light which guided us increased and lit up the horizon. The presence of this fire underwater puzzled me in the highest degree. Was I going toward a natural phenomenon as yet unknown to the savants of the earth? Or even (for this thought crossed my brain) had the hand of man aught to do with this conflagration? Had he fanned this flame? Was I to meet in these depths companions and friends of Captain Nemo whom he was going to visit, and who, like him, led this strange existence? Should I find down there a whole colony of exiles who, weary of the miseries of this earth, had sought and found independence in the deep ocean? All these foolish and unreasonable ideas pursued me. And in this condition of mind, over-excited by the succession of wonders continually passing before my eyes, I should not have been surprised to meet at the bottom of the sea one of those submarine towns of which Captain Nemo dreamed.

Our road grew lighter and lighter. The white glimmer came in rays from the summit of a mountain about 800 feet high. But what I saw was simply a reflection, developed by the clearness of the waters. The source of this inexplicable light was a fire on the opposite side of the mountain.

In the midst of this stony maze furrowing the bottom of the Atlantic, Captain Nemo advanced without hesitation. He knew this dreary road. Doubtless he had often traveled over it, and could not lose himself. I followed him with unshaken confidence. He seemed to me like a genie of the sea; and, as he walked before me, I could not help admiring his stature, which was outlined in black on the luminous horizon.

It was one in the morning when we arrived at the first slopes of the mountain; but to gain access to them we must venture through the difficult paths of a vast copse.

Yes; a copse of dead trees, without leaves, without sap, trees petrified by the action of the water and here and there overtopped by gigantic pines. It was like a coal pit still standing, holding by the roots to the broken soil, and whose branches, like fine black paper cuttings, showed distinctly on the watery ceiling. Picture to yourself a forest in the Hartz hanging onto the sides of the mountain, but a forest swallowed up. The paths were encumbered with seaweed and fucus, between which groveled a whole world of crustacea. I went along, climbing the rocks, striding over extended trunks, breaking the sea bind-weed which hung from one tree to the other; and frightening the fish, which flew from branch to branch. Pressing onward, I felt no fatigue. I followed my guide, who was never tired. What a spectacle! How can I express it? How paint the aspect of those woods and rocks in this medium—their under parts dark and wild, the upper colored with red tints, by that light which the reflecting powers of the waters doubled? We climbed rocks which fell directly after with gigantic bounds and the low growling of an avalanche. To right and left ran long, dark galleries, where sight was lost. Here opened vast glades which the hand of man seemed to have worked; and I sometimes asked myself if some inhabitant of these submarine regions would not suddenly appear to me.

But Captain Nemo was still mounting. I could not stay behind. I followed boldly. My stick gave me good help. A false step would have been dangerous on the narrow passes sloping down to the sides of the gulfs; but I walked with firm step, without feeling any giddiness. Now I jumped a crevice, the depth of which would have made me hesitate had it been among the glaciers on the land; now I ventured on the unsteady trunk of a tree thrown across from one abyss to the other, without looking under my feet, having only eyes to admire the wild sites of this region.

There, monumental rocks, leaning on their regularly cut bases, seemed to defy all laws of equilibrium. From between their stony knees trees sprang, like a jet under heavy pressure, and upheld others which upheld them. Natural towers, large scarps, cut perpendicularly, like a "curtain," inclined at an angle which the laws of gravitation could never have tolerated in terrestrial regions.

Two hours after quitting the *Nautilus* we had crossed the line of trees, and a hundred feet above our heads rose the top of the mountain, which cast a shadow on the brilliant irradiation of the opposite slope. Some petrified shrubs ran fantastically here and there. Fish got up under our feet like birds in the long grass. The massive rocks were rent with impenetrable fractures, deep grottoes, and unfathomable holes, at the bottom of which formidable creatures might be heard moving. My blood curdled when I saw enormous antennae blocking my road, or some frightful claw closing with a noise in the shadow of some cavity. Millions of luminous spots shone brightly in the midst of the darkness. They were the eyes of giant crustacea crouched in their holes; giant lobsters setting themselves up like halberdiers, and moving their claws with the clicking sound of pincers; titanic crabs, pointed like a gun on its carriage; and frightful-looking poulps, interweaving their tentacles like a living nest of serpents.

We had now arrived on the first platform, where other surprises awaited me. Before us lay some picturesque ruins, which betrayed the hand of man and not that of the Creator. There were vast heaps of stone, among which might be traced the vague and shadowy forms of castles and temples, clothed with a world of blossoming zoophytes, and over which, instead of ivy, seaweed and fucus threw a thick vegetable mantle. But what was this portion of the globe which had been swallowed by cataclysms? Who had placed those rocks and stones like cromlechs of prehistoric times? Where was I? Whither had Captain Nemo's fancy hurried me?

I would fain have asked him; not being able to, I stopped him—I seized his arm. But, shaking his head, and pointing to the highest point of the mountain, he seemed to say:

"Come, come along; come higher!"

I followed, and in a few minutes I had climbed to the top, which for a circle of ten yards commanded the whole mass of rock.

I looked down the side we had just climbed. The mountain did not rise more than seven or eight hundred feet above the level of the plain; but on the opposite side it commanded from twice that height the depths of this part of the Atlantic. My eyes ranged far over a large space lit by a violent fulguration. In fact, the mountain was a volcano.

At fifty feet above the peak, in the midst of a rain of stones and scoriae, a large crater was vomiting forth torrents of lava which fell in a cascade of fire into the bosom of the liquid mass. Thus situated, this volcano lit the lower plain like an immense torch, even to the extreme limits of the horizon. I said that the submarine crater threw up lava, but no flames. Flames require the oxygen of the air to feed upon and cannot be developed underwater; but streams of lava, having in themselves the principles of their incandescence, can attain a white heat, fight vigorously against the liquid element, and turn it to vapor by contact.

Rapid currents bearing all these gases in diffusion and torrents of lava slid to the bottom of the mountain like an eruption of Vesuvius on another Terra del Greco.

There indeed under my eyes, ruined, destroyed, lay a town—its roofs open to the sky, its temples fallen, its arches dislocated, its columns lying on the ground, from which one would still recognize the massive character of Tuscan architecture. Further on, some remains of a gigantic aqueduct; here the high base of an Acropolis, with the floating outline of a Parthenon; there traces of a quay, as if an ancient port had formerly abutted on the borders of the ocean, and disappeared with its merchant vessels and its war galleys. Farther on again, long lines of sunken walls and broad, deserted streets—a perfect Pompeii escaped beneath the waters. Such was the sight that Captain Nemo brought before my eyes!

Where was I? Where was I? I must know at any cost. I tried to speak, but Captain Nemo stopped me by a gesture, and, picking up a piece of chalk-stone, advanced to a rock of black basalt, and traced the one word:

## ATLANTIS

What a light shot through my mind! Atlantis! The Atlantis of Plato, that continent denied by Origen and Humbolt, who placed its disappearance among the legendary tales. I had it there now before my eyes, bearing upon it the unexceptionable testimony of its catastrophe. The region thus engulfed was beyond Europe, Asia, and Lybia, beyond the columns of Hercules, where those powerful people, the Atlantides, lived, against whom the first wars of ancient Greeks were waged.

Thus, led by the strangest destiny, I was treading under foot the mountains of this continent, touching with my hand those ruins a thousand generations old and contemporary with the geological epochs. I was walking on the very spot where the contemporaries of the first man had walked.

While I was trying to fix in my mind every detail of this grand landscape, Captain Nemo remained motionless, as if petrified in mute ecstasy, leaning on a mossy stone. Was he dreaming of those generations long since disappeared? Was he asking them the secret of human destiny? Was it here this strange man came to steep himself in historical recollections, and live again this ancient life—he who wanted no modern one? What would I not have given to know his thoughts, to share them, to understand them! We remained for an hour at this place, contemplating the vast plains under the brightness of the lava, which was sometimes wonderfully intense. Rapid tremblings ran along the mountain caused by internal bubblings, deep noise, distinctly transmitted through the liquid medium were echoed with majestic grandeur. At this moment the moon appeared through the mass of waters and threw her pale rays on the buried continent. It was but a gleam, but what an indescribable effect! The captain rose, cast one last look on the immense plain, and then bade me follow him.

We descended the mountain rapidly, and, the mineral forest once passed, I saw the lantern of the *Nautilus* shining like a star. The captain walked straight to it, and we got on board as the first rays of light whitened the surface of the ocean.

## CHAPTER X

### THE SUBMARINE COAL-MINES

The next day, February 20, I awoke very late: the fatigues of the previous night had prolonged my sleep until eleven o'clock. I dressed quickly, and hastened to find the course the *Nautilus* was taking. The instruments showed it to be still toward the south, with a speed of twenty miles an hour and a depth of fifty fathoms.

The species of fish here did not differ much from those already noticed. There were rays of giant size, five yards long, and endowed with great muscular strength, which enabled them to shoot above the waves; sharks of many kinds; among others, one fifteen feet long, with triangular sharp teeth, and whose transparency rendered it almost invisible in the water; brown sagrae; humantins, prism-shaped and clad with a tuberculous hide; sturgeons, resembling their congeners of the Mediterranean; trumpet synganthes a foot and a half long, furnished with grayish bladders, without teeth or tongue, and as supple as snakes.

Among bony fish Conseil noticed some about three yards long, armed at the upper jaw with a piercing sword; other bright-colored creatures, known in the time of Aristotle by the name of the sea dragon, which are dangerous to capture on account of the spikes on their back; also some coryphaenes with brown backs marked with little blue stripes and surrounded by a gold border; some beautiful dorades, and swordfish four-and-twenty feet long, swimming in troops, fierce animals, but rather herbivorous than carnivorous.

About four o'clock, the soil, generally composed of a thick mud mixed with petrified wood, changed by degrees, and it became more stony, and seemed strewn with conglomerate and pieces of basalt, with a sprinkling of lava. I thought that a mountainous region was succeeding the long plains; and accordingly, after a few evolutions of the *Nautilus*, I saw the southerly horizon blocked by a high wall which seemed to close all exit. Its summit evidently passed the level of the ocean. It must be a continent, or at least an island—one of the Canaries, or of the Cape Verde Islands. The bearings not being yet taken, perhaps designedly, I was ignorant of our exact position. In any case, such a wall seemed to me to mark the limits of that Atlantis, of which we had in reality passed over only the smallest part.

Much longer should I have remained at the window admiring the beauties of sea and sky, but the panels closed. At this moment the *Nautilus* arrived at the side of this high, perpendicular wall. What it would do, I could not guess. I returned to my room; it no longer moved. I laid myself down with the full intention of waking after a few hours' sleep; but it was eight o'clock the next day when I entered the saloon. I looked at the manometer. It told me that the *Nautilus* was floating on the surface of the ocean. Besides, I heard steps on the platform. I went to the panel. It was open; but, instead of broad daylight, as I expected, I was surrounded by profound darkness. Where were we? Was I mistaken? Was it still night? No; not a star was shining and night has not that utter darkness.

I knew not what to think, when a voice near me said:

"Is that you, Professor?"

"Ah! Captain," I answered, "where are we?"

"Underground, sir."

"Underground!" I exclaimed. "And the *Nautilus* floating still?"

"It always floats."

"But I do not understand."

"Wait a few minutes, our lantern will be lit, and, if you like light places, you will be satisfied."

I stood on the platform and waited. The darkness was so complete that I could not even see Captain Nemo; but, looking to the zenith, exactly above my head, I seemed to catch an undecided gleam, a kind of twilight filling a circular hole. At this instant the lantern was lit, and its vividness dispelled the faint light. I closed my dazzled eyes for an instant, and then looked again. The *Nautilus* was stationary, floating near a mountain which formed a sort of quay. The lake, then, supporting it was a lake imprisoned by a circle of walls, measuring two miles in diameter and six in circumference. Its level (the manometer showed) could only be the same as the outside level, for there must necessarily be a communication between the lake and the sea. The high partitions, leaning forward on their base, grew into a vaulted roof bearing the shape of an immense funnel turned upside down, the height being about five or six hundred yards. At the summit was a circular orifice, by which I had caught the slight gleam of light, evidently daylight.

"Where are we?" I asked.

"In the very heart of an extinct volcano, the interior of which has been invaded by the sea, after some great convulsion of the earth. While you were sleeping, Professor, the *Nautilus* penetrated to this lagoon by a natural canal, which opens about ten yards beneath the surface of the ocean. This is its harbor of refuge, a sure, commodious, and mysterious one, sheltered from all gales. Show me, if you can, on the coasts of any of your continents or islands, a road which can give such perfect refuge from all storms."

"Certainly," I replied, "you are in safety here, Captain Nemo. Who could reach you in the heart of a volcano? But did I not see an opening at its summit?"

"Yes; its crater, formerly filled with lava, vapor, and flames, and which now gives entrance to the life-giving air we breathe."

"But what is this volcanic mountain?"

"It belongs to one of the numerous islands with which this sea is strewn—to vessels a simple sandbank—to us an immense cavern. Chance led me to discover it, and chance served me well."

"But of what use is this refuge, Captain? The *Nautilus* wants no port."

"No, sir; but it wants electricity to make it move, and the wherewithal to make the electricity—sodium to feed the elements, coal from which to get the sodium, and a coal-mine to supply the coal. And exactly on this spot the sea covers entire forests embedded during the geological periods, now mineralized and transformed into coal; for me they are an inexhaustible mine."

"Your men follow the trade of miners here, then, Captain?"

"Exactly so. These mines extend under the waves like the mines of Newcastle. Here, in their diving dresses, pickaxe and shovel in hand, my men extract the coal, which I do not even ask from the mines of the earth. When I burn this combustible for the manufacture of sodium, the smoke, escaping from the crater of the mountain, gives it the appearance of a still-active volcano."

"And we shall see your companions at work?"

"No; not this time at least; for I am in a hurry to continue our submarine tour of the earth. So I shall content myself with drawing from the reserve of sodium I already possess. The time for loading is one day only, and we continue our voyage. So, if you wish to go over the cavern and make the round of the lagoon, you must take advantage of today, M. Aronnax."

I thanked the captain and went to look for my companions, who had not yet left their cabin. I invited them to follow me without saying where we were. They mounted the platform. Conseil, who was astonished at nothing, seemed to look upon it as quite natural that he should wake under a mountain, after having fallen asleep under the waves. But Ned Land thought of nothing but finding whether the cavern had any exit. After breakfast, about ten o'clock, we went down on to the mountain.

"Here we are, once more on land," said Conseil.

"I do not call this land," said the Canadian. "And besides, we are not on it, but beneath it."

Between the walls of the mountains and the waters of the lake lay a sandy shore which, at its greatest breadth, measured five hundred feet. On this soil one might easily make the tour of the lake. But the base of the high partitions was stony ground, with volcanic locks and enormous pumice stones lying in picturesque heaps. All these detached masses, covered with enamel, polished by the action of the subterraneous fires, shone resplendent by the light of our electric lantern. The mica dust from the shore, rising under our feet, flew like a cloud of sparks. The bottom now rose sensibly, and we soon arrived at long circuitous slopes, or inclined planes, which took us higher by degrees; but we were obliged to walk carefully among these conglomerates, bound by no cement, the feet slipping on the glassy crystal, feldspar, and quartz.

The volcanic nature of this enormous excavation was confirmed on all sides, and I pointed it out to my companions.

"Picture to yourselves," said I, "what this crater must have been when filled with boiling lava, and when the level of the incandescent liquid rose to the orifice of the mountain, as though melted on the top of a hot plate."

"I can picture it perfectly," said Conseil. "But, sir, will you tell me why the Great Architect has suspended operations, and how it is that the furnace is replaced by the quiet waters of the lake?"

"Most probably, Conseil, because some convulsion beneath the ocean produced that very opening which has served as a passage for the *Nautilus*. Then the waters of the Atlantic rushed into the interior of the mountain. There must have been a terrible struggle between the two elements, a struggle which ended in the victory of Neptune. But many ages have run out since then, and the submerged volcano is now a peaceable grotto."

"Very well," replied Ned Land; "I accept the explanation, sir; but, in our own interests, I regret that the opening of which you speak was not made above the level of the sea."

"But, friend Ned," said Conseil, "if the passage had not been under the sea, the *Nautilus* could not have gone through it."

We continued ascending. The steps became more and more perpendicular and narrow. Deep excavations, which we were obliged to cross, cut them here and there; sloping masses had to be turned. We slid upon our knees and crawled along. But Conseil's dexterity and the Canadian's strength surmounted all obstacles. At a height of about thirty-one feet the nature of the ground changed without becoming more practicable. To the conglomerate and trachyte succeeded black basalt, the first dispread in layers full of bubbles, the latter forming regular prisms, placed like a colonnade supporting the spring of the immense vault, an admirable specimen of natural architecture. Between the blocks of basalt wound long streams of lava, long since grown cold, encrusted with bituminous rays; and in some places there were spread large carpets of sulfur. A more powerful light shone through the upper crater, shedding a vague glimmer over these volcanic depressions forever buried in the bosom of this extinguished mountain. But our upward march was soon stopped at a height of about two hundred and fifty feet by impassable obstacles. There was a complete vaulted arch overhanging us, and our ascent was changed to a circular walk. At the last change vegetable life began to struggle with the mineral. Some shrubs, and even some trees, grew from the fractures of the walls. I recognized some euphorbias, with the caustic sugar coming from them; heliotropes, quite incapable of justifying their name, sadly drooped their clusters of flowers, both their color and perfume half gone. Here and there some chrysanthemums grew timidly at the foot of an aloe with long, sickly looking leaves. But between the streams of lava, I saw some little violets still slightly perfumed, and I admit that I smelt them with delight. Perfume is the soul of the flower, and sea flowers have no soul.

We had arrived at the foot of some sturdy dragon trees, which had pushed aside the rocks with their strong roots, when Ned Land exclaimed:

"Ah! Sir, a hive! A hive!"

"A hive!" I replied, with a gesture of incredulity.

"Yes, a hive," repeated the Canadian, "and bees humming around it."

I approached, and was bound to believe my own eyes. There at a hole bored in one of the dragon trees were some thousands of these ingenious insects, so common in all the Canaries, and whose produce is so much esteemed. Naturally enough, the Canadian wished to gather the honey, and I could not well oppose his wish. A quantity of dry leaves, mixed with sulfur, he lit with a spark from his flint, and he began to smoke out the bees. The humming ceased by degrees, and the hive eventually yielded several pounds of the sweetest honey, with which Ned Land filled his haversack.

"When I have mixed this honey with the paste of the artocarpus," said he, "I shall be able to offer you a succulent cake."

"Upon my word," said Conseil, "it will be gingerbread."

"Never mind the gingerbread," said I; "let us continue our interesting walk."

At every turn of the path we were following, the lake appeared in all its length and breadth. The lantern lit up the whole of its peaceable surface, which knew neither ripple nor wave. The *Nautilus* remained perfectly immovable. On the platform, and on the mountain, the ship's crew were working like black shadows clearly carved against the luminous atmosphere. We were now going around the highest crest of the first layers of rock which upheld the roof. I then saw that bees were not the only representatives of the animal kingdom in the interior of this volcano. Birds of prey hovered here and there in the shadows, or fled from their nests on the top of the rocks. There were sparrow hawks, with white breasts, and kestrels, and down the slopes scampered, with their long legs, several fine fat bustards. I leave anyone to imagine the covetousness of the Canadian at the sight of this savory game, and whether he did not regret having no gun. But he did his best to replace the lead by stones, and, after several fruitless attempts, he succeeded in wounding a magnificent bird. To say that he risked his life twenty times before reaching it is but the truth; but he managed so well that the creature joined the honey cakes in his bag. We were now obliged to descend toward the shore, the crest becoming impracticable. Above us the crater seemed to gape like the mouth of a well. From this place the sky could be clearly seen, and clouds, dissipated by the west wind, leaving behind them, even on the summit of the mountain, their misty remnants—certain proof that they were only moderately high, for the volcano did not rise more than eight hundred feet above the level of the ocean. Half an hour after the Canadian's last exploit we had regained the inner shore. Here the flora was represented by large carpets of marine crystal, a little umbelliferous plant very good to pickle, which also bears the name of pierce-stone and sea fennel. Conseil gathered some bundles of it. As to the fauna, it might be counted by thousands of crustacea of all sorts, lobsters, crabs, spider-crabs, chameleon shrimps, and a large number of shells, rockfish, and limpets. Three-quarters of an hour later we had finished our circuitous walk and were on board. The crew had just finished loading the sodium, and the *Nautilus* could have left that instant. But Captain Nemo gave no order. Did he wish to wait until night, and leave the submarine passage secretly? Perhaps so. Whatever it might be, the next day, the *Nautilus*, having left its port, steered clear of all land at a few yards beneath the waves of the Atlantic.

## CHAPTER XI

### THE SARGASSO SEA

That day the *Nautilus* crossed a singular part of the Atlantic Ocean. No one can be ignorant of the existence of a current of warm water known by the name of the Gulf Stream. After leaving the Gulf of Florida, we went in the direction of Spitzbergen. But before entering the Gulf of Mexico, about twenty-five degrees of north latitude, this current divides into two arms, the principal one going toward the coast of Ireland and Norway, while the second bends to the south about the height of the Azores; then, touching the African shore, and describing a lengthened oval, returns to the Antilles. This second arm—it is rather a collar than an arm—surrounds with its circles of warm water that portion of the cold, quiet, immovable ocean called the Sargasso Sea, a perfect lake in the open Atlantic: it takes no less than three years for the great current to pass around it. Such was the region the *Nautilus* was now visiting, a perfect meadow, a close carpet of seaweed, fucus, and tropical berries, so thick and so compact that the stem of a vessel could hardly tear its way through it. And Captain Nemo, not wishing to entangle his screw in this herbaceous mass, kept some yards beneath the surface of the waves. The name Sargasso comes from the Spanish word *sargazzo*, which signifies kelp. This kelp, or berry-plant, is the principal formation of this immense bank. And this is the reason, according to the learned Maury, the author of *The Physical Geography of the Globe*, why these plants unite in the peaceful basin of the Atlantic. The only explanation which can be given, he says, seems to me to result from the experience known to all the world. Place in a vase some fragments of cork or other floating body, and give to the water in the vase a circular movement, the scattered fragments will unite in a group in the center of the liquid surface, that is to say, in the part least agitated. In the phenomenon we are considering, the Atlantic is the vase, the Gulf Stream the circular current, and the Sargasso Sea the central point at which the floating bodies unite.

I share Maury's opinion, and I was able to study the phenomenon in the very midst, where vessels rarely penetrate. Above us floated products of all kinds, heaped up among these brownish plants; trunks of trees torn from the Andes or the Rocky Mountains, and floated by the Amazon or the Mississippi; numerous wrecks, remains of keels, or ships' bottoms, side-planks stove in, and so weighted with shells and barnacles that they could not again rise to the surface. And time will one day justify Maury's other opinion, that these substances thus accumulated for ages will become petrified by the action of the water and will then form inexhaustible coal mines—a precious reserve prepared by far-seeing nature for the moment when men shall have exhausted the mines of continents.

In the midst of this inextricable mass of plants and seaweed, I noticed some charming pink halcyons and actiniae, with their long tentacles trailing after them; medusae, green, red, and blue and the great rhyostoms or Cuvier, the large umbrella of which was bordered and festooned with violet.

All the day of February 22, we passed in the Sargasso Sea, where such fish as are partial to marine plants find abundant nourishment. The next, the ocean had returned to its accustomed aspect. From this time for nineteen days, from February 23 to March 12, the *Nautilus* kept in the middle of the Atlantic, carrying us at a constant speed of a hundred leagues in twenty-four hours. Captain Nemo evidently intended accomplishing his submarine program, and I imagined that he intended, after doubling Cape Horn, to return to the Australian seas of the Pacific. Ned Land had cause for fear. In these large seas, void of islands, we could not attempt to leave the boat. Nor had we any means of opposing Captain Nemo's will. Our only course was to submit; but what we could neither gain by force nor cunning, I liked to think might be obtained by persuasion. This voyage ended, would he not consent to restore our liberty, under an oath never to reveal his existence—an oath of honor which we should have religiously kept? But we must consider that delicate question with the captain. But was I free to claim this liberty? Had he not himself said from the beginning, in the firmest manner, that the secret of his life exacted from him our lasting imprisonment on board the *Nautilus*? And would not my four months' silence appear to him a tacit acceptance of our situation? And would not a return to the subject result in raising suspicions which might be hurtful to our projects, if at some future time a favorable opportunity offered to return to them?

During the nineteen days mentioned above, no incident of any kind happened to signalize our voyage. I saw little of the captain; he was at work. In the library I often found his books left open, especially those on natural history. My work on submarine depths, conned over by him, was covered with marginal notes, often contradicting my theories and systems; but the captain contented himself with thus purging my work; it was very rare for him to discuss it with me. Sometimes I heard the melancholy tones of his organ; but only at night, in the midst of the deepest obscurity, when the *Nautilus* slept upon the deserted ocean. During this part of our voyage we sailed whole days on the surface of the waves. The sea seemed abandoned. A few sailing vessels, on the road to India, were making for the Cape of Good Hope. One day we were followed by the boats of a whaler, who, no doubt, took us for some enormous whale of great price; but Captain Nemo did not wish the worthy fellows to lose their time and trouble, so ended the chase by plunging under the water. Our navigation continued until March 13; that day the *Nautilus* was employed in taking soundings, which greatly interested me. We had then made about 13,000 leagues since our departure from the high seas of the Pacific. The bearings gave us 45° 37' south latitude, and 37° 53' west longitude. It was the same water in which Captain Denham of the *Herald* sounded 7,000 fathoms without finding the bottom. There, too, Lieutenant Parker, of the American frigate *Congress*, could not touch the bottom with 15,140 fathoms. Captain Nemo intended seeking the bottom of the ocean by a diagonal sufficiently lengthened by means of lateral planes placed at an angle of forty-five degrees with the waterline of the *Nautilus*. Then the screw set to work at its maximum speed, its four blades beating the waves with indescribable force. Under this powerful pressure, the hull of the *Nautilus* quivered like a sonorous chord and sank regularly under the water.

At 7,000 fathoms I saw some blackish tops rising from the midst of the waters; but these summits might belong to high mountains like the Himalayas or Mont Blanc, even higher; and the depth of the abyss remained incalculable. The *Nautilus* descended still lower, in spite of the great pressure. I felt the steel plates tremble at the fastenings of the bolts; its bars bent, its partitions groaned; the windows of the saloon seemed to curve under the pressure of the waters. And this firm structure would doubtless have yielded, if, as its captain had said, it had not been capable of resistance like a solid block. We had attained a depth of 16,000 yards (four leagues), and the sides of the *Nautilus* then bore a pressure of 1,600 atmospheres, that is to say, 3,200 pounds to each square two-fifths of an inch of its surface.

"What a situation to be in!" I exclaimed. "To overrun these deep regions where man has never trod! Look, Captain, look at these magnificent rocks, these uninhabited grottoes, these lowest receptacles of the globe, where life is no longer possible! What unknown sights are here! Why should we be unable to preserve a remembrance of them?"

"Would you like to carry away more than the remembrance?" said Captain Nemo.

"What do you mean by those words?"

"I mean to say that nothing is easier than to make a photographic view of this submarine region."

I had not time to express my surprise at this new proposition, when, at Captain Nemo's call, an objective was brought into the saloon. Through the widely opened panel, the liquid mass was bright with electricity, which was distributed with such uniformity that not a shadow, not a gradation, was to be seen in our manufactured light. The *Nautilus* remained motionless, the force of its screw subdued by the inclination of its planes: the instrument was propped on the bottom of the oceanic site, and in a few seconds we had obtained a perfect negative. I here give the positive, from which may be seen those primitive rocks, which have never looked upon the light of heaven; that lowest granite which forms the foundation of the globe; those deep grottoes, woven in the stony mass whose outlines were of such sharpness, and the border lines of which are marked in black, as if done by the brush of some Flemish artist. Beyond that again, a horizon of mountains, an admirable undulating line, forming the prospective of the landscape. I cannot describe the effect of those smooth, black, polished rocks, without moss, without a spot, and of strange forms, standing solidly on the sandy carpet which sparkled under the jets of our electric light.

But, the operation being over, Captain Nemo said, "Let us go up; we must not abuse our position, nor expose the *Nautilus* too long to such great pressure."

"Go up again!" I exclaimed.

"Hold well on."

I had not time to understand why the captain cautioned me thus, when I was thrown forward on to the carpet. At a signal from the captain, its screw was shipped, and its blades raised vertically; the *Nautilus* shot into the air like a balloon, rising with stunning rapidity, and cutting the mass of waters with a sonorous agitation. Nothing was visible; and in four minutes it had shot through the four leagues which separated it from the ocean, and, after emerging like a flying fish, fell, making the waves rebound to an enormous height.

## CHAPTER XII

### CACHALOTS AND WHALES

During the nights of March 13 and 14, the *Nautilus* returned to its southerly course. I fancied that, when on a level with Cape Horn, he would turn the helm westward, in order to beat the Pacific seas, and so complete the tour of the world. He did nothing of the kind, but continued on his way to the southern regions. Where was he going to? To the pole? It was madness! I began to think that the captain's temerity justified Ned Land's fears. For some time past the Canadian had not spoken to me of his projects of flight; he was less communicative, almost silent. I could see that this lengthened imprisonment was weighing upon him, and I felt that rage was burning within him. When he met the captain, his eyes lit up with suppressed anger; and I feared that his natural violence would lead him into some extreme. That day, March 14, Conseil and he came to me in my room. I inquired the cause of their visit.

"A simple question to ask you, sir," replied the Canadian.

"Speak, Ned."

"How many men are there on board the *Nautilus*, do you think?"

"I cannot tell, my friend."

"I should say that its working does not require a large crew."

"Certainly, under existing conditions, ten men, at the most, ought to be enough."

"Well, why should there be any more?"

"Why?" I replied, looking fixedly at Ned Land, whose meaning was easy to guess. "Because," I added, "if my surmises are correct, and if I have well understood the captain's existence, the *Nautilus* is not only a vessel: it is also a place of refuge for those who, like its commander, have broken every tie upon earth."

"Perhaps so," said Conseil, "but, in any case, the *Nautilus* can only contain a certain number of men. Could not you, sir, estimate their maximum?"

"How, Conseil?"

"By calculation; given the size of the vessel, which you know, sir, and consequently the quantity of air it contains, knowing also how much each man expends at a breath, and comparing these results with the fact that the *Nautilus* is obliged to go to the surface every twenty-four hours."

Conseil had not finished the sentence before I saw what he was driving at.

"I understand," said I, "but that calculation, though simple enough, can give but a very uncertain result."

"Never mind," said Ned Land urgently.

"Here it is, then," said I. "In one hour each man consumes the oxygen contained in twenty gallons of air; and in twenty-four, that contained in 480 gallons. We must, therefore find how many times 480 gallons of air the *Nautilus* contains."

"Just so," said Conseil.

"Or," I continued, "the size of the *Nautilus* being 1,500 tons; and one ton holding

200 gallons, it contains 300,000 gallons of air, which, divided by 480, gives a quotient of 625. Which means to say, strictly speaking, that the air contained in the *Nautilus* would suffice for 625 men for twenty-four hours."

"Six hundred and twenty-five!" repeated Ned.

"But remember that all of us, passengers, sailors, and officers included, would not form a tenth part of that number."

"Still too many for three men," murmured Conseil.

The Canadian shook his head, passed his hand across his forehead, and left the room without answering.

"Will you allow me to make one observation, sir?" said Conseil. "Poor Ned is longing for everything that he cannot have. His past life is always present to him; everything that we are forbidden he regrets. His head is full of old recollections. And we must understand him. What has he to do here? Nothing; he is not learned like you, sir; and has not the same taste for the beauties of the sea that we have. He would risk everything to be able to go once more into a tavern in his own country."

Certainly the monotony on board must seem intolerable to the Canadian, accustomed as he was to a life of liberty and activity. Events were rare which could rouse him to any show of spirit; but that day an event did happen which recalled the bright days of the harpooner. About eleven in the morning, being on the surface of the ocean, the *Nautilus* fell in with a troop of whales—an encounter which did not astonish me, knowing that these creatures, hunted to death, had taken refuge in high latitudes.

We were seated on the platform, with a quiet sea. The month of October in those latitudes gave us some lovely autumnal days. It was the Canadian—he could not be mistaken—who signaled a whale on the eastern horizon. Looking attentively, one might see its black back rise and fall with the waves five miles from the *Nautilus*.

"Ah!" exclaimed Ned Land. "If I was on board a whaler, now such a meeting would give me pleasure. It is one of large size. See with what strength its blowholes throw up columns of air and steam! Confound it, why am I bound to these steel plates?"

"What, Ned," said I, "you have not forgotten your old ideas of fishing?"

"Can a whale-fisher ever forget his old trade, sir? Can he ever tire of the emotions caused by such a chase?"

"You have never fished in these seas, Ned?"

"Never, sir; in the northern only, and as much in Bering as in Davis Straits."

"Then the southern whale is still unknown to you. It is the Greenland whale you have hunted up to this time, and that would not risk passing through the warm waters of the equator. Whales are localized, according to their kinds, in certain seas which they never leave. And if one of these creatures went from Bering to Davis Straits, it must be simply because there is a passage from one sea to the other, either on the American or the Asiatic side."

"In that case, as I have never fished in these seas, I do not know the kind of whale frequenting them!"

"I have told you, Ned."

"A greater reason for making their acquaintance," said Conseil.

"Look! Look!" exclaimed the Canadian. "They approach: they aggravate me; they know that I cannot get at them!"

Ned stamped his feet. His hand trembled, as he grasped an imaginary harpoon.

"Are these cetaceans as large as those of the northern seas?" asked he.

"Very nearly, Ned."

"Because I have seen large whales, sir, whales measuring a hundred feet. I have even been told that those of Hullamoch and Umgallick, of the Aleutian Islands, are sometimes a hundred and fifty feet long."

"That seems to me exaggeration. These creatures are only balaeaopterons, provided with dorsal fins; and, like the cachalots, are generally much smaller than the Greenland whale."

"Ah!" exclaimed the Canadian, whose eyes had never left the ocean. "They are coming nearer; they are in the same water as the *Nautilus*."

Then, returning to the conversation, he said:

"You spoke of the cachalot as a small creature. I have heard of gigantic ones. They are intelligent cetacea. It is said of some that they cover themselves with seaweed and fucus, and then are taken for islands. People encamp upon them, and settle there; light a fire—"

"And build houses," said Conseil.

"Yes, joker," said Ned Land. "And one fine day the creature plunges, carrying with it all the inhabitants to the bottom of the sea."

"Something like the travels of Sinbad the Sailor," I replied, laughing.

"Ah!" suddenly exclaimed Ned Land. "It is not one whale; there are ten—there are twenty—it is a whole troop! And I not able to do anything! Hands and feet tied!"

"But, friend Ned," said Conseil, "why do you not ask Captain Nemo's permission to chase them?"

Conseil had not finished his sentence when Ned Land had lowered himself through the panel to seek the captain. A few minutes afterward the two appeared together on the platform.

Captain Nemo watched the troop of cetacea playing on the waters about a mile from the *Nautilus*.

"They are southern whales," said he; "there goes the fortune of a whole fleet of whalers."

"Well, sir," asked the Canadian, "can I not chase them, if only to remind me of my old trade of harpooner?"

"And to what purpose?" replied Captain Nemo. "Only to destroy! We have nothing to do with the whale-oil on board."

"But, sir," continued the Canadian, "in the Red Sea you allowed us to follow the dugong."

"Then it was to procure fresh meat for my crew. Here it would be killing for killing's sake. I know that is a privilege reserved for man, but I do not approve of such murderous pastime. In destroying the southern whale (like the Greenland whale, an inoffensive creature), your traders do a culpable action, Master Land. They have already depopulated the whole of Baffin's Bay, and are annihilating a class of useful animals. Leave the unfortunate cetacea alone. They have plenty of natural enemies— cachalots, swordfish, and sawfish—without you troubling them."

The captain was right. The barbarous and inconsiderate greed of these fishermen will one day cause the disappearance of the last whale in the ocean. Ned Land whistled "Yankee Doodle" between his teeth, thrust his hands into his pockets, and turned his back upon us. But Captain Nemo watched the troop of cetacea, and, addressing me, said:

"I was right in saying that whales had natural enemies enough, without counting man. These will have plenty to do before long. Do you see, M. Aronnax, about eight miles to leeward, those blackish moving points?"

"Yes, Captain," I replied.

"Those are cachalots—terrible animals, which I have met in troops of two or three hundred. As to those, they are cruel, mischievous creatures; they would be right in exterminating them."

The Canadian turned quickly at the last words.

"Well, Captain," said he, "it is still time, in the interest of the whales."

"It is useless to expose one's self, Professor. The *Nautilus* will disperse them. It is armed with a steel spur as good as Master Land's harpoon, I imagine."

The Canadian did not put himself out enough to shrug his shoulders. Attack cetacea with blows of a spur! Who had ever heard of such a thing?

"Wait, M. Aronnax," said Captain Nemo. "We will show you something you have never yet seen. We have no pity for these ferocious creatures. They are nothing but mouth and teeth."

Mouth and teeth! No one could better describe the macrocephalous cachalot, which is sometimes more than seventy-five feet long. Its enormous head occupies one-third of its entire body. Better armed than the whale, whose upper jaw is furnished only with whalebone, it is supplied with twenty-five large tusks, about eight inches long, cylindrical and conical at the top, each weighing two pounds. It is in the upper part of this enormous head, in great cavities divided by cartilages, that is to be found from six to eight hundred pounds of that precious oil called spermaceti. The cachalot is a disagreeable creature, more tadpole than fish, according to Fredol's description. It is badly formed, the whole of its left side being (if we may say it), a "failure," and being only able to see with its right eye. But the formidable troop was nearing us. They had seen the whales and were preparing to attack them. One could judge beforehand that the cachalots would be victorious, not only because they were better built for attack than their inoffensive adversaries, but also because they could remain longer underwater without coming to the surface. There was only just time to go to the help of the whales. The *Nautilus* went underwater. Conseil, Ned Land, and I took our places before the window in the saloon, and Captain Nemo joined the pilot in his cage to work his apparatus as an engine of destruction. Soon I felt the beatings of the screw quicken, and our speed increased. The battle between the cachalots and the whales had already begun when the *Nautilus* arrived. They did not at first show any fear at the sight of this new monster joining in the conflict. But they soon had to guard against its blows. What a battle! The *Nautilus* was nothing but a formidable harpoon, brandished by the hand of its captain. It hurled itself against the fleshy mass, passing through from one part to the other, leaving behind it two quivering halves of the animal. It could not feel the formidable blows from their tails upon its sides, nor the shock which it produced itself, much more. One cachalot killed, it ran at the next, tacked on the spot that it might not miss its prey, going forward and backward, answering to its helm, plunging when the cetacean dived into the deep waters, coming up with it when it returned to the surface, striking it front or sideways, cutting or tearing in all directions and at any pace, piercing it with its terrible spur. What carnage! What a noise on the surface of the waves! What sharp hissing, and what snorting peculiar to these enraged animals! In the midst of these waters, generally so peaceful, their tails made perfect billows. For one hour this wholesale massacre continued, from which the cachalots could not escape. Several times ten or twelve united tried to crush the *Nautilus* by their weight. From the window we could see their enormous mouths, studded with tusks, and their formidable eyes. Ned Land could not contain himself; he threatened and swore at them. We could feel them clinging to our vessel like dogs worrying a wild boar in a copse. But the *Nautilus*, working its screw, carried them here and there, or to the upper levels of the ocean, without caring for their enormous weight, nor the powerful strain on the vessel. At length the mass of cachalots broke up, the waves became quiet, and I felt that we were rising to the surface. The panel opened, and we hurried on to the platform. The sea was covered with mutilated bodies. A formidable explosion could not have divided and torn this fleshy mass with more violence. We were floating amid gigantic bodies, bluish on the back and white underneath, covered with enormous protuberances. Some terrified cachalots were flying toward the horizon. The waves were dyed red for several miles, and the *Nautilus* floated in a sea of blood. Captain Nemo joined us.

"Well, Master Land?" said he.

"Well, sir," replied the Canadian, whose enthusiasm had somewhat calmed; "it is a terrible spectacle, certainly. But I am not a butcher. I am a hunter, and I call this a butchery."

"It is a massacre of mischievous creatures," replied the captain; "and the *Nautilus* is not a butcher's knife."

"I like my harpoon better," said the Canadian.

"Everyone to his own," answered the captain, looking fixedly at Ned Land.

I feared he would commit some act of violence, which would end in sad consequences. But his anger was turned by the sight of a whale which the *Nautilus* had just come up with. The creature had not quite escaped from the cachalot's teeth. I recognized the southern whale by its flat head, which is entirely black. Anatomically, it is distinguished from the white whale and the North Cape whale by the seven cervical vertebrae, and it has two more ribs than its congeners. The unfortunate cetacean was lying on its side, riddled with holes from the bites, and quite dead. From its mutilated fin still hung a young whale which it could not save from the massacre. Its open mouth let the water flow in and out, murmuring like the waves breaking on the shore. Captain Nemo steered close to the corpse of the creature. Two of his men mounted its side, and I saw, not without surprise, that they were drawing from its breasts all the milk which they contained, that is to say, about two or three tons. The captain offered me a cup of the milk, which was still warm. I could not help showing my repugnance to the drink; but he assured me that it was excellent, and not to be distinguished from cow's milk. I tasted it, and was of his opinion. It was a useful reserve to us, for in the shape of salt butter or cheese it would form an agreeable variety from our ordinary food. From that day I noticed with uneasiness that Ned Land's ill-will toward Captain Nemo increased, and I resolved to watch the Canadian's gestures closely.

# CHAPTER XIII

## THE ICEBERG

The *Nautilus* was steadily pursuing its southerly course, following the fiftieth meridian with considerable speed. Did he wish to reach the pole? I did not think so, for every attempt to reach that point had hitherto failed. Again, the season was far advanced, for in the Antarctic regions March 13 corresponds with September 13 of the northern regions, which begin at the equinoctial season. On March 14 I saw floating ice in latitude 55°, merely pale bits of debris from twenty to twenty-five feet long, forming banks over which the sea curled. The *Nautilus* remained on the surface of the ocean. Ned Land, who had fished in the Arctic Seas, was familiar with its icebergs; but Conseil and I admired them for the first time. In the atmosphere toward the southern horizon stretched a white dazzling band. English whalers have given it the name of "ice blink." However thick the clouds may be, it is always visible, and announces the presence of an ice pack or bank. Accordingly, larger blocks soon appeared, whose brilliancy changed with the caprices of the fog. Some of these masses showed green veins, as if long undulating lines had been traced with sulfate of copper; others resembled enormous amethysts with the light shining through them. Some reflected the light of day upon a thousand crystal facets. Others shaded with vivid calcareous reflections resembled a perfect town of marble. The more we neared the south the more these floating islands increased both in number and importance.

At 60° latitude every pass had disappeared. But, seeking carefully, Captain Nemo soon found a narrow opening, through which he boldly slipped, knowing, however, that it would close behind him. Thus, guided by this clever hand, the *Nautilus* passed through all the ice with a precision which quite charmed Conseil; icebergs or mountains, ice fields or smooth plains, seeming to have no limits, drift-ice or floating ice-packs, plains broken up, called palchs when they are circular, and streams when they are made up of long strips. The temperature was very low; the thermometer exposed to the air marked 2° or 3° below zero, but we were warmly clad with fur, at the expense of the sea bear and seal. The interior of the *Nautilus*, warmed regularly by its electric apparatus, defied the most intense cold. Besides, it would only have been necessary to go some yards beneath the waves to find a more bearable temperature. Two months earlier we should have had perpetual daylight in these latitudes; but already we had had three or four hours of night, and by and by there would be six months of darkness in these circumpolar regions. On March 15, we were in the latitude of New Shetland and South Orkney. The captain told me that formerly numerous tribes of seals inhabited them; but that English and American whalers, in their rage for destruction, massacred both old and young; thus, where there was once life and animation, they had left silence and death.

About eight o'clock on the morning of March 16 the *Nautilus*, following the fifty-fifth meridian, cut the Antarctic polar circle. Ice surrounded us on all sides, and closed the horizon. But Captain Nemo went from one opening to another, still going higher. I cannot express my astonishment at the beauties of these new regions. The ice took most surprising forms. Here the grouping formed an Oriental town, with innumerable mosques and minarets; there a fallen city thrown to the earth, as it were, by some convulsion of nature. The whole aspect was constantly changed by the oblique rays of the sun, or lost in the grayish fog amid hurricanes of snow. Detonations and falls were heard on all sides, great overthrows of icebergs, which altered the whole landscape like a diorama. Often seeing no exit, I thought we were definitely prisoners; but, instinct guiding him at the slightest indication, Captain Nemo would discover a new pass. He was never mistaken when he saw the thin threads of bluish water trickling along the ice fields; and I had no doubt that he had already ventured into the midst of these Antarctic seas before. On March 16, however, the ice fields absolutely blocked our road. It was not the iceberg itself, as yet, but vast fields cemented by the cold. But this obstacle could not stop Captain Nemo: he hurled himself against it with frightful violence. The *Nautilus* entered the brittle mass like a wedge, and split it with frightful crackings. It was the battering ram of the ancients hurled by infinite strength. The ice, thrown high in the air, fell like hail around us. By its own power of impulsion our apparatus made a canal for itself; sometimes carried away by its own impetus, it lodged on the ice field, crushing it with its weight, and sometimes buried beneath it, dividing it by a simple pitching movement, producing large rents in it. Violent gales assailed us at this time, accompanied by thick fogs, through which, from one end of the platform to the other, we could see nothing. The wind blew sharply from all parts of the compass, and the snow lay in such hard heaps that we had to break it with blows of a pickaxe. The temperature was always at 5° below zero; every outward part of the *Nautilus* was covered with ice. A rigged vessel would have been entangled in the blocked-up gorges. A vessel without sails, with electricity for its motive power, and wanting no coal, could alone brave such high latitudes. At length, on March 18, after many useless assaults, the *Nautilus* was positively blocked. It was no longer either streams, packs, or ice fields, but an interminable and immovable barrier, formed by mountains soldered together.

"An iceberg!" said the Canadian to me.

I knew that to Ned Land, as well as to all other navigators who had preceded us, this was an inevitable obstacle. The sun appearing for an instant at noon, Captain Nemo took an observation as near as possible, which gave our situation at 51° 30' longitude and 67° 39' of south latitude. We had advanced one degree more in this Antarctic region. Of the liquid surface of the sea there was no longer a glimpse. Under the spur of the *Nautilus* lay stretched a vast plain, entangled with confused blocks. Here and there sharp points and slender needles rising to a height of 200 feet; further on a steep shore, hewn as it were with an axe and clothed with grayish tints; huge mirrors, reflecting a few rays of sunshine, half drowned in the fog. And over this desolate face of nature a stern silence reigned, scarcely broken by the flapping of the wings of petrels and puffins. Everything was frozen—even the noise. The *Nautilus* was then obliged to stop in its adventurous course amid these fields of ice. In spite of our efforts, in spite of the powerful means employed to break up the ice, the *Nautilus* remained immovable. Generally, when we can proceed no further, we have return still open to us; but here return was as impossible as advance, for every pass had closed behind us; and for the few moments when we were stationary, we were likely to be entirely blocked, which did indeed happen about two o'clock in the afternoon, the fresh ice forming around its sides with astonishing rapidity. I was obliged to admit that Captain Nemo was more than imprudent. I was on the platform at that moment. The captain had been observing our situation for some time past, when he said to me:

"Well, sir, what do you think of this?"

"I think that we are caught, Captain."

"So, M. Aronnax, you really think that the *Nautilus* cannot disengage itself?"

"With difficulty, Captain; for the season is already too far advanced for you to reckon on the breaking of the ice."

"Ah! Sir," said Captain Nemo, in an ironical tone, "you will always be the same. You see nothing but difficulties and obstacles. I affirm that not only can the *Nautilus* disengage itself, but also that it can go further still."

"Further to the south?" I asked, looking at the captain.

"Yes, sir; it shall go to the pole."

"To the pole!" I exclaimed, unable to repress a gesture of incredulity.

"Yes," replied the captain, coldly, "to the Antarctic pole—to that unknown point from whence springs every meridian of the globe. You know whether I can do as I please with the *Nautilus*!"

Yes, I knew that. I knew that this man was bold, even to rashness. But to conquer those obstacles which bristled around the South Pole, rendering it more inaccessible than the North, which had not yet been reached by the boldest navigators—was it not a mad enterprise, one which only a maniac would have conceived? It then came into my head to ask Captain Nemo if he had ever discovered that pole which had never yet been trodden by a human creature?

"No, sir," he replied; "but we will discover it together. Where others have failed, I will not fail. I have never yet led my *Nautilus* so far into southern seas; but, I repeat, it shall go further yet."

"I can well believe you, Captain," said I, in a slightly ironical tone. "I believe you! Let us go ahead! There are no obstacles for us! Let us smash this iceberg! Let us blow it up; and, if it resists, let us give the *Nautilus* wings to fly over it!"

"Over it, sir!" said Captain Nemo, quietly; "no, not over it, but under it!"

"Under it!" I exclaimed, a sudden idea of the captain's projects flashing upon my mind. I understood; the wonderful qualities of the *Nautilus* were going to serve us in this superhuman enterprise.

"I see we are beginning to understand one another, sir," said the captain, half smiling. "You begin to see the possibility—I should say the success—of this attempt. That which is impossible for an ordinary vessel is easy to the *Nautilus*. If a continent lies before the pole, it must stop before the continent; but if, on the contrary, the pole is washed by open sea, it will go even to the pole."

"Certainly," said I, carried away by the captain's reasoning; "if the surface of the sea is solidified by the ice, the lower depths are free by the providential law which has placed the maximum of density of the waters of the ocean one degree higher than freezing-point; and, if I am not mistaken, the portion of this iceberg which is above the water is as one to four to that which is below."

"Very nearly, sir; for one foot of iceberg above the sea there are three below it. If these ice mountains are not more than 300 feet above the surface, they are not more than 900 beneath. And what are 900 feet to the *Nautilus?*"

"Nothing, sir."

"It could even seek at greater depths that uniform temperature of seawater, and there brave with impunity the thirty or forty degrees of surface cold."

"Just so, sir—just so," I replied, getting animated.

"The only difficulty," continued Captain Nemo, "is that of remaining several days without renewing our provision of air."

"Is that all? The *Nautilus* has vast reservoirs; we can fill them, and they will supply us with all the oxygen we want."

"Well thought of, M. Aronnax," replied the captain, smiling. "But, not wishing you to accuse me of rashness, I will first give you all my objections."

"Have you any more to make?"

"Only one. It is possible, if the sea exists at the South Pole, that it may be covered; and, consequently, we shall be unable to come to the surface."

"Good, sir! But do you forget that the *Nautilus* is armed with a powerful spur, and could we not send it diagonally against these fields of ice, which would open at the shocks?"

"Ah! Sir, you are full of ideas today."

"Besides, Captain," I added, enthusiastically, "why should we not find the sea open at the South Pole as well as at the North? The frozen poles of the earth do not coincide, either in the southern or in the northern regions; and, until it is proved to the contrary, we may suppose either a continent or an ocean free from ice at these two points of the globe."

"I think so too, M. Aronnax," replied Captain Nemo. "I only wish you to observe that, after having made so many objections to my project, you are now crushing me with arguments in its favor!"

The preparations for this audacious attempt now began. The powerful pumps of the *Nautilus* were working air into the reservoirs and storing it at high pressure. About four o'clock, Captain Nemo announced the closing of the panels on the platform. I threw one last look at the massive iceberg which we were going to cross. The weather was clear, the atmosphere pure enough, the cold very great, being 12° below zero; but, the wind having gone down, this temperature was not so unbearable. About ten men mounted the sides of the *Nautilus*, armed with pickaxes to break the ice around the vessel, which was soon free. The operation was quickly performed, for the fresh ice was still very thin. We all went below. The usual reservoirs were filled with the newly liberated water, and the *Nautilus* soon descended. I had taken my place with Conseil in the saloon; through the open window we could see the lower beds of the Southern Ocean. The thermometer went up, the needle of the compass deviated on the dial. At about 900 feet, as Captain Nemo had foreseen, we were floating beneath the undulating bottom of the iceberg. But the *Nautilus* went lower still—it went to the depth of four hundred fathoms. The temperature of the water at the surface showed twelve degrees, it was now only ten; we had gained two. I need not say the temperature of the *Nautilus* was raised by its heating apparatus to a much higher degree; every maneuver was accomplished with wonderful precision.

"We shall pass it, if you please, sir," said Conseil.

"I believe we shall," I said, in a tone of firm conviction.

In this open sea, the *Nautilus* had taken its course direct to the pole, without leaving the fifty-second meridian. From 67° 30' to 90°, twenty-two degrees and a half of latitude remained to travel; that is, about five hundred leagues. The *Nautilus* kept up a mean speed of twenty-six miles an hour—the speed of an express train. If that was kept up, in forty hours we should reach the pole.

For a part of the night the novelty of the situation kept us at the window. The sea was lit with the electric lantern; but it was deserted; fish did not sojourn in these imprisoned waters; they only found there a passage to take them from the Antarctic Ocean to the open polar sea. Our pace was rapid; we could feel it by the quivering of the long steel body. About two in the morning I took some hours' repose, and Conseil did the same. In crossing the waist I did not meet Captain Nemo: I supposed him to be in the pilot's cage. The next morning, March 19, I took my post once more in the saloon. The electric log told me that the speed of the *Nautilus* had been slackened. It was then going toward the surface; but prudently emptying its reservoirs very slowly. My heart beat fast. Were we going to emerge and regain the open polar atmosphere? No! A shock told me that the *Nautilus* had struck the bottom of the iceberg, still very thick, judging from the deadened sound. We had indeed "struck," to use a sea expression, but in an inverse sense, and at a thousand feet deep. This would give three thousand feet of ice above us; one thousand being above the watermark. The iceberg was then higher than at its borders—not a very reassuring fact. Several times that day the *Nautilus* tried again, and every time it struck the wall which lay like a ceiling above it. Sometimes it met with but 900 yards, only 200 of which rose above the surface. It was twice the height it was when the *Nautilus* had gone under the waves. I carefully noted the different depths, and thus obtained a submarine profile of the chain as it was developed under the water. That night no change had taken place in our situation. Still ice between four and five hundred yards in depth! It was evidently diminishing, but, still, what a thickness between us and the surface of the ocean! It was then eight. According to the daily custom on board the *Nautilus*, its air should have been renewed four hours ago; but I did not suffer much, although Captain Nemo had not yet made any demand upon his reserve of oxygen. My sleep was painful that night; hope and fear besieged me by turns: I rose several times. The groping of the *Nautilus* continued. About three in the morning, I noticed that the lower surface of the iceberg was only about fifty feet deep. One hundred and fifty feet now separated us from the surface of the waters. The iceberg was by degrees becoming an ice field, the mountain a plain. My eyes never left the manometer. We were still rising diagonally to the surface, which sparkled under the electric rays. The iceberg was stretching both above and beneath into lengthening slopes; mile after mile it was getting thinner. At length, at six in the morning of that memorable day, March 19, the door of the saloon opened, and Captain Nemo appeared.

"The sea is open!!" was all he said.

## CHAPTER XIV

### THE SOUTH POLE

I rushed on to the platform. Yes! The open sea, with but a few scattered pieces of ice and moving icebergs—a long stretch of sea; a world of birds in the air, and myriads of fish under those waters, which varied from intense blue to olive green, according to the bottom. The thermometer marked 3°C above zero. It was comparatively spring, shut up as we were behind this iceberg, whose lengthened mass was dimly seen on our northern horizon.

"Are we at the pole?" I asked the captain, with a beating heart.

"I do not know," he replied. "At noon I will take our bearings."

"But will the sun show himself through this fog?" said I, looking at the leaden sky.

"However little it shows, it will be enough," replied the captain.

About ten miles south a solitary island rose to a height of one hundred and four yards. We made for it, but carefully, for the sea might be strewn with banks. One hour afterward we had reached it, two hours later we had made the round of it. It measured four or five miles in circumference. A narrow canal separated it from a considerable stretch of land, perhaps a continent, for we could not see its limits. The existence of this land seemed to give some color to Maury's theory. The ingenious American has remarked that, between the South Pole and the sixtieth parallel, the sea is covered with floating ice of enormous size, which is never met with in the North Atlantic. From this fact he has drawn the conclusion that the Antarctic Circle encloses considerable continents, as icebergs cannot form in open sea, but only on the coasts. According to these calculations, the mass of ice surrounding the southern pole forms a vast cap, the circumference of which must be, at least, 2,500 miles. But the *Nautilus*, for fear of running aground, had stopped about three cable-lengths from a strand over which reared a superb heap of rocks. The boat was launched; the captain, two of his men, bearing instruments, Conseil, and myself were in it. It was ten in the morning. I had not seen Ned Land. Doubtless the Canadian did not wish to admit the presence of the South Pole. A few strokes of the oar brought us to the sand, where we ran ashore. Conseil was going to jump on to the land, when I held him back.

"Sir," said I to Captain Nemo, "to you belongs the honor of first setting foot on this land."

"Yes, sir," said the captain, "and if I do not hesitate to tread this South Pole, it is because, up to this time, no human being has left a trace there."

Saying this, he jumped lightly on to the sand. His heart beat with emotion. He climbed a rock, sloping to a little promontory, and there, with his arms crossed, mute and motionless, and with an eager look, he seemed to take possession of these southern regions. After five minutes passed in this ecstasy, he turned to us.

"When you like, sir."

I landed, followed by Conseil, leaving the two men in the boat. For a long way the soil was composed of a reddish sandy stone, something like crushed brick, scoriae, streams of lava, and pumice stones. One could not mistake its volcanic origin. In some parts, slight curls of smoke emitted a sulfurous smell, proving that the internal fires had lost nothing of their expansive powers, though, having climbed a high acclivity, I could see no volcano for a radius of several miles. We know that in those Antarctic countries, James Ross found two craters, the Erebus and Terror, in full activity, on the 167th meridian, latitude 77° 32'. The vegetation of this desolate continent seemed to me much restricted. Some lichens lay upon the black rocks; some microscopic plants, rudimentary diatomas, a kind of cells placed between two quartz shells; long purple and scarlet weed, supported on little swimming bladders, which the breaking of the waves brought to the shore. These constituted the meager flora of this region. The shore was strewn with mollusks, little mussels, and limpets. I also saw myriads of northern clios, one and a quarter inches long, of which a whale would swallow a whole world at a mouthful; and some perfect sea butterflies, animating the waters on the skirts of the shore.

There appeared on the high bottoms some coral shrubs, of the kind which, according to James Ross, live in the Antarctic seas to the depth of more than 1,000 yards. Then there were little kingfishers and starfish studding the soil. But where life abounded most was in the air. There thousands of birds fluttered and flew of all kinds, deafening us with their cries; others crowded the rock, looking at us as we passed by without fear, and pressing familiarly close by our feet. There were penguins, so agile in the water, heavy and awkward as they are on the ground; they were uttering harsh cries, a large assembly, sober in gesture, but extravagant in clamor. Albatrosses passed in the air, the expanse of their wings being at least four yards and a half, and justly called the vultures of the ocean; some gigantic petrels, and some damiers, a kind of small duck, the underpart of whose body is black and white; then there were a whole series of petrels, some whitish, with brown-bordered wings, others blue, peculiar to the Antarctic seas, and so oily, as I told Conseil, that the inhabitants of the Ferroe Islands had nothing to do before lighting them but to put a wick in.

"A little more," said Conseil, "and they would be perfect lamps! After that, we cannot expect nature to have previously furnished them with wicks!"

About half a mile farther on the soil was riddled with ruffs' nests, a sort of laying ground, out of which many birds were issuing. Captain Nemo had some hundreds hunted. They uttered a cry like the braying of an ass, were about the size of a goose, slate color on the body, white beneath, with a yellow line around their throats; they allowed themselves to be killed with a stone, never trying to escape. But the fog did not lift, and at eleven the sun had not yet shown itself. Its absence made me uneasy. Without it no observations were possible. How, then, could we decide whether we had reached the pole? When I rejoined Captain Nemo, I found him leaning on a piece of rock, silently watching the sky. He seemed impatient and vexed. But what was to be done? This rash and powerful man could not command the sun as he did the sea. Noon arrived without the orb of day showing itself for an instant. We could not even tell its position behind the curtain of fog; and soon the fog turned to snow.

"Till tomorrow," said the captain, quietly, and we returned to the *Nautilus* amid these atmospheric disturbances.

The tempest of snow continued till the next day. It was impossible to remain on the platform. From the saloon, where I was taking notes of incidents happening during this excursion to the polar continent, I could hear the cries of petrels and albatrosses sporting in the midst of this violent storm. The *Nautilus* did not remain motionless, but skirted the coast, advancing ten miles more to the south in the half-light left by the sun as it skirted the edge of the horizon. The next day, March 20, the snow had ceased. The cold was a little greater, the thermometer showing 2° below zero. The fog was rising, and I hoped that that day our observations might be taken. Captain Nemo not having yet appeared, the boat took Conseil and myself to land. The soil was still of the same volcanic nature; everywhere were traces of lava, scoriae, and basalt; but the crater which had vomited them I could not see. Here, as lower down, this continent was alive with myriads of birds. But their rule was now divided with large troops of sea mammals, looking at us with their soft eyes. There were several kinds of seals, some stretched on the earth, some on flakes of ice, many going in and out of the sea. They did not flee at our approach, never having had anything to do with man; and I reckoned that there were provisions there for hundreds of vessels.

"Sir," said Conseil, "will you tell me the names of these creatures?"

"They are seals and morses."

It was now eight in the morning. Four hours remained to us before the sun could be observed with advantage. I directed our steps toward a vast bay cut in the steep granite shore. There, I can aver that earth and ice were lost to sight by the numbers of sea mammals covering them, and I involuntarily sought for old Proteus, the mythological shepherd who watched these immense flocks of Neptune. There were more seals than anything else, forming distinct groups, male and female, the father watching over his family, the mother suckling her little ones, some already strong enough to go a few steps. When they wished to change their place, they took little jumps, made by the contraction of their bodies, and helped awkwardly enough by their imperfect fin, which, as with the lamantin, their cousins, forms a perfect forearm. I should say that, in the water, which is their element—the spine of these creatures is flexible; with smooth and close skin and webbed feet—they swim admirably. In resting on the earth they take the most graceful attitudes. Thus the ancients, observing their soft and expressive looks, which cannot be surpassed by the most beautiful look a woman can give, their clear voluptuous eyes, their charming positions, and the poetry of their manners, metamorphosed them, the male into a triton and the female into a mermaid. I made Conseil notice the considerable development of the lobes of the brain in these interesting cetaceans. No mammal, except man, has such a quantity of brain matter; they are also capable of receiving a certain amount of education, are easily domesticated, and I think, with other naturalists, that if properly taught they would be of great service as fishing dogs. The greater part of them slept on the rocks or on the sand. Among these seals, properly so called, which have no external ears (in which they differ from the otter, whose ears are prominent), I noticed several varieties of seals about three yards long, with a white coat, bulldog heads, armed with teeth in both jaws, four incisors at the top and four at the bottom, and two large canine teeth in the shape of a fleur-de-lis. Among them glided sea elephants, a kind of seal, with short, flexible trunks. The giants of this species measured twenty feet around and ten yards and a half in length; but they did not move as we approached.

"These creatures are not dangerous?" asked Conseil.

"No; not unless you attack them. When they have to defend their young their rage is terrible, and it is not uncommon for them to break the fishing boats to pieces."

"They are quite right," said Conseil.

"I do not say they are not."

Two miles farther on we were stopped by the promontory which shelters the bay from the southerly winds. Beyond it we heard loud bellowings such as a troop of ruminants would produce.

"Good!" said Conseil. "A concert of bulls!"

"No; a concert of morses."

"They are fighting!"

"They are either fighting or playing."

We now began to climb the blackish rocks, amid unforeseen stumbles, and over stones which the ice made slippery. More than once I rolled over at the expense of my loins. Conseil, more prudent or more steady, did not stumble, and helped me up, saying:

"If, sir, you would have the kindness to take wider steps, you would preserve your equilibrium better."

Arrived at the upper ridge of the promontory, I saw a vast white plain covered with morses. They were playing among themselves, and what we heard were bellowings of pleasure, not of anger.

As I passed these curious animals I could examine them leisurely, for they did not move. Their skins were thick and rugged, of a yellowish tint, approaching to red; their hair was short and scant. Some of them were four yards and a quarter long. Quieter and less timid than their cousins of the north, they did not, like them, place sentinels around the outskirts of their encampment. After examining this city of morses, I began to think of returning. It was eleven o'clock, and, if Captain Nemo found the conditions favorable for observations, I wished to be present at the operation. We followed a narrow pathway running along the summit of the steep shore. At half-past eleven we had reached the place where we landed. The boat had run aground, bringing the captain. I saw him standing on a block of basalt, his instruments near him, his eyes fixed on the northern horizon, near which the sun was then describing a lengthened curve. I took my place beside him, and waited without speaking. Noon arrived, and, as before, the sun did not appear. It was a fatality. Observations were still wanting. If not accomplished tomorrow, we must give up all idea of taking any. We were indeed exactly at March 20. Tomorrow, the 21st, would be the equinox; the sun would disappear behind the horizon for six months, and with its disappearance the long polar night would begin. Since the September equinox it had emerged from the northern horizon, rising by lengthened spirals up to December 21. At this period, the summer solstice of the northern regions, it had begun to descend; and tomorrow was to shed its last rays upon them. I communicated my fears and observations to Captain Nemo.

"You are right, M. Aronnax," said he; "if tomorrow I cannot take the altitude of the sun, I shall not be able to do it for six months. But precisely because chance has led me into these seas on the 21st of March, my bearings will be easy to take, if at twelve we can see the sun."

"Why, Captain?"

"Because then the orb of day described such lengthened curves that it is difficult to measure exactly its height above the horizon, and grave errors may be made with instruments."

"What will you do then?"

"I shall only use my chronometer," replied Captain Nemo. "If tomorrow, the 21st of March, the disk of the sun, allowing for refraction, is exactly cut by the northern horizon, it will show that I am at the South Pole."

"Just so," said I. "But this statement is not mathematically correct, because the equinox does not necessarily begin at noon."

"Very likely, sir; but the error will not be a hundred yards and we do not want more. Till tomorrow, then!"

Captain Nemo returned on board. Conseil and I remained to survey the shore, observing and studying until five o'clock. Then I went to bed, not, however, without invoking, like the Indian, the favor of the radiant orb. The next day, March 21, at five in the morning, I mounted the platform. I found Captain Nemo there.

"The weather is lightening a little," said he. "I have some hope. After breakfast we will go on shore and choose a post for observation."

That point settled, I sought Ned Land. I wanted to take him with me. But the obstinate Canadian refused, and I saw that his taciturnity and his bad humor grew day by day. After all, I was not sorry for his obstinacy under the circumstances. Indeed, there were too many seals on shore, and we ought not to lay such temptation in this unreflecting fisherman's way. Breakfast over, we went on shore. The *Nautilus* had gone some miles further up in the night. It was a whole league from the coast, above which reared a sharp peak about five hundred yards high. The boat took with me Captain Nemo, two men of the crew, and the instruments, which consisted of a chronometer, a telescope, and a barometer. While crossing, I saw numerous whales belonging to the three kinds peculiar to the southern seas; the whale, or the English "right whale," which has no dorsal fin; the "humpback," with reeved chest and large, whitish fins, which, in spite of its name, do not form wings; and the finback, of a yellowish brown, the liveliest of all the cetacea. This powerful creature is heard a long way off when he throws to a great height columns of air and vapor, which look like whirlwinds of smoke. These different mammals were disporting themselves in troops in the quiet waters; and I could see that this basin of the Antarctic Pole serves as a place of refuge to the cetacea too closely tracked by the hunters. I also noticed large medusae floating between the reeds.

At nine we landed; the sky was brightening, the clouds were flying to the south, and the fog seemed to be leaving the cold surface of the waters. Captain Nemo went toward the peak, which he doubtless meant to be his observatory. It was a painful ascent over the sharp lava and the pumice stones, in an atmosphere often impregnated with a sulfurous smell from the smoking cracks. For a man unaccustomed to walk on land, the captain climbed the steep slopes with an agility I never saw equaled and which a hunter would have envied. We were two hours getting to the summit of this peak, which was half porphyry and half basalt. From thence we looked upon a vast sea which, toward the north, distinctly traced its boundary line upon the sky. At our feet lay fields of dazzling whiteness. Over our heads a pale azure, free from fog. To the north the disk of the sun seemed like a ball of fire, already horned by the cutting of the horizon. From the bosom of the water rose sheaves of liquid jets by hundreds. In the distance lay the *Nautilus* like a cetacean asleep on the water. Behind us, to the south and east, an immense country and a chaotic heap of rocks and ice, the limits of which were not visible. On arriving at the summit Captain Nemo carefully took the mean height of the barometer, for he would have to consider that in taking his observations. At a quarter to twelve the sun, then seen only by refraction, looked like a golden disk shedding its last rays upon this deserted continent and seas which never man had yet plowed. Captain Nemo, furnished with a lenticular glass which, by means of a mirror, corrected the refraction, watched the orb sinking below the horizon by degrees, following a lengthened diagonal. I held the chronometer. My heart beat fast. If the disappearance of the half-disk of the sun coincided with twelve o'clock on the chronometer, we were at the pole itself.

"Twelve!" I exclaimed.

"The South Pole!" replied Captain Nemo, in a grave voice, handing me the glass, which showed the orb cut in exactly equal parts by the horizon.

I looked at the last rays crowning the peak, and the shadows mounting by degrees up its slopes. At that moment Captain Nemo, resting with his hand on my shoulder, said:

"I, Captain Nemo, on this 21st day of March, 1868, have reached the South Pole on the ninetieth degree; and I take possession of this part of the globe, equal to one-sixth of the known continents."

"In whose name, Captain?"

"In my own, sir!"

Saying which, Captain Nemo unfurled a black banner, bearing an "N" in gold quartered on its bunting. Then, turning toward the orb of day, whose last rays lapped the horizon of the sea, he exclaimed:

"Adieu, sun! Disappear, thou radiant orb! Rest beneath this open sea, and let a night of six months spread its shadows over my new domains!"

# CHAPTER XV

## ACCIDENT OR INCIDENT?

The next day, March 22, at six in the morning, preparations for departure were begun. The last gleams of twilight were melting into night. The cold was great, the constellations shone with wonderful intensity. In the zenith glittered that wondrous Southern Cross—the polar bear of Antarctic regions. The thermometer showed 12° below zero, and when the wind freshened it was most biting. Flakes of ice increased on the open water. The sea seemed everywhere alike. Numerous blackish patches spread on the surface, showing the formation of fresh ice. Evidently the southern basin, frozen during the six winter months, was absolutely inaccessible. What became of the whales in that time? Doubtless they went beneath the icebergs, seeking more practicable seas. As to the seals and morses, accustomed to live in a hard climate, they remained on these icy shores. These creatures have the instinct to break holes in the ice field and to keep them open. To these holes they come for breath; when the birds, driven away by the cold, have emigrated to the north, these sea mammals remain sole masters of the polar continent. But the reservoirs were filling with water, and the *Nautilus* was slowly descending. At 1,000 feet deep it stopped; its screw beat the waves, and it advanced straight toward the north at a speed of fifteen miles an hour. Toward night it was already floating under the immense body of the iceberg. At three in the morning I was awakened by a violent shock. I sat up in my bed and listened in the darkness, when I was thrown into the middle of the room. The *Nautilus*, after having struck, had rebounded violently. I groped along the partition, and by the staircase to the saloon, which was lit by the luminous ceiling. The furniture was upset. Fortunately the windows were firmly set, and had held fast. The pictures on the starboard side, from being no longer vertical, were clinging to the paper, while those of the port side were hanging at least a foot from the wall. The *Nautilus* was lying on its starboard side perfectly motionless. I heard footsteps, and a confusion of voices; but Captain Nemo did not appear. As I was leaving the saloon, Ned Land and Conseil entered.

"What is the matter?" said I, at once.

"I came to ask you, sir," replied Conseil.

"Confound it!" exclaimed the Canadian, "I know well enough! The *Nautilus* has struck; and, judging by the way she lies, I do not think she will right herself as she did the first time in Torres Straits."

"But," I asked, "has she at least come to the surface of the sea?"

"We do not know," said Conseil.

"It is easy to decide," I answered. I consulted the manometer. To my great surprise, it showed a depth of more than 180 fathoms. "What does that mean?" I exclaimed.

"We must ask Captain Nemo," said Conseil.

"But where shall we find him?" said Ned Land.

"Follow me," said I to my companions.

We left the saloon. There was no one in the library. At the center staircase, by the berths of the ship's crew, there was no one. I thought that Captain Nemo must be in the pilot's cage. It was best to wait. We all returned to the saloon. For twenty minutes we remained thus, trying to hear the slightest noise which might be made on board the *Nautilus*, when Captain Nemo entered. He seemed not to see us; his face, generally so impassive, showed signs of uneasiness. He watched the compass silently, then the manometer; and, going to the planisphere, placed his finger on a spot representing the southern seas. I would not interrupt him; but, some minutes later, when he turned toward me, I said, using one of his own expressions in the Torres Straits:

"An incident, Captain?"

"No, sir; an accident this time."

"Serious?"

"Perhaps."

"Is the danger immediate?"

"No."

"The *Nautilus* has stranded?"

"Yes."

"And this has happened—how?"

"From a caprice of nature, not from the ignorance of man. Not a mistake has been made in the working. But we cannot prevent equilibrium from producing its effects. We may brave human laws, but we cannot resist natural ones."

Captain Nemo had chosen a strange moment for uttering this philosophical reflection. On the whole, his answer helped me little.

"May I ask, sir, the cause of this accident?"

"An enormous block of ice, a whole mountain, has turned over," he replied. "When icebergs are undermined at their base by warmer water or reiterated shocks their center of gravity rises, and the whole thing turns over. This is what has happened; one of these blocks, as it fell, struck the *Nautilus*, then, gliding under its hull, raised it with irresistible force, bringing it into beds which are not so thick, where it is lying on its side."

"But can we not get the *Nautilus* off by emptying its reservoirs, that it might regain its equilibrium?"

"That, sir, is being done at this moment. You can hear the pump working. Look at the needle of the manometer; it shows that the *Nautilus* is rising, but the block of ice is floating with it; and, until some obstacle stops its ascending motion, our position cannot be altered."

Indeed, the *Nautilus* still held the same position to starboard; doubtless it would right itself when the block stopped. But at this moment who knows if we may not be frightfully crushed between the two glassy surfaces? I reflected on all the consequences of our position. Captain Nemo never took his eyes off the manometer. Since the fall of the iceberg, the *Nautilus* had risen about a hundred and fifty feet, but it still made the same angle with the perpendicular. Suddenly a slight movement was felt in the hold. Evidently it was righting a little. Things hanging in the saloon were sensibly returning to their normal position. The partitions were nearing the upright. No one spoke. With beating hearts we watched and felt the straightening. The boards became horizontal under our feet. Ten minutes passed.

"At last we have righted!" I exclaimed.

"Yes," said Captain Nemo, going to the door of the saloon.

"But are we floating?" I asked.

"Certainly," he replied; "since the reservoirs are not empty; and, when empty, the *Nautilus* must rise to the surface of the sea."

We were in open sea; but at a distance of about ten yards, on either side of the *Nautilus*, rose a dazzling wall of ice. Above and beneath the same wall. Above, because the lower surface of the iceberg stretched over us like an immense ceiling. Beneath, because the overturned block, having slid by degrees, had found a resting place on the lateral walls, which kept it in that position. The *Nautilus* was really imprisoned in a perfect tunnel of ice more than twenty yards in breadth, filled with quiet water. It was easy to get out of it by going either forward or backward, and then make a free passage under the iceberg, some hundreds of yards deeper. The luminous ceiling had been extinguished, but the saloon was still resplendent with intense light. It was the powerful reflection from the glass partition sent violently back to the sheets of the lantern. I cannot describe the effect of the voltaic rays upon the great blocks so capriciously cut; upon every angle, every ridge, every facet was thrown a different light, according to the nature of the veins running through the ice; a dazzling mine of gems, particularly of sapphires, their blue rays crossing with the green of the emerald. Here and there were opal shades of wonderful softness, running through bright spots like diamonds of fire, the brilliancy of which the eye could not bear. The power of the lantern seemed increased a hundredfold, like a lamp through the lenticular plates of a first-class lighthouse.

"How beautiful! How beautiful!" cried Conseil.

"Yes," I said, "it is a wonderful sight. Is it not, Ned?"

"Yes, confound it! Yes," answered Ned Land, "it is superb! I am mad at being obliged to admit it. No one has ever seen anything like it; but the sight may cost us dear. And, if I must say all, I think we are seeing here things which God never intended man to see."

Ned was right, it was too beautiful. Suddenly a cry from Conseil made me turn.

"What is it?" I asked.

"Shut your eyes, sir! Do not look, sir!" Saying which, Conseil clapped his hands over his eyes.

"But what is the matter, my boy?"

"I am dazzled, blinded."

My eyes turned involuntarily toward the glass, but I could not stand the fire which seemed to devour them. I understood what had happened. The *Nautilus* had put on full speed. All the quiet luster of the ice walls was at once changed into flashes of lightning. The fire from these myriads of diamonds was blinding. It required some time to calm our troubled looks. At last the hands were taken down.

"Faith, I should never have believed it," said Conseil.

It was then five in the morning; and at that moment a shock was felt at the bows of the *Nautilus*. I knew that its spur had struck a block of ice. It must have been a false maneuver, for this submarine tunnel, obstructed by blocks, was not very easy navigation. I thought that Captain Nemo, by changing his course, would either turn these obstacles or else follow the windings of the tunnel. In any case, the road before us could not be entirely blocked. But, contrary to my expectations, the *Nautilus* took a decided retrograde motion.

"We are going backward?" said Conseil.

"Yes," I replied. "This end of the tunnel can have no egress."

"And then?"

"Then," said I, "the working is easy. We must go back again, and go out at the southern opening. That is all."

In speaking thus, I wished to appear more confident than I really was. But the retrograde motion of the *Nautilus* was increasing; and, reversing the screw, it carried us at great speed.

"It will be a hindrance," said Ned.

"What does it matter, some hours more or less, provided we get out at last?"

"Yes," repeated Ned Land, "provided we do get out at last!"

For a short time I walked from the saloon to the library. My companions were silent. I soon threw myself on an ottoman, and took a book, which my eyes overran mechanically. A quarter of an hour after, Conseil, approaching me, said, "Is what you are reading very interesting, sir?"

"Very interesting!" I replied.

"I should think so, sir. It is your own book you are reading."

"My book?"

And indeed I was holding in my hand the work on the *Great Submarine Depths*. I did not even dream of it. I closed the book and returned to my walk. Ned and Conseil rose to go.

"Stay here, my friends," said I, detaining them. "Let us remain together until we are out of this block."

"As you please, sir," Conseil replied.

Some hours passed. I often looked at the instruments hanging from the partition. The manometer showed that the *Nautilus* kept at a constant depth of more than three hundred yards; the compass still pointed to south; the log indicated a speed of twenty miles an hour, which, in such a cramped space, was very great. But Captain Nemo knew that he could not hasten too much, and that minutes were worth ages to us. At twenty-five minutes past eight a second shock took place, this time from behind. I turned pale. My companions were close by my side. I seized Conseil's hand. Our looks expressed our feelings better than words. At this moment the captain entered the saloon. I went up to him.

"Our course is barred southward?" I asked.

"Yes, sir. The iceberg has shifted and closed every outlet."

"We are blocked up then?"

"Yes."

## CHAPTER XVI

### WANT OF AIR

Thus around the *Nautilus*, above and below, was an impenetrable wall of ice. We were prisoners to the iceberg. I watched the captain. His countenance had resumed its habitual imperturbability.

"Gentlemen," he said calmly, "there are two ways of dying in the circumstances in which we are placed." (This puzzling person had the air of a mathematical professor lecturing to his pupils.) "The first is to be crushed; the second is to die of suffocation. I do not speak of the possibility of dying of hunger, for the supply of provisions in the *Nautilus* will certainly last longer than we shall. Let us, then, calculate our chances."

"As to suffocation, Captain," I replied, "that is not to be feared, because our reservoirs are full."

"Just so; but they will only yield two days' supply of air. Now, for thirty-six hours we have been hidden under the water, and already the heavy atmosphere of the *Nautilus* requires renewal. In forty-eight hours our reserve will be exhausted."

"Well, Captain, can we be delivered before forty-eight hours?"

"We will attempt it, at least, by piercing the wall that surrounds us."

"On which side?"

"Sound will tell us. I am going to run the *Nautilus* aground on the lower bank, and my men will attack the iceberg on the side that is least thick."

Captain Nemo went out. Soon I discovered by a hissing noise that the water was entering the reservoirs. The *Nautilus* sank slowly, and rested on the ice at a depth of 350 yards, the depth at which the lower bank was immersed.

"My friends," I said, "our situation is serious, but I rely on your courage and energy."

"Sir," replied the Canadian, "I am ready to do anything for the general safety."

"Good, Ned!" and I held out my hand to the Canadian.

"I will add," he continued, "that, being as handy with the pickaxe as with the harpoon, if I can be useful to the captain, he can command my services."

"He will not refuse your help. Come, Ned!"

I led him to the room where the crew of the *Nautilus* were putting on their cork-jackets. I told the captain of Ned's proposal, which he accepted. The Canadian put on his sea costume, and was ready as soon as his companions. When Ned was dressed, I reentered the drawing room, where the panes of glass were open, and, posted near Conseil, I examined the ambient beds that supported the *Nautilus*. Some instants after, we saw a dozen of the crew set foot on the bank of ice, and among them Ned Land, easily known by his stature. Captain Nemo was with them. Before proceeding to dig the walls, he took the soundings, to be sure of working in the right direction. Long sounding lines were sunk in the side walls, but after fifteen yards they were again stopped by the thick wall. It was useless to attack it on the ceilinglike surface, since the iceberg itself measured more than 400 yards in height. Captain Nemo then sounded the lower surface. There ten yards of wall separated us from the water, so great was the thickness of the ice field. It was necessary, therefore, to cut from it a piece equal in extent to the waterline of the *Nautilus*. There were about 6,000 cubic yards to detach, so as to dig a hole by which we could descend to the ice field. The work had begun immediately and carried on with indefatigable energy. Instead of digging around the *Nautilus* which would have involved greater difficulty, Captain Nemo had an immense trench made at eight yards from the port quarter. Then the men set to work simultaneously with their screws on several points of its circumference. Presently the pickaxe attacked this compact matter vigorously, and large blocks were detached from the mass. By a curious effect of specific gravity, these blocks, lighter than water, fled, so to speak, to the vault of the tunnel, that increased in thickness at the top in proportion as it diminished at the base. But that mattered little, so long as the lower part grew thinner. After two hours' hard work, Ned Land came in exhausted. He and his comrades were replaced by new workers, whom Conseil and I joined. The second lieutenant of the *Nautilus* superintended us. The water seemed singularly cold, but I soon got warm handling the pickaxe. My movements were free enough, although they were made under a pressure of thirty atmospheres. When I reentered, after working two hours, to take some food and rest, I found a perceptible difference between the pure fluid with which the Rouquayrol engine supplied me and the atmosphere of the *Nautilus*, already charged with carbonic acid. The air had not been renewed for forty-eight hours, and its vivifying qualities were considerably enfeebled. However, after a lapse of twelve hours, we had only raised a block of ice one yard thick, on the marked surface, which was about 600 cubic yards! Reckoning that it took twelve hours to accomplish this much it would take five nights and four days to bring this enterprise to a satisfactory conclusion. Five nights and four days! And we have only air enough for two days in the reservoirs! "Without taking into account," said Ned, "that, even if we get out of this infernal prison, we shall also be imprisoned under the iceberg, shut out from all possible communication with the atmosphere." True enough! Who could then foresee the minimum of time necessary for our deliverance? We might be suffocated before the *Nautilus* could regain the surface of the waves? Was it destined to perish in this ice-tomb, with all those it enclosed? The situation was terrible. But everyone had looked the danger in the face, and each was determined to do his duty to the last.

As I expected, during the night a new block a yard square was carried away, and still further sank the immense hollow. But in the morning when, dressed in my cork jacket, I traversed the slushy mass at a temperature of six or seven degrees below zero, I remarked that the side walls were gradually closing in. The beds of water farthest from the trench, that were not warmed by the men's work, showed a tendency to solidification. In presence of this new and imminent danger, what would become of our chances of safety, and how hinder the solidification of this liquid medium, that would burst the partitions of the *Nautilus* like glass?

I did not tell my companions of this new danger. What was the good of damping the energy they displayed in the painful work of escape? But when I went on board again, I told Captain Nemo of this grave complication.

"I know it," he said, in that calm tone which could counteract the most terrible apprehensions. "It is one danger more; but I see no way of escaping it; the only chance of safety is to go quicker than solidification. We must be beforehand with it, that is all."

On this day for several hours I used my pickaxe vigorously. The work kept me up. Besides, to work was to quit the *Nautilus*, and breathe directly the pure air drawn from the reservoirs, and supplied by our apparatus, and to quit the impoverished and vitiated atmosphere. Toward evening the trench was dug one yard deeper. When I returned on board, I was nearly suffocated by the carbonic acid with which the air was filled—ah! If we had only the chemical means to drive away this deleterious gas. We had plenty of oxygen; all this water contained a considerable quantity, and by dissolving it with our powerful piles, it would restore the vivifying fluid. I had thought well over it; but of what good was that, since the carbonic acid produced by our respiration had invaded every part of the vessel? To absorb it, it was necessary to fill some jars with caustic potash, and to shake them incessantly. Now this substance was wanting on board, and nothing could replace it. On that evening, Captain Nemo ought to open the taps of his reservoirs, and let some pure air into the interior of the *Nautilus*; without this precaution we could not get rid of the sense of suffocation. The next day, March 26, I resumed my miner's work in beginning the fifth yard. The side walls and the lower surface of the iceberg thickened visibly. It was evident that they would meet before the *Nautilus* was able to disengage itself. Despair seized me for an instant; my pickaxe nearly fell from my hands. What was the good of digging if I must be suffocated, crushed by the water that was turning into stone? A punishment that the ferocity of the savages even would not have invented! Just then Captain Nemo passed near me. I touched his hand and showed him the walls of our prison. The wall to port had advanced to at least four yards from the hull of the *Nautilus*. The captain understood me, and signed me to follow him. We went on board. I took off my cork jacket and accompanied him into the drawing room.

"M. Aronnax, we must attempt some desperate means, or we shall be sealed up in this solidified water as in cement."

"Yes; but what is to be done?"

"Ah! If my *Nautilus* were strong enough to bear this pressure without being crushed!"

"Well?" I asked, not catching the captain's idea.

"Do you not understand," he replied, "that this congelation of water will help us? Do you not see that by its solidification, it would burst through this field of ice that imprisons us, as, when it freezes, it bursts the hardest stones? Do you not perceive that it would be an agent of safety instead of destruction?"

"Yes, Captain, perhaps. But, whatever resistance to crushing the *Nautilus* possesses, it could not support this terrible pressure, and would be flattened like an iron plate."

"I know it, sir. Therefore we must not reckon on the aid of nature, but on our own exertions. We must stop this solidification. Not only will the side walls be pressed together; but there is not ten feet of water before or behind the *Nautilus*. The congelation gains on us on all sides."

"How long will the air in the reservoirs last for us to breathe on board?"

The captain looked in my face. "After tomorrow they will be empty!"

A cold sweat came over me. However, ought I to have been astonished at the answer? On March 22, the *Nautilus* was in the open polar seas. We were at 26°. For five days we had lived on the reserve on board. And what was left of the respirable air must be kept for the workers. Even now, as I write, my recollection is still so vivid that an involuntary terror seizes me and my lungs seem to be without air. Meanwhile, Captain Nemo reflected silently, and evidently an idea had struck him; but he seemed to reject it. At last, these words escaped his lips:

"Boiling water!" he muttered.

"Boiling water?" I cried.

"Yes, sir. We are enclosed in a space that is relatively confined. Would not jets of boiling water, constantly injected by the pumps, raise the temperature in this part and stay the congelation?"

"Let us try it," I said resolutely.

"Let us try it, Professor."

The thermometer then stood at 7° outside. Captain Nemo took me to the galleys, where the vast distillatory machines stood that furnished the drinkable water by evaporation. They filled these with water, and all the electric heat from the piles was thrown through the worms bathed in the liquid. In a few minutes this water reached 100°. It was directed toward the pumps, while freshwater replaced it in proportion. The heat developed by the troughs was such that cold water, drawn up from the sea after only having gone through the machines, came boiling into the body of the pump. The injection was begun, and three hours after the thermometer marked 6° below zero outside. One degree was gained. Two hours later the thermometer only marked 4°.

"We shall succeed," I said to the captain, after having anxiously watched the result of the operation.

"I think," he answered, "that we shall not be crushed. We have no more suffocation to fear."

During the night the temperature of the water rose to 1° below zero. The injections could not carry it to a higher point. But, as the congelation of the seawater produces at least 2°, I was at least reassured against the dangers of solidification.

The next day, March 27, six yards of ice had been cleared, twelve feet only remaining to be cleared away. There was yet forty-eight hours' work. The air could not be renewed in the interior of the *Nautilus*. And this day would make it worse. An intolerable weight oppressed me. Toward three o'clock in the evening this feeling rose to a violent degree. Yawns dislocated my jaws. My lungs panted as they inhaled this burning fluid, which became rarefied more and more. A moral torpor took hold of me. I was powerless, almost unconscious. My brave Conseil, though exhibiting the same symptoms and suffering in the same manner, never left me. He took my hand and encouraged me, and I heard him murmur, "Oh! If I could only not breathe, so as to leave more air for my master!"

Tears came into my eyes on hearing him speak thus. If our situation to all was intolerable in the interior, with what haste and gladness would we put on our cork jackets to work in our turn! Pickaxes sounded on the frozen ice beds. Our arms ached, the skin was torn off our hands. But what were these fatigues, what did the wounds matter? Vital air came to the lungs! We breathed! We breathed!

All this time no one prolonged his voluntary task beyond the prescribed time. His task accomplished, each one handed in turn to his panting companions the apparatus that supplied him with life. Captain Nemo set the example, and submitted first to this severe discipline. When the time came, he gave up his apparatus to another and returned to the vitiated air on board, calm, unflinching, unmurmuring.

On that day the ordinary work was accomplished with unusual vigor. Only two yards remained to be raised from the surface. Two yards only separated us from the open sea. But the reservoirs were nearly emptied of air. The little that remained ought to be kept for the workers; not a particle for the *Nautilus*. When I went back on board, I was half suffocated. What a night! I know not how to describe it. The next day my breathing was oppressed. Dizziness accompanied the pain in my head and made me like a drunken man. My companions showed the same symptoms. Some of the crew had rattling in the throat.

On that day, the sixth of our imprisonment, Captain Nemo, finding the pickaxes work too slowly, resolved to crush the ice bed that still separated us from the liquid sheet. This man's coolness and energy never forsook him. He subdued his physical pains by moral force.

By his orders the vessel was lightened, that is to say, raised from the ice bed by a change of specific gravity. When it floated they towed it so as to bring it above the immense trench made on the level of the waterline. Then, filling his reservoirs of water, he descended and shut himself up in the hole.

Just then all the crew came on board, and the double door of communication was shut. The *Nautilus* then rested on the bed of ice, which was not one yard thick, and which the sounding leads had perforated in a thousand places. The taps of the reservoirs were then opened, and a hundred cubic yards of water was let in, increasing the weight of the *Nautilus* to 1,800 tons. We waited, we listened, forgetting our sufferings in hope. Our safety depended on this last chance. Notwithstanding the buzzing in my head, I soon heard the humming sound under the hull of the *Nautilus*. The ice cracked with a singular noise, like tearing paper, and the *Nautilus* sank.

"We are off!" murmured Conseil in my ear.

I could not answer him. I seized his hand, and pressed it convulsively. All at once, carried away by its frightful overcharge, the *Nautilus* sank like a bullet under the waters, that is to say, it fell as if it was in a vacuum. Then all the electric force was put on the pumps, that soon began to let the water out of the reservoirs. After some minutes, our fall was stopped. Soon, too, the manometer indicated an ascending movement. The screw, going at full speed, made the iron hull tremble to its very bolts and drew us toward the north. But if this floating under the iceberg is to last another day before we reach the open sea, I shall be dead first.

Half stretched upon a divan in the library, I was suffocating. My face was purple, my lips blue, my faculties suspended. I neither saw nor heard. All notion of time had gone from my mind. My muscles could not contract. I do not know how many hours passed thus, but I was conscious of the agony that was coming over me. I felt as if I was going to die. Suddenly I came to. Some breaths of air penetrated my lungs. Had we risen to the surface of the waves? Were we free of the iceberg? No! Ned and Conseil, my two brave friends, were sacrificing themselves to save me. Some particles of air still remained at the bottom of one apparatus. Instead of using it, they had kept it for me, and, while they were being suffocated, they gave me life, drop by drop. I wanted to push back the thing; they held my hands, and for some moments I breathed freely. I looked at the clock; it was eleven in the morning. It ought to be March 28. The *Nautilus* went at a frightful pace, forty miles an hour. It literally tore through the water. Where was Captain Nemo? Had he succumbed? Were his companions dead with him? At the moment the manometer indicated that we were not more than twenty feet from the surface. A mere plate of ice separated us from the atmosphere. Could we not break it? Perhaps. In any case the *Nautilus* was going to attempt it. I felt that it was in an oblique position, lowering the stern, and raising the bows. The introduction of water had been the means of disturbing its equilibrium. Then, impelled by its powerful screw, it attacked the ice field from beneath like a formidable battering ram. It broke it by backing and then rushing forward against the field, which gradually gave way; and at last, dashing suddenly against it, shot forward on the ice field, that crushed beneath its weight. The panel was opened—one might say torn off—and the pure air came in in abundance to all parts of the *Nautilus*.

## CHAPTER XVII

### FROM CAPE HORN TO THE AMAZON

How I got on to the platform, I have no idea; perhaps the Canadian had carried me there. But I breathed, I inhaled the vivifying sea air. My two companions were getting drunk with the fresh particles. The other unhappy men had been so long without food, that they could not with impunity indulge in the simplest aliments that were given them. We, on the contrary, had no end to restrain ourselves; we could draw this air freely into our lungs, and it was the breeze, the breeze alone, that filled us with this keen enjoyment.

"Ah!" said Conseil. "How delightful this oxygen is! Master need not fear to breathe it. There is enough for everybody."

Ned Land did not speak, but he opened his jaws wide enough to frighten a shark. Our strength soon returned, and, when I looked around me, I saw we were alone on the platform. The foreign seamen in the *Nautilus* were contented with the air that circulated in the interior; none of them had come to drink in the open air.

The first words I spoke were words of gratitude and thankfulness to my two companions. Ned and Conseil had prolonged my life during the last hours of this long agony. All my gratitude could not repay such devotion.

"My friends," said I, "we are bound one to the other forever, and I am under infinite obligations to you."

"Which I shall take advantage of," exclaimed the Canadian.

"What do you mean?" said Conseil.

"I mean that I shall take you with me when I leave this infernal *Nautilus*."

"Well," said Conseil, "after all this, are we going right?"

"Yes," I replied, "for we are going the way of the sun, and here the sun is in the north."

"No doubt," said Ned Land; "but it remains to be seen whether he will bring the ship into the Pacific or the Atlantic Ocean, that is, into frequented or deserted seas."

I could not answer that question, and I feared that Captain Nemo would rather take us to the vast ocean that touches the coasts of Asia and America at the same time. He would thus complete the tour around the submarine world, and return to those waters in which the *Nautilus* could sail freely. We ought, before long, to settle this important point. The *Nautilus* went at a rapid pace. The polar circle was soon passed, and the course shaped for Cape Horn. We were off the American point on March 31, at seven o'clock in the evening. Then all our past sufferings were forgotten. The remembrance of that imprisonment in the ice was effaced from our minds. We only thought of the future. Captain Nemo did not appear again either in the drawing room or on the platform. The point shown each day on the planisphere, and, marked by the lieutenant, showed me the exact direction of the *Nautilus*. Now, on that evening, it was evident, to my great satisfaction, that we were going back to the North by the Atlantic.

The next day, April 1, when the *Nautilus* ascended to the surface some minutes before noon, we sighted land to the west. It was Terra del Fuego, which the first navigators named thus from seeing the quantity of smoke that rose from the natives' huts. The coast seemed low to me, but in the distance rose high mountains. I even thought I had a glimpse of Mount Sarmiento, that rises 2,070 yards above the level of the sea, with a very pointed summit, which, according as it is misty or clear, is a sign of fine or of wet weather. At this moment the peak was clearly defined against the sky. The *Nautilus*, diving again under the water, approached the coast, which was only some few miles off. From the glass windows in the drawing room, I saw long seaweeds and gigantic fuci and varech, of which the open polar sea contains so many specimens, with their sharp polished filaments; they measured about 300 yards in length—real cables, thicker than one's thumb; and, having great tenacity, they are often used as ropes for vessels. Another weed known as velp, with leaves four feet long, buried in the coral concretions, hung at the bottom. It served as nest and food for myriads of crustacea and mollusks, crabs, and cuttlefish. There seals and otters had splendid repasts, eating the flesh of fish with sea vegetables, according to the English fashion. Over this fertile and luxuriant ground the *Nautilus* passed with great rapidity. Toward evening it approached the Falkland group, the rough summits of which I recognized the following day. The depth of the sea was moderate. On the shores our nets brought in beautiful specimens of seaweed, and particularly a certain fucus, the roots of which were filled with the best mussels in the world. Geese and ducks fell by dozens on the platform, and soon took their places in the pantry on board.

When the last heights of the Falklands had disappeared from the horizon, the *Nautilus* sank to between twenty and twenty-five yards, and followed the American coast. Captain Nemo did not show himself. Until April 3 we did not quit the shores of Patagonia, sometimes under the ocean, sometimes at the surface. The *Nautilus* passed beyond the large estuary formed by the Plata, and was, on April 4, fifty-six miles off Uruguay. Its direction was northward, and followed the long windings of the coast of South America. We had then made 1,600 miles since our embarkation in the seas of Japan. About eleven o'clock in the morning the Tropic of Capricorn was crossed on the thirty-seventh meridian, and we passed Cape Frio standing out to sea. Captain Nemo, to Ned Land's great displeasure, did not like the neighborhood of the inhabited coasts of Brazil, for we went at a giddy speed. Not a fish, not a bird of the swiftest kind could follow us, and the natural curiosities of these seas escaped all observation.

This speed was kept up for several days, and in the evening of April 9 we sighted the most westerly point of South America that forms Cape San Roque. But then the *Nautilus* swerved again, and sought the lowest depth of a submarine valley which is between this Cape and Sierra Leone on the African coast. This valley bifurcates to the parallel of the Antilles, and terminates at the mouth by the enormous depression of 9,000 yards. In this place, the geological basin of the ocean forms, as far as the Lesser Antilles, a cliff to three and a half miles perpendicular in height, and, at the parallel of the Cape Verde Islands, another wall not less considerable, that encloses thus all the sunk continent of the Atlantic. The bottom of this immense valley is dotted with some mountains, that give to these submarine places a picturesque aspect. I speak, moreover, from the manuscript charts that were in the library of the *Nautilus*—charts evidently due to Captain Nemo's hand, and made after his personal observations. For two days the desert and deep waters were visited by means of the inclined planes. The *Nautilus* was furnished with long diagonal broadsides which carried it to all elevations. But on April 11 it rose suddenly, and land appeared at the mouth of the Amazon River, a vast estuary, the embouchure of which is so considerable that it freshens the seawater for the distance of several leagues.

The equator was crossed. Twenty miles to the west were the Guianas, a French territory, on which we could have found an easy refuge; but a stiff breeze was blowing, and the furious waves would not have allowed a single boat to face them. Ned Land understood that, no doubt, for he spoke not a word about it. For my part, I made no allusion to his schemes of flight, for I would not urge him to make an attempt that must inevitably fail. I made the time pass pleasantly by interesting studies. During the days of April 11 and 12, the *Nautilus* did not leave the surface of the sea, and the net brought in a marvelous haul of zoophytes, fish, and reptiles. Some zoophytes had been fished up by the chain of the nets; they were for the most part beautiful phyctallines, belonging to the actinidian family, and among other species the phyctalis protexta, peculiar to that part of the ocean, with a little cylindrical trunk, ornamented with vertical lines, speckled with red dots, crowning a marvelous blossoming of tentacles. As to the mollusks, they consisted of some I had already observed—turritellas, olive porphyras, with regular lines intercrossed, with red spots standing out plainly against the flesh; odd pteroceras, like petrified scorpions; translucid hyaleas, argonauts, cuttlefish (excellent eating), and certain species of calmars that naturalists of antiquity have classed among the flying fish, and that serve principally for bait for cod fishing. I had now an opportunity of studying several species of fish on these shores. Among the cartilaginous ones, petromyzons-pricka, a sort of eel, fifteen inches long, with a greenish head, violet fins, gray-blue back, brown belly, silvered and sown with bright spots, the pupil of the eye encircled with gold—a curious animal, that the current of the Amazon had drawn to the sea, for they inhabit freshwaters—tuberculated streaks, with pointed snouts, and a long loose tail, armed with a long jagged sting; little sharks, a yard long, gray and whitish skin, and several rows of teeth, bent back, that are generally known by the name of pantouffles; vespertilios, a kind of red isosceles triangle, half a yard long, to which pectorals are attached by fleshy prolongations that make them look like bats, but that their horny appendage, situated near the nostrils, has given them the name of sea unicorns; lastly, some species of balistae, the curassavian, whose spots were of a brilliant gold color, and the capriscus of clear violet, and with varying shades like a pigeon's throat.

I end here this catalog, which is somewhat dry perhaps, but very exact, with a series of bony fish that I observed in passing belonging to the apteronotes, and whose snout is white as snow, the body of a beautiful black, marked with a very long loose fleshy strip; odontognathes, armed with spikes; sardines nine inches long, glittering with a bright silver light; a species of mackerel provided with two anal fins; centronotes of a blackish tint, that are fished for with torches, long fish, two yards in length, with fat flesh, white and firm, which, when they are fresh, taste like eel, and when dry, like smoked salmon; labres, half red, covered with scales only at the bottom of the dorsal and anal fins; chrysoptera, on which gold and silver blend their brightness with that of the ruby and topaz; golden-tailed spares, the flesh of which is extremely delicate, and whose phosphorescent properties betray them in the midst of the waters; orange-colored spares with long tongues; maigres, with gold caudal fins, dark thorn-tails, anableps of Surinam, etc.

Notwithstanding this "et cetera," I must not omit to mention fish that Conseil will long remember, and with good reason. One of our nets had hauled up a sort of very flat ray fish, which, with the tail cut off, formed a perfect disk, and weighed twenty ounces. It was white underneath, red above, with large round spots of dark blue encircled with black, very glossy skin, terminating in a bilobed fin. Laid out on the platform, it struggled, tried to turn itself by convulsive movements, and made so many efforts, that one last turn had nearly sent it into the sea. But Conseil, not wishing to let the fish go, rushed to it, and, before I could prevent him, had seized it with both hands. In a moment he was overthrown, his legs in the air, and half his body paralyzed, crying:

"Oh! Master, master! Come to me!"

It was the first time the poor boy had spoken to me so familiarly. The Canadian and I took him up, and rubbed his contracted arms till he became sensible. The unfortunate Conseil had attacked a cramp-fish of the most dangerous kind, the cumana. This odd animal, in a medium conductor like water, strikes fish at several yards' distance, so great is the power of its electric organ, the two principal surfaces of which do not measure less than twenty-seven square feet. The next day, April 12, the *Nautilus* approached the Dutch coast, near the mouth of the Maroni. There several groups of sea cows herded together; they were manatees, that, like the dugong and the stellera, belong to the skenian order. These beautiful animals, peaceable and inoffensive, from eighteen to twenty-one feet in length, weigh at least sixteen hundredweight. I told Ned Land and Conseil that provident nature had assigned an important role to these mammalia. Indeed, they, like the seals, are designed to graze on the submarine prairies, and thus destroy the accumulation of weed that obstructs the tropical rivers.

"And do you know," I added, "what has been the result since men have almost entirely annihilated this useful race? That the putrefied weeds have poisoned the air, and the poisoned air causes the yellow fever, that desolates these beautiful countries. Enormous vegetations are multiplied under the torrid seas, and the evil is irresistibly developed from the mouth of the Rio de la Plata to Florida. If we are to believe Toussenel, this plague is nothing to what it would be if the seas were cleaned of whales and seals. Then, infested with poulps, medusae, and cuttlefish, they would become immense centers of infection, since their waves would not possess 'these vast stomachs that God had charged to infest the surface of the seas.'"

However, without disputing these theories, the crew of the *Nautilus* took possession of half-a-dozen manatees. They provisioned the larders with excellent flesh, superior to beef and veal. This sport was not interesting. The manatees allowed themselves to be hit without defending themselves. Several thousand pounds of meat were stored up on board to be dried. On this day, a successful haul of fish increased the stores of the *Nautilus*, so full of game were the seas. They were echeneides belonging to the third family of the malacopterygiens; their flattened discs were composed of transverse movable cartilaginous plates, by which the animal was enabled to create a vacuum, and to adhere to any object like a cupping-glass. The remora that I had observed in the Mediterranean belongs to this species. But the one of which we are speaking was the echeneis osteochera, peculiar to this sea.

The fishing over, the *Nautilus* neared the coast. About here a number of sea turtles were sleeping on the surface of the water. It would have been difficult to capture these precious reptiles, for the least noise awakens them, and their solid shell is proof against the harpoon. But the echeneis effects their capture with extraordinary precision and certainty. This animal is, indeed, a living fishhook, which would make the fortune of an inexperienced fisherman. The crew of the *Nautilus* tied a ring to the tail of these fish, so large as not to encumber their movements, and to this ring a long cord, lashed to the ship's side by the other end.

The echeneids, thrown into the sea, directly began their game, and fixed themselves to the breastplate of the turtles. Their tenacity was such that they were torn rather than let go their hold. Then men hauled them on board, and with them the turtles to which they adhered. They took also several cacouannes a yard long, which weighed 400 pounds. Their carapace covered with large horny plates, thin, transparent, brown, with white and yellow spots, fetch a good price in the market. Besides, they were excellent in an edible point of view, as well as the fresh turtles, which have an exquisite flavor. This day's fishing brought to a close our stay on the shores of the Amazon, and by nightfall the *Nautilus* had regained the high seas.

## CHAPTER XVIII

## THE POULPS

For several days the *Nautilus* kept off from the American coast. Evidently it did not wish to risk the tides of the Gulf of Mexico or of the sea of the Antilles. On April 16, we sighted Martinique and Guadaloupe from a distance of about thirty miles. I saw their tall peaks for an instant. The Canadian, who counted on carrying out his projects in the Gulf, by either landing or hailing one of the numerous boats that coast from one island to another, was quite disheartened. Flight would have been quite practicable, if Ned Land had been able to take possession of the boat without the captain's knowledge. But in the open sea it could not be thought of. The Canadian, Conseil, and I had a long conversation on this subject. For six months we had been prisoners on board the *Nautilus*. We had traveled 17,000 leagues; and, as Ned Land said, there was no reason why it should come to an end. We could hope nothing from the captain of the *Nautilus*, but only from ourselves. Besides, for some time past he had become graver, more retired, less sociable. He seemed to shun me. I met him rarely. Formerly he was pleased to explain the submarine marvels to me; now he left me to my studies, and came no more to the saloon. What change had come over him? For what cause? For my part, I did not wish to bury with me my curious and novel studies. I had now the power to write the true book of the sea; and this book, sooner or later, I wished to see daylight. Then again, in the water by the Antilles, ten yards below the surface of the waters, by open panels, what interesting products I had to enter on my daily notes! There were, among other zoophytes, those known under the name of physalis pelagica, a sort of large oblong bladder, with mother-of-pearl rays, holding out their membranes to the wind, and letting their blue tentacles float like threads of silk; charming medusae to the eye, real nettles to the touch, that distill a corrosive fluid. There were also annelides, a yard and a half long, weighing 600 pounds, the pectoral fin triangular in the midst of a slightly humped back, the eyes fixed in the extremities of the face, beyond the head, and which floated like weft, and looked sometimes like an opaque shutter on our glass window. There were American balistae, which nature has only dressed in black and white; gobies, with yellow fins and prominent jaw; mackerel sixteen feet long, with short-pointed teeth, covered with small scales, belonging to the albicore species. Then, in swarms, appeared gray mullet, covered with stripes of gold from the head to the tail, beating their resplendent fins, like masterpieces of jewelry, consecrated formerly to Diana, particularly sought after by rich Romans, and of which the proverb says, "Whoever takes them does not eat them." Lastly, pomacanthe dorees, ornamented with emerald bands, dressed in velvet and silk passed before our eyes like Veronese lords; spurred spari passed with their pectoral fins; clupanodons fifteen inches long, enveloped in their phosphorescent light; mullet beat the sea with their large jagged tails; red vendaces seemed to mow the waves with their showy pectoral fins; and silvery selenes, worthy of their name, rose on the horizon of the waters like so many moons with whitish rays. On April 20, we had risen to a mean height of 1,500 yards. The land nearest us was the archipelago of the Bahamas. There rose high submarine cliffs covered with large weeds. It was about eleven o'clock when Ned Land drew my attention to a formidable pricking, like the sting of an ant, which was produced by means of large seaweeds.

"Well," I said, "these are proper caverns for poulps, and I should not be astonished to see some of these monsters."

"What!" said Conseil. "Cuttlefish, real cuttlefish of the cephalopod class?"

"No," I said, "poulps of huge dimensions."

"I will never believe that such animals exist," said Ned.

"Well," said Conseil, with the most serious air in the world, "I remember perfectly to have seen a large vessel drawn under the waves by an octopus's arm."

"You saw that?" said the Canadian.

"Yes, Ned."

"With your own eyes?"

"With my own eyes."

"Where, pray, might that be?"

"At St. Malo," answered Conseil.

"In the port?" said Ned, ironically.

"No, in a church," replied Conseil.

"In a church!" cried the Canadian.

"Yes, friend Ned. In a picture representing the poulp in question."

"Good!" said Ned Land, bursting out laughing.

"He is quite right," I said. "I have heard of this picture; but the subject represented is taken from a legend, and you know what to think of legends in the matter of natural history. Besides, when it is a question of monsters, the imagination is apt to run wild. Not only is it supposed that these poulps can draw down vessels, but a certain Olaus Magnus speaks of an octopus a mile long that is more like an island than an animal. It is also said that the Bishop of Nidros was building an altar on an immense rock. Mass finished, the rock began to walk, and returned to the sea. The rock was a poulp. Another Bishop, Pontoppidan, speaks also of a poulp on which a regiment of cavalry could maneuver. Lastly, the ancient naturalists speak of monsters whose mouths were like gulfs, and which were too large to pass through the Straits of Gibraltar."

"But how much is true of these stories?" asked Conseil.

"Nothing, my friends; at least of that which passes the limit of truth to get to fable or legend. Nevertheless, there must be some ground for the imagination of the storytellers. One cannot deny that poulps and cuttlefish exist of a large species, inferior, however, to the cetaceans. Aristotle has stated the dimensions of a cuttlefish as five cubits, or nine feet two inches. Our fishermen frequently see some that are more than four feet long. Some skeletons of poulps are preserved in the museums of Trieste and Montpelier, that measure two yards in length. Besides, according to the calculations of some naturalists, one of these animals only six feet long would have tentacles twenty-seven feet long. That would suffice to make a formidable monster."

"Do they fish for them in these days?" asked Ned.

"If they do not fish for them, sailors see them at least. One of my friends, Captain Paul Bos of Havre, has often affirmed that he met one of these monsters of colossal dimensions in the Indian seas. But the most astonishing fact, and which does not permit of the denial of the existence of these gigantic animals, happened some years ago, in 1861."

"What is the fact?" asked Ned Land.

"This is it. In 1861, to the northeast of Teneriffe, very nearly in the same latitude we are in now, the crew of the dispatch boat *Alector* perceived a monstrous cuttlefish swimming in the waters. Captain Bouguer went near to the animal, and attacked it with harpoon and guns, without much success, for balls and harpoons glided over the soft flesh. After several fruitless attempts the crew tried to pass a slipknot around the body of the mollusk. The noose slipped as far as the tail fins and there stopped. They tried then to haul it on board, but its weight was so considerable that the tightness of the cord separated the tail from the body, and, deprived of this ornament, he disappeared under the water."

"Indeed! Is that a fact?"

"An indisputable fact, my good Ned. They proposed to name this poulp 'Bouguer's cuttlefish.' "

"What length was it?" asked the Canadian.

"Did it not measure about six yards?" said Conseil, who, posted at the window, was examining again the irregular windings of the cliff.

"Precisely," I replied.

"Its head," rejoined Conseil, "was it not crowned with eight tentacles, that beat the water like a nest of serpents?"

"Precisely."

"Had not its eyes, placed at the back of its head, considerable development?"

"Yes, Conseil."

"And was not its mouth like a parrot's beak?"

"Exactly, Conseil."

"Very well! No offense to master," he replied, quietly. "If this is not Bouguer's cuttlefish, it is, at least, one of its brothers."

I looked at Conseil. Ned Land hurried to the window.

"What a horrible beast!" he cried.

I looked in my turn, and could not repress a gesture of disgust. Before my eyes was a horrible monster worthy to figure in the legends of the marvelous. It was an immense cuttlefish, being eight yards long. It swam crossways in the direction of the *Nautilus* with great speed, watching us with its enormous staring green eyes. Its eight arms, or rather feet, fixed to its head, that have given the name of cephalopod to these animals, were twice as long as its body, and were twisted like the furies' hair. One could see the 250 air holes on the inner side of the tentacles. The monster's mouth, a horned beak like a parrot's, opened and shut vertically. Its tongue, a horned substance, furnished with several rows of pointed teeth, came out quivering from this veritable pair of shears. What a freak of nature, a bird's beak on a mollusk! Its spindlelike body formed a fleshy mass that might weigh 4,000 to 5,000 pounds; the varying color changing with great rapidity, according to the irritation of the animal, passed successively from livid gray to reddish-brown. What irritated this mollusk? No doubt the presence of the *Nautilus*, more formidable than itself, and on which its suckers or its jaws had no hold. Yet, what monsters these poulps are! What vitality the Creator has given them! What vigor in their movements! And they possess three hearts! Chance had brought us in presence of this cuttlefish, and I did not wish to lose the opportunity of carefully studying this specimen of cephalopods. I overcame the horror that inspired me, and, taking a pencil, began to draw it.

"Perhaps this is the same which the *Alector* saw," said Conseil.

"No," replied the Canadian, "for this is whole, and the other had lost its tail."

"That is no reason," I replied. "The arms and tails of these animals are re-formed by renewal; and in seven years the tail of Bouguer's cuttlefish has no doubt had time to grow."

By this time other poulps appeared at the port light. I counted seven. They formed a procession after the *Nautilus*, and I heard their beaks gnashing against the iron hull. I continued my work. These monsters kept in the water with such precision that they seemed immovable. Suddenly the *Nautilus* stopped. A shock made it tremble in every plate.

"Have we struck anything?" I asked.

"In any case," replied the Canadian, "we shall be free, for we are floating."

The *Nautilus* was floating, no doubt, but it did not move. A minute passed. Captain Nemo, followed by his lieutenant, entered the drawing room. I had not seen him for some time. He seemed dull. Without noticing or speaking to us, he went to the panel, looked at the poulps, and said something to his lieutenant. The latter went out. Soon the panels were shut. The ceiling was lighted. I went toward the captain.

"A curious collection of poulps?" I said.

"Yes, indeed, Mr. Naturalist," he replied; "and we are going to fight them, man to beast."

I looked at him. I thought I had not heard aright.

"Man to beast?" I repeated.

"Yes, sir. The screw is stopped. I think that the horny jaws of one of the cuttlefish is entangled in the blades. That is what prevents our moving."

"What are you going to do?"

"Rise to the surface, and slaughter this vermin."

"A difficult enterprise."

"Yes, indeed. The electric bullets are powerless against the soft flesh, where they do not find resistance enough to go off. But we shall attack them with the hatchet."

"And the harpoon, sir," said the Canadian, "if you do not refuse my help."

"I will accept it, Master Land."

"We will follow you," I said, and, following Captain Nemo, we went toward the central staircase.

There, about ten men with boarding-hatchets were ready for the attack. Conseil and I took two hatchets; Ned Land seized a harpoon. The *Nautilus* had then risen to the surface. One of the sailors, posted on the top ladder step, unscrewed the bolts of the panels. But hardly were the screws loosed, when the panel rose with great violence, evidently drawn by the suckers of a poulp's arm. Immediately one of these arms slid like a serpent down the opening and twenty others were above. With one blow of the axe, Captain Nemo cut this formidable tentacle, that slid wriggling down the ladder. Just as we were pressing one on the other to reach the platform, two other arms, lashing the air, came down on the seaman placed before Captain Nemo, and lifted him up with irresistible power. Captain Nemo uttered a cry, and rushed out. We hurried after him.

What a scene! The unhappy man, seized by the tentacle and fixed to the suckers, was balanced in the air at the caprice of this enormous trunk. He rattled in his throat, he was stifled, he cried, "Help! Help!" These words, spoken in French, startled me! I had a fellow countryman on board, perhaps several! That heartrending cry! I shall hear it all my life. The unfortunate man was lost. Who could rescue him from that powerful pressure? However, Captain Nemo had rushed to the poulp, and with one blow of the axe had cut through one arm. His lieutenant struggled furiously against other monsters that crept on the flanks of the *Nautilus*. The crew fought with their axes. The Canadian, Conseil, and I buried our weapons in the fleshy masses; a strong smell of musk penetrated the atmosphere. It was horrible!

For one instant, I thought the unhappy man, entangled with the poulp, would be torn from its powerful suction. Seven of the eight arms had been cut off. One only wriggled in the air, brandishing the victim like a feather. But just as Captain Nemo and his lieutenant threw themselves on it, the animal ejected a stream of black liquid. We were blinded with it. When the cloud dispersed, the cuttlefish had disappeared, and my unfortunate countryman with it. Ten or twelve poulps now invaded the platform and sides of the *Nautilus*. We rolled pell-mell into the midst of this nest of serpents, that wriggled on the platform in the waves of blood and ink. It seemed as though these slimy tentacles sprang up like the hydra's heads. Ned Land's harpoon, at each stroke, was plunged into the staring eyes of the cuttlefish. But my bold companion was suddenly overturned by the tentacles of a monster he had not been able to avoid.

Ah! How my heart beat with emotion and horror! The formidable beak of a cuttlefish was open over Ned Land. The unhappy man would be cut in two. I rushed to his succour. But Captain Nemo was before me; his axe disappeared between the two enormous jaws, and, miraculously saved, the Canadian, rising, plunged his harpoon deep into the triple heart of the poulp.

"I owed myself this revenge!" said the captain to the Canadian.

Ned bowed without replying. The combat had lasted a quarter of an hour. The monsters, vanquished and mutilated, left us at last, and disappeared under the waves. Captain Nemo, covered with blood, nearly exhausted, gazed upon the sea that had swallowed up one of his companions, and great tears gathered in his eyes.

## CHAPTER XIX

### THE GULF STREAM

This terrible scene of April 20 none of us can ever forget. I have written it under the influence of violent emotion. Since then I have revised the recital; I have read it to Conseil and to the Canadian. They found it exact as to facts, but insufficient as to effect. To paint such pictures, one must have the pen of the most illustrious of our poets, the author of "The Toilers of the Deep."

I have said that Captain Nemo wept while watching the waves; his grief was great. It was the second companion he had lost since our arrival on board, and what a death! That friend, crushed, stifled, bruised by the dreadful arms of a poulp, pounded by his iron jaws, would not rest with his comrades in the peaceful coral cemetery! In the midst of the struggle, it was the despairing cry uttered by the unfortunate man that had torn my heart. The poor Frenchman, forgetting his conventional language, had taken to his own mother tongue, to utter a last appeal! Among the crew of the *Nautilus*, associated with the body and soul of the captain, recoiling like him from all contact with men, I had a fellow countryman. Did he alone represent France in this mysterious association, evidently composed of individuals of divers nationalities? It was one of these insoluble problems that rose up unceasingly before my mind!

Captain Nemo entered his room, and I saw him no more for some time. But that he was sad and irresolute I could see by the vessel, of which he was the soul, and which received all his impressions. The *Nautilus* did not keep on in its settled course; it floated about like a corpse at the will of the waves. It went at random. He could not tear himself away from the scene of the last struggle, from this sea that had devoured one of his men. Ten days passed thus. It was not till May 1 that the *Nautilus* resumed its northerly course, after having sighted the Bahamas at the mouth of the Bahama Canal. We were then following the current from the largest river to the sea, that has its banks, its fish, and its proper temperatures. I mean the Gulf Stream. It is really a river that flows freely to the middle of the Atlantic, and whose waters do not mix with the ocean waters. It is a salt river, saltier than the surrounding sea. Its mean depth is 1,500 fathoms, its mean breadth ten miles. In certain places the current flows with the speed of two miles and a half an hour. The body of its waters is more considerable than that of all the rivers in the globe. It was on this ocean river that the *Nautilus* then sailed.

This current carried with it all kinds of living things. Argonauts, so common in the Mediterranean, were there in quantities. Of the gristly sort, the most remarkable were the turbot, whose slender tails form nearly the third part of the body, and that looked like large lozenges twenty-five feet long; also, small sharks a yard long, with large heads, short rounded muzzles, pointed teeth in several rows, and whose bodies seemed covered with scales. Among the bony fish I noticed some gray gobies, peculiar to these waters; black giltheads, whose iris shone like fire; sirenes a yard long, with large snouts thickly set with little teeth, that uttered little cries; blue coryphaenes, in gold and silver; parrots, like the rainbows of the ocean, that could rival in color the most beautiful tropical birds; blennies with triangular heads; bluish rhombs destitute of scales; batrachoides covered with yellow transversal bands like a Greek τ; heaps of little gobies spotted with yellow; dipterodons with silvery heads and yellow tails; several specimens of salmon, mugilomores slender in shape, shining with a soft light that Lacépède consecrated to the service of his wife; and lastly, a beautiful fish, the American knight, that, decorated with all the orders and ribbons, frequents the shores of this great nation, that esteems orders and ribbons so little.

I must add that, during the night, the phosphorescent waters of the Gulf Stream rivaled the electric power of our watch-light, especially in the stormy weather that threatened us so frequently. May 8, we were still crossing Cape Hatteras, at the height of the North Caroline. The width of the Gulf Stream there is seventy-five miles, and its depth 210 yards. The *Nautilus* still went at random; all supervision seemed abandoned. I thought that, under these circumstances, escape would be possible. Indeed, the inhabited shores offered anywhere an easy refuge. The sea was incessantly plowed by the steamers that ply between New York or Boston and the Gulf of Mexico, and overrun day and night by the little schooners coasting about the several parts of the American coast. We could hope to be picked up. It was a favorable opportunity, notwithstanding the thirty miles that separated the *Nautilus* from the coasts of the Union. One unfortunate circumstance thwarted the Canadian's plans. The weather was very bad. We were nearing those shores where tempests are so frequent, that country of waterspouts and cyclones actually engendered by the current of the Gulf Stream. To tempt the sea in a frail boat was certain destruction. Ned Land owned this himself. He fretted, seized with nostalgia that flight only could cure.

"Master," he said that day to me, "this must come to an end. I must make a clean breast of it. This Nemo is leaving land and going up to the north. But I declare to you that I have had enough of the South Pole, and I will not follow him to the North."

"What is to be done, Ned, since flight is impracticable just now?"

"We must speak to the captain," said he. "You said nothing when we were in your native seas. I will speak, now we are in mine. When I think that before long the *Nautilus* will be by Nova Scotia, and that there near Newfoundland is a large bay, and into that bay the St. Lawrence empties itself, and that the St. Lawrence is my river, the river by Quebec, my native town—when I think of this, I feel furious, it makes my hair stand on end. Sir, I would rather throw myself into the sea! I will not stay here! I am stifled!"

The Canadian was evidently losing all patience. His vigorous nature could not stand this prolonged imprisonment. His face altered daily; his temper became more surly. I knew what he must suffer, for I was seized with homesickness myself. Nearly seven months had passed without our having had any news from land; Captain Nemo's isolation, his altered spirits, especially since the fight with the poulps, his taciturnity, all made me view things in a different light.

"Well, sir?" said Ned, seeing I did not reply.

"Well, Ned, do you wish me to ask Captain Nemo his intentions concerning us?"

"Yes, sir."

"Although he has already made them known?"

"Yes; I wish it settled finally. Speak for me, in my name only, if you like."

"But I so seldom meet him. He avoids me."

"That is all the more reason for you to go to see him."

I went to my room. From thence I meant to go to Captain Nemo's. It would not do to let this opportunity of meeting him slip. I knocked at the door. No answer. I knocked again, then turned the handle. The door opened, I went in. The captain was there. Bending over his work-table, he had not heard me. Resolved not to go without having spoken, I approached him. He raised his head quickly, frowned, and said roughly, "You here! What do you want?"

"To speak to you, Captain."

"But I am busy, sir; I am working. I leave you at liberty to shut yourself up; cannot I be allowed the same?"

This reception was not encouraging; but I was determined to hear and answer everything.

"Sir," I said coldly, "I have to speak to you on a matter that admits of no delay."

"What is that, sir?" he replied, ironically. "Have you discovered something that has escaped me, or has the sea delivered up any new secrets?"

We were at cross-purposes. But, before I could reply, he showed me an open manuscript on his table, and said, in a more serious tone, "Here, M. Aronnax, is a manuscript written in several languages. It contains the sum of my studies of the sea; and, if it please God, it shall not perish with me. This manuscript, signed with my name, complete with the history of my life, will be shut up in a little floating case. The last survivor of all of us on board the *Nautilus* will throw this case into the sea, and it will go whither it is borne by the waves."

This man's name! His history written by himself! His mystery would then be revealed someday.

"Captain," I said, "I can but approve of the idea that makes you act thus. The result of your studies must not be lost. But the means you employ seem to me to be primitive. Who knows where the winds will carry this case, and in whose hands it will fall? Could you not use some other means? Could not you, or one of yours—"

"Never, sir!" he said, hastily interrupting me.

"But I and my companions are ready to keep this manuscript in store; and, if you will put us at liberty—"

"At liberty?" said the captain, rising.

"Yes, sir; that is the subject on which I wish to question you. For seven months we have been here on board, and I ask you today, in the name of my companions and in my own, if your intention is to keep us here always?"

"M. Aronnax, I will answer you today as I did seven months ago: Whoever enters the *Nautilus* must never quit it."

"You impose actual slavery upon us!"

"Give it what name you please."

"But everywhere the slave has the right to regain his liberty."

"Who denies you this right? Have I ever tried to chain you with an oath?"

He looked at me with his arms crossed.

"Sir," I said, "to return a second time to this subject will be neither to your nor to my taste; but, as we have entered upon it, let us go through with it. I repeat, it is not only myself whom it concerns. Study is to me a relief, a diversion, a passion that could make me forget everything. Like you, I am willing to live obscure, in the frail hope of bequeathing one day, to future time, the result of my labors. But it is otherwise with Ned Land. Every man, worthy of the name, deserves some consideration. Have you thought that love of liberty, hatred of slavery, can give rise to schemes of revenge in a nature like the Canadian's; that he could think, attempt, and try—"

I was silenced; Captain Nemo rose.

"Whatever Ned Land thinks of, attempts, or tries, what does it matter to me? I did not seek him! It is not for my pleasure that I keep him on board! As for you, M. Aronnax, you are one of those who can understand everything, even silence. I have nothing more to say to you. Let this first time you have come to treat of this subject be the last, for a second time I will not listen to you."

I retired. Our situation was critical. I related my conversation to my two companions.

"We know now," said Ned, "that we can expect nothing from this man. The *Nautilus* is nearing Long Island. We will escape, whatever the weather may be."

But the sky became more and more threatening. Symptoms of a hurricane became manifest. The atmosphere was becoming white and misty. On the horizon fine streaks of cirrus clouds were succeeded by masses of cumuli. Other low clouds passed swiftly by. The swollen sea rose in huge billows. The birds disappeared with the exception of the petrels, those friends of the storm. The barometer fell sensibly, and indicated an extreme extension of the vapors. The mixture of the storm glass was decomposed under the influence of the electricity that pervaded the atmosphere. The tempest burst on May 18, just as the *Nautilus* was floating off Long Island, some miles from the port of New York. I can describe this strife of the elements! For, instead of fleeing to the depths of the sea, Captain Nemo, by an unaccountable caprice, would brave it at the surface. The wind blew from the southwest at first. Captain Nemo, during the squalls, had taken his place on the platform. He had made himself fast, to prevent being washed overboard by the monstrous waves. I had hoisted myself up, and made myself fast also, dividing my admiration between the tempest and this extraordinary man who was coping with it. The raging sea was swept by huge cloud drifts, which were actually saturated with the waves. The *Nautilus*, sometimes lying on its side, sometimes standing up like a mast, rolled and pitched terribly. About five o'clock a torrent of rain fell, that lulled neither sea nor wind. The hurricane blew nearly forty leagues an hour. It is under these conditions that it overturns houses, breaks iron gates, displaces twenty-four pounders. However, the *Nautilus*, in the midst of the tempest, confirmed the words of a clever engineer: "There is no well-constructed hull that cannot defy the sea." This was not a resisting rock; it was a steel spindle, obedient and movable, without rigging or masts, that braved its fury with impunity. However, I watched these raging waves attentively. They measured fifteen feet in height, and 150 to 175 yards long, and their speed of propagation was thirty feet per second. Their bulk and power increased with the depth of the water. Such waves as these, at the Hebrides, have displaced a mass weighing 8,400 pounds. They are they which, in the tempest of December 23, 1864, after destroying the town of Yeddo, in Japan, broke the same day on the shores of America. The intensity of the tempest increased with the night. The barometer, as in 1860 at Reunion during a cyclone, fell seven-tenths at the close of day. I saw a large vessel pass the horizon struggling painfully. She was trying to lie to under half steam, to keep up above the waves. It was probably one of the steamers of the line from New York to Liverpool, or Havre. It soon disappeared in the gloom. At ten o'clock in the evening the sky was on fire. The atmosphere was streaked with vivid lightning. I could not bear the brightness of it; while the captain, looking at it, seemed to envy the spirit of the tempest. A terrible noise filled the air, a complex noise, made up of the howls of the crushed waves, the roaring of the wind, and the claps of thunder. The wind veered suddenly to all points of the horizon; and the cyclone, rising in the east, returned after passing by the north, west, and south, in the inverse course pursued by the circular storm of the southern hemisphere. Ah, that Gulf Stream! It deserves its name of the King of Tempests. It is that which causes those formidable cyclones, by the difference of temperature between its air and its currents. A shower of fire had succeeded the rain. The drops of water were changed to sharp spikes. One would have thought that Captain Nemo was courting a death worthy of himself, a death by lightning. As the *Nautilus*, pitching dreadfully, raised its steel spur in the air, it seemed to act as a conductor, and I saw long sparks burst from it. Crushed and without strength I crawled to the panel, opened it, and descended to the saloon. The storm was then at its height. It was impossible to stand upright in the interior of the *Nautilus*. Captain Nemo came down about twelve. I heard the reservoirs filling by degrees, and the *Nautilus* sank slowly beneath the waves. Through the open windows in the saloon I saw large fish terrified, passing like phantoms in the water. Some were struck before my eyes. The *Nautilus* was still descending. I thought that at about eight fathoms deep we should find a calm. But no! The upper beds were too violently agitated for that. We had to seek repose at more than twenty-five fathoms in the bowels of the deep. But there, what quiet, what silence, what peace! Who could have told that such a hurricane had been let loose on the surface of that ocean?

## CHAPTER XX

### FROM LATITUDE 47° 24' TO LONGITUDE 17° 28'

In consequence of the storm, we had been thrown eastward once more. All hope of escape on the shores of New York or St. Lawrence had faded away; and poor Ned, in despair, had isolated himself like Captain Nemo. Conseil and I, however, never left each other. I said that the *Nautilus* had gone aside to the east. I should have said (to be more exact) the northeast. For some days, it wandered first on the surface, and then beneath it, amid those fogs so dreaded by sailors. What accidents are due to these thick fogs! What shocks upon these reefs when the wind drowns the breaking of the waves! What collisions between vessels, in spite of their warning lights, whistles, and alarm bells! And the bottoms of these seas look like a field of battle, where still lie all the conquered of the ocean; some old and already encrusted, others fresh and reflecting from their iron bands and copper plates the brilliancy of our lantern.

On May 15 we were at the extreme south of the bank of Newfoundland. This bank consists of alluvia, or large heaps of organic matter, brought either from the equator by the Gulf Stream, or from the North Pole by the counter-current of cold water which skirts the American coast. There also are heaped up those erratic blocks which are carried along by the broken ice; and close by, a vast charnel house of mollusks, which perish here by millions. The depth of the sea is not great at Newfoundland—not more than some hundreds of fathoms; but toward the south is a depression of 1,500 fathoms. There the Gulf Stream widens. It loses some of its speed and some of its temperature, but it becomes a sea.

It was on May 17, about 500 miles from Heart's Content, at a depth of more than 1,400 fathoms, that I saw the electric cable lying on the bottom. Conseil, to whom I had not mentioned it, thought at first that it was a gigantic sea serpent. But I undeceived the worthy fellow, and by way of consolation related several particulars in the laying of this cable. The first one was laid in the years 1857 and 1858; but, after transmitting about 400 telegrams, would not act any longer. In 1863 the engineers constructed another one, measuring 2,000 miles in length, and weighing 4,500 tons, which was embarked on the *Great Eastern*. This attempt also failed.

On May 25 the *Nautilus*, being at a depth of more than 1,918 fathoms, was on the precise spot where the rupture occurred which ruined the enterprise. It was within 638 miles of the coast of Ireland; and at half-past two in the afternoon they discovered that communication with Europe had ceased. The electricians on board resolved to cut the cable before fishing it up, and at eleven o'clock at night they had recovered the damaged part. They made another point and spliced it, and it was once more submerged. But some days after it broke again, and in the depths of the ocean could not be recaptured. The Americans, however, were not discouraged. Cyrus Field, the bold promoter of the enterprise, as he had sunk all his own fortune, set a new subscription on foot, which was at once answered, and another cable was constructed on better principles. The bundles of conducting wires were each enveloped in gutta-percha, and protected by a wadding of hemp, contained in a metallic covering. The *Great Eastern* sailed on July 13, 1866. The operation worked well. But one incident occurred. Several times in unrolling the cable they observed that nails had recently been forced into it, evidently with the motive of destroying it. Captain Anderson, the officers, and engineers consulted together, and had it posted up that, if the offender was surprised on board, he would be thrown without further trial into the sea. From that time the criminal attempt was never repeated.

On July 23 the *Great Eastern* was not more than 500 miles from Newfoundland, when they telegraphed from Ireland the news of the armistice concluded between Prussia and Austria after Sadowa. On the 27th, in the midst of heavy fogs, they reached the port of Heart's Content. The enterprise was successfully terminated; and for its first despatch, young America addressed old Europe in these words of wisdom, so rarely understood: "Glory to God in the highest, and on earth peace, goodwill toward men."

I did not expect to find the electric cable in its primitive state, such as it was on leaving the manufactory. The long serpent, covered with the remains of shells, bristling with foraminiferae, was encrusted with a strong coating which served as a protection against all boring mollusks. It lay quietly sheltered from the motions of the sea, and under a favorable pressure for the transmission of the electric spark which passes from Europe to America in 0.32 of a second. Doubtless this cable will last for a great length of time, for they find that the gutta-percha covering is improved by the seawater. Besides, on this level, so well chosen, the cable is never so deeply submerged as to cause it to break. The *Nautilus* followed it to the lowest depth, which was more than 2,212 fathoms, and there it lay without any anchorage; and then we reached the spot where the accident had taken place in 1863. The bottom of the ocean then formed a valley about 100 miles broad, in which Mont Blanc might have been placed without its summit appearing above the waves. This valley is closed at the east by a perpendicular wall more than 2,000 yards high. We arrived there on May 28, and the *Nautilus* was then not more than 120 miles from Ireland.

Was Captain Nemo going to land on the British Isles? No. To my great surprise he made for the south, once more coming back toward European seas. In rounding the Emerald Isle, for one instant I caught sight of Cape Clear, and the light which guides the thousands of vessels leaving Glasgow or Liverpool. An important question then arose in my mind. Did the *Nautilus* dare entangle itself in the Manche? Ned Land, who had reappeared since we had been nearing land, did not cease to question me. How could I answer? Captain Nemo remained invisible. After having shown the Canadian a glimpse of American shores, was he going to show me the coast of France?

But the *Nautilus* was still going southward. On May 30, it passed in sight of Land's End, between the extreme point of England and the Scilly Isles, which were left to starboard. If we wished to enter the Manche, he must go straight to the east. He did not do so.

During the whole of May 31, the *Nautilus* described a series of circles on the water, which greatly interested me. It seemed to be seeking a spot it had some trouble in finding. At noon, Captain Nemo himself came to work the ship's log. He spoke no word to me, but seemed gloomier than ever. What could sadden him thus? Was it his proximity to European shores? Had he some recollections of his abandoned country? If not, what did he feel? Remorse or regret? For a long while this thought haunted my mind, and I had a kind of presentiment that before long chance would betray the captain's secrets.

The next day, June 1, the *Nautilus* continued the same process. It was evidently seeking some particular spot in the ocean. Captain Nemo took the sun's altitude as he had done the day before. The sea was beautiful, the sky clear. About eight miles to the east, a large steam vessel could be discerned on the horizon. No flag fluttered from its mast, and I could not discover its nationality. Some minutes before the sun passed the meridian, Captain Nemo took his sextant, and watched with great attention. The perfect rest of the water greatly helped the operation. The *Nautilus* was motionless; it neither rolled nor pitched.

I was on the platform when the altitude was taken, and the captain pronounced these words: "It is here."

He turned and went below. Had he seen the vessel which was changing its course and seemed to be nearing us? I could not tell. I returned to the saloon. The panels closed, I heard the hissing of the water in the reservoirs. The *Nautilus* began to sink, following a vertical line, for its screw communicated no motion to it. Some minutes later it stopped at a depth of more than 420 fathoms, resting on the ground. The luminous ceiling was darkened, then the panels were opened, and through the glass I saw the sea brilliantly illuminated by the rays of our lantern for at least half a mile around us.

I looked to the port side, and saw nothing but an immensity of quiet waters. But to starboard, on the bottom appeared a large protuberance, which at once attracted my attention. One would have thought it a ruin buried under a coating of white shells, much resembling a covering of snow. Upon examining the mass attentively, I could recognize the ever-thickening form of a vessel bare of its masts, which must have sunk. It certainly belonged to past times. This wreck, to be thus encrusted with the lime of the water, must already be able to count many years passed at the bottom of the ocean.

What was this vessel? Why did the *Nautilus* visit its tomb? Could it have been aught but a shipwreck which had drawn it under the water? I knew not what to think, when near me in a slow voice I heard Captain Nemo say:

"At one time this ship was called the *Marseillais*. It carried seventy-four guns, and was launched in 1762. In 1778, on August 13, commanded by La Poype-Vertrieux, it fought boldly against the *Preston*. In 1779, on July 4, it was at the taking of Grenada, with the squadron of Admiral Estaing. In 1781, on September 5, it took part in the battle of Comte de Grasse, in Chesapeake Bay. In 1794, the French Republic changed its name. On April 16 in the same year, it joined the squadron of Villaret Joyeuse, at Brest, being entrusted with the escort of a cargo of corn coming from America, under the command of Admiral Van Stebel. On the 11th and 12th Prairal of the second year, this squadron fell in with an English vessel. Sir, today is the 13th Prairal, the first of June, 1868. It is now seventy-four years ago, day for day on this very spot, in latitude

47° 24', longitude 17° 28', that this vessel, after fighting heroically, losing its three masts, with the water in its hold, and the third of its crew disabled, preferred sinking with its 356 sailors to surrendering; and, nailing its colors to the poop, disappeared under the waves to the cry of 'Long live the Republic!' "

"The *Avenger*!" I exclaimed.

"Yes, sir, the *Avenger*! A good name!" muttered Captain Nemo, crossing his arms.

## CHAPTER XXI

### A HECATOMB

The way of describing this unlooked-for scene, the history of the patriot ship, told at first so coldly, and the emotion with which this strange man pronounced the last words, the name of the *Avenger*, the significance of which could not escape me, all impressed itself deeply on my mind. My eyes did not leave the captain, who, with his hand stretched out to sea, was watching with a glowing eye the glorious wreck. Perhaps I was never to know who he was, from whence he came, or where he was going to, but I saw the man move, and apart from the savant. It was no common misanthropy which had shut Captain Nemo and his companions within the *Nautilus*, but a hatred, either monstrous or sublime, which time could never weaken. Did this hatred still seek for vengeance? The future would soon teach me that. But the *Nautilus* was rising slowly to the surface of the sea, and the form of the *Avenger* disappeared by degrees from my sight. Soon a slight rolling told me that we were in the open air. At that moment a dull boom was heard. I looked at the captain. He did not move.

"Captain?" said I.

He did not answer. I left him and mounted the platform. Conseil and the Canadian were already there.

"Where did that sound come from?" I asked.

"It was a gunshot," replied Ned Land.

I looked in the direction of the vessel I had already seen. It was nearing the *Nautilus*, and we could see that it was putting on steam. It was within six miles of us.

"What is that ship, Ned?"

"By its rigging, and the height of its lower masts," said the Canadian, "I bet she is a ship-of-war. May it reach us; and, if necessary, sink this cursed *Nautilus*."

"Friend Ned," replied Conseil, "what harm can it do to the *Nautilus*? Can it attack it beneath the waves? Can it cannonade us at the bottom of the sea?"

"Tell me, Ned," said I, "can you recognize what country she belongs to?"

The Canadian knitted his eyebrows, dropped his eyelids, and screwed up the corners of his eyes, and for a few moments fixed a piercing look upon the vessel.

"No, sir," he replied. "I cannot tell what nation she belongs to, for she shows no colors. But I can declare she is a man-of-war, for a long pennant flutters from her mainmast."

For a quarter of an hour we watched the ship which was steaming toward us. I could not, however, believe that she could see the *Nautilus* from that distance; and still less that she could know what this submarine engine was. Soon the Canadian informed me that she was a large, armored, two-decker ram. A thick black smoke was pouring from her two funnels. Her closely furled sails were stopped to her yards. She hoisted no flag at her mizzen peak. The distance prevented us from distinguishing the colors of her pennant, which floated like a thin ribbon. She advanced rapidly. If Captain Nemo allowed her to approach, there was a chance of salvation for us.

"Sir," said Ned Land, "if that vessel passes within a mile of us I shall throw myself into the sea, and I should advise you to do the same."

I did not reply to the Canadian's suggestion, but continued watching the ship. Whether English, French, American, or Russian, she would be sure to take us in if we could only reach her. Presently a white smoke burst from the forepart of the vessel; some seconds after, the water, agitated by the fall of a heavy body, splashed the stern of the *Nautilus*, and shortly afterward a loud explosion struck my ear.

"What! They are firing at us!" I exclaimed.

"So please you, sir," said Ned, "they have recognized the unicorn, and they are firing at us."

"But," I exclaimed, "surely they can see that there are men in the case?"

"It is, perhaps, because of that," replied Ned Land, looking at me.

A whole flood of light burst upon my mind. Doubtless they knew now how to believe the stories of the pretended monster. No doubt, on board the *Abraham Lincoln*, when the Canadian struck it with the harpoon, Commander Farragut had recognized in the supposed narwhal a submarine vessel, more dangerous than a supernatural cetacean. Yes, it must have been so; and on every sea they were now seeking this engine of destruction. Terrible indeed! If, as we supposed, Captain Nemo employed the *Nautilus* in works of vengeance. On the night when we were imprisoned in that cell, in the midst of the Indian Ocean, had he not attacked some vessel? The man buried in the coral cemetery, had he not been a victim to the shock caused by the *Nautilus*? Yes, I repeat it, it must be so. One part of the mysterious existence of Captain Nemo had been unveiled; and, if his identity had not been recognized, at least, the nations united against him were no longer hunting a chimerical creature, but a man who had vowed a deadly hatred against them. All the formidable past rose before me. Instead of meeting friends on board the approaching ship, we could only expect pitiless enemies. But the shot rattled about us. Some of them struck the sea and ricocheted, losing themselves in the distance. But none touched the *Nautilus*. The vessel was not more than three miles from us. In spite of the serious cannonade, Captain Nemo did not appear on the platform; but, if one of the conical projectiles had struck the shell of the *Nautilus*, it would have been fatal. The Canadian then said, "Sir, we must do all we can to get out of this dilemma. Let us signal them. They will then, perhaps, understand that we are honest folks."

Ned Land took his handkerchief to wave in the air; but he had scarcely displayed it when he was struck down by an iron hand, and fell, in spite of his great strength, upon the deck.

"Fool!" exclaimed the captain. "Do you wish to be pierced by the spur of the *Nautilus* before it is hurled at this vessel?"

Captain Nemo was terrible to hear; he was still more terrible to see. His face was deadly pale, with a spasm at his heart. For an instant it must have ceased to beat. His pupils were fearfully contracted. He did not speak, he roared, as, with his body thrown forward, he wrung the Canadian's shoulders. Then, leaving him, and turning to the ship of war, whose shot was still raining around him, he exclaimed, with a powerful voice, "Ah, ship of an accursed nation, you know who I am! I do not want your colors to know you by! Look! And I will show you mine!"

And on the forepart of the platform Captain Nemo unfurled a black flag, similar to the one he had placed at the South Pole. At that moment a shot struck the shell of the *Nautilus* obliquely, without piercing it; and, rebounding near the captain, was lost in the sea. He shrugged his shoulders; and, addressing me, said shortly, "Go down, you and your companions, go down!"

"Sir," I cried, "are you going to attack this vessel?"

"Sir, I am going to sink it."

"You will not do that?"

"I shall do it," he replied coldly. "And I advise you not to judge me, sir. Fate has shown you what you ought not to have seen. The attack has begun; go down."

"What is this vessel?"

"You do not know? Very well! So much the better! Its nationality to you, at least, will be a secret. Go down!"

We could but obey. About fifteen of the sailors surrounded the captain, looking with implacable hatred at the vessel nearing them. One could feel that the same desire of vengeance animated every soul. I went down at the moment another projectile struck the *Nautilus*, and I heard the captain exclaim:

"Strike, mad vessel! Shower your useless shot! And then, you will not escape the spur of the *Nautilus*. But it is not here that you shall perish! I would not have your ruins mingle with those of the *Avenger*!"

I reached my room. The captain and his second had remained on the platform. The screw was set in motion, and the *Nautilus*, moving with speed, was soon beyond the reach of the ship's guns. But the pursuit continued, and Captain Nemo contented himself with keeping his distance.

About four in the afternoon, being no longer able to contain my impatience, I went to the central staircase. The panel was open, and I ventured on to the platform. The captain was still walking up and down with an agitated step. He was looking at the ship, which was five or six miles to leeward.

He was going around it like a wild beast, and, drawing it eastward, he allowed them to pursue. But he did not attack. Perhaps he still hesitated? I wished to mediate once more. But I had scarcely spoken, when Captain Nemo imposed silence, saying:

"I am the law, and I am the judge! I am the oppressed, and there is the oppressor! Through him I have lost all that I loved, cherished, and venerated—country, wife, children, father, and mother. I saw all perish! All that I hate is there! Say no more!"

I cast a last look at the man-of-war, which was putting on steam, and rejoined Ned and Conseil.

"We will fly!" I exclaimed.

"Good!" said Ned. "What is this vessel?"

"I do not know; but, whatever it is, it will be sunk before night. In any case, it is better to perish with it, than be made accomplices in a retaliation the justice of which we cannot judge."

"That is my opinion too," said Ned Land, coolly. "Let us wait for night."

Night arrived. Deep silence reigned on board. The compass showed that the *Nautilus* had not altered its course. It was on the surface, rolling slightly. My companions and I resolved to fly when the vessel should be near enough either to hear us or to see us; for the moon, which would be full in two or three days, shone brightly. Once on board the ship, if we could not prevent the blow which threatened it, we could, at least we would, do all that circumstances would allow. Several times I thought the *Nautilus* was preparing for attack; but Captain Nemo contented himself with allowing his adversary to approach, and then fled once more before it.

Part of the night passed without any incident. We watched the opportunity for action. We spoke little, for we were too much moved. Ned Land would have thrown himself into the sea, but I forced him to wait. According to my idea, the *Nautilus* would attack the ship at her waterline, and then it would not only be possible, but easy to fly.

At three in the morning, full of uneasiness, I mounted the platform. Captain Nemo had not left it. He was standing at the fore part near his flag, which a slight breeze displayed above his head. He did not take his eyes from the vessel. The intensity of his look seemed to attract, and fascinate, and draw it onward more surely than if he had been towing it. The moon was then passing the meridian. Jupiter was rising in the east. Amid this peaceful scene of nature, sky and ocean rivaled each other in tranquility, the sea offering to the orbs of night the finest mirror they could ever have in which to reflect their image. As I thought of the deep calm of these elements, compared with all those passions brooding imperceptibly within the *Nautilus*, I shuddered.

The vessel was within two miles of us. It was ever nearing that phosphorescent light which showed the presence of the *Nautilus*. I could see its green and red lights, and its white lantern hanging from the large foremast. An indistinct vibration quivered through its rigging, showing that the furnaces were heated to the uttermost. Sheaves of sparks and red ashes flew from the funnels, shining in the atmosphere like stars.

I remained thus until six in the morning, without Captain Nemo noticing me. The ship stood about a mile and a half from us, and with the first dawn of day the firing began afresh. The moment could not be far off when, the *Nautilus* attacking its adversary, my companions and myself should forever leave this man. I was preparing to go down to remind them, when the second mounted the platform, accompanied by several sailors. Captain Nemo either did not or would not see them. Some steps were taken which might be called the signal for action. They were very simple. The iron balustrade around the platform was lowered, and the lantern and pilot cages were pushed within the shell until they were flush with the deck. The long surface of the steel cigar no longer offered a single point to check its maneuvers. I returned to the saloon. The *Nautilus* still floated; some streaks of light were filtering through the liquid beds. With the undulations of the waves the windows were brightened by the red streaks of the rising sun, and this dreadful day of June 2 had dawned.

At five o'clock, the log showed that the speed of the *Nautilus* was slackening, and I knew that it was allowing them to draw nearer. Besides, the reports were heard more distinctly, and the projectiles, laboring through the ambient water, were extinguished with a strange hissing noise.

"My friends," said I, "the moment is come. One grasp of the hand, and may God protect us!"

Ned Land was resolute, Conseil calm, myself so nervous that I knew not how to contain myself. We all passed into the library; but the moment I pushed the door opening on to the central staircase, I heard the upper panel close sharply. The Canadian rushed on to the stairs, but I stopped him. A well-known hissing noise told me that the water was running into the reservoirs, and in a few minutes the *Nautilus* was some yards beneath the surface of the waves. I understood the maneuver. It was too late to act. The *Nautilus* did not wish to strike at the impenetrable cuirass, but below the waterline, where the metallic covering no longer protected it.

We were again imprisoned, unwilling witnesses of the dreadful drama that was preparing. We had scarcely time to reflect; taking refuge in my room, we looked at each other without speaking. A deep stupor had taken hold of my mind: thought seemed to stand still. I was in that painful state of expectation preceding a dreadful report. I waited, I listened, every sense was merged in that of hearing! The speed of the *Nautilus* was accelerated. It was preparing to rush. The whole ship trembled. Suddenly I screamed. I felt the shock, but comparatively light. I felt the penetrating power of the steel spur. I heard rattlings and scrapings. But the *Nautilus*, carried along by its propelling power, passed through the mass of the vessel like a needle through sailcloth!

I could stand it no longer. Mad, out of my mind, I rushed from my room into the saloon. Captain Nemo was there, mute, gloomy, implacable; he was looking through the port panel. A large mass cast a shadow on the water; and, that it might lose nothing of her agony, the *Nautilus* was going down into the abyss with her. Ten yards from me I saw the open shell, through which the water was rushing with the noise of thunder, then the double line of guns and the netting. The bridge was covered with black, agitated shadows.

The water was rising. The poor creatures were crowding the ratlines, clinging to the masts, struggling under the water. It was a human ant heap overtaken by the sea. Paralyzed, stiffened with anguish, my hair standing on end, with eyes wide open, panting, without breath, and without voice, I too was watching! An irresistible attraction glued me to the glass! Suddenly an explosion took place. The compressed air blew up her decks, as if the magazines had caught fire. Then the unfortunate vessel sank more rapidly. Her topmast, laden with victims, now appeared; then her spars, bending under the weight of men; and, last of all, the top of her mainmast. Then the dark mass disappeared, and with it the dead crew, drawn down by the strong eddy.

I turned to Captain Nemo. That terrible avenger, a perfect archangel of hatred, was still looking. When all was over, he turned to his room, opened the door, and entered. I followed him with my eyes. On the end wall beneath his heroes, I saw the portrait of a woman, still young, and two little children. Captain Nemo looked at them for some moments, stretched his arms toward them, and, kneeling down, burst into deep sobs.

## CHAPTER XXII

### THE LAST WORDS OF CAPTAIN NEMO

The panels had closed on this dreadful vision, but light had not returned to the saloon: all was silence and darkness within the *Nautilus*. At wonderful speed, a hundred feet beneath the water, it was leaving this desolate spot. Whither was it going? To the north or south? Where was the man flying to after such dreadful retaliation? I had returned to my room, where Ned and Conseil had remained silent enough. I felt an insurmountable horror for Captain Nemo. Whatever he had suffered at the hands of these men, he had no right to punish thus. He had made me, if not an accomplice, at least a witness of his vengeance. At eleven the electric light reappeared. I passed into the saloon. It was deserted. I consulted the different instruments. The *Nautilus* was flying northward at the rate of twenty-five miles an hour, now on the surface, and now thirty feet below it. On taking the bearings by the chart, I saw that we were passing the mouth of the Manche, and that our course was hurrying us toward the northern seas at a frightful speed. That night we had crossed two hundred leagues of the Atlantic. The shadows fell, and the sea was covered with darkness until the rising of the moon. I went to my room, but could not sleep. I was troubled with dreadful nightmare. The horrible scene of destruction was continually before my eyes. From that day, who could tell into what part of the North Atlantic basin the *Nautilus* would take us? Still with unaccountable speed. Still in the midst of these northern fogs. Would it touch at Spitzbergen, or on the shores of Nova Zembla? Should we explore those unknown seas, the White Sea, the Sea of Kara, the Gulf of Obi, the Archipelago of Liarrov, and the unknown coast of Asia? I could not say. I could no longer judge of the time that was passing. The clocks had been stopped on board. It seemed, as in polar countries, that night and day no longer followed their regular course. I felt myself being drawn into that strange region where the foundered imagination of Edgar Poe roamed at will. Like the fabulous Gordon Pym, at every moment I expected to see "that veiled human figure, of larger proportions than those of any inhabitant of the earth, thrown across the cataract which defends the approach to the pole." I estimated (though, perhaps, I may be mistaken)—I estimated this adventurous course of the *Nautilus* to have lasted fifteen or twenty days. And I know not how much longer it might have lasted, had it not been for the catastrophe which ended this voyage. Of Captain Nemo I saw nothing whatever now, nor of his second. Not a man of the crew was visible for an instant. The *Nautilus* was almost incessantly underwater. When we came to the surface to renew the air, the panels opened and shut mechanically. There were no more marks on the planisphere. I knew not where we were. And the Canadian, too, his strength and patience at an end, appeared no more. Conseil could not draw a word from him; and, fearing that, in a dreadful fit of madness, he might kill himself, watched him with constant devotion. One morning (what date it was I could not say) I had fallen into a heavy sleep toward the early hours, a sleep both painful and unhealthy, when I suddenly awoke. Ned Land was leaning over me, saying, in a low voice, "We are going to fly." I sat up.

"When shall we go?" I asked.

"Tonight. All inspection on board the *Nautilus* seems to have ceased. All appear to be stupefied. You will be ready, sir?"

"Yes; where are we?"

"In sight of land. I took the reckoning this morning in the fog—twenty miles to the east."

"What country is it?"

"I do not know; but, whatever it is, we will take refuge there."

"Yes, Ned, yes. We will fly tonight, even if the sea should swallow us up."

"The sea is bad, the wind violent, but twenty miles in that light boat of the *Nautilus* does not frighten me. Unknown to the crew, I have been able to procure food and some bottles of water."

"I will follow you."

"But," continued the Canadian, "if I am surprised, I will defend myself; I will force them to kill me."

"We will die together, friend Ned."

I had made up my mind to all. The Canadian left me. I reached the platform, on which I could with difficulty support myself against the shock of the waves. The sky was threatening; but, as land was in those thick brown shadows, we must fly. I returned to the saloon, fearing and yet hoping to see Captain Nemo, wishing and yet not wishing to see him. What could I have said to him? Could I hide the involuntary horror with which he inspired me? No. It was better that I should not meet him face-to-face; better to forget him. And yet—how long seemed that day, the last that I should pass in the *Nautilus*. I remained alone. Ned Land and Conseil avoided speaking, for fear of betraying themselves. At six I dined, but I was not hungry; I forced myself to eat in spite of my disgust, that I might not weaken myself. At half-past six Ned Land came to my room, saying, "We shall not see each other again before our departure. At ten the moon will not be risen. We will profit by the darkness. Come to the boat; Conseil and I will wait for you."

The Canadian went out without giving me time to answer. Wishing to verify the course of the *Nautilus*, I went to the saloon. We were running N.N.E. at frightful speed, and more than fifty yards deep. I cast a last look on these wonders of nature, on the riches of art heaped up in this museum, upon the unrivaled collection destined to perish at the bottom of the sea, with him who had formed it. I wished to fix an indelible impression of it in my mind. I remained an hour thus, bathed in the light of that luminous ceiling, and passing in review those treasures shining under their glasses. Then I returned to my room.

I dressed myself in strong sea clothing. I collected my notes, placing them carefully about me. My heart beat loudly. I could not check its pulsations. Certainly my trouble and agitation would have betrayed me to Captain Nemo's eyes. What was he doing at this moment? I listened at the door of his room. I heard steps. Captain Nemo was there. He had not gone to rest. At every moment I expected to see him appear, and ask me why I wished to fly. I was constantly on the alert. My imagination magnified everything. The impression became at last so poignant that I asked myself if it would not be better to go to the captain's room, see him face-to-face, and brave him with look and gesture.

It was the inspiration of a madman; fortunately I resisted the desire, and stretched myself on my bed to quiet my bodily agitation. My nerves were somewhat calmer, but in my excited brain I saw over again all my existence on board the *Nautilus*; every incident, either happy or unfortunate, which had happened since my disappearance from the *Abraham Lincoln*—the submarine hunt, the Torres Straits, the savages of Papua, the running ashore, the coral cemetery, the passage of Suez, the island of Santorin, the Cretan diver, Vigo Bay, Atlantis, the iceberg, the South Pole, the imprisonment in the ice, the fight among the poulps, the storm in the Gulf Stream, the *Avenger*, and the horrible scene of the vessel sunk with all her crew. All these events passed before my eyes like scenes in a drama. Then Captain Nemo seemed to grow enormously, his features to assume superhuman proportions. He was no longer my equal, but a man of the waters, the genie of the sea.

It was then half-past nine. I held my head between my hands to keep it from bursting. I closed my eyes; I would not think any longer. There was another half-hour to wait, another half-hour of a nightmare, which might drive me mad.

At that moment I heard the distant strains of the organ, a sad harmony to an undefinable chant, the wail of a soul longing to break these earthly bonds. I listened with every sense, scarcely breathing; plunged, like Captain Nemo, in that musical ecstasy, which was drawing him in spirit to the end of life.

Then a sudden thought terrified me. Captain Nemo had left his room. He was in the saloon, which I must cross to fly. There I should meet him for the last time. He would see me, perhaps speak to me. A gesture of his might destroy me, a single word chain me on board.

But ten was about to strike. The moment had come for me to leave my room, and join my companions.

I must not hesitate, even if Captain Nemo himself should rise before me. I opened my door carefully; and even then, as it turned on its hinges, it seemed to me to make a dreadful noise. Perhaps it only existed in my own imagination.

I crept along the dark stairs of the *Nautilus*, stopping at each step to check the beating of my heart. I reached the door of the saloon, and opened it gently. It was plunged in profound darkness. The strains of the organ sounded faintly. Captain Nemo was there. He did not see me. In the full light I do not think he would have noticed me, so entirely was he absorbed in the ecstasy.

I crept along the carpet, avoiding the slightest sound which might betray my presence. I was at least five minutes reaching the door, at the opposite side, opening into the library.

I was going to open it, when a sigh from Captain Nemo nailed me to the spot. I knew that he was rising. I could even see him, for the light from the library came through to the saloon. He came toward me silently, with his arms crossed, gliding like a specter rather than walking. His breast was swelling with sobs; and I heard him murmur these words (the last which ever struck my ear):

"Almighty God! Enough! Enough!"

Was it a confession of remorse which thus escaped from this man's conscience?

In desperation, I rushed through the library, mounted the central staircase, and, following the upper flight, reached the boat. I crept through the opening, which had already admitted my two companions.

"Let us go! Let us go!" I exclaimed.

"Directly!" replied the Canadian.

The orifice in the plates of the *Nautilus* was first closed, and fastened down by means of a false key, with which Ned Land had provided himself; the opening in the boat was also closed. The Canadian began to loosen the bolts which still held us to the submarine boat.

Suddenly a noise was heard. Voices were answering each other loudly. What was the matter? Had they discovered our flight? I felt Ned Land slipping a dagger into my hand.

"Yes," I murmured, "we know how to die!"

The Canadian had stopped in his work. But one word many times repeated, a dreadful word, revealed the cause of the agitation spreading on board the *Nautilus*. It was not we the crew were looking after!

"The maelstrom! The maelstrom!" Could a more dreadful word in a more dreadful situation have sounded in our ears! We were then upon the dangerous coast of Norway. Was the *Nautilus* being drawn into this gulf at the moment our boat was going to leave its sides? We knew that at the tide the pent-up waters between the islands of Ferroe and Lofoten rush with irresistible violence, forming a whirlpool from which no vessel ever escapes. From every point of the horizon enormous waves were meeting, forming a gulf justly called the "Navel of the Ocean," whose power of attraction extends to a distance of twelve miles. There, not only vessels, but whales are sacrificed, as well as white bears from the northern regions.

It is thither that the *Nautilus*, voluntarily or involuntarily, had been run by the captain.

It was describing a spiral, the circumference of which was lessening by degrees, and the boat, which was still fastened to its side, was carried along with giddy speed. I felt that sickly giddiness which arises from long-continued whirling around.

We were in dread. Our horror was at its height, circulation had stopped, all nervous influence was annihilated, and we were covered with cold sweat, like a sweat of agony! And what noise around our frail bark! What roarings repeated by the echo miles away! What an uproar was that of the waters broken on the sharp rocks at the bottom, where the hardest bodies are crushed, and trees worn away, "with all the fur rubbed off," according to the Norwegian phrase!

What a situation to be in! We rocked frightfully. The *Nautilus* defended itself like a human being. Its steel muscles cracked. Sometimes it seemed to stand upright, and we with it!

"We must hold on," said Ned, "and look after the bolts. We may still be saved if we stick to the *Nautilus*."

He had not finished the words, when we heard a crashing noise, the bolts gave way, and the boat, torn from its groove, was hurled like a stone from a sling into the midst of the whirlpool.

My head struck on a piece of iron, and with the violent shock I lost all consciousness.

## CHAPTER XXIII

### CONCLUSION

Thus ends the voyage under the seas. What passed during that night—how the boat escaped from the eddies of the maelstrom—how Ned Land, Conseil, and myself ever came out of the gulf, I cannot tell.

But when I returned to consciousness, I was lying in a fisherman's hut, on the Lofoten Isles. My two companions, safe and sound, were near me holding my hands. We embraced each other heartily.

At that moment we could not think of returning to France. The means of communication between the north of Norway and the south are rare. And I am therefore obliged to wait for the steamboat running monthly from Cape North.

And, among the worthy people who have so kindly received us, I revise my record of these adventures once more. Not a fact has been omitted, not a detail exaggerated. It is a faithful narrative of this incredible expedition in an element inaccessible to man, but to which Progress will one day open a road.

Shall I be believed? I do not know. And it matters little, after all. What I now affirm is, that I have a right to speak of these seas, under which, in less than ten months, I have crossed 20,000 leagues in that submarine tour of the world, which has revealed so many wonders.

But what has become of the *Nautilus?* Did it resist the pressure of the maelstrom? Does Captain Nemo still live? And does he still follow under the ocean those frightful retaliations? Or, did he stop after the last hecatomb?

Will the waves one day carry to him this manuscript containing the history of his life? Shall I ever know the name of this man? Will the missing vessel tell us by its nationality that of Captain Nemo?

I hope so. And I also hope that his powerful vessel has conquered the sea at its most terrible gulf, and that the *Nautilus* has survived where so many other vessels have been lost! If it be so—if Captain Nemo still inhabits the ocean, his adopted country, may hatred be appeased in that savage heart! May the contemplation of so many wonders extinguish forever the spirit of vengeance! May the judge disappear, and the philosopher continue the peaceful exploration of the sea! If his destiny be strange, it is also sublime. Have I not understood it myself? Have I not lived ten months of this unnatural life? And to the question asked by Ecclesiastes three thousand years ago, "That which is far off and exceeding deep, who can find it out?" two men alone of all now living have the right to give an answer:

Captain Nemo and myself.

# Around the World
# in Eighty Days

## CHAPTER I

IN WHICH PHILEAS FOGG AND PASSEPARTOUT ACCEPT EACH OTHER,
THE ONE AS MASTER, THE OTHER AS SERVANT

Mr. Phileas Fogg lived, in 1872, at No. 7, Saville Row, Burlington Gardens, the house in which Sheridan died in 1814. He was one of the most noticeable members of the Reform Club, though he seemed always to avoid attracting attention; an enigmatical personage, about whom little was known, except that he was a polished man of the world. People said that he resembled Byron—at least that his head was Byronic; but he was a bearded, tranquil Byron, who might live on a thousand years without growing old.

Certainly an Englishman, it was more doubtful whether Phileas Fogg was a Londoner. He was never seen on 'Change, nor at the Bank, nor in the counting rooms of the "City"; no ships ever came into London docks of which he was the owner; he had no public employment; he had never been entered at any of the Inns of Court, either at the Temple, or Lincoln's Inn, or Gray's Inn; nor had his voice ever resounded in the Court of Chancery, or in the Exchequer, or the Queen's Bench, or the Ecclesiastical Courts. He certainly was not a manufacturer; nor was he a merchant or a gentleman farmer. His name was strange to the scientific and learned societies, and he never was known to take part in the sage deliberations of the Royal Institution or the London Institution, the Artisan's Association, or the Institution of Arts and Sciences. He belonged, in fact, to none of the numerous societies which swarm in the English capital, from the Harmonic to that of the Entomologists, founded mainly for the purpose of abolishing pernicious insects.

Phileas Fogg was a member of the Reform, and that was all.

The way in which he got admission to this exclusive club was simple enough.

He was recommended by the Barings, with whom he had an open credit. His checks were regularly paid at sight from his account current, which was always flush.

Was Phileas Fogg rich? Undoubtedly. But those who knew him best could not imagine how he had made his fortune, and Mr. Fogg was the last person to whom to apply for the information. He was not lavish, nor, on the contrary, avaricious; for, whenever he knew that money was needed for a noble, useful, or benevolent purpose, he supplied it quietly and sometimes anonymously. He was, in short, the least communicative of men. He talked very little, and seemed all the more mysterious for his taciturn manner. His daily habits were quite open to observation; but whatever he did was so exactly the same thing that he had always done before, that the wits of the curious were fairly puzzled.

Had he traveled? It was likely, for no one seemed to know the world more familiarly; there was no spot so secluded that he did not appear to have an intimate acquaintance with it. He often corrected, with a few clear words, the thousand conjectures advanced by members of the club as to lost and unheard-of travelers, pointing out the true probabilities, and seeming as if gifted with a sort of second sight, so often did events justify his predictions. He must have traveled everywhere, at least in the spirit.

It was at least certain that Phileas Fogg had not absented himself from London for many years. Those who were honored by a better acquaintance with him than the rest, declared that nobody could pretend to have ever seen him anywhere else. His sole pastimes were reading the papers and playing whist. He often won at this game, which, as a silent one, harmonized with his nature; but his winnings never went into his purse, being reserved as a fund for his charities. Mr. Fogg played, not to win, but for the sake of playing. The game was in his eyes a contest, a struggle with a difficulty, yet a motionless, unwearying struggle, congenial to his tastes.

Phileas Fogg was not known to have either wife or children, which may happen to the most honest people; either relatives or near friends, which is certainly more unusual. He lived alone in his house in Saville Row, whither none penetrated. A single domestic sufficed to serve him. He breakfasted and dined at the club, at hours mathematically fixed, in the same room, at the same table, never taking his meals with other members, much less bringing a guest with him; and went home at exactly midnight, only to retire at once to bed. He never used the cozy chambers which the Reform provides for its favored members. He passed ten hours out of the twenty-four in Saville Row, either in sleeping or making his toilet. When he chose to take a walk it was with a regular step in the entrance hall with its mosaic flooring, or in the circular gallery with its dome supported by twenty red porphyry Ionic columns, and illumined by blue painted windows. When he breakfasted or dined all the resources of the club—its kitchens and pantries, its buttery and dairy—aided to crowd his table with their most succulent stores; he was served by the gravest waiters, in dress coats, and shoes with swanskin soles, who proffered the viands in special porcelain, and on the finest linen; club decanters, of a lost mold, contained his sherry, his port, and his cinnamon-spiced claret; while his beverages were refreshingly cooled with ice, brought at great cost from the American lakes.

If to live in this style is to be eccentric, it must be confessed that there is something good in eccentricity.

The mansion in Saville Row, though not sumptuous, was exceedingly comfortable. The habits of its occupant were such as to demand but little from the sole domestic, but Phileas Fogg required him to be almost superhumanly prompt and regular. On this very 2nd of October he had dismissed James Forster, because that luckless youth had brought him shaving-water at eighty-four degrees Fahrenheit instead of eighty-six; and he was awaiting his successor, who was due at the house between eleven and half past.

Phileas Fogg was seated squarely in his armchair, his feet close together like those of a grenadier on parade, his hands resting on his knees, his body straight, his head erect; he was steadily watching a complicated clock which indicated the hours, the minutes, the seconds, the days, the months, and the years. At exactly half past eleven Mr. Fogg would, according to his daily habit, quit Saville Row, and repair to the Reform.

A rap at this moment sounded on the door of the cozy apartment where Phileas Fogg was seated, and James Forster, the dismissed servant, appeared.

"The new servant," said he.

A young man of thirty advanced and bowed.

"You are a Frenchman, I believe," asked Phileas Fogg, "and your name is John?"

"Jean, if monsieur pleases," replied the newcomer. "Jean Passepartout, a surname which has clung to me because I have a natural aptness for going out of one business into another. I believe I'm honest, monsieur, but, to be outspoken, I've had several trades. I've been an itinerant singer, a circus rider, when I used to vault like Leotard, and dance on a rope like Blondin. Then I got to be a professor of gymnastics, so as to make better use of my talents; and then I was a sergeant fireman at Paris, and assisted at many a big fire. But I quitted France five years ago, and, wishing to taste the sweets of domestic life, took service as a valet here in England. Finding myself out of place, and hearing that Monsieur Phileas Fogg was the most exact and settled gentleman in the United Kingdom, I have come to monsieur in the hope of living with him a tranquil life, and forgetting even the name of Passepartout."

"Passepartout suits me," responded Mr. Fogg. "You are well recommended to me; I hear a good report of you. You know my conditions?"

"Yes, monsieur."

"Good! What time is it?"

"Twenty-two minutes after eleven," returned Passepartout, drawing an enormous silver watch from the depths of his pocket.

"You are too slow," said Mr. Fogg.

"Pardon me, monsieur, it is impossible—"

"You are four minutes too slow. No matter; it's enough to mention the error. Now from this moment, twenty-nine minutes after eleven a.m., this Wednesday, 2nd October, you are in my service."

Phileas Fogg got up, took his hat in his left hand, put it on his head with an automatic motion, and went off without a word.

Passepartout heard the street door shut once; it was his new master going out. He heard it shut again; it was his predecessor, James Forster, departing in his turn. Passepartout remained alone in the house in Saville Row.

...

## CHAPTER II

### In Which Passepartout Is Convinced that He Has at Last Found His Ideal

"Faith," muttered Passepartout, somewhat flurried, "I've seen people at Madame Tussaud's as lively as my new master!"

Madame Tussaud's "people," let it be said, are of wax, and are much visited in London; speech is all that is wanting to make them human.

During his brief interview with Mr. Fogg, Passepartout had been carefully observing him. He appeared to be a man about forty years of age, with fine, handsome features, and a tall, well-shaped figure; his hair and whiskers were light, his forehead compact and unwrinkled, his face rather pale, his teeth magnificent. His countenance possessed in the highest degree what physiognomists call "repose in action," a quality of those who act rather than talk. Calm and phlegmatic, with a clear eye, Mr. Fogg seemed a perfect type of that English composure which Angelica Kauffmann has so skillfully represented on canvas. Seen in the various phases of his daily life, he gave the idea of being perfectly well-balanced, as exactly regulated as a Leroy chronometer. Phileas Fogg was, indeed, exactitude personified, and this was betrayed even in the expression of his very hands and feet; for in men, as well as in animals, the limbs themselves are expressive of the passions.

He was so exact that he was never in a hurry, was always ready, and was economical alike of his steps and his motions. He never took one step too many, and always went to his destination by the shortest cut; he made no superfluous gestures, and was never seen to be moved or agitated. He was the most deliberate person in the world, yet always reached his destination at the exact moment.

He lived alone, and, so to speak, outside of every social relation; and as he knew that in this world account must be taken of friction, and that friction retards, he never rubbed against anybody.

As for Passepartout, he was a true Parisian of Paris. Since he had abandoned his own country for England, taking service as a valet, he had in vain searched for a master after his own heart. Passepartout was by no means one of those pert dunces depicted by Moliere with a bold gaze and a nose held high in the air; he was an honest fellow, with a pleasant face, lips a trifle protruding, soft-mannered and serviceable, with a good round head, such as one likes to see on the shoulders of a friend. His eyes were blue, his complexion rubicund, his figure almost portly and well-built, his body muscular, and his physical powers fully developed by the exercises of his younger days. His brown hair was somewhat tumbled; for, while the ancient sculptors are said to have known eighteen methods of arranging Minerva's tresses, Passepartout was familiar with but one of dressing his own: three strokes of a large-tooth comb completed his toilet.

It would be rash to predict how Passepartout's lively nature would agree with Mr. Fogg. It was impossible to tell whether the new servant would turn out as absolutely methodical as his master required; experience alone could solve the question. Passepartout had been a sort of vagrant in his early years, and now yearned for repose; but so far he had failed to find it, though he had already served in ten English houses. But he could not take root in any of these; with chagrin, he found his masters invariably whimsical and irregular, constantly running about the country, or on the lookout for adventure. His last master, young Lord Longferry, Member of Parliament, after passing his nights in the Haymarket taverns, was too often brought home in the morning on policemen's shoulders. Passepartout, desirous of respecting the gentleman whom he served, ventured a mild remonstrance on such conduct; which, being ill-received, he took his leave. Hearing that Mr. Phileas Fogg was looking for a servant, and that his life was one of unbroken regularity, that he neither traveled nor stayed from home overnight, he felt sure that this would be the place he was after. He presented himself, and was accepted, as has been seen.

At half past eleven, then, Passepartout found himself alone in the house in Saville Row. He begun its inspection without delay, scouring it from cellar to garret. So clean, well-arranged, solemn a mansion pleased him; it seemed to him like a snail's shell, lighted and warmed by gas, which sufficed for both these purposes. When Passepartout reached the second story he recognized at once the room which he was to inhabit, and he was well satisfied with it. Electric bells and speaking-tubes afforded communication with the lower stories; while on the mantel stood an electric clock, precisely like that in Mr. Fogg's bedchamber, both beating the same second at the same instant. "That's good, that'll do," said Passepartout to himself.

He suddenly observed, hung over the clock, a card which, upon inspection, proved to be a program of the daily routine of the house. It comprised all that was required of the servant, from eight in the morning, exactly at which hour Phileas Fogg rose, till half past eleven, when he left the house for the Reform Club—all the details of service, the tea and toast at twenty-three minutes past eight, the shaving-water at thirty-seven minutes past nine, and the toilet at twenty minutes before ten. Everything was regulated and foreseen that was to be done from half past eleven a.m. till midnight, the hour at which the methodical gentleman retired.

Mr. Fogg's wardrobe was amply supplied and in the best taste. Each pair of trousers, coat, and vest bore a number, indicating the time of year and season at which they were in turn to be laid out for wearing; and the same system was applied to the master's shoes. In short, the house in Saville Row, which must have been a very temple of disorder and unrest under the illustrious but dissipated Sheridan, was coziness, comfort, and method idealized. There was no study, nor were there books, which would have been quite useless to Mr. Fogg; for at the Reform two libraries, one of general literature and the other of law and politics, were at his service. A moderate-sized safe stood in his bedroom, constructed so as to defy fire as well as burglars; but Passepartout found neither arms nor hunting weapons anywhere; everything betrayed the most tranquil and peaceable habits.

Having scrutinized the house from top to bottom, he rubbed his hands, a broad smile overspread his features, and he said joyfully, "This is just what I wanted! Ah, we shall get on together, Mr. Fogg and I! What a domestic and regular gentleman! A real machine; well, I don't mind serving a machine."

## CHAPTER III

IN WHICH A CONVERSATION TAKES PLACE WHICH
SEEMS LIKELY TO COST PHILEAS FOGG DEAR

Phileas Fogg, having shut the door of his house at half past eleven, and having put his right foot before his left five hundred and seventy-five times, and his left foot before his right five hundred and seventy-six times, reached the Reform Club, an imposing edifice in Pall Mall, which could not have cost less than three millions. He repaired at once to the dining room, the nine windows of which open upon a tasteful garden, where the trees were already gilded with an autumn coloring; and took his place at the habitual table, the cover of which had already been laid for him. His breakfast consisted of a side dish, a broiled fish with Reading sauce, a scarlet slice of roast beef garnished with mushrooms, a rhubarb and gooseberry tart, and a morsel of Cheshire cheese, the whole being washed down with several cups of tea, for which the Reform is famous. He rose at thirteen minutes to one, and directed his steps toward the large hall, a sumptuous apartment adorned with lavishly framed paintings. A flunkey handed him an uncut *Times*, which he proceeded to cut with a skill which betrayed familiarity with this delicate operation. The perusal of this paper absorbed Phileas Fogg until a quarter before four, while the *Standard*, his next task, occupied him till the dinner hour. Dinner passed as breakfast had done, and Mr. Fogg reappeared in the reading room and sat down to the *Pall Mall* at twenty minutes before six. Half an hour later several members of the Reform came in and drew up to the fireplace, where a coal fire was steadily burning. They were Mr. Fogg's usual partners at whist: Andrew Stuart, an engineer; John Sullivan and Samuel Fallentin, bankers; Thomas Flanagan, a brewer; and Gauthier Ralph, one of the directors of the Bank of England—all rich and highly respectable personages, even in a club which comprises the princes of English trade and finance.

"Well, Ralph," said Thomas Flanagan, "what about that robbery?"

"Oh," replied Stuart, "the bank will lose the money."

"On the contrary," broke in Ralph, "I hope we may put our hands on the robber. Skillful detectives have been sent to all the principal ports of America and the Continent, and he'll be a clever fellow if he slips through their fingers."

"But have you got the robber's description?" asked Stuart.

"In the first place, he is no robber at all," returned Ralph, positively.

"What! A fellow who makes off with fifty-five thousand pounds, no robber?"

"No."

"Perhaps he's a manufacturer, then."

"The *Daily Telegraph* says that he is a gentleman."

It was Phileas Fogg, whose head now emerged from behind his newspapers, who made this remark. He bowed to his friends, and entered into the conversation. The affair which formed its subject, and which was town talk, had occurred three days before at the Bank of England. A package of banknotes, to the value of fifty-five thousand pounds, had been taken from the principal cashier's table, that functionary being at the moment engaged in registering the receipt of three shillings and sixpence. Of course, he could not have his eyes everywhere. Let it be observed that the Bank of England reposes a touching confidence in the honesty of the public. There are neither guards nor gratings to protect its treasures; gold, silver, banknotes are freely exposed, at the mercy of the first comer. A keen observer of English customs relates that, being in one of the rooms of the bank one day, he had the curiosity to examine a gold ingot weighing some seven or eight pounds. He took it up, scrutinized it, passed it to his neighbor, he to the next man, and so on until the ingot, going from hand to hand, was transferred to the end of a dark entry; nor did it return to its place for half an hour. Meanwhile, the cashier had not so much as raised his head. But in the present instance things had not gone so smoothly. The package of notes not being found when five o'clock sounded from the ponderous clock in the "drawing office," the amount was passed to the account of profit and loss. As soon as the robbery was discovered, picked detectives hastened off to Liverpool, Glasgow, Havre, Suez, Brindisi, New York, and other ports, inspired by the proffered reward of two thousand pounds, and five percent on the sum that might be recovered. Detectives were also charged with narrowly watching those who arrived at or left London by rail, and a judicial examination was at once entered upon.

There were real grounds for supposing, as the *Daily Telegraph* said, that the thief did not belong to a professional band. On the day of the robbery a well-dressed gentleman of polished manners, and with a well-to-do air, had been observed going to and fro in the paying room where the crime was committed. A description of him was easily procured and sent to the detectives; and some hopeful spirits, of whom Ralph was one, did not despair of his apprehension. The papers and clubs were full of the affair, and everywhere people were discussing the probabilities of a successful pursuit; and the Reform Club was especially agitated, several of its members being bank officials.

Ralph would not concede that the work of the detectives was likely to be in vain, for he thought that the prize offered would greatly stimulate their zeal and activity. But Stuart was far from sharing this confidence; and, as they placed themselves at the whist table, they continued to argue the matter. Stuart and Flanagan played together, while Phileas Fogg had Fallentin for his partner. As the game proceeded the conversation ceased, excepting between the rubbers, when it revived again.

"I maintain," said Stuart, "that the chances are in favor of the thief, who must be a shrewd fellow."

"Well, but where can he fly to?" asked Ralph. "No country is safe for him."

"Pshaw!"

"Where could he go, then?"

"Oh, I don't know that. The world is big enough."

"It was once," said Phileas Fogg, in a low tone. "Cut, sir," he added, handing the cards to Thomas Flanagan.

The discussion fell during the rubber, after which Stuart took up its thread.

"What do you mean by 'once'? Has the world grown smaller?"

"Certainly," returned Ralph. "I agree with Mr. Fogg. The world has grown smaller, since a man can now go round it ten times more quickly than a hundred years ago. And that is why the search for this thief will be more likely to succeed."

"And also why the thief can get away more easily."

"Be so good as to play, Mr. Stuart," said Phileas Fogg.

But the incredulous Stuart was not convinced, and when the hand was finished, said eagerly: "You have a strange way, Ralph, of proving that the world has grown smaller. So, because you can go round it in three months—"

"In eighty days," interrupted Phileas Fogg.

"That is true, gentlemen," added John Sullivan. "Only eighty days, now that the section between Rothal and Allahabad, on the Great Indian Peninsula Railway, has been opened. Here is the estimate made by the *Daily Telegraph*:

| | |
|---|---:|
| From London to Suez via Mont Cenis and Brindisi, by rail and steamboats | 7 days |
| From Suez to Bombay, by steamer | 13 " |
| From Bombay to Calcutta, by rail | 3 " |
| From Calcutta to Hong Kong, by steamer | 13 " |
| From Hong Kong to Yokohama (Japan), by steamer | 6 " |
| From Yokohama to San Francisco, by steamer | 22 " |
| From San Francisco to New York, by rail | 7 " |
| From New York to London, by steamer and rail | 9 " |
| Total | 80 days |

"Yes, in eighty days!" exclaimed Stuart, who in his excitement made a false deal. "But that doesn't take into account bad weather, contrary winds, shipwrecks, railway accidents, and so on."

"All included," returned Phileas Fogg, continuing to play despite the discussion.

"But suppose the Hindoos or Indians pull up the rails," replied Stuart. "Suppose they stop the trains, pillage the luggage vans, and scalp the passengers!"

"All included," calmly retorted Fogg; adding, as he threw down the cards, "Two trumps."

Stuart, whose turn it was to deal, gathered them up, and went on: "You are right, theoretically, Mr. Fogg, but practically—"

"Practically also, Mr. Stuart."

"I'd like to see you do it in eighty days."

"It depends on you. Shall we go?"

"Heaven preserve me! But I would wager four thousand pounds that such a journey, made under these conditions, is impossible."

"Quite possible, on the contrary," returned Mr. Fogg.

"Well, make it, then!"

"The journey round the world in eighty days?"

"Yes."

"I should like nothing better."

"When?"

"At once. Only I warn you that I shall do it at your expense."

"It's absurd!" cried Stuart, who was beginning to be annoyed at the persistence of his friend. "Come, let's go on with the game."

"Deal over again, then," said Phileas Fogg. "There's a false deal."

Stuart took up the pack with a feverish hand; then suddenly put them down again.

"Well, Mr. Fogg," said he, "it shall be so: I will wager the four thousand on it."

"Calm yourself, my dear Stuart," said Fallentin. "It's only a joke."

"When I say I'll wager," returned Stuart, "I mean it."

"All right," said Mr. Fogg; and, turning to the others, he continued: "I have a deposit of twenty thousand at Baring's which I will willingly risk upon it."

"Twenty thousand pounds!" cried Sullivan. "Twenty thousand pounds, which you would lose by a single accidental delay!"

"The unforeseen does not exist," quietly replied Phileas Fogg.

"But, Mr. Fogg, eighty days are only the estimate of the least possible time in which the journey can be made."

"A well-used minimum suffices for everything."

"But, in order not to exceed it, you must jump mathematically from the trains upon the steamers, and from the steamers upon the trains again."

"I will jump—mathematically."

"You are joking."

"A true Englishman doesn't joke when he is talking about so serious a thing as a wager," replied Phileas Fogg, solemnly. "I will bet twenty thousand pounds against anyone who wishes that I will make the tour of the world in eighty days or less; in nineteen hundred and twenty hours, or a hundred and fifteen thousand two hundred minutes. Do you accept?"

"We accept," replied Messrs. Stuart, Fallentin, Sullivan, Flanagan, and Ralph, after consulting each other.

"Good," said Mr. Fogg. "The train leaves for Dover at a quarter before nine. I will take it."

"This very evening?" asked Stuart.

"This very evening," returned Phileas Fogg. He took out and consulted a pocket almanac, and added, "As today is Wednesday, the 2nd of October, I shall be due in London in this very room of the Reform Club, on Saturday, the 21st of December, at a quarter before nine p.m.; or else the twenty thousand pounds, now deposited in my name at Baring's, will belong to you, in fact and in right, gentlemen. Here is a check for the amount."

A memorandum of the wager was at once drawn up and signed by the six parties, during which Phileas Fogg preserved a stoical composure. He certainly did not bet to win, and had only staked the twenty thousand pounds, half of his fortune, because he foresaw that he might have to expend the other half to carry out this difficult, not to say unattainable, project. As for his antagonists, they seemed much agitated; not so much by the value of their stake, as because they had some scruples about betting under conditions so difficult to their friend.

The clock struck seven, and the party offered to suspend the game so that Mr. Fogg might make his preparations for departure.

"I am quite ready now," was his tranquil response. "Diamonds are trumps: be so good as to play, gentlemen."

## CHAPTER IV

### IN WHICH PHILEAS FOGG ASTOUNDS
### PASSEPARTOUT, HIS SERVANT

Having won twenty guineas at whist, and taken leave of his friends, Phileas Fogg, at twenty-five minutes past seven, left the Reform Club.

Passepartout, who had conscientiously studied the program of his duties, was more than surprised to see his master guilty of the inexactness of appearing at this unaccustomed hour; for, according to rule, he was not due in Saville Row until precisely midnight.

Mr. Fogg repaired to his bedroom, and called out, "Passepartout!"

Passepartout did not reply. It could not be he who was called; it was not the right hour.

"Passepartout!" repeated Mr. Fogg, without raising his voice.

Passepartout made his appearance.

"I've called you twice," observed his master.

"But it is not midnight," responded the other, showing his watch.

"I know it; I don't blame you. We start for Dover and Calais in ten minutes."

A puzzled grin overspread Passepartout's round face; clearly he had not comprehended his master.

"Monsieur is going to leave home?"

"Yes," returned Phileas Fogg. "We are going round the world."

Passepartout opened wide his eyes, raised his eyebrows, held up his hands, and seemed about to collapse, so overcome was he with stupefied astonishment.

"Round the world!" he murmured.

"In eighty days," responded Mr. Fogg. "So we haven't a moment to lose."

"But the trunks?" gasped Passepartout, unconsciously swaying his head from right to left.

"We'll have no trunks; only a carpetbag, with two shirts and three pairs of stockings for me, and the same for you. We'll buy our clothes on the way. Bring down my mackintosh and traveling cloak, and some stout shoes, though we shall do little walking. Make haste!"

Passepartout tried to reply, but could not. He went out, mounted to his own room, fell into a chair, and muttered: "That's good, that is! And I, who wanted to remain quiet!"

He mechanically set about making the preparations for departure. Around the world in eighty days! Was his master a fool? No. Was this a joke, then? They were going to Dover; good! To Calais; good again! After all, Passepartout, who had been away from France five years, would not be sorry to set foot on his native soil again. Perhaps they would go as far as Paris, and it would do his eyes good to see Paris once more. But surely a gentleman so chary of his steps would stop there; no doubt—

but, then, it was none the less true that he was going away, this so domestic person hitherto!

By eight o'clock Passepartout had packed the modest carpetbag, containing the wardrobes of his master and himself; then, still troubled in mind, he carefully shut the door of his room, and descended to Mr. Fogg.

Mr. Fogg was quite ready. Under his arm might have been observed a red-bound copy of "Bradshaw's Continental Railway Steam Transit and General Guide," with its timetables showing the arrival and departure of steamers and railways. He took the carpetbag, opened it, and slipped into it a goodly roll of Bank of England notes, which would pass wherever he might go.

"You have forgotten nothing?" asked he.

"Nothing, monsieur."

"My mackintosh and cloak?"

"Here they are."

"Good! Take this carpetbag," handing it to Passepartout. "Take good care of it, for there are twenty thousand pounds in it."

Passepartout nearly dropped the bag, as if the twenty thousand pounds were in gold, and weighed him down.

Master and man then descended, the street door was double-locked, and at the end of Saville Row they took a cab and drove rapidly to Charing Cross. The cab stopped before the railway station at twenty minutes past eight. Passepartout jumped off the box and followed his master, who, after paying the cabman, was about to enter the station, when a poor beggar woman, with a child in her arms, her naked feet smeared with mud, her head covered with a wretched bonnet, from which hung a tattered feather, and her shoulders shrouded in a ragged shawl, approached, and mournfully asked for alms.

Mr. Fogg took out the twenty guineas he had just won at whist, and handed them to the beggar, saying, "Here, my good woman. I'm glad that I met you," and passed on.

Passepartout had a moist sensation about the eyes; his master's action touched his susceptible heart.

Two first-class tickets for Paris having been speedily purchased, Mr. Fogg was crossing the station to the train, when he perceived his five friends of the Reform.

"Well, gentlemen," said he, "I'm off, you see; and, if you will examine my passport when I get back, you will be able to judge whether I have accomplished the journey agreed upon."

"Oh, that would be quite unnecessary, Mr. Fogg," said Ralph politely. "We will trust your word, as a gentleman of honor."

"You do not forget when you are due in London again?" asked Stuart.

"In eighty days; on Saturday, the 21st of December, 1872, at a quarter before nine p.m. Good-bye, gentlemen."

Phileas Fogg and his servant seated themselves in a first-class carriage at twenty minutes before nine; five minutes later the whistle screamed, and the train slowly glided out of the station.

The night was dark, and a fine, steady rain was falling. Phileas Fogg, snugly ensconced in his corner, did not open his lips. Passepartout, not yet recovered from his stupefaction, clung mechanically to the carpetbag, with its enormous treasure.

Just as the train was whirling through Sydenham, Passepartout suddenly uttered a cry of despair.

"What's the matter?" asked Mr. Fogg.

"Alas! In my hurry—I—I forgot—"

"What?"

"To turn off the gas in my room!"

"Very well, young man," returned Mr. Fogg, coolly; "it will burn—at your expense."

# CHAPTER V

### IN WHICH A NEW SPECIES OF FUNDS, UNKNOWN TO THE MONEYED MEN, APPEARS ON 'CHANGE

Phileas Fogg rightly suspected that his departure from London would create a lively sensation at the West End. The news of the bet spread through the Reform Club, and afforded an exciting topic of conversation to its members. From the club it soon got into the papers throughout England. The boasted "tour of the world" was talked about, disputed, argued with as much warmth as if the subject were another Alabama claim. Some took sides with Phileas Fogg, but the large majority shook their heads and declared against him; it was absurd, impossible, they declared, that the tour of the world could be made, except theoretically and on paper, in this minimum of time, and with the existing means of traveling. The *Times, Standard, Morning Post,* and *Daily News,* and twenty other highly respectable newspapers scouted Mr. Fogg's project as madness; the *Daily Telegraph* alone hesitatingly supported him. People in general thought him a lunatic, and blamed his Reform Club friends for having accepted a wager which betrayed the mental aberration of its proposer.

Articles no less passionate than logical appeared on the question, for geography is one of the pet subjects of the English; and the columns devoted to Phileas Fogg's venture were eagerly devoured by all classes of readers. At first some rash individuals, principally of the gentler sex, espoused his cause, which became still more popular when the *Illustrated London News* came out with his portrait, copied from a photograph in the Reform Club. A few readers of the *Daily Telegraph* even dared to say, "Why not, after all? Stranger things have come to pass."

At last a long article appeared, on the 7th of October, in the bulletin of the Royal Geographical Society, which treated the question from every point of view, and demonstrated the utter folly of the enterprise.

Everything, it said, was against the travelers, every obstacle imposed alike by man and by nature. A miraculous agreement of the times of departure and arrival, which was impossible, was absolutely necessary to his success. He might, perhaps, reckon on the arrival of trains at the designated hours, in Europe, where the distances were relatively moderate; but when he calculated upon crossing India in three days, and the United States in seven, could he rely beyond misgiving upon accomplishing his task? There were accidents to machinery, the liability of trains to run off the line, collisions, bad weather, the blocking up by snow—were not all these against Phileas Fogg? Would he not find himself, when traveling by steamer in winter, at the mercy of the winds and fogs? Is it uncommon for the best ocean steamers to be two or three days behind time? But a single delay would suffice to fatally break the chain of communication; should Phileas Fogg once miss, even by an hour, a steamer, he would have to wait for the next, and that would irrevocably render his attempt vain.

This article made a great deal of noise, and, being copied into all the papers, seriously depressed the advocates of the rash tourist.

Everybody knows that England is the world of betting men, who are of a higher class than mere gamblers; to bet is in the English temperament. Not only the members of the Reform, but the general public, made heavy wagers for or against Phileas Fogg, who was set down in the betting books as if he were a racehorse. Bonds were issued, and made their appearance on 'Change; "Phileas Fogg bonds" were offered at par or at a premium, and a great business was done in them. But five days after the article in the bulletin of the Geographical Society appeared, the demand began to subside: "Phileas Fogg" declined. They were offered by packages, at first of five, then of ten, until at last nobody would take less than twenty, fifty, a hundred!

Lord Albemarle, an elderly paralytic gentleman, was now the only advocate of Phileas Fogg left. This noble lord, who was fastened to his chair, would have given his fortune to be able to make the tour of the world, if it took ten years; and he bet five thousand pounds on Phileas Fogg. When the folly as well as the uselessness of the adventure was pointed out to him, he contented himself with replying, "If the thing is feasible, the first to do it ought to be an Englishman."

The Fogg party dwindled more and more, everybody was going against him, and the bets stood a hundred and fifty and two hundred to one; and a week after his departure an incident occurred which deprived him of backers at any price.

The commissioner of police was sitting in his office at nine o'clock one evening, when the following telegraphic dispatch was put into his hands:

SUEZ TO LONDON

Rowan, Commissioner of Police, Scotland Yard:
I've found the bank robber, Phileas Fogg. Send without delay warrant of arrest to Bombay.

FIX, DETECTIVE

The effect of this dispatch was instantaneous. The polished gentleman disappeared to give place to the bank robber. His photograph, which was hung with those of the rest of the members at the Reform Club, was minutely examined, and it betrayed, feature by feature, the description of the robber which had been provided to the police. The mysterious habits of Phileas Fogg were recalled; his solitary ways, his sudden departure; and it seemed clear that, in undertaking a tour round the world on the pretext of a wager, he had had no other end in view than to elude the detectives, and throw them off his track.

## CHAPTER VI

### In Which Fix, the Detective, Betrays
### a Very Natural Impatience

The circumstances under which this telegraphic dispatch about Phileas Fogg was sent were as follows:

The steamer *Mongolia*, belonging to the Peninsular and Oriental Company, built of iron, of two thousand eight hundred tons burden, and five hundred horsepower, was due at eleven o'clock a.m. on Wednesday, the 9th of October, at Suez. The *Mongolia* plied regularly between Brindisi and Bombay via the Suez Canal, and was one of the fastest steamers belonging to the company, always making more than ten knots an hour between Brindisi and Suez, and nine and a half between Suez and Bombay.

Two men were promenading up and down the wharves, among the crowd of natives and strangers who were sojourning at this once-straggling village—now, thanks to the enterprise of M. Lesseps, a fast-growing town. One was the British consul at Suez, who, despite the prophecies of the English government, and the unfavorable predictions of Stephenson, was in the habit of seeing, from his office window, English ships daily passing to and fro on the great canal, by which the old roundabout route from England to India by the Cape of Good Hope was abridged by at least a half. The other was a small, slight-built personage, with a nervous, intelligent face, and bright eyes peering out from under eyebrows which he was incessantly twitching. He was just now manifesting unmistakable signs of impatience, nervously pacing up and down, and unable to stand still for a moment. This was Fix, one of the detectives who had been dispatched from England in search of the bank robber; it was his task to narrowly watch every passenger who arrived at Suez, and to follow up all who seemed to be suspicious characters, or bore a resemblance to the description of the criminal, which he had received two days before from the police headquarters at London. The detective was evidently inspired by the hope of obtaining the splendid reward which would be the prize of success, and awaited with a feverish impatience, easy to understand, the arrival of the steamer *Mongolia*.

"So you say, consul," asked he for the twentieth time, "that this steamer is never behind time?"

"No, Mr. Fix," replied the consul. "She was bespoken yesterday at Port Said, and the rest of the way is of no account to such a craft. I repeat that the *Mongolia* has been in advance of the time required by the company's regulations, and gained the prize awarded for excess of speed."

"Does she come directly from Brindisi?"

"Directly from Brindisi; she takes on the Indian mails there, and she left there Saturday at five p.m. Have patience, Mr. Fix; she will not be late. But really, I don't see how, from the description you have, you will be able to recognize your man, even if he is on board the *Mongolia*."

"A man rather feels the presence of these fellows, consul, than recognizes them. You must have a scent for them, and a scent is like a sixth sense which combines hearing, seeing, and smelling. I've arrested more than one of these gentlemen in my time, and, if my thief is on board, I'll answer for it; he'll not slip through my fingers."

"I hope so, Mr. Fix, for it was a heavy robbery."

"A magnificent robbery, consul; fifty-five thousand pounds! We don't often have such windfalls. Burglars are getting to be so contemptible nowadays! A fellow gets hung for a handful of shillings!"

"Mr. Fix," said the consul, "I like your way of talking, and hope you'll succeed; but I fear you will find it far from easy. Don't you see, the description which you have there has a singular resemblance to an honest man?"

"Consul," remarked the detective, dogmatically, "great robbers always resemble honest folks. Fellows who have rascally faces have only one course to take, and that is to remain honest; otherwise they would be arrested offhand. The artistic thing is, to unmask honest countenances; it's no light task, I admit, but a real art."

Mr. Fix evidently was not wanting in a tinge of self-conceit.

Little by little the scene on the quay became more animated; sailors of various nations, merchants, ship brokers, porters, fellahs bustled to and fro as if the steamer were immediately expected. The weather was clear, and slightly chilly. The minarets of the town loomed above the houses in the pale rays of the sun. A jetty pier, some two thousand yards along, extended into the roadstead. A number of fishing smacks and coasting boats, some retaining the fantastic fashion of ancient galleys, were discernible on the Red Sea.

As he passed among the busy crowd, Fix, according to habit, scrutinized the passers-by with a keen, rapid glance.

It was now half past ten.

"The steamer doesn't come!" he exclaimed, as the port clock struck.

"She can't be far off now," returned his companion.

"How long will she stop at Suez?"

"Four hours; long enough to get in her coal. It is thirteen hundred and ten miles from Suez to Aden, at the other end of the Red Sea, and she has to take in a fresh coal supply."

"And does she go from Suez directly to Bombay?"

"Without putting in anywhere."

"Good!" said Fix. "If the robber is on board he will no doubt get off at Suez, so as to reach the Dutch or French colonies in Asia by some other route. He ought to know that he would not be safe an hour in India, which is English soil."

"Unless," objected the consul, "he is exceptionally shrewd. An English criminal, you know, is always better concealed in London than anywhere else."

This observation furnished the detective food for thought, and meanwhile the consul went away to his office. Fix, left alone, was more impatient than ever, having a presentiment that the robber was on board the *Mongolia*. If he had indeed left London intending to reach the New World, he would naturally take the route via India, which was less watched and more difficult to watch than that of the Atlantic. But Fix's reflections were soon interrupted by a succession of sharp whistles, which announced the arrival of the *Mongolia*. The porters and fellahs rushed down the quay, and a dozen boats pushed off from the shore to go and meet the steamer. Soon her gigantic hull appeared passing along between the banks, and eleven o'clock struck as she anchored in the road. She brought an unusual number of passengers, some of whom remained on deck to scan the picturesque panorama of the town, while the greater part disembarked in the boats, and landed on the quay.

Fix took up a position, and carefully examined each face and figure which made its appearance. Presently one of the passengers, after vigorously pushing his way through the importunate crowd of porters, came up to him and politely asked if he could point out the English consulate, at the same time showing a passport which he wished to have visaed. Fix instinctively took the passport, and with a rapid glance read the description of its bearer. An involuntary motion of surprise nearly escaped him, for the description in the passport was identical with that of the bank robber which he had received from Scotland Yard.

"Is this your passport?" asked he.

"No, it's my master's."

"And your master is——"

"He stayed on board."

"But he must go to the consul's in person, so as to establish his identity."

"Oh, is that necessary?"

"Quite indispensable."

"And where is the consulate?"

"There, on the corner of the square," said Fix, pointing to a house two hundred steps off.

"I'll go and fetch my master, who won't be much pleased, however, to be disturbed."

The passenger bowed to Fix, and returned to the steamer.

# CHAPTER VII

### WHICH ONCE MORE DEMONSTRATES THE USELESSNESS
### OF PASSPORTS AS AIDS TO DETECTIVES

The detective passed down the quay, and rapidly made his way to the consul's office, where he was at once admitted to the presence of that official.

"Consul," said he, without preamble, "I have strong reasons for believing that my man is a passenger on the *Mongolia*." And he narrated what had just passed concerning the passport.

"Well, Mr. Fix," replied the consul, "I shall not be sorry to see the rascal's face; but perhaps he won't come here—that is, if he is the person you suppose him to be. A robber doesn't quite like to leave traces of his flight behind him; and, besides, he is not obliged to have his passport countersigned."

"If he is as shrewd as I think he is, consul, he will come."

"To have his passport visaed?"

"Yes. Passports are only good for annoying honest folks, and aiding in the flight of rogues. I assure you it will be quite the thing for him to do; but I hope you will not visa the passport."

"Why not? If the passport is genuine I have no right to refuse."

"Still, I must keep this man here until I can get a warrant to arrest him from London."

"Ah, that's your lookout. But I cannot—"

The consul did not finish his sentence, for as he spoke a knock was heard at the door, and two strangers entered, one of whom was the servant whom Fix had met on the quay. The other, who was his master, held out his passport with the request that the consul would do him the favor to visa it. The consul took the document and carefully read it, while Fix observed, or rather devoured, the stranger with his eyes from a corner of the room.

"You are Mr. Phileas Fogg?" said the consul, after reading the passport.

"I am."

"And this man is your servant?"

"He is: a Frenchman, named Passepartout."

"You are from London?"

"Yes."

"And you are going—"

"To Bombay."

"Very good, sir. You know that a visa is useless, and that no passport is required?"

"I know it, sir," replied Phileas Fogg; "but I wish to prove, by your visa, that I came by Suez."

"Very well, sir."

The consul proceeded to sign and date the passport, after which he added his official seal. Mr. Fogg paid the customary fee, coldly bowed, and went out, followed by his servant.

"Well?" queried the detective.

"Well, he looks and acts like a perfectly honest man," replied the consul.

"Possibly; but that is not the question. Do you think, consul, that this phlegmatic gentleman resembles, feature by feature, the robber whose description I have received?"

"I concede that; but then, you know, all descriptions—"

"I'll make certain of it," interrupted Fix. "The servant seems to me less mysterious than the master; besides, he's a Frenchman, and can't help talking. Excuse me for a little while, consul."

Fix started off in search of Passepartout.

Meanwhile Mr. Fogg, after leaving the consulate, repaired to the quay, gave some orders to Passepartout, went off to the *Mongolia* in a boat, and descended to his cabin. He took up his notebook, which contained the following memoranda:

> Left London, Wednesday, October 2nd, at 8:45 p.m.
> Reached Paris, Thursday, October 3rd, at 7:20 a.m.
> Left Paris, Thursday, at 8:40 a.m.
> Reached Turin by Mont Cenis, Friday, October 4th, at 6:35 a.m.
> Left Turin, Friday, at 7:20 a.m.
> Arrived at Brindisi, Saturday, October 5th, at 4 p.m.
> Sailed on the *Mongolia*, Saturday, at 5 p.m.
> Reached Suez, Wednesday, October 9th, at 11 a.m.
> Total of hours spent, 158½; or, in days, six days and a half.

These dates were inscribed in an itinerary divided into columns, indicating the month, the day of the month, and the day for the stipulated and actual arrivals at each principal point—Paris, Brindisi, Suez, Bombay, Calcutta, Singapore, Hong Kong, Yokohama, San Francisco, New York, and London—from the 2nd of October to the 21st of December; and giving a space for setting down the gain made or the loss suffered on arrival at each locality. This methodical record thus contained an account of everything needed, and Mr. Fogg always knew whether he was behindhand or in advance of his time. On this Friday, October 9th, he noted his arrival at Suez, and observed that he had as yet neither gained nor lost. He sat down quietly to breakfast in his cabin, never once thinking of inspecting the town, being one of those Englishmen who are wont to see foreign countries through the eyes of their domestics.

# CHAPTER VIII

### In Which Passepartout Talks Rather
### More, Perhaps, Than Is Prudent

Fix soon rejoined Passepartout, who was lounging and looking about on the quay, as if he did not feel that he, at least, was obliged not to see anything.

"Well, my friend," said the detective, coming up with him, "is your passport visaed?"

"Ah, it's you, is it, monsieur?" responded Passepartout. "Thanks, yes, the passport is all right."

"And you are looking about you?"

"Yes; but we travel so fast that I seem to be journeying in a dream. So this is Suez?"

"Yes."

"In Egypt?"

"Certainly, in Egypt."

"And in Africa?"

"In Africa."

"In Africa!" repeated Passepartout. "Just think, monsieur, I had no idea that we should go farther than Paris; and all that I saw of Paris was between twenty minutes past seven and twenty minutes before nine in the morning, between the Northern and the Lyons stations, through the windows of a car, and in a driving rain! How I regret not having seen once more Père la Chaise and the circus in the Champs Élysées!"

"You are in a great hurry, then?"

"I am not, but my master is. By the way, I must buy some shoes and shirts. We came away without trunks, only with a carpetbag."

"I will show you an excellent shop for getting what you want."

"Really, monsieur, you are very kind."

And they walked off together, Passepartout chatting volubly as they went along.

"Above all," said he; "don't let me lose the steamer."

"You have plenty of time; it's only twelve o'clock."

Passepartout pulled out his big watch. "Twelve!" he exclaimed. "Why, it's only eight minutes before ten."

"Your watch is slow."

"My watch? A family watch, monsieur, which has come down from my great-grandfather! It doesn't vary five minutes in the year. It's a perfect chronometer, look you."

"I see how it is," said Fix. "You have kept London time, which is two hours behind that of Suez. You ought to regulate your watch at noon in each country."

"I regulate my watch? Never!"

"Well, then, it will not agree with the sun."

"So much the worse for the sun, monsieur. The sun will be wrong, then!"

And the worthy fellow returned the watch to its fob with a defiant gesture. After a few minutes silence, Fix resumed: "You left London hastily, then?"

"I rather think so! Last Friday at eight o'clock in the evening, Monsieur Fogg came home from his club, and three-quarters of an hour afterward we were off."

"But where is your master going?"

"Always straight ahead. He is going round the world."

"Round the world?" cried Fix.

"Yes, and in eighty days! He says it is on a wager; but, between us, I don't believe a word of it. That wouldn't be common sense. There's something else in the wind."

"Ah! Mr. Fogg is a character, is he?"

"I should say he was."

"Is he rich?"

"No doubt, for he is carrying an enormous sum in brand new banknotes with him. And he doesn't spare the money on the way, either: he has offered a large reward to the engineer of the *Mongolia* if he gets us to Bombay well in advance of time."

"And you have known your master a long time?"

"Why, no; I entered his service the very day we left London."

The effect of these replies upon the already suspicious and excited detective may be imagined. The hasty departure from London soon after the robbery; the large sum carried by Mr. Fogg; his eagerness to reach distant countries; the pretext of an eccentric and foolhardy bet—all confirmed Fix in his theory. He continued to pump poor Passepartout, and learned that he really knew little or nothing of his master, who lived a solitary existence in London, was said to be rich, though no one knew whence came his riches, and was mysterious and impenetrable in his affairs and habits. Fix felt sure that Phileas Fogg would not land at Suez, but was really going on to Bombay.

"Is Bombay far from here?" asked Passepartout.

"Pretty far. It is a ten days' voyage by sea."

"And in what country is Bombay?"

"India."

"In Asia?"

"Certainly."

"The deuce! I was going to tell you there's one thing that worries me—my burner!"

"What burner?"

"My gas burner, which I forgot to turn off, and which is at this moment burning at my expense. I have calculated, monsieur, that I lose two shillings every four and twenty hours, exactly sixpence more than I earn; and you will understand that the longer our journey—"

Did Fix pay any attention to Passepartout's trouble about the gas? It is not probable. He was not listening, but was cogitating a project. Passepartout and he had now reached the shop, where Fix left his companion to make his purchases, after recommending him not to miss the steamer, and hurried back to the consulate. Now that he was fully convinced, Fix had quite recovered his equanimity.

"Consul," said he, "I have no longer any doubt. I have spotted my man. He passes himself off as an odd stick who is going round the world in eighty days."

"Then he's a sharp fellow," returned the consul, "and counts on returning to London after putting the police of the two countries off his track."

"We'll see about that," replied Fix.

"But are you not mistaken?"

"I am not mistaken."

"Why was this robber so anxious to prove, by the visa, that he had passed through Suez?"

"Why? I have no idea; but listen to me."

He reported in a few words the most important parts of his conversation with Passepartout.

"In short," said the consul, "appearances are wholly against this man. And what are you going to do?"

"Send a dispatch to London for a warrant of arrest to be dispatched instantly to Bombay, take passage on board the *Mongolia*, follow my rogue to India, and there, on English ground, arrest him politely, with my warrant in my hand, and my hand on his shoulder."

Having uttered these words with a cool, careless air, the detective took leave of the consul, and repaired to the telegraph office, whence he sent the dispatch which we have seen to the London police office. A quarter of an hour later found Fix, with a small bag in his hand, proceeding on board the *Mongolia*; and, ere many moments longer, the noble steamer rode out at full steam upon the waters of the Red Sea.

## CHAPTER IX

### In Which the Red Sea and the Indian Ocean Prove Propitious to the Designs of Phileas Fogg

The distance between Suez and Aden is precisely thirteen hundred and ten miles, and the regulations of the company allow the steamers one hundred and thirty-eight hours in which to traverse it. The *Mongolia*, thanks to the vigorous exertions of the engineer, seemed likely, so rapid was her speed, to reach her destination considerably within that time. The greater part of the passengers from Brindisi were bound for India; some for Bombay, others for Calcutta by way of Bombay, the nearest route thither, now that a railway crosses the Indian peninsula. Among the passengers was a number of officials and military officers of various grades, the latter being either attached to the regular British forces or commanding the Sepoy troops, and receiving high salaries ever since the central government has assumed the powers of the East India Company: for the sub-lieutenants get 280£, brigadiers, 2,400£, and generals of divisions, 4,000£. What with the military men, a number of rich young Englishmen on their travels, and the hospitable efforts of the purser, the time passed quickly on the *Mongolia*. The best of fare was spread upon the cabin tables at breakfast, lunch, dinner, and the eight o'clock supper, and the ladies scrupulously changed their toilets twice a day; and the hours were whirled away, when the sea was tranquil, with music, dancing, and games.

But the Red Sea is full of caprice, and often boisterous, like most long and narrow gulfs. When the wind came from the African or Asian coast the *Mongolia*, with her long hull, rolled fearfully. Then the ladies speedily disappeared below; the pianos were silent; singing and dancing suddenly ceased. Yet the good ship plowed straight on, unretarded by wind or wave, toward the straits of Bab-el-Mandeb. What was Phileas Fogg doing all this time? It might be thought that, in his anxiety, he would be constantly watching the changes of the wind, the disorderly raging of the billows—every chance, in short, which might force the *Mongolia* to slacken her speed, and thus interrupt his journey. But, if he thought of these possibilities, he did not betray the fact by any outward sign.

Always the same impassible member of the Reform Club, whom no incident could surprise, as unvarying as the ship's chronometers, and seldom having the curiosity even to go upon the deck, he passed through the memorable scenes of the Red Sea with cold indifference; did not care to recognize the historic towns and villages which, along its borders, raised their picturesque outlines against the sky; and betrayed no fear of the dangers of the Arabic Gulf, which the old historians always spoke of with horror, and upon which the ancient navigators never ventured without propitiating the gods by ample sacrifices. How did this eccentric personage pass his time on the *Mongolia*? He made his four hearty meals every day, regardless of the most persistent rolling and pitching on the part of the steamer; and he played whist indefatigably, for he had found partners as enthusiastic in the game as himself. A tax collector, on the way to his post at Goa; the Rev. Decimus Smith, returning to his parish at Bombay; and a brigadier-general of the English army, who was about to rejoin his brigade at Benares, made up the party, and, with Mr. Fogg, played whist by the hour together in absorbing silence.

As for Passepartout, he, too, had escaped seasickness, and took his meals conscientiously in the forward cabin. He rather enjoyed the voyage, for he was well fed and well lodged, took a great interest in the scenes through which they were passing, and consoled himself with the delusion that his master's whim would end at Bombay. He was pleased, on the day after leaving Suez, to find on deck the obliging person with whom he had walked and chatted on the quays.

"If I am not mistaken," said he, approaching this person, with his most amiable smile, "you are the gentleman who so kindly volunteered to guide me at Suez?"

"Ah! I quite recognize you. You are the servant of the strange Englishman—"

"Just so, monsieur—"

"Fix."

"Monsieur Fix," resumed Passepartout, "I'm charmed to find you on board. Where are you bound?"

"Like you, to Bombay."

"That's capital! Have you made this trip before?"

"Several times. I am one of the agents of the Peninsular Company."

"Then you know India?"

"Why yes," replied Fix, who spoke cautiously.

"A curious place, this India?"

"Oh, very curious. Mosques, minarets, temples, fakirs, pagodas, tigers, snakes, elephants! I hope you will have ample time to see the sights."

"I hope so, Monsieur Fix. You see, a man of sound sense ought not to spend his life jumping from a steamer upon a railway train, and from a railway train upon a steamer again, pretending to make the tour of the world in eighty days! No; all these gymnastics, you may be sure, will cease at Bombay."

"And Mr. Fogg is getting on well?" asked Fix, in the most natural tone in the world.

"Quite well, and I too. I eat like a famished ogre; it's the sea air."

"But I never see your master on deck."

"Never; he hasn't the least curiosity."

"Do you know, Mr. Passepartout, that this pretended tour in eighty days may conceal some secret errand—perhaps a diplomatic mission?"

"Faith, Monsieur Fix, I assure you I know nothing about it, nor would I give half a crown to find out."

After this meeting, Passepartout and Fix got into the habit of chatting together, the latter making it a point to gain the worthy man's confidence. He frequently offered him a glass of whiskey or pale ale in the steamer barroom, which Passepartout never failed to accept with graceful alacrity, mentally pronouncing Fix the best of good fellows.

Meanwhile the *Mongolia* was pushing forward rapidly; on the 13th, Mocha, surrounded by its ruined walls whereon date trees were growing, was sighted, and on the mountains beyond were espied vast coffee fields. Passepartout was ravished to behold this celebrated place, and thought that, with its circular walls and dismantled fort, it looked like an immense coffee cup and saucer. The following night they passed through the Strait of Bab-el-Mandeb, which means in Arabic "the Bridge of Tears," and the next day they put in at Steamer Point, northwest of Aden harbor, to take in coal. This matter of fueling steamers is a serious one at such distances from the coal mines; it costs the Peninsular Company some eight hundred thousand pounds a year. In these distant seas, coal is worth three or four pounds sterling a ton.

The *Mongolia* had still sixteen hundred and fifty miles to traverse before reaching Bombay, and was obliged to remain four hours at Steamer Point to coal up. But this delay, as it was foreseen, did not affect Phileas Fogg's program; besides, the *Mongolia*, instead of reaching Aden on the morning of the 15th, when she was due, arrived there on the evening of the 14th, a gain of fifteen hours.

Mr. Fogg and his servant went ashore at Aden to have the passport again visaed; Fix, unobserved, followed them. The visa procured, Mr. Fogg returned on board to resume his former habits; while Passepartout, according to custom, sauntered about among the mixed population of Somalis, Banyans, Parsees, Jews, Arabs, and Europeans who comprise the twenty-five thousand inhabitants of Aden. He gazed with wonder upon the fortifications which make this place the Gibraltar of the Indian Ocean, and the vast cisterns where the English engineers were still at work, two thousand years after the engineers of Solomon.

"Very curious, *very* curious," said Passepartout to himself, on returning to the steamer. "I see that it is by no means useless to travel, if a man wants to see something new." At six p.m. the *Mongolia* slowly moved out of the roadstead, and was soon once more on the Indian Ocean. She had a hundred and sixty-eight hours in which to reach Bombay, and the sea was favorable, the wind being in the northwest, and all sails aiding the engine. The steamer rolled but little, the ladies, in fresh toilets, reappeared on deck, and the singing and dancing were resumed. The trip was being accomplished most successfully, and Passepartout was enchanted with the congenial companion which chance had secured him in the person of the delightful Fix. On Sunday, October 20th, toward noon, they came in sight of the Indian coast: two hours later the pilot came on board. A range of hills lay against the sky in the horizon, and soon the rows of palms which adorn Bombay came distinctly into view. The steamer entered the road formed by the islands in the bay, and at half past four she hauled up at the quays of Bombay.

Phileas Fogg was in the act of finishing the thirty-third rubber of the voyage, and his partner and himself having, by a bold stroke, captured all thirteen of the tricks, concluded this fine campaign with a brilliant victory.

The *Mongolia* was due at Bombay on the 22nd; she arrived on the 20th. This was a gain to Phileas Fogg of two days since his departure from London, and he calmly entered the fact in the itinerary, in the column of gains.

# CHAPTER X

### IN WHICH PASSEPARTOUT IS ONLY TOO GLAD TO
### GET OFF WITH THE LOSS OF HIS SHOES

Everybody knows that the great reversed triangle of land, with its base in the north and its apex in the south, which is called India, embraces fourteen hundred thousand square miles, upon which is spread unequally a population of one hundred and eighty millions of souls. The British Crown exercises a real and despotic dominion over the larger portion of this vast country, and has a governor-general stationed at Calcutta, governors at Madras, Bombay, and in Bengal, and a lieutenant-governor at Agra.

But British India, properly so called, only embraces seven hundred thousand square miles, and a population of from one hundred to one hundred and ten millions of inhabitants. A considerable portion of India is still free from British authority; and there are certain ferocious rajahs in the interior who are absolutely independent. The celebrated East India Company was all-powerful from 1756, when the English first gained a foothold on the spot where now stands the city of Madras, down to the time of the great Sepoy insurrection. It gradually annexed province after province, purchasing them of the native chiefs, whom it seldom paid, and appointed the governor-general and his subordinates, civil and military. But the East India Company has now passed away, leaving the British possessions in India directly under the control of the Crown. The aspect of the country, as well as the manners and distinctions of race, is daily changing.

Formerly one was obliged to travel in India by the old cumbrous methods of going on foot or on horseback, in palanquins or unwieldy coaches; now fast steamboats ply on the Indus and the Ganges, and a great railway, with branch lines joining the main line at many points on its route, traverses the peninsula from Bombay to Calcutta in three days. This railway does not run in a direct line across India. The distance between Bombay and Calcutta, as the bird flies, is only from one thousand to eleven hundred miles; but the deflections of the road increase this distance by more than a third.

The general route of the Great Indian Peninsula Railway is as follows: Leaving Bombay, it passes through Salcette, crossing to the continent opposite Tannah, goes over the chain of the Western Ghauts, runs thence northeast as far as Burhampoor, skirts the nearly independent territory of Bundelcund, ascends to Allahabad, turns thence eastwardly, meeting the Ganges at Benares, then departs from the river a little, and, descending southeastward by Burdivan and the French town of Chandernagor, has its terminus at Calcutta.

The passengers of the *Mongolia* went ashore at half past four p.m.; at exactly eight the train would start for Calcutta.

Mr. Fogg, after bidding good-bye to his whist partners, left the steamer, gave his servant several errands to do, urged it upon him to be at the station promptly at eight, and, with his regular step, which beat to the second, like an astronomical clock, directed his steps to the passport office. As for the wonders of Bombay—its famous city hall, its splendid library, its forts and docks, its bazaars, mosques, synagogues, its Armenian churches, and the noble pagoda on Malabar Hill, with its two polygonal towers—he cared not a straw to see them. He would not deign to examine even the masterpieces of Elephanta, or the mysterious hypogea, concealed southeast from the docks, or those fine remains of Buddhist architecture, the Kanherian grottoes of the island of Salcette.

Having transacted his business at the passport office, Phileas Fogg repaired quietly to the railway station, where he ordered dinner. Among the dishes served up to him, the landlord especially recommended a certain giblet of "native rabbit," on which he prided himself.

Mr. Fogg accordingly tasted the dish, but, despite its spiced sauce, found it far from palatable. He rang for the landlord, and, on his appearance, said, fixing his clear eyes upon him, "Is this rabbit, sir?"

"Yes, my lord," the rogue boldly replied, "rabbit from the jungles."

"And this rabbit did not mew when he was killed?"

"Mew, my lord! What, a rabbit mew! I swear to you—"

"Be so good, landlord, as not to swear, but remember this: cats were formerly considered, in India, as sacred animals. That was a good time."

"For the cats, my lord?"

"Perhaps for the travelers as well!"

After which Mr. Fogg quietly continued his dinner. Fix had gone on shore shortly after Mr. Fogg, and his first destination was the headquarters of the Bombay police. He made himself known as a London detective, told his business at Bombay, and the position of affairs relative to the supposed robber, and nervously asked if a warrant had arrived from London. It had not reached the office; indeed, there had not yet been time for it to arrive. Fix was sorely disappointed, and tried to obtain an order of arrest from the director of the Bombay police. This the director refused, as the matter concerned the London office, which alone could legally deliver the warrant. Fix did not insist, and was fain to resign himself to await the arrival of the important document; but he was determined not to lose sight of the mysterious rogue as long as he stayed in Bombay. He did not doubt for a moment, any more than Passepartout, that Phileas Fogg would remain there, at least until it was time for the warrant to arrive.

Passepartout, however, had no sooner heard his master's orders on leaving the *Mongolia* than he saw at once that they were to leave Bombay as they had done Suez and Paris, and that the journey would be extended at least as far as Calcutta, and perhaps beyond that place. He began to ask himself if this bet that Mr. Fogg talked about was not really in good earnest, and whether his fate was not in truth forcing him, despite his love of repose, around the world in eighty days!

Having purchased the usual quota of shirts and shoes, he took a leisurely promenade about the streets, where crowds of people of many nationalities—Europeans, Persians with pointed caps, Banyas with round turbans, Sindes with square bonnets, Parsees with black miters, and long-robed Armenians—were collected. It happened to be the day of a Parsee festival. These descendants of the sect of Zoroaster—the most thrifty, civilized, intelligent, and austere of the East Indians, among whom are counted the richest native merchants of Bombay—were celebrating a sort of religious carnival, with processions and shows, in the midst of which Indian dancing girls, clothed in rose-colored gauze, looped up with gold and silver, danced airily, but with perfect modesty, to the sound of viols and the clanging of tambourines. It is needless to say that Passepartout watched these curious ceremonies with staring eyes and gaping mouth, and that his countenance was that of the greenest booby imaginable.

Unhappily for his master, as well as himself, his curiosity drew him unconsciously farther off than he intended to go. At last, having seen the Parsee carnival wind away in the distance, he was turning his steps toward the station, when he happened to espy the splendid pagoda on Malabar Hill, and was seized with an irresistible desire to see its interior. He was quite ignorant that it is forbidden to Christians to enter certain Indian temples, and that even the faithful must not go in without first leaving their shoes outside the door. It may be said here that the wise policy of the British government severely punishes a disregard of the practices of the native religions.

Passepartout, however, thinking no harm, went in like a simple tourist, and was soon lost in admiration of the splendid Brahmin ornamentation which everywhere met his eyes, when of a sudden he found himself sprawling on the sacred flagging. He looked up to behold three enraged priests, who forthwith fell upon him; tore off his shoes, and began to beat him with loud, savage exclamations. The agile Frenchman was soon upon his feet again, and lost no time in knocking down two of his long-gowned adversaries with his fists and a vigorous application of his toes; then, rushing out of the pagoda as fast as his legs could carry him, he soon escaped the third priest by mingling with the crowd in the streets.

At five minutes before eight, Passepartout, hatless, shoeless, and having in the squabble lost his package of shirts and shoes, rushed breathlessly into the station.

Fix, who had followed Mr. Fogg to the station, and saw that he was really going to leave Bombay, was there, upon the platform. He had resolved to follow the supposed robber to Calcutta, and farther, if necessary. Passepartout did not observe the detective, who stood in an obscure corner; but Fix heard him relate his adventures in a few words to Mr. Fogg.

"I hope that this will not happen again," said Phileas Fogg coldly, as he got into the train. Poor Passepartout, quite crestfallen, followed his master without a word. Fix was on the point of entering another carriage, when an idea struck him which induced him to alter his plan.

"No, I'll stay," muttered he. "An offense has been committed on Indian soil. I've got my man."

Just then the locomotive gave a sharp screech, and the train passed out into the darkness of the night.

## CHAPTER XI

### IN WHICH PHILEAS FOGG SECURES A CURIOUS MEANS OF CONVEYANCE AT A FABULOUS PRICE

The train had started punctually. Among the passengers were a number of officers, government officials, and opium and indigo merchants, whose business called them to the eastern coast. Passepartout rode in the same carriage with his master, and a third passenger occupied a seat opposite to them. This was Sir Francis Cromarty, one of Mr. Fogg's whist partners on the *Mongolia*, now on his way to join his corps at Benares. Sir Francis was a tall, fair man of fifty, who had greatly distinguished himself in the last Sepoy revolt. He made India his home, only paying brief visits to England at rare intervals; and was almost as familiar as a native with the customs, history, and character of India and its people. But Phileas Fogg, who was not traveling, but only describing a circumference, took no pains to inquire into these subjects; he was a solid body, traversing an orbit around the terrestrial globe, according to the laws of rational mechanics. He was at this moment calculating in his mind the number of hours spent since his departure from London, and, had it been in his nature to make a useless demonstration, would have rubbed his hands for satisfaction. Sir Francis Cromarty had observed the oddity of his traveling companion—although the only opportunity he had for studying him had been while he was dealing the cards, and between two rubbers—and questioned himself whether a human heart really beat beneath this cold exterior, and whether Phileas Fogg had any sense of the beauties of nature. The brigadier-general was free to mentally confess that, of all the eccentric persons he had ever met, none was comparable to this product of the exact sciences.

Phileas Fogg had not concealed from Sir Francis his design of going round the world, nor the circumstances under which he set out; and the general only saw in the wager a useless eccentricity and a lack of sound common sense. In the way this strange gentleman was going on, he would leave the world without having done any good to himself or anybody else.

An hour after leaving Bombay the train had passed the viaducts and the Island of Salcette, and had got into the open country. At Callyan they reached the junction of the branch line which descends toward southeastern India by Kandallah and Pounah; and, passing Pauwell, they entered the defiles of the mountains, with their basalt bases, and their summits crowned with thick and verdant forests. Phileas Fogg and Sir Francis Cromarty exchanged a few words from time to time, and now Sir Francis, reviving the conversation, observed, "Some years ago, Mr. Fogg, you would have met with a delay at this point which would probably have lost you your wager."

"How so, Sir Francis?"

"Because the railway stopped at the base of these mountains, which the passengers were obliged to cross in palanquins or on ponies to Kandallah, on the other side."

"Such a delay would not have deranged my plans in the least," said Mr. Fogg. "I have constantly foreseen the likelihood of certain obstacles."

"But, Mr. Fogg," pursued Sir Francis, "you run the risk of having some difficulty about this worthy fellow's adventure at the pagoda." Passepartout, his feet comfortably wrapped in his traveling blanket, was sound asleep and did not dream that anybody was talking about him. "The government is very severe upon that kind of offense. It takes particular care that the religious customs of the Indians should be respected, and if your servant were caught——"

"Very well, Sir Francis," replied Mr. Fogg; "if he had been caught he would have been condemned and punished, and then would have quietly returned to Europe. I don't see how this affair could have delayed his master."

The conversation fell again. During the night the train left the mountains behind, and passed Nassik, and the next day proceeded over the flat, well-cultivated country of the Khandeish, with its straggling villages, above which rose the minarets of the pagodas. This fertile territory is watered by numerous small rivers and limpid streams, mostly tributaries of the Godavery.

Passepartout, on waking and looking out, could not realize that he was actually crossing India in a railway train. The locomotive, guided by an English engineer and fed with English coal, threw out its smoke upon cotton, coffee, nutmeg, clove, and pepper plantations, while the steam curled in spirals around groups of palm trees, in the midst of which were seen picturesque bungalows, viharis (sort of abandoned monasteries), and marvelous temples enriched by the exhaustless ornamentation of Indian architecture. Then they came upon vast tracts extending to the horizon, with jungles inhabited by snakes and tigers, which fled at the noise of the train; succeeded by forests penetrated by the railway, and still haunted by elephants which, with pensive eyes, gazed at the train as it passed. The travelers crossed, beyond Milligaum, the fatal country so often stained with blood by the sectaries of the goddess Kali. Not far off rose Ellora, with its graceful pagodas, and the famous Aurungabad, capital of the ferocious Aureng-Zeb, now the chief town of one of the detached provinces of the kingdom of the Nizam. It was thereabouts that Feringhea, the Thuggee chief, king of the stranglers, held his sway. These ruffians, united by a secret bond, strangled victims of every age in honor of the goddess Death, without ever shedding blood; there was a period when this part of the country could scarcely be traveled over without corpses being found in every direction. The English government has succeeded in greatly diminishing these murders, though the Thuggees still exist, and pursue the exercise of their horrible rites.

At half past twelve the train stopped at Burhampoor, where Passepartout was able to purchase some Indian slippers, ornamented with false pearls, in which, with evident vanity, he proceeded to encase his feet. The travelers made a hasty breakfast and started off for Assurghur, after skirting for a little the banks of the small river Tapty, which empties into the Gulf of Cambray, near Surat.

Passepartout was now plunged into absorbing reverie. Up to his arrival at Bombay, he had entertained hopes that their journey would end there; but, now that they were plainly whirling across India at full speed, a sudden change had come over the spirit of his dreams. His old vagabond nature returned to him; the fantastic ideas of his youth once more took possession of him. He came to regard his master's project as intended in good earnest, believed in the reality of the bet, and therefore in the tour of the world and the necessity of making it without fail within the designated period. Already he began to worry about possible delays, and accidents which might happen on the way. He recognized himself as being personally interested in the wager, and trembled at the thought that he might have been the means of losing it by his unpardonable folly of the night before. Being much less coolheaded than Mr. Fogg, he was much more restless, counting and recounting the days passed over, uttering maledictions when the train stopped, and accusing it of sluggishness, and mentally blaming Mr. Fogg for not having bribed the engineer. The worthy fellow was ignorant that, while it was possible by such means to hasten the rate of a steamer, it could not be done on the railway.

The train entered the defiles of the Sutpour Mountains, which separate the Khandeish from Bundelcund, toward evening. The next day Sir Francis Cromarty asked Passepartout what time it was; to which, on consulting his watch, he replied that it was three in the morning. This famous timepiece, always regulated on the Greenwich meridian, which was now some seventy-seven degrees westward, was at least four hours slow. Sir Francis corrected Passepartout's time, whereupon the latter made the same remark that he had done to Fix; and upon the general insisting that the watch should be regulated in each new meridian, since he was constantly going eastward, that is in the face of the sun, and therefore the days were shorter by four minutes for each degree gone over, Passepartout obstinately refused to alter his watch, which he kept at London time. It was an innocent delusion which could harm no one.

The train stopped, at eight o'clock, in the midst of a glade some fifteen miles beyond Rothal, where there were several bungalows, and workmen's cabins. The conductor, passing along the carriages, shouted, "Passengers will get out here!"

Phileas Fogg looked at Sir Francis Cromarty for an explanation; but the general could not tell what meant a halt in the midst of this forest of dates and acacias.

Passepartout, not less surprised, rushed out and speedily returned, crying: "Monsieur, no more railway!"

"What do you mean?" asked Sir Francis.

"I mean to say that the train isn't going on."

The general at once stepped out, while Phileas Fogg calmly followed him, and they proceeded together to the conductor.

"Where are we?" asked Sir Francis.

"At the hamlet of Kholby."

"Do we stop here?"

"Certainly. The railway isn't finished."

"What! Not finished?"

"No. There's still a matter of fifty miles to be laid from here to Allahabad, where the line begins again."

"But the papers announced the opening of the railway throughout."

"What would you have, officer? The papers were mistaken."

"Yet you sell tickets from Bombay to Calcutta," retorted Sir Francis, who was growing warm.

"No doubt," replied the conductor; "but the passengers know that they must provide means of transportation for themselves from Kholby to Allahabad."

Sir Francis was furious. Passepartout would willingly have knocked the conductor down, and did not dare to look at his master.

"Sir Francis," said Mr. Fogg quietly, "we will, if you please, look about for some means of conveyance to Allahabad."

"Mr. Fogg, this is a delay greatly to your disadvantage."

"No, Sir Francis; it was foreseen."

"What! You knew that the way—"

"Not at all; but I knew that some obstacle or other would sooner or later arise on my route. Nothing, therefore, is lost. I have two days, which I have already gained, to sacrifice. A steamer leaves Calcutta for Hong Kong at noon, on the 25th. This is the 22nd, and we shall reach Calcutta in time."

There was nothing to say to so confident a response.

It was but too true that the railway came to a termination at this point. The papers were like some watches, which have a way of getting too fast, and had been premature in their announcement of the completion of the line. The greater part of the travelers were aware of this interruption, and, leaving the train, they began to engage such vehicles as the village could provide four-wheeled palkigharis, wagons drawn by zebus, carriages that looked like perambulating pagodas, palanquins, ponies, and whatnot.

Mr. Fogg and Sir Francis Cromarty, after searching the village from end to end, came back without having found anything.

"I shall go afoot," said Phileas Fogg.

Passepartout, who had now rejoined his master, made a wry grimace, as he thought of his magnificent, but too frail, Indian shoes. Happily he too had been looking about him, and, after a moment's hesitation, said, "Monsieur, I think I have found a means of conveyance."

"What?"

"An elephant! An elephant that belongs to an Indian who lives but a hundred steps from here."

"Let's go and see the elephant," replied Mr. Fogg.

They soon reached a small hut, near which, enclosed within some high palings, was the animal in question. An Indian came out of the hut, and, at their request, conducted them within the enclosure. The elephant, which its owner had reared, not for a beast of burden, but for warlike purposes, was half domesticated. The Indian had begun already, by often irritating him, and feeding him every three months on sugar and butter, to impart to him a ferocity not in his nature, this method being often employed by those who train the Indian elephants for battle. Happily, however, for Mr. Fogg, the animal's instruction in this direction had not gone far, and the elephant still preserved his natural gentleness. Kiouni—this was the name of the beast—could doubtless travel rapidly for a long time, and, in default of any other means of conveyance, Mr. Fogg resolved to hire him. But elephants are far from cheap in India, where they are becoming scarce; the males, which alone are suitable for circus shows, are much sought, especially as but few of them are domesticated. When therefore

Mr. Fogg proposed to the Indian to hire Kiouni, he refused point-blank. Mr. Fogg persisted, offering the excessive sum of ten pounds an hour for the loan of the beast to Allahabad. Refused. Twenty pounds? Refused also. Forty pounds? Still refused. Passepartout jumped at each advance; but the Indian declined to be tempted. Yet the offer was an alluring one, for, supposing it took the elephant fifteen hours to reach Allahabad, his owner would receive no less than six hundred pounds sterling.

Phileas Fogg, without getting in the least flurried, then proposed to purchase the animal outright, and at first offered a thousand pounds for him. The Indian, perhaps thinking he was going to make a great bargain, still refused.

Sir Francis Cromarty took Mr. Fogg aside, and begged him to reflect before he went any further; to which that gentleman replied that he was not in the habit of acting rashly, that a bet of twenty thousand pounds was at stake, that the elephant was absolutely necessary to him, and that he would secure him if he had to pay twenty times his value. Returning to the Indian, whose small, sharp eyes, glistening with avarice, betrayed that with him it was only a question of how great a price he could obtain, Mr. Fogg offered first twelve hundred, then fifteen hundred, eighteen hundred, two thousand pounds. Passepartout, usually so rubicund, was fairly white with suspense.

At two thousand pounds the Indian yielded.

"What a price, good heavens!" cried Passepartout. "For an elephant."

It only remained now to find a guide, which was comparatively easy. A young Parsee, with an intelligent face, offered his services, which Mr. Fogg accepted, promising so generous a reward as to materially stimulate his zeal. The elephant was led out and equipped. The Parsee, who was an accomplished elephant driver, covered his back with a sort of saddle cloth, and attached to each of his flanks some curiously uncomfortable howdahs. Phileas Fogg paid the Indian with some banknotes which he extracted from the famous carpetbag, a proceeding that seemed to deprive poor Passepartout of his vitals. Then he offered to carry Sir Francis to Allahabad, which the brigadier gratefully accepted, as one traveler the more would not be likely to fatigue the gigantic beast. Provisions were purchased at Kholby, and, while Sir Francis and Mr. Fogg took the howdahs on either side, Passepartout got astride the saddle-cloth between them. The Parsee perched himself on the elephant's neck, and at nine o'clock they set out from the village, the animal marching off through the dense forest of palms by the shortest cut.

# CHAPTER XII

## IN WHICH PHILEAS FOGG AND HIS COMPANIONS VENTURE ACROSS THE INDIAN FORESTS, AND WHAT ENSUED

In order to shorten the journey, the guide passed to the left of the line where the railway was still in process of being built. This line, owing to the capricious turnings of the Vindhia Mountains, did not pursue a straight course. The Parsee, who was quite familiar with the roads and paths in the district, declared that they would gain twenty miles by striking directly through the forest.

Phileas Fogg and Sir Francis Cromarty, plunged to the neck in the peculiar howdahs provided for them, were horribly jostled by the swift trotting of the elephant, spurred on as he was by the skillful Parsee; but they endured the discomfort with true British phlegm, talking little, and scarcely able to catch a glimpse of each other. As for Passepartout, who was mounted on the beast's back, and received the direct force of each concussion as he trod along, he was very careful, in accordance with his master's advice, to keep his tongue from between his teeth, as it would otherwise have been bitten off short. The worthy fellow bounced from the elephant's neck to his rump, and vaulted like a clown on a springboard; yet he laughed in the midst of his bouncing, and from time to time took a piece of sugar out of his pocket, and inserted it in Kiouni's trunk, who received it without in the least slackening his regular trot.

After two hours the guide stopped the elephant, and gave him an hour for rest, during which Kiouni, after quenching his thirst at a neighboring spring, set to devouring the branches and shrubs round about him. Neither Sir Francis nor Mr. Fogg regretted the delay, and both descended with a feeling of relief. "Why, he's made of iron!" exclaimed the general, gazing admiringly on Kiouni.

"Of forged iron," replied Passepartout, as he set about preparing a hasty breakfast.

At noon the Parsee gave the signal of departure. The country soon presented a very savage aspect. Copses of dates and dwarf palms succeeded the dense forests; then vast, dry plains, dotted with scanty shrubs, and sown with great blocks of syenite. All this portion of Bundelcund, which is little frequented by travelers, is inhabited by a fanatical population, hardened in the most horrible practices of the Hindoo faith. The English have not been able to secure complete dominion over this territory, which is subjected to the influence of rajahs, whom it is almost impossible to reach in their inaccessible mountain fastnesses. The travelers several times saw bands of ferocious Indians, who, when they perceived the elephant striding across-country, made angry and threatening motions. The Parsee avoided them as much as possible. Few animals were observed on the route; even the monkeys hurried from their path with contortions and grimaces which convulsed Passepartout with laughter.

In the midst of his gaiety, however, one thought troubled the worthy servant. What would Mr. Fogg do with the elephant when he got to Allahabad? Would he carry him on with him? Impossible! The cost of transporting him would make him ruinously expensive. Would he sell him, or set him free? The estimable beast certainly deserved some consideration. Should Mr. Fogg choose to make him, Passepartout, a present of Kiouni, he would be very much embarrassed; and these thoughts did not cease worrying him for a long time.

The principal chain of the Vindhias was crossed by eight in the evening, and another halt was made on the northern slope, in a ruined bungalow. They had gone nearly twenty-five miles that day, and an equal distance still separated them from the station of Allahabad.

The night was cold. The Parsee lit a fire in the bungalow with a few dry branches, and the warmth was very grateful, provisions purchased at Kholby sufficed for supper, and the travelers ate ravenously. The conversation, beginning with a few disconnected phrases, soon gave place to loud and steady snores. The guide watched Kiouni, who slept standing, bolstering himself against the trunk of a large tree. Nothing occurred during the night to disturb the slumberers, although occasional growls from panthers and chatterings of monkeys broke the silence; the more formidable beasts made no cries or hostile demonstration against the occupants of the bungalow. Sir Francis slept heavily, like an honest soldier overcome with fatigue. Passepartout was wrapped in uneasy dreams of the bouncing of the day before. As for Mr. Fogg, he slumbered as peacefully as if he had been in his serene mansion in Saville Row.

The journey was resumed at six in the morning; the guide hoped to reach Allahabad by evening. In that case, Mr. Fogg would only lose a part of the forty-eight hours saved since the beginning of the tour. Kiouni, resuming his rapid gait, soon descended the lower spurs of the Vindhias, and toward noon they passed by the village of Kallenger, on the Cani, one of the branches of the Ganges. The guide avoided inhabited places, thinking it safer to keep the open country, which lies along the first depressions of the basin of the great river. Allahabad was now only twelve miles to the northeast. They stopped under a clump of bananas, the fruit of which, as healthy as bread and as succulent as cream, was amply partaken of and appreciated.

At two o'clock the guide entered a thick forest which extended several miles; he preferred to travel under cover of the woods. They had not as yet had any unpleasant encounters, and the journey seemed on the point of being successfully accomplished, when the elephant, becoming restless, suddenly stopped.

It was then four o'clock.

"What's the matter?" asked Sir Francis, putting out his head.

"I don't know, officer," replied the Parsee, listening attentively to a confused murmur which came through the thick branches.

The murmur soon became more distinct; it now seemed like a distant concert of human voices accompanied by brass instruments. Passepartout was all eyes and ears. Mr. Fogg patiently waited without a word. The Parsee jumped to the ground, fastened the elephant to a tree, and plunged into the thicket. He soon returned, saying:

"A procession of Brahmins is coming this way. We must prevent their seeing us, if possible."

The guide unloosed the elephant and led him into a thicket, at the same time asking the travelers not to stir. He held himself ready to bestride the animal at a moment's notice, should flight become necessary; but he evidently thought that the procession of the faithful would pass without perceiving them amid the thick foliage, in which they were wholly concealed.

The discordant tones of the voices and instruments drew nearer, and now droning songs mingled with the sound of the tambourines and cymbals. The head of the procession soon appeared beneath the trees, a hundred paces away; and the strange figures who performed the religious ceremony were easily distinguished through the branches. First came the priests, with miters on their heads, and clothed in long lace robes. They were surrounded by men, women, and children, who sang a kind of lugubrious psalm, interrupted at regular intervals by the tambourines and cymbals; while behind them was drawn a car with large wheels, the spokes of which represented serpents entwined with each other. Upon the car, which was drawn by four richly caparisoned zebus, stood a hideous statue with four arms, the body colored a dull red, with haggard eyes, disheveled hair, protruding tongue, and lips tinted with betel. It stood upright upon the figure of a prostrate and headless giant.

Sir Francis, recognizing the statue, whispered, "The goddess Kali; the goddess of love and death."

"Of death, perhaps," muttered back Passepartout, "but of love—that ugly old hag? Never!"

The Parsee made a motion to keep silence.

A group of old fakirs were capering and making a wild ado round the statue; these were striped with ocher, and covered with cuts whence their blood issued drop by drop—stupid fanatics, who, in the great Indian ceremonies, still throw themselves under the wheels of Juggernaut. Some Brahmins, clad in all the sumptuousness of Oriental apparel, and leading a woman who faltered at every step, followed. This woman was young, and as fair as a European. Her head and neck, shoulders, ears, arms, hands, and toes were loaded down with jewels and gems with bracelets, earrings, and rings; while a tunic bordered with gold, and covered with a light muslin robe, betrayed the outline of her form.

The guards who followed the young woman presented a violent contrast to her, armed as they were with naked sabers hung at their waists, and long damascened pistols, and bearing a corpse on a palanquin. It was the body of an old man, gorgeously arrayed in the habiliments of a rajah, wearing, as in life, a turban embroidered with pearls, a robe of tissue of silk and gold, a scarf of cashmere sewed with diamonds, and the magnificent weapons of a Hindoo prince. Next came the musicians and a rear guard of capering fakirs, whose cries sometimes drowned the noise of the instruments; these closed the procession.

Sir Francis watched the procession with a sad countenance, and, turning to the guide, said, "A suttee."

The Parsee nodded, and put his finger to his lips. The procession slowly wound under the trees, and soon its last ranks disappeared in the depths of the wood. The songs gradually died away; occasionally cries were heard in the distance, until at last all was silence again.

Phileas Fogg had heard what Sir Francis said, and, as soon as the procession had disappeared, asked: "What is a suttee?"

"A suttee," returned the general, "is a human sacrifice, but a voluntary one. The woman you have just seen will be burned tomorrow at the dawn of day."

"Oh, the scoundrels!" cried Passepartout, who could not repress his indignation.

"And the corpse?" asked Mr. Fogg.

"Is that of the prince, her husband," said the guide; "an independent rajah of Bundelcund."

"Is it possible," resumed Phileas Fogg, his voice betraying not the least emotion, "that these barbarous customs still exist in India, and that the English have been unable to put a stop to them?"

"These sacrifices do not occur in the larger portion of India," replied Sir Francis; "but we have no power over these savage territories, and especially here in Bundelcund. The whole district north of the Vindhias is the theater of incessant murders and pillage."

"The poor wretch!" exclaimed Passepartout. "To be burned alive!"

"Yes," returned Sir Francis, "burned alive. And, if she were not, you cannot conceive what treatment she would be obliged to submit to from her relatives. They would shave off her hair, feed her on a scanty allowance of rice, treat her with contempt; she would be looked upon as an unclean creature, and would die in some corner, like a scurvy dog. The prospect of so frightful an existence drives these poor creatures to the sacrifice much more than love or religious fanaticism. Sometimes, however, the sacrifice is really voluntary, and it requires the active interference of the government to prevent it. Several years ago, when I was living at Bombay, a young widow asked permission of the governor to be burned along with her husband's body; but, as you may imagine, he refused. The woman left the town, took refuge with an independent rajah, and there carried out her self-devoted purpose."

While Sir Francis was speaking, the guide shook his head several times, and now said: "The sacrifice which will take place tomorrow at dawn is not a voluntary one."

"How do you know?"

"Everybody knows about this affair in Bundelcund."

"But the wretched creature did not seem to be making any resistance," observed Sir Francis.

"That was because they had intoxicated her with fumes of hemp and opium."

"But where are they taking her?"

"To the pagoda of Pillaji, two miles from here; she will pass the night there."

"And the sacrifice will take place——"

"Tomorrow, at the first light of dawn."

The guide now led the elephant out of the thicket, and leaped upon his neck. Just at the moment that he was about to urge Kiouni forward with a peculiar whistle, Mr. Fogg stopped him, and, turning to Sir Francis Cromarty, said, "Suppose we save this woman."

"Save the woman, Mr. Fogg!"

"I have yet twelve hours to spare; I can devote them to that."

"Why, you are a man of heart!"

"Sometimes," replied Phileas Fogg, quietly; "when I have the time."

## CHAPTER XIII

### In Which Passepartout Receives New Proof
### that Fortune Favors the Brave

The project was a bold one, full of difficulty, perhaps impracticable. Mr. Fogg was going to risk life, or at least liberty, and therefore the success of his tour. But he did not hesitate, and he found in Sir Francis Cromarty an enthusiastic ally.

As for Passepartout, he was ready for anything that might be proposed. His master's idea charmed him; he perceived a heart, a soul, under that icy exterior. He began to love Phileas Fogg.

There remained the guide: what course would he adopt? Would he not take part with the Indians? In default of his assistance, it was necessary to be assured of his neutrality.

Sir Francis frankly put the question to him.

"Officers," replied the guide, "I am a Parsee, and this woman is a Parsee. Command me as you will."

"Excellent!" said Mr. Fogg.

"However," resumed the guide, "it is certain, not only that we shall risk our lives, but horrible tortures, if we are taken."

"That is foreseen," replied Mr. Fogg. "I think we must wait till night before acting."

"I think so," said the guide.

The worthy Indian then gave some account of the victim, who, he said, was a celebrated beauty of the Parsee race, and the daughter of a wealthy Bombay merchant. She had received a thoroughly English education in that city, and, from her manners and intelligence, would be thought an European. Her name was Aouda. Left an orphan, she was married against her will to the old rajah of Bundelcund; and, knowing the fate that awaited her, she escaped, was retaken, and devoted by the rajah's relatives, who had an interest in her death, to the sacrifice from which it seemed she could not escape.

The Parsee's narrative only confirmed Mr. Fogg and his companions in their generous design. It was decided that the guide should direct the elephant toward the pagoda of Pillaji, which he accordingly approached as quickly as possible. They halted, half an hour afterward, in a copse, some five hundred feet from the pagoda, where they were well concealed; but they could hear the groans and cries of the fakirs distinctly.

They then discussed the means of getting at the victim. The guide was familiar with the pagoda of Pillaji, in which, as he declared, the young woman was imprisoned. Could they enter any of its doors while the whole party of Indians was plunged in a drunken sleep, or was it safer to attempt to make a hole in the walls? This could only be determined at the moment and the place themselves; but it was certain that the abduction must be made that night, and not when, at break of day, the victim was led to her funeral pyre. Then no human intervention could save her.

As soon as night fell, about six o'clock, they decided to make a reconnaissance around the pagoda. The cries of the fakirs were just ceasing; the Indians were in the act of plunging themselves into the drunkenness caused by liquid opium mingled with hemp, and it might be possible to slip between them to the temple itself.

The Parsee, leading the others, noiselessly crept through the wood, and in ten minutes they found themselves on the banks of a small stream, whence, by the light of the rosin torches, they perceived a pyre of wood, on the top of which lay the embalmed body of the rajah, which was to be burned with his wife. The pagoda, whose minarets loomed above the trees in the deepening dusk, stood a hundred steps away.

"Come!" whispered the guide.

He slipped more cautiously than ever through the brush, followed by his companions; the silence around was only broken by the low murmuring of the wind among the branches.

Soon the Parsee stopped on the borders of the glade, which was lit up by the torches. The ground was covered by groups of the Indians, motionless in their drunken sleep; it seemed a battlefield strewn with the dead. Men, women, and children lay together.

In the background, among the trees, the pagoda of Pillaji loomed distinctly. Much to the guide's disappointment, the guards of the rajah, lighted by torches, were watching at the doors and marching to and fro with naked sabers; probably the priests, too, were watching within.

The Parsee, now convinced that it was impossible to force an entrance to the temple, advanced no farther, but led his companions back again. Phileas Fogg and Sir Francis Cromarty also saw that nothing could be attempted in that direction. They stopped, and engaged in a whispered colloquy.

"It is only eight now," said the brigadier, "and these guards may also go to sleep."

"It is not impossible," returned the Parsee.

They lay down at the foot of a tree, and waited.

The time seemed long; the guide ever and anon left them to take an observation on the edge of the wood, but the guards watched steadily by the glare of the torches, and a dim light crept through the windows of the pagoda.

They waited till midnight; but no change took place among the guards, and it became apparent that their yielding to sleep could not be counted on. The other plan must be carried out; an opening in the walls of the pagoda must be made. It remained to ascertain whether the priests were watching by the side of their victim as assiduously as were the soldiers at the door.

After a last consultation, the guide announced that he was ready for the attempt, and advanced, followed by the others. They took a roundabout way, so as to get at the pagoda on the rear. They reached the walls about half past twelve, without having met anyone; here there was no guard, nor were there either windows or doors.

The night was dark. The moon, on the wane, scarcely left the horizon, and was covered with heavy clouds; the height of the trees deepened the darkness.

It was not enough to reach the walls; an opening in them must be accomplished, and to attain this purpose the party only had their pocketknives. Happily the temple walls were built of brick and wood, which could be penetrated with little difficulty; after one brick had been taken out, the rest would yield easily.

They set noiselessly to work, and the Parsee on one side and Passepartout on the other began to loosen the bricks so as to make an aperture two feet wide. They were getting on rapidly, when suddenly a cry was heard in the interior of the temple, followed almost instantly by other cries replying from the outside. Passepartout and the guide stopped. Had they been heard? Was the alarm being given? Common prudence urged them to retire, and they did so, followed by Phileas Fogg and Sir Francis. They again hid themselves in the wood, and waited till the disturbance, whatever it might be, ceased, holding themselves ready to resume their attempt without delay. But, awkwardly enough, the guards now appeared at the rear of the temple, and there installed themselves, in readiness to prevent a surprise.

It would be difficult to describe the disappointment of the party, thus interrupted in their work. They could not now reach the victim; how, then, could they save her? Sir Francis shook his fists, Passepartout was beside himself, and the guide gnashed his teeth with rage. The tranquil Fogg waited, without betraying any emotion.

"We have nothing to do but to go away," whispered Sir Francis.

"Nothing but to go away," echoed the guide.

"Stop," said Fogg. "I am only due at Allahabad tomorrow before noon."

"But what can you hope to do?" asked Sir Francis. "In a few hours it will be daylight, and——"

"The chance which now seems lost may present itself at the last moment."

Sir Francis would have liked to read Phileas Fogg's eyes. What was this cool Englishman thinking of? Was he planning to make a rush for the young woman at the very moment of the sacrifice, and boldly snatch her from her executioners?

This would be utter folly, and it was hard to admit that Fogg was such a fool. Sir Francis consented, however, to remain to the end of this terrible drama. The guide led them to the rear of the glade, where they were able to observe the sleeping groups.

Meanwhile Passepartout, who had perched himself on the lower branches of a tree, was resolving an idea which had at first struck him like a flash, and which was now firmly lodged in his brain.

He had commenced by saying to himself, "What folly!" and then he repeated, "Why not, after all? It's a chance, perhaps the only one; and with such sots!" Thinking thus, he slipped, with the suppleness of a serpent, to the lowest branches, the ends of which bent almost to the ground.

The hours passed, and the lighter shades now announced the approach of day, though it was not yet light. This was the moment. The slumbering multitude became animated, the tambourines sounded, songs and cries arose; the hour of the sacrifice had come. The doors of the pagoda swung open, and a bright light escaped from its interior, in the midst of which Mr. Fogg and Sir Francis espied the victim. She seemed, having shaken off the stupor of intoxication, to be striving to escape from her executioner. Sir Francis's heart throbbed; and, convulsively seizing Mr. Fogg's hand, found in it an open knife. Just at this moment the crowd began to move. The young woman had again fallen into a stupor caused by the fumes of hemp, and passed among the fakirs, who escorted her with their wild, religious cries.

Phileas Fogg and his companions, mingling in the rear ranks of the crowd, followed; and in two minutes they reached the banks of the stream, and stopped fifty paces from the pyre, upon which still lay the rajah's corpse. In the semiobscurity they saw the victim, quite senseless, stretched out beside her husband's body. Then a torch was brought, and the wood, heavily soaked with oil, instantly took fire.

At this moment Sir Francis and the guide seized Phileas Fogg, who, in an instant of mad generosity, was about to rush upon the pyre. But he had quickly pushed them aside, when the whole scene suddenly changed. A cry of terror arose. The whole multitude prostrated themselves, terror-stricken, on the ground.

The old rajah was not dead, then, since he rose of a sudden, like a specter, took up his wife in his arms, and descended from the pyre in the midst of the clouds of smoke, which only heightened his ghostly appearance.

Fakirs and soldiers and priests, seized with instant terror, lay there, with their faces on the ground, not daring to lift their eyes and behold such a prodigy.

The inanimate victim was borne along by the vigorous arms which supported her, and which she did not seem in the least to burden. Mr. Fogg and Sir Francis stood erect, the Parsee bowed his head, and Passepartout was, no doubt, scarcely less stupefied.

The resuscitated rajah approached Sir Francis and Mr. Fogg, and, in an abrupt tone, said, "Let us be off!"

It was Passepartout himself, who had slipped upon the pyre in the midst of the smoke and, profiting by the still-overhanging darkness, had delivered the young woman from death! It was Passepartout who, playing his part with a happy audacity, had passed through the crowd amid the general terror.

A moment after all four of the party had disappeared in the woods, and the elephant was bearing them away at a rapid pace. But the cries and noise, and a ball which whizzed through Phileas Fogg's hat, apprised them that the trick had been discovered.

The old rajah's body, indeed, now appeared upon the burning pyre; and the priests, recovered from their terror, perceived that an abduction had taken place. They hastened into the forest, followed by the soldiers, who fired a volley after the fugitives; but the latter rapidly increased the distance between them, and ere long found themselves beyond the reach of the bullets and arrows.

# CHAPTER XIV

### IN WHICH PHILEAS FOGG DESCENDS THE WHOLE LENGTH OF THE BEAUTIFUL VALLEY OF THE GANGES WITHOUT EVER THINKING OF SEEING IT

The rash exploit had been accomplished; and for an hour Passepartout laughed gaily at his success. Sir Francis pressed the worthy fellow's hand, and his master said, "Well done!" which, from him, was high commendation; to which Passepartout replied that all the credit of the affair belonged to Mr. Fogg. As for him, he had only been struck with a "queer" idea; and he laughed to think that for a few moments he, Passepartout, the ex-gymnast, ex-sergeant fireman, had been the spouse of a charming woman, a venerable, embalmed rajah! As for the young Indian woman, she had been unconscious throughout of what was passing, and now, wrapped up in a traveling blanket, was reposing in one of the howdahs.

The elephant, thanks to the skillful guidance of the Parsee, was advancing rapidly through the still-darksome forest, and, an hour after leaving the pagoda, had crossed a vast plain. They made a halt at seven o'clock, the young woman being still in a state of complete prostration. The guide made her drink a little brandy and water, but the drowsiness which stupefied her could not yet be shaken off. Sir Francis, who was familiar with the effects of the intoxication produced by the fumes of hemp, reassured his companions on her account. But he was more disturbed at the prospect of her future fate. He told Phileas Fogg that, should Aouda remain in India, she would inevitably fall again into the hands of her executioners. These fanatics were scattered throughout the county, and would, despite the English police, recover their victim at Madras, Bombay, or Calcutta. She would only be safe by quitting India forever.

Phileas Fogg replied that he would reflect upon the matter.

The station at Allahabad was reached about ten o'clock, and, the interrupted line of railway being resumed, would enable them to reach Calcutta in less than twenty-four hours. Phileas Fogg would thus be able to arrive in time to take the steamer which left Calcutta the next day, October 25th, at noon, for Hong Kong.

The young woman was placed in one of the waiting rooms of the station, while Passepartout was charged with purchasing for her various articles of toilet, a dress, shawl, and some furs, for which his master gave him unlimited credit. Passepartout started off forthwith, and found himself in the streets of Allahabad, that is, the City of God, one of the most venerated in India, being built at the junction of the two sacred rivers, Ganges and Jumna, the waters of which attract pilgrims from every part of the peninsula. The Ganges, according to the legends of the Ramayana, rises in heaven, whence, owing to Brahma's agency, it descends to the earth.

Passepartout made it a point, as he made his purchases, to take a good look at the city. It was formerly defended by a noble fort, which has since become a state prison; its commerce has dwindled away, and Passepartout in vain looked about him for such a bazaar as he used to frequent in Regent Street. At last he came upon an elderly, crusty Jew who sold secondhand articles, and from whom he purchased a dress of Scotch stuff, a large mantle, and a fine otter-skin pelisse, for which he did not hesitate to pay seventy-five pounds. He then returned triumphantly to the station.

The influence to which the priests of Pillaji had subjected Aouda began gradually to yield, and she became more herself, so that her fine eyes resumed all their soft Indian expression.

When the poet-king, Ucaf Uddaul, celebrates the charms of the queen of Ahmehnagara, he speaks thus:

"Her shining tresses, divided in two parts, encircle the harmonious contour of her white and delicate cheeks, brilliant in their glow and freshness. Her ebony brows have the form and charm of the bow of Kama, the god of love, and beneath her long silken lashes the purest reflections and a celestial light swim, as in the sacred lakes of Himalaya, in the black pupils of her great clear eyes. Her teeth, fine, equal, and white, glitter between her smiling lips like dewdrops in a passionflower's half-enveloped breast. Her delicately formed ears, her vermilion hands, her little feet, curved and tender as the lotus bud, glitter with the brilliancy of the loveliest pearls of Ceylon, the most dazzling diamonds of Golconda. Her narrow and supple waist, which a hand may clasp around, sets forth the outline of her rounded figure and the beauty of her bosom, where youth in its flower displays the wealth of its treasures; and beneath the silken folds of her tunic she seems to have been modeled in pure silver by the godlike hand of Vicvarcarma, the immortal sculptor."

It is enough to say, without applying this poetical rhapsody to Aouda, that she was a charming woman, in all the European acceptation of the phrase. She spoke English with great purity, and the guide had not exaggerated in saying that the young Parsee had been transformed by her bringing up.

The train was about to start from Allahabad, and Mr. Fogg proceeded to pay the guide the price agreed upon for his service, and not a farthing more; which astonished Passepartout, who remembered all that his master owed to the guide's devotion. He had, indeed, risked his life in the adventure at Pillaji, and, if he should be caught afterward by the Indians, he would with difficulty escape their vengeance. Kiouni, also, must be disposed of. What should be done with the elephant, which had been so dearly purchased? Phileas Fogg had already determined this question.

"Parsee," said he to the guide, "you have been serviceable and devoted. I have paid for your service, but not for your devotion. Would you like to have this elephant? He is yours."

The guide's eyes glistened.

"Your honor is giving me a fortune!" cried he.

"Take him, guide," returned Mr. Fogg, "and I shall still be your debtor."

"Good!" exclaimed Passepartout. "Take him, friend. Kiouni is a brave and faithful beast." And, going up to the elephant, he gave him several lumps of sugar, saying, "Here, Kiouni, here, here."

The elephant grunted out his satisfaction, and, clasping Passepartout around the waist with his trunk, lifted him as high as his head. Passepartout, not in the least alarmed, caressed the animal, which replaced him gently on the ground.

Soon after, Phileas Fogg, Sir Francis Cromarty, and Passepartout, installed in a carriage with Aouda, who had the best seat, were whirling at full speed toward Benares. It was a run of eighty miles, and was accomplished in two hours. During the journey, the young woman fully recovered her senses. What was her astonishment to find herself in this carriage, on the railway, dressed in European habiliments, and with travelers who were quite strangers to her! Her companions first set about fully reviving her with a little liquor, and then Sir Francis narrated to her what had passed, dwelling upon the courage with which Phileas Fogg had not hesitated to risk his life to save her, and recounting the happy sequel of the venture, the result of Passepartout's rash idea. Mr. Fogg said nothing; while Passepartout, abashed, kept repeating that "it wasn't worth telling."

Aouda pathetically thanked her deliverers, rather with tears than words; her fine eyes interpreted her gratitude better than her lips. Then, as her thoughts strayed back to the scene of the sacrifice, and recalled the dangers which still menaced her, she shuddered with terror.

Phileas Fogg understood what was passing in Aouda's mind, and offered, in order to reassure her, to escort her to Hong Kong, where she might remain safely until the affair was hushed up—an offer which she eagerly and gratefully accepted. She had, it seems, a Parsee relation, who was one of the principal merchants of Hong Kong, which is wholly an English city, though on an island on the Chinese coast.

At half past twelve the train stopped at Benares. The Brahmin legends assert that this city is built on the site of the ancient Casi, which, like Mahomet's tomb, was once suspended between heaven and earth; though the Benares of today, which the Orientalists call the Athens of India, stands quite unpoetically on the solid earth, Passepartout caught glimpses of its brick houses and clay huts, giving an aspect of desolation to the place, as the train entered it.

Benares was Sir Francis Cromarty's destination, the troops he was rejoining being encamped some miles northward of the city. He bade adieu to Phileas Fogg, wishing him all success, and expressing the hope that he would come that way again in a less original but more profitable fashion. Mr. Fogg lightly pressed him by the hand. The parting of Aouda, who did not forget what she owed to Sir Francis, betrayed more warmth; and, as for Passepartout, he received a hearty shake of the hand from the gallant general.

The railway, on leaving Benares, passed for a while along the valley of the Ganges. Through the windows of their carriage the travelers had glimpses of the diversified landscape of Behar, with its mountains clothed in verdure, its fields of barley, wheat, and corn, its jungles peopled with green alligators, its neat villages, and its still thickly leaved forests. Elephants were bathing in the waters of the sacred river, and groups of Indians, despite the advanced season and chilly air, were performing solemnly their pious ablutions. These were fervent Brahmins, the bitterest foes of Buddhism, their deities being Vishnu, the solar god, Shiva, the divine impersonation of natural forces, and Brahma, the supreme ruler of priests and legislators. What would these divinities think of India, anglicized as it is today, with steamers whistling and scudding along the Ganges, frightening the gulls which float upon its surface, the turtles swarming along its banks, and the faithful dwelling upon its borders?

The panorama passed before their eyes like a flash, save when the steam concealed it fitfully from the view; the travelers could scarcely discern the fort of Chupenie, twenty miles southwestward from Benares, the ancient stronghold of the rajahs of Behar; or Ghazipur and its famous rosewater factories; or the tomb of Lord Cornwallis, rising on the left bank of the Ganges; the fortified town of Buxar, or Patna, a large manufacturing and trading place, where is held the principal opium market of India; or Monghir, a more than European town, for it is as English as Manchester or Birmingham, with its iron foundries, edgetool factories, and high chimneys puffing clouds of black smoke heavenward.

Night came on; the train passed on at full speed, in the midst of the roaring of the tigers, bears, and wolves which fled before the locomotive; and the marvels of Bengal, Golconda ruined Gour, Murshedabad, the ancient capital, Burdwan, Hugly, and the French town of Chandernagor, where Passepartout would have been proud to see his country's flag flying, were hidden from their view in the darkness.

Calcutta was reached at seven in the morning, and the packet left for Hong Kong at noon; so that Phileas Fogg had five hours before him.

According to his journal, he was due at Calcutta on the 25th of October, and that was the exact date of his actual arrival. He was therefore neither behindhand nor ahead of time. The two days gained between London and Bombay had been lost, as has been seen, in the journey across India. But it is not to be supposed that Phileas Fogg regretted them.

# CHAPTER XV

## In Which the Bag of Banknotes Disgorges
## Some Thousands of Pounds More

The train entered the station, and Passepartout, jumping out first, was followed by Mr. Fogg, who assisted his fair companion to descend. Phileas Fogg intended to proceed at once to the Hong Kong steamer, in order to get Aouda comfortably settled for the voyage. He was unwilling to leave her while they were still on dangerous ground.

Just as he was leaving the station a policeman came up to him and said, "Mr. Phileas Fogg?"

"I am he."

"Is this man your servant?" added the policeman, pointing to Passepartout.

"Yes."

"Be so good, both of you, as to follow me."

Mr. Fogg betrayed no surprise whatever. The policeman was a representative of the law, and law is sacred to an Englishman. Passepartout tried to reason about the matter, but the policeman tapped him with his stick, and Mr. Fogg made him a signal to obey.

"May this young lady go with us?" asked he.

"She may," replied the policeman.

Mr. Fogg, Aouda, and Passepartout were conducted to a palkigahri, a sort of four-wheeled carriage, drawn by two horses, in which they took their places and were driven away. No one spoke during the twenty minutes which elapsed before they reached their destination. They first passed through the "black town," with its narrow streets, its miserable, dirty huts, and squalid population; then through the "European town," which presented a relief in its bright brick mansions, shaded by coconut trees and bristling with masts, where, although it was early morning, elegantly dressed horsemen and handsome equipages were passing back and forth.

The carriage stopped before a modest-looking house, which, however, did not have the appearance of a private mansion. The policeman having requested his prisoners—for so, truly, they might be called—to descend, conducted them into a room with barred windows, and said: "You will appear before Judge Obadiah at half past eight."

He then retired, and closed the door.

"Why, we are prisoners!" exclaimed Passepartout, falling into a chair.

Aouda, with an emotion she tried to conceal, said to Mr. Fogg: "Sir, you must leave me to my fate! It is on my account that you receive this treatment, it is for having saved me!"

Phileas Fogg contented himself with saying that it was impossible. It was quite unlikely that he should be arrested for preventing a suttee. The complainants would not dare present themselves with such a charge. There was some mistake. Moreover, he would not, in any event, abandon Aouda, but would escort her to Hong Kong.

"But the steamer leaves at noon!" observed Passepartout, nervously.

"We shall be on board by noon," replied his master, placidly.

It was said so positively that Passepartout could not help muttering to himself, "Parbleu, that's certain! Before noon we shall be on board." But he was by no means reassured.

At half past eight the door opened, the policeman appeared, and, requesting them to follow him, led the way to an adjoining hall. It was evidently a courtroom, and a crowd of Europeans and natives already occupied the rear of the apartment.

Mr. Fogg and his two companions took their places on a bench opposite the desks of the magistrate and his clerk. Immediately after, Judge Obadiah, a fat, round man, followed by the clerk, entered. He proceeded to take down a wig which was hanging on a nail, and put it hurriedly on his head.

"The first case," said he. Then, putting his hand to his head, he exclaimed, "Heh! This is not my wig!"

"No, your worship," returned the clerk, "it is mine."

"My dear Mr. Oysterpuff, how can a judge give a wise sentence in a clerk's wig?"

The wigs were exchanged.

Passepartout was getting nervous, for the hands on the face of the big clock over the judge seemed to go around with terrible rapidity.

"The first case," repeated Judge Obadiah.

"Phileas Fogg?" demanded Oysterpuff.

"I am here," replied Mr. Fogg.

"Passepartout?"

"Present," responded Passepartout.

"Good," said the judge. "You have been looked for, prisoners, for two days on the trains from Bombay."

"But of what are we accused?" asked Passepartout, impatiently.

"You are about to be informed."

"I am an English subject, sir," said Mr. Fogg, "and I have the right—"

"Have you been ill treated?"

"Not at all."

"Very well; let the complainants come in."

A door was swung open by order of the judge, and three Indian priests entered.

"That's it," muttered Passepartout; "these are the rogues who were going to burn our young lady."

The priests took their places in front of the judge, and the clerk proceeded to read in a loud voice a complaint of sacrilege against Phileas Fogg and his servant, who were accused of having violated a place held consecrated by the Brahmin religion.

"You hear the charge?" asked the judge.

"Yes, sir," replied Mr. Fogg, consulting his watch, "and I admit it."

"You admit it?"

"I admit it, and I wish to hear these priests admit, in their turn, what they were going to do at the pagoda of Pillaji."

The priests looked at each other; they did not seem to understand what was said.

"Yes," cried Passepartout, warmly; "at the pagoda of Pillaji, where they were on the point of burning their victim."

The judge stared with astonishment, and the priests were stupefied.

"What victim?" said Judge Obadiah. "Burn whom? In Bombay itself?"

"Bombay?" cried Passepartout.

"Certainly. We are not talking of the pagoda of Pillaji, but of the pagoda of Malabar Hill, at Bombay."

"And as a proof," added the clerk, "here are the desecrator's very shoes, which he left behind him."

Whereupon he placed a pair of shoes on his desk.

"My shoes!" cried Passepartout, in his surprise permitting this imprudent exclamation to escape him.

The confusion of master and man, who had quite forgotten the affair at Bombay, for which they were now detained at Calcutta, may be imagined.

Fix, the detective, had foreseen the advantage which Passepartout's escapade gave him, and, delaying his departure for twelve hours, had consulted the priests of Malabar Hill. Knowing that the English authorities dealt very severely with this kind of misdemeanor, he promised them a goodly sum in damages, and sent them forward to Calcutta by the next train. Owing to the delay caused by the rescue of the young widow, Fix and the priests reached the Indian capital before Mr. Fogg and his servant, the magistrates having been already warned by a dispatch to arrest them should they arrive. Fix's disappointment when he learned that Phileas Fogg had not made his appearance in Calcutta may be imagined. He made up his mind that the robber had stopped somewhere on the route and taken refuge in the southern provinces. For twenty-four hours Fix watched the station with feverish anxiety; at last he was rewarded by seeing Mr. Fogg and Passepartout arrive, accompanied by a young woman, whose presence he was wholly at a loss to explain. He hastened for a policeman; and this was how the party came to be arrested and brought before Judge Obadiah.

Had Passepartout been a little less preoccupied, he would have espied the detective ensconced in a corner of the courtroom, watching the proceedings with an interest easily understood; for the warrant had failed to reach him at Calcutta, as it had done at Bombay and Suez.

Judge Obadiah had unfortunately caught Passepartout's rash exclamation, which the poor fellow would have given the world to recall.

"The facts are admitted?" asked the judge.

"Admitted," replied Mr. Fogg, coldly.

"Inasmuch," resumed the judge, "as the English law protects equally and sternly the religions of the Indian people, and as the man Passepartout has admitted that he violated the sacred pagoda of Malabar Hill, at Bombay, on the 20th of October, I condemn the said Passepartout to imprisonment for fifteen days and a fine of three hundred pounds."

"Three hundred pounds!" cried Passepartout, startled at the largeness of the sum.

"Silence!" shouted the constable.

"And inasmuch," continued the judge, "as it is not proved that the act was not done by the connivance of the master with the servant, and as the master in any case must be held responsible for the acts of his paid servant, I condemn Phileas Fogg to a week's imprisonment and a fine of one hundred and fifty pounds."

Fix rubbed his hands softly with satisfaction; if Phileas Fogg could be detained in Calcutta a week, it would be more than time for the warrant to arrive. Passepartout was stupefied. This sentence ruined his master. A wager of twenty thousand pounds lost, because he, like a precious fool, had gone into that abominable pagoda!

Phileas Fogg, as self-composed as if the judgment did not in the least concern him, did not even lift his eyebrows while it was being pronounced. Just as the clerk was calling the next case, he rose, and said, "I offer bail."

"You have that right," returned the judge.

Fix's blood ran cold, but he resumed his composure when he heard the judge announce that the bail required for each prisoner would be one thousand pounds.

"I will pay it at once," said Mr. Fogg, taking a roll of bank bills from the carpetbag, which Passepartout had by him, and placing them on the clerk's desk.

"This sum will be restored to you upon your release from prison," said the judge. "Meanwhile, you are liberated on bail."

"Come!" said Phileas Fogg to his servant.

"But let them at least give me back my shoes!" cried Passepartout angrily.

"Ah, these are pretty dear shoes!" he muttered, as they were handed to him. "More than a thousand pounds apiece; besides, they pinch my feet."

Mr. Fogg, offering his arm to Aouda, then departed, followed by the crestfallen Passepartout. Fix still nourished hopes that the robber would not, after all, leave the two thousand pounds behind him, but would decide to serve out his week in jail, and issued forth on Mr. Fogg's traces. That gentleman took a carriage, and the party were soon landed on one of the quays.

The *Rangoon* was moored half a mile off in the harbor, its signal of departure hoisted at the masthead. Eleven o'clock was striking; Mr. Fogg was an hour in advance of time. Fix saw them leave the carriage and push off in a boat for the steamer, and stamped his feet with disappointment.

"The rascal is off, after all!" he exclaimed. "Two thousand pounds sacrificed! He's as prodigal as a thief! I'll follow him to the end of the world if necessary; but, at the rate he is going on, the stolen money will soon be exhausted."

The detective was not far wrong in making this conjecture. Since leaving London, what with traveling expenses, bribes, the purchase of the elephant, bails, and fines, Mr. Fogg had already spent more than five thousand pounds on the way, and the percentage of the sum recovered from the bank robber promised to the detectives was rapidly diminishing.

# CHAPTER XVI

### IN WHICH FIX DOES NOT SEEM TO UNDERSTAND
### IN THE LEAST WHAT IS SAID TO HIM

The *Rangoon*—one of the Peninsular and Oriental Company's boats plying in the Chinese and Japanese seas—was a screw steamer, built of iron, weighing about seventeen hundred and seventy tons, and with engines of four hundred horsepower. She was as fast, but not as well fitted up, as the *Mongolia*, and Aouda was not as comfortably provided for on board of her as Phileas Fogg could have wished. However, the trip from Calcutta to Hong Kong only comprised some three thousand five hundred miles, occupying from ten to twelve days, and the young woman was not difficult to please.

During the first days of the journey Aouda became better acquainted with her protector, and constantly gave evidence of her deep gratitude for what he had done. The phlegmatic gentleman listened to her, apparently at least, with coldness, neither his voice nor his manner betraying the slightest emotion; but he seemed to be always on the watch that nothing should be wanting to Aouda's comfort. He visited her regularly each day at certain hours, not so much to talk himself, as to sit and hear her talk. He treated her with the strictest politeness, but with the precision of an automaton, the movements of which had been arranged for this purpose. Aouda did not quite know what to make of him, though Passepartout had given her some hints of his master's eccentricity, and made her smile by telling her of the wager which was sending him round the world. After all, she owed Phileas Fogg her life, and she always regarded him through the exalting medium of her gratitude.

Aouda confirmed the Parsee guide's narrative of her touching history. She did, indeed, belong to the highest of the native races of India. Many of the Parsee merchants have made great fortunes there by dealing in cotton; and one of them, Sir Jametsee Jeejeebhoy, was made a baronet by the English government. Aouda was a relative of this great man, and it was his cousin, Jeejeeh, whom she hoped to join at Hong Kong. Whether she would find a protector in him she could not tell; but Mr. Fogg essayed to calm her anxieties, and to assure her that everything would be mathematically—he used the very word—arranged. Aouda fastened her great eyes, "clear as the sacred lakes of the Himalaya," upon him; but the intractable Fogg, as reserved as ever, did not seem at all inclined to throw himself into this lake.

The first few days of the voyage passed prosperously, amid favorable weather and propitious winds, and they soon came in sight of the great Andaman, the principal of the islands in the Bay of Bengal, with its picturesque Saddle Peak, two thousand four hundred feet high, looming above the waters. The steamer passed along near the shores, but the savage Papuans, who are in the lowest scale of humanity, but are not, as has been asserted, cannibals, did not make their appearance.

The panorama of the islands, as they steamed by them, was superb. Vast forests of palms, arecs, bamboo, teakwood, of the gigantic mimosa, and treelike ferns covered the foreground, while behind, the graceful outlines of the mountains were traced against the sky; and along the coasts swarmed by thousands the precious swallows whose nests furnish a luxurious dish to the tables of the Celestial Empire. The varied landscape afforded by the Andaman Islands was soon passed, however, and the *Rangoon* rapidly approached the Straits of Malacca, which gave access to the China seas.

What was detective Fix, so unluckily drawn on from country to country, doing all this while? He had managed to embark on the *Rangoon* at Calcutta without being seen by Passepartout, after leaving orders that, if the warrant should arrive, it should be forwarded to him at Hong Kong; and he hoped to conceal his presence to the end of the voyage. It would have been difficult to explain why he was on board without awakening Passepartout's suspicions, who thought him still at Bombay. But necessity impelled him, nevertheless, to renew his acquaintance with the worthy servant, as will be seen.

All the detective's hopes and wishes were now centered on Hong Kong; for the steamer's stay at Singapore would be too brief to enable him to take any steps there. The arrest must be made at Hong Kong, or the robber would probably escape him forever. Hong Kong was the last English ground on which he would set foot; beyond, China, Japan, America offered to Fogg an almost certain refuge. If the warrant should at last make its appearance at Hong Kong, Fix could arrest him and give him into the hands of the local police, and there would be no further trouble. But beyond Hong Kong, a simple warrant would be of no avail; an extradition warrant would be necessary, and that would result in delays and obstacles, of which the rascal would take advantage to elude justice.

Fix thought over these probabilities during the long hours which he spent in his cabin, and kept repeating to himself, "Now, either the warrant will be at Hong Kong, in which case I shall arrest my man, or it will not be there; and this time it is absolutely necessary that I should delay his departure. I have failed at Bombay, and I have failed at Calcutta; if I fail at Hong Kong, my reputation is lost: Cost what it may, I *must succeed!* But how shall I prevent his departure, if that should turn out to be my last resource?"

Fix made up his mind that, if worst came to worst, he would make a confidant of Passepartout, and tell him what kind of a fellow his master really was. That Passepartout was not Fogg's accomplice, he was very certain. The servant, enlightened by his disclosure, and afraid of being himself implicated in the crime, would doubtless become an ally of the detective. But this method was a dangerous one, only to be employed when everything else had failed. A word from Passepartout to his master would ruin all. The detective was therefore in a sore strait. But suddenly a new idea struck him. The presence of Aouda on the *Rangoon*, in company with Phileas Fogg, gave him new material for reflection.

Who was this woman? What combination of events had made her Fogg's traveling companion? They had evidently met somewhere between Bombay and Calcutta; but where? Had they met accidentally, or had Fogg gone into the interior purposely in quest of this charming damsel? Fix was fairly puzzled. He asked himself whether there had not been a wicked elopement; and this idea so impressed itself upon his mind that he determined to make use of the supposed intrigue. Whether the young woman were married or not, he would be able to create such difficulties for Mr. Fogg at Hong Kong that he could not escape by paying any amount of money.

But could he even wait till they reached Hong Kong? Fogg had an abominable way of jumping from one boat to another, and, before anything could be effected, might get full under way again for Yokohama.

Fix decided that he must warn the English authorities, and signal the *Rangoon* before her arrival. This was easy to do, since the steamer stopped at Singapore, whence there is a telegraphic wire to Hong Kong. He finally resolved, moreover, before acting more positively, to question Passepartout. It would not be difficult to make him talk; and, as there was no time to lose, Fix prepared to make himself known.

It was now the 30th of October, and on the following day the *Rangoon* was due at Singapore.

Fix emerged from his cabin and went on deck. Passepartout was promenading up and down in the forward part of the steamer. The detective rushed forward with every appearance of extreme surprise, and exclaimed, "You here, on the *Rangoon?*"

"What, Monsieur Fix, are you on board?" returned the really astonished Passepartout, recognizing his crony of the *Mongolia*. "Why, I left you at Bombay, and here you are, on the way to Hong Kong! Are you going round the world too?"

"No, no," replied Fix; "I shall stop at Hong Kong—at least for some days."

"Hum!" said Passepartout, who seemed for an instant perplexed. "But how is it I have not seen you on board since we left Calcutta?"

"Oh, a trifle of seasickness—I've been staying in my berth. The Gulf of Bengal does not agree with me as well as the Indian Ocean. And how is Mr. Fogg?"

"As well and as punctual as ever, not a day behind time! But, Monsieur Fix, you don't know that we have a young lady with us."

"A young lady?" replied the detective, not seeming to comprehend what was said.

Passepartout thereupon recounted Aouda's history, the affair at the Bombay pagoda, the purchase of the elephant for two thousand pounds, the rescue, the arrest, and sentence of the Calcutta court, and the restoration of Mr. Fogg and himself to liberty on bail. Fix, who was familiar with the last events, seemed to be equally ignorant of all that Passepartout related; and the latter was charmed to find so interested a listener.

"But does your master propose to carry this young woman to Europe?"

"Not at all. We are simply going to place her under the protection of one of her relatives, a rich merchant at Hong Kong."

"Nothing to be done there," said Fix to himself, concealing his disappointment. "A glass of gin, Mr. Passepartout?"

"Willingly, Monsieur Fix. We must at least have a friendly glass on board the *Rangoon.*"

## CHAPTER XVII

SHOWING WHAT HAPPENED ON THE VOYAGE
FROM SINGAPORE TO HONG KONG

The detective and Passepartout met often on deck after this interview, though Fix was reserved, and did not attempt to induce his companion to divulge any more facts concerning Mr. Fogg. He caught a glimpse of that mysterious gentleman once or twice; but Mr. Fogg usually confined himself to the cabin, where he kept Aouda company, or, according to his inveterate habit, took a hand at whist.

Passepartout began very seriously to conjecture what strange chance kept Fix still on the route that his master was pursuing. It was really worth considering why this certainly very amiable and complacent person, whom he had first met at Suez, had then encountered on board the *Mongolia*, who disembarked at Bombay, which he announced as his destination, and now turned up so unexpectedly on the *Rangoon*, was following Mr. Fogg's tracks step by step. What was Fix's object? Passepartout was ready to wager his Indian shoes—which he religiously preserved—that Fix would also leave Hong Kong at the same time with them, and probably on the same steamer.

Passepartout might have cudgeled his brain for a century without hitting upon the real object which the detective had in view. He never could have imagined that Phileas Fogg was being tracked as a robber around the globe. But, as it is in human nature to attempt the solution of every mystery, Passepartout suddenly discovered an explanation of Fix's movements, which was in truth far from unreasonable. Fix, he thought, could only be an agent of Mr. Fogg's friends at the Reform Club, sent to follow him up, and to ascertain that he really went round the world as had been agreed upon.

"It's clear!" repeated the worthy servant to himself, proud of his shrewdness. "He's a spy sent to keep us in view! That isn't quite the thing, either, to be spying Mr. Fogg, who is so honorable a man! Ah, gentlemen of the Reform, this shall cost you dear!"

Passepartout, enchanted with his discovery, resolved to say nothing to his master, lest he should be justly offended at this mistrust on the part of his adversaries. But he determined to chaff Fix, when he had the chance, with mysterious allusions, which, however, need not betray his real suspicions.

During the afternoon of Wednesday, 30th October, the *Rangoon* entered the Strait of Malacca, which separates the peninsula of that name from Sumatra. The mountainous and craggy islets intercepted the beauties of this noble island from the view of the travelers. The *Rangoon* weighed anchor at Singapore the next day at four a.m., to receive coal, having gained half a day on the prescribed time of her arrival. Phileas Fogg noted this gain in his journal, and then, accompanied by Aouda, who betrayed a desire for a walk on shore, disembarked.

Fix, who suspected Mr. Fogg's every movement, followed them cautiously, without being himself perceived; while Passepartout, laughing in his sleeve at Fix's maneuvers, went about his usual errands.

The island of Singapore is not imposing in aspect, for there are no mountains; yet its appearance is not without attractions. It is a park checkered by pleasant highways and avenues. A handsome carriage, drawn by a sleek pair of New Holland horses, carried Phileas Fogg and Aouda into the midst of rows of palms with brilliant foliage, and of clove trees, whereof the cloves form the heart of a half-open flower. Pepper plants replaced the prickly hedges of European fields; sago bushes, large ferns with gorgeous branches, varied the aspect of this tropical clime; while nutmeg trees in full foliage filled the air with a penetrating perfume. Agile and grinning bands of monkeys skipped about in the trees, nor were tigers wanting in the jungles.

After a drive of two hours through the country, Aouda and Mr. Fogg returned to the town, which is a vast collection of heavy-looking, irregular houses, surrounded by charming gardens rich in tropical fruits and plants; and at ten o'clock they reembarked, closely followed by the detective, who had kept them constantly in sight.

Passepartout, who had been purchasing several dozen mangoes—a fruit as large as good-sized apples, of a dark brown color outside and a bright red within, and whose white pulp, melting in the mouth, affords gourmands a delicious sensation—was waiting for them on deck. He was only too glad to offer some mangoes to Aouda, who thanked him very gracefully for them.

At eleven o'clock the *Rangoon* rode out of Singapore harbor, and in a few hours the high mountains of Malacca, with their forests, inhabited by the most beautifully furred tigers in the world, were lost to view. Singapore is distant some thirteen hundred miles from the island of Hong Kong, which is a little English colony near the Chinese coast. Phileas Fogg hoped to accomplish the journey in six days, so as to be in time for the steamer which would leave on the 6th of November for Yokohama, the principal Japanese port.

The *Rangoon* had a large quota of passengers, many of whom disembarked at Singapore, among them a number of Indians, Ceylonese, Chinamen, Malays, and Portuguese, mostly second-class travelers.

The weather, which had hitherto been fine, changed with the last quarter of the moon. The sea rolled heavily, and the wind at intervals rose almost to a storm, but happily blew from the southwest, and thus aided the steamer's progress. The captain as often as possible put up his sails, and under the double action of steam and sail the vessel made rapid progress along the coasts of Anam and Cochin China. Owing to the defective construction of the *Rangoon*, however, unusual precautions became necessary in unfavorable weather; but the loss of time which resulted from this cause, while it nearly drove Passepartout out of his senses, did not seem to affect his master in the least. Passepartout blamed the captain, the engineer, and the crew, and consigned all who were connected with the ship to the land where the pepper grows. Perhaps the thought of the gas, which was remorselessly burning at his expense in Saville Row, had something to do with his hot impatience.

"You are in a great hurry, then," said Fix to him one day, "to reach Hong Kong?"

"A very great hurry!"

"Mr. Fogg, I suppose, is anxious to catch the steamer for Yokohama?"

"Terribly anxious."

"You believe in this journey around the world, then?"

"Absolutely. Don't you, Mr. Fix?"

"I? I don't believe a word of it."

"You're a sly dog!" said Passepartout, winking at him.

This expression rather disturbed Fix, without his knowing why. Had the Frenchman guessed his real purpose? He knew not what to think. But how could Passepartout have discovered that he was a detective? Yet, in speaking as he did, the man evidently meant more than he expressed.

Passepartout went still further the next day; he could not hold his tongue.

"Mr. Fix," said he, in a bantering tone, "shall we be so unfortunate as to lose you when we get to Hong Kong?"

"Why," responded Fix, a little embarrassed, "I don't know; perhaps—"

"Ah, if you would only go on with us! An agent of the Peninsular Company, you know, can't stop on the way! You were only going to Bombay, and here you are in China. America is not far off, and from America to Europe is only a step."

Fix looked intently at his companion, whose countenance was as serene as possible, and laughed with him. But Passepartout persisted in chaffing him by asking him if he made much by his present occupation.

"Yes, and no," returned Fix; "there is good and bad luck in such things. But you must understand that I don't travel at my own expense."

"Oh, I am quite sure of that!" cried Passepartout, laughing heartily.

Fix, fairly puzzled, descended to his cabin and gave himself up to his reflections. He was evidently suspected; somehow or other the Frenchman had found out that he was a detective. But had he told his master? What part was he playing in all this: was he an accomplice or not? Was the game, then, up? Fix spent several hours turning these things over in his mind, sometimes thinking that all was lost, then persuading himself that Fogg was ignorant of his presence, and then undecided what course it was best to take.

Nevertheless, he preserved his coolness of mind, and at last resolved to deal plainly with Passepartout. If he did not find it practicable to arrest Fogg at Hong Kong, and if Fogg made preparations to leave that last foothold of English territory, he, Fix, would tell Passepartout all. Either the servant was the accomplice of his master, and in this case the master knew of his operations, and he should fail; or else the servant knew nothing about the robbery, and then his interest would be to abandon the robber.

Such was the situation between Fix and Passepartout. Meanwhile Phileas Fogg moved about above them in the most majestic and unconscious indifference. He was passing methodically in his orbit around the world, regardless of the lesser stars which gravitated around him. Yet there was nearby what the astronomers would call a disturbing star, which might have produced an agitation in this gentleman's heart. But no! The charms of Aouda failed to act, to Passepartout's great surprise; and the disturbances, if they existed, would have been more difficult to calculate than those of Uranus which led to the discovery of Neptune.

It was every day an increasing wonder to Passepartout, who read in Aouda's eyes the depths of her gratitude to his master. Phileas Fogg, though brave and gallant, must be, he thought, quite heartless. As to the sentiment which this journey might have awakened in him, there was clearly no trace of such a thing; while poor Passepartout existed in perpetual reveries.

One day he was leaning on the railing of the engine room, and was observing the engine, when a sudden pitch of the steamer threw the screw out of the water. The steam came hissing out of the valves; and this made Passepartout indignant.

"The valves are not sufficiently charged!" he exclaimed. "We are not going. Oh, these English! If this was an American craft, we should blow up, perhaps, but we should at all events go faster!"

# CHAPTER XVIII

### IN WHICH PHILEAS FOGG, PASSEPARTOUT, AND FIX
### GO EACH ABOUT HIS BUSINESS

The weather was bad during the latter days of the voyage. The wind, obstinately remaining in the northwest, blew a gale, and retarded the steamer. The *Rangoon* rolled heavily and the passengers became impatient of the long, monstrous waves which the wind raised before their path. A sort of tempest arose on the 3rd of November, the squall knocking the vessel about with fury, and the waves running high. The *Rangoon* reefed all her sails, and even the rigging proved too much, whistling and shaking amid the squall. The steamer was forced to proceed slowly, and the captain estimated that she would reach Hong Kong twenty hours behind time, and more if the storm lasted.

Phileas Fogg gazed at the tempestuous sea, which seemed to be struggling especially to delay him, with his habitual tranquility. He never changed countenance for an instant, though a delay of twenty hours, by making him too late for the Yokohama boat, would almost inevitably cause the loss of the wager. But this man of nerve manifested neither impatience nor annoyance; it seemed as if the storm were a part of his program, and had been foreseen. Aouda was amazed to find him as calm as he had been from the first time she saw him.

Fix did not look at the state of things in the same light. The storm greatly pleased him. His satisfaction would have been complete had the *Rangoon* been forced to retreat before the violence of wind and waves. Each delay filled him with hope, for it became more and more probable that Fogg would be obliged to remain some days at Hong Kong; and now the heavens themselves became his allies, with the gusts and squalls. It mattered not that they made him seasick—he made no account of this inconvenience; and, while his body was writhing under their effects, his spirit bounded with hopeful exultation.

Passepartout was enraged beyond expression by the unpropitious weather. Everything had gone so well till now! Earth and sea had seemed to be at his master's service; steamers and railways obeyed him; wind and steam united to speed his journey. Had the hour of adversity come? Passepartout was as much excited as if the twenty thousand pounds were to come from his own pocket. The storm exasperated him, the gale made him furious, and he longed to lash the obstinate sea into obedience. Poor fellow! Fix carefully concealed from him his own satisfaction, for, had he betrayed it, Passepartout could scarcely have restrained himself from personal violence.

Passepartout remained on deck as long as the tempest lasted, being unable to remain quiet below, and taking it into his head to aid the progress of the ship by lending a hand with the crew. He overwhelmed the captain, officers, and sailors, who could not help laughing at his impatience, with all sorts of questions. He wanted to know exactly how long the storm was going to last; whereupon he was referred to the barometer, which seemed to have no intention of rising. Passepartout shook it, but with no perceptible effect; for neither shaking nor maledictions could prevail upon it to change its mind.

On the 4th, however, the sea became more calm, and the storm lessened its violence; the wind veered southward, and was once more favorable. Passepartout cleared up with the weather. Some of the sails were unfurled, and the *Rangoon* resumed its most rapid speed. The time lost could not, however, be regained. Land was not signaled until five o'clock on the morning of the 6th; the steamer was due on the 5th. Phileas Fogg was twenty-four hours behindhand, and the Yokohama steamer would, of course, be missed.

The pilot went on board at six, and took his place on the bridge, to guide the *Rangoon* through the channels to the port of Hong Kong. Passepartout longed to ask him if the steamer had left for Yokohama; but he dared not, for he wished to preserve the spark of hope, which still remained till the last moment. He had confided his anxiety to Fix, who—the sly rascal!—tried to console him by saying that Mr. Fogg would be in time if he took the next boat; but this only put Passepartout in a passion.

Mr. Fogg, bolder than his servant, did not hesitate to approach the pilot, and tranquilly ask him if he knew when a steamer would leave Hong Kong for Yokohama.

"At high tide tomorrow morning," answered the pilot.

"Ah!" said Mr. Fogg, without betraying any astonishment.

Passepartout, who heard what passed, would willingly have embraced the pilot, while Fix would have been glad to twist his neck.

"What is the steamer's name?" asked Mr. Fogg.

"The *Carnatic*."

"Ought she not to have gone yesterday?"

"Yes, sir; but they had to repair one of her boilers, and so her departure was postponed till tomorrow."

"Thank you," returned Mr. Fogg, descending mathematically to the saloon.

Passepartout clasped the pilot's hand and shook it heartily in his delight, exclaiming, "Pilot, you are the best of good fellows!"

The pilot probably does not know to this day why his responses won him this enthusiastic greeting. He remounted the bridge, and guided the steamer through the flotilla of junks, tankas, and fishing boats which crowd the harbor of Hong Kong.

At one o'clock the *Rangoon* was at the quay, and the passengers were going ashore.

Chance had strangely favored Phileas Fogg, for had not the *Carnatic* been forced to lie over for repairing her boilers, she would have left on the 6th of November, and the passengers for Japan would have been obliged to await for a week the sailing of the next steamer. Mr. Fogg was, it is true, twenty-four hours behind his time; but this could not seriously imperil the remainder of his tour.

The steamer which crossed the Pacific from Yokohama to San Francisco made a direct connection with that from Hong Kong, and it could not sail until the latter reached Yokohama; and if Mr. Fogg was twenty-four hours late on reaching Yokohama, this time would no doubt be easily regained in the voyage of twenty-two days across the Pacific. He found himself, then, about twenty-four hours behindhand, thirty-five days after leaving London.

The *Carnatic* was announced to leave Hong Kong at five the next morning. Mr. Fogg had sixteen hours in which to attend to his business there, which was to deposit Aouda safely with her wealthy relative.

On landing, he conducted her to a palanquin, in which they repaired to the Club Hotel. A room was engaged for the young woman, and Mr. Fogg, after seeing that she wanted for nothing, set out in search of her cousin Jeejeeh. He instructed Passepartout to remain at the hotel until his return, that Aouda might not be left entirely alone.

Mr. Fogg repaired to the Exchange, where, he did not doubt, everyone would know so wealthy and considerable a personage as the Parsee merchant. Meeting a broker, he made the inquiry, to learn that Jeejeeh had left China two years before, and, retiring from business with an immense fortune, had taken up his residence in Europe—in Holland, the broker thought, with the merchants of which country he had principally traded. Phileas Fogg returned to the hotel, begged a moment's conversation with Aouda, and without more ado, apprised her that Jeejeeh was no longer at Hong Kong, but probably in Holland.

Aouda at first said nothing. She passed her hand across her forehead, and reflected a few moments. Then, in her sweet, soft voice, she said: "What ought I to do, Mr. Fogg?"

"It is very simple," responded the gentleman. "Go on to Europe."

"But I cannot intrude—"

"You do not intrude, nor do you in the least embarrass my project. Passepartout!"

"Monsieur."

"Go to the *Carnatic*, and engage three cabins."

Passepartout, delighted that the young woman, who was very gracious to him, was going to continue the journey with them, went off at a brisk gait to obey his master's order.

## CHAPTER XIX

### In Which Passepartout Takes a Too Great Interest in His Master, and What Comes of It

Hong Kong is an island which came into the possession of the English by the Treaty of Nankin, after the war of 1842; and the colonizing genius of the English has created upon it an important city and an excellent port. The island is situated at the mouth of the Canton River, and is separated by about sixty miles from the Portuguese town of Macao, on the opposite coast. Hong Kong has beaten Macao in the struggle for the Chinese trade, and now the greater part of the transportation of Chinese goods finds its depot at the former place. Docks, hospitals, wharves, a Gothic cathedral, a government house, macadamized streets, give to Hong Kong the appearance of a town in Kent or Surrey transferred by some strange magic to the antipodes.

Passepartout wandered, with his hands in his pockets, toward the Victoria port, gazing as he went at the curious palanquins and other modes of conveyance, and the groups of Chinese, Japanese, and Europeans who passed to and fro in the streets. Hong Kong seemed to him not unlike Bombay, Calcutta, and Singapore, since, like them, it betrayed everywhere the evidence of English supremacy. At the Victoria port he found a confused mass of ships of all nations: English, French, American, and Dutch, men-of-war and trading vessels, Japanese and Chinese junks, sempas, tankas, and flower boats, which formed so many floating parterres. Passepartout noticed in the crowd a number of the natives who seemed very old and were dressed in yellow. On going into a barber's to get shaved he learned that these ancient men were all at least eighty years old, at which age they are permitted to wear yellow, which is the imperial color. Passepartout, without exactly knowing why, thought this very funny.

On reaching the quay where they were to embark on the *Carnatic*, he was not astonished to find Fix walking up and down. The detective seemed very much disturbed and disappointed.

"This is bad," muttered Passepartout, "for the gentlemen of the Reform Club!" He accosted Fix with a merry smile, as if he had not perceived that gentleman's chagrin. The detective had, indeed, good reasons to inveigh against the bad luck which pursued him. The warrant had not come! It was certainly on the way, but as certainly it could not now reach Hong Kong for several days; and, this being the last English territory on Mr. Fogg's route, the robber would escape, unless he could manage to detain him.

"Well, Monsieur Fix," said Passepartout, "have you decided to go with us so far as America?"

"Yes," returned Fix, through his set teeth.

"Good!" exclaimed Passepartout, laughing heartily. "I knew you could not persuade yourself to separate from us. Come and engage your berth."

They entered the steamer office and secured cabins for four persons. The clerk, as he gave them the tickets, informed them that, the repairs on the *Carnatic* having been completed, the steamer would leave that very evening, and not next morning, as had been announced.

"That will suit my master all the better," said Passepartout. "I will go and let him know."

Fix now decided to make a bold move; he resolved to tell Passepartout all. It seemed to be the only possible means of keeping Phileas Fogg several days longer at Hong Kong. He accordingly invited his companion into a tavern which caught his eye on the quay. On entering, they found themselves in a large room handsomely decorated, at the end of which was a large camp bed furnished with cushions. Several persons lay upon this bed in a deep sleep. At the small tables which were arranged about the room some thirty customers were drinking English beer, porter, gin, and brandy; smoking, the while, long red clay pipes stuffed with little balls of opium mingled with essence of rose. From time to time one of the smokers, overcome with the narcotic, would slip under the table, whereupon the waiters, taking him by the head and feet, carried and laid him upon the bed. The bed already supported twenty of these stupefied sots.

Fix and Passepartout saw that they were in a smoking house haunted by those wretched, cadaverous, idiotic creatures to whom the English merchants sell every year the miserable drug called opium, to the amount of one million four hundred thousand pounds—thousands devoted to one of the most despicable vices which afflict humanity! The Chinese government has in vain attempted to deal with the evil by stringent laws. It passed gradually from the rich, to whom it was at first exclusively reserved, to the lower classes, and then its ravages could not be arrested. Opium is smoked everywhere, at all times, by men and women, in the Celestial Empire; and, once accustomed to it, the victims cannot dispense with it, except by suffering horrible bodily contortions and agonies. A great smoker can smoke as many as eight pipes a day; but he dies in five years. It was in one of these dens that Fix and Passepartout, in search of a friendly glass, found themselves. Passepartout had no money, but willingly accepted Fix's invitation in the hope of returning the obligation at some future time.

They ordered two bottles of port, to which the Frenchman did ample justice, while Fix observed him with close attention. They chatted about the journey, and Passepartout was especially merry at the idea that Fix was going to continue it with them. When the bottles were empty, however, he rose to go and tell his master of the change in the time of the sailing of the *Carnatic*.

Fix caught him by the arm, and said, "Wait a moment."

"What for, Mr. Fix?"

"I want to have a serious talk with you."

"A serious talk!" cried Passepartout, drinking up the little wine that was left in the bottom of his glass. "Well, we'll talk about it tomorrow; I haven't time now."

"Stay! What I have to say concerns your master."

Passepartout, at this, looked attentively at his companion. Fix's face seemed to have a singular expression. He resumed his seat.

"What is it that you have to say?"

Fix placed his hand upon Passepartout's arm, and, lowering his voice, said, "You have guessed who I am?"

"Parbleu!" said Passepartout, smiling.

"Then I'm going to tell you everything—"

"Now that I know everything, my friend! Ah! That's very good. But go on, go on. First, though, let me tell you that those gentlemen have put themselves to a useless expense."

"Useless!" said Fix. "You speak confidently. It's clear that you don't know how large the sum is."

"Of course I do," returned Passepartout. "Twenty thousand pounds."

"Fifty-five thousand!" answered Fix, pressing his companion's hand.

"What!" cried the Frenchman. "Has Monsieur Fogg dared—fifty-five thousand pounds! Well, there's all the more reason for not losing an instant," he continued, getting up hastily.

Fix pushed Passepartout back in his chair, and resumed: "Fifty-five thousand pounds; and if I succeed, I get two thousand pounds. If you'll help me, I'll let you have five hundred of them."

"Help you?" cried Passepartout, whose eyes were standing wide open.

"Yes; help me keep Mr. Fogg here for two or three days."

"Why, what are you saying? Those gentlemen are not satisfied with following my master and suspecting his honor, but they must try to put obstacles in his way! I blush for them!"

"What do you mean?"

"I mean that it is a piece of shameful trickery. They might as well waylay Mr. Fogg and put his money in their pockets!"

"That's just what we count on doing."

"It's a conspiracy, then," cried Passepartout, who became more and more excited as the liquor mounted in his head, for he drank without perceiving it. "A real conspiracy! And gentlemen, too. Bah!"

Fix began to be puzzled.

"Members of the Reform Club!" continued Passepartout. "You must know, Monsieur Fix, that my master is an honest man, and that, when he makes a wager, he tries to win it fairly!"

"But who do you think I am?" asked Fix, looking at him intently.

"Parbleu! An agent of the members of the Reform Club, sent out here to interrupt my master's journey. But, though I found you out some time ago, I've taken good care to say nothing about it to Mr. Fogg."

"He knows nothing, then?"

"Nothing," replied Passepartout, again emptying his glass.

The detective passed his hand across his forehead, hesitating before he spoke again. What should he do? Passepartout's mistake seemed sincere, but it made his design more difficult. It was evident that the servant was not the master's accomplice, as Fix had been inclined to suspect.

"Well," said the detective to himself, "as he is not an accomplice, he will help me."

He had no time to lose: Fogg must be detained at Hong Kong, so he resolved to make a clean breast of it.

"Listen to me," said Fix abruptly. "I am not, as you think, an agent of the members of the Reform Club—"

"Bah!" retorted Passepartout, with an air of raillery.

"I am a police detective, sent out here by the London office."

"You, a detective?"

"I will prove it. Here is my commission."

Passepartout was speechless with astonishment when Fix displayed this document, the genuineness of which could not be doubted.

"Mr. Fogg's wager," resumed Fix, "is only a pretext, of which you and the gentlemen of the Reform are dupes. He had a motive for securing your innocent complicity."

"But why?"

"Listen. On the 28th of last September a robbery of fifty-five thousand pounds was committed at the Bank of England by a person whose description was fortunately secured. Here is his description; it answers exactly to that of Mr. Phileas Fogg."

"What nonsense!" cried Passepartout, striking the table with his fist. "My master is the most honorable of men!"

"How can you tell? You know scarcely anything about him. You went into his service the day he came away; and he came away on a foolish pretext, without trunks, and carrying a large amount in banknotes. And yet you are bold enough to assert that he is an honest man!"

"Yes, yes," repeated the poor fellow, mechanically.

"Would you like to be arrested as his accomplice?"

Passepartout, overcome by what he had heard, held his head between his hands, and did not dare to look at the detective. Phileas Fogg, the savior of Aouda, that brave and generous man, a robber! And yet how many presumptions there were against him! Passepartout essayed to reject the suspicions which forced themselves upon his mind; he did not wish to believe that his master was guilty.

"Well, what do you want of me?" said he, at last, with an effort.

"See here," replied Fix; "I have tracked Mr. Fogg to this place, but as yet I have failed to receive the warrant of arrest for which I sent to London. You must help me to keep him here in Hong Kong—"

"I! But I—"

"I will share with you the two thousand pounds reward offered by the Bank of England."

"Never!" replied Passepartout, who tried to rise, but fell back, exhausted in mind and body.

"Mr. Fix," he stammered, "even should what you say be true—if my master is really the robber you are seeking for—which I deny—I have been, am, in his service; I have seen his generosity and goodness; and I will never betray him—not for all the gold in the world. I come from a village where they don't eat that kind of bread!"

"You refuse?"

"I refuse."

"Consider that I've said nothing," said Fix; "and let us drink."

"Yes; let us drink!"

Passepartout felt himself yielding more and more to the effects of the liquor. Fix, seeing that he must, at all hazards, be separated from his master, wished to entirely overcome him. Some pipes full of opium lay upon the table. Fix slipped one into Passepartout's hand. He took it, put it between his lips, lit it, drew several puffs, and his head, becoming heavy under the influence of the narcotic, fell upon the table.

"At last!" said Fix, seeing Passepartout unconscious. "Mr. Fogg will not be informed of the *Carnatic*'s departure; and, if he is, he will have to go without this cursed Frenchman!"

And, after paying his bill, Fix left the tavern.

## CHAPTER XX

### In Which Fix Comes Face-to-Face with Phileas Fogg

While these events were passing at the opium house, Mr. Fogg, unconscious of the danger he was in of losing the steamer, was quietly escorting Aouda about the streets of the English quarter, making the necessary purchases for the long voyage before them. It was all very well for an Englishman like Mr. Fogg to make the tour of the world with a carpetbag; a lady could not be expected to travel comfortably under such conditions. He acquitted his task with characteristic serenity, and invariably replied to the remonstrances of his fair companion, who was confused by his patience and generosity:

"It is in the interest of my journey—a part of my program."

The purchases made, they returned to the hotel, where they dined at a sumptuously served *table d'hote*; after which Aouda, shaking hands with her protector after the English fashion, retired to her room for rest. Mr. Fogg absorbed himself throughout the evening in the perusal of the *Times* and *Illustrated London News*.

Had he been capable of being astonished at anything, it would have been not to see his servant return at bedtime. But, knowing that the steamer was not to leave for Yokohama until the next morning, he did not disturb himself about the matter. When Passepartout did not appear the next morning to answer his master's bell, Mr. Fogg, not betraying the least vexation, contented himself with taking his carpetbag, calling Aouda, and sending for a palanquin.

It was then eight o'clock; at half past nine, it being then high tide, the *Carnatic* would leave the harbor. Mr. Fogg and Aouda got into the palanquin, their luggage being brought after on a wheelbarrow, and half an hour later stepped upon the quay whence they were to embark. Mr. Fogg then learned that the *Carnatic* had sailed the evening before. He had expected to find not only the steamer, but his domestic, and was forced to give up both; but no sign of disappointment appeared on his face, and he merely remarked to Aouda, "It is an accident, madam; nothing more."

At this moment a man who had been observing him attentively approached. It was Fix, who, bowing, addressed Mr. Fogg: "Were you not, like me, sir, a passenger by the *Rangoon*, which arrived yesterday?"

"I was, sir," replied Mr. Fogg coldly. "But I have not the honor—"

"Pardon me; I thought I should find your servant here."

"Do you know where he is, sir?" asked Aouda anxiously.

"What!" responded Fix, feigning surprise. "Is he not with you?"

"No," said Aouda. "He has not made his appearance since yesterday. Could he have gone on board the *Carnatic* without us?"

"Without you, madam?" answered the detective. "Excuse me, did you intend to sail in the *Carnatic*?"

"Yes, sir."

"So did I, madam, and I am excessively disappointed. The *Carnatic*, its repairs being completed, left Hong Kong twelve hours before the stated time, without any notice being given; and we must now wait a week for another steamer."

As he said "a week" Fix felt his heart leap for joy. Fogg detained at Hong Kong for a week! There would be time for the warrant to arrive, and fortune at last favored the representative of the law. His horror may be imagined when he heard Mr. Fogg say, in his placid voice, "But there are other vessels besides the *Carnatic*, it seems to me, in the harbor of Hong Kong."

And, offering his arm to Aouda, he directed his steps toward the docks in search of some craft about to start. Fix, stupefied, followed; it seemed as if he were attached to Mr. Fogg by an invisible thread. Chance, however, appeared really to have abandoned the man it had hitherto served so well. For three hours Phileas Fogg wandered about the docks with the determination, if necessary, to charter a vessel to carry him to Yokohama; but he could only find vessels which were loading or unloading, and which could not therefore set sail. Fix began to hope again.

But Mr. Fogg, far from being discouraged, was continuing his search, resolved not to stop if he had to resort to Macao, when he was accosted by a sailor on one of the wharves.

"Is your honor looking for a boat?"

"Have you a boat ready to sail?"

"Yes, your honor; a pilot boat—No. 43—the best in the harbor."

"Does she go fast?"

"Between eight and nine knots the hour. Will you look at her?"

"Yes."

"Your honor will be satisfied with her. Is it for a sea excursion?"

"No; for a voyage."

"A voyage?"

"Yes, will you agree to take me to Yokohama?"

The sailor leaned on the railing, opened his eyes wide, and said, "Is your honor joking?"

"No. I have missed the *Carnatic*, and I must get to Yokohama by the 14th at the latest, to take the boat for San Francisco."

"I am sorry," said the sailor; "but it is impossible."

"I offer you a hundred pounds per day, and an additional reward of two hundred pounds if I reach Yokohama in time."

"Are you in earnest?"

"Very much so."

The pilot walked away a little distance, and gazed out to sea, evidently struggling between the anxiety to gain a large sum and the fear of venturing so far. Fix was in mortal suspense.

Mr. Fogg turned to Aouda and asked her, "You would not be afraid, would you, madam?"

"Not with you, Mr. Fogg," was her answer.

The pilot now returned, shuffling his hat in his hands.

"Well, pilot?" said Mr. Fogg.

"Well, your honor," replied he, "I could not risk myself, my men, or my little boat of scarcely twenty tons on so long a voyage at this time of year. Besides, we could not reach Yokohama in time, for it is sixteen hundred and sixty miles from Hong Kong."

"Only sixteen hundred," said Mr. Fogg.

"It's the same thing."

Fix breathed more freely.

"But," added the pilot, "it might be arranged another way."

Fix ceased to breathe at all.

"How?" asked Mr. Fogg.

"By going to Nagasaki, at the extreme south of Japan, or even to Shanghai, which is only eight hundred miles from here. In going to Shanghai we should not be forced to sail wide of the Chinese coast, which would be a great advantage, as the currents run northward, and would aid us."

"Pilot," said Mr. Fogg, "I must take the American steamer at Yokohama, and not at Shanghai or Nagasaki."

"Why not?" returned the pilot. "The San Francisco steamer does not start from Yokohama. It puts in at Yokohama and Nagasaki, but it starts from Shanghai."

"You are sure of that?"

"Perfectly."

"And when does the boat leave Shanghai?"

"On the 11th, at seven in the evening. We have, therefore, four days before us, that is ninety-six hours; and in that time, if we had good luck and a southwest wind, and the sea was calm, we could make those eight hundred miles to Shanghai."

"And you could go—"

"In an hour; as soon as provisions could be got aboard and the sails put up."

"It is a bargain. Are you the master of the boat?"

"Yes; John Bunsby, master of the *Tankadere*."

"Would you like some earnest money?"

"If it would not put your honor out—"

"Here are two hundred pounds on account, sir," added Phileas Fogg, turning to Fix. "If you would like to take advantage—"

"Thanks, sir; I was about to ask the favor."

"Very well. In half an hour we shall go on board."

"But poor Passepartout?" urged Aouda, who was much disturbed by the servant's disappearance.

"I shall do all I can to find him," replied Phileas Fogg.

While Fix, in a feverish, nervous state, repaired to the pilot boat, the others directed their course to the police station at Hong Kong. Phileas Fogg there gave Passepartout's description, and left a sum of money to be spent in the search for him. The same formalities having been gone through at the French consulate, and the palanquin having stopped at the hotel for the luggage, which had been sent back there, they returned to the wharf.

It was now three o'clock; and pilot boat No. 43, with its crew on board and its provisions stored away, was ready for departure.

The *Tankadere* was a neat little craft of twenty tons, as gracefully built as if she were a racing yacht. Her shining copper sheathing, her galvanized ironwork, her deck, white as ivory, betrayed the pride taken by John Bunsby in making her presentable. Her two masts leaned a trifle backward; she carried brigantine, foresail, storm jib, and standing jib, and was well rigged for running before the wind; and she seemed capable of brisk speed, which, indeed, she had already proved by gaining several prizes in pilot boat races. The crew of the *Tankadere* was composed of John Bunsby, the master, and four hardy mariners who were familiar with the Chinese seas. John Bunsby, himself a man of forty-five or thereabouts, vigorous, sunburnt, with a sprightly expression of the eye and energetic and self-reliant countenance, would have inspired confidence in the most timid.

Phileas Fogg and Aouda went on board, where they found Fix already installed. Belowdecks was a square cabin, of which the walls bulged out in the form of cots, above a circular divan; in the center was a table provided with a swinging lamp. The accommodation was confined but neat.

"I am sorry to have nothing better to offer you," said Mr. Fogg to Fix, who bowed without responding.

The detective had a feeling akin to humiliation in profiting by the kindness of Mr. Fogg.

"It's certain," thought he, "though rascal as he is, he is a polite one!"

The sails and the English flag were hoisted at ten minutes past three. Mr. Fogg and Aouda, who were seated on deck, cast a last glance at the quay, in the hope of espying Passepartout. Fix was not without his fears lest chance should direct the steps of the unfortunate servant, whom he had so badly treated, in this direction; in which case an explanation the reverse of satisfactory to the detective must have ensued. But the Frenchman did not appear, and, without doubt, was still lying under the stupefying influence of the opium.

John Bunsby, master, at length gave the order to start, and the *Tankadere*, taking the wind under her brigantine, foresail, and standing jib, bounded briskly forward over the waves.

# CHAPTER XXI

### In Which the Master of the *Tankadere* Runs Great Risk of Losing a Reward of Two Hundred Pounds

This voyage of eight hundred miles was a perilous venture on a craft of twenty tons, and at that season of the year. The Chinese seas are usually boisterous, subject to terrible gales of wind, and especially during the equinoxes; and it was now early November.

It would clearly have been to the master's advantage to carry his passengers to Yokohama, since he was paid a certain sum per day; but he would have been rash to attempt such a voyage, and it was imprudent even to attempt to reach Shanghai. But John Bunsby believed in the *Tankadere*, which rode on the waves like a seagull; and perhaps he was not wrong.

Late in the day they passed through the capricious channels of Hong Kong, and the *Tankadere*, impelled by favorable winds, conducted herself admirably.

"I do not need, pilot," said Phileas Fogg, when they got into the open sea, "to advise you to use all possible speed."

"Trust me, your honor. We are carrying all the sail the wind will let us. The poles would add nothing, and are only used when we are going into port."

"It's your trade, not mine, pilot, and I confide in you."

Phileas Fogg, with body erect and legs wide apart, standing like a sailor, gazed without staggering at the swelling waters. The young woman, who was seated aft, was profoundly affected as she looked out upon the ocean, darkening now with the twilight, on which she had ventured in so frail a vessel. Above her head rustled the white sails, which seemed like great white wings. The boat, carried forward by the wind, seemed to be flying in the air.

Night came. The moon was entering her first quarter, and her insufficient light would soon die out in the mist on the horizon. Clouds were rising from the east, and already overcast a part of the heavens.

The pilot had hung out his lights, which was very necessary in these seas crowded with vessels bound landward; for collisions are not uncommon occurrences, and, at the speed she was going, the least shock would shatter the gallant little craft.

Fix, seated in the bow, gave himself up to meditation. He kept apart from his fellow travelers, knowing Mr. Fogg's taciturn tastes; besides, he did not quite like to talk to the man whose favors he had accepted. He was thinking, too, of the future. It seemed certain that Fogg would not stop at Yokohama, but would at once take the boat for San Francisco; and the vast extent of America would ensure him impunity and safety. Fogg's plan appeared to him the simplest in the world. Instead of sailing directly from England to the United States, like a common villain, he had traversed three-quarters of the globe, so as to gain the American continent more surely; and there, after throwing the police off his track, he would quietly enjoy himself with the fortune stolen from the bank. But, once in the United States, what should he, Fix, do? Should he abandon this man? No, a hundred times no! Until he had secured his extradition, he would not lose sight of him for an hour. It was his duty, and he would fulfill it to the end. At all events, there was one thing to be thankful for; Passepartout was not with his master; and it was above all important, after the confidences Fix had imparted to him, that the servant should never have speech with his master.

Phileas Fogg was also thinking of Passepartout, who had so strangely disappeared. Looking at the matter from every point of view, it did not seem to him impossible that, by some mistake, the man might have embarked on the *Carnatic* at the last moment; and this was also Aouda's opinion, who regretted very much the loss of the worthy fellow to whom she owed so much. They might then find him at Yokohama; for, if the *Carnatic* was carrying him thither, it would be easy to ascertain if he had been on board.

A brisk breeze arose about ten o'clock; but, though it might have been prudent to take in a reef, the pilot, after carefully examining the heavens, let the craft remain rigged as before. The *Tankadere* bore sail admirably, as she drew a great deal of water, and everything was prepared for high speed in case of a gale.

Mr. Fogg and Aouda descended into the cabin at midnight, having been already preceded by Fix, who had lain down on one of the cots. The pilot and crew remained on deck all night.

At sunrise the next day, which was November 8th, the boat had made more than one hundred miles. The log indicated a mean speed of between eight and nine miles. The *Tankadere* still carried all sail, and was accomplishing her greatest capacity of speed. If the wind held as it was, the chances would be in her favor. During the day she kept along the coast, where the currents were favorable; the coast, irregular in profile, and visible sometimes across the clearings, was at most five miles distant. The sea was less boisterous, since the wind came off land—a fortunate circumstance for the boat, which would suffer, owing to its small tonnage, by a heavy surge on the sea.

The breeze subsided a little toward noon, and set in from the southwest. The pilot put up his poles, but took them down again within two hours, as the wind freshened up anew.

Mr. Fogg and Aouda, happily unaffected by the roughness of the sea, ate with a good appetite, Fix being invited to share their repast, which he accepted with secret chagrin. To travel at this man's expense and live upon his provisions was not palatable to him. Still, he was obliged to eat, and so he ate.

When the meal was over, he took Mr. Fogg apart, and said, "Sir"—this "sir" scorched his lips, and he had to control himself to avoid collaring this "gentleman"— "Sir, you have been very kind to give me a passage on this boat. But, though my means will not admit of my expending them as freely as you, I must ask to pay my share—"

"Let us not speak of that, sir," replied Mr. Fogg.

"But, if I insist—"

"No, sir," repeated Mr. Fogg, in a tone which did not admit of a reply. "This enters into my general expenses."

Fix, as he bowed, had a stifled feeling, and, going forward, where he ensconced himself, did not open his mouth for the rest of the day.

Meanwhile they were progressing famously, and John Bunsby was in high hope. He several times assured Mr. Fogg that they would reach Shanghai in time; to which that gentleman responded that he counted upon it. The crew set to work in good earnest, inspired by the reward to be gained. There was not a sheet which was not tightened, not a sail which was not vigorously hoisted; not a lurch could be charged to the man at the helm. They worked as desperately as if they were contesting in a Royal Yacht regatta.

By evening, the log showed that two hundred and twenty miles had been accomplished from Hong Kong, and Mr. Fogg might hope that he would be able to reach Yokohama without recording any delay in his journal; in which case, the many misadventures which had overtaken him since he left London would not seriously affect his journey.

The *Tankadere* entered the Straits of Fo-Kien, which separate the island of Formosa from the Chinese coast, in the small hours of the night, and crossed the Tropic of Cancer. The sea was very rough in the straits, full of eddies formed by the countercurrents, and the chopping waves broke her course, while it became very difficult to stand on deck.

At daybreak the wind began to blow hard again, and the heavens seemed to predict a gale. The barometer announced a speedy change, the mercury rising and falling capriciously; the sea also, in the southeast, raised long surges which indicated a tempest. The sun had set the evening before in a red mist, in the midst of the phosphorescent scintillations of the ocean.

John Bunsby long examined the threatening aspect of the heavens, muttering indistinctly between his teeth. At last he said in a low voice to Mr. Fogg, "Shall I speak out to your honor?"

"Of course."

"Well, we are going to have a squall."

"Is the wind north or south?" asked Mr. Fogg quietly.

"South. Look! A typhoon is coming up."

"Glad it's a typhoon from the south, for it will carry us forward."

"Oh, if you take it that way," said John Bunsby, "I've nothing more to say." John Bunsby's suspicions were confirmed. At a less advanced season of the year the typhoon, according to a famous meteorologist, would have passed away like a luminous cascade of electric flame; but in the winter equinox it was to be feared that it would burst upon them with great violence.

The pilot took his precautions in advance. He reefed all sail, the pole masts were dispensed with; all hands went forward to the bows. A single triangular sail, of strong canvas, was hoisted as a storm jib, so as to hold the wind from behind. Then they waited.

John Bunsby had requested his passengers to go below; but this imprisonment in so narrow a space, with little air, and the boat bouncing in the gale, was far from pleasant. Neither Mr. Fogg, Fix, nor Aouda consented to leave the deck.

The storm of rain and wind descended upon them toward eight o'clock. With but its bit of sail, the *Tankadere* was lifted like a feather by a wind, an idea of whose violence can scarcely be given. To compare her speed to four times that of a locomotive going on full steam would be below the truth.

The boat scudded thus northward during the whole day, borne on by monstrous waves, preserving always, fortunately, a speed equal to theirs. Twenty times she seemed almost to be submerged by these mountains of water which rose behind her; but the adroit management of the pilot saved her. The passengers were often bathed in spray, but they submitted to it philosophically. Fix cursed it, no doubt; but Aouda, with her eyes fastened upon her protector, whose coolness amazed her, showed herself worthy of him, and bravely weathered the storm. As for Phileas Fogg, it seemed just as if the typhoon were a part of his program.

Up to this time the *Tankadere* had always held her course to the north; but toward evening the wind, veering three-quarters, bore down from the northwest. The boat, now lying in the trough of the waves, shook and rolled terribly; the sea struck her with fearful violence. At night the tempest increased in violence. John Bunsby saw the approach of darkness and the rising of the storm with dark misgivings. He thought awhile, and then asked his crew if it was not time to slacken speed. After a consultation he approached Mr. Fogg and said, "I think, your honor, that we should do well to make for one of the ports on the coast."

"I think so too."

"Ah!" said the pilot. "But which one?"

"I know of but one," returned Mr. Fogg tranquilly.

"And that is—"

"Shanghai."

The pilot, at first, did not seem to comprehend; he could scarcely realize so much determination and tenacity. Then he cried, "Well—yes! Your honor is right. To Shanghai!"

So the *Tankadere* kept steadily on her northward track.

The night was really terrible; it would be a miracle if the craft did not founder. Twice it could have been all over with her if the crew had not been constantly on the watch. Aouda was exhausted, but did not utter a complaint. More than once Mr. Fogg rushed to protect her from the violence of the waves.

Day reappeared. The tempest still raged with undiminished fury; but the wind now returned to the southeast. It was a favorable change, and the *Tankadere* again bounded forward on this mountainous sea, though the waves crossed each other, and imparted shocks and countershocks which would have crushed a craft less solidly built. From time to time the coast was visible through the broken mist, but no vessel was in sight. The *Tankadere* was alone upon the sea.

There were some signs of a calm at noon, and these became more distinct as the sun descended toward the horizon. The tempest had been as brief as terrific. The passengers, thoroughly exhausted, could now eat a little, and take some repose.

The night was comparatively quiet. Some of the sails were again hoisted, and the speed of the boat was very good. The next morning at dawn they espied the coast, and John Bunsby was able to assert that they were not one hundred miles from Shanghai. A hundred miles, and only one day to traverse them! That very evening Mr. Fogg was due at Shanghai, if he did not wish to miss the steamer to Yokohama. Had there been no storm, during which several hours were lost, they would be at this moment within thirty miles of their destination.

The wind grew decidedly calmer, and happily the sea fell with it. All sails were now hoisted, and at noon the *Tankadere* was within forty-five miles of Shanghai. There remained yet six hours in which to accomplish that distance. All on board feared that it could not be done, and everyone—Phileas Fogg, no doubt, excepted—felt his heart beat with impatience. The boat must keep up an average of nine miles an hour, and the wind was becoming calmer every moment! It was a capricious breeze, coming from the coast, and after it passed the sea became smooth. Still, the *Tankadere* was so light, and her fine sails caught the fickle zephyrs so well, that, with the aid of the currents John Bunsby found himself at six o'clock not more than ten miles from the mouth of Shanghai River. Shanghai itself is situated at least twelve miles up the stream. At seven they were still three miles from Shanghai. The pilot swore an angry oath; the reward of two hundred pounds was evidently on the point of escaping him. He looked at Mr. Fogg. Mr. Fogg was perfectly tranquil; and yet his whole fortune was at this moment at stake.

At this moment, also, a long black funnel, crowned with wreaths of smoke, appeared on the edge of the waters. It was the American steamer, leaving for Yokohama at the appointed time.

"Confound her!" cried John Bunsby, pushing back the rudder with a desperate jerk.

"Signal her!" said Phileas Fogg quietly.

A small brass cannon stood on the forward deck of the *Tankadere*, for making signals in the fogs. It was loaded to the muzzle; but just as the pilot was about to apply a red-hot coal to the touchhole, Mr. Fogg said, "Hoist your flag!"

The flag was run up at half-mast, and, this being the signal of distress, it was hoped that the American steamer, perceiving it, would change her course a little, so as to succour the pilot boat.

"Fire!" said Mr. Fogg. And the booming of the little cannon resounded in the air.

## CHAPTER XXII

IN WHICH PASSEPARTOUT FINDS OUT THAT, EVEN AT THE ANTIPODES,
IT IS CONVENIENT TO HAVE SOME MONEY IN ONE'S POCKET

The *Carnatic*, setting sail from Hong Kong at half past six on the 7th of November, directed her course at full steam toward Japan. She carried a large cargo and a well-filled cabin of passengers. Two staterooms in the rear were, however, unoccupied—those which had been engaged by Phileas Fogg.

The next day a passenger with a half-stupefied eye, staggering gait, and disordered hair was seen to emerge from the second cabin, and to totter to a seat on deck.

It was Passepartout; and what had happened to him was as follows: Shortly after Fix left the opium den, two waiters had lifted the unconscious Passepartout, and had carried him to the bed reserved for the smokers. Three hours later, pursued even in his dreams by a fixed idea, the poor fellow awoke, and struggled against the stupefying influence of the narcotic. The thought of a duty unfulfilled shook off his torpor, and he hurried from the abode of drunkenness. Staggering and holding himself up by keeping against the walls, falling down and creeping up again, and irresistibly impelled by a kind of instinct, he kept crying out, "The *Carnatic*! The *Carnatic*!"

The steamer lay puffing alongside the quay, on the point of starting. Passepartout had but few steps to go; and, rushing upon the plank, he crossed it, and fell unconscious on the deck, just as the *Carnatic* was moving off. Several sailors, who were evidently accustomed to this sort of scene, carried the poor Frenchman down into the second cabin, and Passepartout did not wake until they were one hundred and fifty miles away from China. Thus he found himself the next morning on the deck of the *Carnatic*, and eagerly inhaling the exhilarating sea breeze. The pure air sobered him. He began to collect his sense, which he found a difficult task; but at last he recalled the events of the evening before, Fix's revelation, and the opium house.

"It is evident," said he to himself, "that I have been abominably drunk! What will Mr. Fogg say? At least I have not missed the steamer, which is the most important thing."

Then, as Fix occurred to him: "As for that rascal, I hope we are well rid of him, and that he has not dared, as he proposed, to follow us on board the *Carnatic*. A detective on the track of Mr. Fogg, accused of robbing the Bank of England! Pshaw! Mr. Fogg is no more a robber than I am a murderer."

Should he divulge Fix's real errand to his master? Would it do to tell the part the detective was playing? Would it not be better to wait until Mr. Fogg reached London again, and then impart to him that an agent of the metropolitan police had been following him round the world, and have a good laugh over it? No doubt; at least, it was worth considering. The first thing to do was to find Mr. Fogg, and apologize for his singular behavior.

Passepartout got up and proceeded, as well as he could with the rolling of the steamer, to the afterdeck. He saw no one who resembled either his master or Aouda. "Good!" muttered he. "Aouda has not got up yet, and Mr. Fogg has probably found some partners at whist."

He descended to the saloon. Mr. Fogg was not there. Passepartout had only, however, to ask the purser the number of his master's stateroom. The purser replied that he did not know any passenger by the name of Fogg.

"I beg your pardon," said Passepartout persistently. "He is a tall gentleman, quiet, and not very talkative, and has with him a young lady—"

"There is no young lady on board," interrupted the purser. "Here is a list of the passengers; you may see for yourself."

Passepartout scanned the list, but his master's name was not upon it. All at once an idea struck him.

"Ah! Am I on the *Carnatic*?"

"Yes."

"On the way to Yokohama?"

"Certainly."

Passepartout had for an instant feared that he was on the wrong boat; but, though he was really on the *Carnatic*, his master was not there.

He fell thunderstruck on a seat. He saw it all now. He remembered that the time of sailing had been changed, that he should have informed his master of that fact, and that he had not done so. It was his fault, then, that Mr. Fogg and Aouda had missed the steamer. Yes, but it was still more the fault of the traitor who, in order to separate him from his master, and detain the latter at Hong Kong, had inveigled him into getting drunk! He now saw the detective's trick; and at this moment Mr. Fogg was certainly ruined, his bet was lost, and he himself perhaps arrested and imprisoned! At this thought Passepartout tore his hair. Ah, if Fix ever came within his reach, what a settling of accounts there would be!

After his first depression, Passepartout became calmer, and began to study his situation. It was certainly not an enviable one. He found himself on the way to Japan, and what should he do when he got there? His pocket was empty; he had not a solitary shilling, not so much as a penny. His passage had fortunately been paid for in advance; and he had five or six days in which to decide upon his future course. He fell to at meals with an appetite, and ate for Mr. Fogg, Aouda, and himself. He helped himself as generously as if Japan were a desert, where nothing to eat was to be looked for.

At dawn on the 13th the *Carnatic* entered the port of Yokohama. This is an important port of call in the Pacific, where all the mail steamers and those carrying travelers between North America, China, Japan, and the Oriental islands put in. It is situated in the bay of Yeddo, and at but a short distance from that second capital of the Japanese empire, and the residence of the tycoon, the civil emperor, before the mikado, the spiritual emperor, absorbed his office in his own. The *Carnatic* anchored at the quay near the customhouse, in the midst of a crowd of ships bearing the flags of all nations.

Passepartout went timidly ashore on this so curious territory of the Sons of the Sun. He had nothing better to do than, taking chance for his guide, to wander aimlessly through the streets of Yokohama. He found himself at first in a thoroughly

European quarter, the houses having low fronts, and being adorned with verandas, beneath which he caught glimpses of neat peristyles. This quarter occupied, with its streets, squares, docks, and warehouses, all the space between the "promontory of the treaty" and the river. Here, as at Hong Kong and Calcutta, were mixed crowds of all races, Americans and English, Chinamen and Dutchmen, mostly merchants ready to buy or sell anything. The Frenchman felt himself as much alone among them as if he had dropped down in the midst of Hottentots.

He had, at least, one resource to call on the French and English consuls at Yokohama for assistance. But he shrank from telling the story of his adventures, intimately connected as it was with that of his master; and, before doing so, he determined to exhaust all other means of aid. As chance did not favor him in the European quarter, he penetrated that inhabited by the native Japanese, determined, if necessary, to push on to Yeddo.

The Japanese quarter of Yokohama is called Benten, after the goddess of the sea, who is worshipped on the islands round about. There Passepartout beheld beautiful fir and cedar groves, sacred gates of a singular architecture, bridges half hid in the midst of bamboos and reeds, temples shaded by immense cedar trees, holy retreats where were sheltered Buddhist priests and sectaries of Confucius, and interminable streets, where a perfect harvest of rose-tinted and red-cheeked children, who looked as if they had been cut out of Japanese screens, and who were playing in the midst of short-legged poodles and yellowish cats, might have been gathered.

The streets were crowded with people. Priests were passing in processions, beating their dreary tambourines; police and customhouse officers with pointed hats encrusted with lac and carrying two sabers hung to their waists; soldiers, clad in blue cotton with white stripes, and bearing guns; the mikado's guards, enveloped in silken doubles, hauberks and coats of mail; and numbers of military folk of all ranks—for the military profession is as much respected in Japan as it is despised in China—went hither and thither in groups and pairs. Passepartout saw, too, begging friars, long-robed pilgrims, and simple civilians, with their warped and jet-black hair, big heads, long busts, slender legs, short stature, and complexions varying from copper-color to a dead white, but never yellow, like the Chinese, from whom the Japanese widely differ. He did not fail to observe the curious equipages—carriages and palanquins, barrows supplied with sails, and litters made of bamboo; nor the women—whom he thought not especially handsome—who took little steps with their little feet, whereon they wore canvas shoes, straw sandals, and clogs of worked wood, and who displayed tight-looking eyes, flat chests, teeth fashionably blackened, and gowns crossed with silken scarfs, tied in an enormous knot behind an ornament which the modern Parisian ladies seem to have borrowed from the dames of Japan.

Passepartout wandered for several hours in the midst of this motley crowd, looking in at the windows of the rich and curious shops, the jewelry establishments glittering with quaint Japanese ornaments, the restaurants decked with streamers and banners, the teahouses, where the odorous beverage was being drunk with saki, a liquor concocted from the fermentation of rice, and the comfortable smoking houses, where they were puffing, not opium, which is almost unknown in Japan, but a very fine, stringy tobacco. He went on till he found himself in the fields, in the midst of vast rice plantations. There he saw dazzling camellias expanding themselves, with flowers which were giving forth their last colors and perfumes, not on bushes, but on trees, and within bamboo enclosures, cherry, plum, and apple trees, which the Japanese cultivate rather for their blossoms than their fruit, and which queerly fashioned, grinning scarecrows protected from the sparrows, pigeons, ravens, and other voracious birds. On the branches of the cedars were perched large eagles; amid the foliage of the weeping willows were herons, solemnly standing on one leg; and on every hand were crows, ducks, hawks, wild birds, and a multitude of cranes, which the Japanese consider sacred, and which to their minds symbolize long life and prosperity.

As he was strolling along, Passepartout espied some violets among the shrubs.

"Good!" said he. "I'll have some supper."

But, on smelling them, he found that they were odorless.

"No chance there," thought he.

The worthy fellow had certainly taken good care to eat as hearty a breakfast as possible before leaving the *Carnatic*; but, as he had been walking about all day, the demands of hunger were becoming importunate. He observed that the butchers' stalls contained neither mutton, goat, nor pork; and, knowing also that it is a sacrilege to kill cattle, which are preserved solely for farming, he made up his mind that meat was far from plentiful in Yokohama—nor was he mistaken; and, in default of butcher's meat, he could have wished for a quarter of wild boar or deer, a partridge, or some quails, some game or fish, which, with rice, the Japanese eat almost exclusively. But he found it necessary to keep up a stout heart, and to postpone the meal he craved till the following morning. Night came, and Passepartout reentered the native quarter, where he wandered through the streets, lit by varicolored lanterns, looking on at the dancers, who were executing skillful steps and boundings, and the astrologers who stood in the open air with their telescopes. Then he came to the harbor, which was lit up by the resin torches of the fishermen, who were fishing from their boats.

The streets at last became quiet, and the patrol, the officers of which, in their splendid costumes, and surrounded by their suites, Passepartout thought seemed like ambassadors, succeeded the bustling crowd. Each time a company passed, Passepartout chuckled and said to himself: "Good! Another Japanese embassy departing for Europe!"

## CHAPTER XXIII

### In Which Passepartout's Nose Becomes Outrageously Long

The next morning poor, jaded, famished Passepartout said to himself that he must get something to eat at all hazards, and the sooner he did so the better. He might, indeed, sell his watch; but he would have starved first. Now or never he must use the strong, if not melodious voice which nature had bestowed upon him. He knew several French and English songs, and resolved to try them upon the Japanese, who must be lovers of music, since they were forever pounding on their cymbals, tam-tams, and tambourines, and could not but appreciate European talent.

It was, perhaps, rather early in the morning to get up a concert, and the audience prematurely aroused from their slumbers might not possibly pay their entertainer with coin bearing the mikado's features. Passepartout therefore decided to wait several hours; and, as he was sauntering along, it occurred to him that he would seem rather too well dressed for a wandering artist. The idea struck him to change his garments for clothes more in harmony with his project; by which he might also get a little money to satisfy the immediate cravings of hunger. The resolution taken, it remained to carry it out.

It was only after a long search that Passepartout discovered a native dealer in old clothes, to whom he applied for an exchange. The man liked the European costume, and ere long Passepartout issued from his shop accoutred in an old Japanese coat, and a sort of one-sided turban, faded with long use. A few small pieces of silver, moreover, jingled in his pocket.

"Good!" thought he. "I will imagine I am at the Carnival!"

His first care, after being thus "Japanesed," was to enter a teahouse of modest appearance, and, upon half a bird and a little rice, to breakfast like a man for whom dinner was as yet a problem to be solved.

"Now," thought he, when he had eaten heartily, "I mustn't lose my head. I can't sell this costume again for one still more Japanese. I must consider how to leave this country of the sun, of which I shall not retain the most delightful of memories, as quickly as possible."

It occurred to him to visit the steamers which were about to leave for America. He would offer himself as a cook or servant, in payment of his passage and meals. Once at San Francisco, he would find some means of going on. The difficulty was, how to traverse the four thousand seven hundred miles of the Pacific which lay between Japan and the New World.

Passepartout was not the man to let an idea go begging, and directed his steps toward the docks. But, as he approached them, his project, which at first had seemed so simple, began to grow more and more formidable to his mind. What need would they have of a cook or servant on an American steamer, and what confidence would they put in him, dressed as he was? What references could he give?

As he was reflecting in this wise, his eyes fell upon an immense placard which a sort of clown was carrying through the streets. This placard, which was in English, read as follows:

> ACROBATIC JAPANESE TROUPE,
> HONORABLE WILLIAM BATCULAR, PROPRIETOR,
> LAST PRESENTATIONS,
> PRIOR TO THEIR DEPARTURE TO THE UNITED STATES,
> OF THE LONG NOSES! LONG NOSES!
> UNDER THE DIRECT PATRONAGE OF THE GOD TINGOU!
> GREAT ATTRACTION!

"The United States!" said Passepartout. "That's just what I want!"

He followed the clown, and soon found himself once more in the Japanese quarter. A quarter of an hour later he stopped before a large cabin, adorned with several clusters of streamers, the exterior walls of which were designed to represent, in violent colors and without perspective, a company of jugglers.

This was the Honorable William Batulcar's establishment. That gentleman was a sort of Barnum, the director of a troupe of mountebanks, jugglers, clowns, acrobats, equilibrists, and gymnasts, who, according to the placard, was giving his last performances before leaving the Empire of the Sun for the States of the Union.

Passepartout entered and asked for Mr. Batulcar, who straightway appeared in person.

"What do you want?" said he to Passepartout, whom he at first took for a native.

"Would you like a servant, sir?" asked Passepartout.

"A servant!" cried Mr. Batulcar, caressing the thick gray beard which hung from his chin. "I already have two who are obedient and faithful, have never left me, and serve me for their nourishment and here they are," added he, holding out his two robust arms, furrowed with veins as large as the strings of a bass viol.

"So I can be of no use to you?"

"None."

"The devil! I should so like to cross the Pacific with you!"

"Ah!" said the Honorable Mr. Batulcar. "You are no more a Japanese than I am a monkey! Who are you dressed up in that way?"

"A man dresses as he can."

"That's true. You are a Frenchman, aren't you?"

"Yes; a Parisian of Paris."

"Then you ought to know how to make grimaces?"

"Why," replied Passepartout, a little vexed that his nationality should cause this question, "we Frenchmen know how to make grimaces, it is true, but not any better than the Americans do."

"True. Well, if I can't take you as a servant, I can as a clown. You see, my friend, in France they exhibit foreign clowns, and in foreign parts French clowns."

"Ah!"

"You are pretty strong, eh?"

"Especially after a good meal."

"And you can sing?"

"Yes," returned Passepartout, who had formerly been wont to sing in the streets.

"But can you sing standing on your head, with a top spinning on your left foot, and a saber balanced on your right?"

"Humph! I think so," replied Passepartout, recalling the exercises of his younger days.

"Well, that's enough," said the Honorable William Batulcar.

The engagement was concluded there and then.

Passepartout had at last found something to do. He was engaged to act in the celebrated Japanese troupe. It was not a very dignified position, but within a week he would be on his way to San Francisco.

The performance, so noisily announced by the Honorable Mr. Batulcar, was to commence at three o'clock, and soon the deafening instruments of a Japanese orchestra resounded at the door. Passepartout, though he had not been able to study or rehearse a part, was designated to lend the aid of his sturdy shoulders in the great exhibition of the "human pyramid," executed by the Long Noses of the god Tingou. This "great attraction" was to close the performance.

Before three o'clock the large shed was invaded by the spectators, comprising Europeans and natives, Chinese and Japanese, men, women, and children, who precipitated themselves upon the narrow benches and into the boxes opposite the stage. The musicians took up a position inside, and were vigorously performing on their gongs, tam-tams, flutes, bones, tambourines, and immense drums.

The performance was much like all acrobatic displays; but it must be confessed that the Japanese are the first equilibrists in the world.

One, with a fan and some bits of paper, performed the graceful trick of the butterflies and the flowers; another traced in the air, with the odorous smoke of his pipe, a series of blue words, which composed a compliment to the audience; while a third juggled with some lighted candles, which he extinguished successively as they passed his lips, and relit again without interrupting for an instant his juggling. Another reproduced the most singular combinations with a spinning top; in his hands the revolving tops seemed to be animated with a life of their own in their interminable whirling; they ran over pipe stems, the edges of sabers, wires, and even hairs stretched across the stage; they turned around on the edges of large glasses, crossed bamboo ladders, dispersed into all the corners, and produced strange musical effects by the combination of their various pitches of tone. The jugglers tossed them in the air, threw them like shuttlecocks with wooden battledores, and yet they kept on spinning; they put them into their pockets, and took them out still whirling as before.

It is useless to describe the astonishing performances of the acrobats and gymnasts. The turning on ladders, poles, balls, barrels, &c., was executed with wonderful precision.

But the principal attraction was the exhibition of the Long Noses, a show to which Europe is as yet a stranger.

The Long Noses form a peculiar company, under the direct patronage of the god Tingou. Attired after the fashion of the Middle Ages, they bore upon their shoulders a splendid pair of wings; but what especially distinguished them was the long noses which were fastened to their faces, and the uses which they made of them. These noses were made of bamboo, and were five, six, and even ten feet long, some straight, others curved, some ribboned, and some having imitation warts upon them. It was upon these appendages, fixed tightly on their real noses, that they performed their gymnastic exercises. A dozen of these sectaries of Tingou lay flat upon their backs, while others, dressed to represent lightning rods, came and frolicked on their noses, jumping from one to another, and performing the most skillful leapings and somersaults.

As a last scene, a "human pyramid" had been announced, in which fifty Long Noses were to represent the car of Juggernaut. But, instead of forming a pyramid by mounting each other's shoulders, the artists were to group themselves on top of the noses. It happened that the performer who had hitherto formed the base of the car had quitted the troupe, and as, to fill this part, only strength and adroitness were necessary, Passepartout had been chosen to take his place.

The poor fellow really felt sad when—melancholy reminiscence of his youth!— he donned his costume, adorned with varicolored wings, and fastened to his natural feature a false nose six feet long. But he cheered up when he thought that this nose was winning him something to eat.

He went upon the stage, and took his place beside the rest who were to compose the base of the car of Juggernaut. They all stretched themselves on the floor, their noses pointing to the ceiling. A second group of artists disposed themselves on these long appendages, then a third above these, then a fourth, until a human monument reaching to the very cornices of the theater soon arose on top of the noses. This elicited loud applause, in the midst of which the orchestra was just striking up a deafening air, when the pyramid tottered, the balance was lost, one of the lower noses vanished from the pyramid, and the human monument was shattered like a castle built of cards!

It was Passepartout's fault. Abandoning his position, clearing the footlights without the aid of his wings, and, clambering up to the right-hand gallery, he fell at the feet of one of the spectators, crying, "Ah, my master! My master!"

"You here?"

"Myself."

"Very well; then let us go to the steamer, young man!"

Mr. Fogg, Aouda, and Passepartout passed through the lobby of the theater to the outside, where they encountered the Honorable Mr. Batulcar, furious with rage. He demanded damages for the "breakage" of the pyramid; and Phileas Fogg appeased him by giving him a handful of banknotes.

At half past six, the very hour of departure, Mr. Fogg and Aouda, followed by Passepartout, who in his hurry had retained his wings, and nose six feet long, stepped upon the American steamer.

# CHAPTER XXIV

### DURING WHICH MR. FOGG AND PARTY CROSS THE PACIFIC OCEAN

What happened when the pilot boat came in sight of Shanghai will be easily guessed. The signals made by the *Tankadere* had been seen by the captain of the Yokohama steamer, who, espying the flag at half-mast, had directed his course toward the little craft. Phileas Fogg, after paying the stipulated price of his passage to John Busby, and rewarding that worthy with the additional sum of five hundred and fifty pounds, ascended the steamer with Aouda and Fix; and they started at once for Nagasaki and Yokohama.

They reached their destination on the morning of the 14th of November. Phileas Fogg lost no time in going on board the *Carnatic*, where he learned, to Aouda's great delight—and perhaps to his own, though he betrayed no emotion—that Passepartout, a Frenchman, had really arrived on her the day before.

The San Francisco steamer was announced to leave that very evening, and it became necessary to find Passepartout, if possible, without delay. Mr. Fogg applied in vain to the French and English consuls, and, after wandering through the streets a long time, began to despair of finding his missing servant. Chance, or perhaps a kind of presentiment, at last led him into the Honorable Mr. Batulcar's theater. He certainly would not have recognized Passepartout in the eccentric mountebank's costume; but the latter, lying on his back, perceived his master in the gallery. He could not help starting, which so changed the position of his nose as to bring the "pyramid" pell-mell upon the stage.

All this Passepartout learned from Aouda, who recounted to him what had taken place on the voyage from Hong Kong to Shanghai on the *Tankadere*, in company with one Mr. Fix.

Passepartout did not change countenance on hearing this name. He thought that the time had not yet arrived to divulge to his master what had taken place between the detective and himself; and, in the account he gave of his absence, he simply excused himself for having been overtaken by drunkenness, in smoking opium at a tavern in Hong Kong.

Mr. Fogg heard this narrative coldly, without a word; and then furnished his man with funds necessary to obtain clothing more in harmony with his position. Within an hour the Frenchman had cut off his nose and parted with his wings, and retained nothing about him which recalled the sectary of the god Tingou.

The steamer which was about to depart from Yokohama to San Francisco belonged to the Pacific Mail Steamship Company, and was named the *General Grant*. She was a large paddle-wheel steamer of two thousand five hundred tons; well equipped and very fast. The massive walking beam rose and fell above the deck; at one end a piston rod worked up and down; and at the other was a connecting rod which, in changing the rectilinear motion to a circular one, was directly connected with the shaft of the paddles. The *General Grant* was rigged with three masts, giving a large capacity for sails, and thus materially aiding the steam power. By making twelve miles an hour, she would cross the ocean in twenty-one days. Phileas Fogg was therefore justified in hoping that he would reach San Francisco by the 2nd of December, New York by the 11th, and London on the 20th—thus gaining several hours on the fatal date of the 21st of December.

There was a full complement of passengers on board, among them English, many Americans, a large number of coolies on their way to California, and several East Indian officers, who were spending their vacation in making the tour of the world. Nothing of moment happened on the voyage; the steamer, sustained on its large paddles, rolled but little, and the Pacific almost justified its name. Mr. Fogg was as calm and taciturn as ever. His young companion felt herself more and more attached to him by other ties than gratitude; his silent but generous nature impressed her more than she thought; and it was almost unconsciously that she yielded to emotions which did not seem to have the least effect upon her protector. Aouda took the keenest interest in his plans, and became impatient at any incident which seemed likely to retard his journey.

She often chatted with Passepartout, who did not fail to perceive the state of the lady's heart; and, being the most faithful of domestics, he never exhausted his eulogies of Phileas Fogg's honesty, generosity, and devotion. He took pains to calm Aouda's doubts of a successful termination of the journey, telling her that the most difficult part of it had passed, that now they were beyond the fantastic countries of Japan and China, and were fairly on their way to civilized places again. A railway train from San Francisco to New York, and a transatlantic steamer from New York to Liverpool, would doubtless bring them to the end of this impossible journey round the world within the period agreed upon.

On the ninth day after leaving Yokohama, Phileas Fogg had traversed exactly one half of the terrestrial globe. The *General Grant* passed, on the 23rd of November, the one hundred and eightieth meridian, and was at the very antipodes of London. Mr. Fogg had, it is true, exhausted fifty-two of the eighty days in which he was to complete the tour, and there were only twenty-eight left. But, though he was only halfway by the difference of meridians, he had really gone over two-thirds of the whole journey; for he had been obliged to make long circuits from London to Aden, from Aden to Bombay, from Calcutta to Singapore, and from Singapore to Yokohama. Could he have followed without deviation the fiftieth parallel, which is that of London, the whole distance would only have been about twelve thousand miles; whereas he would be forced, by the irregular methods of locomotion, to traverse twenty-six thousand, of which he had, on the 23rd of November, accomplished seventeen thousand five hundred. And now the course was a straight one, and Fix was no longer there to put obstacles in their way!

It happened also, on the 23rd of November, that Passepartout made a joyful discovery. It will be remembered that the obstinate fellow had insisted on keeping his famous family watch at London time, and on regarding that of the countries he had passed through as quite false and unreliable. Now, on this day, though he had not changed the hands, he found that his watch exactly agreed with the ship's chronometers. His triumph was hilarious. He would have liked to know what Fix would say if he were aboard!

"The rogue told me a lot of stories," repeated Passepartout, "about the meridians, the sun, and the moon! Moon, indeed! Moonshine more likely! If one listened to that sort of people, a pretty sort of time one would keep! I was sure that the sun would someday regulate itself by my watch!"

Passepartout was ignorant that, if the face of his watch had been divided into twenty-four hours, like the Italian clocks, he would have no reason for exultation; for the hands of his watch would then, instead of as now indicating nine o'clock in the morning, indicate nine o'clock in the evening, that is, the twenty-first hour after midnight precisely the difference between London time and that of the one hundred and eightieth meridian. But if Fix had been able to explain this purely physical effect, Passepartout would not have admitted, even if he had comprehended it. Moreover, if the detective had been on board at that moment, Passepartout would have joined issue with him on a quite different subject, and in an entirely different manner.

Where was Fix at that moment?

He was actually on board the *General Grant*.

On reaching Yokohama, the detective, leaving Mr. Fogg, whom he expected to meet again during the day, had repaired at once to the English consulate, where he at last found the warrant of arrest. It had followed him from Bombay, and had come by the *Carnatic*, on which steamer he himself was supposed to be. Fix's disappointment may be imagined when he reflected that the warrant was now useless. Mr. Fogg had left English ground, and it was now necessary to procure his extradition!

"Well," thought Fix, after a moment of anger, "my warrant is not good here, but it will be in England. The rogue evidently intends to return to his own country, thinking he has thrown the police off his track. Good! I will follow him across the Atlantic. As for the money, heaven grant there may be some left! But the fellow has already spent in traveling, rewards, trials, bail, elephants, and all sorts of charges, more than five thousand pounds. Yet, after all, the bank is rich!"

His course decided on, he went on board the *General Grant*, and was there when Mr. Fogg and Aouda arrived. To his utter amazement, he recognized Passepartout, despite his theatrical disguise. He quickly concealed himself in his cabin, to avoid an awkward explanation, and hoped—thanks to the number of passengers—to remain unperceived by Mr. Fogg's servant.

On that very day, however, he met Passepartout face-to-face on the forward deck. The latter, without a word, made a rush for him, grasped him by the throat, and, much to the amusement of a group of Americans, who immediately began to bet on him, administered to the detective a perfect volley of blows, which proved the great superiority of French over English pugilistic skill.

When Passepartout had finished, he found himself relieved and comforted. Fix got up in a somewhat rumpled condition, and, looking at his adversary, coldly said, "Have you done?"

"For this time—yes."

"Then let me have a word with you."

"But I—"

"In your master's interests."

Passepartout seemed to be vanquished by Fix's coolness, for he quietly followed him, and they sat down aside from the rest of the passengers.

"You have given me a thrashing," said Fix. "Good, I expected it. Now, listen to me. Up to this time I have been Mr. Fogg's adversary. I am now in his game."

"Aha!" cried Passepartout. "You are convinced he is an honest man?"

"No," replied Fix coldly, "I think him a rascal. Sh! Don't budge, and let me speak. As long as Mr. Fogg was on English ground, it was for my interest to detain him there until my warrant of arrest arrived. I did everything I could to keep him back. I sent the Bombay priests after him, I got you intoxicated at Hong Kong, I separated you from him, and I made him miss the Yokohama steamer."

Passepartout listened, with closed fists.

"Now," resumed Fix, "Mr. Fogg seems to be going back to England. Well, I will follow him there. But hereafter I will do as much to keep obstacles out of his way as I have done up to this time to put them in his path. I've changed my game, you see, and simply because it was for my interest to change it. Your interest is the same as mine; for it is only in England that you will ascertain whether you are in the service of a criminal or an honest man."

Passepartout listened very attentively to Fix, and was convinced that he spoke with entire good faith.

"Are we friends?" asked the detective.

"Friends? No," replied Passepartout; "but allies, perhaps. At the least sign of treason, however, I'll twist your neck for you."

"Agreed," said the detective quietly.

Eleven days later, on the 3rd of December, the *General Grant* entered the bay of the Golden Gate, and reached San Francisco.

Mr. Fogg had neither gained nor lost a single day.

# CHAPTER XXV

### In Which a Slight Glimpse Is Had of San Francisco

It was seven in the morning when Mr. Fogg, Aouda, and Passepartout set foot upon the American continent, if this name can be given to the floating quay upon which they disembarked. These quays, rising and falling with the tide, thus facilitate the loading and unloading of vessels. Alongside them were clippers of all sizes, steamers of all nationalities, and the steamboats, with several decks rising one above the other, which ply on the Sacramento and its tributaries. There were also heaped up the products of a commerce which extends to Mexico, Chile, Peru, Brazil, Europe, Asia, and all the Pacific islands.

Passepartout, in his joy on reaching at last the American continent, thought he would manifest it by executing a perilous vault in fine style; but, tumbling upon some worm-eaten planks, he fell through them. Put out of countenance by the manner in which he thus "set foot" upon the New World, he uttered a loud cry, which so frightened the innumerable cormorants and pelicans that are always perched upon these movable quays, that they flew noisily away.

Mr. Fogg, on reaching shore, proceeded to find out at what hour the first train left for New York, and learned that this was at six o'clock p.m.; he had, therefore, an entire day to spend in the Californian capital. Taking a carriage at a charge of three dollars, he and Aouda entered it, while Passepartout mounted the box beside the driver, and they set out for the International Hotel.

From his exalted position Passepartout observed with much curiosity the wide streets, the low, evenly ranged houses, the Anglo-Saxon Gothic churches, the great docks, the palatial wooden and brick warehouses, the numerous conveyances, omnibuses, horsecars, and upon the sidewalks, not only Americans and Europeans, but Chinese and Indians. Passepartout was surprised at all he saw. San Francisco was no longer the legendary city of 1849—a city of banditti, assassins, and incendiaries, who had flocked hither in crowds in pursuit of plunder; a paradise of outlaws, where they gambled with gold dust, a revolver in one hand and a bowie knife in the other: it was now a great commercial emporium.

The lofty tower of its city hall overlooked the whole panorama of the streets and avenues, which cut each other at right angles, and in the midst of which appeared pleasant, verdant squares, while beyond appeared the Chinese quarter, seemingly imported from the Celestial Empire in a toy box. Sombreros and red shirts and plumed Indians were rarely to be seen; but there were silk hats and black coats everywhere worn by a multitude of nervously active, gentlemanly looking men. Some of the streets—especially Montgomery Street, which is to San Francisco what Regent Street is to London, the Boulevard des Italiens to Paris, and Broadway to New York—were lined with splendid and spacious stores, which exposed in their windows the products of the entire world.

When Passepartout reached the International Hotel, it did not seem to him as if he had left England at all.

The ground floor of the hotel was occupied by a large bar, a sort of restaurant freely open to all passersby, who might partake of dried beef, oyster soup, biscuits, and cheese without taking out their purses. Payment was made only for the ale, porter, or sherry which was drunk. This seemed "very American" to Passepartout. The hotel refreshment rooms were comfortable, and Mr. Fogg and Aouda, installing themselves at a table, were abundantly served on diminutive plates by negroes of darkest hue.

After breakfast, Mr. Fogg, accompanied by Aouda, started for the English consulate to have his passport visaed. As he was going out, he met Passepartout, who asked him if it would not be well, before taking the train, to purchase some dozens of Enfield rifles and Colt's revolvers. He had been listening to stories of attacks upon the trains by the Sioux and Pawnees. Mr. Fogg thought it a useless precaution, but told him to do as he thought best, and went on to the consulate.

He had not proceeded two hundred steps, however, when, "by the greatest chance in the world," he met Fix. The detective seemed wholly taken by surprise. What! Had Mr. Fogg and himself crossed the Pacific together, and not met on the steamer! At least Fix felt honored to behold once more the gentleman to whom he owed so much, and, as his business recalled him to Europe, he should be delighted to continue the journey in such pleasant company.

Mr. Fogg replied that the honor would be his; and the detective—who was determined not to lose sight of him—begged permission to accompany them in their walk about San Francisco—a request which Mr. Fogg readily granted.

They soon found themselves in Montgomery Street, where a great crowd was collected; the sidewalks, street, horsecar rails, the shop doors, the windows of the houses, and even the roofs, were full of people. Men were going about carrying large posters, and flags and streamers were floating in the wind; while loud cries were heard on every hand.

"Hurrah for Camerfield!"

"Hurrah for Mandiboy!"

It was a political meeting; at least so Fix conjectured, who said to Mr. Fogg, "Perhaps we had better not mingle with the crowd. There may be danger in it."

"Yes," returned Mr. Fogg; "and blows, even if they are political, are still blows."

Fix smiled at this remark; and, in order to be able to see without being jostled about, the party took up a position on the top of a flight of steps situated at the upper end of Montgomery Street. Opposite them, on the other side of the street, between a coal wharf and a petroleum warehouse, a large platform had been erected in the open air, toward which the current of the crowd seemed to be directed.

For what purpose was this meeting? What was the occasion of this excited assemblage? Phileas Fogg could not imagine. Was it to nominate some high official—a governor or member of Congress? It was not improbable, so agitated was the multitude before them.

Just at this moment there was an unusual stir in the human mass. All the hands were raised in the air. Some, tightly closed, seemed to disappear suddenly in the midst of the cries—an energetic way, no doubt, of casting a vote. The crowd swayed back, the banners and flags wavered, disappeared an instant, then reappeared in tatters. The undulations of the human surge reached the steps, while all the heads floundered on the surface like a sea agitated by a squall. Many of the black hats disappeared, and the greater part of the crowd seemed to have diminished in height.

"It is evidently a meeting," said Fix, "and its object must be an exciting one. I should not wonder if it were about the Alabama, despite the fact that that question is settled."

"Perhaps," replied Mr. Fogg, simply.

"At least, there are two champions in presence of each other, the Honorable Mr. Camerfield and the Honorable Mr. Mandiboy."

Aouda, leaning upon Mr. Fogg's arm, observed the tumultuous scene with surprise, while Fix asked a man near him what the cause of it all was. Before the man could reply, a fresh agitation arose; hurrahs and excited shouts were heard; the staffs of the banners began to be used as offensive weapons; and fists flew about in every direction. Thumps were exchanged from the tops of the carriages and omnibuses which had been blocked up in the crowd. Boots and shoes went whirling through the air, and Mr. Fogg thought he even heard the crack of revolvers mingling in the din, the rout approached the stairway, and flowed over the lower step. One of the parties had evidently been repulsed; but the mere lookers-on could not tell whether Mandiboy or Camerfield had gained the upper hand.

"It would be prudent for us to retire," said Fix, who was anxious that Mr. Fogg should not receive any injury, at least until they got back to London. "If there is any question about England in all this, and we were recognized, I fear it would go hard with us."

"An English subject—" began Mr. Fogg.

He did not finish his sentence; for a terrific hubbub now arose on the terrace behind the flight of steps where they stood, and there were frantic shouts of "Hurrah for Mandiboy! Hip, hip, hurrah!"

It was a band of voters coming to the rescue of their allies, and taking the Camerfield forces in flank. Mr. Fogg, Aouda, and Fix found themselves between two fires; it was too late to escape. The torrent of men, armed with loaded canes and sticks, was irresistible. Phileas Fogg and Fix were roughly hustled in their attempts to protect their fair companion; the former, as cool as ever, tried to defend himself with the weapons which nature has placed at the end of every Englishman's arm, but in vain. A big brawny fellow with a red beard, flushed face, and broad shoulders, who seemed to be the chief of the band, raised his clenched fist to strike Mr. Fogg, whom he would have given a crushing blow, had not Fix rushed in and received it in his stead. An enormous bruise immediately made its appearance under the detective's silk hat, which was completely smashed in.

"Yankee!" exclaimed Mr. Fogg, darting a contemptuous look at the ruffian.

"Englishman!" returned the other. "We will meet again!"

"When you please."

"What is your name?"

"Phileas Fogg. And yours?"

"Colonel Stamp Proctor."

The human tide now swept by, after overturning Fix, who speedily got upon his feet again, though with tattered clothes. Happily, he was not seriously hurt. His traveling overcoat was divided into two unequal parts, and his trousers resembled those of certain Indians, which fit less compactly than they are easy to put on. Aouda had escaped unharmed, and Fix alone bore marks of the fray in his black-and-blue bruise.

"Thanks," said Mr. Fogg to the detective, as soon as they were out of the crowd.

"No thanks are necessary," replied. Fix; "but let us go."

"Where?"

"To a tailor's."

Such a visit was, indeed, opportune. The clothing of both Mr. Fogg and Fix was in rags, as if they had themselves been actively engaged in the contest between Camerfield and Mandiboy. An hour after, they were once more suitably attired, and with Aouda returned to the International Hotel.

Passepartout was waiting for his master, armed with half a dozen six-barreled revolvers. When he perceived Fix, he knit his brows; but Aouda having, in a few words, told him of their adventure, his countenance resumed its placid expression. Fix evidently was no longer an enemy, but an ally; he was faithfully keeping his word.

Dinner over, the coach which was to convey the passengers and their luggage to the station drew up to the door. As he was getting in, Mr. Fogg said to Fix, "You have not seen this Colonel Proctor again?"

"No."

"I will come back to America to find him," said Phileas Fogg calmly. "It would not be right for an Englishman to permit himself to be treated in that way, without retaliating."

The detective smiled, but did not reply. It was clear that Mr. Fogg was one of those Englishmen who, while they do not tolerate dueling at home, fight abroad when their honor is attacked.

At a quarter before six the travelers reached the station, and found the train ready to depart. As he was about to enter it, Mr. Fogg called a porter, and said to him: "My friend, was there not some trouble today in San Francisco?"

"It was a political meeting, sir," replied the porter.

"But I thought there was a great deal of disturbance in the streets."

"It was only a meeting assembled for an election."

"The election of a general-in-chief, no doubt?" asked Mr. Fogg.

"No, sir; of a justice of the peace."

Phileas Fogg got into the train, which started off at full speed.

# CHAPTER XXVI

### In Which Phileas Fogg and Party Travel by the Pacific Railroad

"From ocean to ocean"—so say the Americans; and these four words compose the general designation of the "great trunk line" which crosses the entire width of the United States. The Pacific Railroad is, however, really divided into two distinct lines: the Central Pacific, between San Francisco and Ogden, and the Union Pacific, between Ogden and Omaha. Five main lines connect Omaha with New York.

New York and San Francisco are thus united by an uninterrupted metal ribbon, which measures no less than three thousand seven hundred and eighty-six miles. Between Omaha and the Pacific the railway crosses a territory which is still infested by Indians and wild beasts, and a large tract which the Mormons, after they were driven from Illinois in 1845, began to colonize.

The journey from New York to San Francisco consumed, formerly, under the most favorable conditions, at least six months. It is now accomplished in seven days.

It was in 1862 that, in spite of the Southern members of Congress, who wished a more southerly route, it was decided to lay the road between the forty-first and forty-second parallels. President Lincoln himself fixed the end of the line at Omaha, in Nebraska. The work was at once commenced, and pursued with true American energy; nor did the rapidity with which it went on injuriously affect its good execution. The road grew, on the prairies, a mile and a half a day. A locomotive, running on the rails laid down the evening before, brought the rails to be laid on the morrow, and advanced upon them as fast as they were put in position.

The Pacific Railroad is joined by several branches in Iowa, Kansas, Colorado, and Oregon. On leaving Omaha, it passes along the left bank of the Platte River as far as the junction of its northern branch, follows its southern branch, crosses the Laramie territory and the Wasatch Mountains, turns the Great Salt Lake, and reaches Salt Lake City, the Mormon capital, plunges into the Tuilla Valley, across the American desert, Cedar and Humboldt Mountains, the Sierra Nevada, and descends, via Sacramento, to the Pacific—its grade, even on the Rocky Mountains, never exceeding one hundred and twelve feet to the mile.

Such was the road to be traversed in seven days, which would enable Phileas Fogg—at least, so he hoped—to take the Atlantic steamer at New York on the 11th for Liverpool.

The car which he occupied was a sort of long omnibus on eight wheels, and with no compartments in the interior. It was supplied with two rows of seats, perpendicular to the direction of the train on either side of an aisle which conducted to the front and rear platforms. These platforms were found throughout the train, and the passengers were able to pass from one end of the train to the other. It was supplied with saloon cars, balcony cars, restaurants, and smoking cars; theater cars alone were wanting, and they will have these someday.

Book and news dealers, sellers of edibles, drinkables, and cigars, who seemed to have plenty of customers, were continually circulating in the aisles.

The train left Oakland station at six o'clock. It was already night, cold and cheerless, the heavens being overcast with clouds which seemed to threaten snow. The train did not proceed rapidly; counting the stoppages, it did not run more than twenty miles an hour, which was a sufficient speed, however, to enable it to reach Omaha within its designated time.

There was but little conversation in the car, and soon many of the passengers were overcome with sleep. Passepartout found himself beside the detective; but he did not talk to him. After recent events, their relations with each other had grown somewhat cold; there could no longer be mutual sympathy or intimacy between them. Fix's manner had not changed; but Passepartout was very reserved, and ready to strangle his former friend on the slightest provocation.

Snow began to fall an hour after they started, a fine snow, however, which happily could not obstruct the train; nothing could be seen from the windows but a vast, white sheet, against which the smoke of the locomotive had a grayish aspect.

At eight o'clock a steward entered the car and announced that the time for going to bed had arrived; and in a few minutes the car was transformed into a dormitory. The backs of the seats were thrown back, bedsteads carefully packed were rolled out by an ingenious system, berths were suddenly improvised, and each traveler had soon at his disposition a comfortable bed, protected from curious eyes by thick curtains. The sheets were clean and the pillows soft. It only remained to go to bed and sleep, which everybody did—while the train sped on across the state of California.

The country between San Francisco and Sacramento is not very hilly. The Central Pacific, taking Sacramento for its starting point, extends eastward to meet the road from Omaha. The line from San Francisco to Sacramento runs in a northeasterly direction, along the American River, which empties into San Pablo Bay. The one hundred and twenty miles between these cities were accomplished in six hours, and toward midnight, while fast asleep, the travelers passed through Sacramento; so that they saw nothing of that important place, the seat of the state government, with its fine quays, its broad streets, its noble hotels, squares, and churches.

The train, on leaving Sacramento, and passing the junction, Roclin, Auburn, and Colfax, entered the range of the Sierra Nevada. Cisco was reached at seven in the morning; and an hour later the dormitory was transformed into an ordinary car, and the travelers could observe the picturesque beauties of the mountain region through which they were steaming. The railway track wound in and out among the passes, now approaching the mountainsides, now suspended over precipices, avoiding abrupt angles by bold curves, plunging into narrow defiles, which seemed to have no outlet. The locomotive, its great funnel emitting a weird light, with its sharp bell, and its cowcatcher extended like a spur, mingled its shrieks and bellowings with the noise of torrents and cascades, and twined its smoke among the branches of the gigantic pines.

There were few or no bridges or tunnels on the route. The railway turned around the sides of the mountains, and did not attempt to violate nature by taking the shortest cut from one point to another.

The train entered the state of Nevada through the Carson Valley about nine o'clock, going always northeasterly; and at midday reached Reno, where there was a delay of twenty minutes for breakfast.

From this point the road, running along Humboldt River, passed northward for several miles by its banks; then it turned eastward, and kept by the river until it reached the Humboldt Range, nearly at the extreme eastern limit of Nevada.

Having breakfasted, Mr. Fogg and his companions resumed their places in the car, and observed the varied landscape which unfolded itself as they passed along the vast prairies, the mountains lining the horizon, and the creeks, with their frothy, foaming streams. Sometimes a great herd of buffaloes, massing together in the distance, seemed like a movable dam. These innumerable multitudes of ruminating beasts often form an insurmountable obstacle to the passage of the trains; thousands of them have been seen passing over the track for hours together, in compact ranks. The locomotive is then forced to stop and wait till the road is once more clear.

This happened, indeed, to the train in which Mr. Fogg was traveling. About twelve o'clock a troop of ten or twelve thousand head of buffalo encumbered the track. The locomotive, slackening its speed, tried to clear the way with its cowcatcher; but the mass of animals was too great. The buffaloes marched along with a tranquil gait, uttering now and then deafening bellowings. There was no use of interrupting them, for, having taken a particular direction, nothing can moderate and change their course; it is a torrent of living flesh which no dam could contain.

The travelers gazed on this curious spectacle from the platforms; but Phileas Fogg, who had the most reason of all to be in a hurry, remained in his seat, and waited philosophically until it should please the buffaloes to get out of the way.

Passepartout was furious at the delay they occasioned, and longed to discharge his arsenal of revolvers upon them.

"What a country!" cried he. "Mere cattle stop the trains, and go by in a procession, just as if they were not impeding travel! Parbleu! I should like to know if Mr. Fogg foresaw this mishap in his program! And here's an engineer who doesn't dare to run the locomotive into this herd of beasts!"

The engineer did not try to overcome the obstacle, and he was wise. He would have crushed the first buffaloes, no doubt, with the cowcatcher; but the locomotive, however powerful, would soon have been checked, the train would inevitably have been thrown off the track, and would then have been helpless.

The best course was to wait patiently, and regain the lost time by greater speed when the obstacle was removed. The procession of buffaloes lasted three full hours, and it was night before the track was clear. The last ranks of the herd were now passing over the rails, while the first had already disappeared below the southern horizon.

It was eight o'clock when the train passed through the defiles of the Humboldt Range, and half past nine when it penetrated Utah, the region of the Great Salt Lake, the singular colony of the Mormons.

## CHAPTER XXVII

### IN WHICH PASSEPARTOUT UNDERGOES, AT A SPEED OF TWENTY MILES AN HOUR, A COURSE OF MORMON HISTORY

During the night of the 5th of December, the train ran southeasterly for about fifty miles; then rose an equal distance in a northeasterly direction, toward the Great Salt Lake.

Passepartout, about nine o'clock, went out upon the platform to take the air. The weather was cold, the heavens gray, but it was not snowing. The sun's disk, enlarged by the mist, seemed an enormous ring of gold, and Passepartout was amusing himself by calculating its value in pounds sterling, when he was diverted from this interesting study by a strange-looking personage who made his appearance on the platform.

This personage, who had taken the train at Elko, was tall and dark, with black moustache, black stockings, a black silk hat, a black waistcoat, black trousers, a white cravat, and dogskin gloves. He might have been taken for a clergyman. He went from one end of the train to the other, and affixed to the door of each car a notice written in manuscript.

Passepartout approached and read one of these notices, which stated that Elder William Hitch, Mormon missionary, taking advantage of his presence on train No. 48, would deliver a lecture on Mormonism in car No. 117, from eleven to twelve o'clock; and that he invited all who were desirous of being instructed concerning the mysteries of the religion of the "Latter Day Saints" to attend.

"I'll go," said Passepartout to himself. He knew nothing of Mormonism except the custom of polygamy, which is its foundation.

The news quickly spread through the train, which contained about one hundred passengers, thirty of whom, at most, attracted by the notice, ensconced themselves in car No. 117. Passepartout took one of the front seats. Neither Mr. Fogg nor Fix cared to attend.

At the appointed hour Elder William Hitch rose, and, in an irritated voice, as if he had already been contradicted, said, "I tell you that Joe Smith is a martyr, that his brother Hiram is a martyr, and that the persecutions of the United States government against the prophets will also make a martyr of Brigham Young. Who dares to say the contrary?"

No one ventured to gainsay the missionary, whose excited tone contrasted curiously with his naturally calm visage. No doubt his anger arose from the hardships to which the Mormons were actually subjected. The government had just succeeded, with some difficulty, in reducing these independent fanatics to its rule. It had made itself master of Utah, and subjected that territory to the laws of the Union, after imprisoning Brigham Young on a charge of rebellion and polygamy. The disciples of the prophet had since redoubled their efforts, and resisted, by words at least, the authority of Congress. Elder Hitch, as is seen, was trying to make proselytes on the very railway trains.

Then, emphasising his words with his loud voice and frequent gestures, he related the history of the Mormons from biblical times: how that, in Israel, a Mormon prophet of the tribe of Joseph published the annals of the new religion, and bequeathed them to his son Mormon; how, many centuries later, a translation of this precious book, which was written in Egyptian, was made by Joseph Smith Junior, a Vermont farmer, who revealed himself as a mystical prophet in 1825; and how, in short, the celestial messenger appeared to him in an illuminated forest, and gave him the annals of the Lord.

Several of the audience, not being much interested in the missionary's narrative, here left the car; but Elder Hitch, continuing his lecture, related how Smith Junior, with his father, two brothers, and a few disciples, founded the church of the "Latter Day Saints," which, adopted not only in America, but in England, Norway and Sweden, and Germany, counts many artisans, as well as men engaged in the liberal professions, among its members; how a colony was established in Ohio, a temple erected there at a cost of two hundred thousand dollars, and a town built at Kirkland; how Smith became an enterprising banker, and received from a simple mummy showman a papyrus scroll written by Abraham and several famous Egyptians.

The Elder's story became somewhat wearisome, and his audience grew gradually less, until it was reduced to twenty passengers. But this did not disconcert the enthusiast, who proceeded with the story of Joseph Smith's bankruptcy in 1837, and how his ruined creditors gave him a coat of tar and feathers; his reappearance some years afterward, more honorable and honored than ever, at Independence, Missouri, the chief of a flourishing colony of three thousand disciples, and his pursuit thence by outraged Gentiles, and retirement into the Far West.

Ten hearers only were now left, among them honest Passepartout, who was listening with all his ears. Thus he learned that, after long persecutions, Smith reappeared in Illinois, and in 1839 founded a community at Nauvoo, on the Mississippi, numbering twenty-five thousand souls, of which he became mayor, chief justice, and general-in-chief; that he announced himself, in 1843, as a candidate for the presidency of the United States; and that finally, being drawn into ambuscade at Carthage, he was thrown into prison, and assassinated by a band of men disguised in masks.

Passepartout was now the only person left in the car, and the elder, looking him full in the face, reminded him that, two years after the assassination of Joseph Smith, the inspired prophet, Brigham Young, his successor, left Nauvoo for the banks of the Great Salt Lake, where, in the midst of that fertile region, directly on the route of the emigrants who crossed Utah on their way to California, the new colony, thanks to the polygamy practiced by the Mormons, had flourished beyond expectations.

"And this," added Elder William Hitch, "this is why the jealousy of Congress has been aroused against us! Why have the soldiers of the Union invaded the soil of Utah? Why has Brigham Young, our chief, been imprisoned, in contempt of all justice? Shall we yield to force? Never! Driven from Vermont, driven from Illinois, driven from Ohio, driven from Missouri, driven from Utah, we shall yet find some independent territory on which to plant our tents. And you, my brother," continued the elder, fixing his angry eyes upon his single auditor, "will you not plant yours there, too, under the shadow of our flag?"

"No!" replied Passepartout courageously, in his turn retiring from the car, and leaving the elder to preach to vacancy.

During the lecture the train had been making good progress, and toward half past twelve it reached the northwest border of the Great Salt Lake. Thence the passengers could observe the vast extent of this interior sea, which is also called the Dead Sea, and into which flows an American Jordan. It is a picturesque expanse, framed in lofty crags in large strata, encrusted with white salt—a superb sheet of water, which was formerly of larger extent than now, its shores having encroached with the lapse of time, and thus at once reduced its breadth and increased its depth.

The Salt Lake, seventy miles long and thirty-five wide, is situated three miles eight hundred feet above the sea. Quite different from Lake Asphaltite, whose depression is twelve hundred feet below the sea, it contains considerable salt, and one quarter of the weight of its water is solid matter, its specific weight being 1,170, and, after being distilled, 1,000. Fishes are, of course, unable to live in it, and those which descend through the Jordan, the Weber, and other streams soon perish.

The country around the lake was well cultivated, for the Mormons are mostly farmers; while ranches and pens for domesticated animals, fields of wheat, corn, and other cereals, luxuriant prairies, hedges of wild rose, clumps of acacias and milkwort, would have been seen six months later. Now the ground was covered with a thin powdering of snow.

The train reached Ogden at two o'clock, where it rested for six hours. Mr. Fogg and his party had time to pay a visit to Salt Lake City, connected with Ogden by a branch road; and they spent two hours in this strikingly American town, built on the pattern of other cities of the Union, like a checkerboard, "with the somber sadness of right angles," as Victor Hugo expresses it. The founder of the City of the Saints could not escape from the taste for symmetry which distinguishes the Anglo-Saxons. In this strange country, where the people are certainly not up to the level of their institutions, everything is done "squarely"—cities, houses, and follies.

The travelers, then, were promenading, at three o'clock, about the streets of the town built between the banks of the Jordan and the spurs of the Wasatch Range. They saw few or no churches, but the prophet's mansion, the courthouse, and the arsenal, blue-brick houses with verandas and porches, surrounded by gardens bordered with acacias, palms, and locusts. A clay and pebble wall, built in 1853, surrounded the town; and in the principal street were the market and several hotels adorned with pavilions. The place did not seem thickly populated. The streets were almost deserted, except in the vicinity of the temple, which they only reached after having traversed several quarters surrounded by palisades. There were many women, which was easily accounted for by the "peculiar institution" of the Mormons; but it must not be supposed that all the Mormons are polygamists. They are free to marry or not, as they please; but it is worth noting that it is mainly the female citizens of Utah who are anxious to marry, as, according to the Mormon religion, maiden ladies are not admitted to the possession of its highest joys. These poor creatures seemed to be neither well off nor happy. Some—the more well-to-do, no doubt—wore short, open, black silk dresses, under a hood or modest shawl; others were habited in Indian fashion.

Passepartout could not behold without a certain fright these women, charged, in groups, with conferring happiness on a single Mormon. His common sense pitied, above all, the husband. It seemed to him a terrible thing to have to guide so many wives at once across the vicissitudes of life, and to conduct them, as it were, in a body to the Mormon paradise with the prospect of seeing them in the company of the glorious Smith, who doubtless was the chief ornament of that delightful place, to all eternity. He felt decidedly repelled from such a vocation, and he imagined—perhaps he was mistaken—that the fair ones of Salt Lake City cast rather alarming glances on his person. Happily, his stay there was but brief. At four the party found themselves again at the station, took their places in the train, and the whistle sounded for starting. Just at the moment, however, that the locomotive wheels began to move, cries of "Stop! Stop!" were heard.

Trains, like time and tide, stop for no one. The gentleman who uttered the cries was evidently a belated Mormon. He was breathless with running. Happily for him, the station had neither gates nor barriers. He rushed along the track, jumped on the rear platform of the train, and fell, exhausted, into one of the seats.

Passepartout, who had been anxiously watching this amateur gymnast, approached him with lively interest, and learned that he had taken flight after an unpleasant domestic scene.

When the Mormon had recovered his breath, Passepartout ventured to ask him politely how many wives he had; for, from the manner in which he had decamped, it might be thought that he had twenty at least.

"One, sir," replied the Mormon, raising his arms heavenward—"one, and that was enough!"

# CHAPTER XXVIII

## In Which Passepartout Does Not Succeed in
## Making Anybody Listen to Reason

The train, on leaving Great Salt Lake at Ogden, passed northward for an hour as far as Weber River, having completed nearly nine hundred miles from San Francisco. From this point it took an easterly direction toward the jagged Wasatch Mountains. It was in the section included between this range and the Rocky Mountains that the American engineers found the most formidable difficulties in laying the road, and that the government granted a subsidy of forty-eight thousand dollars per mile, instead of sixteen thousand allowed for the work done on the plains. But the engineers, instead of violating nature, avoided its difficulties by winding around, instead of penetrating, the rocks. One tunnel only, fourteen thousand feet in length, was pierced in order to arrive at the great basin.

The track up to this time had reached its highest elevation at the Great Salt Lake. From this point it described a long curve, descending toward Bitter Creek Valley, to rise again to the dividing ridge of the waters between the Atlantic and the Pacific. There were many creeks in this mountainous region, and it was necessary to cross Muddy Creek, Green Creek, and others, upon culverts.

Passepartout grew more and more impatient as they went on, while Fix longed to get out of this difficult region, and was more anxious than Phileas Fogg himself to be beyond the danger of delays and accidents, and set foot on English soil.

At ten o'clock at night the train stopped at Fort Bridger station, and twenty minutes later entered Wyoming Territory, following the valley of Bitter Creek throughout. The next day, December 7th, they stopped for a quarter of an hour at Green River station. Snow had fallen abundantly during the night, but, being mixed with rain, it had half melted, and did not interrupt their progress. The bad weather, however, annoyed Passepartout; for the accumulation of snow, by blocking the wheels of the cars, would certainly have been fatal to Mr. Fogg's tour.

"What an idea!" he said to himself. "Why did my master make this journey in winter? Couldn't he have waited for the good season to increase his chances?"

While the worthy Frenchman was absorbed in the state of the sky and the depression of the temperature, Aouda was experiencing fears from a totally different cause.

Several passengers had got off at Green River, and were walking up and down the platforms; and among these Aouda recognized Colonel Stamp Proctor, the same who had so grossly insulted Phileas Fogg at the San Francisco meeting. Not wishing to be recognized, the young woman drew back from the window, feeling much alarm at her discovery. She was attached to the man who, however coldly, gave her daily evidences of the most absolute devotion. She did not comprehend, perhaps, the depth of the sentiment with which her protector inspired her, which she called gratitude, but which, though she was unconscious of it, was really more than that. Her heart sank within her when she recognized the man whom Mr. Fogg desired, sooner or later, to call to account for his conduct. Chance alone, it was clear, had brought Colonel Proctor on this train; but there he was, and it was necessary, at all hazards, that Phileas Fogg should not perceive his adversary.

Aouda seized a moment when Mr. Fogg was asleep to tell Fix and Passepartout whom she had seen.

"That Proctor on this train!" cried Fix. "Well, reassure yourself, madam; before he settles with Mr. Fogg; he has got to deal with me! It seems to me that I was the more insulted of the two."

"And, besides," added Passepartout, "I'll take charge of him, colonel as he is."

"Mr. Fix," resumed Aouda, "Mr. Fogg will allow no one to avenge him. He said that he would come back to America to find this man. Should he perceive Colonel Proctor, we could not prevent a collision which might have terrible results. He must not see him."

"You are right, madam," replied Fix; "a meeting between them might ruin all. Whether he were victorious or beaten, Mr. Fogg would be delayed, and——"

"And," added Passepartout, "that would play the game of the gentlemen of the Reform Club. In four days we shall be in New York. Well, if my master does not leave this car during those four days, we may hope that chance will not bring him face-to-face with this confounded American. We must, if possible, prevent his stirring out of it."

The conversation dropped. Mr. Fogg had just woke up, and was looking out of the window. Soon after Passepartout, without being heard by his master or Aouda, whispered to the detective, "Would you really fight for him?"

"I would do anything," replied Fix, in a tone which betrayed determined will, "to get him back living to Europe!"

Passepartout felt something like a shudder shoot through his frame, but his confidence in his master remained unbroken.

Was there any means of detaining Mr. Fogg in the car, to avoid a meeting between him and the colonel? It ought not to be a difficult task, since that gentleman was naturally sedentary and little curious. The detective, at least, seemed to have found a way; for, after a few moments, he said to Mr. Fogg, "These are long and slow hours, sir, that we are passing on the railway."

"Yes," replied Mr. Fogg; "but they pass."

"You were in the habit of playing whist," resumed Fix, "on the steamers."

"Yes; but it would be difficult to do so here. I have neither cards nor partners."

"Oh, but we can easily buy some cards, for they are sold on all the American trains. And as for partners, if madam plays——"

"Certainly, sir," Aouda quickly replied; "I understand whist. It is part of an English education."

"I myself have some pretensions to playing a good game. Well, here are three of us, and a dummy——"

"As you please, sir," replied Phileas Fogg, heartily glad to resume his favorite pastime even on the railway.

Passepartout was dispatched in search of the steward, and soon returned with two packs of cards, some pins, counters, and a shelf covered with cloth.

The game commenced. Aouda understood whist sufficiently well, and even received some compliments on her playing from Mr. Fogg. As for the detective, he was simply an adept, and worthy of being matched against his present opponent.

"Now," thought Passepartout, "we've got him. He won't budge."

At eleven in the morning the train had reached the dividing ridge of the waters at Bridger Pass, seven thousand five hundred and twenty-four feet above the level of the sea, one of the highest points attained by the track in crossing the Rocky Mountains. After going about two hundred miles, the travelers at last found themselves on one of those vast plains which extend to the Atlantic, and which nature has made so propitious for laying the iron road.

On the declivity of the Atlantic basin the first streams, branches of the North Platte River, already appeared. The whole northern and eastern horizon was bounded by the immense semicircular curtain which is formed by the southern portion of the Rocky Mountains, the highest being Laramie Peak. Between this and the railway extended vast plains, plentifully irrigated. On the right rose the lower spurs of the mountainous mass which extends southward to the sources of the Arkansas River, one of the great tributaries of the Missouri.

At half past twelve the travelers caught sight for an instant of Fort Halleck, which commands that section; and in a few more hours the Rocky Mountains were crossed. There was reason to hope, then, that no accident would mark the journey through this difficult country. The snow had ceased falling, and the air became crisp and cold. Large birds, frightened by the locomotive, rose and flew off in the distance. No wild beast appeared on the plain. It was a desert in its vast nakedness.

After a comfortable breakfast, served in the car, Mr. Fogg and his partners had just resumed whist, when a violent whistling was heard, and the train stopped. Passepartout put his head out of the door, but saw nothing to cause the delay; no station was in view.

Aouda and Fix feared that Mr. Fogg might take it into his head to get out; but that gentleman contented himself with saying to his servant, "See what is the matter."

Passepartout rushed out of the car. Thirty or forty passengers had already descended, among them Colonel Stamp Proctor.

The train had stopped before a red signal which blocked the way. The engineer and conductor were talking excitedly with a signalman, whom the stationmaster at Medicine Bow, the next stopping place, had sent on before. The passengers drew around and took part in the discussion, in which Colonel Proctor, with his insolent manner, was conspicuous.

Passepartout, joining the group, heard the signalman say, "No! You can't pass. The bridge at Medicine Bow is shaky, and would not bear the weight of the train."

This was a suspension bridge thrown over some rapids, about a mile from the place where they now were. According to the signalman, it was in a ruinous condition, several of the iron wires being broken; and it was impossible to risk the passage. He did not in any way exaggerate the condition of the bridge. It may be taken for granted that, rash as the Americans usually are, when they are prudent there is good reason for it.

Passepartout, not daring to apprise his master of what he heard, listened with set teeth, immovable as a statue.

"Hum!" cried Colonel Proctor. "But we are not going to stay here, I imagine, and take root in the snow?"

"Colonel," replied the conductor, "we have telegraphed to Omaha for a train, but it is not likely that it will reach Medicine Bow is less than six hours."

"Six hours!" cried Passepartout.

"Certainly," returned the conductor. "Besides, it will take us as long as that to reach Medicine Bow on foot."

"But it is only a mile from here," said one of the passengers.

"Yes, but it's on the other side of the river."

"And can't we cross that in a boat?" asked the colonel.

"That's impossible. The creek is swelled by the rains. It is a rapid, and we shall have to make a circuit of ten miles to the north to find a ford."

The colonel launched a volley of oaths, denouncing the railway company and the conductor; and Passepartout, who was furious, was not disinclined to make common cause with him. Here was an obstacle, indeed, which all his master's banknotes could not remove.

There was a general disappointment among the passengers, who, without reckoning the delay, saw themselves compelled to trudge fifteen miles over a plain covered with snow. They grumbled and protested, and would certainly have thus attracted Phileas Fogg's attention if he had not been completely absorbed in his game.

Passepartout found that he could not avoid telling his master what had occurred, and, with hanging head, he was turning toward the car, when the engineer, a true Yankee named Forster, called out, "Gentlemen, perhaps there is a way, after all, to get over."

"On the bridge?" asked a passenger.

"On the bridge."

"With our train?"

"With our train."

Passepartout stopped short, and eagerly listened to the engineer.

"But the bridge is unsafe," urged the conductor.

"No matter," replied Forster; "I think that by putting on the very highest speed we might have a chance of getting over."

"The devil!" muttered Passepartout.

But a number of the passengers were at once attracted by the engineer's proposal, and Colonel Proctor was especially delighted, and found the plan a very feasible one. He told stories about engineers leaping their trains over rivers without bridges, by putting on full steam; and many of those present avowed themselves of the engineer's mind.

"We have fifty chances out of a hundred of getting over," said one.

"Eighty! Ninety!"

Passepartout was astounded, and, though ready to attempt anything to get over Medicine Creek, thought the experiment proposed a little too American. "Besides," thought he, "there's a still more simple way, and it does not even occur to any of these people! Sir," said he aloud to one of the passengers, "the engineer's plan seems to me a little dangerous, but—"

"Eighty chances!" replied the passenger, turning his back on him.

"I know it," said Passepartout, turning to another passenger, "but a simple idea—"

"Ideas are no use," returned the American, shrugging his shoulders, "as the engineer assures us that we can pass."

"Doubtless," urged Passepartout, "we can pass, but perhaps it would be more prudent—"

"What! Prudent!" cried Colonel Proctor, whom this word seemed to excite prodigiously. "At full speed, don't you see, at full speed!"

"I know—I see," repeated Passepartout; "but it would be, if not more prudent, since that word displeases you, at least more natural—"

"Who! What! What's the matter with this fellow?" cried several.

The poor fellow did not know to whom to address himself.

"Are you afraid?" asked Colonel Proctor.

"I afraid? Very well; I will show these people that a Frenchman can be as American as they!"

"All aboard!" cried the conductor.

"Yes, all aboard!" repeated Passepartout, and immediately. "But they can't prevent me from thinking that it would be more natural for us to cross the bridge on foot, and let the train come after!"

But no one heard this sage reflection, nor would anyone have acknowledged its justice. The passengers resumed their places in the cars. Passepartout took his seat without telling what had passed. The whist players were quite absorbed in their game.

The locomotive whistled vigorously; the engineer, reversing the steam, backed the train for nearly a mile—retiring, like a jumper, in order to take a longer leap. Then, with another whistle, he began to move forward; the train increased its speed, and soon its rapidity became frightful; a prolonged screech issued from the locomotive; the piston worked up and down twenty strokes to the second. They perceived that the whole train, rushing on at the rate of a hundred miles an hour, hardly bore upon the rails at all.

And they passed over! It was like a flash. No one saw the bridge. The train leaped, so to speak, from one bank to the other, and the engineer could not stop it until it had gone five miles beyond the station. But scarcely had the train passed the river, when the bridge, completely ruined, fell with a crash into the rapids of Medicine Bow.

## CHAPTER XXIX

### In Which Certain Incidents Are Narrated Which Are Only to Be Met with on American Railroads

The train pursued its course, that evening, without interruption, passing Fort Sanders, crossing Cheyenne Pass, and reaching Evans Pass. The road here attained the highest elevation of the journey, eight thousand and ninety-two feet above the level of the sea. The travelers had now only to descend to the Atlantic by limitless plains, leveled by nature. A branch of the "grand trunk" led off southward to Denver, the capital of Colorado. The country round about is rich in gold and silver, and more than fifty thousand inhabitants are already settled there.

Thirteen hundred and eighty-two miles had been passed over from San Francisco, in three days and three nights; four days and nights more would probably bring them to New York. Phileas Fogg was not as yet behindhand.

During the night Camp Walbach was passed on the left; Lodge Pole Creek ran parallel with the road, marking the boundary between the territories of Wyoming and Colorado. They entered Nebraska at eleven, passed near Sedgwick, and touched at Julesburg, on the southern branch of the Platte River.

It was here that the Union Pacific Railroad was inaugurated on the 23rd of October, 1867, by the chief engineer, General Dodge. Two powerful locomotives, carrying nine cars of invited guests, among whom was Thomas C. Durant, vice president of the road, stopped at this point; cheers were given, the Sioux and Pawnees performed an imitation Indian battle, fireworks were let off, and the first number of the *Railway Pioneer* was printed by a press brought on the train. Thus was celebrated the inauguration of this great railroad, a mighty instrument of progress and civilization, thrown across the desert, and destined to link together cities and towns which do not yet exist. The whistle of the locomotive, more powerful than Amphion's lyre, was about to bid them rise from American soil.

Fort McPherson was left behind at eight in the morning, and three hundred and fifty-seven miles had yet to be traversed before reaching Omaha. The road followed the capricious windings of the southern branch of the Platte River, on its left bank. At nine the train stopped at the important town of North Platte, built between the two arms of the river, which rejoin each other around it and form a single artery, a large tributary whose waters empty into the Missouri a little above Omaha.

The one hundred and first meridian was passed.

Mr. Fogg and his partners had resumed their game; no one—not even the dummy—complained of the length of the trip. Fix had begun by winning several guineas, which he seemed likely to lose; but he showed himself a not-less-eager whist player than Mr. Fogg. During the morning, chance distinctly favored that gentleman. Trumps and honors were showered upon his hands.

Once, having resolved on a bold stroke, he was on the point of playing a spade, when a voice behind him said, "I should play a diamond."

Mr. Fogg, Aouda, and Fix raised their heads, and beheld Colonel Proctor.

Stamp Proctor and Phileas Fogg recognized each other at once.

"Ah! It's you, is it, Englishman?" cried the colonel. "It's you who are going to play a spade!"

"And who plays it," replied Phileas Fogg coolly, throwing down the ten of spades.

"Well, it pleases me to have it diamonds," replied Colonel Proctor, in an insolent tone.

He made a movement as if to seize the card which had just been played, adding, "You don't understand anything about whist."

"Perhaps I do, as well as another," said Phileas Fogg, rising.

"You have only to try, son of John Bull," replied the colonel.

Aouda turned pale, and her blood ran cold. She seized Mr. Fogg's arm and gently pulled him back. Passepartout was ready to pounce upon the American, who was staring insolently at his opponent. But Fix got up and, going to Colonel Proctor, said, "You forget that it is I with whom you have to deal, sir; for it was I whom you not only insulted, but struck!"

"Mr. Fix," said Mr. Fogg, "pardon me, but this affair is mine, and mine only. The colonel has again insulted me, by insisting that I should not play a spade, and he shall give me satisfaction for it."

"When and where you will," replied the American, "and with whatever weapon you choose."

Aouda in vain attempted to retain Mr. Fogg; as vainly did the detective endeavor to make the quarrel his. Passepartout wished to throw the colonel out of the window, but a sign from his master checked him. Phileas Fogg left the car, and the American followed him upon the platform. "Sir," said Mr. Fogg to his adversary, "I am in a great hurry to get back to Europe, and any delay whatever will be greatly to my disadvantage."

"Well, what's that to me?" replied Colonel Proctor.

"Sir," said Mr. Fogg, very politely, "after our meeting at San Francisco, I determined to return to America and find you as soon as I had completed the business which called me to England."

"Really!"

"Will you appoint a meeting for six months hence?"

"Why not ten years hence?"

"I say six months," returned Phileas Fogg; "and I shall be at the place of meeting promptly."

"All this is an evasion," cried Stamp Proctor. "Now or never!"

"Very good. You are going to New York?"

"No."

"To Chicago?"

"No."

"To Omaha?"

"What difference is it to you? Do you know Plum Creek?"

"No," replied Mr. Fogg.

"It's the next station. The train will be there in an hour, and will stop there ten minutes. In ten minutes several revolver shots could be exchanged."

"Very well," said Mr. Fogg. "I will stop at Plum Creek."

"And I guess you'll stay there too," added the American insolently.

"Who knows?" replied Mr. Fogg, returning to the car as coolly as usual. He began to reassure Aouda, telling her that blusterers were never to be feared, and begged Fix to be his second at the approaching duel, a request which the detective could not refuse. Mr. Fogg resumed the interrupted game with perfect calmness.

At eleven o'clock the locomotive's whistle announced that they were approaching Plum Creek station. Mr. Fogg rose and, followed by Fix, went out upon the platform. Passepartout accompanied him, carrying a pair of revolvers. Aouda remained in the car, as pale as death.

The door of the next car opened, and Colonel Proctor appeared on the platform, attended by a Yankee of his own stamp as his second. But just as the combatants were about to step from the train, the conductor hurried up, and shouted, "You can't get off, gentlemen!"

"Why not?" asked the colonel.

"We are twenty minutes late, and we shall not stop."

"But I am going to fight a duel with this gentleman."

"I am sorry," said the conductor; "but we shall be off at once. There's the bell ringing now."

The train started.

"I'm really very sorry, gentlemen," said the conductor. "Under any other circumstances I should have been happy to oblige you. But, after all, as you have not had time to fight here, why not fight as we go along?"

"That wouldn't be convenient, perhaps, for this gentleman," said the colonel, in a jeering tone.

"It would be perfectly so," replied Phileas Fogg.

"Well, we are really in America," thought Passepartout, "and the conductor is a gentleman of the first order!"

So muttering, he followed his master.

The two combatants, their seconds, and the conductor passed through the cars to the rear of the train. The last car was only occupied by a dozen passengers, whom the conductor politely asked if they would not be so kind as to leave it vacant for a few moments, as two gentlemen had an affair of honor to settle. The passengers granted the request with alacrity, and straightway disappeared on the platform.

The car, which was some fifty feet long, was very convenient for their purpose. The adversaries might march on each other in the aisle, and fire at their ease. Never was duel more easily arranged. Mr. Fogg and Colonel Proctor, each provided with two six-barreled revolvers, entered the car. The seconds, remaining outside, shut them in. They were to begin firing at the first whistle of the locomotive. After an interval of two minutes, what remained of the two gentlemen would be taken from the car.

Nothing could be more simple. Indeed, it was all so simple that Fix and Passepartout felt their hearts beating as if they would crack. They were listening for the whistle agreed upon, when suddenly savage cries resounded in the air, accompanied by reports which certainly did not issue from the car where the duelists were. The reports continued in front and the whole length of the train. Cries of terror proceeded from the interior of the cars.

Colonel Proctor and Mr. Fogg, revolvers in hand, hastily quitted their prison, and rushed forward where the noise was most clamorous. They then perceived that the train was attacked by a band of Sioux.

This was not the first attempt of these daring Indians, for more than once they had waylaid trains on the road. A hundred of them had, according to their habit, jumped upon the steps without stopping the train, with the ease of a clown mounting a horse at full gallop.

The Sioux were armed with guns, from which came the reports, to which the passengers, who were almost all armed, responded by revolver shots.

The Indians had first mounted the engine, and half stunned the engineer and stoker with blows from their muskets. A Sioux chief, wishing to stop the train, but not knowing how to work the regulator, had opened wide instead of closing the steam valve, and the locomotive was plunging forward with terrific velocity.

The Sioux had at the same time invaded the cars, skipping like enraged monkeys over the roofs, thrusting open the doors, and fighting hand to hand with the passengers. Penetrating the baggage car, they pillaged it, throwing the trunks out of the train. The cries and shots were constant. The travelers defended themselves bravely; some of the cars were barricaded, and sustained a siege, like moving forts, carried along at a speed of a hundred miles an hour.

Aouda behaved courageously from the first. She defended herself like a true heroine with a revolver, which she shot through the broken windows whenever a savage made his appearance. Twenty Sioux had fallen mortally wounded to the ground, and the wheels crushed those who fell upon the rails as if they had been worms. Several passengers, shot or stunned, lay on the seats.

It was necessary to put an end to the struggle, which had lasted for ten minutes, and which would result in the triumph of the Sioux if the train was not stopped. Fort Kearney station, where there was a garrison, was only two miles distant; but, that once passed, the Sioux would be masters of the train between Fort Kearney and the station beyond.

The conductor was fighting beside Mr. Fogg, when he was shot and fell. At the same moment he cried, "Unless the train is stopped in five minutes, we are lost!"

"It shall be stopped," said Phileas Fogg, preparing to rush from the car.

"Stay, monsieur," cried Passepartout; "I will go."

Mr. Fogg had not time to stop the brave fellow, who, opening a door unperceived by the Indians, succeeded in slipping under the car; and while the struggle continued and the balls whizzed across each other over his head, he made use of his old acrobatic experience, and with amazing agility worked his way under the cars, holding on to the chains, aiding himself by the brakes and edges of the sashes, creeping from one car to another with marvelous skill, and thus gaining the forward end of the train.

There, suspended by one hand between the baggage car and the tender, with the other he loosened the safety chains; but, owing to the traction, he would never have succeeded in unscrewing the yoking bar, had not a violent concussion jolted this bar out. The train, now detached from the engine, remained a little behind, while the locomotive rushed forward with increased speed.

Carried on by the force already acquired, the train still moved for several minutes; but the brakes were worked and at last they stopped, less than a hundred feet from Kearney station.

The soldiers of the fort, attracted by the shots, hurried up; the Sioux had not expected them, and decamped in a body before the train entirely stopped.

But when the passengers counted each other on the station platform, several were found missing; among others the courageous Frenchman, whose devotion had just saved them.

## *CHAPTER XXX*

### In Which Phileas Fogg Simply Does His Duty

Three passengers—including Passepartout—had disappeared. Had they been killed in the struggle? Were they taken prisoners by the Sioux? It was impossible to tell.

There were many wounded, but none mortally. Colonel Proctor was one of the most seriously hurt; he had fought bravely, and a ball had entered his groin. He was carried into the station with the other wounded passengers, to receive such attention as could be of avail.

Aouda was safe; and Phileas Fogg, who had been in the thickest of the fight, had not received a scratch. Fix was slightly wounded in the arm. But Passepartout was not to be found, and tears coursed down Aouda's cheeks.

All the passengers had got out of the train, the wheels of which were stained with blood. From the tires and spokes hung ragged pieces of flesh. As far as the eye could reach on the white plain behind, red trails were visible. The last Sioux were disappearing in the south, along the banks of Republican River.

Mr. Fogg, with folded arms, remained motionless. He had a serious decision to make. Aouda, standing near him, looked at him without speaking, and he understood her look. If his servant was a prisoner, ought he not to risk everything to rescue him from the Indians? "I will find him, living or dead," said he quietly to Aouda.

"Ah, Mr.—Mr. Fogg!" cried she, clasping his hands and covering them with tears.

"Living," added Mr. Fogg, "if we do not lose a moment."

Phileas Fogg, by this resolution, inevitably sacrificed himself; he pronounced his own doom. The delay of a single day would make him lose the steamer at New York, and his bet would be certainly lost. But as he thought, "It is my duty," he did not hesitate.

The commanding officer of Fort Kearney was there. A hundred of his soldiers had placed themselves in a position to defend the station, should the Sioux attack it.

"Sir," said Mr. Fogg to the captain, "three passengers have disappeared."

"Dead?" asked the captain.

"Dead or prisoners; that is the uncertainty which must be solved. Do you propose to pursue the Sioux?"

"That's a serious thing to do, sir," returned the captain. "These Indians may retreat beyond the Arkansas, and I cannot leave the fort unprotected."

"The lives of three men are in question, sir," said Phileas Fogg.

"Doubtless; but can I risk the lives of fifty men to save three?"

"I don't know whether you can, sir; but you ought to do so."

"Nobody here," returned the other, "has a right to teach me my duty."

"Very well," said Mr. Fogg, coldly. "I will go alone."

"You, sir!" cried Fix, coming up. "You go alone in pursuit of the Indians?"

"Would you have me leave this poor fellow to perish—him to whom everyone present owes his life? I shall go."

"No, sir, you shall not go alone," cried the captain, touched in spite of himself. "No! You are a brave man. Thirty volunteers!" he added, turning to the soldiers.

The whole company started forward at once. The captain had only to pick his men. Thirty were chosen, and an old sergeant placed at their head.

"Thanks, captain," said Mr. Fogg.

"Will you let me go with you?" asked Fix.

"Do as you please, sir. But if you wish to do me a favor, you will remain with Aouda. In case anything should happen to me—"

A sudden pallor overspread the detective's face. Separate himself from the man whom he had so persistently followed step by step! Leave him to wander about in this desert! Fix gazed attentively at Mr. Fogg, and, despite his suspicions and of the struggle which was going on within him, he lowered his eyes before that calm and frank look.

"I will stay," said he.

A few moments after, Mr. Fogg pressed the young woman's hand, and, having confided to her his precious carpetbag, went off with the sergeant and his little squad. But, before going, he had said to the soldiers, "My friends, I will divide five thousand dollars among you, if we save the prisoners."

It was then a little past noon.

Aouda retired to a waiting room, and there she waited alone, thinking of the simple and noble generosity, the tranquil courage of Phileas Fogg. He had sacrificed his fortune, and was now risking his life, all without hesitation, from duty, in silence.

Fix did not have the same thoughts, and could scarcely conceal his agitation. He walked feverishly up and down the platform, but soon resumed his outward composure. He now saw the folly of which he had been guilty in letting Fogg go alone. What! This man, whom he had just followed around the world, was permitted now to separate himself from him! He began to accuse and abuse himself, and, as if he were director of police, administered to himself a sound lecture for his greenness.

"I have been an idiot!" he thought. "And this man will see it. He has gone, and won't come back! But how is it that I, Fix, who have in my pocket a warrant for his arrest, have been so fascinated by him? Decidedly, I am nothing but an ass!"

So reasoned the detective, while the hours crept by all too slowly. He did not know what to do. Sometimes he was tempted to tell Aouda all; but he could not doubt how the young woman would receive his confidences. What course should he take? He thought of pursuing Fogg across the vast white plains; it did not seem impossible that he might overtake him. Footsteps were easily printed on the snow! But soon, under a new sheet, every imprint would be effaced.

Fix became discouraged. He felt a sort of insurmountable longing to abandon the game altogether. He could now leave Fort Kearney station, and pursue his journey homeward in peace.

Toward two o'clock in the afternoon, while it was snowing hard, long whistles were heard approaching from the east. A great shadow, preceded by a wild light, slowly advanced, appearing still larger through the mist, which gave it a fantastic aspect. No train was expected from the east, neither had there been time for the succor asked for by telegraph to arrive; the train from Omaha to San Francisco was not due till the next day. The mystery was soon explained.

The locomotive, which was slowly approaching with deafening whistles, was that which, having been detached from the train, had continued its route with such terrific rapidity, carrying off the unconscious engineer and stoker. It had run several miles when, the fire becoming low for want of fuel, the steam had slackened; and it had finally stopped an hour after, some twenty miles beyond Fort Kearney. Neither the engineer nor the stoker was dead, and, after remaining for some time in their swoon, had come to themselves. The train had then stopped. The engineer, when he found himself in the desert, and the locomotive without cars, understood what had happened. He could not imagine how the locomotive had become separated from the train; but he did not doubt that the train left behind was in distress.

He did not hesitate what to do. It would be prudent to continue on to Omaha, for it would be dangerous to return to the train, which the Indians might still be engaged in pillaging. Nevertheless, he began to rebuild the fire in the furnace; the pressure again mounted, and the locomotive returned, running backward to Fort Kearney. This it was which was whistling in the mist.

The travelers were glad to see the locomotive resume its place at the head of the train. They could now continue the journey so terribly interrupted.

Aouda, on seeing the locomotive come up, hurried out of the station, and asked the conductor, "Are you going to start?"

"At once, madam."

"But the prisoners, our unfortunate fellow travelers—"

"I cannot interrupt the trip," replied the conductor. "We are already three hours behind time."

"And when will another train pass here from San Francisco?"

"Tomorrow evening, madam."

"Tomorrow evening! But then it will be too late! We must wait—"

"It is impossible," responded the conductor. "If you wish to go, please get in."

"I will not go," said Aouda.

Fix had heard this conversation. A little while before, when there was no prospect of proceeding on the journey, he had made up his mind to leave Fort Kearney; but now that the train was there, ready to start, and he had only to take his seat in the car, an irresistible influence held him back. The station platform burned his feet, and he could not stir. The conflict in his mind again began; anger and failure stifled him. He wished to struggle on to the end.

Meanwhile the passengers and some of the wounded, among them Colonel Proctor, whose injuries were serious, had taken their places in the train. The buzzing of the overheated boiler was heard, and the steam was escaping from the valves. The engineer whistled, the train started, and soon disappeared, mingling its white smoke with the eddies of the densely falling snow.

The detective had remained behind.

Several hours passed. The weather was dismal, and it was very cold. Fix sat motionless on a bench in the station; he might have been thought asleep. Aouda, despite the storm, kept coming out of the waiting room, going to the end of the platform, and peering through the tempest of snow, as if to pierce the mist which narrowed the horizon around her, and to hear, if possible, some welcome sound. She heard and saw nothing. Then she would return, chilled through, to issue out again after the lapse of a few moments, but always in vain.

Evening came, and the little band had not returned. Where could they be? Had they found the Indians, and were they having a conflict with them, or were they still wandering amid the mist? The commander of the fort was anxious, though he tried to conceal his apprehensions. As night approached, the snow fell less plentifully, but it became intensely cold. Absolute silence rested on the plains. Neither flight of bird nor passing of beast troubled the perfect calm.

Throughout the night Aouda, full of sad forebodings, her heart stifled with anguish, wandered about on the verge of the plains. Her imagination carried her far off, and showed her innumerable dangers. What she suffered through the long hours it would be impossible to describe.

Fix remained stationary in the same place, but did not sleep. Once a man approached and spoke to him, and the detective merely replied by shaking his head.

Thus the night passed. At dawn, the half-extinguished disk of the sun rose above a misty horizon; but it was now possible to recognize objects two miles off. Phileas Fogg and the squad had gone southward; in the south all was still vacancy. It was then seven o'clock.

The captain, who was really alarmed, did not know what course to take.

Should he send another detachment to the rescue of the first? Should he sacrifice more men, with so few chances of saving those already sacrificed? His hesitation did not last long, however. Calling one of his lieutenants, he was on the point of ordering a reconnaissance when gunshots were heard. Was it a signal? The soldiers rushed out of the fort, and half a mile off they perceived a little band returning in good order.

Mr. Fogg was marching at their head, and just behind him were Passepartout and the other two travelers, rescued from the Sioux.

They had met and fought the Indians ten miles south of Fort Kearney. Shortly before the detachment arrived, Passepartout and his companions had begun to struggle with their captors, three of whom the Frenchman had felled with his fists, when his master and the soldiers hastened up to their relief.

All were welcomed with joyful cries. Phileas Fogg distributed the reward he had promised to the soldiers, while Passepartout, not without reason, muttered to himself, "It must certainly be confessed that I cost my master dear!"

Fix, without saying a word, looked at Mr. Fogg, and it would have been difficult to analyze the thoughts which struggled within him. As for Aouda, she took her protector's hand and pressed it in her own, too much moved to speak.

Meanwhile, Passepartout was looking about for the train; he thought he should find it there, ready to start for Omaha, and he hoped that the time lost might be regained.

"The train! The train!" cried he.

"Gone," replied Fix.

"And when does the next train pass here?" said Phileas Fogg.

"Not till this evening."

"Ah!" returned the impassible gentleman quietly.

# CHAPTER XXXI

### IN WHICH FIX THE DETECTIVE CONSIDERABLY FURTHERS
### THE INTERESTS OF PHILEAS FOGG

Phileas Fogg found himself twenty hours behind time. Passepartout, the involuntary cause of this delay, was desperate. He had ruined his master!

At this moment the detective approached Mr. Fogg, and, looking him intently in the face, said:

"Seriously, sir, are you in great haste?"

"Quite seriously."

"I have a purpose in asking," resumed Fix. "Is it absolutely necessary that you should be in New York on the 11th, before nine o'clock in the evening, the time that the steamer leaves for Liverpool?"

"It is absolutely necessary."

"And, if your journey had not been interrupted by these Indians, you would have reached New York on the morning of the 11th?"

"Yes; with eleven hours to spare before the steamer left."

"Good! You are therefore twenty hours behind. Twelve from twenty leaves eight. You must regain eight hours. Do you wish to try to do so?"

"On foot?" asked Mr. Fogg.

"No; on a sleigh," replied Fix. "On a sleigh with sails. A man has proposed such a method to me."

It was the man who had spoken to Fix during the night, and whose offer he had refused.

Phileas Fogg did not reply at once; but Fix having pointed out the man, who was walking up and down in front of the station, Mr. Fogg went up to him. An instant after, Mr. Fogg and the American, whose name was Mudge, entered a hut built just below the fort.

There Mr. Fogg examined a curious vehicle, a kind of frame on two long beams, a little raised in front like the runners of a sleigh, and upon which there was room for five or six persons. A high mast was fixed on the frame, held firmly by metallic lashings, to which was attached a large brigantine sail. This mast held an iron stay upon which to hoist a jib sail. Behind, a sort of rudder served to guide the vehicle. It was, in short, a sleigh rigged like a sloop. During the winter, when the trains are blocked up by the snow, these sleighs make extremely rapid journeys across the frozen plains from one station to another. Provided with more sails than a cutter, and with the wind behind them, they slip over the surface of the prairies with a speed equal if not superior to that of the express trains.

Mr. Fogg readily made a bargain with the owner of this land craft. The wind was favorable, being fresh, and blowing from the west. The snow had hardened, and Mudge was very confident of being able to transport Mr. Fogg in a few hours to

Omaha. Thence the trains eastward run frequently to Chicago and New York. It was not impossible that the lost time might yet be recovered; and such an opportunity was not to be rejected.

Not wishing to expose Aouda to the discomforts of traveling in the open air, Mr. Fogg proposed to leave her with Passepartout at Fort Kearney, the servant taking upon himself to escort her to Europe by a better route and under more favorable conditions. But Aouda refused to separate from Mr. Fogg, and Passepartout was delighted with her decision; for nothing could induce him to leave his master while Fix was with him.

It would be difficult to guess the detective's thoughts. Was this conviction shaken by Phileas Fogg's return, or did he still regard him as an exceedingly shrewd rascal who, his journey round the world completed, would think himself absolutely safe in England? Perhaps Fix's opinion of Phileas Fogg was somewhat modified; but he was nevertheless resolved to do his duty, and to hasten the return of the whole party to England as much as possible.

At eight o'clock the sleigh was ready to start. The passengers took their places on it, and wrapped themselves up closely in their traveling cloaks. The two great sails were hoisted, and under the pressure of the wind the sleigh slid over the hardened snow with a velocity of forty miles an hour.

The distance between Fort Kearney and Omaha, as the birds fly, is at most two hundred miles. If the wind held good, the distance might be traversed in five hours; if no accident happened, the sleigh might reach Omaha by one o'clock.

What a journey! The travelers, huddled close together, could not speak for the cold, intensified by the rapidity at which they were going. The sleigh sped on as lightly as a boat over the waves. When the breeze came skimming the earth, the sleigh seemed to be lifted off the ground by its sails. Mudge, who was at the rudder, kept in a straight line, and by a turn of his hand checked the lurches which the vehicle had a tendency to make. All the sails were up, and the jib was so arranged as not to screen the brigantine. A topmast was hoisted, and another jib, held out to the wind, added its force to the other sails. Although the speed could not be exactly estimated, the sleigh could not be going at less than forty miles an hour.

"If nothing breaks," said Mudge, "we shall get there!"

Mr. Fogg had made it for Mudge's interest to reach Omaha within the time agreed on, by the offer of a handsome reward.

The prairie, across which the sleigh was moving in a straight line, was as flat as a sea. It seemed like a vast frozen lake. The railroad which ran through this section ascended from the southwest to the northwest by Great Island, Columbus, an important Nebraska town, Schuyler, and Fremont, to Omaha. It followed throughout the right bank of the Platte River. The sleigh, shortening this route, took a chord of the arc described by the railway. Mudge was not afraid of being stopped by the Platte River, because it was frozen. The road, then, was quite clear of obstacles, and Phileas Fogg had but two things to fear—an accident to the sleigh, and a change or calm in the wind.

But the breeze, far from lessening its force, blew as if to bend the mast, which, however, the metallic lashings held firmly. These lashings, like the chords of a stringed instrument, resounded as if vibrated by a violin bow. The sleigh slid along in the midst of a plaintively intense melody.

"Those chords give the fifth and the octave," said Mr. Fogg.

These were the only words he uttered during the journey. Aouda, cozily packed in furs and cloaks, was sheltered as much as possible from the attacks of the freezing wind. As for Passepartout, his face was as red as the sun's disk when it sets in the mist, and he laboriously inhaled the biting air. With his natural buoyancy of spirits, he began to hope again. They would reach New York on the evening, if not on the morning, of the 11th, and there was still some chance that it would be before the steamer sailed for Liverpool.

Passepartout even felt a strong desire to grasp his ally, Fix, by the hand. He remembered that it was the detective who procured the sleigh, the only means of reaching Omaha in time; but, checked by some presentiment, he kept his usual reserve. One thing, however, Passepartout would never forget, and that was the sacrifice which Mr. Fogg had made, without hesitation, to rescue him from the Sioux. Mr. Fogg had risked his fortune and his life. No! His servant would never forget that!

While each of the party was absorbed in reflections so different, the sleigh flew past over the vast carpet of snow. The creeks it passed over were not perceived. Fields and streams disappeared under the uniform whiteness. The plain was absolutely deserted. Between the Union Pacific road and the branch which unites Kearney with Saint Joseph, it formed a great uninhabited island. Neither village, station, nor fort appeared. From time to time they sped by some phantomlike tree, whose white skeleton twisted and rattled in the wind. Sometimes flocks of wild birds rose, or bands of gaunt, famished, ferocious prairie wolves ran howling after the sleigh. Passepartout, revolver in hand, held himself ready to fire on those which came too near. Had an accident then happened to the sleigh, the travelers, attacked by these beasts, would have been in the most terrible danger; but it held on its even course, soon gained on the wolves, and ere long left the howling band at a safe distance behind.

About noon Mudge perceived by certain landmarks that he was crossing the Platte River. He said nothing, but he felt certain that he was now within twenty miles of Omaha. In less than an hour he left the rudder and furled his sails, while the sleigh, carried forward by the great impetus the wind had given it, went on half a mile further with its sails unspread.

It stopped at last, and Mudge, pointing to a mass of roofs white with snow, said: "We have got there!"

Arrived! Arrived at the station which is in daily communication, by numerous trains, with the Atlantic seaboard!

Passepartout and Fix jumped off, stretched their stiffened limbs, and aided Mr. Fogg and the young woman to descend from the sleigh. Phileas Fogg generously rewarded Mudge, whose hand Passepartout warmly grasped, and the party directed their steps to the Omaha railway station.

The Pacific Railroad proper finds its terminus at this important Nebraska town. Omaha is connected with Chicago by the Chicago and Rock Island Railroad, which runs directly east, and passes fifty stations.

A train was ready to start when Mr. Fogg and his party reached the station, and they only had time to get into the cars. They had seen nothing of Omaha; but Passepartout confessed to himself that this was not to be regretted, as they were not traveling to see the sights.

The train passed rapidly across the state of Iowa, by Council Bluffs, Des Moines, and Iowa City. During the night it crossed the Mississippi at Davenport, and by Rock Island entered Illinois. The next day, which was the 10th, at four o'clock in the evening, it reached Chicago, already risen from its ruins, and more proudly seated than ever on the borders of its beautiful Lake Michigan.

Nine hundred miles separated Chicago from New York; but trains are not wanting at Chicago. Mr. Fogg passed at once from one to the other, and the locomotive of the Pittsburgh, Fort Wayne, and Chicago Railway left at full speed, as if it fully comprehended that that gentleman had no time to lose. It traversed Indiana, Ohio, Pennsylvania, and New Jersey like a flash, rushing through towns with antique names, some of which had streets and car tracks, but as yet no houses. At last the Hudson came into view; and, at a quarter past eleven in the evening of the 11th, the train stopped in the station on the right bank of the river, before the very pier of the Cunard line.

The *China*, for Liverpool, had started three-quarters of an hour before!

# CHAPTER XXXII

### IN WHICH PHILEAS FOGG ENGAGES IN A
### DIRECT STRUGGLE WITH BAD FORTUNE

The *China*, in leaving, seemed to have carried off Phileas Fogg's last hope. None of the other steamers were able to serve his projects. The Pereire, of the French Transatlantic Company, whose admirable steamers are equal to any in speed and comfort, did not leave until the 14th; the Hamburg boats did not go directly to Liverpool or London, but to Havre; and the additional trip from Havre to Southampton would render Phileas Fogg's last efforts of no avail. The Inman steamer did not depart till the next day, and could not cross the Atlantic in time to save the wager.

Mr. Fogg learned all this in consulting his Bradshaw, which gave him the daily movements of the transatlantic steamers.

Passepartout was crushed; it overwhelmed him to lose the boat by three-quarters of an hour. It was his fault, for, instead of helping his master, he had not ceased putting obstacles in his path! And when he recalled all the incidents of the tour, when he counted up the sums expended in pure loss and on his own account, when he thought that the immense stake, added to the heavy charges of this useless journey, would completely ruin Mr. Fogg, he overwhelmed himself with bitter self-accusations. Mr. Fogg, however, did not reproach him; and, on leaving the Cunard pier, only said: "We will consult about what is best tomorrow. Come."

The party crossed the Hudson in the Jersey City ferryboat, and drove in a carriage to the St. Nicholas Hotel, on Broadway. Rooms were engaged, and the night passed, briefly to Phileas Fogg, who slept profoundly, but very long to Aouda and the others, whose agitation did not permit them to rest.

The next day was the 12th of December. From seven in the morning of the 12th to a quarter before nine in the evening of the 21st there were nine days, thirteen hours, and forty-five minutes. If Phileas Fogg had left in the *China*, one of the fastest steamers on the Atlantic, he would have reached Liverpool, and then London, within the period agreed upon.

Mr. Fogg left the hotel alone, after giving Passepartout instructions to await his return, and inform Aouda to be ready at an instant's notice. He proceeded to the banks of the Hudson, and looked about among the vessels moored or anchored in the river, for any that were about to depart. Several had departure signals, and were preparing to put to sea at morning tide; for in this immense and admirable port there is not one day in a hundred that vessels do not set out for every quarter of the globe. But they were mostly sailing vessels, of which, of course, Phileas Fogg could make no use.

He seemed about to give up all hope, when he espied, anchored at the Battery, a cable's length off at most, a trading vessel, with a screw, well-shaped, whose funnel, puffing a cloud of smoke, indicated that she was getting ready for departure.

Phileas Fogg hailed a boat, got into it, and soon found himself on board the

*Henrietta*, iron-hulled, wood-built above. He ascended to the deck and asked for the captain, who forthwith presented himself. He was a man of fifty, a sort of sea wolf with big eyes, a complexion of oxidized copper, red hair and thick neck, and a growling voice.

"The captain?" asked Mr. Fogg.

"I am the captain."

"I am Phileas Fogg, of London."

"And I am Andrew Speedy, of Cardiff."

"You are going to put to sea?"

"In an hour."

"You are bound for—"

"Bordeaux."

"And your cargo?"

"No freight. Going in ballast."

"Have you any passengers?"

"No passengers. Never have passengers. Too much in the way."

"Is your vessel a swift one?"

"Between eleven and twelve knots. The *Henrietta*, well known."

"Will you carry me and three other persons to Liverpool?"

"To Liverpool? Why not to China?"

"I said Liverpool."

"No!"

"No?"

"No. I am setting out for Bordeaux, and shall go to Bordeaux."

"Money is no object?"

"None."

The captain spoke in a tone which did not admit of a reply.

"But the owners of the *Henrietta*—" resumed Phileas Fogg.

"The owners are myself," replied the captain. "The vessel belongs to me."

"I will freight it for you."

"No."

"I will buy it of you."

"No."

Phileas Fogg did not betray the least disappointment; but the situation was a grave one. It was not at New York as at Hong Kong, nor with the captain of the *Henrietta* as with the captain of the *Tankadere*. Up to this time money had smoothed away every obstacle. Now money failed.

Still, some means must be found to cross the Atlantic on a boat, unless by balloon—which would have been venturesome, besides not being capable of being put in practice. It seemed that Phileas Fogg had an idea, for he said to the captain, "Well, will you carry me to Bordeaux?"

"No, not if you paid me two hundred dollars."

"I offer you two thousand."

"Apiece?"

"Apiece."

"And there are four of you?"

"Four."

Captain Speedy began to scratch his head. There were eight thousand dollars to gain, without changing his route; for which it was well worth conquering the repugnance he had for all kinds of passengers. Besides, passengers at two thousand dollars are no longer passengers but valuable merchandise. "I start at nine o'clock," said Captain Speedy, simply. "Are you and your party ready?"

"We will be on board at nine o'clock," replied, no less simply, Mr. Fogg.

It was half past eight. To disembark from the *Henrietta*, jump into a hack, hurry to the St. Nicholas, and return with Aouda, Passepartout, and even the inseparable Fix was the work of a brief time, and was performed by Mr. Fogg with the coolness which never abandoned him. They were on board when the *Henrietta* made ready to weigh anchor.

When Passepartout heard what this last voyage was going to cost, he uttered a prolonged "Oh!" which extended throughout his vocal gamut.

As for Fix, he said to himself that the Bank of England would certainly not come out of this affair well indemnified. When they reached England, even if Mr. Fogg did not throw some handfuls of bank bills into the sea, more than seven thousand pounds would have been spent!

# CHAPTER XXXIII

### In Which Phileas Fogg Shows Himself Equal to the Occasion

An hour after, the *Henrietta* passed the lighthouse which marks the entrance of the Hudson, turned the point of Sandy Hook, and put to sea. During the day she skirted Long Island, passed Fire Island, and directed her course rapidly eastward.

At noon the next day, a man mounted the bridge to ascertain the vessel's position. It might be thought that this was Captain Speedy. Not the least in the world. It was Phileas Fogg, Esquire. As for Captain Speedy, he was shut up in his cabin under lock and key, and was uttering loud cries, which signified an anger at once pardonable and excessive.

What had happened was very simple. Phileas Fogg wished to go to Liverpool, but the captain would not carry him there. Then Phileas Fogg had taken passage for Bordeaux, and, during the thirty hours he had been on board, had so shrewdly managed with his banknotes that the sailors and stokers, who were only an occasional crew, and were not on the best terms with the captain, went over to him in a body. This was why Phileas Fogg was in command instead of Captain Speedy; why the captain was a prisoner in his cabin; and why, in short, the *Henrietta* was directing her course toward Liverpool. It was very clear, to see Mr. Fogg manage the craft, that he had been a sailor.

How the adventure ended will be seen anon. Aouda was anxious, though she said nothing. As for Passepartout, he thought Mr. Fogg's maneuver simply glorious. The captain had said "between eleven and twelve knots," and the *Henrietta* confirmed his prediction.

If, then—for there were "ifs" still—the sea did not become too boisterous, if the wind did not veer round to the east, if no accident happened to the boat or its machinery, the *Henrietta* might cross the three thousand miles from New York to Liverpool in the nine days, between the 12th and the 21st of December. It is true that, once arrived, the affair on board the *Henrietta*, added to that of the Bank of England, might create more difficulties for Mr. Fogg than he imagined or could desire.

During the first days, they went along smoothly enough. The sea was not very unpropitious, the wind seemed stationary in the northeast, the sails were hoisted, and the *Henrietta* plowed across the waves like a real transatlantic steamer.

Passepartout was delighted. His master's last exploit, the consequences of which he ignored, enchanted him. Never had the crew seen so jolly and dexterous a fellow. He formed warm friendships with the sailors, and amazed them with his acrobatic feats. He thought they managed the vessel like gentlemen, and that the stokers fired up like heroes. His loquacious good humor infected everyone. He had forgotten the past, its vexations and delays. He only thought of the end, so nearly accomplished; and sometimes he boiled over with impatience, as if heated by the furnaces of the *Henrietta*. Often, also, the worthy fellow revolved around Fix, looking at him with a keen, distrustful eye; but he did not speak to him, for their old intimacy no longer existed.

Fix, it must be confessed, understood nothing of what was going on. The conquest of the *Henrietta*, the bribery of the crew, Fogg managing the boat like a skilled seaman, amazed and confused him. He did not know what to think. For, after all, a man who began by stealing fifty-five thousand pounds might end by stealing a vessel; and Fix was not unnaturally inclined to conclude that the *Henrietta* under Fogg's command was not going to Liverpool at all, but to some part of the world where the robber, turned into a pirate, would quietly put himself in safety. The conjecture was at least a plausible one, and the detective began to seriously regret that he had embarked on the affair.

As for Captain Speedy, he continued to howl and growl in his cabin; and Passepartout, whose duty it was to carry him his meals, courageous as he was, took the greatest precautions. Mr. Fogg did not seem even to know that there was a captain on board.

On the 13th they passed the edge of the Banks of Newfoundland, a dangerous locality; during the winter, especially, there are frequent fogs and heavy gales of wind. Ever since the evening before the barometer, suddenly falling, had indicated an approaching change in the atmosphere; and during the night the temperature varied, the cold became sharper, and the wind veered to the southeast.

This was a misfortune. Mr. Fogg, in order not to deviate from his course, furled his sails and increased the force of the steam; but the vessel's speed slackened, owing to the state of the sea, the long waves of which broke against the stern. She pitched violently, and this retarded her progress. The breeze little by little swelled into a tempest, and it was to be feared that the *Henrietta* might not be able to maintain herself upright on the waves.

Passepartout's visage darkened with the skies, and for two days the poor fellow experienced constant fright. But Phileas Fogg was a bold mariner, and knew how to maintain headway against the sea; and he kept on his course without even decreasing his steam. The *Henrietta*, when she could not rise upon the waves, crossed them, swamping her deck, but passing safely. Sometimes the screw rose out of the water, beating its protruding end, when a mountain of water raised the stern above the waves; but the craft always kept straight ahead.

The wind, however, did not grow as boisterous as might have been feared; it was not one of those tempests which burst, and rush on with a speed of ninety miles an hour. It continued fresh, but, unhappily, it remained obstinately in the southeast, rendering the sails useless.

The 16th of December was the seventy-fifth day since Phileas Fogg's departure from London, and the *Henrietta* had not yet been seriously delayed. Half of the voyage was almost accomplished, and the worst localities had been passed. In summer, success would have been well-nigh certain. In winter, they were at the mercy of the bad season. Passepartout said nothing; but he cherished hope in secret, and comforted himself with the reflection that, if the wind failed them, they might still count on the steam.

On this day the engineer came on deck, went up to Mr. Fogg, and began to speak earnestly with him. Without knowing why it was a presentiment, perhaps Passepartout became vaguely uneasy. He would have given one of his ears to hear with the other what the engineer was saying. He finally managed to catch a few words, and was sure he heard his master say, "You are certain of what you tell me?"

"Certain, sir," replied the engineer. "You must remember that, since we started, we have kept up hot fires in all our furnaces, and, though we had coal enough to go on short steam from New York to Bordeaux, we haven't enough to go with all steam from New York to Liverpool."

"I will consider," replied Mr. Fogg.

Passepartout understood it all; he was seized with mortal anxiety. The coal was giving out! "Ah, if my master can get over that," muttered he, "he'll be a famous man!" He could not help imparting to Fix what he had overheard.

"Then you believe that we really are going to Liverpool?"

"Of course."

"Ass!" replied the detective, shrugging his shoulders and turning on his heel.

Passepartout was on the point of vigorously resenting the epithet, the reason of which he could not for the life of him comprehend; but he reflected that the unfortunate Fix was probably very much disappointed and humiliated in his self-esteem, after having so awkwardly followed a false scent around the world, and refrained.

And now what course would Phileas Fogg adopt? It was difficult to imagine. Nevertheless he seemed to have decided upon one, for that evening he sent for the engineer, and said to him, "Feed all the fires until the coal is exhausted."

A few moments after, the funnel of the *Henrietta* vomited forth torrents of smoke. The vessel continued to proceed with all steam on; but on the 18th, the engineer, as he had predicted, announced that the coal would give out in the course of the day.

"Do not let the fires go down," replied Mr. Fogg. "Keep them up to the last. Let the valves be filled."

Toward noon Phileas Fogg, having ascertained their position, called Passepartout, and ordered him to go for Captain Speedy. It was as if the honest fellow had been commanded to unchain a tiger. He went to the poop, saying to himself, "He will be like a madman!"

In a few moments, with cries and oaths, a bomb appeared on the poop deck. The bomb was Captain Speedy. It was clear that he was on the point of bursting. "Where are we?" were the first words his anger permitted him to utter. Had the poor man been an apoplectic, he could never have recovered from his paroxysm of wrath.

"Where are we?" he repeated, with purple face.

"Seven hundred and seven miles from Liverpool," replied Mr. Fogg, with imperturbable calmness.

"Pirate!" cried Captain Speedy.

"I have sent for you, sir——"

"Pickaroon!"

"——sir," continued Mr. Fogg, "to ask you to sell me your vessel."

"No! By all the devils, no!"

"But I shall be obliged to burn her."

"Burn the *Henrietta*!"

"Yes; at least the upper part of her. The coal has given out."

"Burn my vessel!" cried Captain Speedy, who could scarcely pronounce the words. "A vessel worth fifty thousand dollars!"

"Here are sixty thousand," replied Phileas Fogg, handing the captain a roll of bank bills. This had a prodigious effect on Andrew Speedy. An American can scarcely remain unmoved at the sight of sixty thousand dollars. The captain forgot in an instant his anger, his imprisonment, and all his grudges against his passenger. The *Henrietta* was twenty years old; it was a great bargain. The bomb would not go off after all. Mr. Fogg had taken away the match.

"And I shall still have the iron hull," said the captain in a softer tone.

"The iron hull and the engine. Is it agreed?"

"Agreed."

And Andrew Speedy, seizing the banknotes, counted them and consigned them to his pocket.

During this colloquy, Passepartout was as white as a sheet, and Fix seemed on the point of having an apoplectic fit. Nearly twenty thousand pounds had been expended, and Fogg left the hull and engine to the captain, that is, near the whole value of the craft! It was true, however, that fifty-five thousand pounds had been stolen from the bank.

When Andrew Speedy had pocketed the money, Mr. Fogg said to him, "Don't let this astonish you, sir. You must know that I shall lose twenty thousand pounds, unless I arrive in London by a quarter before nine on the evening of the 21st of December. I missed the steamer at New York, and as you refused to take me to Liverpool—"

"And I did well!" cried Andrew Speedy. "For I have gained at least forty thousand dollars by it!" He added, more sedately, "Do you know one thing, Captain—"

"Fogg."

"Captain Fogg, you've got something of the Yankee about you."

And, having paid his passenger what he considered a high compliment, he was going away, when Mr. Fogg said, "The vessel now belongs to me?"

"Certainly, from the keel to the truck of the masts—all the wood, that is."

"Very well. Have the interior seats, bunks, and frames pulled down, and burn them."

It was necessary to have dry wood to keep the steam up to the adequate pressure, and on that day the poop, cabins, bunks, and the spare deck were sacrificed. On the next day, the 19th of December, the masts, rafts, and spars were burned; the crew worked lustily, keeping up the fires. Passepartout hewed, cut, and sawed away with all his might. There was a perfect rage for demolition.

The railings, fittings, the greater part of the deck, and top sides disappeared on the 20th, and the *Henrietta* was now only a flat hulk. But on this day they sighted the Irish coast and Fastnet Light. By ten in the evening they were passing Queenstown. Phileas Fogg had only twenty-four hours more in which to get to London; that length of time was necessary to reach Liverpool, with all steam on. And the steam was about to give out altogether!

"Sir," said Captain Speedy, who was now deeply interested in Mr. Fogg's project, "I really commiserate you. Everything is against you. We are only opposite Queenstown."

"Ah," said Mr. Fogg, "is that place where we see the lights Queenstown?"

"Yes."

"Can we enter the harbor?"

"Not under three hours. Only at high tide."

"Stay," replied Mr. Fogg calmly, without betraying in his features that by a supreme inspiration he was about to attempt once more to conquer ill fortune.

Queenstown is the Irish port at which the transatlantic steamers stop to put off the mails. These mails are carried to Dublin by express trains always held in readiness to start; from Dublin they are sent on to Liverpool by the most rapid boats, and thus gain twelve hours on the Atlantic steamers.

Phileas Fogg counted on gaining twelve hours in the same way. Instead of arriving at Liverpool the next evening by the *Henrietta*, he would be there by noon, and would therefore have time to reach London before a quarter before nine in the evening.

The *Henrietta* entered Queenstown Harbor at one o'clock in the morning, it then being high tide; and Phileas Fogg, after being grasped heartily by the hand by Captain Speedy, left that gentleman on the leveled hulk of his craft, which was still worth half what he had sold it for.

The party went on shore at once. Fix was greatly tempted to arrest Mr. Fogg on the spot; but he did not. Why? What struggle was going on within him? Had he changed his mind about "his man"? Did he understand that he had made a grave mistake? He did not, however, abandon Mr. Fogg. They all got upon the train, which was just ready to start, at half past one; at dawn of day they were in Dublin; and they lost no time in embarking on a steamer which, disdaining to rise upon the waves, invariably cut through them.

Phileas Fogg at last disembarked on the Liverpool quay, at twenty minutes before twelve, 21st December. He was only six hours distant from London.

But at this moment Fix came up, put his hand upon Mr. Fogg's shoulder, and, showing his warrant, said, "You are really Phileas Fogg?"

"I am."

"I arrest you in the queen's name!"

## CHAPTER XXXIV

### In Which Phileas Fogg at Last Reaches London

Phileas Fogg was in prison. He had been shut up in the customhouse, and he was to be transferred to London the next day.

Passepartout, when he saw his master arrested, would have fallen upon Fix had he not been held back by some policemen. Aouda was thunderstruck at the suddenness of an event which she could not understand. Passepartout explained to her how it was that the honest and courageous Fogg was arrested as a robber. The young woman's heart revolted against so heinous a charge, and when she saw that she could attempt to do nothing to save her protector, she wept bitterly.

As for Fix, he had arrested Mr. Fogg because it was his duty, whether Mr. Fogg were guilty or not.

The thought then struck Passepartout that he was the cause of this new misfortune! Had he not concealed Fix's errand from his master? When Fix revealed his true character and purpose, why had he not told Mr. Fogg? If the latter had been warned, he would no doubt have given Fix proof of his innocence, and satisfied him of his mistake; at least, Fix would not have continued his journey at the expense and on the heels of his master, only to arrest him the moment he set foot on English soil. Passepartout wept till he was blind, and felt like blowing his brains out.

Aouda and he had remained, despite the cold, under the portico of the customhouse. Neither wished to leave the place; both were anxious to see Mr. Fogg again.

That gentleman was really ruined, and that at the moment when he was about to attain his end. This arrest was fatal. Having arrived at Liverpool at twenty minutes before twelve on the 21st of December, he had till a quarter before nine that evening to reach the Reform Club, that is, nine hours and a quarter; the journey from Liverpool to London was six hours.

If anyone, at this moment, had entered the customhouse, he would have found Mr. Fogg seated, motionless, calm, and without apparent anger, upon a wooden bench. He was not, it is true, resigned; but this last blow failed to force him into an outward betrayal of any emotion. Was he being devoured by one of those secret rages, all the more terrible because contained, and which only burst forth, with an irresistible force, at the last moment? No one could tell. There he sat, calmly waiting—for what? Did he still cherish hope? Did he still believe, now that the door of this prison was closed upon him, that he would succeed?

However that may have been, Mr. Fogg carefully put his watch upon the table, and observed its advancing hands. Not a word escaped his lips, but his look was singularly set and stern. The situation, in any event, was a terrible one, and might be thus stated: if Phileas Fogg was honest, he was ruined; if he was a knave, he was caught.

Did escape occur to him? Did he examine to see if there were any practicable outlet from his prison? Did he think of escaping from it? Possibly; for once he walked slowly around the room. But the door was locked, and the window heavily barred with iron rods. He sat down again, and drew his journal from his pocket. On the line where these words were written, "21st December, Saturday, Liverpool," he added, "80th day, 11:40 a.m.," and waited.

The customhouse clock struck one. Mr. Fogg observed that his watch was two hours too fast.

Two hours! Admitting that he was at this moment taking an express train, he could reach London and the Reform Club by a quarter before nine p.m. His forehead slightly wrinkled.

At thirty-three minutes past two he heard a singular noise outside, then a hasty opening of doors. Passepartout's voice was audible, and immediately after that of Fix. Phileas Fogg's eyes brightened for an instant.

The door swung open, and he saw Passepartout, Aouda, and Fix, who hurried toward him.

Fix was out of breath, and his hair was in disorder. He could not speak. "Sir," he stammered, "sir—forgive me—most—unfortunate resemblance—robber arrested three days ago—you are free!"

Phileas Fogg was free! He walked to the detective, looked him steadily in the face, and with the only rapid motion he had ever made in his life, or which he ever would make, drew back his arms, and with the precision of a machine knocked Fix down.

"Well hit!" cried Passepartout. "Parbleu! That's what you might call a good application of English fists!"

Fix, who found himself on the floor, did not utter a word. He had only received his deserts. Mr. Fogg, Aouda, and Passepartout left the customhouse without delay, got into a cab, and in a few moments descended at the station.

Phileas Fogg asked if there was an express train about to leave for London. It was forty minutes past two. The express train had left thirty-five minutes before. Phileas Fogg then ordered a special train.

There were several rapid locomotives on hand; but the railway arrangements did not permit the special train to leave until three o'clock.

At that hour Phileas Fogg, having stimulated the engineer by the offer of a generous reward, at last set out toward London with Aouda and his faithful servant.

It was necessary to make the journey in five hours and a half; and this would have been easy on a clear road throughout. But there were forced delays, and when Mr. Fogg stepped from the train at the terminus, all the clocks in London were striking ten minutes before nine.

Having made the tour of the world, he was behindhand five minutes. He had lost the wager!

# CHAPTER XXXV

### IN WHICH PHILEAS FOGG DOES NOT HAVE TO REPEAT
### HIS ORDERS TO PASSEPARTOUT TWICE

The dwellers in Saville Row would have been surprised the next day, if they had been told that Phileas Fogg had returned home. His doors and windows were still closed, no appearance of change was visible.

After leaving the station, Mr. Fogg gave Passepartout instructions to purchase some provisions, and quietly went to his domicile.

He bore his misfortune with his habitual tranquility. Ruined! And by the blundering of the detective! After having steadily traversed that long journey, overcome a hundred obstacles, braved many dangers, and still found time to do some good on his way, to fail near the goal by a sudden event which he could not have foreseen, and against which he was unarmed; it was terrible! But a few pounds were left of the large sum he had carried with him. There only remained of his fortune the twenty thousand pounds deposited at Barings, and this amount he owed to his friends of the Reform Club. So great had been the expense of his tour that, even had he won, it would not have enriched him; and it is probable that he had not sought to enrich himself, being a man who rather laid wagers for honor's sake than for the stake proposed. But this wager totally ruined him.

Mr. Fogg's course, however, was fully decided upon; he knew what remained for him to do.

A room in the house in Saville Row was set apart for Aouda, who was overwhelmed with grief at her protector's misfortune. From the words which Mr. Fogg dropped, she saw that he was meditating some serious project.

Knowing that Englishmen governed by a fixed idea sometimes resort to the desperate expedient of suicide, Passepartout kept a narrow watch upon his master, though he carefully concealed the appearance of so doing.

First of all, the worthy fellow had gone up to his room, and had extinguished the gas burner, which had been burning for eighty days. He had found in the letter box a bill from the gas company, and he thought it more than time to put a stop to this expense, which he had been doomed to bear.

The night passed. Mr. Fogg went to bed, but did he sleep? Aouda did not once close her eyes. Passepartout watched all night, like a faithful dog, at his master's door.

Mr. Fogg called him in the morning, and told him to get Aouda's breakfast, and a cup of tea and a chop for himself. He desired Aouda to excuse him from breakfast and dinner, as his time would be absorbed all day in putting his affairs to rights. In the evening he would ask permission to have a few moments' conversation with the young lady.

Passepartout, having received his orders, had nothing to do but obey them. He looked at his imperturbable master, and could scarcely bring his mind to leave him. His heart was full, and his conscience tortured by remorse; for he accused himself more bitterly than ever of being the cause of the irretrievable disaster. Yes! If he had warned Mr. Fogg, and had betrayed Fix's projects to him, his master would certainly not have given the detective passage to Liverpool, and then—

Passepartout could hold in no longer.

"My master! Mr. Fogg!" he cried. "Why do you not curse me? It was my fault that—"

"I blame no one," returned Phileas Fogg, with perfect calmness. "Go!"

Passepartout left the room, and went to find Aouda, to whom he delivered his master's message.

"Madam," he added, "I can do nothing myself—nothing! I have no influence over my master; but you, perhaps—"

"What influence could I have?" replied Aouda. "Mr. Fogg is influenced by no one. Has he ever understood that my gratitude to him is overflowing? Has he ever read my heart? My friend, he must not be left alone an instant! You say he is going to speak with me this evening?"

"Yes, madam; probably to arrange for your protection and comfort in England."

"We shall see," replied Aouda, becoming suddenly pensive.

Throughout this day (Sunday) the house in Saville Row was as if uninhabited, and Phileas Fogg, for the first time since he had lived in that house, did not set out for his club when the Westminster clock struck half past eleven.

Why should he present himself at the Reform? His friends no longer expected him there. As Phileas Fogg had not appeared in the saloon on the evening before (Saturday, the 21st of December, at a quarter before nine), he had lost his wager. It was not even necessary that he should go to his banker's for the twenty thousand pounds; for his antagonists already had his check in their hands, and they had only to fill it out and send it to the Barings to have the amount transferred to their credit.

Mr. Fogg, therefore, had no reason for going out, and so he remained at home. He shut himself up in his room, and busied himself putting his affairs in order. Passepartout continually ascended and descended the stairs. The hours were long for him. He listened at his master's door, and looked through the keyhole, as if he had a perfect right so to do, and as if he feared that something terrible might happen at any moment. Sometimes he thought of Fix, but no longer in anger. Fix, like all the world, had been mistaken in Phileas Fogg, and had only done his duty in tracking and arresting him; while he, Passepartout . . . this thought haunted him, and he never ceased cursing his miserable folly.

Finding himself too wretched to remain alone, he knocked at Aouda's door, went into her room, seated himself, without speaking, in a corner, and looked ruefully at the young woman. Aouda was still pensive.

About half past seven in the evening Mr. Fogg sent to know if Aouda would receive him, and in a few moments he found himself alone with her.

Phileas Fogg took a chair, and sat down near the fireplace, opposite Aouda. No emotion was visible on his face. Fogg returned was exactly the Fogg who had gone away; there was the same calm, the same impassibility.

He sat several minutes without speaking; then, bending his eyes on Aouda, "Madam," said he, "will you pardon me for bringing you to England?"

"I, Mr. Fogg!" replied Aouda, checking the pulsations of her heart.

"Please let me finish," returned Mr. Fogg. "When I decided to bring you far away from the country which was so unsafe for you, I was rich, and counted on putting a portion of my fortune at your disposal; then your existence would have been free and happy. But now I am ruined."

"I know it, Mr. Fogg," replied Aouda; "and I ask you in my turn, will you forgive me for having followed you, and—who knows?—for having, perhaps, delayed you, and thus contributed to your ruin?"

"Madam, you could not remain in India, and your safety could only be assured by bringing you to such a distance that your persecutors could not take you."

"So, Mr. Fogg," resumed Aouda, "not content with rescuing me from a terrible death, you thought yourself bound to secure my comfort in a foreign land?"

"Yes, madam; but circumstances have been against me. Still, I beg to place the little I have left at your service."

"But what will become of you, Mr. Fogg?"

"As for me, madam," replied the gentleman, coldly, "I have need of nothing."

"But how do you look upon the fate, sir, which awaits you?"

"As I am in the habit of doing."

"At least," said Aouda, "want should not overtake a man like you. Your friends—"

"I have no friends, madam."

"Your relatives—"

"I have no longer any relatives."

"I pity you, then, Mr. Fogg, for solitude is a sad thing, with no heart to which to confide your griefs. They say, though, that misery itself, shared by two sympathetic souls, may be borne with patience."

"They say so, madam."

"Mr. Fogg," said Aouda, rising and seizing his hand, "do you wish at once a kinswoman and friend? Will you have me for your wife?"

Mr. Fogg, at this, rose in his turn. There was an unwonted light in his eyes, and a slight trembling of his lips. Aouda looked into his face. The sincerity, rectitude, firmness, and sweetness of this soft glance of a noble woman, who could dare all to save him to whom she owed all, at first astonished, then penetrated him. He shut his eyes for an instant, as if to avoid her look. When he opened them again, "I love you!" he said, simply. "Yes, by all that is holiest, I love you, and I am entirely yours!"

"Ah!" cried Aouda, pressing his hand to her heart.

Passepartout was summoned and appeared immediately. Mr. Fogg still held Aouda's hand in his own; Passepartout understood, and his big, round face became as radiant as the tropical sun at its zenith.

Mr. Fogg asked him if it was not too late to notify the Reverend Samuel Wilson, of Marylebone parish, that evening.

Passepartout smiled his most genial smile, and said, "Never too late."

It was five minutes past eight.

"Will it be for tomorrow, Monday?"

"For tomorrow, Monday," said Mr. Fogg, turning to Aouda.

"Yes; for tomorrow, Monday," she replied.

Passepartout hurried off as fast as his legs could carry him.

# CHAPTER XXXVI

### IN WHICH PHILEAS FOGG'S NAME IS ONCE MORE AT A PREMIUM ON 'CHANGE

It is time to relate what a change took place in English public opinion when it transpired that the real bank robber, a certain James Strand, had been arrested, on the 17th day of December, at Edinburgh. Three days before, Phileas Fogg had been a criminal who was being desperately followed up by the police; now he was an honorable gentleman, mathematically pursuing his eccentric journey round the world.

The papers resumed their discussion about the wager; all those who had laid bets, for or against him, revived their interest, as if by magic; the "Phileas Fogg bonds" again became negotiable, and many new wagers were made. Phileas Fogg's name was once more at a premium on 'Change.

His five friends of the Reform Club passed these three days in a state of feverish suspense. Would Phileas Fogg, whom they had forgotten, reappear before their eyes! Where was he at this moment? The 17th of December, the day of James Strand's arrest, was the seventy-sixth since Phileas Fogg's departure, and no news of him had been received. Was he dead? Had he abandoned the effort, or was he continuing his journey along the route agreed upon? And would he appear on Saturday, the 21st of December, at a quarter before nine in the evening, on the threshold of the Reform Club saloon?

The anxiety in which, for three days, London society existed, cannot be described. Telegrams were sent to America and Asia for news of Phileas Fogg. Messengers were dispatched to the house in Saville Row morning and evening. No news. The police were ignorant what had become of the detective, Fix, who had so unfortunately followed up a false scent. Bets increased, nevertheless, in number and value. Phileas Fogg, like a racehorse, was drawing near his last turning point. The bonds were quoted, no longer at a hundred below par, but at twenty, at ten, and at five; and paralytic old Lord Albemarle bet even in his favor.

A great crowd was collected in Pall Mall and the neighboring streets on Saturday evening; it seemed like a multitude of brokers permanently established around the Reform Club. Circulation was impeded, and everywhere disputes, discussions, and financial transactions were going on. The police had great difficulty in keeping back the crowd, and as the hour when Phileas Fogg was due approached, the excitement rose to its highest pitch.

The five antagonists of Phileas Fogg had met in the great saloon of the club. John Sullivan and Samuel Fallentin, the bankers; Andrew Stuart, the engineer; Gauthier Ralph, the director of the Bank of England; and Thomas Flanagan, the brewer; one and all waited anxiously.

When the clock indicated twenty minutes past eight, Andrew Stuart got up, saying,

"Gentlemen, in twenty minutes the time agreed upon between Mr. Fogg and ourselves will have expired."

"What time did the last train arrive from Liverpool?" asked Thomas Flanagan.

"At twenty-three minutes past seven," replied Gauthier Ralph; "and the next does not arrive till ten minutes after twelve."

"Well, gentlemen," resumed Andrew Stuart, "if Phileas Fogg had come in the 7:23 train, he would have got here by this time. We can, therefore, regard the bet as won."

"Wait; don't let us be too hasty," replied Samuel Fallentin. "You know that Mr. Fogg is very eccentric. His punctuality is well known; he never arrives too soon, or too late; and I should not be surprised if he appeared before us at the last minute."

"Why," said Andrew Stuart nervously, "if I should see him, I should not believe it was he."

"The fact is," resumed Thomas Flanagan, "Mr. Fogg's project was absurdly foolish. Whatever his punctuality, he could not prevent the delays which were certain to occur; and a delay of only two or three days would be fatal to his tour."

"Observe, too," added John Sullivan, "that we have received no intelligence from him, though there are telegraphic lines all along is route."

"He has lost, gentleman," said Andrew Stuart, "he has a hundred times lost! You know, besides, that the *China*—the only steamer he could have taken from New York to get here in time—arrived yesterday. I have seen a list of the passengers, and the name of Phileas Fogg is not among them. Even if we admit that fortune has favored him, he can scarcely have reached America. I think he will be at least twenty days behindhand, and that Lord Albemarle will lose a cool five thousand."

"It is clear," replied Gauthier Ralph; "and we have nothing to do but to present Mr. Fogg's check at Barings tomorrow."

At this moment, the hands of the club clock pointed to twenty minutes to nine.

"Five minutes more," said Andrew Stuart.

The five gentlemen looked at each other. Their anxiety was becoming intense; but, not wishing to betray it, they readily assented to Mr. Fallentin's proposal of a rubber.

"I wouldn't give up my four thousand of the bet," said Andrew Stuart, as he took his seat, "for three thousand nine hundred and ninety-nine."

The clock indicated eighteen minutes to nine.

The players took up their cards, but could not keep their eyes off the clock. Certainly, however secure they felt, minutes had never seemed so long to them!

"Seventeen minutes to nine," said Thomas Flanagan, as he cut the cards which Ralph handed to him.

Then there was a moment of silence. The great saloon was perfectly quiet; but the murmurs of the crowd outside were heard, with now and then a shrill cry. The pendulum beat the seconds, which each player eagerly counted, as he listened, with mathematical regularity.

"Sixteen minutes to nine!" said John Sullivan, in a voice which betrayed his emotion.

One minute more, and the wager would be won. Andrew Stuart and his partners suspended their game. They left their cards, and counted the seconds.

At the fortieth second, nothing. At the fiftieth, still nothing.

At the fifty-fifth, a loud cry was heard in the street, followed by applause, hurrahs, and some fierce growls.

The players rose from their seats.

At the fifty-seventh second the door of the saloon opened; and the pendulum had not beat the sixtieth second when Phileas Fogg appeared, followed by an excited crowd who had forced their way through the club doors, and in his calm voice, said, "Here I am, gentlemen!"

# CHAPTER XXXVII

### In Which It Is Shown that Phileas Fogg Gained Nothing by His Tour Around the World, Unless It Were Happiness

Yes; Phileas Fogg in person.

The reader will remember that at five minutes past eight in the evening—about five and twenty hours after the arrival of the travelers in London—Passepartout had been sent by his master to engage the services of the Reverend Samuel Wilson in a certain marriage ceremony, which was to take place the next day.

Passepartout went on his errand enchanted. He soon reached the clergyman's house, but found him not at home. Passepartout waited a good twenty minutes, and when he left the reverend gentleman, it was thirty-five minutes past eight. But in what a state he was! With his hair in disorder, and without his hat, he ran along the street as never man was seen to run before, overturning passersby, rushing over the sidewalk like a waterspout.

In three minutes he was in Saville Row again, and staggered back into Mr. Fogg's room.

He could not speak.

"What is the matter?" asked Mr. Fogg.

"My master!" gasped Passepartout. "Marriage—impossible—"

"Impossible?"

"Impossible—for tomorrow."

"Why so?"

"Because tomorrow—is Sunday!"

"Monday," replied Mr. Fogg.

"No—today is Saturday."

"Saturday? Impossible!"

"Yes, yes, yes, yes!" cried Passepartout. "You have made a mistake of one day! We arrived twenty-four hours ahead of time; but there are only ten minutes left!"

Passepartout had seized his master by the collar, and was dragging him along with irresistible force.

Phileas Fogg, thus kidnapped, without having time to think, left his house, jumped into a cab, promised a hundred pounds to the cabman, and, having run over two dogs and overturned five carriages, reached the Reform Club.

The clock indicated a quarter before nine when he appeared in the great saloon.

Phileas Fogg had accomplished the journey round the world in eighty days!

Phileas Fogg had won his wager of twenty thousand pounds!

How was it that a man so exact and fastidious could have made this error of a day? How came he to think that he had arrived in London on Saturday, the twenty-first day of December, when it was really Friday, the twentieth, the seventy-ninth day only from his departure?

The cause of the error is very simple.

Phileas Fogg had, without suspecting it, gained one day on his journey, and this merely because he had traveled constantly *eastward*; he would, on the contrary, have lost a day had he gone in the opposite direction, that is, *westward*.

In journeying eastward he had gone toward the sun, and the days therefore diminished for him as many times four minutes as he crossed degrees in this direction. There are three hundred and sixty degrees on the circumference of the earth; and these three hundred and sixty degrees, multiplied by four minutes, gives precisely twenty-four hours—that is, the day unconsciously gained. In other words, while Phileas Fogg, going eastward, saw the sun pass the meridian *eighty* times, his friends in London only saw it pass the meridian *seventy-nine* times. This is why they awaited him at the Reform Club on Saturday, and not Sunday, as Mr. Fogg thought.

And Passepartout's famous family watch, which had always kept London time, would have betrayed this fact, if it had marked the days as well as the hours and the minutes!

Phileas Fogg, then, had won the twenty thousand pounds; but, as he had spent nearly nineteen thousand on the way, the pecuniary gain was small. His object was, however, to be victorious, and not to win money. He divided the one thousand pounds that remained between Passepartout and the unfortunate Fix, against whom he cherished no grudge. He deducted, however, from Passepartout's share the cost of the gas which had burned in his room for nineteen hundred and twenty hours, for the sake of regularity.

That evening, Mr. Fogg, as tranquil and phlegmatic as ever, said to Aouda: "Is our marriage still agreeable to you?"

"Mr. Fogg," replied she, "it is for me to ask that question. You were ruined, but now you are rich again."

"Pardon me, madam; my fortune belongs to you. If you had not suggested our marriage, my servant would not have gone to the Reverend Samuel Wilson's, I should not have been apprised of my error, and—"

"Dear Mr. Fogg!" said the young woman.

"Dear Aouda!" replied Phileas Fogg.

It need not be said that the marriage took place forty-eight hours after, and that Passepartout, glowing and dazzling, gave the bride away. Had he not saved her, and was he not entitled to this honor?

The next day, as soon as it was light, Passepartout rapped vigorously at his master's door. Mr. Fogg opened it, and asked, "What's the matter, Passepartout?"

"What is it, sir? Why, I've just this instant found out—"

"What?"

"That we might have made the tour of the world in only seventy-eight days."

"No doubt," returned Mr. Fogg, "by not crossing India. But if I had not crossed India, I should not have saved Aouda; she would not have been my wife, and—"

Mr. Fogg quietly shut the door.

Phileas Fogg had won his wager, and had made his journey around the world in eighty days. To do this he had employed every means of conveyance—steamers, railways, carriages, yachts, trading vessels, sleighs, elephants. The eccentric gentleman had throughout displayed all his marvelous qualities of coolness and exactitude. But what then? What had he really gained by all this trouble? What had he brought back from this long and weary journey?

Nothing, say you? Perhaps so; nothing but a charming woman, who, strange as it may appear, made him the happiest of men!

Truly, would you not for less than that make the tour around the world?